D0013133

A MAN BETRAYED

J.V. JONES

ASPECT®

WARNER BOOKS

A Time Warner Company

Copyright © 1996 by J. V. Jones
All rights reserved.

Aspect name and logo are registered trademarks of Warner Books, Inc.

Warner Books, Inc., 1271 Avenue of the Americas, New York, NY 10020

w A Time Warner Company

Printed in the United States of America

First Printing: April 1996

10 9 8 7 6 5 4 3 2 1

Library of Congress Cataloging-in-Publication Data applied for
ISBN: 0-446-67098-7

Book design by H. Roberts
Cover design by Don Puckey
Cover illustration by Darrell Sweet

PRAISE FOR
THE BAKER'S BOY

VOLUME I
IN THE BOOK OF WORDS TRILOGY

"ONE OF THOSE SUCCESS STORIES EVERY WRITER STRIVES FOR.
I finished the book in just three short days . . . there's not a slow spot
in the whole book. I'm eagerly awaiting the next installment,
A Man Betrayed."

—*Fresno County Sun*

"JONES STAMPS IT ALL WITH A DISTINCTIVE TOUCH compounded
largely of sadism and food, a combination that reaches its apex in a
deliciously hedonistic and depraved archbishop. There's so much going
on that the action barely starts in this novel, and an ominous prophecy
promises much more to come."

—**Locus**

"AN EXCITING STORY OF FLOUR, SWEAT, AND TEARS."

—*.net* **magazine**

"*THE BAKER'S BOY* has most of the qualities of a highly successful, popular
fantasy epic . . . a substantial cast and a vivid, colorful landscape. . . .
A REMARKABLY READABLE EPIC."

—*Dragon* **magazine**

"J. V. JONES IS ABOUT TO BECOME ONE OF THE GREAT FANTASY
SUCCESS STORIES OF THE '90s."

—**Mysterious Galaxy Books**

"A COMPLEX TALE OF SORCERY AND SWORDSMANSHIP,
INTRIGUE, AND AFFAIRS OF THE HEART."

—*Library Journal*

Also by J. V. Jones

THE BAKER'S BOY

Published by Warner Books

For Margaret Jones

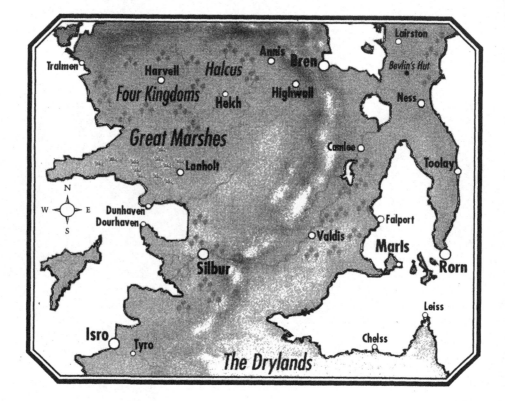

A MAN BETRAYED

Prologue

*T*he girl began to snore gently: a wheezing unpleasant noise that seemed almost a plea for pity. It was the smell of her more than the sound that disturbed him. The fetid and cloying smell that accompanied all her sex. The smell of sweat and urine and discharge. Smells telling, more accurately than any book, the true nature of woman. The secret inner nature that women with all their powers of concealment and dissembling strove to keep hidden away from the eyes of men. And of course they succeeded, for men are easily fooled by outward show; a plump bosom, a flash of teeth, a whiff of scented breath.

But the truth was ever there, for women could never quite rid themselves—despite all the powders and perfumes—of the smell of their own decay.

Kylock rose from his bed, seeking to distance himself from the telling candor that was the stench of women. He would have liked to shake the girl awake and bid her go, but that did not suit his plans, and indeed, after all he had put her through this night, he was not entirely sure that a good shaking would waken her. Oh, the girl would recover: physical resilience was yet another trait of her sex. They outdid and then outlived men.

He moved across the room to where a small copper washbasin waited, as it always did, and began to wash his hands. Scrubbing with a small, but coarse boar's-hair brush, he meticulously cleansed his hands of the taint of woman. Fingers, that a candle length earlier had so eagerly sought out fleshy openings and swellings, were now soaked in the lye-laden water. Kylock took extra care on this occasion. It was a mark of respect for what he would do this night. Not for the person he would do it to, but for the magnitude of what would be done.

He looked at his hands. Pale and long they were; elegant in finger, delicate in shape. Not his father's hands.

A half smile stole across his lips, and he turned his face to the mirror. Not his father's face, not his father's eyes or nose or teeth. With a sudden violent movement he slammed his fist into the mirror. The glass shattered with a satisfying crack and splinter. The girl on the bed momentarily stirred and then, perhaps deciding she was safer in oblivion, settled herself again with a minimum of movement.

The blow had not even drawn blood. Kylock was pleased. It seemed fitting that no blood should be drawn this night. The mirror now presented him with a disjointed array of images. His mother was there as a ghost in the fragments of his features. There was no doubting he was his mother's son. The plane of cheek, the tilt of brow, the swell of lip: they all spoke of his mother.

He didn't bother to search for traces of his father: there would be none to find. There never had been. He was not his father's son. It was as plain as the nose on his face. Indeed, it was the nose that gave everything away: a grim irony, but a truth nonetheless.

Kylock turned from the mirror and readied himself. There were no special requirements. He donned his usual black; so out of place in daylight, so very appropriate at night. The color of secrets and stealth. The color of death. He needed no mirror to tell how very well it became him, how flattering and suitable the hue. Black would suit his mother, too. Like mother like son.

He was so close to where he needed to be, a mere corridor away, but he would not set foot in that hallowed hall, would not feel the cool touch of the bronze doors upon his palms. He must walk a subtler path.

Kylock left his chambers and made his way to the ladies' quarters. Any man who spied him on his way would turn a blind but winking eye, thinking to himself that it was only right that the heir to the Four Kingdoms had the audacity to flaunt the rules by visiting a lady in her chambers after dark.

Kylock had no lady on his mind. He knew an entrance to the passageways was to be found in the ladies' quarters. It was only natural that there be one: where else in the whole castle might a king want to visit more, and yet be seen less doing so?

The king's chancellor had shown him the ways of the castle. One

Winter's Eve, many years before, he had been caught setting the royal hounds on a newly born foal. As punishment, his mother had confined him to his chambers for a week. Thanks to Baralis, he never had to stay there. By opening a wall with a touch of his disfigured fingers, the man had given him the precious gift of secrecy. Even now he could remember the thrill of revelation, the sense that he had found what he had always searched for amidst the stench and the stealth. It had changed his life. So much had been revealed to him, nothing escaped his greedy eye. He'd spied noblemen rutting with chamber maids, heard servants plotting against their masters, and discovered marks from the pox concealed beneath many a great lady's face powder.

Nothing was as it seemed. Corruption and greed lay close to the bone. Flesh masked a world of sins, and by allowing him access to the hidden passages of Castle Harvell, Baralis had shown him the whole tawdry inventory of them.

Kylock located the wall. He imagined he could hear the click of the mechanism as he drew fingers over the stone. An alluring cavity presented itself. Kylock entered and chose his path.

The sudden chill and smell of rot brought visions of his mother. Surely in all eternity there had never been born a greater whore! Queen Arinalda, the beautiful, the aloof; always pretending to be so correct, so impeccable. How far from the truth appearances so often are. The smell was there, though; unmistakable, stronger than in any other woman. She reeked like a whore. Sometimes the smell was so overpowering that he couldn't bear to be in her presence. How many men had his mother slept with? How many lies had she told? How much treachery had she practiced?

That she had slept with men other than the king was obvious. He, Kylock, was proof of that. There was no Harvell blood in him. No fair hair on his head, no short and stocky limbs attached to his body.

His mother had found her pleasures with other men, and he was a result of her lack of control. Women were the weaker sex, and the source of that weakness was their all-consuming lust. They were disgusting: a thin layer of skin stretched over a foul inner self that boasted the same cravings as a beast. He expected the tavern wenches and street girls to give in to these desires, but a queen? His mother, who should have been above every woman in the realm, was a cheap whore. And he was the son of a whore. He could never look in the mirror without the truth staring back at him.

Almost too soon he was there. The nucleus of the castle, the source from which all else flowed, or should have flowed if things were not as they were. The king's chamber.

Kylock released the mechanism and stepped in. The smell of the sick room assailed his senses. The smell of a man slowly losing his body to death. Too slowly.

Quietly, for he knew that the Master of the Bath would be in the adjoining chamber, he stole across the room. His heart was pounding wildly, excitement and fear mixing on every beat. He approached the bed. The crimson silk monstrosity had been home for the king for the last five years. Kylock drew back the curtains and looked upon the face of the man who was not his father.

As he gazed at the king he felt pity. Thanks to the physicians, the man had neither hair nor teeth. He was a pathetic figure with hollowed out cheeks and a constant drool. Kylock saw where the spittle had wetted and stained the pillows, and pity gave way to disgust. This was no king. *His* mother was king. His whore of a mother had been rewarded for her sins by being made sovereign in all but name. He wouldn't have put it past her to have caused the king's illness in the first place. Woman's middle name was treachery.

Well, tonight all things would change. He would not only be ridding the country of a useless king, but also of a fallacious queen. Tomorrow his mother would find herself devoid of her power. There would be a new king, and she would be a fool to try and rule the kingdoms through the reign of this one, too.

Kylock picked up one of the many pillows. His fastidiousness insisted that it be one untouched by the king's drool. There he was, the man who was not his father. *Would I do this if he were my father?* Kylock molded the silken pillow in his hands, smoothing the shape to what he needed. *Yes, I would do it anyway.*

He leaned over the bed. As the shadow of the pillow crossed the king's face, his eyes opened. Kylock took a step back in fright as the light blue eyes of the king looked upon him. A fresh gob of drool rolled down his chin as he tried to speak. Kylock couldn't move. The pillow burned hot in his hands. Eyes of man and boy met. The king's jaw worked slowly, and the drool fell on his chest.

"Kylock, my son." The words were barely intelligible; a mixture of rasp and spittle.

Kylock looked upon the face of the king. The light blue eyes were more lucid than any words: they spoke of love and loyalty and forgiveness. The boy shook his head sadly.

"No, sire. No son of yours." Kylock felt control coming back to his limbs; the pillow was cool once more.

Kylock's beautiful hands pressed the pillow into the toothless, hairless face of King Lesketh. His fingers spread out against the scarlet silk, as he held the pillow firm against the feeble struggling of the king. Lesketh's good arm flayed like a gentle bird. His chest rose and fell, rose and fell, and then rose no more.

Kylock took his first breath as the king was denied his last. He was trembling. His knees felt such weakness, and his stomach fluttered and threatened to turn. He willed himself to be strong: now was not the time for weakness. *He* was king now and he doubted if there would ever be time for weakness again. He lifted the pillow. Death had finally put a stop to Lesketh's drooling. The man who was not his father looked better, more dignified, more noble. More like a king in death than he ever had in life.

Kylock patted the pillow back into shape and placed it, drool stain up, beneath Lesketh's chin. The bedclothes were in disarray; twisted and untidy. He straightened the sheets, drawing them up so they graciously adorned the dead king.

Satisfied that all looked as it should, Kylock took his leave. Down he went, his feet finding the path that his eyes did not see. His sight was full of other images; images of a glorious coronation, of comforting his distraught mother, of winning the war with the Halcus. His reign had started well. He had already performed a great service to his country, ridding it of a weak and sickly king. It was a shame that one of his greatest acts was destined to go unlauded by history. Never mind, he thought, he would give the historians plenty of other things to write about in their dull and spineless books.

He found himself back in his chamber. The girl was there, exactly as he'd left her on the bed. He went straight over to the washbasin and once again cleaned his hands. The smell of death was easier to wash off than the smell of woman.

Drying his hands on a soft cloth, he moved over to his desk. A quick look back served to assure him that the girl was still sound asleep. From under the foot of the desk he took a key. Delicately filigreed in gold, it caught and played with the candlelight. A jeweled box opened upon its turning. With hands long and agile he took the tiny portrait from the box. There she was: beautiful and innocent, far above any other of her sex. Her purity of soul clearly marked on each perfect feature: Catherine of Bren. Not for her a woman's lusts. She was pure and unsullied, the most perfect of women: and she was his.

Just the sight of her likeness threw the girl on the bed into tawdry relief. Catherine would not smell like a whore. She would not be forever damned in hell like other women. Like his mother.

Kylock tenderly replaced the portrait, careful not to scratch its unblemished surface. He was king now. Catherine would be his queen.

Off came his tunic and his fine silk undershirt. His image beckoned him from the shattered mirror, but he paid it no heed. A black desire came upon him, and if he had but looked in the glass he would have seen his eyes glaze over and grow dim. He would not have known himself. There was a hunger within and he had no choice but to feed it, lest it feed itself upon his soul instead. He drew near the bed. The girl moaned and turned away. He stood above her and, with hands that had killed a king, he ripped the linen shift from her back.

Spiraling downward to a place where fear and desire met, Kylock lost himself to his need. The sound of his mother's voice was in his ear and the face of Catherine of Bren in his eye.

One

*A*ll this riding is playing havoc with my rhoids, Grift."

"I know what you mean, Bodger. But it's good for one thing, though."

"What's that, Grift?"

"Regularity, Bodger. There's nothing like a good gallop to have you running for the nearest bush."

"You're a wise man, Grift." Bodger nodded his head in agreement while trying to keep his mule on track. "Of course, I'm not so sure that you were right about us volunteering for this journey to Bren. I had no idea we'd be assigned the worst duty in the whole crew."

"Aye, cleaning up after the horses leaves a lot to be desired, Bodger. It was bound to fall to us, though. You and me being the lowest in rank. I still say that we were lucky to be allowed to come on this mission in the first place. They wouldn't let any old soldiers go along with the royal guard. It's a distinct honor."

"So you keep reminding me, Grift." Bodger looked decidedly skeptical. "I just hope the women in Bren are as willing and comely as you keep saying."

"They most certainly are, Bodger. Have I ever been wrong about women in the past?"

"I've got to give you that, Grift. There's not much you don't know about women."

The two men were bringing up the rear of a large column. They were over eight score in number; five score of royal guard, a score of Maybor's own, together with various camp attendants and packhorses.

"I think I know what makes the Halcus so mean, Grift. This weather is terrible. A blizzard every day and wind so cold it could freeze the juice from a tallow maker's molding."

"Aye, Bodger. Three weeks of this is more than enough for any man. In normal weather we would have been in Bren by now. As it is, we're barely out of Halcus territory. Of course, the chilliest thing around here ain't the weather."

"What d'you mean, Grift?"

"Lord Maybor and Baralis, that's what I mean, Bodger. Those two make the north wind seem like a cool breeze."

"You're right there, Grift. They've been flinging each other looks as dark and deadly as an executioner's hood since the day we started out." Bodger had to pull hard on his reins, as his mule had its own idea of where it wanted to go, and it wasn't along with the pack.

"There's no love lost there, for sure. Have you noticed the way they won't even pitch their tents within a tourney's length of each other?"

"That I have, Grift. Not to mention the fact that Maybor rides at the fore all day, fancying himself a king, while Baralis brings up the rear like a wounded soldier."

"So you think me a wounded soldier, do you?" The two men turned around, startled, as Baralis rode up between them. His face was deathly pale and his eyes glittered harshly with the reflected luster of the snow.

Neither guard spoke: Bodger because he had been almost frightened from his saddle and was trying to right himself, and Grift because he was clever enough to know when it was best *not* to speak.

The king's chancellor continued, a smile threatening but not quite forming, around his thin lips. "Come, come now, gentlemen. Why so tongue-tied all of a sudden?" His beautiful voice belied the coldness of his eyes. "You appeared so talkative only a moment ago. Am I to take it that the north wind has suddenly frozen your tongues? Or is it that you are beginning to regret your glib words?"

Grift could see that Bodger was about to reply, and although his every instinct willed him to remain silent, he knew that if he didn't speak up now, Bodger would get himself into even worse trouble. "My friend here is young, Lord Baralis, and he partook of a little too much ale at breakfast. He meant nothing by his remark. A jest, no more."

The king's chancellor reflected a moment before replying. A gloved hand rubbed idly at his chin. "Youth is a poor excuse for stupidity; ale is an even poorer one." Grift opened his mouth to speak, but Baralis forestalled him with a sudden gesture of the gloved hand. "Nay, man, protest no more. Let the matter rest here, with you in my debt." He met the eyes of both guards, allowing his meaning time to be fully comprehended. Satisfied, he rode forward, his black cloak spread out over the dock of his mare.

So even the camp attendants were gossiping about him! Still, there was solace to be gained in the fact that both of the sniveling dolts were now beholden to him. Baralis had long since learned the value of having people around who were indebted to him. It was a more valuable coinage than gold in a locked chest. One could never tell when one might need to call upon the services of men such as those. After all, guards usually guarded *something* of value.

Oh, but it was cold. Baralis felt chilled to his very soul. He longed for the warmth of his chambers and the comfort of his own fire. It was his hands that suffered the worst. Even now, clad in fur-lined gloves, the wind still cut through to the bone. His weak, deformed hands, so beautiful in youth, were now ruined by his own ambition. The scarred and scant flesh was no match for the wind.

Snow two hands deep covered their path. It shifted with crafty precision with every bluster of air. As a result, the way was treacherous. The foreguard had already lost one horse to lameness. The unfortunate creature had misstepped by only an arm's length, but it was enough for it to find itself in a deep gully masquerading as a benign stretch of snow. They had slaughtered the gelding where it fell.

They were now only a week away from Bren. Yesterday they had crossed the River Emm. There was not a man in the party who hadn't sighed in relief upon traversing the mighty river. Not only was it a great danger in itself, but more importantly, it marked the end of Halcus territory. The company had thought themselves lucky to have successfully traveled through the lands of the enemy for ten days yet remain undetected and unchallenged. Baralis knew differently.

The idea of using his contacts with the Halcus to sabotage the party and slaughter Maybor had been tempting. There was nothing Baralis wanted more than the death of the vain and swaggering lord. It was just too risky, though. A raid on their party could easily get out of hand. He, himself, might be endangered. No, it was better not to chance his own safety. There were other less hazardous ways to rid himself of Maybor.

The lord of the Eastlands had to be eliminated: it was a fact beyond questioning. Baralis would not tolerate any interference with his plans in

Bren. The betrothal negotiations would take subtlety and cunning—two qualities that Maybor was sadly lacking in. More than that, the man was a threat: not just a physical threat—though Baralis did not doubt that his own assassination was never far from the great lord's thoughts—but also a threat to the whole betrothal. Maybor had wanted his daughter to marry Prince Kylock. His failure to secure such a union had embittered him against the new choice for bride.

Baralis scanned the column of men, searching. Near the front, astride a magnificent stallion, he spied the object of his thoughts. Extravagantly robed in scarlet and silver was the lord himself. Even the way Maybor sat his horse told of his over-bloated sense of self-importance. Baralis' lip curled into well-worn lines of contempt at the very sight of him.

He simply could not allow Maybor to reach Bren alive. As king's envoy, the man was actually superior to him! The queen had pulled a dirty trick with that particular appointment. *He*, king's chancellor, the very person who was instrumental in bringing about the match between Prince Kylock and Catherine, should have had preeminence in Bren. Instead the queen had appointed him prince's envoy, and in doing so had made him subservient to Maybor.

He could not and would not endure such an indignity.

The duke of Bren and his fair daughter were *his* concern. Maybor had no business bringing his pot to this fire. Baralis was aware of the politics of both appointments, but the queen would find all her cleverness unrewarded when news of Maybor's demise reached the kingdoms.

There was no doubt about it. Today, this chill and frosty noon, with the north wind blowing like a siren from the abyss, Maybor would meet his death.

Melli knew better than to open the shuttered window. There was a gale coming, and the scant stretch of wood was the only thing between them and its ravages. As it was she wasn't sure the latch would hold. Still, she suspected it might—she had always been lucky that way. The famous Maybor luck had served her family well through the centuries. Or more accurately, it had served the Maybor men well, as they seemed to drain all the luck from their women.

Not her, though. She was the first female of her family to be endowed with that most capricious of gifts.

Melli put her eye to the knot hole and peered out onto the northern plains of Halcus. Almost dazzled by the brilliance of the snow, it took her a moment before she could discern any details of the land. The wind had picked up since she'd last looked and was carrying the snow in its thrall. There was little to be seen: white land against white sky. The snowy expanse was probably grazing pasture in the spring, but for now it was laid out defenseless for winter to take its toll.

The bite of the cold grew too much for her eyes and Melli withdrew her gaze inward. With a scrap of dirty oilcloth she plugged the knot hole. Turning, she caught Jack looking at her, and for some reason her face flushed. Almost against her will, her hand smoothed her hair. It was foolish, she thought, that after being away from the court and its customs for so long she still had the instincts of a court beauty. The women of Castle Harvell had so many rules to live by: rules of conduct, rules of dress, rules of form. Now that Melli had distanced herself from the great court, she realized all the rules could be summed up in one: a woman must at all times strive to please a man.

Even now, after experiencing things that a court beauty could only guess at, Melli found herself falling into the old habits of femininity, most particularly the habit of wanting to look nice for a man.

She smiled at her own folly. Jack, catching the mood of her smile, grinned in response. His keen and handsome face, made all the more appealing by his winter color, caused Melli to feel unaccountably happy. Suddenly she was laughing: bright and high and merry as a tinker. Then Jack joined in. They stood at opposite ends of the small hut that had once been a chicken coop and laughed with each other.

She didn't know why Jack laughed, didn't even know why she herself laughed, she only knew it felt good to do so. And for so long now there had been so little that felt good.

The weather had been against them from the start. Once they crossed into Halcus territory it had become even worse. They had no knowledge of the land and had quickly lost their bearings. That, together with the necessity of changing their course whenever they spotted another human being, had caused them to lose their way. Melli had read tales in her childhood of people taking long journeys guided only by the sun and the stars, but the reality was much different. What the tales failed to tell was that in winter both the sun and the stars didn't put in an appearance for weeks on end. In the daytime the sky was pale and filled with cloud, in the nighttime the sky was dark and filled with cloud.

The result was that they had little idea of where they lay in relation to Bren and Annis. The only thing they knew for sure was that they were still somewhere in Halcus. The fact that they were still in the lands of the enemy had been proven only two days back.

The weather had been getting progressively worse, and Melli had noticed that Jack was still having problems with his injured shoulder. Oh, he tried to hide it, men always did things like that, both in tales *and* reality. He had developed the habit of always slinging his pack over his left shoulder, thereby keeping the strain from his right. Knee-deep in snow they walked, the wind robbing them of what little warmth their clothes could muster. Eventually they came upon a derelict farmhouse. The farmer had long since left, and for good reason: the place had been burnt to the timbers, leaving only a snow-covered ruin.

A storm was threatening. Dark clouds gathered on the horizon and the wind wolfed at their heels. Weary and bone-cold, their spirits soared when behind a clump of bushes they discovered the chicken coop. Located some distance from the farmhouse, the coop had stayed clear of any inflammatory sparks.

Melli knew there would be trouble when the door failed to give and the strain of a latch could clearly be heard within. No door latched itself. Someone else had taken refuge in the coop. Jack's eyes met hers. She could tell he was sizing up just how much she needed shelter. Without cover, the coming storm might be their last. She shook her head slightly: better to walk away. The latched door meant people, and people meant danger. Jack looked at her a second longer, registering her warning, and then turned his gaze to the horizon. The storm lay poised to strike like a predator.

With a sudden, violent gesture, he kicked down the door. The latch gave way. The door collapsed backward, its top hinge failing. In the coop were two men, knives drawn.

The first thing Melli felt was Jack's arm slamming into her chest, pushing her back out of harm's way. She looked up from the snow in time to marvel at how quickly he drew his blade. A pig farmer's blade. Melli could detect the sharp, loamy smell of ale. The two men had been drinking. They moved apart warily, seeking to flank Jack. Jack stepped back from the threshold. Even to Melli's untutored eye it seemed like a smart move. When the men attacked now, they would be forced to come through the doorway one at a time.

The first man came forward. Knife before him, he slashed wildly at the air. Jack fell upon him. It was the only way to describe it. Melli felt she was seeing him for the first time: he was wild with fury. What he lacked in skill, he made up for in rage. It seemed to Melli that Jack was fighting much more than the man beneath him. In the struggle—which the stranger was destined to lose—Jack was fighting against fate and circumstance and even perhaps himself. Every vicious blow was a strike against something less substantial, yet more threatening than his opponent.

The second man moved forward. Melli screamed a warning. "Jack! Look out! He's behind you." He swung around and the man, probably scared at what he saw in Jack's face, fled. He ran awkwardly through the thick snow, leaving deep pits where his feet had stepped.

The first man was dead: a pig-knife to the gut. Jack stood up. He would not look at her. He'd stumbled into the hut and she'd followed, carefully skirting the body and the blood.

Neither had mentioned it since. Melli's thoughts were another matter. Jack was growing more withdrawn. He was as considerate as ever, yet there was something within him that could quickly turn and show an edge. The Halcus soldier had seen the sharpness of it. In a way, Melli was grateful the man had been killed by a knife; the alternative was worse. Jack had a greater potential for destruction within him than an armory of blades.

Melli was secretly intrigued by the thought of sorcery. Oh, she'd been taught as a child that it was evil, and that it was only practiced by those close with the devil. Her father flatly refused to believe in it, saying it was a thing out of legend like dragons and fairies, but she'd heard tales here and there. Tales that told of how at one time, sorcery was common in the Known Lands, and that people who used it were neither good nor bad. Surely Jack was proof of this?

If anything, since she'd witnessed his power the day they'd escaped from the mercenaries, she found herself more attracted to him. Before he had been almost a boy: unsure of himself and awkward, with long legs and long hair. The power he'd drawn seemed to fill him out, like fluid poured into a waterskin. His presence was more compelling, his body more his own. He was maturing fast, and sorcery, with all its accompanying hearsay and heresy, endowed him with an aura that Melli found hard to resist.

Jack had his weaknesses, though. Melli worried in case the bitterness she had glimpsed in his attack upon the Halcus soldier might settle and form part of the man.

Suddenly Melli didn't feel like laughing anymore. She resisted the urge to unplug the knot hole and check the horizon one more time. They had paid dearly for this chicken coop, and there might yet be an even higher price to pay.

As if reading her thoughts, Jack spoke to comfort her. "Don't worry. No one will come," he said. "The soldier can't have gone far, and even if he made it to a village, no one is about to go chasing the enemy in this weather."

It was her fault. If she hadn't spoken up in warning, the man would never have known where they came from. Yet she had, and the sound of the lilting accent of the Four Kingdoms had been clearly heard. If she had only kept silent, the man might have mistaken them for his own. He would, of course, have been no less pleased about having his shelter and his companion taken from him. But such incidents were all too common in both countries, and it might have gone overlooked. Until she spoke.

Now the man who had escaped across the snowy field knew they were from the kingdoms. If he were to make it to a village, he could bring whatever forces were at hand down upon them with just two words: "The enemy."

The Halcus hated the Four Kingdoms with the deep hate that only comes with closeness. Neighbors they had been for centuries, but everyone knows it's one's neighbors one despises the most. The war had raged bitterly for five years now; the same war over the same river that had been fought countless times before. More blood than water flowed along the River Nestor's bitterly disputed banks. The kingdoms had the advantage at the moment: a fact that served to make the Halcus hate them all the more.

"He might not have recognized your accent. You only said a few words." Jack took three strides across the coop and was beside her.

Melli shook her head gently and offered her hand. He took it and they stood side by side, and listened to the sound of the advancing storm. They were trapped here; fleeing under these conditions would surely bring a more certain death than staying put and hoping no one would come. As long as the storm raged, they would be safe. Only fools and the love-sick dared to venture out in a blizzard.

Her hand rested in his. There was no pressure in his touch, but part of her wished that there was. Inexplicably, her thoughts turned toward the king's chancellor, Lord Baralis. And then, as she realized the common thread between the past and the present, she withdrew her hand from Jack's. It was the touch; a touch remembered—many weeks back now— a touch that thrilled and repulsed in one. The memory of Baralis' hand upon her spine. Curious how the mind weaves its associations, sometimes weaving with unlooked-for irony. Two men, both with more than muscle to lend them strength.

Melli wondered if she had offended Jack by withdrawing her hand. She couldn't tell. He was so difficult to read, and the time they'd spent together had only made him more so. She couldn't begin to guess what he thought of her. That he cared for her safety was the only thing she knew for certain. The force with which he had pushed her away from the two men was proof of that.

Still, what did he think of her? A court lady, daughter of Lord Maybor. A noblewoman standing next to a baker's apprentice.

Sometimes Jack was tormented in his sleep. With eyes closed and face slick with sweat, he would toss restlessly on his bedroll, calling words she seldom caught the meaning of. Just over two weeks back, within the shelter of an evergreen wood, he'd had his worst night of all.

Melli had awoken, she knew not why. It was one of those rare nights when the wind had ceased and the cold stopped biting. Instinctively she looked over to Jack. She could tell right away he was having a nightmare. His cheeks were hollow and the tendons on his neck were raised and taut. He became agitated, pushing his cloak and blanket from his body. "No!" he murmured. "No."

Melli sat up, deciding she would go over and wake him. Before she could stand, a chilling sound broke the silence of the wood.

"*Stop!*" cried Jack.

With that cry, the nature of the night and the universe seemed to change. It became more vivid, more intimate, and then more terrible. The torment and the sense of urgency conveyed in that one word made Melli's blood run cold. Jack was silent once more and drifted into a more restful sleep. No such sleep for her that night. The moonlight had withdrawn upon Jack's call and now came the darkness. Melli lay awake through the artificial stillness of the night, afraid that if she fell asleep and then woke in the morning, the world might have changed whilst she slept.

She shuddered and wrapped her cloak closer. Jack was back in his corner, slicing the wet bark from the logs. The hut was too small to have a fire, and with the shutters closed there would be no ventilation, but he prepared one anyway. He didn't like to be idle.

Melli unplugged the knot hole for the tenth time that day. She told herself it was to check on the progress of the storm. But the storm was coming from the east, and Melli's gaze was to the west. Almost blinded by the whiteness, Melli searched for movement from the direction where the second man had headed.

Tavalisk lifted the cloth from the cheese and inhaled deeply. Perfect. Amateurs might first check the look of the cheese, seeing if the blue veining was substantial but still delicate. He knew better. It was the smell that told one all one needed to know. Blue cheese should have no mincing, milk-maid odor. No, this most regal of cheeses should smell like a king. Preferably a dead one. Unfortunately not everyone appreciated the smell of delicate decay wrought by the millions of spores that burrowed their way through the virgin cheese.

Yes, mused the archbishop, the smell was everything. Sharp, tantalizing, challenging, never subtle. It should rise to one's nostrils like a whip to the back: unwanted at first, and then, as one grows accustomed to its particular pleasures, welcomed for all the delights it could bestow.

Tavalisk was a surgeon at his table as he cut into the cheese. With his little silver knife he freed himself a sizable wedge. Once its rind was breached, the odor from the cheese became even more intense. It was almost dizzying. The archbishop was, at such times, as close to religious ecstasy as he was ever likely to get.

A knock sounded upon the door.

"Enter, Gamil." Tavalisk now found that he could tell which of his various aides were awaiting his pleasure just by the sound of their knocking. Needless to say, Gamil had the most annoying knock of all: timid and impatient in one.

"Good day to Your Eminence," offered Gamil, a little less humbly than usual.

"What news this day, Gamil?" Tavalisk did not deign to turn from his cheese.

"Your Eminence will be most interested in the news I bring. Most interested, indeed."

"Gamil, your job is merely to keep me informed. My job is to decide what is interesting." Tavalisk raised the crumbly cheese to his mouth. The sour taste of the mold met his palette. "Come now, Gamil, out with it. Stop sulking like a maiden with no new dress to wear at the dance."

"Well, Your Eminence, do you remember the knight?"

"What night? Was it moonlit or overcast?" The archbishop was beginning to enjoy himself.

"No, Your Eminence. The knight of Valdis, Tawl."

"Oh, you mean the *knight*. Why didn't you say so in the first place? Of course I remember the knight. Handsome chap. No liking for the whip, though, if I remember correctly." Tavalisk was contemplating feeding his cat some of the cheese.

"Does Your Eminence remember we were having him followed as he made his way north?"

"Do you think me a toothless dotard? I most certainly remember. There is nothing," the archbishop showed his teeth, "*nothing*, you hear, that I ever forget. You would do well to remember that, Gamil."

"Please accept my apologies, Your Eminence."

Tavalisk could not resist. "I will accept your apologies, but I won't forget your impertinence." He cut a portion of cheese and held it out to his cat. The creature took one sniff and then beat a hasty retreat. "Carry on with your news, Gamil."

"Well, as you suspected, the knight was headed to Bevlin's cottage."

"Do we know what transpired in that meeting?" Tavalisk was now crouched down by the base of the couch, trying to tempt his cat to eat the cheese.

"We do now, Your Eminence. One of our spies made haste back to the city just to tell us."

"He came himself? This is most unusual. Why could he not send a messenger?" The archbishop had now caught the cat by its neck and was trying to force the cheese into its mouth.

"He deemed the news so monumental, Your Eminence, that he could not risk sharing it with another."

"Hoping for a promotion, is he?"

"I think when Your Eminence finally hears what I have to say," a touch of frustration could be heard in Gamil's voice, "that you might indeed wish to reward the man in some small way."

"Oh, might I? What news could this possibly be? Has Tyren been struck by lightning? Has Kesmont risen from the dead? Or has the knight himself turned out to be Borc incarnate?"

"No, Your Eminence. Bevlin is dead."

Tavalisk released his hold on the cat. He stood up slowly, his weight almost too great to bear. In silence he walked to his desk. Selecting the finest brandy that waited there, he poured himself a brimming glass. It did not occur to him to offer Gamil a cup. Only after he had taken a deep draught of the potent liqueur did he speak.

"Are you sure of what you say? How reliable is this man?"

"The spy in question has worked for you for over ten years, Your Eminence. His loyalty and professionalism are beyond repute."

"How did Bevlin die?"

"Well, our spy turned up at Bevlin's cottage in the early hours of the morning. He looked in through the window and saw the wiseman dead on the bench. Stabbed in the heart. Anyway, he watched and waited, keeping a low profile, and then our knight came into the room. He found the dead body, and then went over the barrel, as they say."

"Over the barrel?"

"Lost his senses, Your Eminence. According to our man, the knight crouched there with the dead man in his arms for over four hours—rocking him back and forth like a baby. Our spy was just about to leave, when the young lowlife who was traveling with the knight came in the room. The boy helped him up and so forth, but then, as soon as he left the knight alone for a minute, the knight was off: galloping into the sunset. The next day, having buried the body and secured the cottage, the boy followed him west. Our spy then made haste to Rorn."

"Who killed the wiseman?"

"That's the strange thing, Your Eminence. Our spy had been watching the cottage from a distance all night. No one came or went after the knight and his boy arrived."

"Our man didn't see the murder?"

"Alas, Your Eminence, even spies must sleep."

The archbishop rimmed his glass with his finger. The smell of cheese, which was being wafted his way due to an open window, was for the moment distasteful to him. He covered the blue-veined round with the cloth, damping the odor.

"So, Gamil, are you saying it was the knight who did this?"

"Yes and no, Your Eminence."

"Meaning?"

"Meaning that his hand might have been upon the blade, but his actions were not his own. His distress when he found the body must attest to the fact that he was an unwilling accomplice."

"Larn." Tavalisk spoke quietly, more to himself than Gamil. "Larn. The knight was there less than two months back. The elders of that island have long had their own agendas, and the most ingenious ways for carrying them out." The archbishop mustered his lips to a plump parody of a smile. "Bevlin has finally paid the price for his interference."

"Larn bears a long grudge, Your Eminence."

"Hmm, you've got to admire them for that." Tavalisk settled back in his chair. "Still, it seems a rather vindictive act. I can't help thinking that there is more to this meal than flavor alone."

"How so, Your Eminence?"

"Larn knows too much for its own good. Thanks to those damned seers, it has a decidedly unfair advantage when it comes to gleaning intelligence. I think that doddering old fool Bevlin was up to something they didn't like."

"If you are right, Your Eminence, then perhaps the knight has some inkling of Bevlin's intent."

Tavalisk nodded slowly. "Are we still tracking him?"

"Yes, Your Eminence. I expect to know in a day or two where he was headed. Bren seems the most likely of places at the moment. If he is there, our spies will keep us informed of his actions."

"Very good. You may go now. I have much to think on." The archbishop poured himself another glass of brandy. Just as his aide reached the door, he called him back. "Before you dash off, Gamil, could you do me one small favor?"

"Certainly, Your Eminence."

"Close all the windows and build me a fire. I am chilled despite the sun." Tavalisk watched as his aide went about piling logs upon the hearth. "No, no, Gamil. That won't do. You must first strip the logs of their bark. I know it will be time-consuming, but there's no point doing a task if you're not prepared to do it properly."

Baralis was among the last to crest the rise. What little protection the slope of the hill had afforded was snatched away, and the north wind cut deeply once more. Absently, he massaged the gloved fingers that held the reins. This journey was yet another toll upon them. The frost had worked its insidious trade upon his joints, robbing him of precious mobility. It seemed that his hands always paid the highest price for his actions.

His position on top of the bluff did offer some consolation for the discomfort of the wind. It gave him a clear view down upon the whole of the column. He spied Maybor immediately. No drab traveler's clothes for him. Even on a long and hazardous journey like this, the portly lord still insisted on being decked out like a peacock. Baralis tasted bile in his mouth. He was not one to spit it out, so he let it run its course upon his tongue, burning the tender flesh. How he hated that man!

He scanned the lay of the land. There were rocks beneath the snow; their jagged edges biting through the white. The downslope was more treacherous than the rise. The path twisted and dipped to accommodate the disorder of the rocks. Baralis could see that the men ahead were picking their paths carefully.

The time was right. Maybor was still only halfway down the slope. A fall from his horse at such a place, amongst a setting of rocks and sudden drops, would surely lead to death. The man's thick and hoary neck would snap like tinderwood when it hit the cold hard earth.

Baralis checked his own path. There would be a short time when he would be in danger, too. Such a drawing as he would perform required great concentration, and so he might need some extra guidance for his horse.

He looked to his flank. Crope was there, sitting miserably on a huge warhorse, hood pulled forward for concealment, not warmth. Baralis knew his servant was hating every minute of this journey. He was shy of people, a natural wariness springing from the way he was usually treated by them. People were afraid of him when alone or in small groups. Once they had a safe number, however, they began to despise him. Even on this trip, the taunting had begun. They called him "the stupid giant" and "scar features." Baralis would have enjoyed burning the skin from their cowardly backs—no one demeaned anything of his—but now was not the time to use indiscreet force.

Now was the time for discreet force. He beckoned Crope forth and the huge man drew close. Baralis motioned to his reins and his servant took them. Not a word was said, not a question asked. They were at the rear with only the packhorses to tell of what transpired.

Once confident that Crope was in charge of his mount, Baralis felt safe to work his drawing. His sight found Maybor and then dropped lower to the man's horse: a beautiful stallion in its prime.

Baralis reached deep within himself. The power, so familiar, yet so intoxicating, flared up to meet him. He felt a wave of nausea followed by the unbearable sense of loss as he forsook himself and entered the beast. The sour tang of horse sweat met his nostrils. Gone at last was the chill of the wind. He knew only warmth.

Pulsing, all-enclosing warmth. Through hair and skin and fat, through muscle and grizzle and bone. Speed was of the essence: danger awaited those who lingered too long in a beast. Quickly he bypassed the belly and all its beguiling intricacies. Up toward the core. He felt the mighty press of the lungs and fought against their powerful suction. The heart beckoned him forth, using its rhythm as a lure. The rest of the body danced to its beat.

Bounded by muscle, snarled with tubes, terrifying in its strength: the heart.

He fell into the pulse of its contractions, became one with the ebb and the flow. Into the hollow he went. A frightening rush of blood and pressure rose to meet him. Through the caverns he traveled, along the channels he sped, until he eventually reached the last. The beginning of the cycle. He found what he came for: a stretch of sinew as tough as old leather, yet thinner, so much thinner, than silk. The valve. He reached out, encircling it with his will. And then rent forth.

Back he snapped like a sapling in a gale. It was so cold and pale, and finally so dark. He tasted the bitter residue of sorcery in his mouth, and then he knew no more.

Maybor was well satisfied with the way things were progressing. He was at the head of eight score of men, counting the attendants, and if he did say so himself, their loyalty—bar only two—was unquestioningly with him.

He saw the respect in the men's eyes and noted their deference to him in all matters. It was just how it should be; after all, he did hold superior rank. He noticed the way the men admired everything from his judgment to his fineness of dress. Not for him a dull traveler's gray. No. He was a great lord and it was fitting that he look the part at all times. Who could guess when they might chance upon someone in this white wilderness whom he might need to impress?

Traveling had definite drawbacks, though. The wind was a devil, and he was quite sure it was blowing the very hair from his scalp. He'd awoken on several mornings to find hair on his pillow. The thought of going bald terrified Maybor, and deciding that it was indeed the fault of the wind, he had taken to wearing a large, furry bearskin hat as protection. At first he had been a little worried about how he might look to his men in such a girlish thing as a hat. But now he'd decided that he looked like a legendary invader from beyond the Northern Ranges and fancied that it added to his mystique.

Borc, but he needed a woman! Three weeks celibate! It was enough to drive a lesser man to perversion. Not him, though. If he couldn't have a woman, then he preferred to drink himself into oblivion each night. Unfortunately oblivion had its price. His head felt dull and heavy from too much ale, and he had to concentrate to sit his stallion in the manner that befitted a lord.

To add to his troubles, the path they were traveling was steep and treacherous. He hated riding downward. He preferred not to see the perils, just take them blindly. However the way was so twisting and precarious that he was forced to bend all his concentration to the task in hand.

They had just come upon a particularly hazardous trail, and were forced to ride one man at a time, when Maybor felt his horse grow skittish. He pulled hard on the reins. This was not the time for the creature to misbehave. He advanced a few feet farther and then he felt the stallion tremble and lurch. The creature tossed its head and tried to buck the lord from his back. Maybor was having none of this and pulled on the reins with all his might. The horse became frantic and broke into a gallop. Maybor could feel the wild pounding of its heart beneath his thighs. Down the path it sprinted, forcing two other riders out of its way. Maybor was becoming scared. He held on as the horse picked up speed.

Then, suddenly, in a scintilla of an instant, the horse dropped beneath him. Maybor was flung forward by the force of his own momentum. He flew through the air and then down the hillside. His body was thrown against rocks and stones. Pain burst into his leg and back. Downward he careened toward a sheer drop.

He saw it coming and knew what it meant. He sped toward his end with a prayer on his lips. Then he hit a rounded boulder. The rock bounced him like a ball and altered his course. Instead of taking the drop, he landed, *crash,* in the middle of a growth of thorny bushes.

His head was reeling, his leg splitting with pain. Thorns bit into his flesh, perilously close to his vitals.

Then the men were upon him, helping him up and fussing and squawking. "Lord Maybor are you all right?" said one sap-faced boy.

"Of course I'm not all right, you fool! I've just been hurled down a hillside!" And then, as two others tried to pull him up, "Careful, you idiots. I am not a wishbone to be pulled."

"Is anything broken, my lord?" ventured one of his captains.

"How in Borc's name would I know if anything is broken? Get me the surgeon."

The captain conferred with a junior for a moment. "The surgeon is awaiting your pleasure where the ground is more stable."

"You mean he is too lily-livered to risk his neck by coming down here." Maybor slapped hard at the man who was trying to free his leg from the bush. "Tell the good surgeon that if he doesn't get down here this instant, I will personally perform on him the only operation I know how to: *castration!*" Maybor made sure his last word had enough strength to carry up the hillside.

Eventually he was freed from the bush and placed on a litter. Two soldiers carried him back to the path. The party had halted and tents were being raised. The first tent up was the surgeon's and Maybor was duly ushered in.

"So tell me, physician. Are there any bones a'broken?" Maybor was in considerable pain, but was not about to betray that fact to anyone else.

"Well, my lord, these things are hard to ascertain—"

"All you damned physicians are the same," interrupted Maybor. "Mincing around the facts. Never committing yourselves to anything more than a maybe. *Aagh!*" The last syllable was uttered as the surgeon removed a long spiky thorn from the lord's posterior. Maybor looked around in time to see a smug expression quickly concealed. "Are they all out, then?"

"Yes, my lord."

"Are you quite sure you wouldn't like a conference to confirm that? It sounded suspiciously like a straight answer to me."

The surgeon was impervious to Maybor's sarcasm. "Perhaps my lord might like to try and stand?" He helped Maybor to his feet, where, to the lord's astonishment, he found he could walk.

"It is as I thought," said the physician. "No bones broken." Maybor was about to point out to the man that he had thought no such thing, when the physician thrust a cup of foul-smelling liquid into his hand.

"Here, drink this," he said.

Maybor downed the concoction in one gulp. It tasted just like his first wife's holk: fishy and lacking the sting of a decent drink. He yawned. "What's this foul brew good for?"

"It's a sleeping draft. It'll make you drowsy in no time."

Maybor felt his lids growing heavy. Suddenly worried, he hobbled back to the stretcher. Laying himself down he said, "Am I that bad that I need to sleep like an old man on his deathbed?" Maybor's eyes began to close of their own accord. Just as he fell into a warm dark trance, he could have sworn he heard the physician reply:

"No, you'll survive either way. But with this method I'll get some peace."

Two

*B*ren, the fortress city. The rock of the north. Set between the mountains and the great lake, Bren was built only for war. The mountains flanked the west and south, the lake lay to the north. The only clear approach to the city was from the eastern plains. And never was there a more carefully constructed site than Bren's eastern wall. It was designed with one basic function: to promote fear in the eyes of all who approached. Its granite towers pierced the clouds, issuing an unspoken challenge to God in his heavens. The mountains, from their position behind the city, seemed to back up this challenge like sentinels.

The outer wall was as smooth as a blade; the individual stones almost undetectable. The mason's art had reached its highest pinnacle in Bren. The walls gleamed with arrogance. They mocked all who approached, saying "scale me if you dare." Cleverly designed recesses caught shadows in the morning sun. A sharp eye could detect their presence, but a keen mind only guess at their uses.

Probably for pouring hot oil and the like, thought Nabber. Or to conceal a well-placed archer. He whistled in appreciation. They had no such fancy stuff in Rorn.

The boy joined the throng of people lining up to enter the city. He took off his cloak, reversed it so that the scarlet lining was on the inside once more, and put it back on. He had need of some coinage, and at such times it was best not to be too conspicuous.

He did a quick scan of the people waiting to walk through the gate. Not much prospecting here, that was sure. A distinctly mottled and poor-looking lot; farmers and beggars and worse. Not a plump and well-fed merchant among them. Just his luck, he'd picked the wrong gate.

"Here you," he cried to the tall, lanky guard who was on his side of the gate. "Yes, you, string-o-beans."

"What d'you think you're doing addressing the duke's guard in that manner?"

"Sorry, my friend. I meant no offense. Where I come from, calling a man string-o-beans is considered a compliment." Nabber beamed brightly at the guard and waited for the inevitable question.

"Where d'you come from then?"

"Rorn. The finest city in the east. A place where men who are as unusually tall and lanky as yourself are in great demand with the women."

The guard's face registered interest and disbelief in equal measure. He sighed heavily. "What d'you want?"

"Information, my good friend."

"Not a spy, are you?"

"Of course I am. Been sent by the archbishop of Rorn himself."

"All right, all right. None of that lip, or I won't let you pass."

Nabber smiled his winning smile. "Where do all the merchants enter the city?"

"What's that to you?"

"I lost my gaffer, that's what." Nabber was never caught short of a quick story. "Fur merchant, he is. I wondered where the best place to look for him is."

"The northeast gate is where all the merchants pass. Two courtyards south is the traders' market. You might find him there."

"I'm in your debt, my friend," said Nabber. "Though I wonder if I might impose upon your extensive knowledge of the city for a moment longer."

The guard fell for the flattery. "Go on."

"Well, situated as you are, in a most important post, you must see a lot of the people who enter the city?"

"That I do."

"Well, there's an acquaintance of mine, whom I have good reason to believe may have come this way. I wonder if you might have seen him."

The guard's face hardened. "I'm not supposed to give out information like that to foreigners. Who passes these gates is Bren's business, not yours."

"Suppose I was to tell you that this man has robbed a great deal of money from my gaffer? We both know that there ain't anyone more wealthy or generous than a fur merchant." Nabber resisted the urge to speak further and allowed the guard to come to his own conclusions. Which he did.

"Reward, is there?"

"Ssh, my friend. Speak that word any louder and half the city will be after it."

"How big is this reward?"

"I don't like to mention exact figures, if you know what I mean." Nabber waited until the guard nodded. "But suffice to say, there'd be enough to set you up real nice for your retirement. Even go to Rorn, you could. A man as handsome as yourself is wasted in this city."

"How do I know you're speaking the truth?"

"Do I look clever enough to fool you?"

The only answer the guard could possibly give was "No."

"Right," said Nabber. "This man I'm looking for is taller than you, but not as lanky. Broad, he is, and well muscled. Blond hair, blue eyes, handsome, if you like that kind of thing. Wearing a cloak like myself, he would be."

"What would he be doing wearing a cloak like yours?" The guard was suspicious.

"He stole it from my gaffer, of course. My gaffer always likes to dress me like himself, says it makes for better business recognition." Nabber sent a silent prayer of thanks to the fictional fur merchant who was turning out to be so useful.

The guard took a step back, scratched his chin, looked at Nabber, looked at the ground, looked toward the east. Finally he spoke. "There *was* a man fitting your description. Entered the city on horseback about five days ago. Tall and blond, he was. Right mean-looking, too." He thought a moment longer. "And come to think of it, he did have a cloak like yours. I remember the bright red lining."

It took all of Nabber's considerable powers of self-control to stop himself from heaving a massive sigh of relief. The memory of Swift's voice echoed in his ear: *"Nonchalance, boy, never show interest. Let them think you're a fool, rather than know you're a rogue."*

Nabber shrugged. "Could be our man. Do you happen to know which part of the city he headed for?"

The guard looked a little disappointed at Nabber's casualness. "There's no way of knowing that, boy. In a city the size of Bren, a man might go unseen for a lifetime."

"Five days ago, you say? Is there anywhere in the city where a man with a strong arm and a skill for using weapons might head?"

"In my experience, men like that blond no-hope end up in one of two places: the brothel or the fight pit."

"Where might I find either of those establishments?"

"On any street corner in the west of the city."

Nabber was itching to be on his way. "So, my friend, give me your name so I can let my gaffer know who it was who gave me the tip-off."

"Longtoad."

"My, my. I see you have a name as handsome as your figure. Well, Longtoad, I'll be sure to pass on the good word." Nabber sketched a hasty bow and was about to retreat when the guard laid a hand upon his shoulder, gripping his flesh through the cloak.

"Not so fast, you little devil. I want to know the name of your gaffer the fur merchant—and your own name, for that matter."

"Steady on the fabric, Longtoad. This cloak cost a fortune." The guard relaxed his hold. "Now then, my gaffer's name is Master Beaverpelt, and me, I'm known as Woolyhair. Just ask any fur trader; the name Beaverpelt is a byword for quality throughout the Known Lands."

The guard released his grip on the boy. "Beaverpelt. Ain't never heard a name like that before. You mark my words, boy, if I find you've been oiling my rag, I'll hunt you down, then string you up. Now move along sharpish."

Nabber saluted the guard and then slipped into the crowd. He crossed the threshold of the east gate and entered the city of Bren. The first thing he did was sniff the air. Nothing. Where was the smell? Rorn reeked of filth and the sea—where was Bren's smell? He took another deep breath, drawing the air into his nostrils like a connoisseur. There was no smell. How could Bren call itself a city and yet have no odor of its own? Nabber had been to Toolay, Ness, and Rainhill: they all had their own unique smells. He was disappointed. The stench of a city was its signature; a way to tell the nature of the place and its people. To Nabber's mind, there was something decidedly furtive about a city that had no smell.

A man jostled against him, muttering curses and warnings. He was tall and dark, his tunic stretching tautly across a finely muscled chest. Nabber couldn't help himself. With one fast and fluid motion, he reached inside the man's tunic. His hands closed around a bundle. He snatched his arm back and then turned into the crowd. He didn't look back. Swift had warned him many times about the dangers of looking back. He didn't speed his pace, either, once again heeding Swift's advice: *"Be a professional at all times, boy . The moment you break into a run is the moment you admit your guilt."*

Nabber went with the crowd as far as it suited him and then slipped into a timely alleyway. Bren might have no smell, but at least it boasted some decently dark and fiendish passages. Nabber began to feel more at his ease as he walked through the gaps between buildings: this was familiar territory.

He trod paths that had been trodden many times before by people more desperate than himself, and fell under shadows that had cloaked those with more need for concealment than a simple pocket from Rorn. Nabber was right at home. He came across other people lurking in the alleyways and either tipped them a nod if they looked friendly, or averted his eyes if they looked dangerous.

Finally he came upon a suitably isolated recess. Crouching down, he reached in his sack and pulled out the bundle. This was the best part, right before the unraveling, when anticipation met need. With practiced hands he undressed the package. The cold glint of silver met his eye. He was disappointed; better the warm glow of gold. Still, coinage was coinage. Pity about the mark, though, for he had the look of one who held gold somewhere on his person. Probably strapped to his thigh, close to his vitals. Few pockets were ever desperate enough to venture *there*.

Nabber sighed with the regret and rummaged through the contents of the sack. A lot could be learned about a man from the bundle he carried. This one would have eaten a cold—and Nabber discovered rather tasteless—game pie for dinner. However, the man was used to good things, for the bundle was lined with silk. He'd also been hoping to get lucky, for there was a sheep's bladder beneath the pie, oiled and ready to use. The man either had an aversion for fatherhood or a fear of the ghones.

Nabber pulled absently on the bladder, deciding its worth. There was no resale value, but he was loath to throw anything away, so he tucked it into his pack. Perhaps he could give it to Tawl when he found him. A handsome man like his friend always had women a'queing. Unfortunately the women who were the most willing were usually the most catching. A man had need of a sheath with girls like that.

Nabber was just about to discard the bundle when something blue and shiny caught his eye. Closer inspection revealed a tiny miniature tucked away in the corner. He freed it from its hiding place and brought it into the light. He whistled in appreciation. The girl in the painting was quite a beauty: golden hair, blue eyes, lips as soft as freshly hung tripe. The dark man with the muscles had a fine taste in ladies, if not food. Flipping the miniature over revealed writing on the other side. Nabber was no scholar, so the text remained unread, but he could recognize crosses that marked kisses as quick as the next man. With a shrug, he pocketed the portrait and turned his eyes to the pie.

Nabber finished it off and wondered what his next move should be. He had need of more money, as his contingency had been sadly depleted due to his stay in Rainhill. Dicing had ever been his downfall, that together with his tendency to order extravagant meals at even more extravagant inns, had rendered him penniless. He'd even had to sell his pony. Though, granted that wasn't a great sacrifice. Never had there been a more mutually agreeable parting than the one between Nabber and his horse.

So, he needed coinage. And a few well-worn silvers just weren't enough for a boy with expensive tastes like himself. He also needed to find the knight.

Tawl was somewhere in the city, he was almost certain of it. The guard at the gate had merely confirmed his suspicions. Nabber had followed the knight's trail for over three weeks now, visiting villages that Tawl had passed through, following paths that Tawl had ridden on. Nabber had talked to countless strangers about the knight, and if they'd seen him pass they remembered a man with golden hair and dangerously blank eyes.

Tawl needed him. It wasn't in the boy's nature to ask too many questions, so he didn't dwell on the reason why. He just knew that the knight was in trouble and required rescuing. Nabber was the one who would step in and do the job.

He knew that Tawl had been on some heroic quest, the sort that knights were always on, and he feared that his friend might have given up his duty. Nabber considered it his responsibility to put the knight back on track. It was different for him: once a lowlife, always a lowlife. He had no desire to be anything other than a pocket, unless of course it was to be a *rich* pocket. But Tawl, well, he was noble and honorable, and it just wasn't right that he should go astray. Who could tell? By helping his friend, he might be helping himself. Quests were notorious money spinners.

He looked up past the darkened buildings to the sky above. It was already past midday; time to get a move on. In his experience, it was at about this time that merchants, with a full morning of trading behind them and before they'd had chance to spend their profits in the taverns, had the fullest pockets. Nabber struck a path toward the northeast gate, where, if memory served him, the traders' market was held. Opportunity beckoned and he was never one to ignore the call.

"I'm just going out for a minute. I need to stretch my legs." Jack knew Melli would protest.

"But the blizzard's still raging. You'll catch your death," she said. "Can't you wait and see if it clears up a little first?"

She was worried about him, he could tell from the set of her mouth: soft lips drawn to a hard line. Well, she would just have to worry; he needed some air. Four days holed up in a chicken coop had taken their toll. He had to be outside, see the expanse of the land rather than the enclosure of the walls. He needed to be by himself.

He didn't want to hurt Melli by telling her that, so he said, "Nature calls."

A flush came to her cheeks, but even her embarrassment at the mention of such an indelicate subject was not enough to forestall a warning. "Don't venture far."

Jack couldn't help but smile—a man could love a woman like that. "Don't worry," he said, "I won't be gone long." Their eyes met and, as if something in her gaze compelled him, he stretched out his hand. It hung in the air between them until her hand stretched out to meet it. Her fingers were cool and her touch light, but it was enough for Jack, who knew little of such things. He resisted the urge to squeeze and enfold her hand: he didn't want to risk rejection. So he withdrew quickly and, he knew, awkwardly from her touch.

They had been together many months now, and although shared danger had brought them closer, there would always be a distance between them. She was a noblewoman and he was a baker's boy, and they could travel hand in hand for a lifetime and still end up a world apart.

Night after night they had spent huddled close with only a stretch of blanket between them. Jack knew how she smelled in the morning; he'd seen her laugh and shout, but never cry. He knew just enough about her to realize that she would never be for him. There would be no future in a relationship between them; love, there might be, but that wouldn't be enough for either of them. He needed a girl who he could hug and kiss and fight with. A girl with spirit, like Melli, but one who didn't make him feel as if he were a clumsy country boy.

Jack turned to the door and began to force it back against the wind. A

flurry of snow gusted forth into the chicken coop. Jack looked back at
Melli before stepping out into the blizzard. She didn't smile. She stood
rigid with the gale blowing at her dark hair. Too beautiful by far for him.

The door closed with the cut of the wind the moment he let it go. Biting, terrible cold assaulted him, rife and sparring snow blinded him. He'd
only walked a few steps when his foot kicked something hard. He
crouched down and felt what it was. The body of the man he'd killed four
days ago. It had to be moved. For Melli. He wouldn't let the first thing she
saw once the storm passed be a dead man.

Hands already graying with cold sought out the collar of the dead
man's tunic. The body was embedded deep within the snow and took all
of Jack's strength to free it. With grim determination, he began to drag the
body along the ground. The snow was nearly two feet deep and the corpse
cleaved through it like a plow.

Another man dead. How many more would he kill? At least this had
been a clean death. No taint of sorcery had marked this man's end. He'd
killed with a blade and there was more dignity in the death because of it.
Or was he fooling himself? Did it make any difference to the Halcus soldier? Sorcery or blade, he was still dead. The mourning would be the
same.

Jack's arms began to ache. His back felt like it would break. His hands
had passed through gray to blue, and he knew enough about the cold to
realize that frostbite would soon follow. Dragging the man's body through
the snow was his penance. Master Frallit had told him many times that a
man should pay for his mistakes. If he cut too much butter into the dough
and it baked closer to a cake than a loaf, the master baker would allow him
nothing to eat for a week except the ruined bread. Jack had resented Frallit's hard ways at the time, but now he grasped on to the idea of atonement
with an eagerness born of self-reproach.

He was a baker's boy, not a murderer. Everything was so different
from what he was used to. It was as if his life was no longer under his control. Ever since the morning when he'd burned the loaves, he found himself doing things out of character. He had killed someone for shelter. What
gave him the right to put his needs above someone else's? There was
Melli, of course: he would have killed a hundred men to give her safe
haven. But if he were honest, it was more than just Melli. Four days back,
when he'd forced the door of the chicken coop and found two men poised
with knives drawn, he'd discovered something very hard and unemotional inside of himself: the will to survive.

It was what had driven him through the freezing plains of Halcus, and what would make him continue on no matter what he faced. Perhaps the incident with the loaves hadn't changed him in any way, merely brought something out in him that was already there. His mother was strong. Even toward the end, when her body failed, her strength of will was breathtaking. She refused the help of the physicians and would not take anything to dull the pain that might dull her wits as well.

Only in her case it seemed as if she didn't want to survive.

Jack's fingers were frozen to the dead man's collar, but it was not the cold that chilled to the bone. A fragment of memory, more tenuous than a wisp of snow, filtered down through the accumulated recollections of eight years past. A snatch of conversation, not meant for his ears:

"She's a tough one, that's for sure."

"Aye, but if she won't let them slice her, she'll be a gonna just the same."

"Not a chance of that, friend. She won't even take a poultice to stay the growth, let alone take a knife to cut it out."

He hadn't even understood it at the time, and the years had conspired to make him forget, but today, dragging a body to a place fit for the dead, he realized what it meant: *his mother had wanted to die*. Her will, so much more than a match for his own, had been directed toward death not survival.

The wind keened sharp and relentless. The dead man pulled at his back. He was so weary; there was too much he didn't understand. If he looked for answers, he found heartache instead. Why had she wanted to die? Was her life in the castle so bad? Or was he just a worthless son? He missed her so much. She was the only person who was truly his, only now it seemed she'd forsaken him. Just as his father had done.

It would be so easy to give everything up, to lie down in the snow beside the dead man and keep him company in the world beyond. Jack stopped for a moment, watching the cool cheek of the horizon, as he tried to swallow the lump in his throat. There was no question, really; he had to continue. Fate was at his heels and it guided his feet forward to the dance.

On Jack walked, the dead man in his wake, back doubled up with the burden.

The wind was with him, bearing him along from the coop. It blustered and howled, hamming up its part in the drama, and the snow formed a backdrop with its silent display. Jack looked back. He was now a fair distance from the little wooden shack. It wasn't far enough. He couldn't leave the body within sight of the coop. He owed it to the dead man.

Finally he came upon a copse of trees that were camouflaging a slight depression in the land. He drew close, breath short and ragged from the strain of dragging the body, and saw that a frozen pond formed the center of the dip. This was where he would leave his burden.

He slid down the slope and the dead man followed. The ice was as hard as stone. Jack pushed the body toward the middle of the surface and folded the dead man's arms across his chest. He stood above him and watched as snow gathered once more upon the cold flesh. The body began to take on the look of a stone carving. The snow shone upon the flesh like silver filings: adorning, ennobling. Satisfied that he had managed to give the man at least a semblance of dignity, Jack turned and scaled the slope.

Only when he reached the top did he allow his hands the shelter of his cloak. As he emerged from the tangle of bush and tree, he spied the coop in the distance. Something dark moving from the west caught his eye. He couldn't gain perspective for a moment and thought it was a flock of birds, or a even a herd of cattle. His vision crystallized, and in that instant his heart missed a beat. The sensation was nothing like the dreamy descriptions given by love poets. It was hard, jolting, throwing his whole body out of kilter, unsettling his very core.

The dark mass was mounted men, the Halcus, and they were heading toward the chicken coop. Toward Melli.

One step forward and then Jack felt the sliver of a blade upon his throat.

"Take another step and you're dead."

Melli was beginning to feel worried. Jack had been gone too long. There had been something odd about him when he left, and for one horrible moment she'd had the feeling that she wouldn't be seeing him again. Such fancies were pure foolishness, she told herself as she paced the meager length of the coop.

The past weeks had been the most strenuous in her life, taking their toll not only from her body but her mind as well. She dreaded to think what the rigors of winter had done to her face and was glad there was no mirror to confirm her suspicions. More important than that, though, was the loss of her peace of mind. Such an overused and undervalued phrase. Peace of mind was as simple as falling asleep and knowing there would be a hot drink waiting when you awoke, and as precious as seeing your worth in the eyes of the ones that you loved. It was, when one got down to the root of it, the assurance of stability. The comfort of knowing things would always being the same. Now, for her, there were no such assurances.

She unplugged the knot hole and looked out onto the blank snow, looking north and then west. She didn't believe her eyes at first. Although she had looked to the west for the past four days with the sole intent of spotting the enemy, now that she actually saw them coming, they seemed to be an appalling trick of fate. Like a child, she had supposed that watching for them would keep them away. She did not have time to mourn the loss of yet another stolen assurance.

Judging from their distance, she had a minute or two to make ready. Melli could not allow herself to think of Jack, she must think only of herself. She was the measure of her own worth now, and the subtle and unbendable arrogance that only comes to those who are born into a world of high privilege enabled her to value herself highly.

Rummaging through her scant possessions, she found the small food knife that the old woman pig farmer had given her. It was half the size of the pig-gutting knife and not nearly as sharp. There was no sense in her challenging a whole group of men with such a weapon. She decided to conceal the knife and use it later when the odds against her lessened. That was if the odds were given a chance to lessen.

Melli wouldn't allow herself to think like that. She would not give in to fear. She would meet the enemy with head held high. Let them know that the women of the Four Kingdoms were a force to be reckoned with, just like the men.

She hid the knife in her bodice, thinking luck was once again with her. She was still wearing the old-fashioned dress that the pig farmer had given her. Unlike her own stylish court dresses, this had an out-of-date boned corset. So stiff and dense was the area between waist and breast that the hardness of a small knife might go undetected among the bones.

The noise of the riders could now be heard and Melli grew afraid. Her hands fluttered nervously to her face and then her bodice. Her cloak! She would put on her cloak. She could barely tie the fastening, so violently were her hands shaking. Her stomach was an empty hollow and it pulled at her nerves like hunger.

The door burst open. Two men stood in the threshold and more behind them. "Where is the bastard?" demanded the first, the tallest.

Melli clasped her hands tightly together, tilted her chin, and said with all the bravado she could muster, "Which bastard?"

The man's face momentarily registered confusion. He was quick to recover his equilibrium. "Don't trade words with me, girl, lest you'll speak yourself into the grave." He dropped his voice an octave lower and Melli recognized the modulated tones of unquestioned authority. "Now then. Tell me where the boy is who killed one of my men." An abrupt hand gesture brought the second man forward. He was wielding a leather-bound club.

"Why, gentlemen, I was hoping you'd be able to tell me where he is, for I'm damned if I know." Melli could see surprise on the men's faces. She seized her advantage and continued. "Walked out on me, he did, just this morning. Stole all my money. When you eventually find him, I'd be glad if you could give him a few extra blows just for me."

Another man forced his way in—the place was getting decidedly crowded—and Melli recognized him as the one who had escaped from the coop four days back. Her heart sunk as he said, "Don't believe a word of it, Captain. She cried a warning to the mad devil. She's in league with him."

A trace of contempt could be seen in the face of the captain as his man spoke. "Well, girl," he said. "What have you to say to that?"

Melli got the distinct impression he knew she was lying and was merely amusing himself at her expense. She soldiered on regardless. "What is there to say, sir? Have you never disliked a man yet pulled him from the path of a horse anyway?"

The leader grunted. "I see the women of the kingdoms are as slick-tongued as the men are thick-headed."

"I can't speak for the men of my country," said Melli. "But on behalf of the women, I thank you. It must be a nice change for you to talk to a woman who does not whine like a goat."

The leader burst out laughing at this allusion to the complaining nature usually ascribed to the women of Halcus. He was about to speak when a voice called from behind:

"Captain! There's tracks in the snow. Looks as if something's been dragged away."

"The villain robbed my supplies," said Melli quickly. "Took a whole winter's worth of cheeses." She guessed Jack had done away with the body and knew that now was not a good time to mention it.

The captain ignored her comments. "How old are the tracks?"

"Fresh, I would say, sir. No more than an hour or two old."

"Well, follow them, you blasted fool! Take an extra five men." He turned to Melli. "I'll wait here with this little vixen. The rest of you outside."

Jack moved his head a fraction to look at his assailant. As he did so, he felt something press against the side of his throat. Only when a warm trickle of blood rolled down his neck did he realize he'd been cut. He was too numb from the cold to feel pain, so he had no way of telling how deep the wound was. A second knife pressed against his back.

"Don't move, or I'll kill you." The voice that spoke had an edge as hard as a blade. Jack stood perfectly still. The only thing he could see of the man was the white of his breath in the cool air.

Jack watched the riders approaching the coop. There were a full score of them. The wind, which had whipped and cut all morning, beating the snow into a frenzy, seemed to take a malicious delight in suddenly calming, allowing him a clear view of the little shack. He held his breath as the riders slowed and dismounted, and then one man kicked the wooden door open. Jack felt a pressure growing within: familiar, loathsome, yet strangely compelling. The taste was in his mouth, like copper, like blood: sorcery. It had been many weeks since he'd last felt its swell. He would not give in to it. As if seconding his unspoken resolution, his attacker jabbed the knife into his back. The press of the blade against his spine halted its flow.

Although he could not see the face of the man, he sensed a tension from him, perhaps in the increasing pressure of the knife. It occurred to Jack that although he spoke with the harsh tones of the Halcus, the man was not one of the group below and, in fact, did not want to be spotted by them.

Jack looked on as three men entered the coop. He could almost picture the scene. He had no doubt that Melli would meet the Halcus with dignity. She was, above all else, proud. But for all his confidence in her bearing, he knew it would mean nothing to hardened soldiers. They would do whatever they wanted.

At that moment the chicken coop, which was no more than a spot on Jack's vision, formed the center of his universe. If only he knew what was happening. If only he hadn't left. The tension became unbearable. He had to go to her. Or at least try.

He sprang forward. Free from the knife for only an instant, his attacker sprang with him. Before Jack knew it, the blade was against his body once more. Strange how the metal was warm despite the cold.

"Don't think you can run from me." The voice again, low and hard. "Is the girl in the shack worth losing your life over?"

Jack was just comprehending the threat behind the man's words when the scene below changed. Six men had mounted their horses and were beginning to follow the dead man's trail in the snow.

"Come." The man pushed Jack before him, forcing him in the opposite direction from the approaching riders. Jack caught a glimpse of one of his blades: it was curved and blackened, combining deadliness with show.

The pressure of sorcery which had been so overwhelming only minutes before had now dissipated, leaving a sick feeling in Jack's stomach. Strangely, he drew courage from its absence; it was better to meet his fate with his body as his sole weapon. Not entirely true. He remembered the pig-gutting knife tucked into the front of his belt. He would have a weapon after all. With stealth that would make a pickpocket proud, Jack drew his knife. He felt the lick of the blade upon his belly: the edge was still keen.

His attacker was quickening the pace. Hooves could now be heard plowing their way through the virgin snow. They emerged from the cover of the trees and two horses awaited.

"Get on the mare." The man accompanied this order with a push of his knife. Jack turned, blade in hand, and slashed at him. He was surprised to find a large but portly red-haired man as his foe. "You waste my time, boy," the man said, a trace of annoyance mixed with something suspiciously like amusement. "Well, come at me if you must, but make it fast. There's men approaching."

Jack suddenly felt rather foolish. He had no skill with the blade, and the man before him, although heavyset, seemed to have all the confidence and skill of a master. He moved his substantial weight from foot to foot with the grace of a dancer. Both short knife and curved sword drew subtle shapes of encouragement in the air. "Come, boy, don't prolong the inevitable."

Jack lunged forward, pig-gutting knife at what he hoped to be a threatening angle. The curved blade knocked the knife from his hand with a bone-shattering jolt. In that instant the short knife was upon his throat.

The man shook his head. "You shouldn't have been distracted by the sword, boy. It's the short knife that will always find you." He turned his head, intent on listening for the advancing riders. They were close now. "Well, I'm afraid I'm going to have to take drastic measures." With a flip of his wrist, the curved blade jumped into the air, spun around, and then landed blade in palm. Jack watched as the short knife was drawn back. Then unexpectedly, he felt a powerful blow to the back of his head. His skull cracked loudly, and the world began to fade away.

The last thing he heard before he passed out was the man saying: "Of course, you should never have been fooled by the short knife. It's the sword that will always get you."

"So," said the captain, "now that we're alone, perhaps you can tell me what a Four Kingdom's noblewoman is doing roaming around Halcus." He permitted his mouth the curve of smugness, while his fingers traced the line of his mustache, reworking the grease and making it gleam once more.

Melli was beginning to regret her flippant manner; all her clever words had led to this. If she hadn't piqued his interest, she would probably be outside being gagged and bound, and judging from her previous experiences with men, that would most definitely be preferable.

The coop now seemed unbearably small. The captain, leathers creaking with every breath, filled the room with the force of his presence rather than the fact of his body.

"Your tongue appears to have lost its speed," he said. "Am I to take it that you can't put on a performance without an audience?"

Melli knew the danger in being thought a noblewoman of the enemy. She would be tortured and raped, then when there was little of her left, she would be ransomed. Every day the enemy waited on the payment would mean one less finger. Two years ago the Lady Varella had been kidnapped from her husband's estates along the River Nestor. When she had finally been returned, she had only two fingers left. Three months later the woman had taken her life. Unable to grasp a dagger or measure poison, she had thrown herself into the bullpen and had been gored on the horns of her husband's mightiest bull. Melli shuddered at the remembrance. *She* would not be returned home fingerless.

She smiled coquettishly and thrust forward her bosom. "Why, sir, you do me an honor thinking me nobly born. Though of course my grandfather's uncle on my mother's side was said to be nephew of a squire." Melli judged a simpering giggle was in order and acted accordingly. "So, as you can see, I do have some claims on the blood."

"You expect me to believe this?" The captain's handsome face grew dangerous. "You think me foolish enough not to know when I'm in the presence of a woman of the blood? You need to work on your acting, my lady. Your voice gives everything away." He moved toward Melli and grasped her arm. The smell of leather and sweat surrounded her. "Give me the truth now, or pay the price for your lies."

Melli took shallow breaths. She didn't want to draw in his scent: such a personal thing, the smell of another. "You are a clever man, sir." Melli stretched a slow smile, giving herself time to think. "I am indeed a noble-woman . . . of sorts." She knew she had to devalue herself, to become a less alluring prize. The Lady Varella's husband had been a wealthy man, with an even wealthier family. "I am the daughter of Erin, Lord of Luff." Melli picked a well-known, poverty-stricken lord as her father. Besides his poverty, Luff was famous for his promiscuity and had fathered many bas-tards. "I am not of his wife's issue," she said, bowing her head.

"Luff's bastard, eh?" The captain squeezed her arm tighter. "Then what are you doing in Halcus?"

"I'm on my way to Annis. My father has a cousin there who is a dress-maker, and I am to be apprenticed."

"If your father thinks so little of you to send you to a trade, why then would he bother to have you versed in courtly manners?"

"*We* are not barbarians in the kingdoms."

The captain raised his hand and slapped her. Although she'd been expecting it, the blow still sent her reeling. She fell back against the wall of the coop and landed awkwardly in the matted straw. Her cheek was bright with pain, and when blood flowed to her skin it stung like vinegar.

"Watch your tongue, bitch." The captain stood over her, his elegant mustache framing his cruel mouth. "Seems you are of little worth, I best take my rewards where I find them." He leaned over her, his leathers straining and creaking, his mouth wet with saliva and mustache grease.

Melli was cornered. The walls were a prison, and the scratch of the dry straw was a torture. His mouth was on hers and tooth knocked against tooth. His lean tongue was in her mouth; its presence revolted her and she bit down upon it. The captain's free arm whipped back. Pain exploded in her abdomen. He punched her again, lower this time, in the vulnerable flesh between her hips.

"Don't act like a coy virgin with me," he said. "A daughter of a bas-tard has no business with shows of virtue. You've had men aplenty before." His hands were running down her bodice, searching for the ties.

The knife! She couldn't let him find the knife. She had to distract him.

"I am a virgin," she cried. To her own ears, this, the first truth that she had uttered in his presence, had the clear ring of conviction about it.

The captain backed away, almost imperceptibly. He reached out and took her chin in his hand, tilting her face to meet his. "Look at me and say that again."

"I am a virgin." Melli could not understand the man's sudden change of demeanor.

"I believe you speak the truth." He stood up and smoothed down his leather tunic. "So not all the women of the kingdoms rut like beasts, eh?" His eyes sharpened from the dullness of lust to the brightness of greed. Melli had lived long enough with her father to know when a man's face showed the knowledge of profit to be made. She was suddenly nervous, fearing that she had made a terrible error.

"What's it to you that I am a virgin?"

"I'm not about to answer questions from a bastard's daughter." A banging at the door diverted his attention. "Come."

The man who wielded the leather-bound club entered the coop. He spied Melli on the floor and smirked.

"Get up, bitch!" commanded the captain. He then turned his attention back to his second. "Have you picked up the murderer?"

"No. He got away."

"What d'you mean, got away?" The captain's voice was chilling in its calmness. "How can someone on foot outrun six mounted men?"

"He had some help. A red-haired man had two horses waiting. They rode like the devil."

"Red-haired, you say?" The captain's hand was back smoothing his mustache.

The second nodded. "There was something strange about the whole business. The boy was slumped over his horse."

"Was he wounded?"

"It's hard to say."

"You mean you never got close enough to get a good look." The captain shot a glance at Melli. "I suppose it would be useless to ask you about this red-haired man?"

Melli was experiencing a whirl of emotions: wonder at Jack escaping, worry that he might be hurt, curiosity over who the red-haired man might be, and fear about what bearing the incident might have on her own circumstances. To make things worse, the pain in her stomach and lower abdomen was excruciating. "I know nothing of a red-haired man."

"Mm." The captain appeared to make a decision. "Very well. For now we'll head back to the village. We'll mount a proper search for the boy once the storm gives."

"Why the rush, Captain?" said the second. "Why not finish your business here?" He looked pointedly at Melli. "And then maybe you'll be generous enough to share your fortune."

"No one will touch the girl. Understand, no one." The captain eyed the puzzled face of his second. "She is a virgin, Jared."

The second nodded with comprehension. "A mighty fine-looking one, at that."

"She's been court trained, too."

The second whistled. "Quite a prize."

The captain turned his attention back to Melli. "Can I trust you to ride on your own, or will I have to bind you like a thief?"

The exchange between the two men had filled Melli with apprehension. The combination of worry and punches made her feel sick. She was determined to show neither fear nor pain. "I will ride alone," she said.

Three

I tell you, Grift, being at the back is the worst thing. All we do all day is walk through piles of horse dung."

"Aye, Bodger. I know what you mean, but horse dung has its uses."

"What uses are those, Grift?"

"It can stop a woman from getting with child, Bodger."

"How does it work, Grift? Does it stop your seed from hitting the mark?"

"No, Bodger. Once it's up there, it smells so bad that it puts a man right off." Grift chuckled merrily. "Ain't nothing like not doing it for ensuring you won't become an unwilling father."

Bodger tried out his new skeptical look: raising his left eyebrow, while keeping his right one level.

"What's the matter, Bodger? You look like you're in the throes of painful indigestion."

Bodger quickly changed to an expression he was more comfortable with. "Mighty queer thing—Maybor's horse dropping dead the other day."

"Aye, but that wasn't the strangest thing to happen that morning, Bodger. Did you notice the way that Baralis near fell off his horse right about the time that Maybor's stallion hit the deck?"

"Aye. I saw that hooded giant Crope lift him right up and lay him on the ground. It was just as well that the captain decided to make camp then and there, for Lord Baralis was one man who wasn't fit for a full day's ride."

The attention of both men was diverted by the sound of swift horses approaching from behind.

"It's the two rear watches, Grift. Looks like they're bringing someone in."

"Damn! I hope it's not trouble with the Halcus."

"No, Grift. The third man's no Halcus." Bodger twisted in his saddle to get a better look at the approaching riders. "He's royal guard."

"Are you sure, Bodger?"

"Blue and gold under his cloak, Grift."

"I tell you, Bodger, if a lone member of the guard has been sent to catch up with us, it means trouble."

"What sort of trouble, Grift?"

"The worst sort, Bodger."

The two men fell into silence as the three riders passed them. The face of the newcomer was grim and unreadable in the thin light of morning. Grift saw a black-cloaked man break off from the column and make his way to the fore, where the riders were headed. "I see Lord Baralis is anxious to be let in on the news, Bodger," he murmured.

The column, abuzz with the arrival of the messenger, slowed to a halt. Grift looked on as the riders approached the front, where Maybor and his captains rode. The riders came to a halt. The messenger saluted. Words were spoken. Lord Baralis approached, and he and Lord Maybor were drawn aside by the messenger. Grift had a clear view of all three men, but could not hear what words were exchanged. Both lords looked tense and drawn. After hearing the man speak, Maybor nodded. The messenger drew closer to the column. In a loud and ringing voice, he proclaimed:

"The king is dead. Long live the king. Long live Kylock."

Jack was handed a chicken leg. "Eat," commanded the red-haired man, who he now knew to be called Rovas.

Jack had just awakened to find himself in a small three-roomed cottage. A fire burned brightly in the hearth and there were pots on the boil. From the light stealing in through the cracks in the shutters, Jack could tell it was midmorning. The collar of his tunic was rubbing against the cut on his neck, and his head was splitting with pain.

He looked at the leg of chicken. It seemed a strange breakfast, but he knew little of the ways of the Halcus. Most people in the kingdoms thought the Halcus were foul-mouthed barbarians. He took a bite of the chicken: it was tender and sharply spiced.

"Good, eh?" prompted Rovas, who was salting his own portion with an admirable lack of restraint. Salt was obviously not as expensive here as it was in the kingdoms. The red-haired man noticed Jack's gaze. "Not much salt in the kingdoms these days, eh?" he said. "What with those damned knights of Valdis controlling the supply, and then the war . . ." He shook his head. "There's not enough salt around to keep a powderer in business."

Jack, noting a certain smugness to the man's words, said, "You appear to be faring well."

"Isn't that always the way, though? A war means different things to different people. Take me: never had so much salt on my table since the war began. It's one of the perks. Here." Rovas pushed the salt bowl toward Jack. "By rights you should take some, seeing's this comes from a shipment that was bound for the kingdoms."

"So you're a thief?"

The man laughed: a robust and glorious sound. "Yes, you could say that. You could also say I'm a brigand, a bandit, a smuggler, a black-marketeer. Take your pick. I prefer to be called a beneficiary, though."

"Beneficiary?"

"Of the war." Rovas smiled, showing large, white teeth. "This war is one big wheat field ripe for the harvest. It would be a shame to let all the grain go rotten on the stalk, so I farm off the excess."

Jack knew self-serving rhetoric when he heard it. "Stealing other people's grain is the work of a weasel, not a farmer."

Rovas laughed again. "A weasel, eh? Just one more name to add to my list."

The red-haired man settled back to enjoy his breakfast. Despite his good humor, Jack could detect a certain nervousness in his bearing. His eyes kept flicking to the door as if he were expecting somebody. And, indeed, a few minutes later the door opened. A woman walked in. She was mature in years, but tall and finely featured. Disappointment flashed across Rovas' face.

"Have you seen any sign of her?" he asked the woman.

"No." They exchanged a tense look. The woman's face held accusation. Her hand twisted the fabric of her dress.

"I shouldn't have left her there," Rovas said.

"Doing things you should not is quite a habit with you," retorted the woman.

Jack tried to grasp what was familiar in the woman's voice. She didn't sound like Rovas, she sounded more like . . . Melli! That was it. She had the same kind of voice as the women at court. An accent like his own, but with the clipped and modulated tones of a noblewoman. He wondered how a woman of the kingdoms had come to live in the lap of the enemy.

"I begged her to ride at my back," said Rovas, "but she insisted I go alone."

"It was a close call?"

"Not so close that my horse couldn't have borne two."

The woman's knuckles were white as she grasped her skirts. "How many were there?"

"A score turned up at the coop. Six came after me and the boy." Rovas had apparently lost his appetite; he dropped the half-eaten chicken leg on the platter. "The last I saw of her, she was hiding in the gorse. It was freezing out there, Magra. If the soldiers didn't find her, the frost certainly did." He stood up and made his way to the fire.

"Do you think she will do anything foolish?" The woman looked quickly toward Jack.

Rovas' eyes followed her gaze. "I hope not. Someone else can do the job now."

Jack saw the look the two exchanged: it was loaded with silent messages. A conspirator's glance. He was beginning to feel wary. He wanted to be back with Melli again, to be on his way.

The woman called Magra poured herself a cup of steaming holk. She warmed her hands on its curves. Turning toward Jack, she said, "So this is the murderer?"

She looked at him closely, even to the point of drawing a candle nearer. Jack felt uncomfortable under her scrutiny, but made a point of meeting her gaze. After a moment she spoke up. "You have a look about you, boy, that is familiar to me."

Jack dreaded the coming question. In his experience remarks like that always led to inquiries about a person's family. He had no intention of sharing the shame of his parentage with the aloof and self-possessed woman standing next to him. He was saved the task of evasion by Rovas.

"Come, Magra," he said. "Sit down. You won't make your daughter come any faster by bothering the boy."

The woman gave him one final look. Despite the coldness of her eyes, Jack found himself feeling sorry for her. She was worried about her daughter, and he was merely providing a distraction. Sighing heavily, the woman lost a measure of her rigid poise; instantly appearing older and smaller. Drawing close to the fire, she sat upon a three-legged stool. Rovas crossed over to her and laid his huge hand upon her shoulder. Magra drew away from the touch, and Rovas was left standing awkwardly with his arm held out. He turned and rested his weight against the fireplace. As he did so, the woman's hand flitted up for an instant in a tiny gesture of reconciliation that went unseen. The two stayed that way for some time, the candle burning down a notch, the fire blazing on.

The door latch broke the spell. It rattled, then lifted, and a girl stepped into the room. No, once in the light, she was more than a girl. She was a woman. Jack looked on as Rovas and Magra rushed over to her. Rovas reached her first, his arms reaching out to envelop her in a bear hug. She was so slight, easily mistakable for a young girl, but Jack saw that she was older than he, probably by three or four years. She turned to her mother. There was a formality between the two women that was absent between her and Rovas. Still, there was a moistness to the mother's eyes. "I have been too long at the fire," she said when her daughter noticed.

"So," said Rovas, beaming brightly. "What kept you?"

All three broke into an uneasy laugh. To Jack, it was as if he were not in the room. He felt as if he was intruding; these were not his friends, these were not his joys to share. If anything, the arrival of the girl had made him angry. *They* were all right. The girl had made it back safely, their lives were unchanged. What about Melli?

"So, you see," the girl was saying, "I had to wait it out overnight, or the guard set to watch the chicken coop might have spotted me."

The girl had been within sight of the chicken coop! Things were beginning to fall into place: Rovas had brought him here on her horse, so she had been forced to hide from the soldiers, and then make it back on foot. Questions jumped to Jack's lips. Why had they taken him? Why had they acted against their own countrymen? And what did they want with him? More important than all that was the fact that the girl who just walked in had spent the night near the chicken coop.

"What happened to the girl in the coop?" he demanded, surprised at the venom in his voice.

All three turned to look at him. Jack caught the quick exchange of glances between Rovas and the girl—a warning given and received.

"She is dead," said the girl. "The captain ordered her to be clubbed to death, as befits an accomplice to murder."

Melliandra. His daughter would have been queen this day. What a fool she had been to run away. What a fool *he* had been to let her get away. She was a jewel, cut for royalty, polished for power, a fitting adornment for a king. He had not seen her in so long; how he missed her quick wit and sparkling eyes.

Feeling old and saddened, Maybor drew his cloak close. The snow had turned to sleet and was driving into his face. He was waiting for the tents to be erected. The tidings that the messenger brought were of such import that it was decided to set up camp then and there, and travel no more this day. This arrangement suited Maybor nicely; not only did he want to question the messenger further about the circumstances leading to the king's death, but also, since the fall from his horse and his subsequent painful landing in a thorn bush, riding had become rather painful. He was quite sure the physician hadn't pulled out all the thorns from his backside. It would be just like their kind. If they couldn't kill you outright with their cures, they always had other ways to make you suffer.

As for his horse dropping dead under him, well, just wait till he returned to Harvell. The horse dealer who'd sold him the stallion would find himself in line for a flogging if he didn't return the two hundred golds. Maybor grunted, sending whitened breath into the air. He would see to it that the dealer was flogged even after the money was returned; someone had to pay for his humiliation.

Maybor glanced toward Baralis. The black-cloaked lord was hovering like a vulture. It was obvious that he wanted to be the first to question the messenger. He probably supposed that as king's chancellor he had that right, but *he*, Maybor, was head of this party and he would decide the rules.

The steward came forward and informed him his tent was ready. Maybor instructed the man to fetch the messenger as soon as he was refreshed and out of his riding clothes.

"But, sir," said the steward, "Lord Baralis has requested his presence first."

Maybor pulled a gold coin from his doublet and pressed it into the soft flesh of the man's palm. "Here. See to it that the messenger comes to me first." The steward nodded and dashed off. Loyalty was one means of ensuring one's orders were carried out. Gold was another.

He stepped into his tent and set about stripping off his outer clothes. Just as he was struggling with the awkward back fastenings of his tunic, Baralis entered.

"Should I call a servant to help you?" he said, moving forward, his lips parting to show a rare glimpse of tooth. "I can see you're having trouble with those laces. I must say, I find it quite admirable the way you endure being laced into a garment like a girl." Baralis crossed over to the low table that had been set with food and drink, and poured himself a glass of wine.

Maybor was furious, but he had enough presence of mind to realize that he would look quite ridiculous getting angry while only half-dressed. He settled for an indignant snort and hurriedly donned one of his fur-lined robes.

In the wake of restored dignity came anger. "What in Borc's name are you doing here?" he demanded. "Leave my tent this instant."

"Or else?" Baralis didn't bother to look up. He was intent upon choosing a piece of dried fruit.

Maybor hated the cool arrogance of the man. "Come, now, Baralis. Is your memory so short that you can't recall how handy I am with a sword?"

"My memory is faultless, Maybor. However I don't perceive an old man with a sword to be much of a threat."

Old man! Maybor was prevented from issuing a scathing reply by the arrival of the messenger. The young man had changed his clothes and shaven his beard.

"I am pleased to find you both here," he said tactfully.

"Yes, it was good of Lord Maybor to offer his tent for this meeting," said Baralis. "Would you care for some refreshment?"

Maybor did not like this one bit. Baralis was acting like a benevolent host, and by doing so was giving the messenger the idea that he was in charge. Maybor decided to play the king's chancellor at his own game.

"Seeing as you are playing mother, Baralis, pour me a glass of wine and slice me some venison." He watched with glee as Baralis was obliged to comply with his request. "Such thin slices. I can see you have no taste for red meat." Baralis handed the platter to him. The meat was tough, but the look of indignation on Baralis' face was tenderizer enough.

"So, tell me, young man. What are you called?" Maybor was not going to allow Baralis to take the lead again.

"My name is Durvil, sir." The young man looked nervous. The undercurrent of hostility in the tent had not gone unnoticed.

"Well, Durvil. Tell me the exact manner of the king's death."

"He died in his sleep, my lord. A most peaceful death by all accounts. He was found by the Master of the Bath in the morning. He was already stiff and cold."

"Was the Master of the Bath present in the king's chamber all through the night?" asked Baralis.

"The Master of the Bath sleeps in a room just off the king's chamber, my lord."

"Foul play wasn't suspected?"

"No, Lord Baralis. No one could gain access to the king's chamber without being spotted by the royal guard."

"But still, the Master of the Bath was asleep all night?"

"Yes."

Maybor wondered why Baralis was so concerned with the possibility of foul play. The king had been a doddering, slavering invalid for over five years now; it was no surprise that he had finally done the decent thing and dropped dead. "Exactly how many days ago did this happen?" he asked.

"A week after you left, sir."

"So the king has been dead almost three weeks, then?"

"Yes, sir."

"How did the queen take the news?" asked Baralis. Maybor was rankled; the king's chancellor was asking better questions than he.

"The queen was most distressed. She locked herself up with the body and would not let anyone tend to it for over a day. In the end, the king had to order that she be taken away by force."

The king. It was a shock to hear it: Kylock now a king.

"Is the queen well? She is not being held?" Baralis again, always rooting deeper.

"No, sir. The king would not do such a thing to his mother." There was indignation in the messenger's words—already the new king was commanding a measure of loyalty. "The day I left, His Majesty was bidding her a fond farewell."

"Farewell?"

"Yes. The queen elected to leave the court and retire to her castle in the Northlands."

"Does it not strike you as strange that a woman, no longer young, would risk her health by embarking on such a long journey in the frozen grip of winter?"

Maybor had to admit that Baralis had a point there.

"No, sir. Kylock assured the court that it was what she wanted. He sent a handsome detachment of the royal guard to escort her."

"Hmm." Baralis allowed this skeptical syllable to hang in the air a moment before saying, "And what of Kylock? Does he still wish the proposed betrothal between himself and Catherine of Bren to go ahead?"

"Yes, indeed, my lord. He is most anxious for the union."

The look of relief on Baralis' face was fleeting but unmistakable.

"Surely now that Kylock is king, he has no need for two envoys?" An idea was beginning to form in Maybor's mind.

"His Majesty expressly bid me state that he still wanted both of you to serve as his envoys."

"I am king's envoy," said Maybor, feeling rather pleased with himself. "Lord Baralis is prince's envoy. Only there is no longer any prince."

"I beg your pardon, Lord Maybor," said Baralis, "but I believe I was appointed *Kylock's* envoy."

"Did the king express any wishes on the matter of who between us would take precedence?" Maybor was thinking that if Kylock had said nothing on the matter, that would mean things would go on as they were, with him as the superior envoy.

"King Kylock expressed the wish that you sort out such matters amicably between yourselves. He is confident in both your abilities to strike a favorable contract."

Maybor was not entirely happy with this reply, and he expected Baralis felt the same way. His confidence was still high, though. He was, after all, king's envoy. He took a deep draught of wine and settled back amidst the silken cushions.

He was surprised by Baralis' next question. "What were Kylock's first actions upon becoming king?"

"The king did everything expected of him, my lord. He kept vigil in the great hall and prayed for God's guidance."

"I don't want to know about all the ceremonies he was obliged to perform for show. Has he passed any laws? Taken any actions? Ordered any executions?" Maybor detected a certain anxiety behind Baralis' words.

"I was sent out two days after the king's death." The messenger's tone was one of subtle reprimand. "Kylock had not taken any actions. He was deep in mourning for his father."

"What of the war?" persisted Baralis.

"I believe the king did express the wish that the war finally be won."

Baralis, having squeezed this information out of the messenger, seemed to withdraw into himself. Maybor couldn't figure out what was so important about the statement. Surely it was only fitting that Kylock state his commitment to winning the war with the Halcus. If things had turned out differently, and he had been Kylock's father-in-law, he would have urged the new king to win the war as quickly as possible. In fact, it was high time the Halcus were sent back to their filth-ridden hovels once and for all. He had missed too many apple-growing seasons because of them.

"If you will excuse me, my lords, I will retire," said the messenger. "I have ridden a long journey and am weary to the bone."

Maybor nodded his assent, and the messenger bowed and then left.

Baralis stood up, smoothing his robes with his crooked hands. "I bid you good day, Lord Maybor," he said with a thin show of courtesy. As he passed by Maybor, he forced something cool and smooth into the lord's hands. "I believe you dropped this earlier."

After he'd left, Maybor opened his palm. In it was a gold coin. He did not need to look at it closely to know it was the same one he had given to the steward outside the tent an hour before.

Tavalisk was eating blood pudding. True, it was a peasant dish and therefore low on his list of culinary favorites, but every now and then he felt the need to delve into the fare of his childhood. His servants knew nothing about this, of course. He told them he occasionally ate such things as blood pudding and tripe to feel empathy for the peasants who were forced to live on such foods. He made sure this excuse was well publicized, and what had been a liability—his occasional yearning for foods from his impoverished youth—had now turned into an asset. The people of Rorn admired his attempts to eat as they ate; it added to his reputation as a man of the people. And Rorn was a city that was at the mercy of its people.

Tavalisk cut himself a portion of the pudding, marveling in its rich, black color. Blood, when dripped from a carcass, usually a freshly slaughtered lamb, was stirred over a flame until it thickened and turned black. Chunks of fat and seasonings were added, and the ingredients were then stuffed into a casing and boiled. When prepared correctly, the pudding should have a dense grainy texture that spoke of the grave.

Tavalisk spit out a chunk of fat. He was only interested in the blood.

The archbishop knew he should be a happy man; the interfering old fool Bevlin was finally out of the way. The wiseman had been a thorn in his side for years. Only now he found himself feeling rather apprehensive about the future: Bevlin was gone, events in Bren were moving swiftly, and the Knights of Valdis were a constant thorn in his side. Trouble that had been simmering for months, even years, seemed close to coming to the boil.

More and more, Tavalisk found his thoughts heading north toward Bren. The coming drama would be staged in that most deadly of cities. If Marod was right, *he* would have a leading part in what was to come. A tiny smile pulled at the corner of the archbishop's mouth. If Marod was wrong, then damn him! He'd still steal the show anyway.

A knock sounded and Gamil entered carrying Tavalisk's cat. Gamil's face was sporting a vicious and still bleeding scratch.

"I finally located your cat, Your Eminence."

"What took you so long? You've been gone for hours."

"The cat was hiding on the compost heap at the far end of the gardens, Your Eminence. It was most reluctant to be brought back."

The archbishop tempted the cat forward with a morsel of pudding. "Really, Gamil, it's most inconsiderate of you to bleed on my best silk rug."

Gamil hastily daubed the blood from his face with the corner of his robe. "I apologize for bleeding, Your Eminence."

"Good. Now, what news have you?"

"Well, our spies have tracked the knight as far as Bren. Apparently the young man is not acting like himself."

"Who, pray tell, is he acting like, then?" Bren again: its very name was enough to make the archbishop's heart beat faster. He reluctantly pushed the dish of pudding to one side; his physician had told him he was slightly overweight and should consider eating less. Advised him to take up music instead. Music, indeed!

"He's acting like a scoundrel, Your Eminence. Womanizing, drinking, brawling: causing trouble with every step."

"So he's actually having some fun for a change. He needed to loosen up a little, if you ask me. He was a little too noble for his own good." Tavalisk lifted a pudgy arm to the light. The porcelain-pale flesh wobbled like aspic.

"You don't think me fat, do you, Gamil?"

"No, Your Eminence. You have a most . . ." Gamil paused as he searched for the right phrase, ". . . a most magnitudinous bearing."

"Magnitudinous." The archbishop liked the sound of the word on his lips. "I think you're right, Gamil. I'm a long way from fat, I'm magnitudinous." He favored his aide with a smile. "So, back to other matters. What else have you for me this day?"

"Not much, Your Eminence. The young boy is still following the knight, and we still don't know why Larn arranged the assassination of Bevlin."

"Really, Gamil, sometimes I think you have the mental capacity of that pudding over there. It's obvious to me why Larn had Bevlin bumped off. Bevlin had been trying to put an end to the practices on the island for years now. The old fool was never happy unless he was imposing his moral values upon others. Personally, I think there is nothing wrong with being bound to a rock. I hear they get fed regular meals."

"Your Eminence is a great humanitarian."

"Alas, Gamil, it is a weight I have to bear." Tavalisk took a swing at the cat, sending it flying into the air. If *he* couldn't have any more pudding, then neither could his cat. "Any news of the knights?"

"Tyren is said to be fuming over the expulsions, Your Eminence. He may not take things as passively as we thought."

"*We* thought, Gamil. *We* thought no such thing. *I* thought they would be likely to treat the expulsions as a gauntlet thrown in their face, and it seems I was right. They will rise to the challenge."

"That could mean war, Your Eminence."

"Perhaps. We will have to wait and see how the north reacts." The archbishop smiled. "Anyway, I fear the whole thing may have been fated from the start."

"What gives Your Eminence cause for such thought?"

Tavalisk looked at Gamil a moment, considering. His fingers strayed to the book on his desk. These days Marod was never far from his reach. His aide looked a little too eager for Tavalisk's liking, so he shrugged negligently. " 'Tis nothing, merely a hunch," he said. "You must never forget that I am archbishop, Gamil, and therefore blessed with divine insight from time to time." He was not ready to share his revelation just yet. "Be sure to keep a careful eye on Valdis and Bren in the coming months, Gamil."

"Certainly, Your Eminence. If there is nothing further, I will take my leave."

"Just a quick word of advice before you go, Gamil. I'd get that cut seen to, if I were you. With a face such as yours, you can ill afford yet another disfigurement."

The door opened, and something was thrown at her. Melli panicked for a moment, thinking it a knife or a club. The object missed and landed on the ground beside her. It was a loaf of bread. Her captors were being most generous with their food. She had already been served three meals that day. Melli got the distinct impression she was being fattened like a feast-day goose. The way they were going, she'd be served buttermilk and pig fat next, to promote a shiny coat.

Melli was in a small, dark root cellar. She was alone and bitterly cold. She had been brought here the day before. The company had ridden up to a large garrison, and the captain had led her beneath the innermost building. He left strict orders with the guards to keep her well fed and not to come near her. The guards had complied. She had only seen their shadowy forms in the doorway as they pushed platters of food into the cellar.

She had spent a cold and lonely night huddled in a corner for warmth. Her one comfort was that at least Jack was free. Melli had noticed how little he liked being holed up in the chicken coop for a few days. To be stuck here, with no power to open the door, might have been too much for him.

Not for her, though. She was getting quite used to captivity. One way or another, she had been a captive all her life.

Melli knew she was lucky. She had talked herself out of the fate of Lady Varella. Whatever happened next, she could take comfort in the fact that she would have all ten fingers left to deal with it. Melli tore open the loaf and began to chew on the rubbery and over-yeasted bread. For the first time it occurred to her that what happened to Lady Varella was as much the fault of the kingdoms as the Halcus. If her husband had welcomed her back lovingly, instead of making her feel like a useless, hideous invalid, then she wouldn't have been driven to suicide. A woman in the kingdoms was only as valuable as her appearance, and a woman with two fingers couldn't even make herself useful at the spinning wheel—as was expected of those with no claim to beauty. So Varella had no value, and she knew it, and did the only decent thing she could do: remove the burden from her husband and family.

Melli heard the scuttle of a cockroach. As a child she'd been afraid of them. It was considered becoming for a lady to make a pretty show of terror whenever an insect was spotted. Young girls even went so far as to *choose* a specific insect that they simply could not bear the sight of. The smaller and more pathetic the insect, the more refined the lady. Melli stomped on the creature with her foot. Judging from the substantial cracking noise, it must have been a big one.

The door opened again. What next, she thought, a five-course dinner? A man stepped into the doorway; he was haloed by the light. The creaking of leathers told her what her eyes could not see: it was the captain.

"I hope my men are treating you well," he said.

"About as well as a farmer treats his prize heifer."

The captain laughed and stepped into the room. "Borc, 'tis cold in here. Have they refused you blankets?"

"I never asked."

"By my leave, you are a proud wench! It will prove your downfall if you do not stay the flow."

"If you have come here to exchange character flaws with me," said Melli, "then I suggest arrogance as one of yours."

The captain laughed once more. His hand stole to his gleaming mustache, which Melli was beginning to suspect served to hide less than perfect teeth.

She was desperate to know what was going to happen to her, but didn't want to betray her anxiety to the captain. Instead, she said, "I hope you don't plan to keep me here long, as the dark robs me of my appetite and good looks. I'm sure you wouldn't like an ugly, scrawny stray on your hands."

"My dear lady, you do yourself an injustice. I would say your beauty is enhanced by the dark, like a wine in a cellar."

"Some wines turn to vinegar if left too long."

"You will not be left too long. By the morrow you will be on your way."

"Which way is that?"

"Eastward is the usual route." The captain shrugged. "Whatever way, it is no concern of yours."

"How so?" Melli was beginning to feel anger at his smugness.

"Spoils of war, my dear. You're mine to do with how I please." With that the captain executed a singularly contemptuous bow and walked over to the door. "And it pleases me to make a healthy profit." He stepped from the room and closed and locked the door behind him.

Melli's hand stole toward her side. She felt the fabric of her dress and then the hardness of the boned corset. Just above her waist, her fingers found what they'd been searching for: the knife. It was still there, pressed against her rib cage. Blood-warm and metal-smooth, it was now her only comfort; whatever happened next, at least she had a blade.

Four

"*R*otten lamb! Rotten pork! Bring your rotten meat here!"

Nabber was intrigued by this call and pushed through the crowds toward the man who was shouting. "What d'you want with rotten meat?" he asked. Nabber was always open to the possibility of a new ploy.

"Have you got any?"

"No."

"Well, don't stand around wasting my time then."

"I could get some, though. If you make it worth my while."

"Don't be stupid, boy. There's no money in rotten meat. It's charity. For the lepers."

"You give your lepers rotten meat?" The man nodded and Nabber continued, admiringly, "You treat your lepers well in Bren, we give 'em nothing in Rorn."

"The duke is famous for his good works." The man smiled the smile of the morally superior and urged Nabber along.

Nabber was beginning to like Bren. At first it had seemed like a cold fish of a city when compared to his beloved Rorn, but it was beginning to grow on him. Now that he'd been in the city for a few days, he realized he had been wrong about there being no smell. Bren did have an odor: a subtle festering. Once his young nostrils finally picked up on this he began to feel decidedly more at home. In fact, he was now starting to think that there was really little difference between the two cities. Bren was just cleverer when it came to hiding its flaws.

Of course the cold was an entirely different matter. He just wasn't born for the snow. True, a man could wear a most handsome cloak in the cold, but it just wasn't enough. Thanks to a well-to-do but unsuspecting salt merchant, he had managed to procure some rather fine pigskin gloves. They were far too big, however, and hung limply on his hands like just-milked cow's udders. So he didn't wear them. He prided himself on being well turned out: Swift would have expected no less.

He had the beginnings of a healthy contingency once more. Bren was an affluent city. The traders' market was proving to be fertile ground. Oh, Bren had pockets of its own, but from what he'd seen, they were sadly lacking in finesse. A quick snatch and grab. What skill was there in that? Swift, had he been dead—which was quite possible, given his risky line of business—would have turned in his grave.

Nabber forced his way through the crowds. Due to his diminutive size and the great clamor of people, he couldn't see where he was going. This was only a problem when he bumped his shin painfully against a stone fountain. "Borc's breath!" he muttered, rubbing his leg. "What's the use of all these fountains?" Since he'd been here, he'd noticed that there was hardly a street corner that didn't boast a fountain or a decorative pool. Only they didn't look very decorative with their dark, bird-dropping-stained stone. In fact, they looked rather depressing. Doubtless the man who'd built the city had a great love of water, either that or he took a fiendish delight in placing fountains just where they'd cause the most inconvenience. Like here.

Nabber was beginning to feel a little annoyed; his shin was throbbing and he was having no luck locating Tawl.

The trouble was that tall, golden-haired men just weren't as rare here as they were in Rorn. He'd asked people if they'd seen a golden-haired stranger and had been sent on various forays to all four corners of the city. So far he'd found a sheepherder from Ness, a fortune-teller from Lanholt, and a pimp from Dourhaven. But no Tawl. The pimp had been most accommodating, though, even offered to help him look. But the man hinted at the time-honored tradition of a favor for a favor, and Nabber didn't think he'd be willing to oblige with what might be asked.

So that left him nowhere. Well, more exactly, it left him at the foot of an inconvenient and ugly fountain.

It was early morning, and the day offered thin light and sharp breezes. Bren was yet another city of early risers, and the streets were already crowded with people going about their business. Commerce was the great and invisible bond that held the city together. Nabber could feel its pull, and it was like a caress to him. He hurried on his way to the traders' market.

The pickpocket's art lay in its subtlety. The secret was in the touch, and the trick was to make your victim believe that it was purely accidental. The touch could range from a gentle brushing of an arm to a plunderous fall into the crowd. Body contact was what counted. Nabber could turn a pat on the shoulder into a delve into a tunic, an arm outstretched to steady himself into an exploration of a purse. The art of the pocket was similar to that of the magician: it was all sleight of hand. A magician had his flick of the wrist, a pocket had his furtive fingerings.

The most important skill to those who valued their art—and Nabber, having been taught by an expert, counted himself among their number—was the lift. If a man had a goodly weight of coins nestled in his tunic, he would feel their loss as keenly as a missing tooth if the lift wasn't done right. The pocket must withdraw swiftly, but also carefully. He mustn't lift the package too quickly away from the body. The pressure should be gradually diminished, lest the body detect the sudden change.

Of course, a distraction round about this time helped, and Nabber made a point of picking a mark who was either engrossed in conversation, in a hurry to be on his way, or watching a spectacle. Pretty young ladies were the most reliable spectacle. A man will forget what time of day it is when a shapely figure walks past.

There were other techniques: ways of slipping rings from fingers and bracelets from wrists, ways of taking knives from scabbards and fur from collars. There was more than one way to rob a mark.

The best thing about pocketing to Nabber was the way no one was hurt. It was not a violent or threatening crime. It didn't even deprive a man of all his worldly goods, like robbing his house would. It just left a man short of coinage and trinkets. And to Nabber, it was a matter of honor that he always picked people who could well afford to replace both.

By midmorning his tunic was sporting some unusual but profitable bulges. Nabber could tell from the soft clink of metals against his belly that gold had been acquired. Gold had a sound all of its own, and music could be heard in its janglings.

Once he'd confirmed this supposition—a quick trip down a long alleyway—he decided a fine breakfast was in order. He had a fancy for nice surroundings and a blazing fire. He spied a group of rich-looking merchants, one of whom was familiar and would doubtless find himself short later in the day, and decided to follow them. The plump ones always knew where the best eating was.

He was led to a well-kept inn name of Cobb's Cranny. A rosy-cheeked man came forward to greet the merchants. He was all welcomes and solicitudes, bringing warm blankets and hot toddies, ordering the fire to be bellowed and the tables to be laid. His air of genial supervision led Nabber to conclude that the host was none other than Cobb himself.

Once the merchants were settled to his satisfaction, the innkeeper turned his attention to Nabber. "Servants round the back, boy."

"I'm afraid you're mistaken, sir," said Nabber. "I am no servant. But I will gladly take my business elsewhere, though I've heard the name of Cobb's Cranny on many a well-fed man's lips and was hoping to try your famous special." Nabber knew he was on a safe bet with the famous special. There was not an inn or hostelry in the whole of the Known Lands that did not boast a famous special.

The innkeeper relented. "I must ask to see your money first, young man." Nabber pulled out one gold coin. The innkeeper nodded. "Now would you care for the special boiled or fried?"

"I've been told fried is best."

Nabber settled himself in a comfortable upholstered chair that was as close to the fire as he could manage, since the merchants had formed a barricade around it. He poured himself a glass of bitter and foamy ale and settled down to enjoy himself.

Now, quite apart from his skills as a pocket, Nabber had another accomplishment he was proud of. He had what was known in Rorn as "big ears." That is to say, he had the hearing of a fox. His time as a lookout had honed this skill to a fine art. Everyone knew lookouts should be more accurately termed listenouts. Down in the darkened streets of Rorn, under the mantle of the night, you heard a man before you saw him.

Nabber could never pass up an opportunity to practice this skill and had been an uninvited party to countless conversations in taverns too numerous to mention. You could never tell when a casual remark between two companions might prove profitable. Not that profit was his only motive, though it was the only honorable one. The truth was that Nabber was just plain curious.

He sat back in his comfortable chair and listened to the conversation between the merchants. They were talking about the proposed marriage of the duke's daughter.

"I tell you, Fengott," said the fat one, "I'm not so sure about the whole thing. What do we want with a prince from the Four Kingdoms coming here and ruling our city? Bren's doing just fine without him."

"The duke seems set on it, though. I must say, I don't think he's got any intention of letting Prince Kylock come here and take his place. As I see it, the duke intends to use the kingdoms as his personal stockpile. Grain and timber we'll have aplenty."

"Aye," said the third one. "A marriage for the duke's convenience, that's all."

"From what I've heard that prince will be getting quite a handful." The fat man looked around and then lowered his voice. " 'Tis rumored that Catherine's no blushing virgin."

"I wouldn't say that in the duke's hearing, if I were you, Pulrod," said the one named Fengott. "A man would be sent to the gallows for such talk."

"Aye, but not before he'd been tortured first," chipped in the third one.

Nabber lost track of the conversation as the innkeeper brought him a huge steaming bowl of fried goose feet. Goose feet! His stomach turned at the sight of them. All that talk in Rorn about northerners being barbarians was obviously true.

"Eat up," said the man who could be Cobb. "There's plenty more where they came from."

Nabber wasn't generally a fussy eater, but he drew the line at trotters, tongues, and feet. The innkeeper hovered over him, anxiously awaiting his first taste. Nabber took a deep breath and buried his face in his hands.

"What's the matter, my boy?" The innkeeper was instantly concerned.

"It's the goose feet," said Nabber, shoulders shaking. "I thought I'd be able to face them after all this time, but the sight of them reminds me too much of my dead mother."

"She had feet like a goose?"

Nabber buried his head deeper. "No, she used to cook them for me— just like this. They were my favorites. The sight of them is more than I can bear."

The innkeeper ordered the bowl to be removed. He placed a comforting hand on Nabber's shoulder. "I understand, my boy. I'll have something else prepared, no extra cost."

"Thank you, kind sir. I'm most grateful. Could you make sure it's pork or lamb?"

Goose feet! What sort of place has goose feet as its special? Nabber took a draught of ale and waited upon his second course. His ears strayed back to the merchants.

"The pits have been dead this season," said the one named Fengott. "It's hardly worth placing a bet. I haven't seen a good fight all month."

"You're right. There's been no decent challengers to the duke's champion for half a year now. They're all fighting like women who don't want their dresses creased."

"I did see someone who might be promising," said the fat one.

"When?"

"Just last night. Big golden-haired fellow, not from round here by all accounts. He fought like a madman. Tore his opponent's arm off right before my very eyes."

"What's his name?"

"No one knows. Some say he's a knight. He keeps a rag bound to his forearm. You know, the place where knights are branded with their circles."

"He can't be a knight," said the third one. "They're not allowed to fight for profit." The other men grunted in agreement.

"Where was he fighting?" asked Fengott. "I wouldn't mind taking a look at him."

"Chapel Lane is where I saw him, but I think he's a free lance, so can fight where he pleases."

"Well, I'll keep an eye out for him. I'm always looking for a fair wager."

"Here, have you seen that new road they're building . . ."

Nabber withdrew his hearing and sat very still. Before him a dish of spiced lamb went unnoticed. The fighter was Tawl. He was sure of it. But where there should have been gladness, there was despair instead. What had become of his friend? The man he knew would never fight in a pit like a mercenary. Nabber knew it was time he faced the truth. Tawl had murdered Bevlin. He had stowed this fact in the deepest recess of his mind, hoping it would eventually be forgotten. But truths, particularly ugly ones, burrowed like worms and eventually found their way to the surface.

Still, Tawl was his friend, and friendship was sacred. At the tenderest spot in his still young heart, Nabber could not believe Tawl had acted willingly.

He laid a gold coin on the table—more than enough to cover the cost of the geese feet as well as the spiced lamb—and took his leave. He asked a passerby the way to Chapel Lane and set his path accordingly.

Jack sat alone on the straw-filled pallet that was now his bed. They had given him a room of his own; judging from the furnishings it was normally the women's bedchamber. He didn't know what they wanted with him. He suspected he'd merely been caught up in some internal squabble between the Halcus. None of that mattered. Melli was dead.

"She's dead," the girl had said. Her voice cold and without compassion. So similar to the last time he'd heard those words.

His mother had died when he was nine summers old. A growth forming first in her breast and then spreading to her lungs. She coughed up blood for a full year before her death. She tried to hide the bloodstained rags from him, stuffing them deep within her embroidery basket while he slept. Only he wasn't asleep. He couldn't fall asleep until he'd seen the rags and made sure they were no more bloodied than normal. But too often they were. So he would wash them for her; rubbing the stain against the stone by the light of a midnight candle. The next morning he'd rise early and take the drying rags from the grate. After he'd softened them by rubbing the fabric against his palm, he'd slip them into her basket. When his mother wakened, she would find the newly cleaned strips, and they could both pretend for a while that there had never been any blood.

It got so bad near the end that rags weren't enough, so he ripped up his tunics to give to her. At the very end, she was kept from him. Whispered words of warning barred her door. Jack's only consolation was the light that stole from under the panel. As long as it shone, the candles still burned, and while they burned, she still lived.

Crope was the last to talk to his mother. Even now, Jack could remember the huge giant emerging from the doorway, tears in his eyes, hand in his tunic. How he hated Crope for being called to her side. No call came for him.

For three days he was not allowed to see her. And then there was nothing to see. The light disappeared from under the door. The cellar steward's wife came. "She's dead," she said. "No use getting upset. Make yourself useful by scrubbing those pots. You wouldn't want to turn into a burden."

So he'd scrubbed pots the day his mother died, and scoured the floors the next. It had helped, in a way, for a tired and aching boy, whose fingertips bled from using course brushes, had little time or strength to think of his mother. He realized half a year later that he could no longer remember what she looked like before the illness. He'd scrubbed the memory clean away along with the pots and the pans.

Jack's fist came crashing down on the side of the pallet. The wood cracked and splintered. Melli was dead. He would not forget her with the same faithless haste. It was all his fault. He should never have left her to deal with the body. He should never have killed the man in the first place.

The girl called Tarissa stepped into the room. "What's going on?"

Jack regarded her coldly and said nothing. She spotted where the wood had been punched. "You did that?" Her voice was flat, neutral in more ways than one. Neutral in its careful lack of emotion, and neutral in its dialect. She had neither the kingdom's lilt of her mother, nor the Halcus accent of Rovas.

"Look, I'm sorry about the girl," she said.

"Are you?" Her sympathy made him angry. "Or was it just part of your plan?" Jack could still feel the pressure of Melli's last touch upon his hand. The memory of their final parting was new and painful, and he ground his knuckles into the splintered wood.

"Plan?"

Again Jack's fist came down upon the wood. The girl stepped back, momentarily frightened. "Innocence doesn't suit you," he said. "Don't expect me to believe that you and Rovas were up near the frozen pond for the good of your health." The splinters drew blood. Why had they saved *him*, not Melli? His life was worthless. No one would mourn his passing. But Melli, she might have been a queen. She was beautiful and proud, and the day he'd turned against the mercenaries and blasted them with a mixture of rage and sorcery, she had saved his life. With his mind gone and his body failing, Melli had dragged him for leagues across the forest to find shelter.

"What's done is done." Tarissa shrugged. "We did not bring about the death of the girl. You have yourself and a certain Halcus captain to blame for that."

"What is this captain's name?"

Rovas entered the room and Tarissa fell under his shadow. "I will not tell you his name yet," he said.

"Why not?" Jack had the feeling they were both acting. That the whole scene had been arranged, and by asking this question, he was playing into their hands.

"Because you might do something foolish, when, given time and preparation you could do something wise instead."

So here it was: the proposal. Skillfully cast, expertly baited. All that remained was for him to take the lure.

"So that's why you brought me here," said Jack, "to do *something wise?*"

"No," said Rovas. "I brought you here to save your life. You know you would have died trying to help the girl."

"And you expect a favor for a favor?" Jack stood up. He was more than a match for Rovas in height. "Well, I'm sorry, but you'll get no gratitude from me."

Tarissa took a speaking breath, but Rovas stopped her from using it. "I expect nothing from you," he said. "You are free to go."

A silence followed. Jack sensed that Tarissa was unhappy with Rovas' words. He knew better—Rovas was still acting. The words were merely a dramatic feint. Like all things hollow, they were more sound than substance.

"But," said Rovas, "I can't guarantee your safety once you leave this cottage. You murdered a Halcus soldier and will be tracked and hunted like a blooded stag."

"And you will give them the scent?"

"Me, no. Tarissa, I think I can speak for, and she wouldn't, either. But her mother . . ." Rovas shook his head. "Magra has no love of anyone from her former country. She is a bitter woman, and bitterness turns to spite when long in the belly."

"I see that the word free has little meaning when dropped from your lips." Jack wiped his bloodied knuckles on his tunic.

Rovas watched him carefully, his eyes flicking down to the blood. He was not oblivious to the threat implied by Jack's action.

When he spoke again, his tone was calming. "Stay here, and I promise that by the time you come to leave, you will be better able to take care of yourself. Whether it be evading the soldiers, or extracting revenge from their captain."

That was what Rovas was after, Jack was sure of it. He wanted the captain murdered and needed him to do it. He decided not to let Rovas know just how transparent he was being. "You are right," he said. "I have need of training. You saw only two days back that I have little skill with a blade. If I am to escape from this country alive, then I must be able to defend myself."

"So you'll stay?"

"As long as it suits me."

The change in Rovas' manner was overwhelming in its completeness. The huge man stepped forward and embraced Jack. The smells of garlic and sword oil wafted from his tunic. In the throes of the powerful and heavily scented embrace, Jack spied Tarissa over Rovas' shoulder. The girl's face was as cool as ever, only now her lips were drawn into a grudging smile. There was something familiar about her features. Something known or remembered. Before he could grasp at what it was, she turned and left.

They were drawing close to the mountains, and the land, as if practicing for its great feat of elevation, had begun to slope and fall. Baralis could not spy the peaks of the Great Divide, for the clouds and the snow conspired to keep their heights hidden. But he knew they were there. They called to him. Their ancient and venerable songs, without words or music, carrying their messages to all who could perceive them. In this modern world of metal plows and water clocks, that number was not many.

Baralis could hear them. The messages were an unconceited statement of might. A generous warning from that which was without prejudice. Their songs told that they were a power to be dealt with, and one crossed at one's own risk. A toll might be taken for passage.

Bren lay on the other side of the mountains. Baralis knew what kind of city it was. He knew the turn of the streets. He'd seen the sparkle of water in its fountains. Bren was a dangerous city. Dangerous in its pride. Its children were taught that Bren was the most beautiful, the most pure, and the most powerful city in the Known Lands. Not for them the festering passions of Rorn, not for them the overcultured languor of Annis. No, they were alone in their perfection. Their city was cleaner, more industrious, and stronger than any other.

Such pride is always dangerous. When a person is sure he knows the best way, he is seldom content until he has made converts out of others. So it was with Bren. Baralis drew his lips into a cynical line. Only conversion, when undertaken by the good duke took the form of annexation.

The duke of Bren had started modestly enough: surrounding villages were brought into the fold, small rivers were claimed. Then towns were invited to join with them—the invitations always so thoughtfully accompanied by a legion or two of Bren's armies. Since the duke had been in power, the maps of the Known Lands had changed. Bren, which twenty years before had been a fair-sized city surrounded by many towns, now stood alone.

And the duke wanted more.

Baralis knew all this, and it did not worry him. He and the duke had the same aims, for the time being.

He stroked the mane of his horse; such a beautiful creature, so gentle, so obedient. Not at all like that arrogant, preening, and now dead stallion of Maybor's.

He looked to where Maybor led the column. The great lord was now riding his captain's gelding and looked most uncomfortable doing so. Doubtless the fall from his horse had rendered him somewhat infirm. Baralis was beginning to think that Maybor could not be killed. At least not in one fell swoop. Perhaps his best course would be to slowly debilitate the man. Certainly the poison on his robes and now the fall from his horse had left their marks. Maybe he should just carry on trying to murder him until the old philanderer was so overcome with various injuries and afflictions that he dropped dead of his own accord.

Baralis smiled, his lips following the curve of his thoughts: Maybor was a naive fool if he thought he would be the superior envoy now that King Lesketh was in his grave.

And what a premature grave it was.

Someone had a hand in the king's death, he was sure of it. From the very beginning of the king's affliction, right from the impact of the double-notched arrow, Baralis had controlled the man's illness. Controlled the progress of poison on the flesh, controlled the wasting of muscle and then mind, and, when it suited him, controlled the semblance of recovery. He was the architect of the king's illness, and it was an insidious construction designed to be brought down on his bidding. The king had not been due for death.

Only now he was dead. Despite what the messenger said, despite the presence of the Master of the Bath and the royal guard, someone had gained access to the king's chamber. Baralis was almost certain of who it was: Kylock, once prince and now king.

So the boy had made his first move. He should have expected it. Kylock would not be content living in the shadow of an invalid king and a too-powerful queen. Baralis could almost be pleased with this youthful show of initiative, as long as the boy didn't make any more rash moves.

Of course he would have preferred that in his absence the court be run by the queen. She was a woman who knew the value of stability, and stability was just what Baralis needed until the marriage between Kylock and Catherine of Bren was consummated. Only then should the combined might of Bren and the kingdoms show its teeth. Now he was worried in case Kylock should take it upon himself to win the war with the Halcus— a victory that Baralis knew could be won by a determined leader—and by doing so, draw the eyes of the world northward before the alliance was in place. A world made nervous by an aggressive new king would look much more critically upon a proposed alliance between the two mightiest states in the north.

There was some consolation to be gained in the fact that the armies of the kingdoms were badly depleted. Five years of war rendered even the best of soldiers battle weary. Still, it was a situation that would need careful monitoring.

Kylock was his creature. Murdering the king was simply proof of it.

The deed would have been done once the marriage had taken place. All Kylock did was anticipate the need. He had been rash, yes, but he'd carried it off! Fooling court and queen into believing the king's death was a natural progression of his illness. Baralis couldn't help but feel a little proud. Not a father's pride, rather pride of ownership.

There was much he didn't know about Kylock. The boy had power, he was certain of it. He was also equally certain he could not use it. The drugs he provided acted as a suppressant. Kylock took them willingly, thinking they provided him with insight into the world of darkness. All they did was drive him nearer to madness. And that was the way Baralis wanted it. So much easier to control a man whose power of reasoning had been eroded by subtle shifts of poison about the brain.

The drug inhibited the swell of sorcery in the mind. Sorcery came from the mind and the gut; it met and became potent in the mouth. Kylock could draw power from the belly, but his will could not form the intent. He was like a wheel that could not turn for want of grease.

It had to be so. Baralis could not risk the future king's reputation being sullied by rumors of sorcery.

There was another, more personal reason for administering the drug. 'Twould be dangerous if Kylock turned out to be more powerful than himself. It was difficult to gauge these things, but the signs were there: he was conceived on a night of reckoning, when fate itself danced its way into his seed. Fate aside, blood alone would ensure the passing down of sorcery's particular gifts. And Baralis' blood had ever been potent.

The wind picked up and there was bite to its bluster. Baralis pulled his collar close about his neck, seeking to quiet his misgivings along with the cold. Kylock was addicted to the drug. He would continue to take it in Baralis' absence. There was nothing to be concerned about; he was merely tired, no more. Endless hours in the saddle combined with the relentless chill of wind and snow had worn him down. He was anxious to be over the mountains and into the city. Ambition and intrigue were his lifeblood, and the long journey eastward had forestalled both.

By murdering the king, Kylock may have made his job more difficult, but he was always one to rise to a challenge.

Melli sat at the foot of the stairs and waited. She knew it was now well past morning. The light stealing beneath the doorway grew steadily weaker and would soon be replaced by the even paler glow of candlelight. Even this late in winter the days were still short.

She had sat here for many hours now, knowing the delicate terror of anticipation. At every sign of movement from above, Melli would grow tense; her hands fluttered nervously, one to smooth her dress, another to check her blade. Once she was sure the knife had not slipped from its position between living skin and dead bone, she would compose herself. It was important not to look afraid. Only they never came, and so Melli had more time to think the worst.

She wondered what the delay could mean. She knew the captain had intended her to be taken away in the morning, and now it seemed his plans were either delayed or changed. Melli stood and waited.

As the hours went by and her limbs grew stiff with stillness and cold, Melli wondered what had become of Jack. In the weeks they'd spent with each other, she had come to rely on him. She had watched him gradually changing, growing more sure of himself, and at the same time more distant. She was quite confident that he'd survive on his own. In fact, he would probably do better now that he didn't have her to worry about.

The lock turned, and Melli's thoughts snapped back to herself. She stood up and faced the door. Her heart quickened and her stomach reeled. The door opened and two men were silhouetted in its frame. One was tall and well proportioned: the captain. The other was slight and oddly shaped.

"There she is," said the captain, making no move to enter the room. "I told you she was a beauty."

"Bring her up into the light." The voice of the second man was thin and high, lacking in emotion.

The captain made a snort of protest, but complied with the man's wishes. He descended the steps and grabbed Melli by the wrist. Twisting her arm to ensure compliance, he forced her up the stairs. She was led past the man in the doorway and into the light.

She had to squint at first. The light was too bright.

The captain slapped her hard on the cheek. "Stop squinting, girl!" he ordered.

Melli did not have time to wonder at this curious command, as the second man moved close and began prodding her with a long, thin finger. She shrank back in distaste. The man was badly disfigured. One side of his face was slack; there was no muscle to fill out the cheek. His left eyelid drooped nearly shut, and his half-mouth rested in a flaccid sneer.

"Too skinny," he said, the lips on his good side curling up slightly. He shook his head. "Too skinny."

The captain looked at the man with barely disguised distaste. "You're mistaken, sir. There is meat to the bones."

The man made a doubting sound with tooth and spittle as he circled Melli. She noticed that his left arm lay limp at his side; the fingers curled close to the palm. His left leg dragged as he walked.

He continued prodding her with his good hand. A finger came up to her cheek, and its long, yellow nails drew a furrow in her skin. "Not as young as you promised," he said.

The captain shrugged. "She is young enough, Fiscel, and you know it."

The man ignored this comment and slipped his fingernail between Melli's lips. Melli was forced to open her mouth as his nail pressed against the tender flesh. She tasted her own blood. He ran his finger along her teeth and pulled her lips back to see the gums.

Apparently satisfied with what he saw, he turned his attention to her body. Melli felt the guilty pressure of the knife at her side. Detection of the hidden weapon seemed imminent. Through the fabric of her dress, the man named Fiscel squeezed the swell of her breast. This indignity was too much for Melli to bear and she raised her arm to strike him. With surprising speed Fiscel caught her arm, and with unexpected strength he forced it to her side. He made a strange sound in his throat, and it took Melli a moment to realize he was laughing. His face was close to hers. She smelled the sick-sweet odor of his breath. It occurred to Melli that if she could divert his attention long enough, he might not resume his prodding of her body, and her knife might go undetected.

She decided to become her own saleswoman. "I am, I assure you, sir, well rounded. There is no bone on me that is without its fair measure of meat. I see no need to poke me as if I were a newly set cheese."

The captain, who was becoming impatient with all the proddings and examinations, seemed pleased at this statement. "See, Fiscel. I told you she has the bearing of a noblewoman."

Melli took this opportunity to step away from her inspector. To her delight, Fiscel let her go and turned his attention to the captain.

"I will take her," he said. "Though she is a disappointment to me."

The captain seemed unaffected by this pronouncement; he leaned back against the wall, placing a foot on an empty beer barrel. With his oiled mustache and softly beaten leathers, he was a picture of dashing elegance. He was well aware of the contrast between himself and the other man, and Melli saw that he was using his physical superiority as part threat, part bargaining tool. "I'm afraid I have you at a disadvantage, sir," he said.

"What disadvantage is that?"

"When you first arrived and were taking a glass of mulled wine, I took the liberty of having one of my men, inspect your . . . how should I put it? . . . your wares. He told me you had two other girls, and that, although young, they were lacking in beauty and bearing." The captain permitted himself to look a little smug.

Fiscel waived his good arm dismissively. "Captain, your low tricks are as misguided as they are predictable. Those two girls are no concern of yours, and their charms, or lack of them, have no bearing on this deal." The flesh-trader—for Melli now knew without a doubt that he was one— was obviously well used to verbal parrying. "I am in half a mind to leave the girl. She is pretty, yes, but no longer young and has a violent disposition."

"The girl is not yet past her eighteenth year, and violence when called spirit is often attractive in a woman." The captain had now given up his nonchalant pose. Melli almost felt sorry for him. He was in the presence of one who would surely outwit him.

"The girl might be thought young here in the north," said Fiscel, "but in the Far South, she would be considered an old maid. She is many years past first blood."

Melli strove to hide her embarrassment at the mention of such an intimate subject by a man. In all her life, she'd never heard a man make any references to a woman's cycle, and she thought it a subject they had no knowledge of.

"Fiscel, you and I both know that not all your dealings are done in the Far South. I have heard that you do business in places as near as Annis and Bren. This girl is still young in the eyes of such cities." The captain was allowing his temper to show. "The girl is beautiful, nobly born, fine figured, and she knows courtly manners. Do not try to tell me that she is an old maid barely worth your attention."

"You say she is a virgin?"

"You have my word."

Fiscel made a peculiar doubting noise, which had the effect of spraying the limp side of his lips with spittle. "The girl is no great find. She is skinny, dark-eyed, and small breasted. I will give you a hundred less than you're asking."

"The girl is pale-skinned, blue-eyed, and well-hipped. I will take no less than my original price."

Melli was beginning to feel most indignant at being talked about so callously. Although she disliked the flesh-trader's comments, she could see there was some truth to them.

"The girl is simply not worth three hundred golds," said Fiscel. "Her hair is too dark, her chin is too forward, and she is too tall. Why, her very height alone will cut down the number of potential buyers—men insist on being taller than their women."

Melli had the distinct feeling that Fiscel could come up with belittling things to say about her until winter's end. She took some comfort in the fact that he would probably be no less insulting if he were face to face with the greatest beauties of the day.

"I will take two fifty, no less." Apparently, the good captain had succumbed to this last tirade; either that, or he'd run out of good points with which to counter the insults.

"Take two twenty-five and you have a deal." Fiscel smiled: a dreadful sight, as only half his face complied with his wishes.

The captain rolled the fine points of his mustache and did not bother to conceal his repulsion. "Two forty."

"Two thirty."

"Done."

Fiscel held out his long-nailed hand to clasp on the deal. The captain brushed the surrounding air, but did not touch it. He glanced over at Melli, a strange look not without regret. "You have got yourself a good deal, Fiscel."

The flesh-trader shrugged. "She will do." He unclasped his belt, and for one awful moment, Melli wondered if he was going to flog or rape her. He did neither. Instead he twisted the broad leather belt until a split in the inner lining became apparent, dipped his fingers into the split, and drew out two fifty-gold bars. These he handed to the captain, who duly tested them with a scrape of his knife. Fiscel replaced the belt. "You will receive the rest once I have confirmed your word."

"Word?"

"Your word that she is a virgin. Just as you tested the gold, I must test the girl."

The captain did not look pleased, but Melli really didn't give a damn. What test was this? Her face flushed with anger, but she forced herself to be calm. Maybe if she were left alone with Fiscel, she would have a chance to use her knife.

"It is nothing to be concerned with, captain," he was saying. "I will take her to the inn with me, and once certain delicacies have been ascertained, I will pay my due. I will, of course, expect a complete refund if the girl has been used." Fiscel's good eye narrowed sharply. "Perhaps, if such an unhappy situation arises, I might be persuaded to take the girl off your hands for the odd thirty golds."

The captain reluctantly agreed. "I will set a guard by the inn, in case you decide upon a late-night departure."

"You are too kind." Fiscel came as close to a bow as his twisted frame could muster. He turned to Melli. "Follow me, girl. I am most anxious that this matter be settled tonight."

Five

Darkness came early to Bren. The sun slipped behind the western mountains, and the city fell victim to their shadows. On cold winter nights such as this, mist rose from the great lake and cloaked the city in its icy pall.

Those who braved the chill streets of Bren did so in search of what diversions the darkened city afforded. Bren was not a city of music or culture, high cuisine or clever conversation. Bren was a city of power. A city that knew the value of a strong army and that praised the worth of a strong man. A night's entertainment for a man of Bren—the women didn't count—consisted of a skin or two of cheap ale, some wagering at the fighting pits and, if he had a few extra coppers left, an hour's worth of whoring.

The whores of Bren didn't roam the streets or ply the taverns, it was too cold for walking, particularly in the sort of clothes they chose to wear. Instead, they worked the brothels. These brothels were to be found close to the fighting pits. A man who wins at wagering will likely feel the need of a woman to celebrate. The man who loses needs a woman for commiseration. Not that women were the only sex on offer, though Bren, as a soldiering city, officially frowned upon anything that was not considered manly.

Still, most men were drawn from their homes at night, leaving the warmth of the embered hearth for the cold promise of the streets. Once sufficiently numbed against winter's chill by a skin or two of ale, they would gather around the pits, hungry for the sight of blood.

The fighting pits had been present in Bren before there were any walls, before it was even a city, when it had just been an ambitious town. Some said the pits first started Bren's craving for bloodshed, others said it was merely a symptom of what had always been present. The men of Bren cared little for such debates: intellectual pursuits were for the priest and the weaklings. Fighting was what counted.

The pits were circular in shape, roughly four men across, and less than a man deep. The crowd gathered around the edge and laid bets on whatever fight was taking place. Tradition held that the victor of the fight was thrown one-third of all money bet. However, this was usually not adhered to unless the fighter was either especially good, or had enforcers in the crowd. The rules of conflict were simple: the only weapon allowed was the short-bladed hand knife, and once in the pit anything was considered fair game. Victory could be claimed by either death, unconsciousness, or submission.

In olden days, long metal spikes had jutted from the walls of the pit, and the idea was to impale one's victim. Too many people died that way— though the victors always got their third—and the practice had stopped from lack of willing participants. It was rumored that such matches could still be found, if one knew the right people and were willing to pay the price.

Tawl lifted the skin to his lips and drank deeply of the cheap ale. He then swung the skin above his head and poured the remainder over his hair and face. The crowd was bigger than last night. No doubt the story of the man whose arm he tore off had spread. Nothing like a maiming for bringing in the crowds. He could see the men looking his way, see their eyes appraising him and their whispering lips discussing him. He could feel their excitement, their desire for blood and guts and bone. He was repulsed by them.

But he would give them what they wanted. He checked the linen wrap around his arm. The cloth was closely bound; it would not slip. He had brought dishonor upon himself, but he would not willingly bring it upon the knighthood. He'd tried to rid himself of the mark: he burned his flesh and then rubbed sawdust into the wound; he'd scored the skin with the edge of his sword, drawing a cross in blood. The circles still remained. They taunted him with their presence and shamed him with what they stood for. He was no longer a knight, but the circles would give him no peace.

His eyes strayed to his hands. There was blood beneath his nails; whose, he did not know. Perhaps one-arm, perhaps the man before, or the man before that, perhaps even Bevlin. It didn't matter. Blood was a fitting adornment.

Corsella came and sat beside him. The deep cleft of her bosom, which was exposed to the night air, was goose-pimpled. Tawl absently ran his blood-stained fingers over the puckered flesh. "Did you bring more ale?"

Corsella, who was young from a distance but aged with nearness, nodded. "I did, Tawl." She hesitated a moment, and then took a deep breath. "I think you should wait until the fight's over before you take any more."

Anger flared in Tawl, and he smacked the woman full on the lips. *"Give me the ale, bitch!"*

Quick tears flared but didn't fall. Blood trickled from the corner of her mouth. She passed the skin without a word. He drank more than he'd intended, just to spite her. The ale gave him no joy, merely dulled his senses further. Of late that was the most he could hope for.

He looked over to the other side of the pit. A man, naked from the waist up, was being rubbed with goose fat: his opponent. He was of average height yet well muscled, his skin still smooth with youth. His face was beautiful, but not without arrogance. Tawl had seen his kind before. He had made a name for himself in his village and had come to the city hoping to repeat his triumph. The crowd was clearly impressed by the boy's looks. They cheered as he presented himself for their admiration. The goose fat, which was supposed to make it harder to get a hold of him, served to show off his body to its best advantage.

Tawl knew what the crowd was thinking. They looked at him and the boy, and then money changed hands with wolflike speed. They expected the boy to win, but not before the golden-haired stranger had put up quite a fight. Perhaps, if they were lucky, someone might end up maimed or dead. Tawl took another draught of ale. Men would lose money betting against him this night.

He stripped off his leather tunic, and Corsella ventured forward with a pot of goose fat. He shook his head. He wasn't going to be greased like a lamb for the spit. Nor would he take off his linen undershirt; he wasn't about to give the crowd the added spectacle of a chest covered with scars left by torture. They'd have to pay more if they wanted to see those.

The boy stepped down into the pit. The crowd applauded his smooth-skinned scowl and cheered when his muscles caught the light. He seemed very young to Tawl.

Cries of street vendors could be heard above the noise of the appraising crowd:

"Roasted chestnuts! Red hot! Warm your hands and your belly. If the fight gets boring you can always throw 'em."

"Extra strong barley ale! Half a skin only two silvers. One drink will make the fight look good and your wife look beautiful."

"Pork joints! Hot from the ovens. A safer bet than any fighter."

The crowd quieted as Tawl stood up. All eyes were upon him, and he fancied he saw regret in the faces of some who bet against him. Too bad. He made his way to the edge of the pit and jumped down to the stone floor below. The crowd was disappointed. The boy, whose name was Handris, was putting on a show, displaying his muscles and his noble profile to their best advantage. Tawl merely paced the pit, head down, ignoring the crowd and his posturing opponent.

A red swath of fabric was raised and then dropped into the pit. The fight had begun.

The boy circled, looking for weak points. That was his first mistake. With every step he unknowingly showed his own weaknesses. Tawl was a hawk on the wing. His years of training and experience came back to him like a gift. He evaluated his opponent almost without realizing what he did. The boy was nervous—that was good. He knew how to carry his knife, though. His arms were well muscled, but his flank and back were weak. Just above his belt there was a slight discoloration: an old wound or bruise—probably still tender.

Tawl stood and let the boy come to him. The boy swung forward with his knife. An instant later he twisted round, kicking out with the back of his heel. Tawl was forced to step away from the knife and in doing so left himself open for the kick. Pain exploded in his shin. The boy's second mistake was not to use his advantage. He let the appreciation of the crowd fill his ears and his mind. Tawl pounced forward. His knife provided a distraction while he elbowed the boy's jaw. The boy's head snapped back. Tawl allowed him no chance to steady himself. He was on him again; a punch to the gut and then a rake of the knife along the boy's arm.

At the sight of blood, the crowd *ah*'ed in appreciation. Doubtless more money was wagered.

The boy was quick to right himself. He had the lightning reflexes of youth. He sprang forward and the force of his momentum carried them both to the ground. He brought his knife up and pushed for Tawl's face. That was his third mistake—too much reliance on his blade. Tawl raised his knee with all the force he could muster and slammed it into his opponent's thigh. The boy reacted violently, and his knife cut into Tawl's shoulder. Bright blood soaked through the linen.

The boy was still on top of him, his knife poised for further thrusts. Something in the way the boy held the blade reminded Tawl of a long shadow once cast in Bevlin's hut. He tried to force the vision of the dead man from him. But when he succeeded, he found the image of his sisters lying beneath. He was worthless. He'd failed his family, his knighthood, and Bevlin. Anger became his weapon and his shield. A rage came upon him, and suddenly he was no longer fighting a boy, he was fighting against fate. Fighting against Larn and its lies, fighting against his ambition and what it had made him.

He flung the boy from him. He landed badly on his back. Tawl was over him in an instant. He threw away his blade—it reminded him too much of the long-shadowed night. The crowd was in a frenzy. There was fear in the eyes of the boy. Tawl went for his throat, his fingers enclosing the muscled column. He felt the graze of the boy's knife upon his flank. Not relieving his grip for an instant, Tawl knocked it from his hand, using his elbow like a club. He kicked the knife away.

With his free arm, he punched the boy time and time again. He knew no self-restraint. The only thing that mattered was getting the demons off his back. Even then he knew they would give him no peace. The boy's face became a bloody pulp. The crack of broken bones sobered the now silent crowd.

Tawl took a deep breath. When he let it out, he tried to let go of his rage. It was hard; with rage came forgetfulness and even perhaps the semblance, no matter how temporary, that he was in control. Only he wasn't, either way.

He got to his feet and stood back from the lifeless body of the boy. The only noise in the chill night was the sound of his own breath, quick and ragged. The crowd was waiting. At first Tawl didn't understand why. Then he saw the red swath. It was lying near the wall of the pit. He went over and picked it up. He held it aloft for the crowd to see: the sign of victory.

The crowd erupted into a riot of shouting and calling. Whether in delight or damnation, Tawl didn't care. He felt something hard hit his shoulder, and then something at his back. The crowd was throwing coins. Silver and gold. Soon the bottom of the pit was aglow with the sparkle of coinage.

The boy's friends came and dragged the body away. Tawl wasn't sure if he was dead or alive. Corsella was lowered into the pit and busied herself loading coins into her sack. All this time Tawl hadn't moved, the red swath was still in his hand, its bright corners flapping in the breeze.

Melli followed Fiscel out of the garrison. The man's walk was almost comical; he lurched from good leg to bad like a drunken cripple. His breathing was weak and irregular, and was accompanied by a straining rasp of a sound that emanated from deep within his chest. The smell of him filled her with revulsion. The overbearing sweetness of exotic perfume barely masked the stench of the sickbed beneath.

Even though Melli was a head taller than Fiscel, she wasn't sure that she could manage to overpower him. Her wrist was still throbbing from earlier, when he had shown her the force of his tight-fingered grip. Melli rubbed the sore spot. Fiscel's body had power despite the look of it. She was not really worried about his strength: it was his appearance that disturbed her the most. His face was a grotesque mask; his good eye was quick and vulpine, his bad eye watery and dim. He was physically repulsive, and it was this, more than any hidden strength, that she was afraid of.

A guard drew back the heavy wooden door and Melli stepped out into the dark Halcus night. The wind brought tears to her eyes, and the terrible cold froze them on her cheeks.

Fiscel grabbed her arm. His long fingernails dug into her flesh. He led her forward. At first she could see nothing, then as her eyes grew accustomed to the dark, she made out a shape in the blackness. It was a wagon, and three horses were harnessed to it. Two of the horses were large and heavy, and one was slender of back and limb: a rider's horse. A man dressed in a cloak of gray was attending to them.

Fiscel brought her to the back of the wagon. He rapped sharply on the wood and the door swung open. Melli felt the flesh-trader's hands upon her backside as he pushed her up the step and into the wagon. The door was closed after her, and she found herself in the company of two other women.

The smell of bitter almonds filled her nostrils. The wagon was lit by a small oil lamp. There was barely enough space to contain the four straw pallets that lay aside each other. A brief stretch of Isro carpet and several smooth-sided chests were the only other contents.

The two women were not surprised at her sudden entrance. They lounged on a pallet drinking hot liquid from brass-encased glasses. One of the women, who was dusky skinned and raven haired, indicated that she should sit. Melli was inclined to ignore the languid gesture, but the wagon lurched forward and she found herself unsteady on her feet. The raven-haired woman smiled an I-told-you-so.

The wagon began to move more steadily and Melli settled herself on the pallet nearest the door. The raven-haired woman nodded to the pale-haired girl, obviously an order to pour another cup of liqueur, for the girl took up the silver pot and filled a glass with the steaming, clear liquid. Melli took the cup by its brass handle. The metal was warm to the touch, but not as hot as the glass beneath.

The sharp but fragrant vapors slipped into nose and lung, working their subtle magic of relaxation and comfort. The jostling of the wagon, the itch of the straw, the ache of her muscles, they all seemed to recede into the background. Melli took a sip from the cup. The liquid scalded her tongue. She felt it burn all the way to her belly. Then the warming began. She felt her body growing heavy and warm. Her fingers swelled with hot blood, her face became flushed, and she could feel her heart racing to keep up with her thoughts.

The raven-haired woman smiled an encouragement. The pale-haired girl sent a warning.

Melli drained her cup, welcoming its heat on her tongue. The wagon came to an abrupt stop. A minute or two later there was a rap on the wood. The door was opened again and Fiscel stood there, one shoulder higher than the other. He beckoned Melli forward. The pale-haired girl stepped ahead of her.

"No, Lorra," said Fiscel to the girl. "You will spend the night here in the wagon. Estis will watch over you."

"You mean I don't get to stay at the inn and have a decent supper." The girl sounded peevish.

"You will do as I say." Fiscel's tone brought an end to the matter. Then, turning toward the raven-haired woman, he said, "Come, Alysha." The raven-haired woman poured some of the almond liqueur into a flask, picked up an embroidered sack, and followed him out.

Melli found herself in the cold once more, but this time she was oblivious to its touch. They were in the center of a small town. Light peeked from shuttered windows, smoke rose from snow-laden rooftops, and a lone dog barked an angry lament.

Melli was led to the narrow doorway of a tavern named the Dairyman. Behind her, the wagon rumbled away. Fiscel pushed her into the bright lights and warm air of the tavern. A room full of men stared at them.

"Keep your mouth shut," warned Fiscel. He left her by the door in the care of the raven-haired woman, Alysha. The flesh-trader made his ungainly way to the bar, sparking many a disgusted look as he did so. He spoke with the innkeeper and money changed hands. A second exchange with the tavern girl prompted further largesse. Finally, Fiscel turned to

Alysha and nodded. Melli was guided forward, toward a low door at the back of the room. The motion drew the eye of every man present, and the room fell silent as they passed.

Fiscel tapped impatiently with his walking stick and threw Melli an accusation of a glance. It was as if he blamed her for being an object of attention.

Melli was feeling most peculiar. Blood coursed through her veins at an alarming rate; she was giddy with its speed and richness. Her body felt heavy and feverish, and somewhere deep within she felt an unnamable need.

With Fiscel to the front, and Alysha to the back, she was led up a curved staircase to the floor above. The tavern girl appeared and showed them to their rooms. One was large and comfortable, with a full-sized bed, the other small and cramped with two pallets. The tavern girl bobbed a curtsy and promised to be back soon with food.

Melli struck a path toward the smaller room, but Fiscel laid a restraining hand upon her arm. "No, my pretty," he said, his voice thin and mocking. "Why so eager to be rid of me? We should spend some time together. Get to know each other."

Alysha opened the door of the largest room and sat on the bed. She patted the covers, inviting Melli to join her. Melli declined and sat on a wooden bench near the unlit fireplace. As she did so, she heard the soft laughter of the raven-haired woman. Fiscel smiled, the good side of his mouth revealing his bad teeth.

"I propose we eat first, and then, when we're all relaxed, we can get down to the business of the night." He turned to Alysha. "I see you have brought a flask of nais with you, my precious one. Pour our new friend a cup before it grows cold."

Nabber watched as Tawl stepped from the pit. The golden-haired knight was oblivious to the praise and back-slapping. A wealthy-looking man stepped forward and tried to engage him in conversation. Tawl brushed him aside. Another man who was watching the knight closely seemed familiar to Nabber. It took him a moment to realize it was the very first person he'd pocketed upon entering the city. The man with the portrait of the golden-haired girl. Yes, it was him all right. His chest was as broad as his head was narrow. His dark, plumply lidded eyes never left Tawl for an instant.

The knight was still clutching the victory marker. Even from Nabber's position at the opposite side of the pit, he could see the force with which Tawl was holding on to the swath. His knuckles were white.

In all his days, Nabber had never witnessed a fight like the one he'd just seen. It was almost as if Tawl were possessed. His eyes glazed over, and he didn't seem to know what he was doing, nor how to stop himself. Nabber was sure he wasn't the only person in the crowd who'd felt disturbed at the sight. It was as if they'd been allowed a glimpse of something shocking and intensely private. A spell had been cast this night, and the man in the blood-stained undershirt whom he used to call his friend had been the sorcerer.

Nabber had watched as the crowd grew more and more excited. More than just blood thirst, it was the fascination of seeing a fellow human laid bare. Those primitive instincts, which the world commands be hidden, had been on show this night. Nabber shook his head slowly. Men would pay good money for the chance to see such savagery again.

Already a fair sum of coinage had been thrown into the pit. Gold and silver, no copper. Nabber felt that the crowd only needed the smallest measure of encouragement to throw more. Their generosity needed a little prompting, that was all. He might have even done it himself if it weren't for the fact that a fleshy woman with hair of a particularly unnatural shade of yellow was quickly putting what coinage there was into a sack.

Dual instincts warred within Nabber. There was money to be made here, lots of money. No doubt about it. But it would be money gained from the loss of a man's honor. Now a dilemma such as this would have been no problem in the past; coinage was coinage, and acquiring it was the most noble of pursuits. However, Nabber only had to look over to where Tawl stood—distant and immeasurably changed—to know that there were other things in the world just as important as money, and helping a friend was one of them.

The hairs on Nabber's arm stood on end. This was, without a doubt, his noblest moment. He felt quite proud of himself; he would help his friend. Still, if there was money to be made while doing so, he was not about to turn it down.

Nabber watched as the yellow-haired woman scrambled from the pit and went to join Tawl. He said something to her, and the woman pulled a half-skin of ale from her sack. Tawl snatched it from her and drained it flat. The woman handed him his tunic, but he brushed it aside. He grabbed hold of her arm and they made their way free of the crowd.

It was bitterly cold on the streets of Bren. The mist from the great lake had begun to gather and thicken. Nabber was chilled even with his cloak, jerkin, tunic, waistcoat, shirt, and undershirt on—Rorn had been a much easier city to dress for—and he wondered how Tawl could manage with just a layer of linen between him and the cold.

He didn't like any of it: the fighting, the drinking, the woman with yellow hair. It wasn't that he disapproved of those sort of things. No, indeed, he was an open-minded man of the world. It was just that it didn't seem right for Tawl to be doing them. Tawl was a knight, and knights were supposed to be better than everyone else.

Nabber followed the knight and his lady as they made their way through the city. The district began to change for the worst and Nabber began to feel more at home. Prostitutes clothed in low-cut dresses stood in brothel doorways and called to passersby. They promised exotic delights, curvaceous bodies, and cheap rates. They even called to Nabber:

"Over here, dearie. Special rate for first-timers."

"Give me a chance, little one, and I'll show you where everything goes."

He smiled politely at the offers, but shook his head, just like Swift had taught him. Not that Swift himself ever shook his head at a prostitute. After all, he'd say, what else was a man's contingency for?

Some of the calls were less flattering.

"Bugger off, you little snot! You're scaring the punters."

"Stop gawking, peep-boy! If you can't pay, don't look."

"I don't give lessons, baby-face. Come back when you've filled out your britches."

Nabber was immune to this sort of heckling. The prostitutes in Rorn had far sharper tongues.

He hung back a little from Tawl, keeping his distance. For some reason, which he could not name, he didn't want to make contact with the knight just yet. Eventually the pair slowed down and entered a brightly lit building. The red-painted shutters confirmed it was another brothel.

Nabber slipped down the side of the building. He waded through the filth of kitchen refuse and emptied chamberpots until he found what he was looking for: a way to see inside. The shutter was closed to keep out the cold and the smell, but the wood was badly warped. There was a convenient split running down its length. Nabber put his eye to the wood.

Smoke filled the room. Candles burned low and the fire was well banked with ashes. Groups of men and woman lounged on chairs and benches. Food, fried but now cold, congealed unnoticed on platters. There was fondling and drinking, both men and women showing more enthusiasm for the latter. The women's dresses were unlaced and their bosoms, both small and large, went mostly unnoticed.

Nabber looked on as Tawl and his ladyfriend entered the room. She pushed a path through the drunkenness and cleared a bench for them to sit on. Tawl immediately called for ale, his voice harsher than Nabber remembered. Ale came and food along with it. The knight ignored the food and drank the ale from the jug. The girl whispered something to him, perhaps a caution for his drinking, and Tawl smacked her in the chest. Nabber was shocked.

The girl appeared quite used to this sort of treatment and didn't make a move to leave. She took a portion of fried chicken and set about tearing at it with large but even teeth. Nabber saw her exchange a seemingly casual glance with a small-eyed woman. The woman edged nearer, and the girl slipped her the sack. Tawl was drinking heavily and saw none of this.

The small-eyed woman left the room and returned a few moments later. Tawl's sack was still in her hand, but it looked slimmer now. She crossed the room, paused a second in front of the mirror to pat her heavily powdered hair, and then returned the sack to the girl. Although Nabber had no way of knowing, he was almost certain that the bundle now contained substantially less of Tawl's gold. Indignation rose in his breast. Robbing was normally fair game to him, but this was down right deceitful. The girl with the bright yellow hair had set Tawl up. And it probably wasn't the first time.

But it would be the last. No one robbed a friend of his and got away with it. No one.

Nabber looked toward Tawl. The knight's head was down. He seemed absorbed in something. It took Nabber a moment to realize that he was intent upon his arm. He was rewinding the cloth that bound his forearm. The cloth that served to hide his circles. With movements made slow by drink, Tawl wound the cloth, his fingers binding the fabric deep into his flesh. The bandage slipped and Nabber was shocked by what lay underneath: a portion of flesh as big as a fist was burned. The flesh was raised and blistered. The scar which ran through his circles had reopened and formed a ribbon of red through the black.

Tawl began to rewind the cloth. He wasn't a man concerned with bandaging an injury, he was a man intent on hiding his shame. By covering his circles it was as if Tawl were trying to hide the past, to bandage it out of sight.

Nabber moved away from the window. He felt a confusion of unfamiliar emotions. There was a pressure in his throat and an aching in his chest. The sight of Tawl, sitting alone in the sordid whorehouse quietly binding his circles, was too painful to bear. He turned his back on the window and made his way to the street. Time to get a little sleep. He would return in the morning when the knight was sober.

He walked back up the road, past the brothels and their prostitutes. If they called to him, this time he didn't hear them.

Melli, who usually prided herself on a healthy appetite and had not eaten for at least half a day, found the food held no interest for her.

Fiscel and Alysha had been the perfect hosts, solicitous and polite. Her plate was never empty, her glass always full. Melli hadn't actually tested how quickly they brought more food, but when it came to refilling her glass, they showed the speed and intent of swooping kestrels.

Thinking of birds of prey, Melli noticed that Fiscel had the eye of a predator. His gaze was sharp, focused, cold as metal. That was his good eye, of course. His bad eye had the look of the prey. Melli giggled merrily and wondered why she only had such witty thoughts when she'd been drinking. A small, detached part of her argued that perhaps she did have such thoughts when sober, only they didn't seem so amusing to a sound mind and a dry belly.

She most definitely had a wet belly now. Wet Belly Melli! She laughed brightly and Fiscel laughed, too. The flesh-trader looked so repulsive when he laughed that the sight of him made Melli laugh more. The raven-haired Alysha just smiled, a smile soft with all the guile and complicity that women of the Far South were famous for.

Fiscel refilled her cup. The brimming glass was unsteady in her hand and wine spilled on the rush-covered floor. Melli bent forward to see how much wine was lost. As her head came up, she caught a glance and a nod exchanged between her hosts. Alysha moved toward the foot of the bed. Strangely, amidst all her feelings of drunken glee and growing trepidation, Melli found herself envying the older woman. She moved like a temptress. The beauty that was denied in her face flourished in the ravishing but effortless grace of her movements. Melli felt like a country bumpkin in her presence.

With arms so fluid as to seem almost without bone, Alysha reached for the embroidered sack. A pull on the thread revealed its contents: rope, coiled like a snake. Something glinted in the center of the coil.

Melli tried to focus upon the shiny object, but her eyes refused to do her bidding.

Fiscel settled back in his comfortable chair. He had the satisfied look of a connoisseur about to enjoy a feast. Wet Belly Melli was beginning to feel like Melli On a Spit.

The bright flash of metal drew her eye and turned her stomach. Alysha drew a blade from her belt. Its haft was encrusted with pearls. The dark-haired woman knelt before the rope and began to cut its length. She was adept with a blade and even managed to endow the business of rope cutting with a certain capable elegance.

When she'd finished there were four lengths of rope. Up came the beautiful neck, revealing a half smile on the unlovely face. "Come," she beckoned, the first word she'd spoken in Melli's presence. "Come and join me. I will promise not to hurt you." A voice to match her movements, not her face. A beautiful, husky voice that hinted of things exotic and forbidden.

Melli was suddenly afraid. She looked to the door and saw that Fiscel caught the action. His good hand lay resting upon his walking stick. The end of the stick was formed by a large swelling of wood a fist thick. Melli understood the threat even before the flesh-trader's fingers enclosed the weighted end. She looked back to Alysha, who was sitting patiently on the bed. The dark-haired woman raised a hand of invitation. She was playing the game as if Melli had free will. Melli knew there was no choice; the invitation nothing but an order in disguise.

As if reading her thoughts, the woman said, "Come willingly to me now and I will be gentle. Refuse and I may have to hurt you." There was bone to the flesh after all, and tough meat beneath.

Drinking all that almond liqueur followed by numerous glasses of cheap wine had been a terrible mistake. Melli was pretty sure that she was in no state to make a run for it, or to put up a fight. There was one option, though.

She began to scream at the top of her voice. Melli was pleasantly surprised at how loud and jarring a sound came from her lips.

She didn't see the blow coming. She felt the excruciating impact, heard the thud of wood against her skull. Tears came to her eyes and spittle to her lips. Stumbling forward, she fell into the waiting arms of Alysha. The woman dragged her onto the bed.

Melli's head was caught in a spiral of pain and heaviness. She was tempted to give in and pass out. Forcing herself to stay conscious, she focused on the pain rather than the heaviness. The back of her head throbbed like a hive. Even in her dull and drunken state she realized the blow had been placed with care; a knock on the back of the head would leave no noticeable scars or bruises. Her hair would cover the consequences. Fiscel was obviously a man who treated his merchandise with due consideration. Melli felt a certain spiteful delight in the fact that she was already marked goods. Six welts on her back would bring her desirability—and very probably her price—right down.

Alysha bent over her and began to spread her arms. Melli could do nothing; it was taking all her concentration just keeping the room in focus. The raven-haired woman drew her arm out to the side and then above her head. She reached over for the length of rope and tied Melli's wrist to the bedpost. The rope was soft against her wrist, its touch nearly a caress. Alysha pulled hard on the silken rope and the caress became a vise. Fear and bile bubbled within Melli's stomach. She felt the mix burn in her throat. Once both arms were secure, Alysha's cool touch fell upon Melli's leg, drawing it out and to the side. The rope found one ankle and then the other.

Melli was spread-eagled on the bed. She raised her head, an achievement in itself considering it weighed twice as much as normal. Fiscel was back on his well-cushioned chair, and Alysha stood above her, knife in hand.

The dark-haired woman wielded the blade like a professional. One moment its tip rested against Melli's bodice, the next it was slicing a path down her dress.

The knife! Melli felt it fall from her skin along with the fabric. She waited, breath in body, for its discovery. A few seconds passed, and she risked raising her head once more. Alysha was sitting cross-legged on the floor, it looked as if she was polishing something. Melli glanced down at her dress. The fabric of her bodice lay unfurled on both sides like opened petals. Most of the knife was concealed under the dress, but the edge of the hilt could be seen jutting from the folds. Melli shifted her body slightly, and fabric and knife fell toward her. Next, she raised her back and shoulders, and the knife slipped down toward her waist. When she lay flat once more, the knife was hidden beneath her.

She was allowed no time to enjoy her triumph. Alysha came and sat by the foot of the bed, between her legs. In her hand she was holding what looked to Melli to be a smooth piece of glass. Melli felt her undergarments fall away from her skin. She flushed with shame.

"Such a pretty body," said Alysha. "Not as skinny as I thought. You would render a fair amount of fat."

Melli raised her head as Alysha lowered hers. The woman was kneeling between her legs and looking at her most private parts. Melli could not bear the indignity and shifted angrily against the ropes. She felt her knife slide against her back, and then the sting of the blade as it cut into her skin. Terrified she might do more damage to herself, she lay as still as the dead.

Alysha murmured words of calming in her soft, faraway voice. Melli felt something smooth and cool press gently against her sex. She saw the woman's lips move as if in prayer. What was spoken had more weight than words. The air from Alysha's mouth reached out toward her, probing. Melli became afraid. She'd heard many tales of sorcery, even seen it once herself, but this—so much less powerful than Jack's drawing—seemed an unbearable intrusion. She shifted against the ropes, suddenly not caring if her knife was revealed. Magic was inside of her; its presence warming as it searched. Every fiber of her soul fought against it. Every cell of her body felt violated.

Alysha mouthed a few words and the force withdrew, becoming air once more upon her tongue. "The hymen is intact," she said. "The girl is still a virgin." As she stood up, her legs faltered and she was forced to steady herself against the wall.

"Are you sure?" asked Fiscel.

"Of course I am," Alysha snapped. "The girl has a hymen as tough as old leather. She will need quite a breaking."

"There will be plenty of blood?"

"More than usual."

"Good. She will fetch a high price." Fiscel's smile was warm with anticipation. "My southern beauty never lets me down. You have so many talents, my dear, I don't know what I'd do without you." He poured a glass of nais and handed it to the woman. "Why, your hand is shaking, Alysha. What is the matter?"

Alysha looked quickly toward Melli. "There is something about that girl, Fiscel," she whispered.

Melli was trying very hard not to fall asleep, but she felt so weak. Her eyes had stopped focusing and her thoughts had followed suit. Slowly, despite all her efforts, her eyelids began to close.

"What do you mean, my precious?" asked Fiscel.

"Her fate is strong. It fought against the sorcery, nearly forcing it back upon me before I was ready. And her womb . . ." Alysha shook her head. "Her womb waits for a child who will bring both war and peace."

Traff spat out the wad of snatch. It was not a good blend, too bitter by far. He spat a few more times for good measure. A man needs a clean mouth.

He watched the shadowed cottage. The lights had gone out some time ago. The old woman would be fast asleep by now. Still, he would wait a few minutes longer, just to be sure. Surprise was as good a weapon as the keenest knife.

He passed the time by grinding the chewed snatch into the snow with the heel of his boot. Perhaps he might give up snatch all together. He'd heard that it rotted the teeth. In the past he wouldn't have cared one way or another about rotted teeth. Bad breath and toothache were for women and priests to fret over. But now he had other things to consider—his pretty young bride-to-be for instance.

Lady Melliandra, daughter of Lord Maybor and once betrothed to King Kylock, was to be his. Her father had sold her to him, along with two hundred pieces of gold. The great lord had struck a lame deal. He, Traff, had given away a little information, nothing more. Lord Maybor, however, had given away his only daughter. The old fool was in his dotage. So desperate had he been to hear about Baralis' scheming that he'd lost his powers of judgment. And as a result, the delicious Melli was his.

All he had to do now was to find her.

That was what brought him here tonight, to a small cottage set back from Harvell's eastern road. A cottage that was owned by an old woman who was a pig farmer.

The old crow deserved a beating just for the fact that she'd not turned her farm over to the authorities like she was supposed to. An old widow woman had no business running a farm, depriving a man of making a legitimate livelihood. She would be hanged if the word got out—and make no mistake, the word would get out—only by then she might be too stiff for a hanging.

Traff stepped out from his hiding place in the bushes and made his way toward the cottage. His blade was tucked in his belt and pressed against his thigh like a second manhood. He drew the knife from its resting place and his body mourned the loss. It was a fine knife, long and thin-bladed. A knife for fighting, or for killing.

He approached the cottage from behind, slipping between the barn and the sty. The smell of pigs filled his nostrils, and Traff found himself wishing he still had a mouthful of snatch, bad or otherwise. The pigs caught his scent and grunted nervously.

He fell under the shadow of the cottage and made for the door. Pushing it gently, he tested its strength: good hinges and a firm bolt. He moved away. Moving toward the front of the building, he tried every window shutter until he found one with rusted hinges. Breaking in was going to be noisy. Traff shrugged. The woman was old and probably deaf. He shouldered into the shutter with all his strength. The hinges cracked like kindling. The shutter fell into the cottage, taking the linen curtain with it. It crashed against the floor. Wincing at the noise, Traff climbed into the cottage.

Borc, but it was dark! He stood for a moment allowing his eyes to grow used to the blackness. He was in the kitchen. On the far side lay the door to the bedchamber. He adjusted his grip on the knife and then made his way across the room. The door was not bolted and swung back to his touch. In the darkness he could make out a white figure on the bed. It took him a moment to realize that the old woman was sitting up and that she had a knife in her hand.

"Don't come any closer," she said. "I bought this knife last week, and I've a hankering to test the blade."

Traff laughed. It really was quite absurd. Did the old crow have no idea just how ridiculous she sounded? The woman made a quick movement and then he felt something tear into his shoulder. The bitch had thrown the knife! Anger flared within Traff. He crossed the room in one leap. Grabbing the woman by her scrawny neck, he pressed his thumb into her throat. The feel of old flesh repulsed him. Blood sprinkled onto the covers and the floor. His blood.

"Not so brave now, old hag." Traff pushed his thumb against her windpipe. With his other hand he performed a showy maneuver with his knife, making sure the blade caught what little light was in the room. The woman's eyes glittered in unison with the blade. Traff was beginning to feel more relaxed now that he was back in charge. The wound on his shoulder didn't feel too deep. He had been wearing his leathers and they would have taken some of the bite from the knife.

"Now then, all I want you to do is answer a few questions for me. You'll be all right as long as you tell me the truth." Traff's tone was that of a parent admonishing a naughty child. "I've been talking to a friend of yours. He told me that you had two visitors stay here about five weeks back. Is this true?" Traff eased his grip on the woman's throat to give her a chance to confirm what he was saying. The woman didn't as much as blink an eye. Traff jabbed the haft of his blade into her chest. The woman coughed and spluttered. "I'll take that as a yes," he said.

"Were their names Melli and Jack?" Another thrust of the haft. The woman stifled her coughs this time. Traff was quickly depleting what little store of patience he'd been blessed with. "Look here, bitch, you answer my questions or I'll cut off both your hands and set fire to your precious pig sty." To illustrate his willingness to perform the former of these two threats, Traff drew the blade against her wrist. Dark blood welled to the surface in a thin line. She bled well for an old one.

"Now then, let's move along." He was the indulgent parent again. "What I need to know is where they were headed." Traff eased the point of the blade into the woman's open wound and absently drew back the skin.

"They headed east." The old woman sighed as she spoke. A single tear glistened forth in the darkness.

"Good, but not good enough." Traff scraped his blade against the intricate bunching of bones in the woman's wrist. "Where in the east?"

"Bresketh."

"No such place, old woman." One quick flick of the knife and the tendon connecting one bone to another was severed.

The woman cried out. "They told me Bresketh."

Traff got the distinct impression the woman was telling the truth. He tried a different tactic. "They might have told you Bresketh, but where do you think they were headed?" No reply. "Answer me, old woman, or your pigs will be crackling before the night is over."

"Bren. I think they were heading to Bren."

Traff smiled. "One last question. Did the boy Jack ever lay a finger on the girl?"

"I don't know what you mean."

Traff was pleased to note that the old woman now sounded afraid. "Let me explain, then," he said. "Melli is my betrothed, and it would make me very angry if she was as much as touched by another man." Traff continued working his knife into the open wound on the old woman's wrist. "Very angry, indeed."

"He never laid a finger on her. I swear."

"Good." Traff brought the knife to the woman's throat and slit her windpipe.

He wiped his hands and knife clean on her nightgown and then stood up. He was sorely tempted to put a flame to the sty, but he'd promised her "friend" that he could have the pigs, and he was a man of his word. When it suited him.

Now all that remained was to find a candle and then ransack the place. The old crow was bound to have a stash of gold somewhere. After a good night's rest and a hearty bacon breakfast, he would begin the journey east. Melli was his betrothed, and he would track her down wherever she was.

Six

*T*hey were making their way toward the pass. The path began to narrow and steepen as it wound its way up into the mountains. To either side lay huge banks of snow; virgin white, they gleamed with silent menace. The air, which was already ice-cold, had begun to thin out, and Maybor's damaged lungs had to strain for every precious load of oxygen.

Damn Baralis! He was responsible for this. Before the incident on Winter's Eve, he'd had the staying power of a man half his age. His lungs had been the mightiest of bellows, and now, thanks to Baralis and his foul poisons, they were as full of holes as a cheese-maker's cloth.

At least the wind was at rest. For the first time in this cursed journey the air was still, bestowing an unlooked-for blessing upon his weary bones.

If all went well and the pass was met by midafternoon, they would be in Bren in three days time. Maybor was impatient to gain the city. He was tired of traveling, sick of looking at snow and the back end of horses and, most importantly, he was anxious to be among civilization again. Bren promised all the delights of a modern city: fine food and strong ale, cheap women, and skilled tailors. He would find a tailor first. It was high time he had some decent robes made. His lungs had not been the only casualty of Winter's Eve: his wardrobe had to be destroyed. Now he had barely enough clothes to impress a tavern wench. Baralis had a lot to answer for.

Maybor turned his horse, a treacherous move on so narrow a path, and headed back along the length of the column. It was time he and Baralis sorted out a few things. Confronting the man here, along the cliffs and drops of the Great Divide, would give him the advantage. There was no greater horseman than he; no man could guide and control a horse as well. Baralis possessed no such skill. If Maybor judged right, the king's chancellor would be feeling just a little nervous at the moment, a little preoccupied with having to ride his horse along the hazardous snow-covered trail.

What better time to test the man's verbal acuity? And if Baralis' horse happened to lose its footing in the heat of debate, and plunge itself and its rider down into the snowy abyss of the mountain, that would merely be a regrettable accident.

The path was only wide enough to accommodate two riders abreast. Even so, Baralis chose to ride alone, or perhaps no one was willing to ride at his flank. Maybor had noted the way all the soldiers gave the king's chancellor a wide berth; they were afraid of him, though they would never admit it. Maybor could understand their fear; he more than anyone else knew just how dangerous Baralis could be.

Moving down along the column caused considerable inconvenience to the riders as they were forced to make way for the man and his horse. Maybor eventually pulled alongside Baralis.

"So, Maybor, to what do I owe this unexpected pleasure?" Baralis was as calm and aloof as ever.

Maybor had to admire the way the man could speak in such low tones and yet have all his words clearly understood. "I think you know what brings me here," he replied. "There are still some matters that need to be resolved between us."

"Matters to be resolved, indeed! Since when did you become a statesman, Maybor? Last I heard, your talents ran to women and murder. I didn't realize you were also an aspiring politician."

"Taunt me not, Baralis. As you have just pointed out, one of my talents *is* murder."

"Is that a threat, Maybor?" Baralis didn't wait for a reply. "Because if it is, then it's a naive one. You may have a little talent as far as murder is concerned, but you are merely a skilled amateur when compared to me." A little of the sting was robbed from the man's words as he was forced to rein his horse tightly to guide the creature around a sharp turn in the path.

"Not so great with a horse, though?" Maybor could not resist the jibe. He rounded the curve with the grace of Borc himself. One quick look to the left confirmed that the snowbank had given way to a sheer drop. To the right, the snow still rose like a mighty hillside. Maybor brought his horse closer to Baralis' mount, forcing the man to ride nearer the edge.

"Enough of this quibbling, Maybor. Cut to the bone. What did you come here to say?"

"I came here to tell you that I will be the superior envoy in Bren. I am king's envoy."

"I didn't know you could speak with the dead, Maybor."

"What d'you mean?"

"Well, correct me if I'm wrong, but you were appointed King Lesketh's envoy. Lesketh, as we both know is now cold in his grave, and unless you have developed a way to converse with his spirit, you have no rights in Bren."

Baralis' mocking tone raised a knot of fury in Maybor's gut. How he hated the arrogance of the man! He edged his mount more to the left. The two horses were so close their bellies were almost touching. Baralis was forced to pull on his reins to slow his mount.

"What's the matter, Baralis? Surely you aren't afraid of a little drop?"

"Don't play games with me, Maybor. You wouldn't want to lose another horse."

Maybor met the cold challenge of Baralis' eyes. There was an unflinching insolence in their gray depths. Maybor sat back in his saddle. He couldn't really believe what the man had said. He was claiming responsibility for killing his beloved stallion. And while he'd been riding it, no less! No, it couldn't be true.

Suddenly a cold wind blasted Maybor's face. A terrifying rumbling came in its wake. The mountainside was moving. A whole bank of snow was shifting.

"Avalanche!" someone cried.

The air was filled with the crashing of snow. Maybor rode forward in panic. The snow slid down in one mighty sheet, smashing into the path. The noise was deafening. There was chaos along the column. Men rode in fear for their lives. One man rode himself right off the cliffside. Chunks of snow and ice shot through the air like crossbolts.

Finally the snow came to rest, leaving a deadly silence as its obituary. White powder floated down on the party like a pall.

The column had congregated around the bend in the path. No one could see the damage done by the avalanche. They were short both men and supplies. The avalanche had caught the last of the column. Maybor looked around, suddenly hopeful. Baralis was still among the living. He cursed himself; he should have used the distraction to push the king's chancellor from the cliff!

No one dared move. Maybor's eyes were racing over the remaining supplies. Not one of the barrels had his mark upon it. Damn it! He'd lost three score casks of Nestor Gold. It was to have been his personal gift to the duke of Bren.

"My cider!" he exclaimed loudly. Maybe the men could dig it out.

"Crope!" The name was uttered with quiet anguish. The voice belonged to Baralis.

Maybor spun around. Baralis was moving toward the bend in the path, oblivious to the rest of the party. Maybor did a quick scan of the men. The huge lumbering idiot was nowhere to be seen.

"Lord Baralis!" shouted the captain. "You can't go back there, it won't be safe. Wait an hour or two and give the snow time to settle before we dig the men out."

"They will be long dead by then," murmured Baralis.

"I will send some men to accompany you," said the captain, moving forward.

"I will go, too," cried Maybor. He wasn't about to let Baralis pick through all the supplies with no one watching.

Baralis turned to face the party. His skin gleamed like polished marble. His gaze surveyed the men, meeting the eyes of each one in turn. *"Ride on!"* he commanded, his compelling voice carrying the authority of a king. "Ride on! I will deal with this danger alone!"

Such was the force of his voice that, after a short pause, the men began to turn their horses and make their way along the path. Maybor was powerless to stop them. The compulsion to obey was too strong. He watched as Baralis dismounted and made his way around the bend toward the avalanche site. Maybor was tempted to follow, but the threat of danger was too real and he didn't like the idea of his hide being permanently buried beneath a mountain of snow.

The party rode for a few minutes before the path widened sufficiently to make camp. The men were silent, their faces grave and tense. The captain ordered a head count.

Maybor did not doubt where the thoughts of all the men lay. Everyone was wondering what was happening at the avalanche site. A few minutes passed and then something strange happened: a warm wind rippled through the camp. Maybor told himself he'd imagined it, but the puzzled faces of others confirmed its presence. Again the air gusted warm and fast. There was a cracking, shifting noise. And then the unmistakable aroma of cooking meat.

Even as Maybor was disturbed at the smell, his mouth betrayed him by watering. He looked up, but the face of every man in the party was cast down, all intent on keeping their own counsel. It was as if to look at someone else might cause the strange goings-on to solidify into reality.

A length of time passed; Maybor had no way of gauging its measure. The air was cold once more. A chill breeze held the smell of well-done meat in its keep. The only noise was the sound of someone tapping a barrel—a man with enough good sense to realize that now was exactly the right time for a stiff drink.

Then, just as the ale began to flow, Maybor spotted Baralis approaching the campsite. He was walking, leading his horse by its reins. Lying over the mare's back was the body of a man. Size and width alone confirmed that it was Crope. The king's chancellor drew near. He was leaning heavily against the mare. The body on the horse shifted slightly; Crope was still alive.

The captain looked to Baralis.

He nodded, his face grim. "Go now," he said. "Rescue those who are left. Most are dead. I have done what I can."

Maybor could read the questions on the captain's face, but something stronger than curiosity forced the man to hold his tongue: fear.

Baralis led his horse to a sheltered section of the path. He ordered a guard to help lay Crope's body on the ground. Maybor could clearly see the strain on the face of the king's chancellor. He was exhausted, his shoulders drooping, his hands shaking. Reaching inside his cloak, he pulled out a small glass vial. He swallowed the contents like a man dying of thirst. His weight was against the horse, and without its support Maybor suspected Baralis would collapse.

The captain began to organize a group of men to accompany him to the avalanche site. Maybor insisted on going along to inspect the damage. A few minutes later, they rode up to the place where the snow lay across the path. The smell of meat tantalized the palate. Maybor hurried forward.

A portion of the snow had entirely melted away. Water pooled and then dripped from the path. Barrels and bodies were uncovered. The snow-melt formed a rough circle. At the center was the body of a horse and its rider. They were joined as one; their bodies scorched and blackened. Cooked to a crisp. Maybor heard the sound of more than one man vomiting.

Never had it been more difficult to deny the existence of sorcery. The very air was thick with it. Maybor rolled his phlegm and spat out the taste of meat and magecraft. "Come on now, men," he cried, purposefully sounding harsh. "There are still some alive. Now is not the time for shows of womanly weakness."

The soldiers began to clear away what remained of the snow and free the few men who were still moving. Past the melt-site, Maybor noticed a mound of snow that looked to have several barrels embedded in it. If he wasn't mistaken, his mark was upon them. "Before you deal with the dead," he called, "free my cider. Five gold pieces to the man who brings me the most barrels."

It was time for his midmorning snack. He had a fancy for some meat. Hot, sizzling fat surrounding delicate pink flesh: charred on the outside, tender within. Tavalisk had to stop himself from pulling the bell chord and summoning forth a huge joint of lamb.

He was watching his diet. His physician—Borc rot his soul—had lectured him on the dangers of overeating. None of the dreary recitation had any effect on the archbishop until the foul charlatan had mentioned the fact that overeating could lead to early death. Early death was one thing that Tavalisk most definitely wanted to avoid. What was the point of amassing great stashes of gold and land if one wasn't going to live to enjoy them?

Consequently he was trying his best to cut down on his eating. Instead of his usual three-course breakfast—eggs and bacon, followed by kippers and rolls, followed by cold pea soup—he now had only two courses. Needless to say, it was the pea soup that was bidden a fond farewell. Still, it was a sacrifice, and such uncharacteristic self-denial was hard for Tavalisk to bear. In fact, it made him rather angry.

The physician had prescribed music as a distraction. Now, the archbishop was as fond of music as the next man, and music might indeed tame savage beasts and so forth, but when it came to his stomach, a jaunty tune—no matter how well played—just couldn't stop his overactive bile from burning away at his gut.

A knock was heard at the door. The wood rang of Gamil. "Enter," called Tavalisk, taking up his lyre. He strummed with studied indolence, his mind firmly on food.

"I wish Your Eminence joy of the day."

"There is little joy in this day, Gamil." The archbishop suddenly hated his aide; the man probably had three courses for *his* breakfast. "Quickly tell me what petty intelligences you have and then be off. I am already tiring of your presence."

"Well, Your Eminence, do you remember the man who spied on the knight for us?"

"Of course I do, Gamil. I am too young for my dotage just yet. You mean my spy, the one who waited outside Bevlin's hut and saw the dead body the next morning?" The smell of cooking wafted gently through the open window. Tavalisk strummed faster on his lyre.

"The man has been seen keeping low company, Your Eminence."

"Just how low, Gamil?"

"He's been talking with friends of the Old Man."

"Hmm. That low, eh?"

"Yes, Your Eminence. He was spotted in the whoring quarter emerging from one of the Old Man's lairs, accompanied by two cronies."

Tavalisk looked over to the bowl of fruit, the only food in the room. Peaches and plums mocked him with their pink plumpness. How he hated the cruelty of fruit! He fingered his lyre with increased vigor. "And did this man leave with a heavy purse?"

"I can't exactly say, Your Eminence. But straight after leaving the Old Man's lair, he made his way to the market district and bought himself two new robes."

"Wool or silk?"

"Silk, Your Eminence."

"Ah, then we have our answer. Our man has sold his information to the Old Man."

"Your Eminence is as wise as he is musical."

"So you've noticed my playing, then, Gamil?" Tavalisk broke into a new and very loud tune on his lyre.

"Your Eminence's playing leaves me at a loss for words."

"That is always the way with the great masters, Gamil. They move one to emotion, not to speeches." The archbishop finished off his tune with a suitably theatrical flourish. Even to his biased ears he could tell he hadn't quite hit all the right notes. Still, genius was measured by more than purely technical skills alone.

"So, Gamil," he said, laying down his lyre, "how well did the Old Man know Bevlin?"

"We know they corresponded at irregular intervals, Your Eminence. The last time we were aware of an exchange of letters was just after the knight returned from Larn."

"It seems to me, Gamil, that the Old Man won't be pleased that his good friend Bevlin was bumped off by someone he tried to help."

"Indeed, Your Eminence. The Old Man is known for his loyalty to his friends."

"What action do you think he might take?"

"Who can tell, Your Eminence?" said Gamil with a slight shrug.

"*You* can tell, Gamil. That's what I pay you for."

"These things are difficult to predict Your Eminence. Perhaps the Old Man might seek revenge for Bevlin's death by having the knight assassinated."

"Hmm. The situation bears watching. Keep an eye to the gates and ports. I will be interested in knowing if any of the Old Man's cronies leave the city."

"Yes, Your Eminence."

Tavalisk pulled on the bell rope; he needed food. Playing the lyre had honed an edge to his appetite. No wonder so many of the great masters were as fat as pigs.

"I think it would be wise to pick up our man, Gamil. I can't allow one of my spies to turn traitor and get away with it. And who knows, once his tongue is sufficiently loosened by the rack, we might find out just what the Old Man is planning to do about Bevlin's death." The archbishop put down the lyre. Something about its shape reminded him of pomegranates—his favorite fruit. "Is there anything else?"

"A rather unsettling rumor about Tyren has reached my ears, Your Eminence."

"How unsettling, Gamil?"

"I've heard that he's ordered the knights to intercept and seize all of Rorn's cargoes that are headed to the north."

"This is intolerable! Who does that gold-greedy bigot think he is?" The archbishop pulled on the bell rope again. He now had need of a drink as well as a meal. "I need this confirmed as soon as possible, Gamil. If it is true I will have to come up with a suitable form of retaliation."

If a war was coming, let no one say that Rorn was slow from the stables. The archbishop smiled a tiny smile. The whole thing was really quite stimulating. The Known Lands had been too long without a decent conflict, and as long as it was waged in the north, both he and Rorn would be safe from its ravages.

"I shall endeavor to find the fact behind the fiction, Your Eminence. If there's nothing further, I will take my leave."

"I was rather hoping you would stay, Gamil. After a quick snack, I was planning to play all of Shuge's masterworks, and I'm anxious for your opinion on my fingerings."

"But Shuge's masterworks run to some five hours or more, Your Eminence."

"I know, Gamil. It will be a real treat for such an avid music lover as yourself."

There were six sacks of grain in the kitchen and Rovas was busy turning them into eight. Jack watched as the seasoned smuggler practiced one of the less ethical tricks of his trade. He poured a portion of the barley grain into a new sack until it was quarter full, then he took a quantity of what looked to be wood shavings and poured them into the sack. Next he topped the sack up with more grain and tied it with a length of twine.

"Couldn't that do a person harm?" asked Jack.

Rovas smiled showing wide teeth in a wide mouth. "There's people who'd put worse than wood shavings in grain, boy."

"Such as?"

"Ground bones, soil, sand." Rovas made an expansive gesture with his arm. "The people who get this grain should count themselves lucky. I've taken the trouble to shave the wood real fine. No one will choke on it, and I've heard that it's good for the digestion."

"Better for your pocket, though."

"What's the point of a man doing business if he can't make a little profit?" Rovas reached over to Jack and tousled his hair. "You're young yet, boy, and you don't know the ways of the world. Commerce is and always has been its driving force." He slung one of the sacks of grain over his shoulder. "You've got a lot to learn, Jack, and if I do say so myself, I'm the man to teach you." With that he stepped outside and began loading the grain onto his cart.

Once he had finished, he turned to Magra, who was spinning by the fire. "Come, woman," he said. "Accompany me to market like a good wife would." Rovas then addressed Jack. "You see, boy, potential customers will think a seller more honest if they see he is a family man."

"Perhaps I should go along as your son, then," said Jack with a hint of amusement, "just to complete the family circle."

Rovas slapped Jack on the back. "You're learning fast, boy. But I'll have to decline. I've known these buyers for many years now, and a long lost son might prove a little difficult for them to swallow."

"So might those eight sacks of grain."

Rovas laughed heartily and even the normally hostile Magra managed a snort of amusement. The smuggler buckled his belt and slipped a knife and a sword under the leather. "When I get back, boy," he said, "I'll start teaching you how to use a blade like a real man." He winked merrily and then was off, Magra trailing after him.

Jack breathed a sigh of relief. It was good to be on his own. It seemed as if he'd had no chance to think since he'd heard that Melli was dead. He moved closer to the fire and poured himself a cup of mulled cider. The sweet and heady fragrance of apples tugged at his senses, evoking memories of his life in Castle Harvell. The kitchens were often filled with the scent of apples, either with baking or cider-making. There was such simplicity then; no dangers, no worries, no guilt.

He ran his hand over the thick and bristling growth on his chin and neck. It had been many days since he'd had a shave. The last time had been the day the Halcus soldiers came to the coop . . . the day that Melli was murdered.

Jack threw the cup into the fire where it smashed against the back wall—*he should have been there!* It should have been he, not Melli, who was clubbed to death. He had failed the only person who'd ever relied upon him. He cupped his face in his hands, pressing his fingertips deep into his temples. The pain of guilt became a tangible pressure. He felt it build up, demanding release. A sharp metallic taste slivered along his tongue.

The shelving that hung above the fire suddenly rattled and then gave way, sending all the pots and pans that were hanging from it plunging into the flames. Jack stepped back in horror. He heard a door open behind him and Tarissa walked in.

"What in Borc's name have you done?" she cried, dashing forward to salvage what was probably a week's worth of food from the fire. "Don't just stand there, help me!" She grabbed hold of the metal poker and speared the haunch of mutton with its tip. "It's badly charred, but the meat will be all right," she said. "Wrap a rag around your hand and save what pots you can."

Jack obeyed her orders and pulled several pots from the fire. Most were empty, their contents spilt and then lost to the flames.

"The stew and porridge!" cried Tarissa, but it was too late. Those two most staple of foods sizzled on the embers.

Jack pulled the last of the pans from the fire. He managed to salvage a pot full of beets, two roasting turnips, and a string of sausages.

"What happened?" demanded Tarissa. She was obviously upset. Angry tears gleamed in her eyes. A family's wealth was judged by its supply of food.

"I don't know," Jack said. "The shelf just collapsed." He wasn't being honest, he knew what had happened: as his anger and frustration flared, the shelf had given way. The two were related, there was no doubt in his mind, and it was sorcery that provided the connection. He supposed he should be thankful that no one was hurt. Only he didn't feel very thankful at the moment, just tired and confused.

"Here, let me look at your hand. The rag is badly scorched." Tarissa sat beside him on the bench and unwrapped the rag. The flesh beneath was livid red. Tarissa's face softened into remorse. "I'm sorry, Jack," she said. "I shouldn't have asked you to put your hand in the fire. Please forgive me." Her fingers hovered above the burn and then lightly touched his wrist.

Jack could not meet her eyes. Blistering pain swelled in his hand. He almost welcomed the sensation. It diverted his thoughts from the truth. Sorcery accompanied him, and like a shadow it would follow him to the grave.

Tarissa began searching in cabinets for ointments to put on his skin. He was deeply moved by her sudden change in demeanor. Her kindness was an unexpected gift. Jack sat and let her rub salve onto his wounds. Her touch was gentle, as if she were afraid to hurt him further. He looked at her face. Her lashes were long and fair, her nose short with a tiny bump, her lips pink and full. She was beautiful, not perfect, just beautiful. She looked up and their eyes met. For a brief second Jack was puzzled by what he saw. There was something about her that was known to him. Delicate hazel eyes, an intricate mingling of brown and green, met his.

Her lips moved the barest instance: an invitation as bold as open arms. He leaned forward and kissed her, a chaste kiss made less so by the plumpness of both sets of lips. Jack felt her tender flesh give way and then envelop him. He reached out with his arm to draw her near, but she backed away. She stood up awkwardly and would not look at him.

"It was you that made the shelf give way." A statement.

Jack looked to the floor. "I never laid a hand upon it."

"I know." Tarissa smiled with tantalizing assurance.

Jack could think of no reply. There was little point in lying; she had guessed the truth. Instead he asked, "Is Tarissa your full name?"

She laughed outright at this blatant attempt to change the subject, yet seemed happy to go along with it. "My full name is Tarissyna," she said.

Jack felt his spirits lighten. She knew the truth but didn't condemn him: her second gift to him. "Tarissyna is a noblewoman's name in the kingdoms."

She shrugged. "Perhaps, but I've lived in Halcus most of my life, and my name counts for little here."

"When did you leave the kingdoms?"

"I was a babe in arms when my mother brought me here." There was an edge to her voice. It took Jack a moment to realize it was bitterness.

"Why did Magra leave?"

"She was not wanted. She was an inconvenience to people in high places. By staying she risked death."

"And you?"

Tarissa laughed coldly. "They wanted me dead more than my mother."

"But you were just a baby."

"Wars have been waged over babies." Tarissa turned away and began to brush the remains of the food from the hearth.

Jack could tell she wanted to say no more. She had told him just enough to pique his interest, and he found himself more puzzled than ever. He could still feel the press of her lips against his. It acted like a reprimand, reminding him not to question too deeply, after all she had done no less for him. By dropping the subject of the shelf falling into the fire, she had saved him from awkward questions. He would do no less for her.

Jack knelt beside her, helping to scrape the burnt stew from the grate. He looked at Tarissa, and she looked at him. Their mutual secrets, only hinted at, never told, acted as a bond between them. And when their arms brushed together as they cleaned up the fireplace, neither was inclined to be the first to pull away.

A short time later, when the grate shone like a newly minted coin, the door burst open and in came Rovas and Magra. The older woman sniffed the room like a bloodhound and then made straight for the fire. "What has happened here?" she cried. Even in anger, her voice carried the elegant modulated tones of a noblewoman. Her eyes darted to Jack.

Tarissa spoke before Jack could stop her. "There was a little accident, Mother. I was stirring the stew when the whole shelf came down."

"How can that be?" asked Rovas. "I nailed that up good and strong before winter set in."

"Hmm, I think we have our answer, then," said Magra. "If ever a man lacked practical skills, it is you, Rovas Widegirth."

"Less of the wide girth, woman. You know as well as I do that to be a successful merchant you need to appear prosperous. There's nothing like a big belly for showing a man's got money to spend."

Jack wondered what a woman like Magra was doing with a man like Rovas. They were total opposites. Magra was refined; her speech, her appearance, even the words she chose, spoke of nobility, yet Rovas was a self-confessed rogue. It didn't make any sense.

"No need to worry," Rovas was saying. "There's plenty more where that came from. How can I call myself a smuggler and not have some hidden stashes?" He turned to Jack. "Come with me, boy. You can help me dig up the vegetable garden. I buried a chest of salted beef there. The only problem is, I can't remember exactly where."

As Jack left the cottage, he caught Tarissa's eye. He sent her a look of thanks. She had saved him from some difficult questions.

Rovas spotted the burn mark on his hand. "How'd you do that, boy?"

"I was helping Tarissa save the pots from the flame."

"Right hand, eh? Never mind, that won't stop me teaching you the blade. A true fighter knows how to wield a knife with both hands. This way your left can have a head start."

Nabber made his way along Bren's busy streets. Traders and beggars called to him. He bought a stuffed pork pie from a street merchant and tossed a handful of coppers toward a cripple and his blind mother. The speed with which the mother found the coins was nothing short of miraculous for a blind woman. Nabber smiled brightly her way. He knew she could see, but he admired her skill anyway. The way her eyes rolled wildly in her sockets was truly the work of a dedicated artiste.

He bit into his pie. It was delicious, hot and juicy, with at least a passing resemblance to pork.

It was a beautiful day, that is, for a place as cold as Bren. The sky was light blue and clear, the air crisp and fresh. Something was going on in the city, he was sure of it. To the north of the city, where all the fancy buildings and the duke's palace were situated, the streets were being cleaned and banners were being hung. Probably expecting important visitors, Nabber concluded. Affairs of state didn't concern him, however. He had one mission on his mind today: he was going to help Tawl.

He passed a market stall where hand mirrors were being sold. He picked one up and had a quick look at himself. "S'truth!" he muttered to his reflection. He hastily smoothed back his hair with a handful of spit. To think he'd gone following Tawl last night with the hair of a wild man. His collar was none too clean, either. Swift would be disappointed. *"Always wear a clean camlet,"* he would say. *"You'll look less like a scoundrel that way."* Nabber could see the wisdom of Swift's words. Though he still wasn't sure what a camlet was.

He was tempted to pocket the mirror—it would make a fine addition to his personal grooming accoutrements—but the stall-holder had a mean eye, and Nabber prided himself on knowing when *not* to take chances.

The sun followed him to the west of the city. It was late afternoon and Nabber wondered if he should have made an effort to find Tawl earlier. The problem was that the best pickings were to be found before noon, and he'd been reluctant to give up a day's earnings. Swift would have thought him foolish. So here he was, best part of the day over, bag full of coinage in his tunic, on his way to find the knight.

He took a turn onto Brotheling Street and made his way toward the place where he'd last seen Tawl. The smell was more accurate a guide than any map. Each building had its own characteristic odor, and Nabber honed in on the one he remembered from last night. The place looked rather dismal in the daylight; the timbers were rotting and the paint was peeling. It just went to show how generous the night was with its favors. The building had looked like a palace under its patronage.

Nabber knocked boldly on the door.

"Go away, you're too early," came the reply.

"I'm looking for a man, name of Tawl. He's a fighter." Nabber was forced to shout at the wood, for the door had not been opened.

"No one here named Tawl. Now get lost!"

"He was here last night. Big fellow, golden hair, bandage on his arm."

"What's in it for me?"

Nabber began to feel more comfortable talking to the faceless voice; information for coinage was a concept he was more than familiar with. "Two silvers if you know where he is."

"Ain't worth my breath."

"Five silvers then." This was turning out to be more expensive than he hoped. Still, it all helped the cash circulate. Swift had given him long lectures on the importance of circulation.

"Done." The door was opened and a small-eyed woman emerged. Nabber recognized her at once as being the woman who had stolen Tawl's gold. "Let's see the spark of your silver."

Nabber brought out the promised coinage. "May I be so bold as to ask the name of such a fine-looking woman as yourself?"

The woman looked taken aback by this request. She patted her elaborately coifed hair, and said, "I'm Madame Thornypurse to you, young man."

Powder from her head swirled into the air, and Nabber had to fight the urge to sneeze. "So, Madame Thornypurse, which way was the gentleman headed?"

"Not a friend of yours, is he?" The woman's voice was as shrill as a mating goose.

"No, madame," said Nabber. "Never met him before in my life. I'm merely a messenger."

Madame Thornypurse sniffed in approval. "The man you're looking for has gone drinking in the Duke's Fancy. It's a tavern on Skinners Lane. Now hand over the cash."

"It was a pleasure doing business with you, madame," said Nabber with a little bow as he passed her the coinage. Swift himself would have been impressed at the speed with which the money disappeared into her bodice. Nearly as quickly, the door was shut in his face.

Nabber sneezed heavily; the hair powder finally proved too irritating to ignore. He then made his way along Bren's busy streets. He soon found the Duke's Fancy. It was a tall and brightly colored building. A group of men were dicing in the doorway. Nabber was tempted to join them, for he loved to dice more than he liked to eat, but he passed them by, pausing only once or twice to see how the dice were landing. It was really quite a pity he was on a mission, as the dice were landing with the grace of a goddess. A man could circulate a lot of coinage with dice as sweet as those.

He entered the tavern and pushed his way through the throngs of revelers. The air was thick with the smells of hops, yeast, and sweat: a fine drinking man's odor.

Nabber caught the flash of straw yellow hair: it was the woman who'd collected Tawl's money for him the night before, and then passed it on to old Thornypurse. Indignation swelled in his breast and he stepped toward her. She was calling loudly for more ale and was being enthusiastically cheered on by a group of men and women. The ale came—a whole barrel of it—and she reached into a sack to pay the innkeeper. It was Tawl's sack. The woman was buying drinks for Borc knows how many people, and paying for them with Tawl's money!

The knight was still nowhere in sight. Nabber's eyes followed the sack. As always, his hands were ahead of his brain. The straw-haired woman was distracted for only an instant as she raised her cup in toast, but it was enough. Nabber slid the sack from the table. With fingers that never faltered for an instant, he bundled it into his cloak. Now was not the time to revel in the thrill of the snatch, so he bowed his head low and made for the door.

A second later the cry went up: "My gold! Someone's stole my gold!"

Nabber had to stop himself from shouting out that it wasn't her gold at all. He kept calm. He could see the door. Only a few steps and he'd be gone. There was some disturbance in the crowd behind him. He couldn't afford to look back. He pushed the last of the people out of the way and made it to the doorway. Still not sure if he'd been fingered, he began to saunter slowly down the street. He was just about to break out into a nonchalant whistle when he heard the telltale sign of footsteps behind him. Nabber quickly abandoned all attempts to appear blameless and started to run as fast as his legs could carry him.

Swift, while being a thief of great sophistication, had known of the occasional need for a quick escape. Nabber followed his instructions: *"Never run in a straight line. Take every turn that crosses your path, always head to where the crowd is at its thickest . . . and move like the wind."* Down streets and alleys he fled, through markets and gatherings he charged. The footsteps still followed. He dived into an alleyway, good and dark, and ran up its length. It ended in a stone wall. Nabber drew a deep breath. It was too tall to scale; he'd just have to blaze a path backward. Quickly he scanned his brain for any words of wisdom that Swift might have imparted on this particular predicament. He came up blank. Nabber was forced to conclude that Swift would never have been stupid enough to run up a blind alleyway.

Knees trembling from fatigue more than fright, Nabber turned to face his pursuer. The man was silhouetted against the light. He moved forward and the sunlight shone on his hair. Golden hair. It was Tawl.

A long moment passed. The sun retreated with the tact of a diplomat, leaving man and boy alone. A low wind gusted down the alleyway. It toyed with the filth, picking up more smell than substance.

Tawl stood and looked at Nabber, his great chest heaving, his hair the color of dark gold. There was no expression to be read on his face. Without a word he began to move away.

To Nabber's amazement the knight turned and started to retrace his steps down the alleyway. Tawl's pace was slow and his head was bowed. Nabber couldn't bear it an instant longer. "Tawl!" he cried. "Wait." He saw the knight hesitate for the briefest instant, and then, without turning round, he shook his head. At the sight of this small, almost negligent gesture, Nabber felt his throat grow tight. Tawl was walking away from him.

Swift had warned him many times about the dangers of friendship: *"Never let a man get close enough to rob your purse,"* he would say. Having no friends himself, merely accomplices, Swift was a person who put little value on friendship. Up until the time he'd met Tawl, Nabber had been inclined to agree with him. But Swift wasn't always right. Yes, he could turn a phrase more smoothly than a milkmaid churning butter, yet for all his cleverness he could trust no one. And no one trusted him. Suddenly the idea of ending up like Swift—a man who asked you what you wanted before asking your name—didn't seem as enticing to Nabber as it had in the past.

He ran after Tawl and put a hand on his arm. "Tawl, it's me! Nabber."

"Get away from me, boy." Tawl's words were as sharp as blades. He pulled his arm free and continued walking.

"Here," said Nabber, handing him the sack. "Take your loot back. I only robbed it to stop your ladyfriend from spending it all."

The knight pushed the sack away. "I don't need you as my keeper. Have it yourself. There's plenty more where that came from."

"You mean you plan on staying in Bren?"

"My plans are not your concern, boy." Tawl quickened his pace, but Nabber kept to his side.

"What about your quest? The boy . . ." Nabber was about to say, "the boy who Bevlin sent you to look for," but stopped himself. Now wasn't a good time to mention the dead wiseman.

Tawl swung around. *"Leave me be!"*

There was such venom in the knight's words that Nabber actually took a step back. He got his first close look at his friend's face. Tawl had aged. Lines that had been mere suggestions a month earlier had deepened and set. Anger blazed across his features, but there was something more in his eyes. It was shame. As if realizing he'd been found out, Tawl lowered his eyes and turned back to his path. His footsteps echoed softly as he walked away.

Nabber was tempted to give him up; the man wanted no one's help. It was getting late and the idea of a hot supper at a fine tavern was most appealing. He watched Tawl reach the end of the passageway and turn onto the street. Just before he passed out of sight, Tawl ran his fingers through his hair. It was a simple movement, one Nabber had seen him do a hundred times before. The familiarity of the action made Nabber realize how well he'd come to know Tawl. The knight was his only friend, and they were both a long way from home. Supper began to seem less important.

He hurried after Tawl. It had been a mistake to approach him in such a forthright manner, asking about the quest, telling him he was being cheated of his money. If he was ever to get the knight back to his old self, he'd have to try a more subtle technique. Tawl obviously wanted to forget the past, forget the wiseman, forget the search for the boy, forget even himself. Well, he'd make sure that Tawl wasn't allowed to forget. The one thing that he was sure of was the fact that the knight had lived to find the boy. It had been his sole purpose, and for him to give up on it so completely struck Nabber as being unspeakably tragic.

For tonight, though, it would be best if he just kept watch on him. He'd bide his time and wait for a suitable opportunity to get back in the knight's good graces.

Nabber stepped onto the street. He paused a minute to buy a pastry from a street trader—missing out on a hot supper was one thing, but going without anything to eat at all was quite another—and then struck a path back toward the Duke's Fancy.

Seven

Of course, Bodger, there's really only one way to tell if a woman's a virgin."

"You mean apart from them having straight hair, Grift?"

"That one's an old wives' tale, Bodger."

"I've got to agree with you there, Grift. Ever since you've been wearing those extra-tight hose, you could easily be mistaken for an old wife."

"Hmm, I wear them strictly for therapeutical reasons, Bodger. With vitals as delicate as mine, the first gust of wind sends them north, and once they're there, it's murder to get them back."

"Aye, Grift, you're famous for your temperamental vitals."

"Do you want me to impart my worldly wisdom or not, Bodger? Other men would pay good money to be taught by a master such as myself."

"Go on, then. What's the real way to tell if a woman's a virgin?"

"You have to put her in a room with a badger, Bodger."

"A badger?"

"Aye, Bodger, a badger." Grift sat back on his mule and made himself as comfortable as a man on a mule can be. "You take the badger, Bodger, lock it in a room with the girl you're testing. You leave them alone for a couple of hours, and then go and see what's happened."

"What's supposed to happen, Grift?"

"Well, Bodger, if the badger falls asleep in the corner, then the girl's been around the haystack, if you know what I mean. But if the badger comes and curls up on her lap, then she's a virgin good and true."

"What if the badger bites the girl, Grift?"

"Then the girl will catch the ground pox, and no one will care either way, Bodger."

Bodger nodded judiciously; Grift had a point there. The two men were at the back of the column, making their way down a wide but steep mountain path. The air was silent and brittle. No birds called, no winds blew.

"You had a close call yesterday, Bodger."

"I was lucky to be brought out from under the avalanche, Grift."

"I don't think luck had much to do with it, Bodger. Lord Baralis makes his own luck." Although Grift was sorely tempted to ask Bodger exactly what had happened at the avalanche site the day before, he knew it was wise not to do so. No one who'd been pulled out from under the snow had talked about it. In fact, no one in the entire party had mentioned the incident. People were pretending it never happened. By the time they reached Bren, it would be gone from everyone's memory. Six men had died.

Hearing a noise behind him, Grift looked around. "Here, Bodger, Crope's finally caught up with us. That's him joining the rear now."

"Aye, Grift. He'd be hard to mistake down a deep tunnel. I wonder why he insisted on hanging back at the avalanche site this morning."

"Let's find out why, Bodger." The two men pulled aside from the column and waited until Baralis' servant was abreast of them.

"Nasty bruise that, Crope," said Bodger, motioning toward Crope's forehead.

"Hurts real bad," replied Crope in his low and gentle voice.

"Is that why you didn't ride with us first thing, then? Because you weren't up to it?"

Crope shook his head at Grift. "No, I had to go digging."

"Burying treasure, Crope?" Grift winked at Bodger.

"No, Grift," Crope said, oblivious to Grift's sarcasm. "I lost my box in the 'lanche. Slipped right out of my pocket, it did. Took me a long time to find it." Crope smiled and patted the square-shaped bulge in his tunic. "It's back where it belongs now."

"Why, Crope, you amaze me," said Grift. "I don't believe I've ever heard you say so many words in one go. That box must be pretty important to spark such an outpouring of verbal eloquence."

Crope's face lost its smile. "None of your business, Grift. I wants to be on my own now." With that Crope pulled on his reins to slow his mount, and Bodger and Grift rode ahead.

"Well, Bodger," said Grift, "if I know Crope, he's probably keeping his old toenail clippings in that mysterious box of his."

"Aye, Grift. Either that or his nasal hair."

"He'd need a bigger box for that, Bodger!"

Bodger nodded his head judiciously. "Still, Crope risked riding through the pass on his own just to save that box."

"The pass wasn't as bad as I thought it would be, Bodger. We were over it in no time."

"Aye, Grift. If the weather holds, we'll be in Bren in two days time."

"It's when we reach Bren that the real drama will begin, Bodger."

"How so, Grift?"

"Well, no one in Bren knows yet that Kylock is now king. If you ask me, Bodger, the people there will get mighty jittery when they find that out. Betrothing a girl to a prince is an entirely different matter than betrothing her to a king."

"I thought it would be more of an honor, Grift."

"Bren's not a city that likes to be upstaged; it needs to be the dominant force in any alliance. Mark my words, Bodger, there'll be trouble when we reach our destination."

The sun disappeared behind a bank of clouds. Night was pushing its suit and the day would soon succumb.

It was cold in the garden and the snow crackled underfoot like long-dead leaves. The breath of the two men could be seen whitening, crystallizing. When they drew close, which they did from time to time, there was a certain intimacy in the crossing of their breaths.

Jack was amazed by Rovas' stamina. Although the man was possibly twenty years older than himself, he moved with the speed of a stag and fought with the endurance of an ox. Jack was feeling at a distinct disadvantage. They were fighting with long staffs—a weapon that tested a man's strength more than his reflexes. Jack was beginning to realize how very little he knew about combat. Up until this point his only weapon had been a pig-gutting knife, and although it had helped him kill a man, it had been frenzy not skill that had placed the blade.

The wood came together with a blunt cracking sound. Once again Rovas pushed him back. Jack turned his staff. His opponent was faster and the wood met again. Rovas chuckled. "Waste of a blow, boy. Shouldn't have bothered." With a lightning quick movement he disengaged his staff, took a step back, released his fore-grip, and used the staff as a spear. He slashed at Jack's shoulder. Jack was totally unprepared and went down, his head meeting rocks beneath the snow.

"You said I had to hold the staff with both hands." Jack got to his feet, brushing the snow from his tunic.

"Did I?" Rovas was nonchalant. "Well, that just goes to show that you should play by no man's rules except your own." The huge man looked quite alarming; his face was bright red and he was sweating with gusto.

"So I should trust no one."

"Just one person: yourself."

Jack handed Rovas his staff and the two made their way back toward the cottage. It had been an exhausting day. Rovas had woken him at dawn and they'd spent most of the light hours in the garden fighting. The bearded smuggler was a good teacher. He had a vast stock of weapons ranging from the leather-bound clubs favored by the Halcus, to the seemingly dainty—but Jack had learned deadly—thin-bladed swords of Isro. There was not one weapon in his collection that Rovas couldn't use or offer some useful advice on.

Rovas stopped by the small outbuilding that was attached to the cottage. "Fancy helping me stuff the kidneys?" he asked. "The women can't abide messing around with the internals."

Jack tried hard not to look bewildered.

Rovas laughed heartily and opened the door, pausing to strike up a lantern. The smell of newly butchered meat filled Jack's nostrils. The light gleamed upon the offal. Liver rested in platters pooled with blood. Kidneys waited coyly in baskets, scenting the air with their distinct perfume. "Beautiful, eh?" prompted Rovas.

Jack was beginning to think that Rovas was slightly mad. How could a man possibly find such a sight appealing? He nodded his head slightly, in what he hoped was a noncommittal manner.

Rovas smiled brightly, showing teeth as large as pebbles. "There's loot in this room, boy. There's people around Helch who haven't seen as much as a single sausage all winter. They'll pay good money for a pound or two of prime offal."

So that was it. Rovas wasn't mad after all, merely greedy. "Where did all this meat come from?" asked Jack.

Rovas beckoned him closer, and when he spoke his voice was a theatrical whisper. "From a good friend of mine, name of Lucy."

Lucy. Jack reeled at the sound of it. His mother's name. Such a common calling. Hundreds of girls in every city in the Known Lands answered to its light, musical sound. Strange how he'd gone so long without hearing it spoken. It brought back a yearning for the past, for a time when he'd rest his head against his mother's chest and the world held no secrets, just promises.

She had worked so hard. Even now he could smell the ash, see its grayish bloom upon her face and touch the burns upon her fingers. She had been an ash maid in the kitchens; raking through the cinders in the morning, banking down the embers at night. The staff was merciless, it was always:

"More wind in the bellows, Lucy."

"Lucy, bring more logs from the pile."

"Clean the ash from the grate, Lucy, and while you're about it, make it shine."

Only Lucy wasn't her real name. Jack could never pinpoint the exact moment when he discovered this; it was more a gradual realization.

From as early as he could remember he spent his days in the kitchen. He tried to be as "quiet as a mouse and as little trouble as a laying hen," for when he got into trouble his mother was punished for him. He'd totter under one of the huge trestle tables, find the rind of an apple, or the scrape from a carrot to chew upon, and settle down to view the goings-on. The kitchen was a place of wonders; cooking smells filled his nostrils, the clang of copper pots and complaints filled his ears, and the sight of food tempted his young eyes.

He'd spend hours lost in daydreams. The butcher's cleaving knife became Borc's ax, Master Frallit's apron would become the Knights of Valdis' banner, and the stool by the fire where his mother sat became a throne.

When his mother grew tired, as she did more and more the year before she took to her bed, Jack would help her with the fires. One time when they both had their backs to the kitchen, scrubbing the burn from the grate, the head cook called out: "Lucy, clean the stove when you've finished there." His mother never looked round. The cook called again, louder. "Lucy! The stove needs a cleaning." Jack had to shake his mother's arm to get her attention.

From that day on he watched her more closely. There were many times when she failed to respond to her name. Later, before the end, when he was older and she was weaker, Jack challenged her about it. "What are you really called, Mother?" he asked. He'd chosen his time with cruel precision. She was too ill to feign surprise—he felt ashamed of that now.

She sighed and said, "I will not lie to you, Jack. Lucy is not my given name, it was chosen for me by another later." He tried to get her to say more, pleading at first, and when that failed, shouting. Sick as she was, her strength of will remained firm and her lips remained closed. Rather than lie to him, she had told him nothing instead.

Rovas, bearing offal, brought Jack back to the present. He was glad of it, there were too many questions in the past.

"The trouble with the kidneys, Jack," he said, "is that they're a little . . . how should I put it? . . . a little light."

"Light?"

"Too many to a pound, if you know what I mean." Rovas smiled like a guileful child.

"So you intend on making them heavier." Jack was beginning to catch the man's meaning.

Rovas nodded enthusiastically. "You're a bright boy," he said. "Now this is what we do." The smuggler placed a kidney upon an empty platter and then whipped out his knife. "One tiny cut, here, just above the tendon." He opened the kidney like a surgeon, and then held the incision open with the knife-point. "Just pass me that jar over there, boy." Rovas indicated a large container on a shelf. "Careful, it's quite a weight."

Jack swung the jar from the shelf and nearly dropped it. Master Frallit's baking stones were heavy, but at least they were large. "What's in this?" he asked.

"Lead, of course. Heavy as a mountain, soft as a good cheese. Reach in and grab me a chunk. A fair-sized one, mind. We don't want it getting stuck in anybody's throat."

Jack handed Rovas a piece of the gray metal, and the man wasted no time inserting it into the middle of the kidney. He carefully closed the cut, molding it back to its original appearance, and then gave it to Jack to feel. "Not a bad job, if I do say so myself."

"This could kill a man," said Jack, testing its weight in the palm of his hand.

"So could going without meat all winter." Rovas shrugged. "A man's got to make a living, and the chances are the metal will be found before the kidney reaches the pot." He caught Jack's disapproving look. "It's the way of the world, boy. If I didn't do it, someone else would. Halcus has been through some hard times since the war with the kingdoms started, and things look set to get worse. It won't be long before Bren is pushing us from the other side. If someone like me comes along and brings supplies to people who wouldn't normally get them, then it's only fair I take a decent profit for my troubles."

"What do you mean about Bren pushing from the other side?" Jack wasn't about to challenge Rovas on his way of doing business. The man would never admit he was doing anything wrong.

"Haven't you heard? Your country is joining with Bren, and if you ask me, it means trouble for more than just us here in Halcus. Annis, Highwall, even Ness—everyone's nervous. People are afraid that Bren is using the Four Kingdoms to help them dominate the north." Rovas spat reflectively. "Just this morning I heard news that Highwall is busy training an army in readiness. That's one city that won't wait for an attack like a rabbit down a hole."

This was the first Jack had heard about a war. The kingdoms joining with Bren? Events had moved swiftly since he left the castle. "Kylock is going to marry . . ." Jack struggled to remember the name of the duke's daughter, "Catherine of Bren?"

Rovas nodded. "War's acoming."

War. It might never have happened if Melli had married Kylock as she had been supposed to. She would never have been killed, either. Jack put the kidney on the platter and tried to wipe his hands free of the blood. The stain smeared and thinned, but would not come off. Looking down at his bloodied hands, Jack couldn't help feeling that he was somehow responsible for what was to come. It was foolishness, he told himself. He'd never influenced Melli in any way; she had already decided not to marry Kylock before they met.

Feeling guilty, yet not understanding why, prompted Jack to attack Rovas. He wanted to share the blame. "You should be pleased if war breaks out," he said, his voice rising in anger. "More fighting will mean more profit."

For one brief instant Jack thought Rovas would hit him. The man's body became tense, his hand moved abruptly from his side. He controlled himself, though. Jack could clearly see him working to regain his good humor. With an effort Rovas shrugged and said, "Skirmishes along the border are one thing, boy, a full-blown war is quite another. Yes, there's more money to be made, but there's more chance of being killed before you spend it!" By the time he'd finished the last sentence, Rovas was back to his old self. Jack was almost sorry; he wanted a fight.

"Here," said Rovas, distracting Jack's thoughts by handing him the platter of kidneys. "Stuff these for me. I've had enough of war for one day. I'm off to get my supper." With that he left the hut, shutting the door behind him.

The thought of war had stirred something within Jack. The kingdoms joining with Bren? Why did the news matter so much? And why did it make him want to pick a fight with a man who would surely have beaten him? For the first time since leaving the castle, Jack felt restless. The familiar yearning to take off and leave everything behind was upon him. The platter felt like a dead weight in his hands. The smell of the kidneys was unbearable. He shoved the platter away and opened the door.

The chill night air cooled Jack's face. The familiar yearning, but also the familiar frustration. He had nowhere to go.

Rovas' footsteps formed an arc in the snow. Jack's eye followed the curve to where it ended: the entrance to the cottage. The people inside were his only connection to the world: Rovas, Magra, Tarissa. They were not what they seemed. Magra and Tarissa had secrets to keep. The same thing that made the mother bitter had made the daughter strong. Then there was Rovas, who only minutes earlier had nearly slipped and shown the edge beneath the padding. They had the look of a family, but not the feel of one.

Even the cottage had the look of home about it: candlelight slipping out from the shutters, smoke spiraling up from the roof, the polished door offering a welcome. It was no place for him to stay. Jack suddenly felt tired. He couldn't foresee a time when he'd ever have a proper home again. Traveling with Melli had made him forget how alone he was. As long as she was with him all his worries had been for her. Keeping Melli safe and warm and well fed was all that mattered. Now that she was gone, his thoughts turned inward once more.

For many months now his destination had been Bren. There was no reason behind it other than it felt right to head east. Now more than ever, with the news of war still ringing in his ears, he felt the need to be there. But he wouldn't go. Not yet, anyway. He wasn't ready. He had no skills at fighting, and if he were going to a place of war, it would be better to be prepared. And then there was Melli. Jack couldn't bear the thought of going without trying to make amends; her death was too important to be casually forgotten. Leaving now would diminish her. Nearly ten years ago, when his mother died, he'd carried on as if nothing had happened, barely sparing a breath to mourn her. He wouldn't make the same mistake again.

Jack closed the door and the expanse of the night retreated. He would stay and learn. Rovas was using him—the man obviously had his own reason to want the Halcus captain dead—so *he* would use Rovas. He would learn all the smuggler could teach.

Reaching for his knife, Jack turned back to the kidneys. He suddenly felt sorry for the Halcus; leaded meat was the least of their problems.

The stars were out in Bren. Bells, muffled by damp and darkness, tolled the hour of midnight. Oil lamps cast their light into the fray, gaining an ally in the snow, which reflected then magnified their meager assault.

The crowd was restless. They had been kept waiting too long. Blood was what they craved. They had come to see the golden-haired stranger fight. A man who looked like an angel yet fought like a devil. Rumors abounded: he was a nobleman who'd fallen from grace; he was a warrior from beyond the northern ranges; he was a knight on a quest. The blend of mystery, romance, and danger was a heady mix to the people of Bren. They turned out in unheard-of numbers to see the object of so much speculation.

Nobles, taking tipples from silver flasks, rubbed shoulders with tradesmen swigging from tankards and peasants slurping from skins. There were even some women present, hoods pulled over their heads to hide their identities and thick cloaks pulled close to conceal their femininity.

Nabber surveyed the crowd. Pickings were rich tonight. He was astute enough to know that the real cash lay not in the hands and pockets of the nobility, but in the pouches of the tradesmen. The nobles were notoriously tight of fist, whereas the merchants were eager to spend and came prepared. Although he'd made a promise to himself that he wouldn't do any prospecting, Nabber found the pull of easy cash hard to ignore. He pocketed almost without conscious thought, as a man might scratch an itch. A few silver coins here, a jeweled dagger there. The peasants he left alone, never forgetting Swift's words: *"Only the lowest kind of scoundrel steals from the poor."*

Still, he hadn't come here tonight for financial gain. He'd come to keep an eye on Tawl. The knight was keeping the people waiting. His opponent, a man as broad as he was tall, was making his impatience known. He was already greased and in the pit, and Tawl hadn't even shown up yet.

At last there was a hush. The crowd parted and from their midst emerged Tawl. He made his way to the foot of the pit and ripped off his tunic. Gasps of awe escaped from those nearby as his muscled but scarred torso was revealed. Nabber felt such pain at seeing his friend revealed in all his fallen magnificence before the crowd that he could hardly bear to look.

"I've killed men before now for keeping me waiting." It was Tawl's opponent, shouting up from the pit in an attempt to bring the crowd's attention back to himself.

The crowd was pleased by this warning and looked to Tawl for a suitably menacing reply. When it came, they had to strain to hear the words:

"Then you kill too lightly, my friend."

The crowd was silent. Tears came to Nabber's eyes. He alone knew the anguish behind Tawl's words—words that were more a reproach to himself than his opponent. Nabber, who had never aspired to anything more than a comfortable life, began to comprehend the tragedy of a man who had failed to live up to his own ideals.

A cry went up, "Let the fight begin!" and Tawl jumped into the pit.

The betting, which had been a lackluster affair before the knight's appearance, began to take on the look of a feeding frenzy. As the two fighters circled each other, odds were shouted and bets were laid. Nabber took a moment to size up Tawl's opponent. He was a large man, wide and well muscled, with no lard to slow him down. Someone nearby offered five golds on him to win. Nabber could not resist; in his eyes the fight had only one outcome. Tawl would prevail.

"I'll take you up on that, kind sir," he said, feeling a twinge of guilt.

"Done!" replied the man. They exchanged markers—notched sticks— and Nabber moved away.

In the pit, the fighters were locked together. Taut muscles, perfectly balanced, strained for supremacy. Tawl's knife was close to his foe's belly. Nabber felt a ripple of indignation on spotting the knife of his opponent. It was longer than a hand knife, a fist longer. The man was not playing fair.

"Ten golds on the scarred stranger," he cried to no one in particular. It was his way of backing up Tawl.

"Make it twenty and you're on." The voice of a nobleman.

"We have a deal." Another exchange of markers, this time with a polite bow, and then Nabber stepped back into the crowd.

The fighters were well matched at first. Each man executing a seemingly effortless array of feints and thrusts. The fight gained momentum and an edge of anger honed the skills of both men. Tawl was forced to parry a blow with his forearm, and his opponent's blade cut through to bone. Blood welled slick and dark in the lamplight. The crowd cheered. Nabber, always the businessman, knew a good opportunity when he saw one: everyone thought that Tawl had lost his advantage.

"Who'll give me two to one on the stranger?"

Nabber was inundated with takers and collected markers like fallen leaves. The problem was that by the time he'd finished his dealings, the fight had taken a turn from bad to worse. Tawl's arm was drenched in blood and lay limp at his side. He was backed up against the wall of the pit, his opponent's knife at his throat. Tension was so high that most of the crowd had actually stopped betting. Nabber willed his knees not to give way under him.

"I'll give you five to one on the stranger," hissed someone in his ear. To Nabber, the idea of betting at such a time seemed appalling. He turned around and kicked the man hard in the shins.

The subsequent need for a quick escape prevented Nabber from seeing what happened next. Suddenly the crowd went wild, stamping their feet and calling at the top of their voices. When Nabber managed to get close to the pit once more, he found the balance of power changed. Tawl had his opponent up against the wall of the pit. The man's knife lay on the ground. Tawl's knife was at his throat. The eyes of the knight were dangerously blank. The knife blade shook with tension as both men fought over its course. It hovered and wavered, close enough to flesh to draw blood, yet not near enough to slice muscle and tendon.

Tawl's opponent gathered his strength and in one brilliant move pushed the knife away from his throat. The knight was forced to step back. The last thing the dark-haired man saw was Tawl stepping forward. Freed from the stalemate, Tawl pivoted to the side and fell upon his opponent's flank. He sliced the man open from belly to groin.

The crowd was shocked. It had happened too fast. Where was the skill? The finesse? A moment passed while they decided how to respond. Nabber was disturbed at the sheer violence of Tawl's attack. His opponent was lying in his own blood, his entrails seeping from the wound. Even now, Nabber knew with all his heart that he couldn't abandon his friend. It wasn't Tawl who he'd just watched fight: it was someone else. He gathered his breath deep within his lungs and let out a cry:

"To the victor!"

The crowd followed his lead. The stalemate had been broken and Bren was happy once again to cheer the winning side. The noise was dizzying and the sparkle of coinage was dazzling. The dead man was soon covered with silver. Nabber took his markers from his tunic and began to look around for his debtors. He spotted the nobleman in the distance, trying to slink away unnoticed. Nabber spat with disgust. He should have known better than to bet with anyone of the blood. They were notoriously absent losers.

He had just decided to cut his losses when someone tapped him on the shoulder. Nabber didn't look round at first; it certainly wouldn't be anyone eager to pay their bets. For a brief second his heart thrilled, perhaps it was Tawl. He spun around. The man wasn't Tawl, but he was familiar all the same.

"Well met, my friend," said the stranger. " 'Twas a good fight, eh?" It was the man he'd pocketed his first day in Bren: the huge chest, the wide arms, the shiny black hair.

Nabber suppressed his natural desire to run. There was no way the man could prove it was him. Then he remembered the portrait. It was tucked under his belt and would give him away as surely as falling leaves gave away autumn. He remained outwardly calm despite the turmoil within. "Not a bad fight. Though I've seen better in Rorn."

"Is that where your friend is from?" The stranger's eyes glanced toward the pit. "Rorn?"

Nabber was immediately on the defensive. "What makes you think he's a friend of mine?"

"I watched you working the crowd for him. Quite a job—reviving the betting and then saving his skin at the end." The stranger smiled, showing white teeth. "Nice trick that—having a boy in the crowd."

"I ain't nobody's boy," said Nabber.

"I saw you follow him the other night," said the man. "After he beat that young lance from out of town."

Nabber decided to change tactics. "What's it to you?"

The man shrugged, his whole body becoming taut for the barest instant. Nabber suddenly realized what he was dealing with: a contender.

"Perhaps I should introduce myself," he said. "I'm Blayze, the duke's champion."

Impressed, but determined not to show it, Nabber said, "My, my, shouldn't you be busy defending the duke, then, rather than hanging around on street corners?"

The man ignored the jibe—Nabber had to give him credit for that. "I like to keep an eye on the competition, and your golden-haired friend is the only decent fighter I've seen in a long while."

"Just as well for you, really."

Another shrug. "Makes no difference to me, boy, I beat all comers." He was confident without being arrogant, and well spoken—for a fighter.

"Need a decent fight, do you," said Nabber, "to help raise your favor?"

The man who he now knew to be called Blayze, pulled away a little. "I'm not about to waste my time talking with a boy whose tongue is quicker than his wits. Now, unless you're willing to admit you know the lance who just won in the pit, I'm off." He turned and began to walk away.

"Tawl," shouted Nabber. "His name is Tawl and he's from the Lowlands." Friendship was one thing, but on a night like this when the coinage shone brighter than any oil lamp, it was difficult to believe that anything mattered more than money and its making. Besides, what was the harm of telling Blayze a name?

The man carried on walking. "Arrange a meet for me. Two days from now at sundown by the three golden fountains." He never turned around to discover if his words had been heard, he merely slipped into the crowd. A few seconds later, Nabber spotted him making his way down the street. He was accompanied by a slight figure who was both cloaked and hooded.

Nabber took all his markers and snapped them. No chance of finding who they belonged to now. No chance of finding Tawl, either. The knight had left the pit. Even if he *were* to find Tawl, he would never agree to come to a meeting set up by him. It was probably for the best. Blayze had the look of a man who wasn't used to losing; a full compliment of front teeth and a straight nose were rare sights in fighters. And the body! Nabber whistled in appreciation. More muscles than a shipful of sailors. Tawl wouldn't stand a chance.

Or would he? Nabber began to make his way toward Brotheling Street. Tawl had a unique talent that owed more to rage than to muscle, so perhaps the outcome was anything but certain. One thing that *was* certain, though, was that there was loot to be made here. Plenty of it. The duke's champion fighting the latest sensation in Bren, Nabber could almost hear the sound of money spinning about the pit. This was just the sort of earner that Swift spent his days dreaming of—and it was his for the taking!

As Nabber walked up the street, he felt an unfamiliar sensation. Like bellyache, only higher and deeper, it formed a tight band around his chest. He tried ignoring the feeling at first and set his thoughts upon solving the problem of how he was going to get Tawl to agree to a meet with Blayze. However, the pain wouldn't go away. It niggled and chided and allowed him no peace. Despite his attempts to pass it off as an unusually high case of indigestion, Nabber knew in his heart it was guilt.

Melli drifted through the hazy clouds between waking and sleeping. Some tiny still-lucid part of her brain hinted that sleep was best. Some large still-active part of her belly *swore* that it was.

Cheap Halcus wine and exotic southern liqueurs didn't mix. She'd paid the price for their incompatibility all day. Rolling along a bumpy road in a wagon that was obviously built before Borc's first coming hadn't helped much, either. She was sick and feeling sorry for herself.

Her brain defied her stomach and set a course for full waking. Without opening her eyes, she was aware that it was late. The light filtering through the tissue of her eyelids was low and golden; candlelight, and the cries of owls and wolves had found their way into her dreams for some time now. The smell of incense and almonds was as strong as ever, and she realized, rather belatedly, the wagon was no longer moving.

She heard the door open and then felt a flurry of cold air race in. Fiscel's voice said: "Alysha, I want a word alone." Melli kept her eyes closed and lay very still.

"Lorra." It was Alysha's low and alluring voice. "Go outside for a while."

"But it's cold and dark. I was nearly asleep—"

"Go now," said Alysha, cutting the young girl's complaints short. "Or I will make you stay out the whole night."

"You wouldn't dare."

Alysha laughed. "You're no great prize, Lorra. Your flesh would fetch as much dead as alive."

Melli tried hard not to shudder, but the coldness of the woman's words was too much. The sound of the door slamming was testament to their sting. Lorra had obviously decided not to take Alysha up on her threat.

Fiscel spoke softly, "Is the new girl all right?"

The rustle of silk suggested a shrug. "She will live. Her stomach reacted to the herbs in the nais, that's all."

"Are you sure she is asleep?"

"She hasn't stirred all day."

"Good," said Fiscel. "We must talk about what you saw last night."

Melli now realized what the dull pressure was in her abdomen: she badly needed to relieve herself. Having grasped this, she became desperate and slowly curled her body into a ball.

The voices of both people had dropped even lower. Alysha was speaking. "She is trouble. It is bad luck to even travel with her."

"What makes you so sure of this? How do I know that what you say isn't a drunken woman's fancy?"

"You know me better than that, Fiscel," hissed Alysha. "Only last winter I saved your skin by warning you when the storm would hit. Ignore my warning this time at your own risk." The chink of glasses was followed by the pouring of liquid. The sound was torture to Melli's bladder.

"What are you saying, then?"

"I'm saying that we should sell her as soon as possible, lest we become victims of her fate."

"But I had plans to take her across the drylands," said Fiscel. "One such as her would be worth a fortune in Hanatta."

"Hanatta is months away. I say we get rid of her before the moon wanes."

Why was she such a liability? Melli cast her mind back to the evening before. There was drinking, a little eating, more drinking and then— Melli's body stiffened under the light wool blanket—then there was the testing. A wave of nausea rippled through her body. She swallowed hard to keep the bile from her mouth. That foul woman had done something to her, something dirty and shocking. Her eyes stung and she was forced to open them the barest fraction to let out the tears. In that one second, she glimpsed Fiscel and Alysha; they were distorted by the salt water and looked like monsters. Melli, who had long prided herself on her fearlessness, suddenly felt alone and afraid.

Her knife, which for days now had been her main source of comfort, began to seem like a useless toy. Even now she could feel its metal-coolness against her side. Only Borc knew how she had managed to hold on to it after the dress-splitting of the night before. But it wasn't important anymore. These two people, who were calmly discussing her fate in much the same way as her father must have done while arranging her betrothal to Kylock, had the power of life or death over her. That sort of power could not be challenged by a knife.

Apparently she did have another weapon, though. They were wary of her. Alysha must have discovered something during her testing and Melli doubted that it was the ghones.

"We pass Highwall tomorrow. You know people there." It was Alysha again.

"No," said Fiscel. "Too close to the initial transaction. Word could reach the good captain, and our guarantee of safe passage through Halcus might be withdrawn." There was a faint rustle as Fiscel adjusted his position. "If you're so set on being rid of her, then the best I can do is Bren. If the weather holds, we'll be there in less than a week."

"The same contact as before?"

"Yes. He'll pay a fair price, but our friend in Hanatta would pay us double."

"If we ever reach Hanatta." Alysha's voice became harsh. "Where I come from, we call people like her thieves. Their fates are so strong they bend others into their service. And what they can't bend they steal."

Melli was shocked. What was in her that was so dangerous? For some reason her thoughts turned to Jack. She remembered the day in the pig farmer's cottage when she'd been given a glimpse into the future. Jack's future. If Alysha had uncovered some of this, then it was Jack's fate she was seeing, not hers. Or was she fooling herself? Melli ran through what little she remembered of the vision. She had been there alongside him!

She was out of her depth. Fate, visions, sorcery: it was all madness. Her father had spent a lifetime denying such things existed. She loved him for that. Strange to believe that before meeting Jack she would have agreed with him.

Melli turned her attention back to the two people who were deciding what would become of her.

"We'll head for Bren, then," Fiscel was saying. "While we're there I'll pick up a replacement."

"As you wish."

Silk rustled softly at first and then the light from the candle dimmed as someone passed in front of it. There was a peculiar slurping sound followed by a sharp intake of breath. Melli risked opening her eyes. Alysha was naked from the waist up and Fiscel was kissing her breasts. The raven-haired woman seemed impervious to the caress and stood, back straight as a spear, staring straight ahead. Melli closed her eyes again. She'd seen enough.

There was no way of knowing how long she lay awake, listening to the small, desperate noises of Fiscel's lovemaking. But when it was over and Lorra returned to the wagon once more, she'd never been more grateful for silence.

Eight

Maybor cursed his stays for the third time in less than an hour. He cursed his dead horse, too. He thought for a few minutes and then cursed Baralis as well.

They were approaching Bren. The city walls gleamed like steel. In their shadows awaited the cause of Maybor's bad temper: the delegation sent to greet them. Only minutes now before they met. Crucial minutes when people who counted would make their judgments. And here he was, sitting on a horse that was not his own, with a blanket tucked beneath the saddle to cushion his backside, dressed in the same cloak he'd been wearing for nearly a week!

Baralis, Borc rot his soul, had destroyed the trunk that carried his magnificent ermine cloak when rescuing Crope from the avalanche. What was one dead servant compared to the loss of a fine cloak? Still, at least the rest of his new and hastily made wardrobe was intact, and a man only needed a cloak if he intended to venture out into the cold.

Maybor urged his horse forward; he wanted no one to doubt that he was leader of this party. Horns sounded and the delegation from Bren swept forward to meet him.

"We wish you welcome on this fine day, Lord Maybor," said the herald. "Your presence does honor to our city."

"It is I who am honored to be here," replied Maybor, pleased that they knew who he was.

"We beg the privilege of accompanying you to the palace, where the duke awaits."

"I am content to follow your lead." Maybor inclined his head graciously, took up a position at the front of the delegation, and rode into the city of Bren.

It was nothing like he had expected. The sheer scale of the place overwhelmed him; it made Harvell seem like a backwater. The roads were laid with cobble and stone. Tall buildings crowded close, and people lined the streets in their thousands. Soldiers were everywhere, accompanying their entourage, keeping back the crowds, their longswords hooked but not sheathed at their waists. The duke was obviously a man who understood the value of a silent threat.

The sound of people cheering was music to Maybor's ears. He had not wanted this match, but it was plain to see that there was glory in it, and he was determined to have his share. He waved to the crowd and they responded with vigor, calling and waving their banners. There was a likeness painted on many of these banners and it took Maybor a while to realize that the handsome smiling face was supposed to be Kylock. Handsome the new king might be, but he couldn't recall ever having seen him smile.

Before he knew it they were approaching the palace gates. The drab browns and grays of the crowd gave way to the deep blue of the ceremonial guard. The gates swung open and Maybor found himself looking at the granite stronghold that formed the duke's palace. He took a sharp intake of breath; an ill-advised move, for his still tender lungs were not used to such force and retaliated by contracting violently.

Caught between the awe inspired by the palace and the inconvenience of stifling a coughing fit, Maybor came face-to-face with the duke. Garon of Bren wore the blue of his soldiers and the same naked sword at his waist. He was lean like a fighter, and his most imposing feature was his elegant hooked nose. The duke brought his horse alongside of Maybor's and held out his arm in welcome. The two men clasped hands in the military fashion, each careful to show no weakness of grip. The courtyard was packed with people; everyone from noblemen to grooms was silent, eager to hear what passed between the two.

"I bid you welcome, friend," said the duke.

Maybor was aware that all eyes were upon him. He searched his mind for just the right words to impress the court of Bren. "On behalf of His Royal Highness King Kylock, sovereign of the Four Kingdoms," he said, "I am honored to accept your hospitality."

The fool, thought Baralis, as the crowd began to murmur nervously. Now was neither the time nor place to let Bren know that the old king was dead.

The duke's face paled visibly. There wasn't a man in the courtyard who didn't notice it. Baralis knew the duke well; he wasn't the kind of man to show any emotion in public, and the fact that his face had paled was a sign more telling than a murderous rage. Maybor would die for this!

The news would be around the city before they sat down for the welcoming feast. *Kylock is now a king,* they would say, *and the duke was shocked to hear it!*

Baralis urged his horse forward. All eyes were drawn by the movement. Maybor sent him a look filled with loathing—the man had no sense of discretion. The duke acknowledged his presence with a slight incline of his head. When he spoke his voice was cold.

"Lord Baralis, perhaps you can tell me when King Lesketh died."

Baralis looked into the calculating eyes of a hawk. "The king died peacefully in his sleep two weeks after we left Harvell, Your Grace. A messenger was dispatched with the news."

"His Highness begged me to inform you that he is still eager for the match." It was Maybor, determined not be left out of the reckoning.

The Hawk of Bren—for that was how he was known to his enemies—ignored Maybor's comments. Raising a gloved hand, he turned his horse and made his way back toward the palace. His retinue followed him through to the inner courtyard. Baralis and Maybor were borne along with the crowd.

The duke had ill liked learning of Lesketh's death along with the stableboys and grooms. It should have been handled differently. The duke should have heard the news in private, and it should have been left for him to decide how and when to tell his people.

Baralis rubbed his aching hands together. Perhaps there was something to be gained from the slackness of Maybor's tongue. The duke was a proud man and would not look kindly on anyone who made him look a fool. Baralis searched for the duke's figure in the crowd. He had dismounted and was giving instructions to his equerry. Once finished he slipped away through a small side door. Not wasting a second, Baralis dismounted and followed him.

This was the old part of the palace. The damp stone proclaimed its age. Many centuries ago it had been a fortress and then a castle and later a mighty citadel. Baralis marveled at the skill of the artisans; they had created a magnificent disguise. The structure had the look of a gracious palace, but it was fortified for war.

The whole city was ringed with walls. Like a tree each ring marked growth, each successive duke had strengthened the battlements in a thousand small and unassuming ways. It would be a foolish army that underestimated the defenses of the city of Bren.

Baralis reached out and touched the stone wall; it was almost a caress.

"Do I detect a trace of proprietorship in your touch, Lord Baralis?" It was the duke, his voice was cold and without humor.

"No," said Baralis, turning to face him. "Merely admiration."

"Then I suppose I should feel flattered," said the duke. "Not threatened."

He was quick, too quick. Baralis searched for a way to draw the conversation away from such a dangerous, and fundamental, subject. "I am here to offer my apologies for Lord Maybor's indiscretion."

"Apologies hold no interest to me, Lord Baralis. Has Kylock taken any action against the Halcus?"

The Hawk had gone straight for the heart. Already he was considering the effect of Kylock's kingship on his northern neighbors. Baralis was well pleased that they were alone: there was no one here to contradict the lie. "Petty border squabbles are of little interest to Kylock. His eyes are turned inward to the court."

The duke was not convinced. "The city of Bren thought it was getting a prince."

"And how long did you expect him to keep that title? It was no secret that Lesketh had more use for a sickbed than a crown."

"I expected Kylock to stay a prince until the marriage was consummated." The duke took a step forward and his face emerged from shadow. "Let's name trouble plainly, Lord Baralis. The north is already nervous of this match. Kylock being crowned is ill tidings. Kylock winning battles is a threat."

"I haven't noticed you playing peacemaker."

"Bren's policies are my concern, not yours," said the duke.

"Even when those policies affect everyone in the southeast?" Baralis was not so easily intimidated into silence. "Tyren was lucky to find an ally in Bren, as he's sadly lacking in friends elsewhere."

"The knights are being persecuted. Bren offers them safe haven."

"Tell me, Your Grace," said Baralis, "since when did joining Bren's forces on the battlefield count as safe haven?"

The duke's face hardened to muscle. There was no fat to fill out either lip or cheek. "Tyren is free to do as he wishes. No one forced him to aid my causes."

"Such a convenient little friendship. You make sure that no one interferes with their trade and they help fight and finance your battles." The duke was about to speak, but Baralis raised a warning hand and halted the words in his throat. "Do not talk to me about the nervousness of the north, Your Grace, when well you know that it is *Bren* they are wary of, not the kingdoms."

The duke's hand encircled the hilt of his sword. Jewels flashed between his fingers. "Lord Baralis," he said, "I will give you this warning once, and I advise you to heed it well. Do not make the mistake of challenging me. You may hold power at Harvell, but here in Bren *my* will is law. I tell you now, this marriage will go ahead only if I see fit to let it. And no second-rate nobleman from a court too long stagnant will influence me either way." The duke turned on his heels and walked away, leaving Baralis to swallow his words.

Tavalisk was fingering his flute. He felt too weak to blow. Four days of cutting down on his food had damned near finished him off! Hunger made him vicious. Already this afternoon he had planned a suitable program of punishment for his physicians, a new method of torture for all the knights in his dungeons, and a way to fine all musicians. This burst of brilliance had only served to hone his appetite further, and now the archbishop's mind was firmly on his next meal.

His one and only consolation was at his side: *The Book of Words* by Marod. If ever he needed a good reason to live as long as possible, all he had to do was glance at the book to find one. Conflict in the Known Lands was almost certain and according to Marod, he, Tavalisk, had a key part in its outcome. The archbishop had no intention of dying before he'd had a chance to play his role to the fullest.

With that thought in mind, he pulled his bell cord. The physicians were wrong: missing supper would kill him more quickly than a thousand feasts.

Unfortunately his aide answered the call. "Gamil, I rang in the hope I might be fed, not bored."

"I thought the physicians had advised a diet of bread and music, Your Eminence."

"I've had enough of music this week to last me a lifetime. I swear I will have every musician in Rorn flogged and strung." Tavalisk smiled sweetly. "Do you play, Gamil?"

"Alas, Your Eminence, I have no skill with music."

"One day you must tell me exactly where your skills lie. I, for one, have seen no evidence of anything special except an extraordinary capacity to annoy me." The archbishop reached over and jabbed his cat with his flute. The creature hissed most rewardingly. Music did have its uses, after all. "Since you're here, Gamil, you might as well tell me what you learned on your latest foray."

"The spy has been brought in, Your Eminence. I took the liberty of questioning him—"

"You took the liberty, Gamil!" interrupted Tavalisk, annoyed that he'd missed out on the fun of a good torture. "You mean you had someone interrogated without my knowledge or consent?"

"I thought Your Eminence would be pleased by my initiative."

"If I'd wanted initiative, Gamil, I would never have employed you in the first place." Tavalisk's little finger was caught in one of the air holes of the flute. Realizing that this was not a good time to look undignified, he buried his hand and the attached instrument beneath his robe. "One more lapse like this and I will be forced to take the *initiative* of having you dismissed. Now carry on."

Gamil's face was a study of barely concealed malice. "The Old Man has sent two of his cronies to Bren. Apparently they left the city two days back."

"Hmm. Then revenge for Bevlin's death is imminent. The Old Man is obviously seeking to assassinate the knight." Tavalisk was busily trying to work his finger free of the flute. "Did our former spy show any remorse for his treachery?"

"Just before the rack dislocated his left arm, he did express a degree of repentance."

"That is gratifying to hear, Gamil. I must commend you on your judicious use of torture." Tavalisk suspected he had pushed his aide a little far and was seeking to neutralize the threat. "Anything else?"

"The Knights of Valdis are becoming bolder, Your Eminence. Ever since they gained Bren's support, they have done nothing but cause us trouble. The rumors about them seizing all of Rorn's cargoes heading north are true. Ten cartloads of salted fish and seventy bolts of finest silk were taken just past Ness."

Tavalisk was pleased to hear it. Now at last he could take firm action against Tyren and his circular friends. And he was just in the right sort of mood to take the offensive. "Send letters out to Toolay, Marls, and Camlee, demanding that they each supply five hundred troops to help guarantee the safe passage of southern cargoes. Tell them that Rorn will be committing a similar number." The archbishop considered for a moment. "Rorn's five hundred will have orders to kill any knights they encounter— even ones who are not engaged in the confiscation of goods."

"But, Your Eminence, the other powers won't agree to patrol the trade routes if Rorn is acting out a personal vendetta."

"The other powers won't know about the order until it is too late. When one of our men finally butchers a knight on neutral territory, he will not be seen as acting for Rorn alone."

"Thereby implicating the other southern powers."

"Exactly, Gamil! Toolay and Marls might as well save their breath; nothing indicts more surely than a vigorous denial. Anyway, there'll probably be little time for finger pointing; these things have an uncanny way of escalating." The archbishop managed a wistful sigh.

"Your Eminence is most cunning."

"Thank you, Gamil." In his excitement, Tavalisk had stuffed his finger even deeper into the flute. Beneath the fabric of his cloak, he tried desperately to pull the two apart. "Of course, this will require delicate handling."

Gamil's eyes strayed to the archbishop's lap. He looked bemused for a moment, and then said finally, "Indeed it will."

"I don't intend to drag the south into a war that by all rights is the north's affair," said Tavalisk. "No. Let the north fight it out between themselves, I am merely seeking the means of bringing matters to a head. If things work out well, our southern friends will be eager to go along with any plan that promises to keep the knights away from their doorsteps."

"Your Eminence is playing a dangerous game."

"They are the only sort worth playing, Gamil."

Tavalisk dismissed his aide. He was too caught up in the thrill of politicking to set him the usual demeaning task. Once the door was closed, the archbishop turned his attention to the flute. Realizing he would never get his finger out by pulling, he smashed the instrument against the desk. The wood cracked, and as he freed himself the splinters drew blood. Tavalisk shrugged, brought his finger to his lips, and began to suck on the bloody tip. It would do until he got his next meal.

Forty-nine, fifty, done. Jack straightened his back and his vertebrae clicked in protest; he'd been bent over too long for their liking. Six blades, each drawn fifty times over the whetstone. He tested the sharpness of the last by splitting a strand of his hair. He'd done a good job.

Rovas had insisted that he learn how to take care of his large armory of weapons. So Jack had spent much of the day nailing leather to clubs, greasing blades, restringing bows, and filing the rust from spearheads. He enjoyed the simple discipline of having tasks to do, especially now, when, unlike his time at the castle, he was free to walk away if he pleased. It felt good to use his muscles, to sweat, to ache, and to work without having to think.

Jack brushed the hair from his forehead. It was much too long. Frallit would have reached for his knife at the mere sight of it. Jack paused, blade in hand, and wondered whether to hack it off. It was thick and wild and the winter sun had scattered gold amidst the brown. When the knife fell, it sliced leather, not hair. Jack cut a strip of cowhide and used it to tie his mane at the back. He didn't need to conform to anyone's rules now.

Satisfied by this small act of independence, he made his way back to the cottage. Strange how only two days ago he'd felt an overpowering urge to leave. He still couldn't understand the reason why. What was Bren to him? Even now he could remember the urgency; it had been just like the times at Castle Harvell, when he'd lain awake through the night, desperate to find adventure and purpose, yet by the time morning came the urgency had gone.

The cottage was a welcome haven from the cold. The fire burned brightly, casting a glow of kinship on its surroundings. Magra sat in a tall chair, sewing, while Tarissa tended the stew. Jack was filled with a sudden envy for Rovas. The man had this sight to come home to every night: two women waiting for him, logs on the fire, and hot food above it.

Rovas himself was engaged in one of his many dubious practices. He was blowing air into legs of mutton. Inflating the tendons like a bellows made the meat appear fatter and more succulent than it actually was. Jack was well pleased that the smuggler-cum-con-artist hadn't asked him to do that particular job.

Magra began to lay food on the table: crusty bread, roasted chickens stuffed with apples and hazelnuts, rabbit stew, and turnips braised in cider. The one thing that a smuggler was always sure of was good food on his table. They sat down and picked up their knives. As in most country households there was no talking whilst eating.

Jack still hadn't managed to figure out what held these three people together. At first he'd assumed that Rovas and Magra were man and wife, but he'd since learned that was not the case. They were a curious group: Magra with her elegant manners and cool demeanor, Rovas with his bluff

good humor and disregard for the niceties of life, and Tarissa falling
somewhere in between the two. Lacking her mother's noble ways, she
was softer, more easygoing, yet she still retained something of Magra's
character. Her pride, perhaps.

The food was delicious, flavored with strong herbs and seasonings
favored by the Halcus. Jack used the opportunity of sitting around the
table to steal glances at Tarissa. He'd had no chance to talk to her since
the day he'd sent a week's worth of food into the fire. He still remembered
her kiss. Kisses he'd had before: Castle Harvell was full of young maids
willing to give a young lad a teasing peck on the lips, some even offering
their tongues and tender breasts. He'd even kissed the daughter of a lord,
Melli. But Tarissa's kiss had meant more. It held all the power and mystery that only an older woman could bestow.

Jack supposed that she was at least five years older than he. She was
of medium height and full figured, with hips that curved more wickedly
than any young girl's. He watched her as she ate. She had an appetite to
match Melli's, tearing away at chicken bones and washing the meat down
with cup after cup of cider. Unlike Melli, however, Tarissa helped prepare
what she ate. The pies and the broth were made by her own hand. She knew
how to keep a flame on the fire and how to bank the ashes overnight. Her
hands were callused, her arms were muscled, and her face was freckled by
the sun. Tarissa was no highborn lady; she was used to hard work and fresh
air. Jack admired her as she wrapped the remains of the cheese in a cloth
she first dampened with ale. He could be friends with a girl like this.

Only he wasn't sure if friendship would be enough. His gaze moved
upward to her face. He saw her lips were glistening with chicken fat. The
cider had flushed her cheeks, and the heat of food and fire had brought
moisture to her skin. A droplet of sweat gathered mass in the dip of her
neck. When heavy enough it trickled downward to her breast. Jack followed its progress as it slipped down the pale skin, eventually sequester-
ing itself beneath the fabric of her dress.

Tarissa looked up and caught the object of his gaze. To his horror he
felt himself blushing.

"It is hot in here, isn't it?" Tarissa's smile was that of a woman who
knew her charms were being appreciated.

Jack was thankful that she'd provided him with an excuse for turning
red, but he was still embarrassed at being caught staring at her breasts. To
cover this he uttered the first words that sprung to his lips. "A little too hot
for me, I fear. I think I might take a brief stroll outside."

"That sounds like a good idea," said Tarissa. "I'll join you."

Jack was too surprised to think of a reply. His problem was solved when Magra spoke up. "It's too late for you to be going out, Tarissa," she said.

"Aye, too cold as well," added Rovas.

Jack could tell that Magra and Rovas were just using excuses to mask the fact that neither of them wanted Tarissa to be alone with him. Which was rather odd, since he'd been alone with her three days earlier. Tarissa, however, had no intention of having her wishes curtailed. "Nonsense," she said. "I'll wrap up well and we'll only go as far as the gate." She favored Jack with an intriguer's smile.

Together they walked toward the door, Tarissa pausing to don her cloak. Jack felt the pressure of disapproving gazes. For some reason Rovas looked more annoyed than Magra.

Night had fallen while they ate. The sky was dark: there was neither moon nor stars to relieve the blackness. They didn't make it as far as the gate. They sat on the wall that formed part of the dairy shed. The only light was a glimmer escaping from the shuttered window of the cottage.

Tarissa turned to Jack. "So you like my breasts, eh?"

Jack smiled despite himself, liking her forthrightness, and at the same time thrilled by the sudden intimacy. With that one sentence, she had become, in his eyes, a woman of the world—daring and openly sexual. He cursed himself for not being able to think of a suitably gallant and risqué reply.

Tarissa, for her part, didn't seem the least put out by his silence. "You do admit you were looking at me over the dinner table?"

"Would you be offended if I said yes?"

"I'd be more offended if you said no. A woman likes to feel she is attractive."

"Surely you don't need my looks to confirm that."

Tarissa smiled, the curve of her cheek catching the shuttered light. "How old are you, Jack?"

"One and twenty," he lied.

"Well, you're tall enough for it, and broad as can be hoped, but your face tells a different story from your body." She laughed. A warm and pretty sound, that was, in Jack's opinion, exactly what the night needed to make up for the lack of stars.

"I'm eighteen."

"Aah." Tarissa settled herself comfortably on the wall. "Do you want to know how old I am?"

"No."

At last he'd said something that pleased her. She leaned forward. Her cloak fell apart; the cleft of her breast was deep with shadows. Gently, she pressed her mouth against his. Her lips were soft and still salty with chicken fat. Her tongue was cidered and succulent. Their bodies drew close with little prompting. Jack's hand strayed to the meat of her hips. His saliva washed her palate clean and he tasted the woman beneath the meal. Tarissa pulled back abruptly. Her breath came heavily, emphasizing the swell of her breast. There was a look to her face that Jack could not comprehend. She gently eased his hands from her hips.

"Perhaps you are too young for me after all."

It was a cruel blow, which she was well aware of, for her eyes carefully avoided him. Jack was confused but not surprised. He'd spent plenty of time listening to Grift's advice about women, and the one thing the castle guard was consistent about was that women had been born to confound men. Jack knew Tarissa had been more than willing: her tongue had been his guide. Thwarted desire turned to anger.

"Why did you pull away?" he demanded, grabbing hold of her wrist.

"I already told you. Or do you need me to repeat it twice, like a nurse to an infant?"

Jack's arm was up in an instant. Only a great feat of willpower stopped him from slapping her. And she knew it.

"Tell me the truth," he said, his other hand still holding on to her wrist. "What am I to you?" It became clear to Jack that his demand went deeper than what had happened between them this night. "Ever since I've been here, I've heard nothing but lies and evasions. Why are you so interested in murdering the captain who killed Melli? And what really happened to her?" Jack was shaking. "You were there the day she was murdered. Tell me what you saw."

Tarissa turned back to the light. "Let go of my wrist, and then I will tell you what I can."

Jack obliged, and seeing the red marks that he'd raised on her flesh, he felt a measure of remorse. This he hid as well as he could; anger was getting him further than moderation.

An owl called out. Its baleful cry announcing the darkest hours of the night, hours given to witchcraft and deception and worse. The wind, which had been a cold but gentle breeze, showed its teeth and gnawed at Jack's bones. Tarissa spoke:

"I didn't see much the day your friend died. I had to keep myself hidden. I couldn't risk being picked up by the Halcus guard. I was a distance away, in the trees that surrounded the pond where you laid the dead man to rest. I saw the riders approaching. Two men, the captain and his deputy, entered the coop, closing the door behind them. They were in there less than an hour, and when they came out, there was blood on the deputy's club.

"Later on, when the riders had withdrawn, I went down to the coop. The girl Melli lay dead on the floor."

Jack's stomach constricted and his throat became dry: Melli had suffered more than he thought. He should have been the one to die. He should never have left her alone that day. His thoughts turned abruptly, as if his mind was defending itself against the torments of guilt. "The body is still there, then?"

"No, no," said Tarissa quickly. She would not meet Jack's eye. "The captain sent two soldiers out the next day to pick up the body."

The owl called again. To Jack, it was as if the unseen predator was confirming his doubts. Tarissa was not telling the whole truth. He studied her as best he could in the darkness. Her eyes were downcast, a tendon on her neck quivered delicately, but it was her hands that gave her away. She was clutching the fabric of her dress with such force that the fabric was beginning to rip.

Jack reached for Tarissa's shoulders and began to shake her. *"I want the truth!"*

"Easy now, Jack." It was Rovas. His voice was a thickly buttered warning.

Tarissa stepped back and looked toward Rovas. "Go on in, Tarissa," he said. She stood defiant. "I would speak with Jack man-to-man. Now be gone." Tarissa held her position a moment longer and then made her way back to the cottage. Both men watched in silence until the door was closed behind her.

Rovas turned to Jack. "You touch one hair on her head again, and as Borc is my witness, I will kill you!"

Jack was almost pleased by the threat; his anger now had a legitimate challenge. "I wouldn't be so sure that you could."

"You're no match for me, boy." Rovas was contemptuous. "You're nothing more than an overgrown sapling. You can barely hold a blade."

"There are things more dangerous than any weapon."

Rovas looked at him keenly, eyes narrowing to slits in his brawny face. Moments passed while the two men stood against each other. Then, to Jack's surprise, Rovas slapped him hard on the back.

"You have a nice way with intimidation, Jack," he said. "Have you ever considered joining the Halcus? Intimidation is the one element of soldiering they take seriously." Rovas laughed merrily at his own joke.

Jack could feel the smuggler's will upon him, encouraging him to laugh along. He obliged, but not because he found the joke amusing.

The laughter died as abruptly as it started. Rovas placed a paternal hand upon Jack's arm. "Listen, my friend. You were right when you said Tarissa wasn't telling you the truth. But don't blame her; she spoke only to spare your feelings." Rovas took a deep breath, drawing the darkness of night into his lungs. "The girl was raped and then beaten. When Tarissa found her, her head had been cut off." One final squeeze of his arm, and Rovas was off, back to the cottage.

The owl called again. Jack barely heard its cry. He leaned against the wall and wept.

Nine

Baralis walked over to the window. He unlatched the shutter and gazed upon the Great Lake. The northern wall of the duke's palace rose from water, not from soil. Early morning mist robbed the lake's surface of its gleam and stole both scale and grandeur from the view. The worst of the mist's sins, however, was the damp.

Baralis rubbed his hands. They ached with a pain so biting he wished he could cut them off. He considered going to the head of the duke's household and demanding that his rooms be changed for ones with a more southerly position. He decided against it. It would be perceived as a sign of weakness and the duke, who was both physically and mentally strong, might use the knowledge to his advantage. Better to suffer than to be thought a weakling.

He called for Crope to lay out his robes of state and bring a shine to his chain of office. Maybor was right, prince's envoy was now a worthless title. It was time to be known as king's chancellor.

The welcoming feast was to be held tonight. The duke had been thoughtful in delaying it a day to give the weary travelers time to rest. Baralis' lip curled at the breach. Canceling the feast had been an act of caution, not courtesy. The good duke would spend today seeing how Bren took the news of Kylock's recent elevation. Only when he had assured himself that there was still enough support for the match would he give the order to his staff.

The Hawk still wanted his prey. Oh, he called a fine warning, but Baralis could tell the difference between genuine reluctance and merely the show of it. The duke needed an alliance with the kingdoms; not only did he have no male heir, but the city consumed grain and timber at such a rate that it could no longer support itself. By allying with the knights he was courting trouble in the south, and by annexing bordering towns and villages he was courting trouble in the north. To top it all off, he wanted to be named a king. An alliance with the kingdoms would bring wealth, might, and titles his way.

The duke might not be pleased that Kylock now had sovereignty, but he wouldn't let that displeasure spoil the match. It just suited him to pretend that it would.

Baralis made his way down toward the center of the palace. His steps were slow and he paused many times to admire the skill of the masons, who had managed to make walls so thick seem so graceful. Less than a year from now it would be *he*, not the duke, who presided over this domain. Even now, as he descended the stairs to greet his host, Crope was above in his rooms, unpacking the poisons that would kill him.

No sudden and suspicious end for the Hawk. Soon after the marriage of Catherine and Kylock was consummated, the duke would start to complain of a slight biliousness of the gut. Months would pass and the duke's ailment would gradually worsen. There would be cramps and vomiting and then blood in the urine. By this time poison would be suspected and the duke would eat nothing that had not been tested. 'Twould be too late. The poison—a drink shared in celebration with the king's chancellor to mark the night his daughter was bedded—would have gnawed so deeply into stomach and liver that nothing but Borc's grace could save him.

He had Tavalisk to thank for the poison. The information he'd gleaned from the archbishop's library was well worth the price of the loan. What was one war, if it helped him win another, more glorious, one?

The poison was as subtle as the silken rugs of Isro and as deadly as their blades. One drink was enough: it settled in the gut and gradually corrupted the tissue that cradled it. The sharp taste would be a problem, but by choosing to administer it on a night of celebration, Baralis was hoping to pass it off as a traditional bridal drink, complete with exotic herbs and spices.

That was all in the future, though; for the time being he needed to concentrate on finalizing the betrothal. It had been foolish of him to challenge the duke yesterday—Maybor's stupidity had been catching. He had to ingratiate himself with the duke and his court. There were worries to be allayed and problems to be smoothed over, and when all else failed there were bribes to be given.

Baralis reached the magnificent visitors gallery. Domed ceilings were currently the latest fashion in the south, and the duke's palace boasted the only one in the north. Voices floated across its lofty expanse. There was no mistaking the rough-barrel sound of Maybor.

"So you see, Your Grace, Kylock is planning to finish the war once and for all."

"Indeed, Lord Maybor," came the duke's low and deceptively smooth voice. "I am gratified to hear it."

Baralis crossed the tiled floor with the speed of a panther. He ignored Maybor and bowed to the duke. "Good morning, Your Grace."

"Lord Baralis, I trust you slept well?" The duke didn't wait for an answer. "My steward felt that the north wing might be a little damp. I told him only you could be the judge of that."

"My rooms are more than satisfactory."

"Good," said the duke. "The king's envoy has just been telling me of Kylock's wish that the war with the Halcus be won as soon as possible."

"He'll be planning to send more troops to the border," chipped in Maybor.

Baralis felt hate so potent it nearly turned to sorcery on his lips. He took a calming breath to control himself. Not since adolescence had he come so close to drawing out of sheer emotion. Maybor was acting like a malicious fiend; he was well aware that the slightest hint of aggression from Kylock would endanger the match. Not only that, the man was inventing details of his own! He didn't have the slightest idea whether or not Kylock intended to send more troops to the front. To make matters worse, here was the duke picking the man's brains like a glutton at a feast and flattering him all the while by calling him king's envoy!

"As king's chancellor," said Baralis, "*I* will be the first to know when Kylock decides to move against the Halcus." Time to play Maybor at his own game. If lies were called for, let no one find him wanting. "Kylock begged me to assure Your Grace that although, as Lord Maybor has just stated, he wishes to win the war, he will take no action until the marriage vows have been spoken."

Maybor's mouth opened in protest but, probably unable to find a suitably diplomatic way of contradicting him, he closed it again.

The duke did not look pleased. "As you gentlemen seem to be having some difficulty agreeing on an official version of Kylock's policies," he said, "I think I will leave you alone and let you fight it out amongst yourselves." With that the duke bowed smartly and left.

Baralis and Maybor stared at each other until the sound of the duke's footsteps receded to nothing more than a distant flapping.

Maybor waggled his finger and tutted. "Been leading His Grace astray, I see," he said. "I considered it my duty as king's envoy to put him straight."

This was too much for Baralis. The drawing was on his tongue in an instant. It slivered through the air with the force of his intent. A second later Maybor was doubled up in pain. "If you ever, *ever*, make me look a fool again," hissed Baralis to the curve of the man's back, "I swear that I will smite you down where you stand." Satisfied that his threat had been heeded, Baralis withdrew the sorcery.

A servant walked past and glanced their way. Maybor straightened up, his breathing quick and strained, his face purple. *"You will regret this day in hell,"* he rasped.

Baralis almost admired the way the great lord mastered his pain by walking away with head held high.

The drawing had been a warning blow, nothing more. It was never wise to draw directly against another. There was always a chance that a man's will could interfere, causing the power to snap back with the momentum of a strung bow. Sorcerers had died that way. Some drawings could be easily done: a compulsion upon the muscles to prevent them from contracting, a delving into the mind to search for answers, a survey of the tissue to find diseases. But they were all instances that caused no harm to the body, their effects purely temporary. If one wanted a man dead it was far wiser, and safer, to use a method other than sorcery to kill him.

Sorcery served better as accomplice than assassin.

Winter's Eve had been the exception. When the flash of a blade had warned of immediate danger, learning gave way to instinct—and Baralis had paid the price for it.

Dumb creatures were a lot easier to harm, though there was danger even then. Drawing himself into Maybor's horse had been a risk. Sorcery acted like an infection: it triggered the body's natural defenses. Animals, particularly large ones, had been known to fight off drawings. During his time in the Far South, Baralis once watched a man die who was trying to cause harm to a bear.

He had traveled to Hanatta a month after his mother's funeral. The small farming community where he'd lived hadn't suspected that he was responsible for her death. They shook their heads and called it a natural miscarriage. His masters had known, though. Her corpse stank of sorcery.

But what could they do? He was a child who had made a childish mistake. They wanted to be rid of him all the same. So they coated their desire in a layer of concern: *"We can teach you no more, Baralis, your skills are beyond us. In the Far South there is much to learn."* They hoped he would never come back.

Thirteen, he was. Sent on a journey across the drylands and then over the mountains and into the tropics. He'd traveled with a pilgrimage of knights and priests. A week before they reached Hanatta, he murdered a man. This time with intent. Rain beat down upon leather hides, but that was not what woke him. A man's hand reaching for the smoothness of thigh beneath the coarseness of blanket did. The dagger, a parting gift from his father, slid into the man's belly like a marker into a barrel of ale. Sorcery honed the blade, but his hand held the haft.

The next morning they found him: fast asleep with a dead man at his side. The air was so humid that the blood was still wet on his thighs.

For the second time that year he was pronounced free of guilt. Who would condemn a boy for taking measure against such an act? Just like his masters, the pilgrims couldn't wait to be rid of him.

Hanatta was a city so foreign, so completely different from anything he'd ever known, that it scared and thrilled in one. People so striking that to look at them was a joy, jostling past others so disfigured that Baralis wondered how they survived. He soon found the man to whom the letter of introduction was addressed. He'd read the letter hundreds of miles earlier. It was an unmistakable warning: . . . *Baralis is brilliant, yet needs to be taught kindness and humanity, else he turn into something that we all might regret.*

The masters at Leiss had badly miscalculated. The man they sent him to was concerned with ability, nothing else. Moral niceties were pushed aside in the pursuit of knowledge. Four glorious years of experimentation and discovery followed. There was nothing they didn't try. No drawing was too heinous, no ritual too bloody, no animal too valuable to lose.

The sorcery of the Far South was different from that of Leiss. More subtle, less reliant on potions and physical strength, and infinitely more sophisticated. He learned how to make creatures his own, and perfected the skill of entering and then searching the body. Looking back now, he realized that the manuscript at Leiss which contained the means of his mother's death had probably come from Hanatta.

Danger was a constant companion. His hands suffered their first disfigurement when he laid them upon an oxen and tried to get her to drop her calf. It was before her time and she fought the compulsion with all her strength. Nature was on her side. The thread broke, and before he knew it his hands were burning. The energy from the drawing demanded an outlet. His flesh bore the scars to this day.

Still, it was nothing compared to what he saw later in an open air bearbaiting ring close to the meat market.

Bearbaiting could be seen on every street corner in Hanatta. It was the city's favorite pastime, and fortunes were won or lost on the performance of a hound. Baralis enjoyed the spectacle of blood and carnage. He liked watching the faces of the spectators as the dogs harried the bear. This night the crowd was anxious; high on nais and a week of fasting, they were eager for excitement.

The hounds belonged to a man of great wealth and importance. The collars around their necks were beaten gold. They were inbred for carnage: thick-necked, strong-jawed, with teeth that gripped till death. Loosed into the enclosure, they drew circles about the bear, working together to agitate and confuse.

All went well at first. One of the hounds drew close, distracting the bear while the other approached from the side. The beast let out a mighty squeal as the hound's teeth sank into the flesh of its foreleg. The bear raised up on its hind legs and the dog left the ground. Wild with frenzy, it swung its mighty paws in a half-circle and the dog lost its grip. The sheer force of the bear's momentum sent the hound flying to the far side of the enclosure. The crack of its skull was clearly heard. One dog left and its wealthy owner was getting nervous.

Baralis saw the man searching the crowd for a face. A moment later he nodded to a man dressed like a beggar, and soon after Baralis felt the beginning of a drawing. Straightaway he realized what was happening: a sorcerer was attempting to weaken the bear. His mistake was to do it too gradually. He needed to make it look natural, to mimic the signs of fatigue. At first he did a good job, slowing the creature down by restricting the blood flow to its heart. Then the bear became frightened. It ignored the remaining dog and crashed into the fence. The crowd scattered and all but one got away. A young boy was trapped beneath the tangle of wood that had been the enclosure. The bear, shaking and in pain, fell upon its victim.

The sorcerer tried to withdraw. Desperation marked the intent. With the crowd screaming and the bear tearing the boy limb from limb, the drawing began to turn. Blood frenzy was upon the bear. The power of instinct fought for the beast. Will to survive met with silent knowledge accumulated over hundreds of centuries—and struck with the force of a whip. The bear's blood pumped fast and furious, smashing through the sorcerer's clasp.

No one paid any attention to the beggar in the crowd. The raging bear was a greater spectacle. The man in rags fell to the ground, foaming at the mouth. His body was racked by spasms and blood seeped from his nose and ears and eyes. A minute later he was dead, his skull split by the backlash of the drawing.

It was never wise to spend too long in any creature. If a deed were to be done, then let it be done swiftly. He'd given Maybor's horse no chance to react, slipping in with the grace of a dancer and then striking with the speed of a storm. He'd learned caution that day by the meat market. There was little glory in coming to the same end as the sorcerer who had drawn upon the bear.

Nabber scraped the dung from his shoes and cursed all animals, especially horses. The problem with following someone was that your eyes had to be on your mark, not your feet. Now, filth was as much part of city life as markets and merchants, and Nabber usually had no opinion on it, but only this morning he'd taken it upon himself to lift a very splendid and very flimsy pair of silk shoes. Swift had once said, *"A pocket's shoes are his greatest defense,"* and always advocated cloth, not leather, for those on the game. Silk was indisputably silent, but it also had the unfortunate tendency to soak through with urine and slops the minute a man walked out the door.

Still, they were an excellent fit and he had other more important things to occupy his mind than the stains on his shoes.

Tawl was drinking in the tavern opposite. There had to be some way to get him to come to the meeting. Loot wouldn't be enough, or would it? Minutes earlier the knight had walked into the Brimming Bucket accompanied by the woman with straw yellow hair and the lady proprietor of the brothel, Madame Thornypurse. If there were ever any females who liked money better than those two did, then Nabber had never met them.

Action was called for, and with shoes squelching at every step, he crossed the street and entered the tavern. The Brimming Bucket would have been more aptly named the Leaking Bucket, for there was ale everywhere and it wasn't confined to the cups and the barrels. Nabber's shoes found themselves in a foamy puddle a wrist deep. People were shouting and singing and brawling. Two women were arm wrestling, a group of men were busy swapping insults, and one man was holding a cup full of beer to his eye.

Kylock, Kylock, Kylock. The name was on everyone's lips. Even the men who were insulting each other were speaking it. "You're as devious as Kylock and as ugly as his father's corpse," said one of them, receiving grunts of appreciation from the crowd.

"You should speak the name of our future king with respect," piped up another.

"Kylock will never be king here!"

"The duke wouldn't let him."

"The duke won't live forever."

"Catherine will rule Bren, not Kylock."

"She'll marry him, use his armies, rape his country, and then send him back to his mother!"

"Aye!" came the voice of the crowd as one.

Nabber had little interest in such worldly matters. Whoever was ruler in Bren made no difference to him. Loot was what counted, not kings. He pushed through the crowds, kicking shins and stomping on toes when people refused to move out of his way. He soon heard the shrill voice of Madame Thornypurse.

"My sister will be arriving next month," she said. "Couldn't bear staying in the kingdoms a moment longer. The place is such a backwater, you know." The good lady spotted Nabber. "You're the messenger from the other day, aren't you, boy?" She patted the back of her heavily powdered hair and smiled. "I never forget a face."

"A good memory is the least of your charms, Madame Thornypurse," replied Nabber with a short bow. It never hurt to flatter the ladies—even the ugly ones.

"Such a fine young man." Her eyes narrowed for a moment. "Another message to deliver?"

"As perceptive as you are beautiful." An idea was beginning to form in Nabber's head. "Is the knight here?"

"Just over yonder with my daughter, Corsella."

So that was what the thieving, dyed-haired, hanger-on was called. "I just can't believe it," he said.

Madame Thornypurse looked confused. "Believe what?"

"I can't believe that you're her mother." Nabber smiled winningly. "Tell me the truth. You're sisters, aren't you?"

Simpering like a girl a third of her age, Madame Thornypurse said, "You're not the first to ask me that. It's the rat oil, you know."

"Rat oil?"

"Yes, very expensive. You have to squeeze a lot of rats to get even half a cup."

Nabber was feeling decidedly out of his depth. He hadn't got the slightest clue what rat oil was. He proceeded with caution. "It's worth the expense."

"I rub it into my face twice a day."

That explained a lot of things.

"Should I call the knight over?" she asked.

Nabber shook his head and looked down at his feet.

"What's the matter, young man?" said Madame Thornypurse. "I detect a little reluctance on your part."

"You are a perceptive woman. I *am* a little nervous about approaching him." Nabber got the reply he'd hoped for:

"Can I help in any way?"

"Madame Thornypurse, I wouldn't dream of burdening you with a matter of such . . ." Nabber made a great show of choosing the right word ". . . importance."

"Importance?"

"And profit."

Madame Thornypurse's entire body quivered at the word profit. She took a step forward and laid a proprietorial hand upon his shoulder. "Tell me everything, my dear boy."

"You've heard of Blayze, the duke's champion?" Madame Thornypurse nodded eagerly. "Well, he's interested in meeting with your friend, the knight."

"He wants a fight?" cried Madame Thornypurse.

"Ssh. Don't tell half the tavern."

Madame Thornypurse looked suitably contrite. "Go on."

"There's no need to tell you," said Nabber, "of the vast sums of money that will change hands on such a venture."

"No need at all," she whispered.

"Now this is strictly confidential." Nabber could feel Madame Thornypurse's fingers digging into his shoulder. "If the knight dies—and let's face it, there's a good chance of that—someone will have to bury him."

The girlish glow of greed faded from the good lady's face. "*Bury* him?"

"As the knight has no family in the city, whoever agrees to care for his body will take his portion of the spoils."

"The knight is like a son to me!" cried Madame Thornypurse. "I would consider it my duty to care for his dearly beloved corpse."

"You are a remarkable woman," said Nabber. "Now, let's get down to business. The knight needs to meet Blayze tonight at sundown by the three golden fountains. Can you arrange for him to be there?"

"As my life depended on it."

"Good. Until we meet again, fair lady." Nabber quickly looked toward Tawl. The knight was downing yet another skin of ale, oblivious to his surroundings. "Let him drink all he wants. It will make for smoother negotiations."

Madame Thornypurse nodded judiciously and held out her hand to be kissed. Nabber reluctantly obliged, thoughts of rat oil uppermost in his mind, and then made his way from the tavern. He struck a path toward the three golden fountains. If his plan was to work, he needed to have a few words with the duke's champion before Tawl did.

Rovas burst into the cottage. "The rumors are true: Lesketh is dead and Kylock means to win the war."

The effect of Rovas' words on Magra and Tarissa was profound. Mother and daughter looked straight at each other. All color drained from Magra's face. Tarissa stood up, sending her sewing flying into the air and went to kneel beside her mother. She took and kissed her hand. Magra pulled away. "When did this happen?" she asked. Her voice was high and strained. Jack thought she sounded angry.

"He died in his sleep over a month ago now." Rovas looked away.

Silence followed. No one moved. The fire sent shadows dancing across the room. Tarissa's face was buried in her hands. Magra sat very straight, her eyes focused on a point far in the distance. Rovas and Tarissa seemed to be waiting for her to break the silence.

Finally she did. She stood up and walked toward the fire. Her back was straight and rigid. "Kylock will win the war," she said.

Despite the weight of the words, everyone in the room seemed to draw a sigh of relief. Jack got the distinct feeling that Magra had somehow changed the subject. Yet the dead king and Kylock *were* the subject.

"How will this affect his marriage to Catherine of Bren?" asked Tarissa, jumping in to fill the silence. Her question was for Rovas, but she looked at Jack. She was checking to see how the strange scene had affected him. He gave nothing away. She smiled gently, and Jack, even though he realized she had some other motive, found himself smiling back. Tarissa was the most seductive-looking woman he had ever seen. Jack's mind began to drift away from thoughts of asking questions.

"I've a feeling the marriage will go ahead regardless," Rovas was saying. "Things have progressed so far that to halt them now would cause embarrassment to both parties." The smuggler looked weary. He poured himself a tankard of ale and downed it in one.

The three continued talking, discussing the war and its possible effects, yet Jack no longer heard them. He was watching, not listening.

Tarissa was speaking, her soft and lovely mouth assuming countless beautiful forms. Jack recalled the feel and the taste of it. The memory took his breath away. Why had she pulled back from him last night, when only moments earlier she had invited him forward? There was no answer, and if Grift's counsel was anything to go by, that was not unusual with women. The castle guard had warned him many times about the perils of romance: *"If you're as confused as a peacock in a snowstorm, then things are going well,"* he would say. *"But, if you're as carefree as a barnacle on a rock, then there's trouble acoming for sure."*

Jack had little experience with women, but he knew enough to suspect that Grift was not always right. Still, what did he expect? He'd kissed a woman older and wiser than himself. A voluptuous, tempting woman with eyes of hazeled gold. He felt a little ashamed of his thoughts; they talked of war while he thought of lust.

Taking his eyes from Tarissa, he noticed Rovas looking at him. The smuggler flashed a warning, and for half a second Jack was convinced that he was reading his mind. For some reason, Rovas didn't want him having anything to do with Tarissa. Earlier that day, when he'd been out in the back field practicing with the long sword, it had been Magra who brought his midday meal. At first Jack thought it was because Tarissa was avoiding him, but now, seeing the hostile look in Rovas' eye, he wondered whether it was because the smuggler had ordered her to stay away from him.

Jack decided to test his theory. He stretched his arms and stood up. "My body's as stiff as a week-old loaf. I'm going for a walk before it gets dark." He looked directly as Tarissa: "Do you want to join me?"

That one simple question sent a wave of looks, warnings, counter-warnings, and unreadable expressions crisscrossing among the three.

Tarissa took a deep breath. "I think that I might." She looked to her mother, appealing for help.

"It's nearly suppertime, girl," said Rovas. "You have to help your mother with the meal."

Everyone waited on Magra. The woman was staring at the smuggler. Her face held a warning that Jack couldn't understand. *Didn't want* to understand. "I can get supper on my own," she said. "You go ahead, Tarissa, but don't be long."

The tension between Magra and Rovas was unmistakable. It crackled as fiercely as the fire, but was as invisible as its heat. The smuggler wanted to speak up against her, that was plain to see, but she was Tarissa's mother and therefore had final say. She was scared, though, and not the only one: her daughter's hand shook as she tied the laces on her cloak.

Crack! Rovas kicked over the timber scuttle, sending chopped logs careening over the floor. "What are you waiting for?" he cried. "If you're getting supper, *then damn well get it now!*"

Tarissa was at her mother's side in an instant. "I won't go out, I'll stay and—"

"No," said Magra, "you and Jack take a walk."

"But—"

"Go now," she said, her tone inviting no contradiction. Standing up, she started to pick the logs from the floor. Rovas had his back to the room and was facing the fire. He didn't turn to look as they left.

The cool air blasted against Jack. Its freshness on his lips made him aware of a sour taste in his mouth: sorcery. Rovas had been lucky. He held his hand out, not sure if he needed comfort, or if he was trying to give it. Tarissa clasped it tightly and motive no longer mattered.

They walked in silence: an unspoken agreement not to speak until they were free of the cottage. The sky dimmed and the wind shifted, pushing them on their way. Jack's head felt as heavy as one of Frallit's baking stones. He hadn't even been aware that something was building inside of him. He was confused by the scene he'd just witnessed, and angry at Rovas for losing his temper. So angry he'd been ready to lash out. The frightening part was that sorcery was becoming so familiar to him that he no longer noticed its presence. One step toward Tarissa and Rovas would have been dead. Jack was sure of it. He'd done no less for Melli.

Jack's thoughts turned in midstep. Everything darkened. Nothing mattered except staying and killing the man who had raped and then murdered Melli. Rovas didn't matter, wild plans to run off to where the action was didn't matter, even Tarissa with her soft brown hair and fingers callused by swordplay didn't matter.

"Jack, you're hurting me." Tarissa pulled her hand away.

Startled, Jack said, "I'm sorry, I was thinking about . . ." He couldn't say "Melli," couldn't speak her name out loud. Even thinking it brought back the horror of Rovas' words: *"When Tarissa found her, her head had been cut off."* To say it would risk the words becoming an image.

"Your mind is on your friend," Tarissa said. She turned to face him; Jack saw the mirror-image of his eyes in hers. "I'm sorry . . ."

He waited. The sky waited, the wind in the trees waited. She had something else to say. Only she didn't say it. She said something else, but it wasn't what she'd started.

". . . I'm sorry about Rovas just now."

"He is very protective toward you. Like a father." Jack watched Tarissa's expression. He was almost glad when it gave nothing away.

"We have no one else except him," she said. "He took us in when we were penniless, cared for us all these years. He asks so little in return."

"What does he want from me, then?"

"I think you know that. He wants you to kill the captain."

"Why?" Strange, but by asking these questions, Jack got the impression that he was letting Tarissa off the hook.

"He and Rovas were friends once," she said. "Or rather, business associates. A smuggler needs contacts in the military, you know, to stop awkward searches and confiscations. To turn a blind eye. Anyway, the captain started to get greedy, asking for a share of the profits rather than a flat fee. Well, Rovas refused to pay it, and now he can't transport his goods to Helch without the captain ordering them to be seized."

"So he wants me to rid him of his problem."

"Your problem, too."

Jack didn't bother to hide his bitterness. "It looks like I came along at just the right time."

"More for me than for Rovas." Tarissa took a few steps forward and turned her face to the wind. "I was supposed to kill the captain that day."

The night turned sharply into something else. Darker and deeper and bounded like a cave, Jack felt it change for the worst. "Why you?"

Tarissa drew her shawl close. She looked down. "Jack, don't make me answer that."

His hand was up. He grabbed her shoulders and swung her round to face him. "Why you? Rovas was up on the rise that day. He could have shot the captain himself."

Still looking down, Tarissa shook her head. "I'm a better shot with a longbow."

"You're lying."

Tarissa pulled free of him. Turning her back, she cried, "All right! All right! If you must know, he threatened to throw Mother and me out of the house unless I did it for him."

Stunned, all Jack could do was look at the back of Tarissa's head. How could a man do such a thing? How could Rovas threaten someone he loved? Tarissa's shoulders were shaking. She was crying. Jack wanted to put his arms around her, to protect her, but just as he moved forward, a thought glimmered darkly into existence. Before he knew what he was doing, he spoke it out loud, his lips forming the words less than a hand's length from her ear:

"Rovas wanted you to murder the captain to bind you more closely to him. Once you did it, he would always have something to hold over you. You and Magra could never leave him for fear that he might tell someone what you did. The deed wasn't as important as the power it gave him."

Tarissa had stopped shaking. Slowly she turned around. "You shouldn't have said that, Jack. It's not true. It's just not true." Her voice was high, almost hysterical. Tears rolled down her cheek. "Never say that again. Never." With that she ran away, shawl flapping behind her, head down to avoid the wind.

Jack watched her go. What he said had been true, and they both knew it.

Ten

One last drink might do it. Tawl took a swig from the skin: a golden brew and probably one he'd paid dearly for. It didn't matter. What *did* matter was forgetting. It was the only thing he lived for.

Yet no matter how much he drank, how ruthlessly he fought, how hard he tried, he couldn't forget. Anna and Sara, the baby, and then Bevlin—each one had placed their trust in him, and he'd betrayed them all. He'd failed as a man, as a brother, and as a knight. Everything that he held dear was gone and the shell that remained felt as cold and as deep as a grave. Except it wasn't a grave, for there at least was peace. Or so the wisemen said.

How many days, weeks, months had passed since Bevlin's death was impossible to say. Everything blurred into one, and the only things that changed were the faces of the men he fought and the quality of the ale.

It was having less and less effect, though. Three skins he'd drunk tonight, but his arm was steady as an oak, his steps sure as a bailiff's and his mind as clear and as sharp as a sliver of glass.

His body had the look of a traitor. It mocked him with its vigor; muscles were hard, skin was taut, and tendons were poised to spring. None of it was right. He was half a man and it was fitting that he look like one.

Two images were at the center of his being, seared into his retina as surely as his circles were seared into flesh. Whenever he looked at anyone or anything he saw them first. Everything filtered through them: the small, burnt plot of ground that marked the place where the cottage had stood, and the dead man covered in blood. No amount of fighting or ale could make them go away. There'd been a saying at Valdis: *A man pays in the next life for his sins, a knight pays in both.* Tawl hadn't understood it at the time. He did now.

"Come on, Tawl. We'll be late if you don't hurry." Corsella grabbed his arm and steered him down the street. She made the mistake of thinking he was drunk. He wished he was.

"I think there's time for him to finish the skin, my precious," said Madame Thornypurse. The woman was up to something. She'd taken his knife away and was now encouraging him to drink his fill.

They fell under the shadow of the palace and moved toward the center of a large, flagged square. Three fountains, gurgling and embellished with gold, one man dark and well built. He stepped forward and bowed.

"Good evening, ladies." And to Tawl, "Well met, friend."

Tawl spoke over the simpering of the women. "I'm no friend of yours."

"Then allow me to introduce myself. I'm Blayze, duke's champion." The man waited, obviously used to impressing people with his title.

Tawl ignored him and turned to Madame Thornypurse. "So this is what your scheme is. Arranging a fight with me as the centerpiece. Haven't you earned enough from me already?"

"My dear Tawl, I only have your interests at heart." Madame Thornypurse's hand fluttered like a wounded butterfly to her throat.

Blayze raised a beautifully arched brow. "I hardly blame your reluctance, Tawl. It is never easy to contemplate defeat."

Madame Thornypurse and her daughter sighed in agreement.

"Trying to goad me, eh?" said Tawl. "Cheap tactics from a man who wears such expensive clothes."

Blayze was not insulted. He studied the cuff on his embroidered tunic. "Victory bought them for me. You, too, could win such rewards." He shrugged. "Of course, you might find yourself in a shroud."

"Popularity flagging, is it? Need a decent victory over an opponent worthy of you?" Tawl began to walk away. "Well, you can forget about me, I'm not prepared to be anyone's path to glory."

"That really doesn't surprise me, my friend. From what I've heard, glory isn't your strong suit."

Tawl spun around. "What have you heard?"

"I've heard you're a Knight of Valdis, and that fighting in the pits is the least of your sins."

Tawl was at his throat in an instant. He knew that was what the man wanted, but it made no difference. His failure was too new a wound to be salted. His hands grabbed oiled and scented skin. The muscles beneath were iron. The two women squawked and panicked like scared hens. Blayze's neck was his. He squeezed the two weakest points under the jaw, pressing them together. He felt a quick jab at his side. A blade, smoothly drawn.

"Step away," said the champion. His rasping words were backed up by a second, more threatening jab.

From the corner of his eye, Tawl saw two guards approaching, spears in hand. Probably alerted by the women's screams. Tawl let Blayze go, hating his cowardice as he did so. Even now, when there was nothing to live for, his first instinct was to save himself. For what?

Blayze waved the guards away. "Now is neither the time nor place for this," he said to Tawl. "One week from now, I'll be waiting for you in the pit just south of the palace. There we can finish what we started." He made a show of wiping the blood from his knife. "Unless, of course, you place no value on honor."

"There is little honor in drawing a blade on an unarmed man." Tawl suddenly felt tired. What did it matter? "I'll be there. Though you might find the odds too even for your liking."

"A good fight, fairly fought, that's all I'm after."

Tawl didn't care what the man was saying anymore, he wanted to be away. He needed a drink. Night had fallen, and it was the worst sort: still and cloudless. The stars were a thousand pointing fingers. He walked away, desperate to be alone. Nothing mattered except escaping to a place where he could forget. No longer could lovemaking divert his thoughts. Drinking and fighting were all that was left. So he would do what he could, and perhaps, Borc willing, his next fight might be his last.

Maybor spat out a mouthful of meat. It was tough and tasteless, probably peacock. He hated such fancy stuff. Where was the venison, the pork, the beef? In front of the duke, no doubt. There was one man who wouldn't be eating overstuffed, overfluffed, overdone fowl. The duke ate his meat red and bloody.

Maybor surveyed the huge banqueting table. Laden with candles and platters, tankards and bones, around it sat the highest nobility of Bren. The men were a drab and short-haired lot. Not a beard or a bright color between them. They obviously took their lead from the duke, who favored the unadorned style of the military. Even now the man had his sword at the table. And what a splendid and posturing weapon it was. Maybor thought he might get himself one; it drew the eye more certainly than the most elaborately embroidered silk.

At least the women didn't follow His Grace's example. Beautifully molded dresses traced curves as tempting as anything the kingdoms had to offer. Their voices were a little harsh, but their waists were full, and their hips sported more meat than a brace of dead peacocks. More than one of these tempting creatures had looked his way, and who could blame them? Amongst such dull men, he stood out like a king. Bren might be famous for its tailors, but its weavers and dyemakers must work in the dark.

"Was the breast not to your liking?" It was Catherine herself. In a room full of beautiful women, she found no equal. Maybor had harbored every intention of scorning her, but here, sitting by her side, fingers resting upon the same trencher, he found himself dazzled. The portrait painter had done her an injustice: she was magnificent. Her skin glowed, her hair shone, her lips were formed by angels. An untouched princess poised to become a woman.

For an instant Maybor was bemused by her comment, but quickly realized she was referring to the fowl. "I have little taste for peacock, my lady."

"Then we must see that you are meated." She clapped her hands and a servant hovered close. "Venison for the lord."

A huge platter of meat was laid before Maybor. He made a great show of picking out the fattest joint and handing it to Catherine.

"Sir, you do me honor."

"Lady, it is honor enough to be in your presence." Maybor felt inordinately pleased with himself: he'd said and done just the right thing. Baralis had heard him, too. The king's chancellor gave him a look filled with malice. He was sitting next to the duke's aged mother, a woman as deaf and ugly as she was old and wrinkled.

Baralis was going to die. There was no question about it. The how and the when were all that needed deciding. He could allow no one to do what he did this morning and get away with it. No one. All his tricks and fancies wouldn't save him. The king's chancellor would rest long in the grave.

Oh, but the pain had been worth it! He'd made Baralis look a fool and a liar. If anything, Bren was turning out to be his city; the duke was courting his favor, and Catherine was attending to his every need like a dutiful daughter. Even the man to his left, the great and wealthy Lord Cravin, was treating him with the respect he deserved.

Catherine was talking with the man on her right, so Maybor took the chance of broaching the subject that was on everyone's mind, but on no one's lips. "Tell me, Lord Cravin, how is Bren taking the news of Kylock's sovereignty?"

Lord Cravin cleaned the sauce from his fingers with meticulous care. Although he was looking down, Maybor got the uncanny feeling that he was checking every man in the room to see where their attentions lay, listening for the sound of bated breath. The lord reached over for a flagon of wine and spoke, his words an expertly fired arrow with Maybor as the only target, "Not bad enough."

The possibility of intrigue opened like a rare and seductive bloom. Maybor was heady with its scent. *Careful, must be careful*, he warned himself. Quick to learn, he mimicked Lord Cravin's nonchalance by plucking the feathers from what remained of the peacock. "Things will go as planned, then?"

"Unless someone is bold enough to change their course." Cravin handed Maybor a platter of spiced eels.

"We must meet some time to discuss our—" Maybor noticed Catherine was no longer talking to the man at her side.

"Discontent," said Cravin, stepping in, "with the eels?"

"Yes," Maybor said. "They are not as slippery as I like them."

"Then let me wet them a little for you," said Catherine. She took up a silver tureen and poured cameline sauce into the dish. "I trust they'll slip down your throat more easily now, Lord Maybor."

Maybor studied the girl and could find nothing but innocent concern on her face. His attentions were suddenly distracted by Baralis standing up, goblet in hand.

"Ladies and gentlemen of the court," he said, the subtle power in his voice silencing the room in an instant. "May I propose a toast to the fairest and most gracious maiden in the whole of the Northern Territories: Catherine of Bren."

The crowd had no choice but to second him. They raised their glasses and shouted *"Aye!"*

Baralis hadn't finished. "A second toast to the greatest of leaders and the most inspired of generals: the duke of Bren." Once again the crowd backed him.

He was leading them along as surely as a shepherd guides his sheep. Maybor guessed what was coming next. The man was a master of manipulation.

"And a final toast," said Baralis. "To a union more glorious, more noble, and more magnificent than any joining in the history of the Known Lands: the marriage of Kylock, sovereign of the Four Kingdoms, and Catherine of Bren."

The crowd rose to meet him. Shouting and banging, their enthusiasm was so contagious that even Maybor found his foot tapping along. Baralis had done a fine job; he had taken a court that was reluctant and whipped them into a frenzy of self-congratulation. Who, looking around this room now, could honestly say that Bren was against the marriage?

Those who looked closely at the duke's face, perhaps. His hand was a little stiff as he raised his glass, his smile a tad reluctant. The man did not enjoy watching his court being manipulated. Maybor rubbed his stubbled chin. There were possibilities here. Chinks that could be made into breaches. The betrothal would stick—Baralis had made sure of that tonight—but the marriage was a long way off. Much might happen over the coming months. For one thing, Kylock could win the war with the Halcus, that would certainly make everyone nervous. The duke might change his mind, for another. And then there was the latest development: intrigue.

Maybor glanced toward Lord Cravin. The man was cheering along with all the gusto of a well-polished actor. A wise move, and one he could learn by. It was best to seem in favor of the match for the time being. The most effective strike was an unexpected one. Maybor took up his cup and toasted the betrothal. If the wine was a little bitter on his tongue, he let no one know it.

Catherine of Bren unpinned the pearl circlet from her hair and slipped the pearl earrings from her lobes. She looked at herself in the mirror and her lips curved to half a smile. It had been an interesting evening.

Sitting between two fools—one boring, one vain.

The king's envoy had failed to impress her. He'd passed the time spitting, plucking feathers, and flirting, but the king's chancellor . . . Catherine's smile spread . . . now there was a man to be reckoned with. Until yesterday it was Lord Baralis, not Lord Maybor, who she was due to sit next to at the banquet. Apparently her father was punishing him for something. Could Lord Baralis help it that the old and doddering King Lesketh had finally popped off?

Yes, an interesting evening. She'd played the part of dumb female well: her guests' cups were never empty, their vanities constantly flattered, and their meats well moistened with sauce. Catherine began to untie the lacings on her dress. Lord Cravin had so discreetly let his displeasure be known, hoping to find an ally in Lord Maybor. It wasn't important; there was nothing they could do to halt the match. Just seeing how cleverly Lord Baralis had handled the court made her confident of that.

She would be a queen not of one but two countries.

A timid knock was heard upon her door. "Go away, Stasia, I will undress myself. Do not disturb me till morning."

Catherine hooked her hands beneath the neckline of her dress and pulled the heavily brocaded silk away from her body. Next came the linen shift beneath. As she drew it over her head, the material caught against the belt. The shift ripped in two. "Damn!" she muttered, cursing the iron monstrosity that rested upon her hips: her maiden's belt.

Molded from two ribbons of iron, dull and heavy, yet snake-close to her body, it was the bane of her existence. Made to her exact and most intimate measurements, it combined the skills of a craftsman with the guile of an armorer. Like the very palace itself, she was alluring on the outside, but impregnable within. The belt rubbed against her belly and buttocks constantly, raising welts and chafe-sores. The first year of wearing it she'd nearly died of an infection, so it had been sent back to the forge to be made anew. What emerged was something more delicate, yet just as monstrous.

Five years she'd endured it. Five years of not being able to bathe or relieve herself properly. Five years of sweat, rust, and humiliation.

No one wore them anymore—if indeed anyone ever had—they were a thing of the past, read about in stories, giggled about whilst embroidering. Still, here she was, the highest-ranking female in the greatest court in the Known Lands, trussed up as surely as a felon in the stocks. Her father was keen on keeping up the traditions of his ancestors, traditions that warned of the weak nature and insatiable sexual appetites of the women of Bren. She would never forgive him for it.

Though it did have its advantages. As long as she wore it she was above suspicion. Catherine gently caressed the metal. Ancient runes of warding were etched upon the curve. She had learned long ago that they had no power to guard. She began to concentrate upon the point where lock and solder met, gently warming the join. She could taste the metal on her tongue. It excited her. Nausea threatened, but she ignored it. The tiny pinpoint of metal shifted and grew pliable with the heat. Catherine drew a little more. All of the belt was now warm to the touch. The heat between her legs excited her further.

Instinctively, she knew the exact moment when the solder would give. She pulled upon the hinge and the belt opened enough for her to slip it over her hips and step from it. 'Twas a foolish man who thought his valuables were safe just because he locked the door.

Her legs were weak, threatening to give way beneath her. She stumbled to her bed, feeling triumphant and lightheaded. Where was Blayze? She wanted him now.

Pouring herself a glass of red, she settled back to wait. The duke had done her a service by forcing the maiden's belt upon her: she had been obliged to learn sorcery to escape from it. Her handmaiden Stasia had an aunt who had knowledge of such things. Of course, Catherine hid her real intent, saying she was interested in metals because her jewelry so often broke. A weak excuse, but who would dare contradict the duke's daughter? Especially an old woman who was breaking ancient laws by practicing sorcery.

At first the woman had told her she had no talent, that it was passed down in the blood and that the house of Bren had been gifted with real power, not magic. There was a little there, though. Probably from her mother's side. Not much, just a trace, but sufficient to work with. So she had learned enough to weaken the solder and a few other tricks that were useful to know. The old crow had died a few months back and Catherine had found herself a little restless since. She missed the thrill of new knowledge and the danger of discovery.

Running her hands down her thighs, she admired the smoothness of her body. Such long legs, such pale, unblemished skin. The only thing that marred the length was the small birthmark that rested just above her ankle. The sign of the hawk, borne by all men and women of the house of Bren. It marked her as her father's daughter. An irrefutable sign of her lineage—and she wore it with pride.

A triple knock upon the shutter. About time. She didn't bother to cover her nakedness as she crossed over to the window. Unhooking the latch, she stood back and watched as the duke's champion climbed through the gap.

"Where have you been?" she demanded. Blayze reached out to kiss her, but she pulled away. There was ale on his breath.

"Arranging a few things." His eyes were upon her breasts. Catherine covered them with her hands.

"What things?"

"My fight with the yellow-haired stranger from out of town." He walked over to the trestle table and poured himself a glass of wine. He stood for a moment, perfectly aware that he cut a fine figure in a new tunic and with glass in hand. "Everything went well. It's on for next week."

"My father will be glad to hear it. He was hoping to entertain his guests with a spectacle."

"Then he'll get one." Blayze seemed rather pleased with himself. He sat on the bed and slapped his thigh, beckoning her to join him. Another time she might have held out, but the sorcery still ran hot in her blood. She came over and sat on his lap. He was strong and well muscled; a fighter, not a courtier.

"So tell me about your challenger," she said.

"A loser. A fallen knight who's been lucky in his choice of opponents. I can't understand what all the fuss is about."

"So you're sure to win?"

"I nearly killed him where he stood. We met outside the palace by the three fountains," said Blayze. "The man went for my throat."

Catherine thought for a moment. "You can't afford to lose this fight," she said.

"No chance of that."

"But I've heard that all of Bren is talking about him."

Blayze pushed her away. "Then they're talking about someone who's not worthy of their breath."

Catherine moved toward him, offering her breasts to be kissed. He was angry, so he was rough, and that was the way she wanted it. Their lovemaking was fierce, a wrestling match of tumbles and holds. Blayze pinned her to the bed whilst his tongue traced the red marks left by the maiden's belt. His saliva stung the still-tender flesh, but it made her desire him all the more.

Later, when the candles guttered in the remains of the wax, and when they lay exhausted on the bed, Catherine sought out Blayze's hand. She felt tender toward him. She would soon go on and marry someone else. A glorious future was hers, but Blayze had nothing except his title as duke's champion. Such an honor, dependent solely upon physical prowess, was by its very nature purely transitory.

"You will win, won't you?" she said.

Blayze was affectionate, kissing her wrists. "Of course I will, my love. There's no need to worry."

"But I do worry. What if this man lands a lucky blow?" She thought for a moment that she'd pushed too far. Blayze stood up and started getting dressed. "I'm sorry, I didn't mean to offend you."

He turned toward her and said softly, "Catherine, do you really think I would leave something as important as this to chance?"

The words thrilled her. "What have you planned?"

"I can beat this lance blindfolded, but as you said, there's always the chance of a lucky blow." Blayze paused and Catherine nodded her encouragement. "So I had a quiet word with the landlady of the inn he's staying at—though inn might be too generous a description."

"The woman runs a brothel?"

Blayze nodded. "Aye, so she knows the value of the duke's own coinage. Anyway, she's going to poison his food. He'll have slowed down quite considerably by the night of the contest."

Catherine stood up and put her arms around Blayze. Kissing him full on the lips, she used her tongue as a lure: she wanted him again. Men were always more interesting when they used their wits as well as their muscle.

Eleven

*I*t was early morning in the cottage. Tarissa was busy stoking the fire and Magra was at the table peeling turnips. Rovas, silent and moody for some days now, had gone out an hour earlier, muttering that he wouldn't be back before nightfall. Jack was glad; the place was more peaceful without him. It was nice just to sit and enjoy the pleasures of mulled holk while taking in the sounds and smells of the beginning of the day.

Broth was slowly warming, its delicate fragrance competing with the cinnamon from the holk. Long-dried herbs hung from the rafters and the warmth from the fire sweetened their smell. Brushing and scraping, chopping and mixing; the sounds of the kitchen were a familiar comfort. The women had smiled at him earlier when he'd taken up a knife and started slicing onions. He didn't see anything unusual about it; in the kitchens at Castle Harvell, a boy who was idle was asking for a beating.

The sword that Rovas had given him stood resting against the pickling vat. As a baker's boy he had always been strong; kneading enough dough to feed the castle each day soon put muscle on a man's arms and chest, but using the longsword required new muscles and new strength. His back had to bear the considerable weight of the blade, and his flank the brunt of the thrust. Jack's legs were aching, too. Rovas spent a lot of time explaining balance, not just centering the blade upon the body, but also balancing upper strength with lower. "When wielding a longsword a man's in danger of becoming top heavy," he would say. "You need muscle on your thighs to even out the weight." So the smuggler had him running up hills and barrel rolling.

Ever since Jack had defied him by taking a walk with Tarissa, Rovas had used their training sessions as a form of punishment. Practice had become dangerous. Rovas was remarkably skilled with the blade, light on his feet, firm with his grip, and always quick to thrust. Jack had no chance against him. Sitting here in the kitchen chopping pork bones for the broth, he only had to look down at his arms to see the full extent of Rovas' hostility over the past three days. His arms were covered in cuts and bruises.

He was getting better, though. Yesterday the smuggler had tried to make him look a fool by forcing him back against a tree. Jack had rallied his strength and somehow managed to land a decent blow. His blade grazed the length of Rovas' sword and came to rest in the flesh of his wrist. The look of indignant surprise made the later thrashing worth it.

Jack didn't know what to make of this strange household that he found himself in. Tensions ran deep, yet he didn't know what caused them, or why his presence seemed to aggravate them further. Magra was a dilemma. Proud and cold as the greatest courtier, he thought at first she was against him, but only minutes before they'd shared a joke about the onions and she'd patted his shoulder gently. He couldn't pretend to know about such things—after all, what experience did he have of anything except baking and beatings—but he got the distinct impression that Magra was being nice to him merely to spite Rovas.

One thing was certain: both Magra and Tarissa were afraid of the wide and usually jaunty smuggler. They laughed and teased him, but they each stepped carefully, as if frightened of waking a sleeping bear.

Another thing certain was that he had to stay here. Now more than ever. Tarissa had lied when she said Rovas had given so much, yet asked for so little in return. Expecting her to kill a man for him was currency of the highest tender. What kind of man would do such a thing to a girl who was as good as his daughter? Leaving was out of the question. If he left now, Tarissa would never be free of Rovas. They would become accomplices in murder, bound together by shared secrets, fear, and guilt.

Jack glanced quickly at her. Tarissa was putting the bellows to the fire. Her sleeves were rolled up and the muscles on her arms pushed against her skin. Her face was illuminated by the flames. The golden light suited her. She looked young and strong and self-possessed. Jack's hands curled up to a fist. How could Rovas have expected her to kill someone? How could he have forced this honest and hard-working girl into acting as his assassin?

Jack felt hatred swell in his stomach. It suited him to let it build.

Rovas lived to control the women in this cottage. He wanted to have the power of life and death over them. He wanted to make Tarissa his partner in crime.

Tarissa put down the bellows and smiled Jack's way. "I've blown a gale on that fire," she said, "and it still looks fit to die." She had ash on her nose and in her hair. A single curl fell across her cheek and she blew it away like a feather. She was so straightforward, no airs or graces. Nothing hidden.

Jack found it hard to return her smile, but he did. And as his lips stretched then curved, there was no question in his mind that he would have to kill the Halcus captain. He couldn't let Rovas corrupt and then blackmail this spirited girl before him.

Magra stood up. The spell of hate and vows was broken. "I'm going to take a walk to Lark's Farm," she said. "It's about time we had some fresh eggs."

This was a surprise. Jack and Tarissa exchanged looks. She was as baffled as he. There was no explanation other than Magra wanted to leave them alone. She knew Rovas would be gone all day. Putting on a cloak of scarlet wool, she fastened it at her throat. Jack saw for the first time what she must have looked like twenty years earlier: a breathtaking beauty. Taller and more slender than her daughter, Magra's bearing was as much a part of her attraction as her finely chiseled face.

Tarissa noticed he was looking at her mother. She smiled, and he saw that she was proud. There was so much Jack wanted to know. Why had they fled from the kingdoms? How had they come to be here? And why did deep lines of bitterness mark the beauty of Magra's face?

Before she left, she threw a look at her daughter, an uneasy mix of warning and resignation.

As soon as the door was closed Jack walked over to Tarissa. He couldn't help himself, he wanted to be close to her. She didn't move away. Meeting his gaze, she said, "What are you going to do now, Jack?" Her words were taunting, but her eyes sparkled an invitation.

Jack was overwhelmed by her closeness. He had a sudden mad desire to take her in his arms.

Tarissa smiled slowly. "Another kiss, perhaps. Or are you going to surprise me?"

Jack knew a challenge when he heard one. He stepped forward. Drawing his hands around her waist, he lifted her into his arms. Tarissa's seductive smile was gone in an instant. She screamed and giggled and then punched him. He told her she had a good punch, *for a girl*. And she hit him even more. Finally he let her go.

Like two children with no supervision, they ran around the kitchen, fighting and laughing and breaking odd pieces of pottery. Everything was funny: the broth, the fire, the half-peeled turnips. The novelty of being alone together in the cottage was so overwhelming that it left them light-headed.

Tarissa wrestled free of him. "You smell of onions," she said.

"Thank you," replied Jack. "I made a special effort."

She kicked his shin and dashed away with the speed of a hare. He chased her around the kitchen, dredging up the rushes with every step. Tarissa had never looked more splendid: color in her cheeks, hair wild and curling, and breasts heaving. Jack felt a little ashamed of noticing such things, and he tried not to, but they drew his eye and engaged his thoughts—constantly.

She caught him at it again and laughed out loud. Jack, hearing amusement not derision, laughed with her. Her eyes sparkled. He was enchanted by her confidence and the sheer earthiness of her. She was no great unapproachable lady. He felt no awkwardness around her. She may have been brought up in a different country, but she lived in his world. It was a world where kitchens were the only rooms that counted, where friends gathered around the fire, and where hard work was shared as readily as tall tales at supper.

They stopped for a moment and Tarissa offered her hand to be kissed. Jack's heart was beating fast. Her hands were sturdy; the nails were short and not as clean as they should be. The palms were crisscrossed with tiny scars from practicing with the sword, and six perfectly formed and totally irresistible calluses graced her fingers. Bypassing the smooth white skin on the top of her hand, he kissed the calluses instead. Tarissa couldn't stop giggling, so he kissed them all again.

She was a delight to be with. Gone was the scared girl of three nights back, gone was the haughty woman he'd first kissed. Rovas had made a fatal mistake: by trying to keep them apart he had drawn them closer. Three days of being unable to talk or hardly look at each other had driven them to this. They were strangers before, now they were united in intrigue.

Tarissa giggled as he kissed her calluses one more time. She begged him to stop, and when he wouldn't, she pulled at his hair and bit his earlobe.

Gradually, the biting turned into something softer, and wetter. Jack had to physically stop himself from crushing her. Her tongue traced the journey from ear to mouth. Her breasts were within reach and nothing, nothing, could prevent him from caressing them. A small murmur of encouragement thrilled him more than any touch. Tarissa became the older woman again, guiding, teaching, sure of herself in every way.

Jack moved his hand upward, needing to feel skin rather than fabric. Tarissa pulled away. "We're moving too quickly," she said, unable to look him straight in the face.

At that moment all that Grift had ever told him about women seemed true. They were false, heartless, and confusing enough to drive a man wild. Why was there nothing in his life that was simple and straightforward? His past, his future, his abilities, and now this failed attempt at lovemaking. More frustrated than angry, he pushed his hair back and sighed. "What did I do wrong?"

She surprised him by smiling gently. "You have such beautiful hair." Leaning forward, she pushed back the strands that he'd missed. "I'm sorry, Jack. Your excitement was infectious. It carried me to a place where I wasn't ready to be." She held out her hand and he took it.

How could he hate her? The passion drained from his body, leaving a residue of tenderness. "Then I'm sorry, too." He smiled as he spoke. Grift had told him many times that women were notorious for having a man apologize when he'd done nothing wrong. Jack didn't mind, though. The one thing Grift had *forgotten* to tell him was that it was all worth it.

"Rovas is making us act like lovesick fools," said Tarissa, "yet we hardly know each other. You say you lived at Castle Harvell, but I don't know what you did there, or why you left, or who your family are."

There it was, the question he'd dreaded all his life, its asking always inevitable. Family was what counted. It defined who a person was and where he had come from. Ultimately a man was judged by it. So what did that make him? With a mother commonly thought to be a whore and a father who didn't exist, he had nothing to boast about. And a lot to be ashamed of.

Now was not the time to talk of family. Jack made an effort to keep the mood light. He stood up, pulling Tarissa with him, and said, "You mean I forgot to tell you I was an apprentice baker?"

"A baker?" Tarissa was delighted.

Jack steered her in the direction of the table. "Yes, a baker. I think it's about time I impressed you with my skills." He sat her down by the large, trestled work-top and began to pull out flour and water and fat. Next he went over to the fire and placed the baking stone in the center of the flame.

"What are you going to make?" asked Tarissa, elbows on the table, engrossed in what he was doing.

He rubbed his chin for a moment and then smiled. "Something sweet, I think." Jack worked quickly, adding everything he could find to the dough: dried fruit and peel, honey, cinnamon. After a while he looked up. Tarissa was watching him with quiet intent. "Come and help me knead the dough," he said. She shook her head. Jack was not about to be put off so easily. He stopped what he was doing and reached across the table. "Give me your hands." The moment she held them out, he took hold of them and rubbed the dough from his fingers onto hers. "Looks like you might as well do some kneading now," he said. "A little more dough will make no difference."

Tarissa pulled a face, but came and stood beside him. Jack stepped behind her and placed her hands on the dough. Slowly, he taught her how to knead and then roll it, explaining that every dough has a different texture and showing the right way to test for it. He guided her fingers and directed her arms.

Jack was acutely aware of her nearness. The curve of her neck was the most tempting sight he'd ever seen. The feel of her hands beneath his was a joy to be savored. The dough was soon forgotten and all that counted was touching and being close.

A rattle of the door and in walked Magra. Jack and Tarissa stopped what they were doing immediately. Like lovers caught kissing, they both blushed with guilt.

"Baking, I see," said Magra.

"Jack was just teaching me how to knead dough," said Tarissa, hastily scraping the flour from her fingers.

"So Jack's a baker, is he?" Magra slammed the egg basket down on the table. "Well, that's about as good as I can expect, stuck here in the borderlands."

Jack was more confused than ever. He thought Magra had gone out with the sole intent of leaving them alone. Now here she was, clearly unhappy with the result. Magra obviously considered him to be beneath her daughter. Why then had she conspired to bring them closer?

Tarissa moved over to the wash basin and began to clean her hands. Jack finished shaping the dough. He turned it onto the baking stone and then covered it with a large copper pot. This was the nearest most cottages could get to an oven: heat would rise from the stone and be caught in the pot. He didn't hold high hopes for the sweet loaf; the yeast had had little time to work, so the bread would be heavy.

Glancing toward Tarissa, a thought dark with possibilities occurred to Jack. Perhaps Magra was reluctantly bringing them together because the alternative was worse.

Uneasy with the direction his mind was traveling, and afraid where his thoughts might eventually lead, Jack quickly cleaned up the table and made his way outside. The borrowed sword was in his hand. He felt the need to do something physical. Rovas had hung an empty beer barrel from a tree, so when it was swung, Jack could practice dodging and feigning. Jack set it swinging, but dodging wasn't on his mind. He wielded the sword and stabbed the barrel over and over again. Splinters flew through the air. Jack hardly saw them. He was determined to destroy the barrel. The metal hoops raked against his sword, damaging the blade, but the wood gave way like butter. Thrust after thrust he aimed, the man who had hung the barrel his imaginary target.

"No, Bodger. The women of Bren like their men short and hairy."

"So you're in with a chance, then, Grift."

"We both are, Bodger."

"I may be short, Grift, but I'm definitely not hairy."

"You seen the back of your neck lately? I wouldn't want to be around you come a full moon."

"You don't believe all those old wives' tales about werewolves, do you, Grift?"

"Have you noticed, Bodger, that it's always the old wives who live the longest?"

"What d'you mean, Grift?"

"I mean, Bodger, that they live that long because they know all the perils. You won't catch an old wife going out on a full moon without a supply of prunes."

"Prunes, Grift?"

"Aye, prunes, Bodger. The deadliest of fruits."

"How so, Grift?"

"Well, there's two things werewolves want to do with women: rollick 'em and then eat 'em. And I don't know if you've ever rollicked a girl who's been pruning, Bodger, but let me tell you, it ain't pleasant."

Bodger shook his head sagely. "What about the eating part, Grift?"

"No one likes the taste of prunes, Bodger. Not even werewolves."

The two men toasted to Grift's good sense and settled back in their chairs.

"So who told you about the women of Bren, Grift?"

"Gatekeeper, name of Longtoad. Apparently it's the women of *Rorn* who go for tall men. Anyway, he told me a few interesting things about the duke."

"What about the duke, Grift?"

"By all accounts the man has the sexual appetite of an owl, Bodger. He just about lives for rollickin'. But he's fussy, if you know what I mean."

"Fussy?"

"Aye. He's got a deep fear of catching the ghones. According to Longtoad, that's how his father died. The late duke hit the deck soon after his plums did. So the current duke only rollicks women who have never been touched."

"Ugly women, is that, Grift?"

"No, you fool, virgins. It's the only certain way of ensuring a girl ain't got the ghones." Grift finished his ale. "Well, Bodger, I think it's time we were going, those pews won't clean themselves."

"It was an inspired move of yours, Grift, to get in with the chaplain. If it wasn't for that, we'd be stuck in the stables looking after the horses."

"Aye, Bodger. My powers of persuasion are matched only by the power of my intellect."

Every eighth step there was horse dung. A mathematical oddity, but true nonetheless. Perhaps horses got together to arrange it like that, because there was just enough distance between droppings to lure a man into a false sense of security and then *splat!* Dung on his shoes.

Nabber was spending a lot of time looking at his feet. He told himself it was because of the dangers of dirt, but really it was because he was feeling a strange new emotion: guilt. He'd heard about guilt before, stories of people being stricken with it, of sorrow and madness. Swift himself had adamantly maintained that *"guilt is the death of a pocket,"* so Nabber had come to the logical conclusion that it was a sort of vague disease that could kill a man unless he found a cure.

It was all Tawl's fault. Somehow the knight had managed to give him a bad dose of guilt. Here he was, man of the world, doing what every self-respecting dealer was supposed to do—make deals—yet he was feeling as if he'd committed the crime of the century. It had gotten so bad that he could hardly look a man in the face and had taken to looking at the ground with all the intent of a smircher looking for gold.

Everything had been going fine until he'd gotten the rat oil woman involved. After that it had gone downhill faster than a greased archbishop. What had possessed him to tell that smug dandy of a fighter, Blayze, that Tawl had a shameful past? It had seemed like inspiration from the gods at the time—a sure way of goading the knight into agreeing to the match. It had worked, too. From his vantage point behind a tree at the corner of the square, he'd seen it all: the discussion, the tussle, the women, and the guards. He'd even heard Tawl say he was up for the fight. What was the matter, then? Why did he feel so bad?

Looking back, Nabber tried to pinpoint the exact moment when he'd begun to feel the first pangs of guilt.

It was about the time when Tawl wandered off alone, leaving Madame Thornypurse and her straw-haired daughter Corsella to talk to Blayze. Big ears weren't enough to hear what passed between the three. That in itself was a bad sign: according to Swift, *"the worse the plot, the quieter the plotting."* Something had gone down there by the three golden fountains—Nabber was sure of it—and it boded no good for the knight.

Guilt had been festering ever since, and he had to do something about it before it killed him.

Nabber's feet picked a path to Brotheling Street. The loot in his pack jangling as he walked. Each clink of coinage served to irritate his already chronic condition. He'd done well by Blayze. The man had given him twenty golds, not to mention the ten silvers he'd pocketed while the champion was counting out the payment. Also not to mention the gold he'd pocketed from Madame Thornypurse herself whilst they were talking in the Brimming Bucket—there was one lady who knew how to conceal her valuables! After all, it was only fair that he reclaimed as much of Tawl's gold as possible, and Nabber was quite certain that the pouchful of loot suspended from Madame Thornypurse's underdrawers rightly belonged to the knight. So, all things considered, he'd made a pretty profit from the whole affair.

That was only part of the problem. What if the knight lost the fight? Or worse, what if he died? He, Nabber, would be left holding the loot, and as he was already suffering from chronic guilt, such a blow would surely finish him off.

Best to make sure it never happened. To save the knight would be the same as saving himself.

He arrived by the red-shuttered building. For some reason, knocking at the door didn't seem like a good idea, so Nabber slipped down the adjoining alleyway and sought out the warped window casing that had proven so useful many nights earlier.

The place was decidedly dark and dingy inside. Too early for business, a few tired-looking girls lounged around on benches, intent on getting drunk before the punters arrived. Madame Thornypurse was nowhere to be seen. A flash of bright hair marked Corsella, busy rubbing rouge into her sour, little face. Disappointed, Nabber was about to turn away when he heard the unmistakable sound of someone retching—a familiar noise to a boy who at one time had the dubious privilege of living next door to the most notorious mass poisoner in Rorn: Master Sourgill, the proprietor of Sourgill's Fresh Fish Tavern.

The retching was followed by a painful, hacking cough, and then Corsella piped up: "Ssh, Tawl, you'll wake Mother."

The knight was obviously in an adjoining room, so Nabber worked his way around to the back of the building. The smell, which had been bad enough in the alleyway, rose to the level of an overpowering stench. The source was an open ditch. It ran along the length of the street and was filled with things so appalling that even Nabber didn't care to look at them.

Finding an eye-hole was not as easy as he'd hoped. Eventually he pulled some sick-looking greenery from its place on a ledge. The resulting fissure was crawling with spiders, but provided a view into the back of the building.

Tawl was crouched on the floor, shivering from head to foot. For a brief moment Nabber was transported back to Bevlin's cottage, to the time when the knight rocked the dead man in his arms. The shock of remembrance cooled his skin and set his hands trembling. The young pickpocket was suddenly struck with the sense that he was dealing with things far beyond his ken. His life had always been straightforward: see it, want it, take it. There was profit, food, and dicing. Yet on the other side of the wall crouched a man to whom none of that mattered, and strangely, Nabber felt drawn to him for that very reason. He had no word for love, no inkling how to use it. Friendship was all that his experiences had allowed. So the extreme anger he felt toward the person who had done this—for he was no fool and guessed that a certain rodent-oiled hand was responsible—he attributed to that one familiar concept.

The guilt was so bad he thought he would be struck down where he stood. It was most definitely time to pay the lady of the house an unexpected visit.

"Thank you, my man, just leave it on the table." Maybor waved a languorous dismissal. The second the door was closed, however, he fell on the box like a wolf on a fawn. Messages from the kingdoms.

Several dull scrolls from his overseer concerned with dwindling winter supplies, a note from his servant Crandle advising him that he was still too ill to make the journey to Bren, and then the interesting stuff. A letter from Kedrac, and a missive, complete with ribbons and wax, written in a hand that he had seen only once before. The last time the letter had been delivered by an eagle.

Maybor turned to his son's letter first. The handwriting was large and familiar, so it was relatively easy for him to read.

Good. Kedrac had seen sense over the chambermaid affair, stating that, *"No woman, especially a dead one, should be allowed power enough to break the bonds between father and son."*

The boy knew how to choose his words. Maybor was well pleased. Kedrac was now his again and, with Melliandra gone perhaps never to return, he valued what remained of his family more highly. As he read on, joy turned to excitement. Kedrac was talking about the new king. Apparently Kylock was turning out to be quite a leader: *"Father, he is brilliant. His plan for defeating the Halcus is both daring and inspired. He intends to send a battalion into enemy territory and attack the border forces from the rear."*

Maybor drew a hand to his face and scratched his chin reflectively. If Kylock succeeded, it would certainly put an end to the stalemate, though it seemed rather an aggressive act for a country whose only concern was supposed to be securing its borders. Baralis would not be pleased about this.

As he folded his son's letter, a wicked smile stretched across Maybor's lips. Kedrac had provided him with an interesting morsel to let drop upon the duke's plate. He was going to have to be careful with his politicking. No one must know that he was against the match, not even his son, for it seemed from the letter that Kedrac admired his sovereign. Perhaps was even privy to Kylock's inner council: plans of attack were a covert business. Yes, discretion was most definitely called for. Best not to risk the anger of the newly crowned king.

On to the next letter. Waxed, but not sealed. According to Crandle, it had arrived a few days after he'd left for Bren. With fingers a little stiffer than he'd like, Maybor unraveled the scroll. Damned foreign handwriting! All loops and fancy dangles—a man could ruin his eyesight just deciphering it.

Slowly the words took shape. It was the second letter from the mysterious would-be conspirator from a city far in the south. Only not so mysterious now: *"You rightly guessed that I am a man of the Church. Ask yourself this, then: who is the only man of God who holds power worth the wielding?"* It had to be the archbishop of Rorn. A small yet very intense thrill passed down Maybor's back. He was intriguing on a grand scale now. Reading on, he found more to his liking: *"The union between Bren and the kingdoms will cast a broad shadow over the north. He who is responsible for the joining will guide its progress."* And then, further down the page: *"If you harbor the desire to oppose the match, you will find the might of the south behind you."* The archbishop was obviously not a man to parry words like a love poet.

Maybor put down the letter and took up his cup. All in all, two very interesting exchanges. He felt as if he'd been endowed with new power. There was danger here, though. The worst kind: personal danger. To be a thorn in Baralis' side was one thing, to risk his own lands and position was quite another. His step must be light and his voice as quiet and beguiling as an angel.

Dipping quill into ink, he set about writing a reply to the letter from the east. The task took many hours, Maybor learning subtlety as he wrote.

Nabber knocked loudly on the door. "Open up! Open up! Duke's business."

Corsella, freshly rouged and all the worse for it, answered. She took one look at him, and said, "Bugger off, you little snot."

Foot in the door, Nabber pressed his advantage. "I'm a friend of your mother's. I was talking with her the other day in the Brimming Bucket. It was me who arranged the fight for Tawl."

"You do look sort of familiar. Who are you, then?" Corsella, while matching Madame Thornypurse in looks, obviously fell short of her mother's intelligence. Which suited Nabber nicely.

"I'm Blayze's brother . . ." Nabber searched for an appropriate name ". . . Scorch. And I must have a word with your mother as soon as possible."

Corsella simpered in memory of the handsome champion. "You don't look like him."

"Aah, well, he's got my father's nose. Mine came from a distant uncle."

"Hmm."

"Look, I really don't care whether you believe me or not, but how will your mother react when she finds you closed the door on the duke's own messenger?"

Madame Thornypurse was obviously less than a loving mother, for Corsella thought for a moment, and then said, "You better come in."

She led him through to the large open room he'd spied on from the alleyway. The lounging ladies merely ignored him. A large man who he'd never noticed before was sitting in the corner putting an edge to his blade. Nabber was silently praying that Tawl would stay in the back of the house; now was not the time to be recognized. A few minutes later Corsella returned.

"Mother will see you in her chamber."

Madame Thornypurse in her bedclothes was a sight to be reckoned with. Wearing a white sleeping gown and cap, she looked like a hideous, vengeful angel. There was a vaguely putrid smell in the room, probably the rat oil.

Nabber was nervous, but determined not to show it. He took up her hand and kissed it. "Good evening, fair lady."

The fair lady was having none of it. She snatched back her hand. "You never told me you were Blayze's brother."

Nabber shrugged. "There was no point in telling you." He thought for a second, then added, "Besides, everyone in Bren knows of me, I assumed you would, too." That seemed to do it. The skepticism drained from Madame Thornypurse's face.

"So what do you want?"

"Well, you know you and my brother arranged to . . ." Nabber let the sentence dangle, hoping that Madame Thornypurse would finish it for him.

"Give the knight a few doses of poison?" she prompted.

Nabber sucked in his breath. Nothing in his whole life had made him as angry as those casually dropped words. This woman was poisoning Tawl!

Before he knew it, his knife was in his hand. He cursed its shortness. Madame Thornypurse screamed and tried to scramble away. Nabber was hardly aware of what he was doing. He wanted to hurt this woman badly. She cowered back in the bedclothes. Her slippered foot protruded from the sheets. With one mighty thrust, Nabber stabbed it. Blood spurted from the wound. Madame Thornypurse wailed hysterically.

Corsella and the man who'd been tending his blade burst into the room. The man was wielding his newly sharpened knife. Corsella screamed and went to swipe at Nabber. Nabber dodged and found himself face-to-face with the blade.

Madame Thornypurse was holding her foot and screaming, "Kill the little bastard!"

As feet seemed to be working for him, Nabber stamped hard on the knife-man's toes. "Aagh," cried the man, making the error of thrusting his blade at the same time he was clutching his toe. Nabber shot past him in an instant. Corsella grabbed hold of his hair and tried to wrestle him to the ground. Nabber didn't like anyone touching his hair, and he punched Corsella hard in the stomach.

Screams of mother and daughter filled the air. Just as he reached the door, the knife-man caught up with him. His face was murderous. He grabbed Nabber's arm and twisted it hard behind his back. Nabber heard a crack as it was dislodged from the joint. The pain brought tears to his eyes. The knife-man brought the blade to his throat. "I'm gonna slice you to ribbons," he said, pushing the knife forward.

In that instant someone entered the room. Nabber heard the sliver of a knife leaving its sheath. And then a voice, familiar, "You touch that boy and you'll die before you draw your next breath." It was Tawl.

Blood wet and sticky trickled down Nabber's chest. The blade had found flesh. Nabber felt faint with shock: *his flesh.*

The knife-man backed away slowly. Mother and daughter were quiet. Tawl's expression was enough to frighten anyone into silence. Deadly silence.

The second the blade was drawn back from his chest, Nabber felt strong arms about him. Their touch was the most comforting thing he'd ever felt. He promptly fainted. The last thing he was aware of was the reassuring smell of the knight as he carried him from the brothel.

Twelve

*N*abber became aware of a dull pain in his shoulder. He shifted slightly, hoping to ease it, but could find no relief. Apart from that he was fairly comfortable; there was straw, not fresh but not soiled, dim light, warmth, and the unmistakable smell of horse dung. If he was in a stable, he didn't want to know about it. Horses were not his favorite animals.

Memories filtered through his mind. How could he have been so foolish as to have stabbed Madame Thornypurse? Where was his brain? And then, suddenly anxious: where was his sack? Nabber opened his eyes immediately and looked around in the straw. No sign of it and, to make matters worse, he *was* in a stable. Wooden stalls rose up about him and various tack, bits, bridles, and other baffling horsy things, hung from nails like holy relics. And there! Horses blowing and nickering.

As he tried to stand up, pain shot through his shoulder. His left arm wasn't responding the way it should; it hung limply at his side, the upper tendons badly strained. Everything came back to him: the knife-man, the blade to his throat, Tawl to the rescue. With his good arm he felt his throat. It was bandaged, and something that smelled bad, which probably meant it was doing good, was smeared on either side of the cloth.

The stall door opened and in walked Tawl. Nabber had only seen him from the back the day before so he was shocked at the change in the knight's appearance. His skin was pale and dark hollows surrounded his eyes. "How are you feeling?" he asked, placing various pots and packages down on the floor.

Nabber only had one thought on his mind. "Where's my sack?"

"Must be back at Thornypurse's." Rather firmly, Tawl took Nabber by the shoulders and forced him to sit back down again. "Your left arm is out of the socket."

"We've got to go back and get my sack. There's a fortune in gold inside it."

Tawl ignored what he said, closed his hand about Nabber's wrist, and then pulled sharply. With his other hand, the knight forced the joint back into the socket.

Nabber screamed loudly at this indignity. The pain was excruciating. His vision blurred and his head started reeling. Still, his thoughts were on his sack. "My contingency's gone. It took me months to . . . *Aagh!*" he cried as an arm's length of muscle protested at being moved. Wisely, he decided to let the newly fixed limb rest at his side. "Took me months to build that contingency. We've got to get it back."

Tawl shook his head. "You're not going back there."

"Well, you go, then."

"If I ever decide to go back there, it will be on my own business, not yours." A hard edge to the knight's voice stopped Nabber from pressing further. He tried a different approach instead.

"They were poisoning you."

"Yes. I thought so after I was sick two days in a row."

"Blayze put them up to it."

Tawl seemed tired, almost disinterested. "Makes sense. Though I doubt if he intended Thornypurse to nearly kill me. It wouldn't look so good—him beating a man who can barely stand."

For the first time, Nabber realized that Tawl was ill. Here he was acting like a big baby over a sore arm and a flesh wound, while the knight had probably been given enough poison to kill a brothelful of whores.

"Here," said Tawl, handing him a freshly baked loaf. "Eat this, it will help keep your strength up."

"What about you, the poison?"

"I'll be all right. I caught it before it was too late."

Nabber was skeptical. "How can you be sure?"

The knight looked down, intent on unwrapping the bundles. At first, Nabber didn't think he was going to reply. Then after a moment he spoke. His voice was quiet, and he never once lifted his gaze from the floor. "I learned about poisons at Valdis. How to identify them, how to treat their effects. Thornypurse gave me hemlock: a mistake only a novice would make. A thumbnail of leaf can kill a man, and Blayze wanted me weakened, not dead.

"I knew there was something wrong the next morning." Tawl shrugged. "At Valdis you learn to monitor your body closely. I felt something eating away at my stomach, so I readied some charcoal and swallowed it."

"Swallowed charcoal!" Nabber was disgusted.

Tawl managed a smile. "When it's prepared right, it forces a man to expel the contents of his stomach."

Nabber nodded. "I heard you throwing up, all right, if that's what you mean."

"I was rid of the poison before it was too late. Another debt I owe to Valdis." The knight raised a hunk of bread to his lips, but didn't bite off any. He put it down untouched. Nabber noticed how badly his arms were shaking. The fact that Tawl had somehow managed to carry him from the brothel seemed nothing short of a miracle. "Anyway, it looks like Blayze will end up with what he wants: a vulnerable opponent."

"You can't mean you're still going to fight him?" Nabber was horrified. "The fight's only two days away. You're in no fit state to—"

"You're not my keeper, boy," said Tawl. "I gave my word and I'll keep it."

There was no way Nabber could let this happen. The knight wouldn't stand a chance against the duke's champion. Blayze was fit and healthy, with muscles like a prize bull, whereas Tawl looked ready for the sickbed. It was suicide! This was one of those rare moments when the truth was called for. Nabber took a deep breath. "Look, I'll go to Blayze and tell him the deal's off. I was the one who got Madame Thornypurse to drag you to the meeting in the first place. It was all my idea." He squirmed in readiness for a verbal thrashing.

Tawl's voice was gentle. "It makes no difference now, Nabber. What has been agreed upon cannot be undone."

A strong wave of guilt hit Nabber—just when he thought he was free of it, as well. "But you could get killed."

"Better to die than risk dishonor." Tawl seemed to regret his words the moment they left his mouth. Abruptly, he stood up. "Eat your food and get some rest. I'll be back before dark."

"I think you're the one who needs rest."

Tawl opened the door. "I need a lot of things, Nabber, but right now I'll make do with a drink." The knight dropped the latch and left Nabber alone in the hay.

Bailor, head of the duke's household, sat in the most comfortable room in the duke's palace: his own. For seventeen years now, ever since

His Grace had come to power, it had not been considered fashionable to have chambers more luxurious than the duke. This had proven rather difficult for the court to bear, as the duke was an austere man with more liking for simplicity than sophistication.

Though he didn't mind the show of it. Indeed, the palace itself was more magnificent than ever: two beautiful new courtyards, a domed ceiling, fountains, and stained glass. The building of beautiful distractions had served to conceal the building of greater fortifications. Arrow loops had been recut to run lengthwise, square towers were pulled down and round ones built in their place. All the roofs had been raised to a slope and the crenellations along the battlements had been shuttered with iron. Yes, the duke was a man of simple tastes: invasion and protection.

And women.

Bailor stood up and went over to the window. It was shuttered with wood, but hinges were currently being cast that were strong enough to take the weight of metal sheets. The ladies would not like those. Not that the ladies counted in Bren.

It was time to do business. Bailor had noticed of late that the duke grew rapidly bored of the women that were brought to him. They were all beautiful—a few exquisitely so—most to some degree cultured, and every one of them was young and willing. Now, normally Bailor wouldn't mind His Grace's short attention span, after all, what the duke finished with one day was his the next, but the man was becoming irritable, blaming him for picking women with no life, no intelligence. What did His Grace expect? He had neither the time nor inclination to bother with wooings and clandestine affairs. He simply wanted to bed a woman and have done with it; yet he still expected, indeed demanded, that these women be fine and cultured like the ladies of the court.

Bailor spent a good part of every day searching for such women. He had contacts in Camlee, Annis, and Highwall, knew flesh-traders from Tyro and Chelss, was friends with impoverished nobles with young daughters, and had spies in all the convents. Everything he had—his high position, his fine rooms, his well-stocked coffers, and his wide-ranging responsibilities— depended solely on his ability to find women for the duke.

Daughters of the high nobility would not go near the man. The risk to their precious reputations was too great: the duke had never been known to compensate a girl for her shame. Of course, the truly difficult part was ensuring that these women were virgins. The duke insisted on that above anything else.

Altogther it made for a difficult task, but one that the head of the duke's household would never dream of relinquishing to another. It formed the foundation of his power base.

Bailor had started young: carrying love notes between lovers as a boy. One day a certain young lady of high birth had pleaded with him for his help. She was in love, but her feelings were not returned. She was desperate, cried prettily and was willing to pay. Five golds it cost her for the love potion. Such substances were frowned upon in Bren as the devil's handiwork and no decent woman dared to use them. He'd never looked back. Drugs, potions, erotica, young women, and young boys: he could get anything for anybody. The court depended on him and paid handsomely for his silence.

Quickly, Bailor shrugged off the silk he wore around his chambers and donned the wool and linen expected of a man of his ranking. He had learned long ago that not only was it wise to appear modest, but it made for better bargaining, as well.

He made his way down to the small reception room he called his own. It was as sparse as his private rooms were sumptuous. A man was waiting for him. A deformed and ugly cripple: Fiscel the flesh-trader.

"No need to get up, my friend," he said, repulsed at the sight of the man struggling from a chair. "How are you this day?"

"I am well. The pass was smooth." Tiny drops of spittle sprayed over the desk. Bailor resisted the urge to draw his hand away.

"What have you for me today? A girl from Annis, perhaps?" Of all the northern cities, Annis had the reputation for the most beautiful women.

"No, from the kingdoms." Fiscel's high voice grated upon Bailor's nerves.

"Women from the kingdoms are plain and bad tempered."

"Not his one, she's a beauty. Court trained, too."

"A nobleman's daughter?"

Fiscel nodded. "A nobleman's bastard."

"Well, bring her in, then." The head of the duke's household was becoming impatient.

"Come now, Bailor. You know I like to set a minimum before I let you see the goods."

"How much?"

Fiscel leaned back in his chair. "Five hundred golds."

"Don't be ridiculous. There's no way I can guarantee that as a minimum." It was an outrageous price, three times what was normally asked.

The flesh-trader's hand closed about his walking stick as he braced himself to stand. "Very well, then. I will take my business elsewhere."

Bailor's interest was now piqued. He couldn't let the man leave without seeing the woman who could command such a minimum. Putting an arm on the man's shoulder, he said, "There's no rush, my friend. Stay and take a cup of wine."

"Like you, Bailor, I don't drink during negotiations."

Both men had each other's measure.

"Three hundred golds," said Bailor, "and I'll see her this instant."

"Five hundred golds or you'll see her not at all."

This was not the way negotiations normally went. Somewhere along the way, he'd lost control. Damn Fiscel! The truth was that he now desperately wanted to see the girl. Perhaps this one might engage the duke's interest longer than a week. "Four hundred, then. That's my final offer."

"Then this is my final refusal." Fiscel's good eye gleamed with cunning. "Look, Bailor, you and I have known each other for many years. Would I demand such a price without first being sure of the value of my goods?"

"Very well, five hundred minimum, but I don't promise I'll purchase."

Fiscel stood up. "You'll purchase."

Alysha's long and elegant fingers bit into her flesh like talons. Not once had she loosened her grip since they'd entered the palace. Melli hated the woman. She had spent hours this morning being scrubbed and plucked like a pheasant for the table; there was a new dress, ribbons for her hair, and pearls for wrist and throat. Alysha had been merciless; coarse brushes, tweezers, toothpicks, and caustic ointments were her instruments of torture.

Fiscel was returning. The sight of him limping across the courtyard sent a tremor of apprehension up Melli's spine. Alysha's grip became tighter, and she was forced forward to meet him.

"Did he agree to the minimum?" Alysha's voice betrayed uncharacteristic concern.

Fiscel was out of breath. He leaned heavily on his stick. "Yes. Follow me. We must display while the man is still curious."

Display! Melli did not like the sound of this one bit. She stood her ground and refused to be moved. They were in one of the palace courtyards and a few noblemen were walking around the shrubs and fountains. She could shout to them, tell them that she was a nobleman's daughter and demand that they help her. Only she was a long way from home and the name Maybor would mean nothing to the people of Bren. Even if it did, Melli couldn't be sure that her father wouldn't just disown her.

She was trapped. Fiscel and Alysha watched her constantly. She hadn't been allowed out of the wagon for over a week. Everything, including using the chamberpot, had to be done in full view of Alysha's sly and smiling face. At first Melli had been on her guard, looking for chances to run away, constantly feeling for her knife, but no opportunities occurred and gradually her watchfulness was replaced with planning. Melli had given a lot of thought to escape, and she had decided that her best option was to wait until she was sold. The man who bought her would get no interest on his investment. She would be gone before he could lay a hand upon her.

At least that was the plan up until a few hours ago. When they entered Bren late last night, she hadn't expected to be taken to the duke's palace. Escaping from here was not going to be easy. It looked open enough—servants coming and going, courtiers strolling about—yet guards were posted on every corner and the portcullis smelled of newly rubbed oil.

Alysha's grip bit to the bone and Melli stepped forward. As they crossed the castle grounds, people turned to stare at them, and many a knowing look was flashed their way. Eventually they came to a small wooden doorway just past the entrance to the kitchens. Fiscel turned abruptly and raised his stick to Melli's chest.

"One smart word out of you, my precious, and I'll beat your ribs to splinters." And then to Alysha: "You stay here."

Melli was pushed through the doorway, Fiscel following behind. They entered a small cramped room that was lit by four candles. A plump man, plainly dressed, sat behind a wooden table.

"Here she is, Bailor. Did I overestimate her charms?"

The stranger stood up, his face registering no emotion. He caught hold of Melli's arm and drew her toward the light of the candles. Dressed plainly he might be, but he smelled of expensive oils. Melli tried hard to keep calm during the scrutiny. Strangely, it helped that the man didn't seem too impressed by her. If he'd been smiling and gloating, it would have been a different matter.

After a while, the man turned to Fiscel. "I'll take her," he said.

The flesh-trader licked a speckle of drool from his lips. "Aah, but we haven't agreed to a price."

"Five hundred was the price." Judging by the man's voice, Melli realized that he was more than a common servant.

"Five hundred was the *minimum*," corrected Fiscel. "We both know she is worth more than that." He contemplated the knotted end of his stick. "Say, eight hundred."

"This is ridiculous, you know I'm not authorized to pay such an amount, His Grace—"

"Save your breath, Bailor," interrupted Fiscel. "You're not bargaining with some local brothel-keeper now. You can pay, we both know it."

Melli's hand rubbed against the bodice of her dress. The knife still sang beneath. Amidst all this madness, nothing seemed as sane as the blade. Fiscel would get his way, she did not doubt it. She should be pleased; here was a chance to rid herself of the abominable twosome and finally escape. Why then were her hands shaking and her legs so weak they could hardly bear her weight?

"Very well, Fiscel," the man was saying. "I'll take her for eight." He looked Melli up and down one final time. "Are you sure she's a virgin?"

Now the deal was done, Fiscel was at his most humble. He bowed profusely and the good half of his mouth came close to a smile. "She was tested by my girl, Alysha, who's from the Far South."

This explanation seemed to satisfy the man. Obviously women of the Far South were famous for more than just duplicity and facial hair.

The man left the room, closing the door behind him.

"Made a handsome profit out of me, didn't you?" Melli realized she now had nothing to fear from Fiscel. "If I were you, I'd take it straight to a surgeon and ask him to sew up the slack side of your mouth."

The flesh-trader grabbed hold of her hair. He pulled on it so forcefully that Melli's neck snapped back. "If you try and run away from here, I swear I will hunt you down and slay you." There was a world of malice in Fiscel's good eye.

Melli pulled away from him, hardly caring if she left a fistful of hair behind. She looked at him coldly, and said, "What makes you so sure I won't do the same to you?"

The door opened again and Melli turned her back as the gold changed hands. The true magnitude of what was happening to her was beginning to sink in. The two men in this room were buying and selling her! She, Maybor's daughter, once promised to a prince, had been bargained for like a bolt of Marls' silk. Running away from Castle Harvell had proven fruitless, for here she was, hundreds of leagues to the east, in a city she had no knowledge of, in a position a thousand times more degrading than being married against her will.

"Farewell, my precious." It was Fiscel, acting the part of a benevolent patron. "I trust you will remember my advice."

"Don't worry, Fiscel," said Melli, "I will never forget a single thing you said or did to me."

The flesh-trader sent her a warning glance, but Melli didn't deign to acknowledge it. The moment the door was closed, she turned to the stranger. "So, who paid a king's ransom for me?"

The man smiled; he seemed relieved to be rid of Fiscel. "Why, you are honored, my dear. You will be sent to His Grace."

Melli was confused. His Grace was a title usually given to younger brother's of kings, yet in Bren there was no king . . . only a duke. Comprehension dawned, and the stranger nodded in delight.

"Yes, my dear, you belong to the duke of Bren." Gently, he took her hand. Melli was almost glad of it. The shock of hearing she had been purchased by the most powerful man in the north had sent her head reeling. "Let me introduce myself. I'm Bailor, head of the duke's household. And what is your name?"

"Melli." She leaned against him for support. This seemed to please him and he patted her arm gently.

"Melli from where?"

"Deepwood. Melli of Deepwood."

"Aah." The syllable was hung with doubt. "Well, Melli of Deepwood, as long as you're good and do what I tell you, your stay here will be a pleasure for both of us." A slight leer spoiled Bailor's attempt at pleasantry. "Now, I'll show you to your room and let you have a little rest."

Melli was relieved. For the first time in many days, she would finally be alone.

"So, Your Grace, when do you intend to set a marriage date?" Baralis brought the cup to his lips, but no wine met his tongue. They were in the duke's chambers, a sparse set of rooms with no rugs to cushion the stone, nor linen to soften the light. Baralis was determined to have answers. He was not prepared to let the Hawk circle cautiously any longer. It was time he came to land.

"The betrothal has not yet been finalized." The duke didn't even bother with the pretense of drinking. His cup lay untouched on the table.

"The betrothal can be formalized by proxy. We can settle this matter here and now." Baralis altered the tone of his voice, mixing grit with the oil. "Unless you care to ignore your court's affirmation of the match."

The duke stood up and pulled his sword from his belt. He drew the blade to the light and began to examine the edge. "Quite a politician, aren't you, Baralis? But here in Bren we value strength, not smoothness of tongue."

"In the kingdoms we value straight answers."

To Baralis' surprise, the duke seemed pleased with this retort. He put down his sword and then swung around. "Well, seeing you value straight answers, you might like to give me one. Is it true that Kylock is planning a new offensive on Halcus?"

Baralis cursed Maybor. Yesterday they both received messages from the kingdoms, and it appeared that the man had wasted no time telling the duke about Kylock's intentions. "So the king is seeking to strengthen his borders. What is wrong with that?"

"It sounded more like an invasion," said the duke, cool as ever, "than a simple border defense."

"Who can blame Kylock for wanting the border dispute to be settled once and for all? It's raged for over five years now. He wants to present his new bride with a country both prosperous and secure."

"A fine sentiment, Baralis."

"Catherine will be a queen, Your Grace."

"Would you have her an empress, too?"

There it was: the heart of the matter. How much did the Hawk suspect? And if he did guess at the plan for a northern empire, how willing was he to go along with it?

Baralis decided it was wise to back away from the subject. The duke was not the sort of man to be fooled by fine words of glory. "Whenever two powers join as one, there is always a risk of what is created being called an empire."

The duke drew his thin lips to an even thinner line. "Before I set a marriage date, certain stipulations need to be agreed upon."

Baralis did not permit himself even the tiniest show of relief at the duke's apparent willingness to drop such a dangerous subject. "Those are matters for the lawyers, Your Grace."

"Surely you and I can decide upon a few things among ourselves, King's Chancellor." The use of his title was almost a challenge.

Although wary, Baralis had little choice but to ask: "What things, Your Grace?"

"Timber and grain tributes to start with, and then perhaps you could give me a written guarantee that the resources of Bren will be used in no war that is not of our own making." The duke smiled, his first of the meeting. "Your powers of proxy can surely cover these little details."

The duke was shrewd. Asking for timber and grain tributes was nothing short of blackmail. It also gave him something tangible to show to his people—a direct benefit of the match. As for the other matter—a written guarantee—well, he could have one. Who would be around to enforce it once His Grace had died a painful death? "What level of resources do you require?"

"I realize it's difficult to transport grain and timber over the mountains, so I will limit the tribute to three times a year. Say, five thousand bushels of grain and nine hundred weight of timber."

Baralis brought his cup to his lips and actually swallowed. The amount the duke was asking was too high. "I agree," he said. Nothing was going to prevent this marriage from taking place.

"And the guarantee?"

"I will have it drawn up by the morrow."

"Good," said the duke. "I think that's everything, so I will let you take your leave. You may consider the betrothal formalized."

A young girl, ravishing to behold, with hair red and pale skin, entered the room. She saw the two talking and quickly left. Before she closed the door, Baralis spied a large bed in the adjoining room.

"And the marriage date?"

"Let's wait and see the ink upon the paper before we engrave the date in stone."

Baralis was becoming impatient. "Keep the groom waiting too long and his ardor might cool."

"Push the bride too quickly and she might frighten and run away." The duke came and stood beside him. "I will give you a date within the month. Now, I have other matters to see to." He bowed slightly. "I trust you will come and watch my champion fight the night after tomorrow. 'Tis put on in your honor."

"Of course, it will be interesting to see the best that Bren has to offer."

"You won't be disappointed," said the duke.

Tavalisk was eating brains. An overrated dish that required a lot of sauce to make palatable. The archbishop was his own cook today, and he suspected the brains were slightly overdone, for he'd been chewing the last piece for several minutes and it still wasn't ready to swallow.

He hated fast days. The Church recognized about forty fasts a year.

They were supposed to cleanse the spirit, elevate the mind, and expunge the body. In reality, they just drove everyone to sin. Only prisoners and zealots fasted on holy days. But, as in everything, appearances had to be kept up; the kitchens were deserted, the butcher's blocks were dry, and behind shuttered windows a city full of people ate furtively in the dark.

Tavalisk glanced over to his lyre. Yesterday, in a fit of temper, he'd stepped on it. The action, while producing his best ever note, had sadly flattened the instrument, rendering it unplayable. The tambourine had met a similar, but slightly more rewarding end, and his cat was now limping because of it. He'd finally given up on music. Food had tempted like a courtesan, and music's charms had paled under its lure.

In walked Gamil without as much as a knock. The man was getting above himself. "Your Eminence, the rumors are true."

"What rumors, Gamil? Rorn has enough of them to set a fishwife whispering for a year." Tavalisk seasoned the brains in the pot. "Talking of fishwives, how's your dear mother?"

"Long dead, Your Eminence."

The archbishop fished out a portion of brain and tested it between his fingers. "Good, good. Give her my regards."

"Lesketh is dead. Kylock is now king."

Tavalisk dropped the brain back into the pot. "Fair or foul?"

"By all accounts, Your Eminence, the poor man died in his sleep."

"Foul, then." The archbishop poured himself a cup of wine. "Now when Catherine marries Kylock it will be a true joining of powers. Two such well-positioned points from which to dominate the north. Baralis is a clever dog, I'll give him that."

"How can you be so sure that is his plan, Your Eminence?"

"Marod predicted it, Gamil: *When two mighty powers join as one.*" Tavalisk took a long draught of wine. "We are witnessing the birth of the dark empire."

"What can we do to prevent it from happening, Your Eminence?"

"More than you think, Gamil. There is nothing more vulnerable than a newborn." The archbishop stirred the pot. "We can get the knights in trouble for one thing, make friends in Bren for another, and most importantly we can alert the other northern powers to Baralis' ambitions—perhaps even offer our support if it's needed."

"But I don't understand how stirring trouble with the knights will aid your cause."

"*Our* cause, Gamil," corrected Tavalisk. "Unless of course you fancy living in a world were there is no Church to pay your salary." Tavalisk was feeling rather smug.

"I don't understand, Your Eminence."

The archbishop shook his head sadly. "Oh, Gamil, you do disappoint me. You've obviously never read Marod's *Book of Words*. According to him, the dark empire will bring with it the end of the Church. 'The temples will fall,' he said." Tavalisk looked quickly at his aide. That was quite enough for the moment; he'd let Gamil chew a little before giving him the full meal. "As for the knights, those hypocrites are in with the duke of Bren. Some of them even fought in his last skirmish: the massacre at Luncorn. That pathetic little town paid dearly for its attempt at independence."

Tavalisk speared a portion of gray matter and dipped it into the garlic butter. With so many convoluted loops and folds, brains were made for sauce. "Goading Tyren is our best way to get the south interested in what's happening in the north. The knights are aggressively pursuing our trade, and the duke is helping them all the way. If Bren becomes more powerful then so, by association, do the knights."

The archbishop took the pan off the heat. The brains were now so tough that they'd be put to better use on the hull of a battleship. "Anyway, how is our four-city force doing? Slain any knights yet?"

"No, Your Eminence."

"How unfortunate."

"But there was an exchange, Your Eminence. Just north of Camlee. We seized eight wagonloads of goods."

"Where are those goods now, Gamil?"

"They are being held in Camlee, awaiting further instructions."

Tavalisk smiled, plump lips parting to show a glimpse of tiny white teeth. "Distribute the goods evenly between Camlee, Marls, and Toolay. Rorn will have none of them. Make sure the details of the split are well spread."

"But I don't understand, Your Eminence."

"Really Gamil, like a tree you grow thicker by the day. Tyren is going to be looking to lay blame, and the cities that are holding the goods will look the guiltiest. I want Tyren and his northern playmates to think that *all* of the south is against him. With Marls, Camlee, and Toolay dividing the spoils, it certainly looks that way. And no one can say that Rorn instigated the whole affair as we haven't got a bean to show for it." Tavalisk took a sip of wine. "Everything is going beautifully. All we need now is a good slaughter. I'm thinking one knight is no longer enough. Let's murder a troop of them."

"I'll pass on Your Eminence's wishes."

"Discreet as ever, Gamil."

"Of course, Your Eminence. If there is nothing more, I will take my leave."

Tavalisk stood up and handed the pot containing the braised brains to his aide. "Seeing as no one's working in the kitchens today, Gamil, just run down and prepare me a light dinner: meat, fish, pastries—you know what I like."

Gamil hid his annoyance badly. He stalked out of the room, broth splashing from the pan. The archbishop *tut-tutted*; his aide would have to clean up the stains when he returned.

Thirteen

*T*he steel drew sparks when it met. Rovas was fighting like a demon. His face was red, and sweat scattered at every turn of his head. "Thrust, thrust!" he cried. Air burned in Jack's lungs. Frustration, not skill, was placing the blade. He was desperate to get near the man, and Rovas, well aware of this, was goading him to it. Again and again Jack lunged forward only to find his target had neatly sidestepped.

They were practicing in the meadow just south of the cottage. The blows exchanged had long since lost the caution of a training bout. The blood snaking down Jack's arm was proof of that.

Spring was close and the snow no longer crackled underfoot. The sound of running water could be heard in the distance and green spikes of grass cut through the white. Jack had no time to appreciate the changes of the season. Rovas was bent on defeating him. "Come on," he goaded. "Take a go at me." Jack obliged the man. He thrust forward, bracing his body for the blow.

Steel screeched upon steel. Rovas was forced to step back. Jack remembered the smuggler's words: *"Press any advantage, no matter how small."* He snatched his blade upward, forcing Rovas to raise both arms in defense. Quick as a flash, Jack was in with the dagger. A rake across the wrist forced the man to drop his shortsword. Kicking it away, Jack ensured the smuggler wouldn't get it back. The man was left with his dagger.

Jack considered his options. Rovas was fond of saying: *"Surprise is the greatest weapon,"* so surprise him he would. He flung his dagger toward the smuggler's chest. His aim was bad, but that didn't matter. The man was forced to turn to the side. Jack lunged forward and pressed the point of his shortsword to Rovas' chest. Rovas was forced to raise both arms in a sign of submission.

Jack had to resist the temptation to smile. It was sweet indeed to see the smuggler at a loss for both words *and* moves. "Do you surrender?" he said, voice betraying no emotion.

Rovas bowed his head and did not look up as he mumbled, "I do."

Removing his blade from the man's chest, Jack said, "Quite a fight, eh, Rovas?" He offered the smuggler his hand, but it wasn't taken.

"Think you're smart now, don't you?" Rovas said. He walked over to where his shortsword lay on the ground. "But that was just a lucky trick, nothing more."

Jack sat on the ground. He didn't care that the wet snow soaked through his britches. His hair was plastered to his face and he brushed it back. The stretch of leather with which he normally tied it was nowhere to be seen. "Would you judge me ready?"

"With shortsword maybe. The longsword needs work and your bow skills are poor."

Jack smiled. "You're a great flatterer."

Rovas smiled with him. "Flattery only leads to one thing in my book."

"What's that?"

"Fools." They both laughed and the tension that had built steadily over the past week was broken. "You did good, lad," said Rovas when they stopped.

"When do I get the captain's name?"

Rovas stood up. "Come help me paint some fish and I'll explain a few things."

Jack followed him to the smuggler's hut. This time the place smelled of fish rather than offal. "Here," said Rovas handing him a cloth. "Hold that against the wound." He then turned his attention to the fish. "These need to be at market by noon."

"Judging by the smell, they should have been there yesterday." Jack winced as he pressed the cloth into the cut.

"No matter, it's looks that count."

Jack noticed a pig's carcass had been set to hang, throat down. The blood had drained into a large bowl. Rovas took the bowl, set it on the table, and then plunged his hands into the blood. Hands dripping with partly coagulated blood, the smuggler brushed them against the fish. The fish, which had been a sickly flesh color, began to take on the look of a fresh catch.

"Now, about this captain," said Rovas as he continued to paint the fish. "He's situated in a garrison that holds twenty score of troops, so he's not going to be easy to get to. You're going to have to enter the place at night, find him, do away with him, and then shift yourself out of there sharpish."

Jack was surprised; he hadn't reckoned on this. "Is there any other way? Why can't I take him by surprise when he's away from the garrison?"

"You won't get near him. He never goes anywhere without a score of guards. They'd have you down in an instant."

Logical, but some shred of instinct deep within Jack warned him to doubt the smuggler's words. "I could pick him out with a bow."

Rovas shook his head. "No, lad, you're no archer. One misplaced arrow and the captain's guard would be down on you like vultures. My plan's best. Catch him when he's vulnerable. Sneak in, sneak out." The smuggler was up to his elbows in blood. "Besides, I know the garrison like the back of my hand; there's a couple of useful tunnels in there. Help you escape real fast, they will."

Jack was still suspicious. "If they'll help me escape, why won't they help me enter?"

"Tunnels like that are always bolted on the inside." There was a trace of woodenness in Rovas' voice, as if he'd uttered a set piece from a play. Perhaps aware of this himself, he hurried on in a more natural tone: "We'll pick a feast night, that way all the soldiers will be the worse for ale. Spring Blessing begins next week, so everyone's guard will be lowered by drink. It'll be perfect."

Wary, but not sure why, Jack tried to throw Rovas off guard. "Tarissa told me the reason why you wanted the captain dead."

The smuggler looked up from his work. "Did she, eh? Well, it wasn't her business to."

Jack was tempted to tell him that he knew Tarissa was supposed to kill the captain, but he stopped himself. Saying the words would only make him angry, and for the moment he was after information, not conflict. "So you and the captain were business partners?"

"Aye, and then the bastard got greedy. I pulled out of the arrangement, and now he's stooped to blackmail. Ten golds a month it costs me to stop him from running to the authorities." All the fish were now glowing with health thanks to the pig's blood, so Rovas wiped his hands on a cloth. "He's bleeding me dry."

"And the night of Spring Blessing you'll be rid of your problem." Despite the warning voice in his head, Jack was excited. The time was drawing near. Only when the Halcus captain was out of the way would he be free to live his own life, to go where he wanted and to do whatever he chose. He already knew where he wanted to go: Bren. His thoughts kept returning to the city. Even before Rovas had told him about Catherine of Bren's marriage to Kylock, Jack had felt a desire to go there. Sometimes in his dreams he saw a city with high battlements, nestled by the foot of a great mountain. It was Bren, he was certain of it.

"Any news of the new king?" asked Jack.

"There's rumors he's planning a full-scale invasion. If it's true he'll probably wait for full spring." Rovas rolled his phlegm, then spat. "No one in the north is taking any chances, though, especially Halcus. Smithies are making more money than's good for them, and every wisp of a lad over thirteen is busy practicing with a sword. The garrisons have been overrun with men wanting to join up and have a go at the kingdoms." The smuggler ran his hands across his beard. "Or Bren, or both."

Jack helped Rovas load the baskets of fish onto his wagon. The sun broke through the clouds and the wind died down to a breeze. "So war is coming?" asked Jack.

"The minute Kylock invades Halcus there's no going back. Powers will line up on both sides, and once that happens war is inevitable. The scale of the thing is the question. If it's just a dispute between northern powers it might be settled, but if cities like Camlee and Ness become involved, then they'll drag the south along with them." Rovas sat up on the wagon and took hold of the reins. "The south has been looking for a chance to crack down on the knights for over a decade now, and a northern war will provide it with a convenient opportunity."

"So the war could spread south?" Jack felt foolish, he had no idea that matters in the Known Lands were so sensitive. He was beginning to realize just how isolated the kingdoms had been.

"Not so sure of that," said Rovas. "The south will be hoping that the war can be contained in the north. They won't like the idea of any of their dainty white cities being sullied by carnage." The smuggler pulled on the reins and the wagon lurched forward. "Mark my words, boy. We're being led as surely as lambs to the slaughter, and there are those who would shape an empire from our blood."

The wagon trundled away. Jack was shaking, and he hardly knew why. Rovas' words had stirred something within him. *An empire of blood.* The world began to spin around him. The sky came close and formed an arc above his body. He stumbled to the ground, sick, disorientated. The snow burned his fingers and the sun burned his soul. *An empire of blood.* Colors ran: green, blue, white; they all bled to crimson. Jack brought his hand to his eyes and tried to keep out the light. Madness came to fill the void. A thousand images beat like tiny insect wings. *An empire of blood.* A city with high battlements. A man with golden hair. A baby crying in a locked room. And Melli, Melli was there, but just as quickly, she was gone. So many more sights impossible to define: blood the only common thread.

Wet, his hands were wet. Panic brought him round. He opened his eyes and forced the sky back to its place. Colors refocused and the snow was cool beneath him. Tears, not blood, streaked across his palms.

Jack braced himself to stand. Nausea rose up like sorcery, both bitter to the taste. He had to concentrate to keep his legs from bending at the joint. Step by shaky step, he made his way toward the cottage. It felt as if the world had softened and shown its middle. His heart was still racing at the sight. *An empire of blood.* Yet what did it have to do with him? He was a baker, not a savior. He stopped in his tracks. How could he think, even for a minute, that he had some part to play in what was to come? Yet the images he'd seen had the unmistakable feel of a message. Or a warning. Surely warnings were only sent to people who could make a difference?

Sighing heavily, Jack tried to dismiss it all as nonsense. The fight with Rovas, followed by the bloodstained fish—it was easy to see how his mind might have deluded him. The latch on the door seemed impossibly heavy. It finally gave way and he found himself in the warmth of the cottage. Magra and Tarissa both looked up from their work. As soon as they saw his face they rushed toward him. Jack fell into Tarissa's arms. She pulled him close to the fire, and her words of gentle comfort were the last thing that he heard.

Melli paced the length of the room. Her reflection drew her eye despite her attempts to ignore it. She looked pale and older. The bones on her face had sharpened to angles and subtle lines traced her once-smooth brow. Nineteen this spring, but there would be no treats or fancy ribbons to mark her anniversary. A slight smile thinned her lips. Her father would miss giving her gifts. That was the one thing he delighted in more than anything else; he would buy her dresses, hand mirrors, carved boxes, slippers—all chosen with no thought to cost. If nothing else, he had always sought to please her.

She wondered where he was now and what he was doing. Probably at his estate in the Eastlands preparing for spring planting. Well, that was what he officially did, anyway; in reality he got drunk every night and went off hunting everyday. The overseer saw to the land. Melli caught another glimpse of her reflection: there were tears in her eyes now.

She missed her father. She missed his proud, possessive love.

Scolding herself for her frailty, Melli brushed away the tears before they had chance to fall. She was strong—Maybor had given her that—and she had a low tolerance for weakness, both in herself and others. Strength in a person attracted her more than looks or titles or money. Looking back, she began to realize why the young men of the court had failed to catch her interest: they had no power, no experience, no guile.

Her thoughts turned before she could stop them. Baralis. There was a man to put others in the shade. Even now, months later, Melli could still feel his breath in her lungs. She had been breathing it ever since. Once she had heard a physician say that air became flesh in the body. Did that mean part of her was created by Baralis?

Melli carefully avoided her reflection this time; she was afraid of seeing a flush upon her face. Why did her mind insist on coming up with such nonsense? Trying to divert her thoughts as far away from the subject of Baralis as possible, she found herself thinking of Jack. What had become of him? He was alive and well; she knew it as surely as she knew her own name. Fate hadn't chosen him to let him die amongst the enemy.

Melli took a deep breath as her thoughts raced toward the very thing she had been trying to avoid for days: Alysha's words to Fiscel when they both thought she was asleep: *"Where I come from, we call people like her thieves. Their fates are so strong they bend others into their service. And what they can't bend they steal."* Had fate chosen her, as well?

A soft knock on the door was a welcome interruption. "Enter," she called, falling into the old habits of a court lady. Bailor walked in the room. He was dressed more finely than the last time she saw him. The silks were well tailored, but the overelaborate style suited neither the roundness of his belly nor the spindliness of his legs. He looked toward the empty food tray that rested upon the bed.

"A healthy appetite, I see."

"If you're worried about my figure, bring me less next time. Like a good milk cow, I eat all that's set in front of me." Gone was Melli's nervousness of the day before. She was ready to challenge anyone or anything that came before her. Plenty of food, a good bed, a night of total privacy, and the absence of Fiscel and Alysha had all combined to invigorate her flagging spirit.

"No, no, my dear," said Bailor. "You misunderstand me; it was a compliment. The duke is fond of women who eat with their bellies, not their waists."

Melli had encountered men like Bailor before; although servants, they were used to being treated well by everyone, including noblemen. They gained power over courtiers by discreetly supplying them with whatever illicit commodities or diversions were currently in fashion. Castle Harvell boasted more than its fair share of such enterprising individuals.

"So when will I meet His Grace?" said Melli with what she hoped was a pretty smile. It would do her no harm to befriend the man.

The smile provoked a little anxious vanity on Bailor's part. He sucked in his stomach and smoothed down his tunic. "That's what I came to talk to you about. Tomorrow night there is a big event happening in Bren. The duke's champion is fighting the mysterious golden-haired stranger—half the city will be watching. His Grace will be in attendance with two important foreign dignitaries. Usually after such affairs the duke likes to retire to his chambers for . . . how should I put it? A little feminine comfort."

"So bloodshed whets his appetite."

"I wouldn't put it quite so crudely," said Bailor.

"No. That wouldn't be your style." Realizing that she had spoken before thinking, Melli worked quickly to mend her error: "You're a man of too great a sensibility to stoop to such coarseness."

Bailor seemed pleased with the compliment. The belly receded even further into the silk. "And you're a lady of obvious breeding. Tell me, who are your family?"

A strong warning flashed through Melli's mind. He was trying to catch her out: she had already told him where she was from. She cursed her foolishness. Here she was acting like a great lady when she was supposed to be a minor nobleman's bastard. No one must find out she was Maybor's daughter. She had already shamed her father enough by running away; she would not shame him further by claiming his name. Another thought occurred to her: Bailor was exactly the sort of man who would blackmail her father if he ever discovered the truth. Maybor would pay dearly to prevent the news of his daughter's disgrace reaching the ears of the court.

Remembering the lie she used on the Halcus captain, Melli said, "My father is Lord Luff of the Four Kingdoms. My mother was a servant girl from Deepwood."

"Aah." Understanding dawned on Bailor's face. "I see, I see. The kingdoms, eh? Your king looks set to marry Catherine."

"King?" Melli felt a deep hollow in the pit of her stomach.

"Yes." Bailor beamed. "Didn't you know? Lesketh is dead, and Kylock is now king."

She had to sit down. Her first thought was for her father. He would be taking this hard; by all rights his daughter should be a queen this day. *She* should be a queen this day. Melli tried to shrug it off, but the reality was so weighty it bore her down. The power that could have been hers! Regret wormed its way into her brain and she was helpless to stop it. Only months earlier she had assumed that Kylock and Maybor would divide up whatever power was bestowed upon her. Now she realized that power was never given, it was taken. By leaving the castle she had stopped her father from controlling her destiny. She had taken the power for herself. If she were queen today, it would be more than in name alone.

The image of Kylock worked to slow her regrets. No, she didn't want to be married to him. His dark and handsome face had never displayed anything except scorn, and his lips were molded for cruelty. Catherine of Bren was welcome to him.

"My dear Melli," said Bailor, "are you all right? You look quite pale."

It took Melli a moment to settle herself; her mind was spinning around the throne. "Yes, just a little dizzy. You know how women are."

Bailor nodded his head. "You're not called the delicate sex for nothing."

Melli quickly scanned her repertoire and came up with a simpering smile. "When will the marriage take place?"

"Not for many months, I should think." Bailor headed toward the door. "Anyway, there's no need to concern your pretty head with such matters. I expect you to be prepared if I call on you tomorrow night."

Melli wasn't ready for him to leave, there was something else she wanted to ask him. "Is there any chance that I might take a walk in the grounds? The fresh air will improve my looks."

Bailor waggled his finger. "I don't think so, my dear, not just yet. Let's wait and see how you and the duke get along first, before we talk of favors."

Melli couldn't quite muster a second simper. "Never mind, it's too cold for walks at the moment."

"I know." The look Bailor gave her was an unmistakable warning. "I'll be off now. If you need a new dress or any other baubles, ask the guard to send for Veena; she will get you what you need." He closed the door behind him and Melli clearly heard the sound of the bolt being drawn on the other side.

Damn, he'd seen right through her! *A walk in the grounds*. How could she have been so stupid? Bailor's use of the word *guard* was no coincidence. Now he was going to watch her like a hawk. Angry at herself, Melli stamped her foot and looked for something to throw across the room. She took a pewter cup from the tray and was just about to hurl it at the mirror when she caught sight of her reflection: she looked just like her father. Face red, chin tilted, eyes flashing—it was Maybor through and through.

Melli let the cup drop from her hands and fell on the bed. She'd run a long way only to find that her father had been with her all the time. Smiling gently, she curled up in the covers. Her thoughts darted like mayflies and it was a long time before she found any rest.

Tawl entered the stall and threw two full skins of ale on the floor. Straight away he crossed over to Nabber, and without saying a word, he unwrapped the bandage from around his neck. He looked at the wound, felt around it for bloating, and then took a leather pouch from his tunic. Scooping a portion of the herb and grease mixture in his fingers, Tawl proceeded to smear it around the wound. Once finished, he retied the bandage and then turned his attention to Nabber's injured arm. "Does this hurt?" he asked, lifting it gently.

Nabber squawked indignantly. "Are you trying to kill me? Of course it hurts."

Tawl laughed. "You'll live. That arm will be back to normal in a few days."

"Better had be, my friend, that's my pocketin' arm." Nabber was feeling a little annoyed at being poked and prodded. Tawl was taking the physicianing too far. "Thanks to you I'll be needing to do even more prospecting when I'm better. How could you save me and not my sack?"

"What was in your sack?"

"Why, loot of course. Gold, coinage, jewels—all good stuff."

"No, Nabber," said the knight softly. "Not all the good stuff."

"What d'you mean? Was anything saved?"

"Something more valuable than gold." Tawl sat down in the hay. Nabber prayed that he wouldn't reach for one of the skins, but he did. He took off the cap, but didn't bring it to his lips. "What you did in the brothel was worth more than the greatest treasure: you risked everything to save a friend." The knight looked Nabber in the eye. "Nothing matters in life as much as protecting the people you love."

The words burned Nabber like a flame. He couldn't look any longer into the knight's face. The truth of Tawl's pain was too unbearable to see. It was too naked, too revealing. Nabber suddenly felt very small. His first reaction was to deny himself: he didn't deserve any praise. "I was the one who got you into the whole thing in the first place. If it wasn't for me, you would never have been poisoned—"

Tawl shook his head. "None of that matters. What counts is that you were there."

"If doing one good thing can cancel out a hoard of bad stuff, then why aren't you trying to find the boy?" The second the words were out of his mouth, Nabber knew he'd gone too far. With one simple sentence he'd raised Bevlin from the grave.

The knight surprised him with his gentleness. "No longer a boy, Nabber. Five years is enough to make a man."

Gaining courage, Nabber persisted: "Then why don't we find him? I'll help you—you know, with coinage and the like. It will be just like old times."

"There's no going back to old times."

"But—"

"You know nothing," Tawl was becoming angry. "*Nothing.* A world of good deeds isn't enough to cancel out what I have done."

The desperation in the knight's voice was enough to stop Nabber's tongue. He should never have spoken so carelessly in the first place. A small part of him wondered what else Tawl had gone through, for the pain he was experiencing seemed to have more than one source. Nabber wanted to reach out to him, to help him, to put his arms around him. Swift would have frowned on such softness, though. So he spoke instead. "You should put some of that ointment on your arm. A burn like that could get infected."

"It'll be all right. It's more than a few weeks old now."

Nabber stood up. "No, I insist. If you're going to fight tomorrow night, there's a chance it might reopen if it's too dry and stretched." He went over and knelt beside the knight. Expecting to be brushed aside, he was surprised when Tawl held out his arm.

"I suppose if you're going to be my second, you might as well start now."

The memory of Swift's disapproving face was the only thing that stopped Nabber from giving away his joy. Tawl's second! It was the greatest, the highest, the best and only honor he'd ever been given. Pride swelled in his heart as he unwound the knight's bandage. His hands shook with excitement over his newly bestowed title.

What he saw beneath the linen put a stop to his elation. Close up, the burn was appalling. The surface was puckered and raised, and there was a slit of weeping flesh where the skin had been burned away. It took all of Nabber's considerable talent for stoicism to keep the shock from his face. Down the length of the burn, cutting through the circles like an arrow through a target, ran Tawl's old scar. Only it no longer looked old. It looked bright and biting and newly given.

Fourteen

A full moon shone down on the city of Bren. The wind sent the mist from the lake northward to the frozen wastes. The stars were set in a clear sky, yet five thousand people hardly noticed. A ring of torches sent smoke into the crowds, and their brightness formed the center of the night.

A halo of light surrounded the pit. Casting outward, it grazed across the faces of all who had come, drawing everyone under its thrall. People were quiet, subdued, dressed in their best with rings on their fingers and jeweled daggers at their belts. Not one hawker plied his trade. The only noise was the whip of the wager, and never had Bren been so anxious to bet.

Maybor drew his furs close. Spring might be on its way, but tonight, in this city, winter was king. The duke would be here soon. The court waited in their gilded enclosure anxious for him to arrive. Baralis was here, standing alone, dressed in black, his features masked by shadow. Maybor was well pleased that the man had decided not to take his official seat; it meant he would have the Hawk to himself.

He had a good view of both fighters. The duke's champion had bared his chest for the benefit of the crowd. Grease was being worked into his muscles, and bound around his forehead were the colors of Bren. A fine specimen, broad and thickly muscled, a bit like he'd been in his youth. Maybor glanced toward the other man: tall and golden haired, he stood alone. There were dark circles under his eyes and a bandage about his arm. There was no doubt in Maybor's mind which of the two his money would be on.

It was a good thing, not allowing women to the pit, he thought as he surveyed the all male crowd. Fights were men's affairs and there would be no feminine flapping to spoil the night.

People kept looking his way. He must cut a fine figure with new fur-trimmed cloak and his gift from the duke at his side. A fine, gray boar-hound lay at his feet. Its small eyes never rested, its flattened ears moved with every sound, and its huge jaws waited like a trap ready to be sprung. Maybor stroked the creature's head absently. It was quite an honor to be given one of the duke's own hounds. The Hawk had brought it himself soon after he'd been told about Kylock's invasion plans. A suitable payment for such privileged information. Maybor smiled. The duke had doubtless enjoyed flaunting that particular morsel in front of Baralis.

And here he was now, walking across the courtyard escorted by twelve armed guards. The duke of Bren's appearance set the crowd buzzing. No fancy ceremonial robes for the Hawk. He was dressed, as always, in military blue. Maybor couldn't quite keep a disapproving glint from his eye: the man had no sense of show.

The duke made straight for the court enclosure. He bowed first to Maybor and then Baralis. He stepped upon the raised dais and waited for the noise of the crowd to stop. Every eye was upon him. Silence came and the duke raised his right arm. Both fighters made their way forward. Positioned as they were on opposite sides of the pit, they arrived in front of the Hawk at exactly the same time.

Maybor, who was sitting behind the duke, saw everything clearly. The champion presented his knife first. The Hawk took it and measured the size of the blade against his forearm. Satisfied, he gave it back: "May Borc bring you glory," he said. He repeated the ritual with the blond stranger, but his blessing lacked the power of the first.

Both men had their seconds with them. Behind the champion stood a man who could only be his brother. Not quite as handsome or as well-muscled as Blayze, he walked with a pronounced limp. He was currently whispering to his brother, and his inward slanting teeth caught the light. On the other side was a boy, barely old enough to hold a sword, his right arm resting in a sling. A poor choice for a fighter's keeper.

The fighters and their seconds withdrew. They wasted no energy exchanging glances. Once they had taken up their positions by the pit, a cry went up:

"Fighting tonight for the honor of Bren is Blayze, duke's champion." The crowd cheered loud and long. Finally, when they stopped the crier began again. "And his challenger is Tawl, knight of Valdis."

Before the crowd could react, the golden-haired fighter raised his arm. "No, my friend," he said. "Not from Valdis."

Wisps of excitement raced through the crowd. "But I have been told—" began the crier.

"*I* tell you that I am from the Lowlands."

Maybor had to admit that there was a compelling force to the man's words. He rubbed his hands together. Things were taking an interesting turn. A little drama before the match was salt for the meat.

"Very well, sir," said the crier. "In Bren we take a man on his word." He then turned and addressed the crowd: "And the duke's challenger is Tawl, from the Lowlands." The announcement met with more whispering than cheering.

Both men jumped into the pit. A red scarf was raised and the crier looked to the duke for a sign. Still standing, the duke raised his right arm. He made a fist, and then with one sharp movement, he brought it to his chest. The scarf dropped into the pit.

Nabber watched as they circled around each other. No chance of Tawl spotting any weaknesses with Blayze. There was every chance that Blayze would notice how pale and drawn the knight looked, however. The burn on Tawl's right arm was vulnerable, too, but he hid it well. Most people assumed the bandage was there to hide his circles—even now, after he'd stated that he wasn't from Valdis. Nabber guessed it had cost Tawl a lot to deny his knighthood.

Blayze lunged forward with his knife. Tawl feinted to one side, but just as quickly he was back. Knife arm now down, Blayze was vulnerable. The knight drew back his weapon as if ready for a strike and then punched Blayze square in the face with his left fist. The crowd was stunned. They hissed at the indignity of the move.

The champion went reeling backward. Tawl pounced, trying to floor him, but he hadn't counted on the sheer physical strength of the champion. The man hardly swayed. He pushed Tawl away with such force that the knight had to struggle to keep his footing. Nabber could clearly see the sweat on Tawl's brow. The crowd was frantic, betting with the frenzy of locusts on a field of grain.

Blayze sauntered over to where Tawl was recovering. The torchlight gleamed on the grease. He raised a finger to his chin and prodded the flesh. A small gesture, designed to provoke. A challenge to Tawl to try punching him again. The knight leapt forward. Blayze was ready for him.

Up went his elbow, smashing into Tawl's jaw. It was a risky move, for the knight's blade was close to his flank. The force of the blow was so great that all Tawl could do was rake the blade down the champion's side. It was barely enough to draw blood.

Blayze gave Tawl no time to recover. Altering the grip on his knife, he stabbed at the knight's chest. The two fighters were so close it was impossible to see what happened. Then Blayze backed away and the light fell on Tawl. His linen undershirt was stained with blood. The crowd cheered wildly. A huge knot twisted in Nabber's stomach: the stain was growing larger.

Glancing toward the court enclosure, Nabber looked upon the face of the duke. He was a man well pleased with what he saw.

There was no respite for Tawl. Blayze hounded him, and Tawl was forced to back away. Nabber wanted to shout out, *"He was poisoned!"* but he knew the knight's sense of honor would prevent him from making it known. Nabber respected that. It was what set Tawl apart from every man he'd ever known.

It was hard to gauge just how bad the wound was. More telling than the blood was the fact that the knight had slowed down. He was in the center of the pit and Blayze was circling like a vulture. The champion kept making quick feints and lunges, hoping to entice Tawl into letting down his guard. He was taunting him, too, saying that from what he'd heard he wasn't surprised that Tawl no longer wanted to be known as a knight. Nabber felt truly ashamed. *He* had given Blayze that particular weapon.

The blood reached Tawl's waist. His breathing was sharp and fast. Sweat ran down his nose and cheeks, and still he managed to keep the champion at bay. The crowd was not happy with this lull in the fight; they hissed and jeered at Tawl for taking evasive action rather than attacking.

Blayze was losing patience. He was anxious for an exchange to show off his skills. He shouted loudly, "I say you are a knight and I'm the one to prove it!" A cheer went up from the crowd. A series of fast moves dazzled the audience and served to confuse Tawl. Blayze's knife traced intricate patterns in the air. Each flash of the blade was a warning.

He made his move. A quick strike with the knife caught Tawl's right arm. The bandage was slit down the middle. Blayze stepped back and Tawl's bandage fell to the ground.

"Aah!" A sharp intake of breath united the crowd. The circles were there for everyone to see. The circles, the burn, and the scar. Nabber felt a deep pain in his chest; he could hardly bear to look at Tawl. His vision

thinned and blurred. Tears streaked down his face unnoticed. It was all his fault.

Tawl raised his eyes from his circles and faced the crowd. People who had been jeering stopped. There was something in the knight's face that compelled silence. Golden hair gleamed in the torchlight and the blood-stained tunic became an emblem. His voice, when it came, rent through the fabric of the night, changing its very texture: "I no longer count myself a knight," he said softly. "I am not worthy of Valdis."

The words brimmed with truth and anguish. The crowd shifted nervously—one man's tragedy had been revealed and they were unsure how to react. Blayze decided for them. Unhappy with the shift of emphasis from himself to the knight, he attacked.

Jumping on his back, he brought the knight to the ground. Tawl drew up his arms and legs and sprang backward. Blayze failed to find his footing and stumbled to the ground. Tawl pounced like a mountain lion. He brought his left knee down hard on Blayze's wrist. The bone cracked and the champion lost his grip on his knife. Tawl kicked it away, out of reach. Shifting his position, he pinned Blayze to the ground. By fixing his weight on the champion's thighs, he prevented the man from leaping up.

The crowd was stunned and thrilled in one. Cheers and hisses were heard in equal measure. Nabber promised Borc that he'd never pocket another man in his life as long as Tawl won the fight.

Tawl's blade came down. Blayze struggled to keep it from his throat. He was fighting a losing battle. With his right wrist broken, the champion was attempting to fend off the knife. Tawl's sword arm might be burned, but it was still more than a match for Blayze's left.

Just as the tip of the blade pierced the skin, something happened. Tawl wavered. His arm shook and then his body convulsed. His left arm shot to his chest and he lost his grip on the champion.

The air quivered with sorcery. Every hair on Baralis' body prickled with it. Someone was drawing power upon the golden-haired fighter. It was in his lungs like a cancer. Baralis sent out his awareness: he had to discover who was foolish enough to attempt such a feat.

He was a blind man feeling for edges. The drawing was weak, unfocused, the work of an amateur. He followed the trail to a pinpoint in the crowd. A slight, cloaked figure was the source.

Baralis felt the fighter flex his will. It was a tangible force and it was backed up by fate. Its strength was breathtaking. A warning flashed deep within Baralis. This man, this golden-haired fighter who once was a knight, had a destiny so urgent that it wouldn't let him succumb to the shock of the drawing. He was fighting it tooth and nail. Baralis had heard about such men during his stay in the Far South. It was said that their fates would repel all interference—especially from sorcery. Thieves, they were called, but he couldn't remember why.

Even as his hold on the blade wavered, the knight still fought on. The sorcerer was weakening. The power tautened like a drawn bow, ready to snap back. Inexperienced the cloaked figure might be, but he had still drawn enough to burn the skin off his own face.

The sharp tang of sorcery brought saliva to Baralis' mouth. He looked closely at the instigator. So small, so slight: it was a woman! Excited curiosity won over caution and Baralis shaped a compulsion on his very next breath. Weaving with subtle precision, he worked it below the thread of the drawing. An instant later the cloaked figure turned and looked at him. With the cries of the crowd sounding in his ears and the taste of sorcery still fresh upon his tongue, Baralis recognized the face of Catherine of Bren.

The knight's will fought back with deadly force. In that instant, Catherine lost control of the drawing. A fraction of a second later, Baralis sent out a drawing of his own. Not pausing to think, he directed every fiber of his soul toward the space between Catherine and the knight. The drawing broke. Baralis heard the sound of it snapping through the air. He sped to meet it. There wasn't enough time to brace himself. It smashed against him with the force of a storm. His mind was torn from his body and then he fell into the dark.

Nabber felt certain that Tawl was a goner. The knight's seizure had given Blayze enough time to recover both his strength and his blade. The champion took the knife in his left and slashed at Tawl's face. Tawl was doubled up with pain, but he just managed to turn away. The blade sliced his ear. Blayze moved forward again, preparing to strike. The crowd cheered him on. Victory was in sight.

All of a sudden, Tawl appeared to recover. He straightened his back and dropped his arm from his chest. He looked into Blayze's eyes and smiled. A second later he kicked in the champion's kneecaps. Both of them. The man fell to the ground. Tawl was on him in an instant. He punched an elbow into his face, breaking his nose. Blood splattered the features of both men. Tawl surprised the crowd by throwing away his knife. He took Blayze's forehead in both hands and smashed his skull into the ground. Again and again the man's head was brought down upon the stone flooring. The crowd was horrified. All eyes were on the pool of blood which surrounded the champion's face.

Nabber felt a sudden tug on his arm. He tore his gaze away from the pit and found himself face-to-face with the girl in the portrait. *"Make him stop!"* she screamed. One swift second to put everything into place—she was obviously the champion's sweetheart—another second to ponder on the exaggeration of the artist—the girl looked a lot more haggard in person—and then he was off, leaping into the pit like a hero to the rescue.

He ran straight up to Tawl. The knight was in a blood frenzy, aware of nothing except the need to destroy. Nabber put a hand upon his arm and said gently, "Come on, Tawl, time to stop. No need to fight anymore." The knight looked up. His eyes were glazed, unfocused. Nabber realized he was far away in another place, fighting a fight that could never be won. "Please, Tawl, for me. Please stop." Tawl hesitated; his eyes cleared. He stopped and let Nabber pull him away. Standing up, he began to make his way from the pit.

The crowd waited in silence. In took Nabber a moment to realize what they were waiting for. The red scarf of victory still lay on the ground. Instinctively, he knew Tawl would never raise it. As his second, he could do it for him. Nabber picked up the red marker from the floor and held it above his head. As he did so, he looked for the hooded girl from the portrait. She was nowhere to be seen.

Maybor watched as the young boy raised the scarf over his head and the crowd broke into an uneasy applause. It was turning out to be a most interesting evening. By far the high spot had been some five minutes earlier, when Baralis had collapsed where he stood. One minute the king's chancellor was his usual contemptible self, stealing glances from the side like an uninvited guest, and the next he'd turned as pale as pig lard and his legs gave way under him. He was quickly borne away by a handful of servants, his body as still as a corpse.

The matter caused little commotion. The duke barely looked up from the fight. Sick envoys were obviously not a priority when the honor of Bren was at stake.

Maybor was hoping that some enterprising courtiers had taken it into their heads to poison the man. Either that or he'd been stricken with a fatal seizure. Indeed, seizures seemed the order of the night. The golden-haired fighter had definitely succumbed to some sort of attack. Strange how he recovered just after Baralis collapsed.

Unable to keep the smile from his face, Maybor uncapped his flask and took a hearty swig of brandy. Yes, it was a night of rare drama and intrigue, and the show wasn't even over yet.

The duke was not a happy man. A muscle was pumping in his cheek and his eyes were as cold and as dark as the Great Lake he claimed for his own. The crowd was looking to him for a sign, a gesture, no matter how small, that would give them some indication of how best to react. The Hawk was giving little away. He stood up and acknowledged the red marker with the briefest of nods.

"Bring the victor before me," he cried.

A few moments passed. To Maybor's eyes it looked as if the young boy had to practically drag the knight forward. Eventually the two stood before the duke. The wound on the fighter's chest had been quickly bound. Judging from the amount of blood on his tunic, the blade must have cut deep between the bones. The man looked sick, almost fevered; his skin had a gray cast to it and his brow was slick with sweat. The circles that had caused such an uproar were no longer on show. A length of green silk covered the spot where they lay. The boy's shirt, which was a matching color, was sporting a missing sleeve.

The crowd hushed in anticipation. "I will ask you one question," said the duke to the knight. "Are you free of your obligation to Valdis?"

Time slowed. The moon shone a pale light upon the dais and the faces of five thousand people were turned toward the knight.

"I have long forsaken Valdis," he said.

"So you count yourself a free man?"

"I do."

"Then I ask you to take a pledge and be named as my champion."

A ripple of shock rose from the crowd.

The knight looked toward his second. He made a small gesture with his hand, and then said, "I am willing to take the pledge."

As close as he was to the duke, Maybor could not tell what he was thinking. The Hawk took a deep breath and then spoke in a voice designed to ring the city with its echoes. "Repeat after me: I, Tawl of the Lowlands, do solemnly pledge to protect the duke and his heirs with all the strength of my body and the force of my spirit until Borc himself calls me to rest."

A minute of silence passed and then the knight repeated the oath.

Fifteen

*T*he man with golden hair was at the center of the city. The high battlements closed about him like the sharp teeth of a predator. He was never getting out of there.

Jack awoke. He was confused, disorientated. An ember in the fire suddenly burst into flame. Never had a dream seemed so vivid, so true, so tragic. Jack was overcome with a sense of loss. He felt alone, abandoned, as if he'd been left to fend for himself in an uncertain world. The golden-haired stranger had deserted him. Jack knew he would never see him in his dreams again.

Strange, but although the man had appeared to him only once before, he seemed to be a symbol of something. Something fundamental and precious like hope.

Jack was cold to the core. He drew the covers close, but how could a blanket warm the marrow of his bones? The embers ran out of fuel. The fire petered to nothing; a dark shell with a glint of red at its heart. There was no way of telling the time. He might have been asleep for hours, or minutes or seconds. The kitchen was quiet, dark except for the banking fire. Rovas slept in the larder, and Magra and Tarissa slept in the room behind the chimney.

Jack stood up and went over to the window. He unlatched the shutter and looked out at the night. The sky seemed impossibly large. Stars vied with a full moon, but nothing was as compelling as the dark. He was truly alone now. What did it mean? Why was the man with golden hair so important? And what would happen now that he had gone? Jack ran his hands through his hair. He'd barely had a chance to recover from what happened yesterday, when his dreams had abducted his body, and now this. He looked to the sky for answers, but the impartial silence of the heavens was his only reply.

A floorboard creaked behind him. "Jack, are you all right?" came Tarissa's voice.

He didn't turn. "No. Something has changed. I don't know what."

"Was it another vision?" Tarissa rested her arm upon his shoulder.

"A dream, a vision—I don't know."

"Come and sit down. I'll make up the fire."

She was so close he could feel her breath on the back of his neck. Its warmth drew him in. He was so cold and she alone could warm him. He turned toward her, following her breath to its source. Her mouth was open as if somehow she understood what he needed. She came to meet him. Her substance was an antidote to the vast emptiness of space, and her warmth expelled the cold like a flame.

Lips met, skin touched. A pull upon a strand and Tarissa's nightgown fell to the floor. Her nakedness was a gift. The moonlight gleamed upon her flesh, but it was to the shadows that his tongue was drawn. The exquisite dip where the throat joined the body, the heavy underside of her breasts, and the fragrant moistness of the hairs beneath her arm. He couldn't touch her enough. He needed to feel part of her, to help dull his sense of loss and to be saved from the anguish of being alone.

His urgency was so great it drove them to a place where nothing mattered, only the wetness of saliva and the soft edges where flesh became hollows. Tarissa made her body an offering, sacrificing herself to the force of his need.

As soon as the maid had left, Melli turned toward the mirror and rubbed the rouge from her face. There was no way she was going to be garnished like a dish at a banquet. Off with the dress, too. Ever since her brief stay with Mistress Greal, Melli had taken a deep disliking to the color red. She didn't care a jot whether or not she looked nice for the duke.

As she changed back into the dress given to her by Fiscel, she checked again to see that her knife was still in place. The hardness of the metal pleased her. The duke would get quite a fright if he tried to come too close. Not that she had any intention of letting matters get that far. She looked at her reflection: what else could she do to make herself unappealing? A flash of inspiration came to her and she spent the next ten minutes biting her nails to the quick.

It really was getting rather late, well past midnight by her reckoning. Perhaps His Grace had gone off the idea of feminine diversions. She hadn't heard from Bailor all day, but the fact that he had sent a girl to tend to her appearance was a sign that she might still be called upon despite the lateness of the hour.

There was a small part of her that hoped the call would come. Try as she might to deny it, the thought of a confrontation with the duke excited her. He was said to be the most powerful man in the north. It would be interesting to see what kind of man lay behind the reputation. Melli scolded her imagination and deliberately focused on a disturbing thought to punish herself. If the man was as brutal as was rumored, then how would he react to being challenged in his own chambers with a knife?

A knock at the door was followed by the drawing of a bolt. In walked Bailor. He took a long look at her, and then said, "If you take the gilding from the lily, the flower still remains."

Melli felt a flush upon her face. He had seen right through her attempt to make herself unappealing. Determined not to admit her tactics, she feigned innocence. "I decided not to wear the red dress, the color doesn't become me."

"Aah. And your nails, did their length not become you, either?"

"I broke one and thought it wise to make the rest even."

"And the rouge?"

"Pale cheeks are the height of beauty in the kingdoms."

Bailor actually laughed. "You are going to be quite a surprise to the His Grace. I can't decide which is the quicker: your tongue or your wits."

Melli tried to look indignant. "Are you calling me a liar, sir?"

"You're no shrinking violet, that's for sure." He gave her an appraising look. "You will do just the way you are. Follow me."

Now the moment had finally come, Melli found that she wasn't the least bit excited, just nervous. She let Bailor lead her out of the room. They walked along a series of galleries and then down many flights of stairs. The farther they descended, the more worried Melli became. Surely the duke's chamber would be situated high in the palace? She stopped in her tracks. "Where are you taking me?" she demanded.

"For a bastard daughter, you have quite an air about you," said Bailor, looking at her sharply. Melli dropped her gaze to the floor. "There's no need to worry," he continued. "The duke values discretion in all things, especially matters of a personal nature. There is a tunnel in the servants' chapel that leads to his chambers."

"How very convenient to have both sin and salvation within such easy reach." Melli was relieved. She didn't doubt his words for an instant. Castle Harvell was riddled with tunnels, and there was no reason to believe that the duke's palace would not boast a few of its own.

"Did the fight go well?" she asked as they approached a low wooden doorway.

Bailor wheeled around. "Under no circumstances must you mention the fight to His Grace."

"Why?"

"He lost his champion tonight."

"Was the man killed?"

"Worse than killed. His brains were smashed out of his skull." Bailor's voice was grim. "He is barely alive. The physicians are doing what they can, but there is little hope that he'll live through the night."

"And the victor, what has become of him?"

"His fate plays a stronger tune. The duke appointed him his new champion." Bailor glanced around before placing his hand on the door. "He had little choice really, what with the court and the foreign envoys looking on. He is a proud man and to have his champion defeated in such a way was quite upsetting for him. So whatever you do, don't mention the fight to him." He looked to Melli for her assent, but at that instant the door swung open.

"Thought I heard voices. It's a little late for a service, though." Straight away Melli recognized the accent of the kingdoms. Instinctively she turned her head away from the man to whom the voice belonged.

"You are not the normal guard," said Bailor. "What are you doing in the chapel at this hour?"

"Me and my friend here have been doing a little work for the chaplain." The guard indicated a second man standing behind him. "We were just finishing off polishing the floors." There were a bucket and some cloths on the floor behind them.

"I would advise you not to work so late in the future." said Bailor. "Now let me pass."

They walked into the chapel, Melli keeping her head bent low toward the floor. Her heart was beating wildly. She was almost certain that the guards were from Castle Harvell. They could recognize her in an instant.

"What's your name, man?" asked Bailor to the one who had opened the door.

"Grift, sir, and my companion here is Bodger."

"Well, Grift, I trust you know the value of a still tongue?"

"You can count on me and Bodger, sir."

"I'm pleased to hear it." Bailor took hold of Melli's arm. "I think it's time you gentlemen retired for the evening."

The one called Grift nodded judiciously. "Of course, sir, say no more. Me and Bodger will be on our way." With that he and the second guard made their way toward the main entrance to the chapel.

Bailor waited until the door was closed behind them. "Drunken fools," he said under his breath. He then guided Melli toward the altar.

Hanging behind the altar were several painted panels charting Borc's progress from shepherd to hero to god. Bailor went straight to the middle panel and pressed against the left side. The whole thing swung open like a door. Startled, Melli jumped back. Her nerves were on edge; the incident with the guards had left her badly shaken.

"Follow me," said Bailor.

They traveled up a narrow, spiral staircase. They must have been expected, thought Melli, for the stairway was lit with torches. Up and around they went, burrowing into the heart of the palace. Eventually they came to a door. Bailor knocked lightly and the door was opened by a guard wearing military blue. The man nodded curtly and let them pass. They walked through the small anteroom and into a large but sparsely furnished chamber. One man stood alone by an unshuttered window.

Bailor cleared his throat. "Your Grace, may I present Melli of Deepwood."

The man turned and looked at Melli. Never in all her life had she received such a look: cold and appraising, it seemed to strip her bare and then discard what was left.

"Take her away," he said.

"But, sir—"

"I said take her away."

Anger rose within Melli. No one dismissed her so brusquely. "Do what the man said, Bailor. After all, he's had quite an upsetting evening— best to let him mourn his champion alone." She spun around and began to walk back the way they'd come.

The duke was on her in an instant. He slapped her across the face. Melli reeled with the force of the blow. She struggled to keep her footing.

Once she was stable, she drew herself up to her full height, looked the duke straight in the eye, and said: "It's a pity your champion couldn't muster such a blow, else the fight might have ended quite differently."

Flint gray eyes reappraised her. Without looking at Bailor, he said, "Leave us alone."

Melli heard the sound of footsteps receding into the distance. Determined not to be the first to look away, she held her gaze firm. The duke took a brief step forward and Melli couldn't stop herself from flinching.

"Not as tough as you seem," said the duke with a stretch of lip that might have passed for a smile.

"Well, I'm sure you're looking to make someone pay for tonight. I've probably come at just the right time." She tilted her chin. "If you're going to beat me, I should warn you, I will fight back."

"I don't doubt that you would." The duke turned and went over to a large wooden table. He poured a single glass of wine. "Here," he said, "take this."

Melli was out of her depth, but determined not to show it. "I think I'll have to refuse," she said. "After all, it's probably poisoned and I have no intention of making it easier for you to overpower me."

The duke brought the glass to his lips and took a mouthful of the wine. Melli thought he would offer her the rest, but he merely returned the cup to the table. "There's no such place as Deepwood," he said.

"You are obviously unfamiliar with the kingdoms."

"I know every inch of it like the back of my hand." The words were more statement than boast. It frightened Melli to hear them.

"Why are you so interested in the kingdoms?"

The duke's response was as quick as a lash. "Why are you lying about where you are from?"

Melli looked around the room. She spied a wooden desk in the corner and walked toward it. She needed to give herself time before replying. Such a bare room; the stone floor was beautifully cut, but there were no rugs to warm the foot or please the eye. The walls were hung with nothing but swords. It was not going to be easy to fool the duke. His wits were sharp and he was the sort of man who was used to getting answers. She was determined to rise to the challenge. "I lie and say I'm from Deepwood because it shocks people less than telling them the truth. I'm a bastard from the wrong side of the bed."

"You have a bastard's temper, I'll give you that."

"You slap a woman like one."

The duke laughed outright. "Do all women in the kingdoms have nettles for tongues?"

"You tell me, seeing as you know the place so well." Melli wondered if she'd gone too far. The duke's knowledge of her country was no laughing matter. Lying on the desk there were maps and charts. The forests of the kingdoms were circled like treasure.

The duke saw where her eyes had rested, yet made no attempt to cover the charts. "It is not unusual," he said, "if you are about to ally with a country, to make a study of its geography."

"And resources?"

The duke shrugged. "It is no secret that Bren needs timber. What is the point of allying with a country unless there is something to be gained at the join?"

"So what do the kingdoms gain?"

"Access to the most powerful army in the Known Lands."

Melli shuddered. The heat left her face. A gap opened up in her consciousness and she struggled with all her might not to spiral toward it: in its middle lay prophecy. Just like the time at the pig farmer's cottage when she had lost herself to its guile, it beckoned her forth with all the promise of what the future would hold. Only she didn't want to see it. A future where the most powerful army in the Known Lands played a part would not make for a pretty picture. Melli forced her mind to focus on the present, and the breach that held the future collapsed upon itself unseen.

She was holding on to the desk so tightly her knuckles were white. The marriage between Kylock and Catherine went so much deeper than nuptials and wedding feasts.

"Go now," said the duke. "The guard will show you back to your chamber."

Melli was weak and disorientated. The desk was the only thing that kept her standing. The duke's cold dismissal didn't seem to make any sense. Or had he seen something in her face? Seconds had passed, yet it felt like she had run up a high hill and was now breathless at the top. The duke was waiting, impatient for her to be gone.

She risked a step forward. Her legs did not fail her. There was a large door with bronze carvings at the opposite end of the room and she made her way toward it.

The duke stopped her. "You will go the way you came," he said.

Melli could barely remember. She needed to be alone, to rest, to sleep—to forget. The duke guided her toward the small side door where she had first entered. The same guard waited in the anteroom. He took hold of her arm, and when she next looked round the duke had gone.

The journey back to her room seemed endless. She forced her feet to find the steps. By the time they had arrived at the chapel, her thoughts were racing. The jolt she'd received from the foretelling might have left her body weak, but her mind was quick to recover.

The night had not gone at all as she planned. The knife was still in its place by her side, yet not once had she considered pulling it out. The very idea seemed ludicrous. The duke was much more solid and intimidating than she had counted on, not to mention the fact that his chambers were obviously well guarded. There would be no chance for a quick escape. Her plan would need rethinking. Still, it had been an interesting encounter: the most powerful man in the north was no fool, yet she had managed to fool him all the same. She was not surprised that Jack hadn't liked talking about his family, for the mention of the word *bastard* seemed to bring most inquiries to a halt.

The guard led Melli to her room. The minute the bolt was drawn on the other side of the door, she threw herself on the bed. Melli hugged the pillow to her body. It had been exhilarating to trade words with the most powerful man in the north.

The tavern was emptying out for the night, only drunks and fools remained. Bitter smoke rose from cheap tallow and the rushes were alive with vermin. Traff crushed a rat beneath his boot; the bones made a pleasing cracking noise when kicked. The creature landed on the opposite side of the room. Right by the feet of the man he was going to murder.

He hated the Halcus. They were dirty, dog-eating scum. A week back he had been jumped, and the bastards had stolen his horse. They beat him and left him for dead. Now it was time to return the favor. Already this evening he'd eaten a large and overpriced meal, drank three skins of ale, and had just ordered a bed for the night. What he needed now was the money to pay for it. And that fat and greasy Halcus merchant slouching drunkenly across the room was the one who was going to oblige.

Traff stood up and made his way to the merchant's table. "Good evening, my friend. Fancy a cup of ale?"

The merchant looked him up and down. "Not from round here, are you?"

Traff nodded as he sat down. "From Silbur originally."

"What you doing here, then?"

He wanted to put his fist into the man's fat, nosy face. "Looking for action against the kingdoms or Bren."

"You're too far east for the kingdoms," said the merchant, "and it's too early to tell if there's a war coming with Bren."

Dangerously close to losing his temper, Traff said, "You caught me out, my friend. I'm on a mission for a certain wealthy lord."

The merchant's interest visibly increased. "Which wealthy lord?"

"Can't say, but there might be something in it for you if you can help me out a little." Traff moved closer. "I'm looking for a woman."

"What is she to the lord?" The merchant's breath reeked of onions.

"Trouble, if you get my drift." Traff waited until the man nodded and then continued. "She's pale skinned, dark haired, talks with a kingdoms' accent."

"Is she tall?" asked the merchant becoming excited. "And comely?"

Traff nodded. "A rare beauty. Why, have you seen her?"

"A girl matching her description was in town about three weeks back. She stopped the night in this tavern. I saw her with my own eyes. Caused quite a scandal, by all accounts. The man she was traveling with murdered a soldier, and she was caught by Captain Vanly."

Traff worked to conceal his excitement. This was the first word he'd heard of Melli since he left the kingdoms. "Where is she now?"

"Vanly sold her." The merchant drew excited little breaths. "It was the talk of the town. He made quite a profit, you know—because she was a virgin."

"Who bought her?"

"Flesh-trader, name of Fiscel. Last I heard, he was traveling east."

"Toward Bren?"

The merchant shrugged. "He'll probably pass that way to pick up a few extra girls, but I doubt if he'll stop. There's more money to be made in the Far South."

"What happened to the boy she was with?"

"Got clean away." The merchant's eyes narrowed. "What about that little something for myself you promised?"

Traff had been waiting for this. "There's five golds if it's her that you saw. Outside in my wagon I have a portrait of her. Come and take a look at it and then we'll call the matter settled."

The merchant nearly leapt from his chair. On the way out of the door, Traff called to the tavern maid, "Back in five minutes."

The night was cold and clear. Their breaths plumed smoke in the air.

As they rounded the corner, Traff drew his knife. Seeing no wagon, the merchant turned, puzzled. Seeing the blade, he made to scream. The sound never left his lips. With one hand Traff grabbed the man's forelock and yanked his head back, with the other he slit his throat. The body stiffened for an instant and then fell backward. Traff caught it and drew it to the ground.

He took a quick look around. It was too late for passersby. Tearing at the dead man's clothing, he started looking for loot. He couldn't find any. The body was heavy, awkward, hard to move. In his anger, Traff took his knife and sliced the man's clothes to ribbons. As the bloodstained tunic fell away, Traff spotted a pouch tied below the dead man's belly. He seized it eagerly. It contained a couple of golds, five silvers, and a large, finely cut ruby. A fair haul.

His intention had been to hide the body and spend the night in the inn, but that now seemed too risky, and the idea of moving the fat man didn't appeal to him at all. He kicked the corpse a couple of times for good measure and then made his way out of town. Bren was his destination. He'd be able to pick up Melli's trail there.

Traff whistled a tune as he walked. It was a fine night; his betrothed was alive and well and still a virgin. He couldn't hope for anything more.

Sixteen

Jack was woken by Rovas shaking him roughly. "Sleeping a bit late, aren't you?" he said.

Jack was thrown into an immediate panic. Where was Tarissa? Where were her clothes? What sort of state had they left the kitchen in? Had they even bothered to close the shutter? Jack scanned his surroundings. Everything was as it should be: his pallet was neat, the kitchen was tidy, and the shutter was firmly closed. A sigh of relief escaped him. Too late he realized Rovas was watching.

The smuggler's eyes narrowed sharply. "Were you up in the night?"

"What makes you say that?" His second mistake: answering a question with a question.

"The fire has gone out. Someone has stirred the life out of the ashes."

"Oh, that. It got a little cold about midnight." Jack stood up and splashed some water on his face. Although his back was toward Rovas, he could tell that the man was looking at him. He didn't feel in the mood to play games. What had happened last night was too precious, too intimate, to be spoiled by ugly suspicions. Jack turned on Rovas. "If you have something to say, come out and say it."

The smuggler regarded Jack coolly. "I do have something to say and this is it: keep your hands, your eyes, and your mind away from Tarissa."

"Or else?"

"I'll kill you."

Both men turned as the side door opened. Tarissa walked in, carrying a basket of washing. She took in the scene and walked straight over to

Jack. Slapping him hard on the face, she said, "You kept Mother and me awake half the night with your pacing around. Next time you can't sleep at least try to be quiet." She was magnificent: eyes flashing, cheeks flushed, her whole body trembling with anger. Jack wanted to kiss her. He could see the effect her outburst was having on Rovas. The man looked first astonished, then confused, and finally decidedly sheepish. "I don't know what you're smiling about, Rovas," she said. "It's normally your snoring that haunts my dreams."

"I don't snore, woman," he replied.

"No, and you're a good and honest shopkeeper, too."

All three of them laughed. Rovas patted Jack on the shoulder in way of an apology. Jack's first instinct was to pull away, but Tarissa flashed him a warning glance. She had not gone to the trouble of putting on a performance for it to be ruined by the supporting cast. He made an effort for her and accepted the smuggler's touch. Looking up, Jack saw Magra in the doorway. Her face was an unreadable mask.

"Well, I've got to be off," said Rovas. "There's a man in town who's spent the last three days carving peppercorns out of wood, he should have enough by now to double my pepper weight and triple my profits." He tucked a loaf of bread in his belt and made his way toward the door. "I'll be back before dark."

As soon as the door was closed, Magra said to Tarissa, "I suppose you're rather pleased with yourself. You were having quite some fun making Rovas look a fool."

"Mother I—"

Jack interrupted. "It's not Tarissa's fault."

"I know." The older woman looked suddenly tired. She sat down by the fire and poured herself a cup of mulled holk. "Jack, we owe Rovas more than you can imagine. Over twenty years ago, when he was not much older than a boy himself, he took us in: me a hated foreigner and Tarissa just a babe in arms. We can never repay him for that. Never."

Tarissa was looking down at the floor. A flush of guilt rose up her neck. "I'm sorry, Mother." She reached for Jack's hand and squeezed it gently. It was a gesture intended to silence him. She didn't want him contradicting anything that was said about Rovas.

Magra shook her head. "No, you were right to do what you did. It was for the best."

Jack's thoughts returned to the night when Rovas kicked the wood scuttle across the room. Magra was right: it was for the best. Not for himself—Rovas didn't frighten *him*—but for the two women who had no choice but to live with the man. Jack wanted to take them away, both of them, and give them a home free of guilt and obligation. Rovas would stop at nothing to keep control of his makeshift family—blackmail, murder, coercion—and it was time someone brought an end to his twenty-year reign of terror.

Last night had changed everything. Tarissa had given herself to him. There was no other way to describe it; she had sensed his grief and in one beautiful, selfless gesture she used her body to ease the pain.

After need, came passion. How long they spent cradled between the rushes and the moonlight Jack would never know. It had seemed like an eternity. And later, much later, there had been hours when Tarissa lay sleeping in his arms. Yet she still had time to steal away, gather up her clothes, tidy the pallet, and close the reproachful shutter. This morning she had saved him again.

For the first time in his life he had a true debt to repay. Falk had given him gifts just as precious as Tarissa's, but he had denied him the honor of repaying them. Not so with Tarissa. Jack's mind raced forward. He would take her away from the cottage, work to give her a new home, good food, and fine clothes. There would be no trip to Bren, no wandering off to find action and adventure. That wasn't important now.

Something had happened last night. He couldn't begin to understand what, but it had changed everything. For months now he had felt as if he were being pulled forward, pulled toward events and places that were not of his choosing. This morning the tension had gone.

Other things mattered now. All his life he had wanted a family, and here, in front of his eyes, there was one for the taking. Why hadn't he seen it sooner? Tarissa could be his. Once the Halcus captain was done away with, he would be able to do whatever he wanted. He could move to Annis or Highwall and get a job as a baker. With the money from that and a little scribing on the side, it wouldn't be long before he could send for Tarissa and Magra.

As Jack was busy planning, there was a small part of his mind that stayed detached. It warned him that he was working to fill the void that had been created last night. So what if he was? Fate had set him free, and what he did with his life now was no one's concern but his own.

"No, Bodger, the way to tell if a man has the staying power of a stallion isn't by seeing if he eats his greens."

"But Longtoad says the more greens a man eats, the better able he is to satisfy the wenches."

"There ain't no way that a man with the figure of a spring onion is going to be able to satisfy the wenches more than once in a bedding. No, Bodger. Take it from me, the true sign of staying power is nasal hair."

"Nasal hair, Grift?"

"Nasal hair, Bodger. The more hair that dangles down from a man's snifter, the better able he is to wear out the wenches. Take Master Frallit— he has more hair up one of his nostrils than the entire royal guard has under their armpits, and you'll never meet a man whose loaf rises quicker after the first kneading."

"I see you have quite a head growing up there yourself, Grift."

"Thank you, Bodger. You wouldn't do too bad yourself if you stopped trimming them."

"But I've never trimmed my nasal hair, Grift."

"Ah, well, your best hope then is to concentrate on quality rather than quantity."

Bodger quickly hid his shortcomings by taking a deep draught of ale. "Do you think we'll get into trouble for being in the chapel last night, Grift?"

"I don't think so, Bodger. The chaplain set us to guard the door. He can hardly complain if we nipped inside for a quick toddle of holy spirits."

"We did clean the floor as well, Grift."

"Aye, you did a fine job with those tiles, Bodger."

"When will the normal guards take over the watch, Grift?"

"We are the normal guards now, Bodger. The chaplain said we've got the job as long as we keep quiet about him being drunk as a pheasant every night before six."

"He did tell us to keep out of the chapel, though."

"Bodger, if you think I'm going to be spending every night hunkering down in a doorway, when I could be kipping in a pew, then you're sadly mistaken."

"What d'you think those two were up to last night, Grift?"

"It wasn't midnight mass, that's for sure, Bodger. If you ask me, I think there's some kind of passageway from the chapel that leads somewhere high and mighty. That girl was too noble to be dallying with the shifty-looking chap who escorted her. She was obviously destined to keep company with a lord."

"Did you notice anything familiar about her, Grift?"

"Like what, Bodger?"

"Well, I don't know about you, but to me she looked the spitting image of Maybor's daughter, the Lady Melliandra."

"One day soon, Bodger, I'm going to have to give you my theory on men with bad eyesight. The girl looked nothing like her; you must have had a little too much of the chaplain's extra-strong brandy."

"I suppose you're right, Grift. Anyway, what about men with bad eyesight?"

"Aah, well, Bodger, men with bad eyesight are notorious for . . ."

"Master, there is a lady to see you," said Crope.

Layers of pain peeled away and left raw and stinging flesh beneath. Each breath was a victory, each thought was a blade in his heart. He had taken the blow full on his chest. It had hit him like a flight of blazing arrows, searing through skin and muscle and precious tissue. The burning was intolerable. Even now, with perceptions dulled by precious drugs, he could feel it trying to claim his flesh for its own.

Oh, but it was worth it. He would not change a thing. The lady who waited to see him would be the most important woman in all of history and her life had to be saved at all cost. If Catherine of Bren had died last night, his plans would have faded to dust.

Such a foolish, arrogant girl to think that she could draw sorcery as easily as she exerted her will. A child playing with fire. Even now she probably had no idea of the risk she had taken. The backlash was devastating; it bore no relation to the initial drawing. It had been honed and focused like the edge of a blade. Going in, it had been a cheap trick, a mischief-making ripple, nothing more. Yet the golden-haired knight had altered its nature. By fighting the drawing, his body acted like a prism, condensing the power to a fine point. Coming out it was a deadly force. And Catherine of Bren, who was destined to be queen of the Four Kingdoms, had been its target.

There was no doubt in Baralis' mind that she would have been incinerated on the spot. The only thing that saved her was the speed of his reflexes. By sending his own drawing out, he had managed to divert the force. He had taken the backlash upon himself. There had been no other way; split seconds never made for clever strategy. With barely an instant to ready himself for the blow, he'd done what he could—the beginnings of a shielding, nothing more. Still, he had survived while Catherine would not have stood a chance. Survival wasn't only in his blood, it was in every cell, in every nerve, in every breath of his body. It would take more than a failed knight with an actively fighting fate to finish *him* off.

The combination of pain and drugs was dizzying. His head reeled and his body protested even the slightest of movements. Under the covers lay bandages and under the bandages lay burns. The skin on his chest was seared like a piece of meat. It would take weeks, even months, to recover. Still there were options. He might be weak, but his powers of sorcery were already recovering. The drawing he performed last night was nothing: a tangent sent out to divert, a tilt upon a table. As long as he didn't do anything too physical, too challenging, he might still draw upon his source.

There were certain techniques that he'd learned in the wild expanse of the Great Plains. Techniques that specialized in using a person's life force as a stepping stone to recovery. A gentle drawing was all that was needed. The victim provided his own fuel. It had to be done; he could not afford to spend the next few months confined to a sickbed like an invalid. He needed new skin for his chest.

"Inform the lady I cannot see her now, Crope," said Baralis softly. "Tell her I beg her forgiveness but I am . . ." He thought for a moment. Was it better to hide his weakness, or was there more profit to be gained from playing the martyr? ". . . too ill to receive visitors." Catherine might emerge more pliable after she'd stewed a while in her own guilty juices.

"But, master, it is the duke's daughter," said Crope, obviously worried about turning away such an elevated visitor.

"Send her away." Yes, let her sit and worry for a while. She would be most anxious that he not reveal last night's little episode to her father. After all, there could be only one reason why she wanted the duke's champion to win the fight. Sweet Catherine was not as innocent as she looked. Baralis managed a wisp of a smile. Things may have turned out for the best: he now had a measure of power over the duke's daughter. The fact that she had turned up at his chambers so early in the morning was a sure sign that she was worried he might use it.

Crope returned. Every heavy step reverberated in the tender tissue of Baralis' chest. "She has gone, master, but she begged me . . ." the huge giant struggled over the exact wording ". . . she begged me to give you her deepest sympathy."

"Good." He had expected no less. A fit of coughing wracked his already frail body. The pain was distant, like a scene viewed through mist.

Although the drugs were strong, they could only mask, not heal. There was so much to be done; the betrothal was due to be finalized, the marriage date had not been set, the court of Bren was still nervous of the match, and at any moment Kylock could take it into his head to invade Halcus and put everything in jeopardy. Now more than ever he needed to be fit to fight.

Baralis cursed the knight. Any one else would have succumbed to the drawing, either that or sent it back in its original amateurish form. Absorbing such a blow would have left Baralis with nothing more than a headache and a mild chest pain. Instead he'd ended up with a section of skin burnt from his body. When he'd watched the man die in Hanatta, the original drawing had been strong and true; not so with Catherine's feeble attempt. The knight must have a strong fate indeed to send it back with such force. It suddenly occurred to Baralis that he didn't know the outcome of the fight.

"Crope," he called, too weak to raise his voice above a whisper. "Who won the fight last night?"

"The knight did, master. Blayze was beaten good and proper." Crope smiled, pleased to be a source of information. He busied himself preparing a mixture of wine fortified with herbs. For the first time Baralis realized that his servant had probably been awake all through the night tending him.

"Go take some rest, Crope," he said.

The man shook his head adamantly. "No, master. I stay here until you're better."

"Very well, but you must sleep later. Tomorrow I will need your special help." If he was going to perform a quick healing, he would need Crope to find him a victim. It could wait for a day, though; he was not strong enough just yet to perform the necessary drawing.

Baralis' thoughts returned to the knight. "How did the duke react when his champion lost?"

"He made the knight his new champion on the spot."

A small piece of the puzzle fell into place: the knight was obviously fated to be the defender of the duke's heir. He would need watching. Who could tell what part he might have to play? Baralis tried to keep his mind focused. His job was to search out anyone or anything that might have some bearing on what was to come. He cast his thoughts back to the instant when the power had hit him. The memory was fire and brimstone, yet amidst the pain something was revealed: a glimpse of the man who had shaped the sending. Every hair on Baralis' body prickled against the sheets. Powerful people were involved in the knight's fate. Tavalisk, Larn, Bevlin. The three emerged like ghosts from the backlash.

What did it mean? Bevlin was a name he hadn't heard in over ten years; a mystic who spent his days sifting through old prophesies and predicting doom with spiteful glee. Larn, a place of power and seering; and lastly Tavalisk, the greatest mischief-maker in the Known Lands. How did they all fit in with the knight?

Baralis shifted impatiently against the sheets. He needed to be well; people needed contacting, motives had to be discovered. Nothing could be left to chance. Never in his life had he felt so frustrated. The only thing he could do today was rest. How he despised his own frailty. "Bring me the red-stoppered jar," he called to Crope. In it was his most potent sleeping draught; if he couldn't act, then he might as well be insensible to the world. When he next woke up, he would be stronger, able to work as well as think. His hand trembled as he brought the jar to his lips. Never had there been so much for him to do.

Melli had found a large beetle scurrying across the floor of her room and was busy making its life miserable. She was decidedly bored. What had her life come to when the only way of passing the time was to torment a poor unsuspecting insect? There was always eating, of course. She let the beetle scurry off and turned her attention to the breakfast tray. The bacon and sausages had all been eaten while hot, and only cold roast fowl remained. That and some rather soft and yeasty-tasting bread. The jug of wine was well watered, so there was little chance of getting drunk to relieve the tedium. All in all, it was not a very appetizing selection. The kitchens of Bren were sadly lacking in creativity.

So was the person who'd furnished her room: bare stone walls and floors, a bed, a chest, a mirror, and a washstand. From the circular sweep of the walls, Melli judged that she was in a tower, or a turret. There was a high, narrow window, but the view was of nothing but sky.

Tearing off a chunk of the loaf, Melli fell back on the bed and began to chew on the moist and doughy bread. Last night had proven quite entertaining, indeed. The duke had not been what she expected. He was arrogant, yes, but also rather interesting. She liked the way he dressed plainly, not indulging himself in satins and silks. Growing up with her father, Melli had grown used to men who spent as much time and money on their appearances as the greatest of court beauties. In fact, all of Queen Arinalda's court had been centered around the importance of show. Not so with Bren. The duke didn't seem interested in finery. His clothes were plain, his rooms were bare, and if the food was anything to go by, his staff was not chosen for their skills at the hearth.

Melli had to admit that she was a little impressed with his knowledge of the kingdoms, and perhaps a little intimidated, too. With all his charts and lists, he had been like a merchant keeping stock of his assets. He was obviously expecting to take the leading role in the alliance. And he was the sort of man who got what he expected.

The bolt whirred softly and then the door swung open. "Quite an appetite, I see," said the duke.

Melli, who had been lying spread-eagled on the bed, scrambled to compose herself. In the split second that it took her to sit up, surprise turned to indignation. "How dare you walk in here unannounced!" she cried. Her words were not quite as cutting as she hoped due to the mouthful of bread she was still chewing.

"I dare because I own this palace and all that is in it, including you, my lady of Deepwood."

"Is paying the only way you can get a woman?" Melli was up off the bed in an instant—if he was going to slap her this time, she was not going to make it easy by being a sitting target.

"I see a good night's rest has failed to mellow your tongue." The duke was cool, perhaps even a little amused. It was difficult to tell.

"I see a good night's rest has failed to improve your manners." Now that she had recovered from the shock of him actually visiting her, Melli was beginning to feel rather exhilarated. It was a welcome change from taunting beetles. "To what do I owe this pleasure? Have you come here to interrogate me about my homeland? Perhaps I know the locations of some forests you failed to circle."

The duke smiled. "I doubt it." He walked into the room. Although not a large man, his presence seemed to fill the remaining space. Melli felt as if she could barely move without touching him. "I have come to apologize."

Melli actually laughed. The idea of this imperious, unemotional man apologizing to her seemed ludicrous. "For slapping me, I suppose?"

"No, you deserved that. I came to apologize for dismissing you so abruptly, especially after you appeared to be taken ill."

Taken ill? Melli was confused for a moment, until she realized he was referring to the few minutes that she'd spent fighting off the fore-telling. The sight of her grabbing hold of the desk for support must have been a little strange, to say the least. Melli tried to play the incident down.

"I was tired, nothing more."

"Aah," said the duke. "If I remember correctly, your tiredness came on just after the mention of Bren's armies."

"Did it? I really can't recall." Melli didn't like the way the subject was progressing. "Anyway, I accept your apology. Though I think you owe me another one for barging in here without as much as a knock to reveal your approach." The apology was just an excuse, she was certain of it. The duke didn't strike her as a man who would waste his breath on such a trifle.

"A second apology is out of the question," he said. "I rarely have cause to regret my actions." His hand rested on the hilt of his sword. It seemed strange that a man would wear such a keen blade and not shield it with a scabbard, unless, of course, his aim was to intimidate. The duke looked around the room. "Bailor told me that you asked if you could take a walk in the grounds."

"And if I did?"

"Tomorrow I will be leaving for my hunting lodge in the mountains. You will accompany me."

Melli didn't know whether to be annoyed at his arrogance, or excited by the prospect of leaving the palace. Before she had a chance to decide how to react, the duke made his way to the door.

He bowed—a curt, soldierly gesture. "Until tomorrow," he said, and then left.

The jug of wine was in her hand before the bolt had been fully drawn. Watered or not, she needed a drink. It was without a doubt the most insipid mix she'd ever tasted, and it required a good half a jug to produce any effects.

What was the man up to? An apology? Very unlikely. He had just ordered her to accompany him on a trip; if courtesy was his motive, then he surely would have taken the trouble to veil the order in the polite guise of an invitation. No. The good duke had another motive, and as the wine slowly worked its way into her bloodstream, warming her skin and loosening her thoughts, she began to realize what it was.

A knock preceded the second drawing of the bolt. In walked Bailor. Melli didn't feel inclined to right herself this time. Instead, she lounged on the bed, pouring the last of the wine into her cup.

Bailor looked a little saddened at what he saw. "A pretty girl like yourself shouldn't be drinking so much before noon."

"Your concern touches me deeply," Melli said. "I'm sure the wine which accompanies my next tray will owe a greater debt to the well rather than the vintner."

Ignoring what she said, Bailor began to pace around the room. He was wearing a rather fine robe in green silk and it flapped behind him like a broken wing. "The duke appears quite taken with you, my dear."

Melli looked Bailor straight in the eye and said, "I know." It was the only possible explanation for the lame excuse and the trip to the hunting lodge. Why hadn't it occurred to her sooner? At Castle Harvell she had grown accustomed to the attentions of men, why should Bren, or for that matter, its duke, be any different?

"He summoned me to an audience only this morning," Bailor continued, rubbing his hands together in excitement, "asking about you. Who you are, where you came from. I wouldn't be surprised if he called for you again today."

"He just left."

Bailor's already prominent eyes bulged further. "He came here!"

"Yes," said Melli with a casual shrug. She was beginning to enjoy herself. "He just came by to invite me to his hunting lodge in the mountains."

"The lodge!" Bailor uttered the words as if he were referring to a holy temple. "His Grace never invites women to the lodge." He took the jug from the table and raised it to his lips before realizing it was empty. "What did he say to you?"

"First of all he apologized for his rudeness—"

"Borc spare us all!" Bailor had actually joined her on the bed and began to fan himself with the corner of his robe. "The duke never apologizes. What have you done to him? Are you a witch?"

Melli laughed; she was beginning to like Bailor a lot more now that his demeanor was less detached. She handed him her cup. There was still a little wine at the bottom. He took it from her and downed it in one go.

"The duke is due to leave first thing in the morning. You must have some suitable clothes. I will send for Veena. Do you ride?"

"Of course."

"Good, good. Do you hunt, by any chance?"

How could the daughter of the greatest huntsman in the kingdoms not hunt? It was a point of pride to Maybor that all his sons and even his daughter were chasing boars before other children had learned how to sit a horse. "I have hunted once or twice. But surely there will be little game in the mountains?"

"The lodge is on a slope forming part of a mighty valley. There is a lake and many animals gather there to drink: bears, mountain lions, deer."

"Who else is going?"

"Not many, I think. It will only be a short trip—two or three days at the most. You will obviously be expected to keep a low profile. The duke does not like to draw attention to his personal affairs."

"I doubt if I'll be hunting, then." Melli was disappointed. It had been a long time since she last knew the thrill of the chase.

Bailor stood up. "Hmm, perhaps he may be a little less guarded without the eyes of the court upon him. There's no way of knowing, as he's never taken a lady to his lodge before. Either way, I will make sure that he knows you can hunt. It will certainly come as a pleasant surprise to him."

Melli realized that she had gone up in value in Bailor's eyes. The man was almost skipping around the room. She would have liked to ask him about the location of the lodge, but thought it best to hold her tongue. Bailor was no fool; he would be quick to guess her motives. Instead, she asked, "What else did the duke want to know about me?"

"He asked about your parents, who your father was, how you came to my attention, that sort of thing."

Checking out her story. "And he never normally inquires about his purchases?"

"Very rarely. It is a great honor to be singled out by him."

Try as she might, Melli couldn't quite keep the sneer from her lips. She was daughter of the wealthiest lord in the kingdoms, nearly betrothed to a prince. The honor of being the duke's latest dalliance was a dubious one at best.

"Well, I must be on my way," said Bailor. "I will see that Veena brings you all you need." He looked almost too happy, and a thought occurred to Melli. "Does the duke have other women?"

"He is a man with strong physical needs."

"What becomes of the women he is no longer interested in?"

"Several things. Some of them are sold again, a couple stay on in the palace as ladies maids, and a few are given the freedom to go where they please."

"Yet first they go to you?" Melli took the fact that Bailor couldn't meet her eye as confirmation. "Tell me, has the duke just bid farewell to his previous favorite?"

"Earlier this morning he did express the wish that he had no desire to see Shanella again." Bailor was clearly uncomfortable, as he brought the subject round to her again. "Another good sign for you, Melli, my dear."

"Not a bad one for you, either, Bailor," said Melli as he closed the door.

Seventeen

*N*abber hated mornings. The earlier in the morning, the more he hated it. As a pocket it was his time-honored duty to be up and about for the dawn markets, but never once in all his years of prospecting could he truthfully say that he'd enjoyed being up with the lark. Now, stuck in this dungeon of a palace, in a room close to the kitchens and the brewery, with an ear-splitting array of noises going in the background, and little chance of slipping out for a healthy spot of pocketing, he hated mornings more than ever.

There was only one reason why he was putting up with such unpromising conditions: they were better for Tawl. There were physicians here; one had cauterized and bandaged Tawl's chest wound, another had dressed the burn on his arm with a cooling herbal poultice. A third man had given him a sleeping draught that had kept him unconscious for nearly a full day, and a pretty maid kept bringing food and ale to fortify the patient's strength. Not that Tawl got to see much of the ale, though. Well, a pocket had to have some compensations to make up for the boredom.

The knight was sleeping now; it was probably for the best. The burn, the poison, the wound, and the fight had all taken their various tolls, and his body needed rest more than the cleverest of potions.

If rest was what he was getting. Nabber had been awakened several times in the night by Tawl crying out in his sleep. He mumbled words in a foreign tongue, called out two names that sounded like Anna and Sara, and once, when the night was at its darkest, his whole body was racked with silent sobs. Nabber had sat beside him on the bed, put his arms around Tawl's shoulders, and stayed with him until the sobbing stopped.

Dawn slipped through the room like a thief, stealing the shadows from the corners and overpowering the light from the candles. Judging from the noise, the palace staff had been up for some hours. The smells of fermenting hops and freshly baked bread vied for the nostrils, and heat from the great ovens warmed the air like a long-lit fire.

They had been brought here just after Tawl had sworn his oath. The knight had started to stumble away from the court enclosure, blind to all who were watching, blood soaking through his makeshift bandage. The duke made a small gesture with his arm and a man had stepped forward. Dressed in loose silks that didn't quite succeed in hiding his huge belly, he was most insistent that the knight accompany him to the palace. Tawl didn't have the strength to put up a fight. He let himself be led away. The fat man had no interest in Nabber, but by adamantly refusing to let Tawl out of his sight and threatening to scream at the top of his lungs if he was crossed, Nabber succeeded in having himself included in the invitation.

So here they were, guests of the good duke himself. It was an improvement on the stables—anyplace that didn't contain horses was better than *there*—but it was sorely lacking in profit potential. Ever since he'd left his sack at Madame Thornypurse's, Nabber's mind had been on his contingency, or rather his sad lack of it. He needed to be out doing business, filling his empty coffers, and helping Bren's cash to circulate properly.

The palace was probably full to the rafters with loot, but the snag was the guest obligation. You couldn't rob from your host; it just wasn't honorable. Swift, who himself had played host to many fellow villains in his time, had warned Nabber most strongly about the sacred bond between guest and host: *"You can drink him dry, insult his good name, and even rollick his wife, but you must never, ever, steal from your host."* It was a touching sentiment and one that never failed to bring a lump to Nabber's throat. Robbing from the palace, therefore, was out of the question.

If he'd been here under another pretext, it would have been a different matter altogether. Nabber scratched his chin as a rather sneaky possibility occurred to him. Swift had never mentioned anything about taking a nosy around your host's abode to see where he kept his valuables. No, there was definitely no rule to cover that one. Perhaps later he might do a little reconnaissance, purely out of professional interest, of course, nothing more. A man could learn a lot from a casual stroll past a strong room.

Nabber was interrupted from his reverie by the door being flung open. A young woman stood in the doorway. It was the same one who had begged him to stop the fight two nights back: the girl in the portrait. She saw Tawl lying asleep on the bed and walked into the room, closing the door behind her. As she came closer, Nabber saw that there were tears streaming down her face. "How is he?" she demanded.

Nabber brushed down his tunic and slicked back his hair. Judging by the way she was dressed, she was a great lady indeed. The other night she had been wearing a plain wool cloak; today she wore satin and pearls. "Not well, miss. He slept all of yesterday."

A small, anguished sound escaped from her lips. She lunged toward Tawl. It took Nabber a second to realize that the object that glinted in her hand was a dagger. Quick as a flash, Nabber sped to meet her. He grabbed hold of her wrist and forced the blade from her grip. Her breath smelled of brandy, and there was a stain running down the front of her dress. Her muscles had no strength to fight him. Bursting into a fresh rush of tears, she mumbled over and over again, "I hate him, I hate him."

Nabber had a good idea of what must've happened: Blayze had probably died.

After a moment the girl seemed to pull herself together. She wiped the tears from her eyes with the sleeve of her dress and crossed the remaining distance to Tawl's bed. Nabber watched her warily, ready to spring if she tried to harm him in any way. She shook the knight's shoulder. Tawl's eyes opened. The legacy of the sleeping draught could clearly be seen in his slowly focusing gaze. Drawing her face breath-close to his, she whispered softly, "I will see you dead for what you did the other night."

Nabber held his breath. Tawl looked into the eyes of the girl. "I am already damned, my lady," he said. "Death can only bring me peace."

The girl spat on him.

Nabber caught hold of her arm. "Leave him alone, he's been through enough," he cried, trying to pull her away.

She shook herself free of his grip and turned back to face the knight. "You have not seen the last of me, Tawl of the Lowlands." The words chilled Nabber to the bone. She stood for a moment, trembling with the force of her own hate, and then swung around and stalked out of the room.

Tawl sat up slowly. He brought his feet to the floor and pushed back the covers. "In Borc's name, what have I done?" he said.

Nabber could think of no reply. There was no explanation. Tawl had beaten a man to the point of death and sworn an oath that he had not been free to swear. Nabber didn't know much about the Knights of Valdis, but he knew that Tawl must have broken some terrible law by vowing to be the duke's champion. He had forsaken the knighthood and there was no going back. Nabber wished with all his heart that the fight had never been fought.

The door opened for a second time—did no one knock in Bren? In walked the duke himself. His lean body was cloaked, ready for a journey. His face was cold and unreadable. "What was my daughter doing here?"

Nabber hid his surprise well. *The duke's daughter?* That was certainly unexpected. Before he could think of anything to say, Tawl stepped in.

"She came here to inquire about my health," he said.

He should have expected no less. Even now, with his ties to Valdis newly broken, Tawl still had the instincts of a knight: gallantry, protectiveness, a lady's honor to be saved at all cost. For some reason Nabber felt his spirits picking up.

The duke seemed to accept this explanation. "And how *is* your health?"

"Better for the skill of your physicians."

"Good." The duke turned his back to the wall. "You fought hard the other night. More than anything else, I admire a man who refuses to give in to defeat."

"Blayze was a worthy opponent."

"Yes, he served me well. He died early this morning. It is fitting that he is gone; there would have been no future for him here. Bren does not look upon failure lightly." The duke was silent a moment, his gaze cast down to the floor. "I admit that I was reluctant to take your oath, but now I see that it was for the best. You won. You are the better man." He spun around to face Tawl. "I will never ask you why you left the knighthood, but hear this: your first loyalty is now to me, and I will be no cheap second to Valdis."

"My oath stands. I am yours to command." Tawl's voice was firm and true.

"I am well pleased," said the duke. "Now, I am about to leave for a short hunting trip. When I return I expect to find you ready to take your place at my side."

"It will be so."

The duke held out his hand and Tawl clasped it. The two stood together for a moment, and then the duke turned and left.

For the first time since he'd come to Bren, Nabber began to think that there was hope for his friend. It had been a long time since he'd last seen Tawl so resolute.

Maybor knocked at Baralis' door. He was due to accompany the duke on a hunting trip to the mountains and was therefore anxious to do two things: first, he wanted to make sure that Baralis had not had a miraculous recovery in the night; and second, if the king's chancellor did come round, he wanted him to be made aware of the fact that the duke had issued him a grave insult. No exclusive mountain trip for Baralis, not even an invitation.

Receiving no reply, Maybor knocked again. It really was quite delicious. *"Just a few trusted companions and myself,"* the duke had said. He, Maybor, had been honored amongst the few. Baralis, in turn, had been dishonored by the omission. Maybor considered it his duty to deliver the cutting blow. Too bad it wouldn't be a fatal one.

A couple of days hunting was just what he needed. Fresh air in his lungs, a fine mount between his thighs, and a well-tooled spear in his hand. It was the perfect chance to show off his skill at the chase. Just yesterday his new wardrobe had been delivered from the tailors; it boasted a fine selection of cloaks and tunics that were sure to impress all who looked upon them. The hunting trip would be a great personal success.

He was anxious to get a look at some mountain game, as well. The kingdoms didn't have anything as exciting as mountain lions. He certainly hoped it wasn't too early in spring for them.

Where was that imbecile Crope? One final knock, and if there was no answer this time he was going in.

The door swung open and the great man's servant answered. He was holding a pot in one hand and what looked to be a linen undershirt in the other. Maybor had dealt with Crope in the past and knew that there was little point in trying to force his way through. "How is your master?" he demanded.

"Sleeping."

"No, you idiot, I want to know how he is."

"He is sleeping."

Maybor was coming close to losing his temper. He spoke very loudly, as if talking to the deaf. "I want to know if there has been any improvement in your master's health."

"He has been sleeping since yesterday morning."

Borc, but the man was ugly! His face was as slack as a drawstring purse, his eyes were beady and close, his whiskers were the size of matching broomheads, and his nasal hair was a startling shade of red. Specimens like him should be strangled at birth. "What happened to your master on the night of the fight? What made him collapse?"

Crope considered for a moment. "He was taken ill, sir."

He was stupid as well as ugly. There was little point in pursuing the subject any further. Crope was too well trained to give anything away. "If your master awakes, inform him that, unlike myself, he was not invited to hunt with the duke at his private lodge in the mountains. Have you got that?"

"Yes."

"Repeat it back to me." Maybor listened as Crope recited the sentence back to him. "Good. Be sure he gets the message." He turned and was just about to walk away when an idea came to him. "Is that your master's?" he demanded, pointing to the linen shift Crope was holding. As soon as the man nodded, Maybor leapt forward and grabbed it from him. Taken by surprise, Crope had no chance to stop him. Maybor smiled triumphantly at the bewildered servant and then began to walk away.

He tucked the shift in his tunic and pondered on what little he had learned from Crope. If Baralis had been sleeping all day, then the illness must be serious indeed. Knowing the king's chancellor, though, he wasn't about to die from it. His scrawny neck was too durable by far. Maybor wrapped his hands in his cloak as he made his way through the damp north wing. There had to be some way to get to the man. Baralis couldn't be allowed to continue ruining his prospects and humiliating him in public. There was a growing list of debts that needed repaying: several attempts on his life, the death of his horse, the thwarting of his ambitions and, lastly, the disappearance of his daughter.

Maybor felt a tightness in his throat and slowed down his step. What had become of Melliandra? His precious, beautiful jewel. He had been a fool. He should never have tried to force her to marry Kylock. She was headstrong and stubborn and proud—just like himself—and he should have handled the situation differently. Maybor stopped by an arrow loop and stared out onto the calm gray waters of the Great Lake. Where was she? Probably somewhere far away, frightened to come forward because she feared his wrath. Traff was supposed to be looking for her, but Maybor wasn't sure that he wanted his daughter to be found by Baralis' ex-mercenary. The man was dangerous, unpredictable, and he believed that Melliandra was now his property.

How could he have promised his daughter's hand in marriage to a

mercenary? Maybor leaned heavily against the wet stone wall as he realized the full extent of his stupidity. It was all Baralis' fault; once that man
had started scheming, nothing else had mattered but beating him at his
own game. What a mess he'd made of everything!

Self-recrimination was a new and painful experience for Maybor. He
was not a man given to looking inward: action was what counted. An idea
occurred to him: he would write to Kedrac and have him send messages
out to every town and village in the Four Kingdoms. He would offer a
reward of five hundred golds for information leading to his daughter's
recovery. No, he could do more than that; he would issue a public declaration, forgiving Melliandra for her disobedience and promising that if she
were to come forward she would be received once more into the loving
bosom of her family.

Maybor's mind was racing; he would send the letter this day. He was
determined to have his daughter back. She might not marry a king, but
there were plenty of rich nobles here in Bren who would be pleased to
have her. He could see her now: her blue eyes dark and fiery, her skin as
pale as snow. Oh, she was a beauty, no doubt about it. After all, she'd been
lucky enough to take after him, not her mother.

Having decided upon a course of action, Maybor could barely contain
his excitement. Melliandra would be safely back at Castle Harvell within
a matter of weeks. His step was light and he hummed a jaunty tune, the
words of which had long eluded him. It was still early morning; if he hurried, he could get the letter written and sent before he left for the hunt.

Just as he was about to enter his chambers, someone cut in front of
him. "Lord Maybor, may I have a word?"

It was Lord Cravin, the man who had sat beside him at the welcoming banquet. "Certainly. Step inside my chambers."

Cravin shook his head. "No. I would prefer it if you would walk with
me for a minute."

That was telling. Obviously Castle Harvell wasn't the only place
where the walls had ears. Maybor nodded briefly, enjoying his sudden fall
into the silk-lined pit of intrigue.

Cravin led the way. He was a distinguished-looking man. Like the
duke, his nose was finely hooked. There was gray at his temples and his
hair was cut close to the skull. Only when they reached a discreet tree-
lined forecourt did he deem it fitting to speak. "The duke will be leaving
the city for the next few days. I hear you are to accompany him?"

"And if I am?"

" 'Twould be better if you stayed. There is bigger game to be had, here, in the palace."

"Meaning?"

"With the duke away, we can talk freely. It is time we discussed our mutual interests."

This was a dilemma for Maybor: he loved hunting. "Can we not talk on my return?"

"You can talk all you like," said Cravin. "I, however, would never be foolish enough to say anything if I thought there was a chance that it could find its way into the duke's ear."

"To cancel my trip now may offend His Grace." Maybor was tempted by the idea of secret liaisons and plotting, but he was even more tempted by the idea of ingratiating himself with the duke. A few good hunts' worth of shared danger and they'd be friends for life.

"The duke will not notice your absence. His eye is on more unpredictable game than mountain lions."

"Women?" Maybor could barely keep the longing from his voice. It had been a long time since he'd last felt the rounded belly of a well-proportioned wench. He had no idea how a man went about procuring women in a foreign city. All the serving girls he'd seen were either too old or too skinny.

"One woman in particular. I hear the duke's latest dalliance has stirred his jaded fancy." Cravin's eyes narrowed. "Have you a wish for a little feminine comfort yourself, Lord Maybor?"

"I am a man of considerable appetites."

"I could send several young ladies to your chamber tonight."

That certainly shifted the balance. Hunting could wait. Right now the thought of a good bedding was much more appealing. "I will send my regrets to the duke. I feel a slight fever coming on."

Cravin bowed his head. "I will contact you in due course."

"Until then." Maybor returned the bow, and then as an afterthought he added, "Be sure to send the women all at once."

Acknowledging the request with the coolest of smiles, Cravin turned and set a course for the palace.

Maybor stood for a moment in the forecourt. The breeze from the lake was sharp but not cold. Things were getting interesting. He'd go back to his chambers, write a letter to his son concerning Melliandra, take a short nap to recover his strength, and then prepare for a night of lustful diversions. Intrigue would merely be spice for the joint.

As he made his way back to his chambers, Maybor remembered the bulge in his tunic: Baralis' undershirt. He smiled broadly. There'd be mischief as well as merriment.

Despite her determination to be disdainful of new clothes, Melli couldn't quite help admiring herself in the mirror. She had to admit that the color and style suited her rather well. Blue had long been her favorite color, and the embroidery which chased along the hem of the dress was beautiful to behold. Seashells and starfish swam amongst a sea of silken thread. The work was obviously done in Toolay, so it must have cost a pretty penny indeed. Bailor was sparing no expense.

There was one problem with her new dress, though: its soft bodice made it difficult to conceal her knife. Melli sat down on the edge of the bed. Did she really need a weapon? The situation she now found herself in was so much different than she imagined. In many ways there seemed to be less danger. Although the duke was a powerful man, she couldn't imagine him trying to force himself upon her. Surely he was too honorable for that? But then, Edrad at the inn in Duvitt had seemed like an honorable man, too. Melli began to bind the blade of the knife with a length of cloth. It was better to take no chances.

The old woman who lived on a pig farm, and whose name they never knew, had given her this knife. As long as she had it, Melli felt safe. By now, it was more like a talisman than a weapon.

She tucked the sheathed blade in her bodice and tried to position it where it would attract the least attention. For the first time in her life, Melli wished that she had a larger chest. Lady Helliarna's daughter, Carinnela, had breasts the size of serving platters. She could probably conceal an entire armory down *her* bodice!

A soft knock was followed by the entrance of Bailor. He smiled broadly. "Good morning, my dear."

Melli couldn't help but smile back. He looked quite dazzling in his latest robe: a fully sheened silk of burnished gold. She could see her face in the fabric that stretched across his belly.

"A fine dawn this morning, my dear. It promises to be a perfect day for travel." He reached over and patted her shoulder. "And you are looking quite lovely, I see."

"So are you, Bailor."

He seemed well pleased at the compliment. "Why, thank you, my dear. The silk came all the way from Isro." Sucking in his belly a little for good measure, he briefly checked his reflection in the mirror.

Melli found herself liking Bailor; he always seemed in good spirits and he treated her kindly when he had no reason to. "To what do I owe this pleasure?"

"His Grace awaits."

She had expected his answer, but it still sent a chill up her spine. The next few days would change her life, she was certain of it. She might escape from the duke, murder him, run into a long lost friend of her father's, or even *talk* her way to freedom. Anything could happen. And, as Melli fastened the pin on her cloak and went down to meet the duke, she prayed it would be for the best.

Tarissa was vicious. She fought dirty and she wasn't above using her feminine charms to her advantage. She and Jack were in the south field, and they were sparring with short blades. This was the first time Jack had ever fought with Tarissa, and he'd made the grave mistake of making allowances because she was a girl. Her calluses were earned with blood. And judging from the wicked slash she'd just delivered to his wrist, she would soon be sporting a few more in his honor.

Tarissa flashed a tremulous, worried smile. Jack, who was on the offensive, felt sorry for her and began to back away. It was a mistake and he was annoyed with himself for not realizing it sooner. Tarissa was in like lightning. A sharp blow to his already injured wrist, and his blade was in the air before he knew it. Tarissa sprang forward like a cat and caught the knife by its handle before it reached the ground.

"Ha!" she cried from the mud. "Ha!"

The sight of her triumphant grin was the most annoying and the most exquisite thing he'd ever seen in his life.

"So Rovas thinks you're ready, eh?" she said, waving his knife in his face. "Let's hope there are no women in the garrison. You're a fool as far as helpless damsels go."

Jack joined her in the mud. "A fool, am I?" With a quick sweep of his left hand, he disarmed Tarissa of both knives and then quickly pinned her to the ground. "Act helpless now."

Tarissa pursed her lips as an invitation to a kiss. There was no way he could resist her, and he leaned forward to meet her lips. The next thing he knew she had her hand on his throat. "Don't think I need to, do I?"

They rolled and kicked in the mud, laughing and pinching and trying to pull each other's shoes off. This was the first time they had been alone in two days and Jack was relishing every minute of it.

Rovas had left for market an hour back and Magra, busy with spring cleaning, had given her permission for them to take a short walk together. Earlier, as they had walked hand in hand to the practice field, Jack decided he would not mention what had happened between them the other night unless Tarissa brought up the subject first.

Scrambling up from the ground, Tarissa offered her hand. "Come on," she said. "It's time we got cleaned up."

At first Jack thought they would head back to the cottage, but Tarissa skimmed past the building and led him down the back and through the trees. The earth was soft underfoot. The past few days had been warm enough to melt much of the snow and the soil had drunk itself sodden. A slight breeze cut past their faces, but it wasn't enough to dry the mud on their cheeks.

"Down here," said Tarissa as she pushed through some bushes and slid down a rocky embankment. Jack followed her. At the bottom of the incline was a stream that broke into a waterfall and then formed a pool of the clearest, brightest water he had ever seen. Snow still lay white in the shadows, but the water's edge was ringed in green and yellow. Daffodils, golden and glorious, swayed softly on the breeze.

"Isn't it beautiful?"

"Perfect," said Jack.

The water played lightly on the rocks, dancing and tinkling and flashing like crystal. Two willows trailed their naked branches into the pool, and somewhere in the undergrowth the first courting calls of spring could be heard.

Tarissa took Jack's hand and led him to the water's edge. She slipped off her shoes and dipped a toe in the water. Pulling a face, she quickly withdrew. "It's colder than it looks." The light reflecting from the water's surface sparkled upon her features. There was gold to match the daffodils in the hazel of her eyes. A streak of dirt rested upon the curve of her cheek. Jack pulled off his waistcoat and plunged it into the water. Wringing it out, he raised the damp cloth to her face. Gently, he began to rub the mud from her cheek. Tarissa's skin was as smooth and warm as brass about a lantern, and the mark came off with the lightest of touches. Next he moved to her hands, spreading out her fingers to reach the soil that hid between. Every so often, he would pause and dip the waistcoat in the water to wash away the dirt. Lastly, he came to her legs. He drew her dress up to her knees and ran the cloth down the length of her calf. Ankles, toes, and arches were cleaned with tender care. He didn't stop until every last speck of dirt was gone.

Jack looked up to see that Tarissa had tears in her eyes. "What's the matter?" he asked.

"I'm sorry, Jack."

"For what?"

She didn't reply. She reached out to kiss him instead. Jack tasted the salt tears on her lips. What did she have to be sorry about? He didn't understand. The memory of the other evening flashed through Jack's mind and he was helpless to stop it. All questions faded into insignificance as she moved her body closer. His hands encircled her waist. The flesh to either side was the most tempting of distractions.

A second later she pulled away. Jack got the distinct impression that he'd just fallen victim to another of Tarissa's fighting feints.

"What was Melli to you?" she asked, diverting his thoughts a second time.

Jack thought for a moment, and then said, "She was a friend."

"And she was running away, too?"

How was Tarissa able to guess so much? He hadn't told her he was running away. He was surprised at the turn the conversation was taking. Why in this beautiful, intimate place did Tarissa choose to talk about the past? "We were both afraid of what would become of us if we stayed in Castle Harvell." He didn't want to lie to her, but wasn't ready to tell the truth, either.

"Was it something to do with what happened to you the other day, when you came in the cottage and collapsed by the fire?" Tarissa took his hand and drew it to her lap. "Jack, I know that you're different from other people. That much has been obvious ever since you made the shelf fall into the fire. Why can't you tell me about yourself? Is the truth so damning?"

Jack leaned over the edge of the pool. Two faces were reflected upon the water's surface. It took a split second to discern which one was his. Under the gentle light of the shaded grove, both faces looked the same. Suddenly he knew he could tell her anything. He felt closer to Tarissa than anyone else. She was generous and kind; he could trust his secrets with her.

"One morning, many months ago now, I burnt the first batch of morning loaves. I was frantic—the master baker has beaten the hides off boys for less. I felt a pain in my head, and the next thing I knew, I was lying on the ground and the loaves were no longer burnt, just browning." Jack looked up to check on how Tarissa was taking the story. She smiled a soft encouragement. He continued:

"It was sorcery, so I had no choice but to leave the castle. I couldn't risk being stoned." There was more to tell, and Tarissa knew it; she left the silence for him to fill.

"For months now I've felt as if I were being pulled along. Forced into situations where I had little control, taking steps that I felt weren't mine to choose. Something was drawing me forward, but I don't know why, or where I was headed. When Rovas told that there was a chance Halcus might go to war against Bren, something snapped inside of me. I wanted to put down everything and dash away to where the action was. The other day when I got ill, Rovas said something about an empire of blood—" Jack hesitated for a moment; even now the words still haunted him. "Tarissa, when I heard him say it, it was like a blade in my soul. My legs gave way, the world seemed to crowd around me. I thought I was going mad."

He was shaking now, the memory almost more than he could bare. "I felt as if I was being punished for failing to understand."

"Failing to understand what?" Tarissa asked.

Jack managed a wiry smile. "I don't know. Perhaps I was meant to play a part in the war."

"*Was* meant to?"

Tarissa was quick, more than a match for him; she'd put her finger on the heart of the matter. "Yes. *Was* meant to. Something happened to me the other night, I don't know what, but I feel free now. It's as if I've been living with my hands tied behind my back and suddenly the ties have been cut."

"That was the night I came to you." It was not a question.

"I don't know what I would have done without you," said Jack. He caught hold of Tarissa's hand and brought her fingers to his lips. "You saved me that night. Whoever cut the ties left me with an open wound, and you were there to stop the bleeding. I will never forget what you did. Never."

Tarissa leaned forward and kissed his forehead. "I would do anything for you."

Hearing those words, Jack understood the meaning of truth and friendship. There was not a doubt in his mind: she *would* do anything for him. And he would do anything for her. Jack realized he loved the chestnut-haired girl at his side. He brought her close and held her until the willows cast their shadows into the pool.

The day was drawing to a close by the time they headed back. It was cold now and the breeze was trying hard to be a wind. The lights from the cottage could be seen in the distance, and both of them were reluctant to reach their destination. Tarissa had her arm through his and every couple of steps they would pause for kissing.

"Now that you're free to do as you please," she said, "what will you do?"

This was a subject that had been on Jack's mind constantly for the past two days. There was only one thing he was certain of: Tarissa had to come with him no matter what he did. He had come to the cottage with two skills to his name—baking and scribing—and he would leave with a third: fighting. Somehow among the three he should be able to make a living for Tarissa and himself. The question was, where to start from? He would never go back to the kingdoms, and he now had no desire to see the city of his dreams. So Bren was not an option. Despite his stay here, Halcus was, and always would be, enemy territory. That left Annis and Highwall.

Highwall was a fortress city. Named for the size of its battlements, it was almost a match for its greatest rival, Bren. It was famous for producing the best weapons in the north and the skill of its engineers was legendary. If war was coming, then Highwall would be certain to play a major part.

Annis, on the other hand, was said to be a place of beauty and learning, of craftsmen and artisans and artists. Jack remembered his mother had a bracelet carved from bone. It was intricately crafted and inlaid with silver and quartz. When he asked her about where it came from, she said it was made in Annis. Perhaps he would head there, then. Not because he thought he would learn anything new about his mother—she had bought the bracelet from a tradesmen visiting Castle Harvell, or so she said—but because it was obviously a city that valued honest skills and fine workmanship. And, if he couldn't get a job as a baker or a scribe, then sooner or later his newly acquired ability with a blade would come in useful. Annis might not be famous for soldiering, but its people would fight if they believed themselves threatened.

"I think we will head for Annis," he said.

"We?"

Jack felt a little abashed. He grinned, probably rather sheepishly. "Well, I was hoping—"

"Hoping, were you?" interrupted Tarissa, stopping in her tracks and putting hands to hips. "Next time perhaps you should ask before you hope." Her voice was brutal, but her eyes gave her away.

Jack swept her off the ground. She scratched; she kicked; she screamed. "Are you coming with me to Annis?" he asked, still holding her firmly. "Or will I have to throw you down the hill?"

Tarissa's feet were kicking air. Her face was beet-root red. "We're not on a hill," she cried.

"Well, I'll just have to carry you until I find one, then." Jack slung her over his shoulder as if she were a sack of grain and began walking back the way they'd come. Tarissa screamed afresh, kneed him in the chest, and pummeled his back with her fists.

Jack began to whistle and broke into a run, or as close as he could manage under the circumstances.

This seemed to have the desired effect, for Tarissa stopped fighting and shouted, "All right, all right, I'll come with you to Annis. Just put me down!"

Jack held her firm. "Is that a promise?"

"Yes!" Tarissa was on the ground in an instant. A second later she was chasing him back toward the cottage.

In his whole life, Jack could not remember ever being so happy. He had been worried in case Tarissa hadn't wanted to come with him; after all, the only life she knew was here in Halcus. Rovas was many things: a liar, a user, and a bully, but he provided well for his family, and Tarissa would be giving up a life of comfort and stability. She was taking a risk coming with him. There was no telling what Rovas might do when he found out that she and her mother were gone. He considered them his property, and he wouldn't take kindly to them taking off without his permission

Jack kissed Tarissa lightly on the cheek. He would not let her down.

There was nothing he wouldn't do for her. Jack's mind raced ahead of his legs. He would work day and night. Surely someone would employ him as a baker. In the evenings he could scribe by candlelight. He no longer felt worried about people discovering he wasn't normal: sorcery seemed a thing of the past. If anything happened again, he felt confident he could control it. As long as he had Tarissa, he could do anything.

There would be problems, though. He had no letters of introduction, no proof of his trade. Money would be very tight and they might have to live roughly for a while. And then there was Magra. She had to come with them; Tarissa would have it no other way. They were mother and daughter, and Jack understood the value of family. There would be three in the party for Annis.

Jack knew it was a great responsibility that he was taking on, but he felt as if he needed to do it, not only for Tarissa, but for himself. Two nights back something had happened; it was almost as if a part of him had been taken away. He felt lighter and more free than he had in months, yet the sensation of weightlessness, of having no ties, no responsibility and no fate, left him with a feeling akin to hunger. There had to be a meaning to his life. He didn't want to drift aimlessly with no purpose or commitments, with nothing to worry about but feeding and clothing himself. His back was built to bear more.

Tarissa and Magra would be his purpose. He would spend all his waking hours working to give them everything they needed. It would be a welcome burden.

After a minute or so of being chased, Jack decided to let himself be caught. Tarissa ran toward him, giggling and cursing and out of breath. "So I'm forced to go with you to Annis?"

"You wouldn't want to break your promise."

"I wouldn't want to be without you." She raised her head and kissed him softly. "I love you, Jack," she said, taking his hand and leading him back toward the cottage.

Eighteen

*R*ovas was waiting for them. A bench lay upturned on the floor and Magra was busy mopping up what looked to be the remains of a bowl of stew. Jack was instantly on guard.

"Where have you been?" demanded Rovas, his voice dangerously low.

"I have already told you that," said Magra, looking up from the floor and speaking very precisely. "I sent Jack to look for Tarissa. I was worried about her. She had been out on her own too long."

Magra was giving them an excuse. Judging from the shaking of her hands and the disorderly state of the cottage, she had just been subject to one of Rovas' temper tantrums. The beginning of a matching anger began to rise within Jack. Magra and Tarissa were his family now and he wouldn't stand for anyone upsetting them.

Jack moved forward and came to stand directly opposite Rovas. Although smaller than him, the smuggler was twice as wide. He was barely two feet away and his breath reeked of ale. "Well, we're back now," said Jack, turning his voice to a threat. "So there's no need for you to worry."

The two men looked at each other. Rovas' eyes were filled with loathing. Jack didn't want to think about the reason why the man hated him so much. Such thoughts were best kept in the dark. He was aware of a buildup of tension within his head and a burning sensation in his throat. Sorcery or fear—it was hard to tell. Whatever it was, he worked to keep it under control. Afraid that his bile might carry a sting more deadly than acid, Jack made a determined effort to stop his stomach from contracting. He wanted to deal with Rovas alone. With muscle, not sorcery as his weapon.

Rovas backed away.

Sighs of relief could be heard from Tarissa and Magra. Part of Jack wanted to sigh along with them, but he stood firm, never once taking his eyes off the smuggler. He was suspicious: Rovas was not a man to back down lightly.

"Well, Jack," he said. "It's obvious you're ready to avenge your sweetheart's death. Aggression like that will come in useful when it comes to dealing with Captain Vanly."

"He's the man who murdered Melli?" Jack was tense. He had managed to control the swell of sorcery, but at what cost? His heart was beating wildly and he was aware of a warm trickle of blood running from his nose.

"Murdered and raped her, then cut off her head." Rovas' lip curled to a sneer. A sharp intake of breath sounded from Tarissa.

The words were a finely aimed barb. Jack covered the space between him and the smuggler, his hands grabbing for the man's throat. Rovas was ready. A mighty punch sent his head reeling. The two men fell on the floor. Pots and pans scattered about them. Jack hit his jaw on the side of the table and the smuggler landed on top of him. Tarissa was screaming. Sorcery was building. Rovas had got hold of a knife.

Then someone threw cold water over them. Jack looked up. Magra stood above him like a goddess, an empty bucket in her hand. She bent down and started beating them both with the wooden bucket. Her fine features were wild with fury. Jack could see where Tarissa got her physical strength from; the blows were fierce and biting. He and Rovas submitted to the beating like naughty children. After a while, however, Rovas clearly had enough.

"Leave me be, woman," he said. "I'll be black-and-blue tomorrow."

"I hope you are," cried Magra. "And that goes for you, too!" she said, turning to Jack.

Rovas smiled ruefully and held out his hand. "Come on, lad, I'm sorry for speaking out of turn. I don't know what got into me." Jack could feel the considerable force of Rovas' charm working upon him. "No hard feelings, eh?"

To keep the peace for Magra and Tarissa's sake, Jack took the smuggler's hand. "No hard feelings," he lied. The tension in the room collapsed upon itself, leaving relief in its wake.

Rovas helped Jack to stand up. The sorcery, for there had been no mistaking its metallic tang, seemed to have dissipated naturally this time. Although beating quickly, his heart now felt under less strain. The nosebleed had stopped.

Magra had swapped the bucket for a pitcher of ale and poured them both a brimming cup. Jack took the offered cup and downed it in one. "So when do I see to Vanly?"

Rovas wiped the froth from his upper lip. "The day after tomorrow. I just got word that Kylock has invaded western Halcus, so it won't be long before Vanly is called to the front."

Jack dropped his beer mug. *Kylock invading Halcus.* He never heard the sound of the mug crashing to the floor. At the mention of Kylock's name, something pulled sharply at Jack's thoughts, causing them to refocus on Bren and the war, and then, unexpectedly, on the man with golden hair. It seemed the thread hadn't been severed after all.

Baralis warmed the oil in a crucible over the flame. When it reached the desired temperature, he added a dull gray powder to the mix. His hands shook with fatigue. The pain in his joints was unbearable. The pain in his chest was torture.

Crope had laid out the body on the bed. The unfortunate girl, whoever she was, had been lured here with promises of gold. Baralis didn't bother to ask where she came from. She was a whore, that much was obvious, and judging from her coarsely dyed yellow hair, she was a low-class one at that. She would not be missed.

They were in a small inn in the whoring quarter. It was shabby and flea-ridden. The rushes on the floor stank of mold and the stains on the bedclothes told of sex and blood and urine. A place where no questions were asked once the innkeeper had tested the worth of one's gold. The journey here had been almost intolerable. Crope had to carry him from the palace and lift him into the waiting litter. All the time, the skin on his chest was weeping into the bandage. Pain had accompanied every footfall of the litter carriers. It had all been necessary, though. Even with the duke away, Baralis could not risk anyone at the palace discovering what he was up to. Too many hostile eyes waited eagerly for his downfall.

"It's not enough to place the cloth over her face," he said to Crope. "It must be tied, so she cannot see." The girl was unconscious, but if she were to wake, as she surely would, it would be better if she didn't see what was happening to her. "Bind her hands together, as well." Baralis had watched the effects of fear on many people, and he'd seen enough to know that extreme terror could sometimes provoke great feats of strength, so he was taking no chances. This girl had to die so that he might regain his strength. He needed new skin for his chest.

The powder had dissolved in the oil. A light scum floated on the surface and Baralis drew it off with a spoon. He allowed a drop of water to fall into the crucible; it hissed and skittered. Good, the oil was ready. He picked up the crucible by its long tapering handle and carried it toward the bed. Pushing back the cloth from the girl's forehead, he poured the oil over her scalp.

The girl convulsed. A low groan gurgled in her throat and then her jaw started working on a scream. The wad of cloth in her mouth stopped the sound from escaping. Her body thrashed wildly on the bed and under the cloth her eyes opened. The fine linen gave away every terrified blink. A fatty, meaty smell filled the air as the oil burned its way into her flesh.

Baralis stood and watched. After a few moments the powder that was borne on the oil began to work its commission. The girl settled down, her jaw no longer straining to be heard. One scarred finger scraped along the crucible's edge, and the last drop of oil was brought to Baralis' lips. He let it fall under his tongue. It was cool now, but bitter all the same. Quickly, so quickly it worked. The room blurred sharply and then refocused, more vivid and more menacing than before. The girl became known to him. Her seedy little life appeared in patches before him. She was no different than a thousand whores: greedy, vain, pathetic.

The drawing would be half sorcery, half alchemy. A particularly potent mix, which was still practiced amongst the nomads who roamed the Great Plains. In those ancient grasslands, where survival depended on the whims of nature and the speed of a spear, hunters were second only to God. The herdsmen tended the herds, while the hunters rode out on their swift and graceful horses and slew any man or beast that was a threat. If a hunter were maimed or injured, a herdsman would forfeit his life. The sorcery created by the sacrifice would save him. It was a hard law, but one Baralis had come to respect during the year he'd spent with the nomads. Survival of the tribe was all that counted.

Set apart from the civilized world that encircled them, the nomads had managed to keep and cultivate their magic. The elders held generations worth of knowledge in their heads. Nothing was recorded: methods and ingredients were passed from father to son. Their sorcery was thick with earth and blood. Crude and powerful, it depended on the flesh and bones of sacrifice. Even the lacus, that most fetid of potions which could cure a man of a hundred different ailments, was the product of ritual slaying. A score of goats and one newly born child went into its making. Squeezing the animals' stomachs rendered a pale silvery liquid, but it was the sacrifice of the child that gave the lacus its life. Without it, the lacus was as insipid as milk.

The nomads kept their secrets close. Few knew of the true nature of their magic. When he arrived on the Great Plains, fresh from his time in the Far South, the skills of the herdsmen had seemed crude and blundering compared to the heady, subtle magic of Hanatta. He knew differently now. They were closer to the source: blood and belly, earth and nature; the mind and its intellect almost disregarded. Sacrifice took the place of thought.

Baralis readied the blade. There was a balance to all things, and the knife must be as warm and as salted as the skin it would cut. Crope hovered behind like an anxious nursemaid. He would be there to catch him when he fell.

The herdsmen had saved his life. He had left Hanatta in disgrace. His teacher thought his niece was too young for amorous advances. Thirteen, she was, her pubis barely downed, her hips newly curving, yet the girl was ready all the same. There was more seduction than modesty in her coyly given glances. His teacher had discovered them together. There was blood on the girl's thighs and a matching stain on his lips. Baralis left for the north the next day.

Journeys had always proven dangerous for him, and this one was no exception. He fell in with a group of traveling musicians; they were headed for the court at Castle Harvell in order to perform at the betrothal ceremony of Arinalda and Lesketh. It was during this time, listening to what the minstrels knew about the Four Kingdoms, hearing how King Lesketh was weak and cared more for hunting than for politics, that ideas began to grow in Baralis' mind. By all accounts, the country was lacking in firm leadership and there were great opportunities for those with the ambition to take them.

It would be four more years before he found his way to the kingdoms. Their party was attacked by bandits one hundred leagues north of Silbur. They were outnumbered three to one. Baralis made the mistake of performing a defensive drawing. The attackers were superstitious fools; they thought he was a devil and the minstrels were his minions. They slaughtered everyone in the party except him. Devils would not die by the blade.

Beaten and bound, they dragged him to their camp. They jeered and taunted, and when they grew bored they resorted to torture. His hands were thrust into hot coals, not once, but many times. He felt the pain even to this day. Eventually they tired of him and carried him out to a rocky plain and left him there to die.

The luck of the devil saved him. Delirious with exposure and thirst, too weak for even the simplest drawing, Baralis came so close to death he could smell it. He reeked like carrion. Visited by visions, on the edge of madness, the stars gave him glimpses of greatness. There was much to learn on oblivion's cusp. He saw it all. Fate unraveled itself before him; it tantalized with an image of the north that was ripe for the taking and chastised with the threat of death and obscurity.

By the time the nomads found him, he'd done his deal with the devil. Or fate, or whatever it was that played one man or one country off against another and then waited to see who would win. He became a force of nature on the plains while he lay dying, and the two men who eventually found him had no choice but to bow to his fate. They brought him to the heart of the tribe. Once there, the elders tended him as if he were a hunter, and in many ways he was. Burning with a newly discovered cause, they called him "the chosen one" and offered up their resources like gifts to a god.

One year to the day he spent with them. Unconcerned with good or evil, the herdsmen respected strength, fertility, and fate. His time with them honed his body and spirit and filled his mind with ancient learning. He emerged from the plains with a mission and the means to carry it out.

Baralis forced his mind to the present and focused it upon the girl. She lay still now, her eyes closed, the linen still wet with her tears. The powdered oil was a bond shared, but the blade was for her alone.

Oh, the pain was intolerable. His chest, its muscles and the tender tissue beneath, all damaged to save the life of a silly girl. Catherine of Bren would find herself with a considerable debt to pay.

With hands that were steady despite the pain, Baralis took the blade and slit the fabric of his victim's dress. Chest and breast and belly were revealed by the taper's light. Not quite as young as he would have liked, yet still of an age when the skin would smooth quickly from a pinch.

"Turn her for me," he ordered. Her back would provide a more appropriate stretch of skin. Crope stepped forward and did his bidding. "Good. Now bring me the second container." Baralis' eyes rested upon the girl's back. It was just what he needed.

Crope fumbled around by the table until he found the freshly pestled leaf. "Is this the one, master?"

Baralis nodded. "Hold it for me." He bent over the girl and nicked the flesh at the base of her spine. Blood welled bright and gaudy. It ran along the salted blade and into the waiting pot. The sap of the leaf rose to meet it. Baralis bit hard on the tip of his tongue. The taste from the oil filled his mouth. His own blood dripped into the mix and the potion was complete. He stirred it once with bare fingers and then drew his power into the pot.

Such weakness, it made him sway where he stood. Crope waited in the shadows, arms ready if needed. The potion took sorcery's spark and became greater than the sum of its parts. Baralis leaned over and smeared it onto the skin of the girl's back. Immediately he felt a corresponding burn upon his chest. The pain reached new heights of torment. The girl upon the bed began to move. The blade drew itself to her skin, Baralis merely its keeper.

Around her back it traced a course, across the neck, along the arms and above the buttocks. The girl arched her spine to meet it. Baralis began to lose himself; he felt every cut of the knife. Head pounding, hands soaked in blood, Baralis wavered as the darkness beckoned. He knew a single, terrifying pain and then the girl, beautiful in her abandon, was his.

Backward he fell. Past and present no longer held meaning. His chest blazed like an inferno and his flesh was consumed by the flames.

From somewhere he heard a voice: "Pretty necklace has owls. Can I keep it, master?"

Baralis never knew if he nodded or shook his head.

Maybor was pleasantly pickled. Life was good, but the ale was better. A drink in his hand, two girls in his bed: who could want for anything more? One young lady lay eyes closed, bottom up, worn out by the breadth of his passion. The other girl, a saucy vixen if ever there was one, was eyeing him up for another go around the maypole.

He wasn't quite up to it yet.

In fact, now that he'd had a brothel keeper's fill, his urges had receded along with his codpiece. His mind was still active, though, even if his fishing rod wasn't.

He stood up, modestly covering his vitals with a huge cushion. Shakindra was the name of the boar-hound the duke had given him. Maybor had shortened it to Shark. *"Shark,"* he called, moving toward the bedside chest. "Here, boy." Maybor chose to ignore the fact that Shark was actually a girl.

"I'm telling you now, matey," piped up the vixen from the bed, "I ain't gonna do no kinky stuff, not for any amount of money."

Maybor ignored the girl and beamed at the dog. "Good boy. Good boy." At first he'd been a little wary of the scary-looking creature, but now, seeing it come toward him, tail wagging, eyes bright with intelligence, Maybor began to feel rather fond of it. The dog came up and licked his face. "Who's a big bastard, then, eh?" said Maybor fondly. He reached into the chest. "Got something for my big boy. Something to get his teethy-weethy into." Pulling out Baralis' linen undershirt, Maybor stuffed it against Shark's muzzle. *"Kill, boy. Kill."*

Shark growled like a hound from hell and tore the shirt into shreds. The dog's jaws frothed in frenzy; its chest shook with intent. After the creature had destroyed the shirt, it continued to worry away at the remains as if they were a threat to its life. Maybor smiled, well pleased. Shark was aptly named.

After a few moments he turned his attention back to the vixen on the bed. What was it she said about kinky stuff?

Melli hitched up her dress and rubbed fragrant oils into her thighs. The ladies at Castle Harvell had told her many times that such preparations were essential for lovemaking. Apparently men liked nothing better than to follow their hands and their noses up to the flower with the honey. Melli hated such silly talk: flowers with honey, indeed! The ladies at Castle Harvell should call a spade a spade!

Melli breathed a sigh of relief as the oil worked its fancy upon her flesh, soothing, cooling, easing the pain. Lovemaking might not be on her mind, but rider's chafe was on her thighs. Six hours in the saddle! It was enough to make even the most hardened rider walk bowlegged for a week.

Oh, the scenery was breathtaking: all purple mountains heavily topped with snow, and lush green meadows in the first flush of spring, but it wasn't quite enough to offset the strain of the ride. She was sorely out of practice. At one time riding had been like second nature; however, once a girl's blood flowed it was considered unseemly to ride astride in the company of men. Another silly court custom! And one she was pleased to say hadn't been adopted for the journey to the lodge. In fact, the duke himself had helped her onto the horse, cupping his hand in readiness for a foot meant to mount, not sit.

Unfortunately that was the only gallant thing His Grace had done all day. For the entire six hours he had ignored her; she rode at the back along with servants and supplies. No one had spoken to her, they just stared and whispered amongst themselves. It was a fair-sized party, nearly twenty in all: the duke and four other noblemen, several grooms, two dog handlers, an array of men servants and kitchen staff, and a lady's maid, who Melli presumed was meant to attend upon her. She didn't count the armed guards in the numbers.

Bailor did not accompany them. Melli had hoped he would, for he was the nearest thing that she had to a friend in Bren. They had arrived at the lodge by midafternoon, and the first thing the duke did was change his horse and ride out on a hunt—so she'd had no one to talk to all day.

The lady's maid came in the room. Besides Melli, she was the only other female in the party. Obviously such trips were usually for men alone.

The girl bobbed a reluctant curtsy. "I'm supposed to see to you, lady," she said. The word *lady* carried all the effect of a verbal sneer.

"Well, you could have come sooner," snapped Melli, upset by the girl's manner. "I've been on my own for hours."

"Didn't think you'd want anything until now." The girl picked up the jar of fragrant oil and sniffed the contents. "The duke said you are to join him in his private apartments for supper. So I suppose you'll need seeing to."

For some reason Melli felt close to tears. No one, not even Mistress Greal, had treated her with the contempt that this serving girl did. The worst thing was that she had no defense: she was little more than a slave and much less than a prostitute. Anger was her only recourse. "Leave me now. I do not require anything from you. If you should happen to see His Grace, then kindly tell him I have dismissed you because of your insolence."

That certainly seemed to do the trick. The girl instantly recognized and then reacted to the nobility in her voice. She actually re-curtsied. "I'm sorry, miss. I didn't mean to offend you."

That was exactly what you meant to do, thought Melli. "Very well, I will let the matter pass this time. Please fetch me a measure of red wine and some bread and cheese. I haven't eaten anything since this morning, and I've no intention of waiting upon the duke's call before I line my belly." Ever since arriving at the hunting lodge, Melli had been alone in her room, unregarded and unfed. So much for hunting and feasting! "And when you come back, you can help me change. I've little desire to please His Grace, but I've even less desire to sit here any longer in a dress that reeks of horse sweat. Now run along and be quick about it." It was so easy to fall into the old ways of court. Servants had to be treated harshly in order to gain their respect.

"Yes, miss." The girl performed a hasty curtsy and was off, now eager to do her bidding.

An hour later Melli was nibbling on the last of the cheese while being laced into her gown.

"Oh, miss," cried the girl, "if you eat another morsel, the seams will surely rip."

"Well, don't tie the laces so tight then, Nessa, for I intend to eat some more when I see the duke."

"Yes, Nessa," came an amused, sardonic voice. "I will be feeding your lady with the game I caught earlier. 'Twas a large beast and will need plenty of belly."

It was the duke. Both women looked around, startled. Nessa immediately dropped to the floor in a low curtsy. Melli barely inclined her head.

"Really, sir! Are all the men in Bren as bad mannered as you? For I pity the women if they are." Melli turned to Nessa. "Get off the floor, girl, and finish my laces. His Grace won't mind waiting, as he surely came hoping for a show."

Nessa reluctantly left the floor and finished her work on the dress. Melli could feel her hands shaking.

The duke seemed not in the least offended by her words, and this rankled Melli further, as they were intended to do just that. He walked about the room with an air of proprietorship, pausing to stoke the fire and then pour himself a quarter glass of wine. Out of the corner of her eye, Melli noticed that whilst the glass reached his lips, the level of liquid never fell.

"Nessa and I had an interesting little conversation about half an hour back," he said. "She tells me you are quite the high lady with your orders and chastisements."

Nessa shot Melli a "forgive me" glance. Melli was not about to forgive anyone. First she turned to the duke. "Next time, instead of a lady's maid, perhaps you could send a scribe to help me dress. He might not be able to improve my looks, but at least he can record what I have to say word for word."

And then to Nessa: "As for you, my girl, I'd be careful with that tongue of yours. Things that loose have a nasty habit of falling off." Melli was seething.

The duke's face showed no emotion. "Leave us," he said to Nessa. The girl almost raced from the room. When she had gone he held out his arm. "Come, I will accompany you to my chambers. The meat is growing cold."

"And if I refuse?"

"Then I will be forced to carry you there."

Melli did not doubt that he could. He was a strong man; his arms bore the muscles of a soldier, not a duke. She was just about to issue a scathing reply when she caught herself: she'd been such a fool! Acting like a great lady with no thought of where it might lead. She was supposed to be the illegitimate daughter of a minor lord, yet here she was not only taking servants to task, but reprimanding the duke himself as well. He was already suspicious; a man of his standing never stooped to questioning maid servants without good cause. Melli cursed her stupidity! He had all but accused her of being a high-born lady, and instead of denying the charge, she had, by both words and attitude, practically admitted to it.

She blamed her father. Maybor's blood had long been thick with arrogance, it was no wonder that hers was, too.

Determined to make no more mistakes, Melli quietly took the duke's arm. He was surprised by her submission—a slight raising of his eyebrows gave him away—but he walked her out of the room without a word.

The lodge was modestly named. It was huge. Built from pine and cedar timbers, it gave more of an impression of warmth than the palace. They walked along a high-ceilinged corridor that was painted with hunting murals, down a short flight of stairs, and then along a lengthy corridor that ended in a beautifully carved doorway. The duke opened the door and bid her enter his chambers.

He didn't stand on ceremony. He sat down at one end of a solid pine table and motioned that Melli should sit at the other. The duke had been right when he said the meat was getting cold, for a huge haunch of something lay steaming on a platter. One servant waited upon them. To calm her nerves, Melli took a deep draught of wine. It was a mistake, for the drink was fortified and stronger than she was used to. The duke noted her surprise. "Bring the lady some water," he commanded the servant.

Melli didn't know why this annoyed her, but it did nonetheless. "Tell your man not to waste his time, I will take my wine as it comes." She knew it was a mistake—coming so soon after her just-sworn resolution to be meek—but the duke's arrogant demeanor brought out the devil in her.

"So be it," he said, and waved his arm in dismissal. The servant left the room. He turned back to Melli. "Try the meat." It was as good as an order.

Melli hacked off a fair-sized portion of the crackled and roasted flesh. It was delicious: juicy, bloody, marbled with fat. She couldn't remember the last time she'd tasted anything so wonderful.

"Good?" prompted the duke. He sat back in his chair, regarding her as if she were a moth in a jar. A full cup of wine rested in his hand. The servant had not refilled it once.

"It's a little tough. What did you say it was?"

"I didn't. It *was* a young and fleet-footed buck."

"Tastes more like an old and slow-stepping stag."

The duke threw his head back and laughed. He slammed his cup on the table. "By Borc! You are an annoying wench!" He didn't sound in the least bit annoyed; in fact, he sounded rather pleased. "Tell me, did you get that tongue of yours from your father or your mother?"

A tiny warning sounded in Melli's head. An innocent question? Or was he trying to catch her out? Why couldn't she keep her mouth shut? "From my father, I think."

"Hmm, that was Lord Luff, wasn't it?"

Melli was growing nervous. "Yes."

"Strange. I met the man once. He didn't strike me as being particularly quick witted."

He could be bluffing, but it was best not to put it to the test. "Aah, well my mother was no shrinking violet, either. I could have got it from her."

The duke's demeanor visibly changed. He looked at her coldly. "You are lying," he said.

Try as she might, Melli could not stop the heat from rushing to her face. There was nothing for her to do but stand up and turn her reddening face to the fire. A second later she felt the duke's hands upon her shoulders.

"Look at me," he ordered. He gripped her flesh so hard that Melli had no choice but to obey.

Melli turned toward him. Her own guilt was clearly reflected in his flint gray eyes. He reached up and, for one moment, she thought he would hit her. Instead he took her chin in his hand. He smelled like the game he had hunted. Squeezing his fingers into her cheek, he said: "Tell me who your father is." His voice was low and menacing, it allowed no space for falsehood or evasion.

Panicking, knowing she had only seconds, Melli searched for a convincing lie. It was too late for backtracking.

Annoyed at her hesitation, the duke dug his fingertips deeper into her cheeks. *"Tell me,"* he hissed.

A knock sounded at the door. The duke did not take his eyes off Melli for an instant. "Do not disturb me," he called.

"Your Grace," came a muffled voice, "there is important news. A messenger has come from the court."

The duke swore and pushed Melli back toward the fire. "Come," he cried, voice harsh and impatient.

Even as she struggled to find her footing, Melli breathed a sigh of relief. Her shin caught against the grate. It was red-hot and she pinned her lips together to keep from crying out. She hated him!

In walked two men. Melli recognized one of them from the journey; the other still had his cloak and leathers on. Neither of them as much as glanced at her.

"Your Grace, Kylock has invaded Halcus."

"When did this happen?"

"A week ago," said the cloaked one. "Pigeons arrived at Bren today."

"What are his numbers?"

"Two battalions, with another following."

The duke clenched his fists. "That is no border-keeping force. The man means to take more than the River Nestor. Is there any news of the battle?"

"No news yet, Your Grace. But Kylock had surprise on his side. The Halcus expected him to wait until full spring."

A small, dry laugh escaped from the duke's throat. "Then the Halcus are fools." He started to pace about the room. When he next spoke, it was more to himself than the two men. "Kylock has moved quickly, his father has barely been dead a month. There wasn't enough time for him to train an army, yet the fact that the Halcus are badly undermanned will work in his favor." He addressed the messenger. "Who in Bren knows about this?"

"No one except the handlers, Lord Cravin, and myself, Your Grace."

The duke turned to the second man. "I want you to ride back to Bren tonight. No one is to know about this until I return."

"Yes, Your Grace," said the man. He bowed and left the room.

"You," he said to the messenger, "will do me the favor of accompanying this lady back to her room. Your news has given me much to think on."

The man bowed and made his way toward Melli. He looked tired, but friendly, and he offered his arm. The duke didn't even bother to look at her as she left.

Nineteen

*T*avalisk was sorting through his morning communications. The letter from He Who Is Most Holy was hardly worth the parchment it was written on. His Holiness, Borc rot his spineless soul, was becoming nervous about events in the north. He had heard about the four-city force that had been sent out to protect southern trade, and he thought it might be perceived as—how did he put it? The archbishop skimmed the page: *"as a hostile act, sure to inflame tensions that are already dangerously asmoulder."*

Tavalisk dropped the letter. His Holiness should keep his nose out of world affairs and stick to what he knows best: praying and poetry. He should have had the courage to excommunicate the Knights of Valdis years ago. It was nothing short of a disgrace that they were allowed to worship the same God and the same savior. Let them invent a God of their own, he thought. Though they were welcome to the savior: Borc's legend grew shoddier by the day.

If *he* were in His Holiness' position, he would have had the knights hounded as heretics throughout the entire continent. All their lands would be annexed, their business interests would be confiscated, and their leader would be burned at the stake. Tyren was such a greasy little individual he would take to the flame like a fatted calf.

Tavalisk settled back in his chair and picked at the remains of his breakfast. Oh, to go back to those glorious days when He Who Is Most Holy had wielded real power. Armies marched on his orders and leaders waited upon his every word. Over the past four hundred years the Church had declined like a decrepit old man. His Holiness was the latest in a long line of weak-kneed, over-philosophizing, under-opinionated fools! Why, the only reason that he, Tavalisk, had power was that he had the guts to take it. Before him the archbishop's seat at Rorn had been nothing but a heavily cushioned footstool. He had made it a throne.

If Marod's *Book of Words* was anything to go by, even the feeble remains of the Church were in danger. There was little doubt that the line *The temples will fall,* heralded the downfall of the Church. And, knowing that snake Baralis, it was likely to happen sooner rather than later.

Despite the early hour, Tavalisk poured himself a small measure of brandy. He could not allow the northern empire to flourish. The Knights of Valdis would like nothing better than to destroy the Church as it existed and appoint themselves as leaders of the faith. Where would that leave him? On the streets, powerless. This was such an alarming thought that the archbishop downed his drink in one. At least he wouldn't be penniless. A certain treasure-filled mansion, in a discreet street not a stone's throw away from where he sat, was proof of that. But wealth without power was like food without salt: dull and unappetizing. No, he simply couldn't allow it to happen. His Holiness was obviously going to be no help: he was so busy keeping a middle course that he was becoming as thin and predictable as the line he was treading. He would have to do it all himself.

Indeed, that was his destiny. Tavalisk's hands brushed against the cover of Marod as an idea occurred to him. Surely if he managed to save the Church, greater glory could be his. He would become the ultimate defender of the Faith. The clergy would be so grateful, his name so exalted, he could make a successful bid to takeover His Holiness' position.

Tavalisk, in his excitement, took the *Book of Words* and brought it to his lips. Marod was a genius. The rewards for following his predictions were greater than he ever imagined. He could become leader of the Church!

A knock at the door caused the archbishop to hastily place Marod on the table. It wouldn't do for him to be caught kissing books—people might get the wrong idea and think he had returned to his scholarly past! "Enter," he called.

In walked Gamil. "Your Eminence, there is important news."

Tavalisk was still basking in the glow of future glories, so he felt inclined to deal benignly with his aide. "Is there, indeed? Then you'd better sit down and tell me what it is."

Never once in his ten years of devoted service had Gamil ever been asked to sit down in the archbishop's presence. He looked decidedly wary. "Is Your Eminence feeling well?"

"Never better." The archbishop beamed. "Come along, Gamil. Don't stand there all agape like a wife who's just caught her husband bedding another woman. Tell me your news."

Gamil did not sit. "I've just received word that our four-city force has had an unfriendly exchange with the knights."

"Were there any casualties?" asked Tavalisk, rubbing his hands together in glee.

"Yes, Your Eminence. On both sides. Two of our men lost their lives and twenty of the knights. Valdis was outnumbered five to one."

"Excellent! Excellent!" Tavalisk poured brandy into two glasses, one of which he handed to his aide. "News like this is worth celebrating. Marls, Camlee, and Toolay have now stuck their heads up so high that there's no going back. Mark my words, Gamil, this will be the start of open conflict between the south and Valdis. Tyren is probably seething as we speak."

Gamil looked at the drink the archbishop had just given him as if it were poison. "Forming the four-city force was a very clever idea, Your Eminence."

"Not just clever, Gamil, brilliant." Tavalisk made an encouraging gesture with his hand, prompting his aide to drink up. "So, tell me, how did this altercation happen?"

"Our scouts spotted a small group of knights traveling just north of Camlee. They hurried back to the camp, telling the other soldiers that they'd been fired at by the knights. Apparently, all the men in the camp were so bored with sitting around whittling wood all day and guarding the odd cargo train, that they seized upon this information as a good excuse to go and slice some skin. By all accounts there was quite a bloodbath. The heads of the dead knights were mounted on stakes by the roadside. No one passing from the north to the south can fail to see them."

Tavalisk smiled widely. His Holiness certainly had cause to worry: there was nothing more inflammatory than a head on a stake. Everything was coming together beautifully, the battle lines were being drawn and the time was fast approaching when everyone who counted would be forced to choose their side. The events that had just occurred north of Camlee had practically forced the south into declaring their position. They could hardly oppose the knights without opposing Bren, and by implication, the kingdoms as well.

Or could they? At this point, the south might argue that their quarrel was exclusively with the knights. Tavalisk rubbed his chin. Perhaps matters required a little more help. "Gamil, were the knights guarding any cargo at the time of the attack?"

"Yes, Your Eminence. Several wagonloads of fine cloth bound for Bren."

"Perfect. It couldn't be better." The archbishop's mind raced across the possibilities and reached for the best like a cherry-picker at the tree. "I think it's time we started a rumor, Gamil."

"Another plague, Your Eminence?"

"No. Something more subtle than a plague." Tavalisk stood up and walked over to the window. "We know that Catherine of Bren is due to be married soon to King Kylock."

"Yes."

"And what do all brides need?"

"A groom."

"No, you fool! They need a wedding dress. What if the cargo that we seized had contained the cloth that was due to be made into Catherine's bridal gown?"

"But the duke of Bren would know otherwise, Your Eminence."

"That doesn't matter, Gamil. Don't you see? If we claim to have seized their beloved Catherine's wedding dress, it will be a humiliation for Bren regardless of whether it's true or not. It's as good as burning their flag. Once word gets out, it will look as if the south is opposed to the knights *and* Bren. The seized wedding dress will become a thrown gauntlet."

"I will start the rumor today, Your Eminence."

"Knowing you as I do, Gamil, I'm sure half the city will know about it by sundown." The archbishop waved a negligent dismissal. He felt too pleased with himself to bother issuing a menial task or an insult. Besides, Gamil needed to conserve all his energy for his tongue.

"So how big is the garrison?" Jack's voice was blunt. In reality he was scared. He was just beginning to realize the immensity and danger of the task he had sworn to do.

He and Rovas were sitting face-to-face across the kitchen table. The women had left them alone, muttering about herbs to be gathered.

"There's over twenty score of soldiers stationed there full-time," said Rovas. "The number increases depending on the time of year and where the trouble spots are. At this point, everyone's eyes are to the west. Kylock's invasion has taken them all by surprise."

"So they'll be on their guard?

Rovas gave him a shrewd look. "Not stuck out here in the east, they won't. They'll be so busy training and recruiting and putting edges on their blades that they wouldn't even notice Borc himself arriving for his second coming."

Jack took a sip of his ale to give himself time to think. Rovas was downplaying the dangers. He couldn't really blame the man for doing so; after all, there was no way he would agree to steal into the garrison if he thought twenty score of soldiers would be armed and waiting. Still, it gave Jack cause to be wary: what other perils might Rovas choose to minimize or ignore? "How many men are set to guard at night?"

"Outside there are four pairs. One pair mounts the garrison, two guard the main gate, and one guards the service entrance at the rear." The smuggler spoke with assurance and Jack had no cause to doubt him.

"How are they armed?"

"The ones on the battlements have crossbows. All the others have spears and short swords."

Jack nodded. "What about inside?"

"That's more difficult to say." Rovas pulled in his cheeks and made a slight sucking sound. His face was red and peeling. Too much ale, sun, and wind had caused the blood vessels to break on his nose. "I won't lie to you, Jack," he said, endowing his deep voice with a measure of affection. "There could be as many as ten pairs. And I can't say for certain where they'll be stationed. They could be practically anywhere."

Jack wondered when he had become so suspicious. To him, Rovas' attempt at disarming truthfulness seemed calculated to win his trust. Strange to think that only a few months earlier, when he was working as a baker's boy in Castle Harvell, he had taken everyone on their word. Trust was now a thing of the past.

It was easy to forget what Rovas really did for a living. He was a smuggler, a con artist, and a thief. He preyed on people who were poor and hungry and sold them goods that were an insult to their meager purses. Rovas liked to project an air of rakish good humor, but he wasn't a rake at all. He was a villain.

He had tried to force Tarissa to murder a man. The same man whose murder they now sat around the table plotting. Rovas had found someone else to do his dirty work for him. Jack shifted to the edge of his seat. He needed to be wary of every word that left the smuggler's lips. "So what's the best way to gain entry?"

"The service entrance. There's no need to force your way in. I'll give you a barrel of ale with the mark of the local inn upon it." Rovas leaned forward as he told Jack of his plan. "It's Spring Blessing, so they'll be wanting all the ale they can get. There'll be all sorts passing through that door tomorrow night: whores, cooks, musicians. You don't say a word. That accent of yours will give you away in an instant. Simply turn up at the door with the ale and they'll let you through. No one will pay the slightest attention to a dumb and unarmed tavern boy."

"Unarmed?"

"Aye, you'll be a stranger to them, so they'll search you for sure. Your weapon will be strapped to the inside of the ale barrel. It'll be a little wet, but deadly nonetheless." Rovas was looking rather pleased with himself. "O' course you'll have to find a pick or a bar to get inside the barrel, but that shouldn't be difficult. At worst you can simply smash it against a wall. If anyone comes, just pretend you dropped it. Chances are that everyone will be so drunk that they won't even care."

The plan sounded feasible, yet Jack found it hard to accept that it would be so easy. On feastdays at Castle Harvell, the guards who were on duty were strictly forbidden to drink. "Everyone won't be drinking, though?" he prompted.

Rovas moved back and the light from the candle fell from his face. "The only ones who won't be tippling will be the four pairs of external guards." He looked straight at Jack from the shadows, challenging him to question his word.

How much could he believe? Rovas was a practiced liar: anyone who could pass off fish painted with blood as a fresh catch had to have a tongue that dripped oil. Yet Jack knew he had no choice but to accept what Rovas said. There was little chance he was going to catch the man out, and, all things considered, the smuggler *did* want Vanly murdered. So why would he lie about the dangers?

Jack was afraid. He was playing at being tough, nothing more. What had he ever done in his life that readied him for this? Oh, he could handle a blade now, but he was still happier kneading dough than attacking an opponent. Jack smiled despite himself; that wasn't quite true anymore. It felt right to have a sword in his hand. He'd learned fast, almost as if it were second nature. Already he was developing the ability to know what his opponent's next move would be even before he made it. Rovas had told him to watch the eyes of his opponent if he wanted to see what they'd try next, but Jack had learned that wasn't quite enough. You had to watch the line of their muscles to see which were ready to contract, and you had to memorize all the moves that had gone before: a man was always anxious to pull something new from his hat.

In many ways baking had prepared him for fighting: long hours had honed his endurance, working under Frallit had given him a strong sense of self-discipline, and kneading dough for six hours a day and hauling sacks of grain from the granary had given him arms of steel.

Nothing had prepared him for stealing into a garrison, though. Nothing made him ready to kill a man in cold blood and then make an escape. Nothing. If it wasn't for Tarissa, he might not have gone through with it. Melli was dead. Revenge paled beside that one, irrefutable fact. If anyone was to blame for her death, it was *he*, not Vanly. To kill the man in her name would be as good as a lie. So he would do it for Tarissa, instead.

"How do I know the guards will let me into the garrison with the ale? They might just take it from me." Jack knew his only safeguard with Rovas was to question every detail.

"That's easy. I'll make sure you get a barrel with an Isro tap. No one except tavern-keepers knows how to open them. They'll have to let you in if they want the ale to flow." Rovas smiled charmingly. "And believe me, they'll want the ale to flow. There's nothing like Isro Amber for putting a fire in the blood."

"Where will Vanly be?"

Rovas' whole face lit up at the question; he'd obviously been eagerly awaiting it for some time. "Aah, well, that's where my inside information comes in. I know for a fact that a troop of dancing girls are currently on their way from Helch to the garrison. Now, these dancing girls are little more than whores, and one of them is said to be so beautiful that men fall to their knees at the very sight of her. Knowing the good captain as I do, he'll be spending the evening trying to bed her." Rovas winked merrily. "And knowing the dancing girls of Helch as I do, he won't have to try very hard."

"So he'll be alone except for this one girl?"

"I'm almost certain of it. He'll eat with his men in the mess hall about sundown. He'll get drunk by downing a few skins of ale, and get randy by watching the Helch girls dance. Then he'll retire for the evening with the most beautiful girl in the room on his arm."

"How do I find his quarters?" asked Jack. They were coming to the most dangerous part; entering the garrison wouldn't be that difficult, but if he were caught wandering around the officers' quarters it would mean certain capture. Or worse.

Rovas spilled a heap of flour onto the table. He spread it out flat with the palm of his hand and then proceeded to draw a rough sketch of the garrison in the powder. "Here," he said, tracing the outline of the south wall, "is the service entrance. You simply turn to your left, head along the east wall until you come to a covered arcade." Rovas accompanied each word with a corresponding line in the flour. "At the end of the arcade is a set of double doors, pass through these, take the short flight of stairs on your right, and the first door you come to will be Vanly's sleeping quarters."

Jack was not looking at the map. He was watching Rovas' face instead, searching for the slightest sign that what the smuggler said was a lie. He didn't find one. There was one glaring omission, though: the officers' quarters were bound to be guarded. Jack didn't believe that Rovas had innocently overlooked that fact. "What about guards?"

Rovas shrugged. "There might be a pair of them guarding the double doors. If you wait long enough, you'll be able to slip by when they change. Who knows, they might be so drunk that they let you sail past. With that long hair of yours they might even think you're an officer's friend—if you get my drift. Though you're a little too tall and muscley for the normal type." Rovas laughed at his own wit. "Anyway, the point is it's Spring Blessing; wine and women will be on everyone's mind, and those who aren't thinking about merriment will be worried about the war in the west. We couldn't pick a better time to make our move."

It was time for the most important question of all. "How do I escape?" Jack watched Rovas like a hawk. Of all the things the man was likely to lie about, this was the only one that really counted. Jack knew he would be at his most vulnerable once the deed was done.

Rovas looked Jack straight in the eye. "There's a tunnel leading from Vanly's quarters all the way out into the woods."

"Why can't I use it to get in?" Jack had already heard the answer, but he wanted to make sure anyway.

"It'll be bolted on the inside."

"How do you know about this tunnel?"

"You forget, Jack. I used to be in business with the man. We used that tunnel all the time to take goods back and forth." Rovas brushed his hands over the flour, cleaning the slate for another sketch. "It was built at the same time as the garrison. It's not unusual to have escape tunnels situated in an officer's quarters in case of the need for quick escape. If the garrison was ever under siege, it would be used to smuggle food and supplies through." A fat finger traced the corner of the garrison. "Look, here's

Vanly's quarters. The entrance to the tunnel is located under the bed. The floorboards are hinged and underneath is a barred trapdoor. Once you raise the trapdoor, you're looking at an eight-foot drop, so be careful: don't jump blindly, or you could break a leg. Lower yourself feet first. It'll be pitch-black in there. You could take a candle, but it would just slow you down. Best to work in the dark. There's only one way to go, so you won't get lost."

Rovas traced a curved line leading out from the garrison. "The tunnel itself is about four feet high, so it won't be easy going. It's long, too. It doesn't slant straight to the woods, because a stream cuts through its path, so the tunnel has to curve to avoid it. When you reach the other end, it's going to take all your strength to shift the opening. A large rock lies atop the entrance. So don't be fooled into thinking it's just a case of raising another trapdoor. There are footholds cut in the timber; hike yourself up and push with all your might."

Jack found it difficult to doubt what Rovas was saying. The man seemed to have a lot of convincing details at his disposal. Still, he pushed to find holes in the man's story. "I thought you'd be waiting for me."

"I will, just not in the woods. A patrol comes around about once an hour. It's too much of a risk for me to wait—I have no way of knowing how long you'll be." Rovas poked away at the flour, indicating the woods. "See here at the edge, where the stream grazes the trees, that's where I'll be waiting with a spare horse."

"Won't a man with a spare horse look suspicious?"

"Aye, lad, you might be right. Though I'd hoped to go unnoticed, it's a pretty remote area by the stream. The guards only patrol the center of the woods, because they know there's a tunnel there."

"Then they'll be watching the tunnel entrance?" Somehow, Jack knew Rovas would have a convincing answer ready. He wasn't disappointed.

"No, lad. Only the officers know the exact location of the tunnel. It wouldn't do to have every soldier in the garrison knowing how to sneak in and out whenever they pleased." Rovas rubbed the stubble on his chin. "Come to think of it, the guards might not even know there's a tunnel. There's no need to tell them the real reason why they have to keep an eye on the woods."

Jack searched for any lack of logic or inconsistencies in Rovas' story, but could find none. But there was one way to call his bluff. "Take me to the tunnel entrance tonight."

Rovas didn't flinch. "Very well, as you wish. We'll have to wait until the small hours, though. If we were spotted, we'd have to call the whole thing off."

"It's all right, it doesn't matter." Jack was satisfied—there was no reason to go there now. If Rovas had hesitated even for an instant, it would have been a different story. Feeling more relaxed, Jack asked one final question. "How do I know I can trust you, and that I won't end up getting caught or killed?"

Rovas' light blue eyes looked straight into his. "Magra and Tarissa would never forgive me if you didn't come back."

Maybor was waiting by an open drain just off the butcher's courtyard. Apparently the duke's palace didn't have need of a middens. All their chamberpots were emptied straight into the lake. A sorry arrangement if ever there was one. How was a man to conduct a discreet meeting without a ghastly smell to put off potential eavesdroppers? There was small consolation to be found in the fact that there was a distinctly unpleasant odor emanating from the drain. Blood and decomposing entrails might not smell quite as bad as a middens, but at least they drew the same amount of flies.

Here was the man now. Lord Cravin did not look at all pleased to be summoned to such an inauspicious spot. Still, the man managed to step over the bloody carcasses with a certain amount of grace. He was wearing rather fine shoes, as well. Maybor saw Cravin's discomfort as a personal advantage; he had successfully thrown the man off guard.

"Well met, Maybor," said Cravin a little testily. "If I'd known you had such a fondness for carnage, I would have suggested meeting in the sanitarium, that way you could have watched *people* having their limbs hacked off."

"No, farm animals will do just fine." Maybor picked up a slice of what looked to be a pig's ear with the toe of his boot and flipped it into the gutter.

Cravin appeared to calm himself. "I trust you found the ladies to your liking?"

"More than adequate, my friend." Maybor was feeling rather superior. "Though the second girl was a little skinny for my taste. Her hips were like a lentil grower's feast; pleasant enough, but lacking in meat. As for the first—"

"Enough," hissed Cravin. "I did not come here to discuss the female form." He took a step closer, the right half of his face falling under the shadow cast by his hooked nose. "Hear my piece now, or walk away from this meeting with nothing but the blood on your boots to show for it."

"I'm listening."

"How well do you know Lord Baralis?"

The question took Maybor by surprise. His first instinct was to be guarded. "I could tell you a thing or two."

"Then you're aware that he's a dangerous man with dangerous ambitions?" Cravin's eyes shone shrewd like a hawk.

Maybor, feeling uncharacteristically cautious, merely nodded.

"The marriage between Catherine and Kylock is no spur of the moment affair. Baralis has planned for it for over a decade—perhaps even longer."

"And how would you know this?" Maybor had decided his policy: say nothing and let the lord from Bren spill his guts.

"For ten years now Baralis has crushed, murdered, or suppressed any party who sought Kylock's hand in marriage."

Melliandra! Maybor's thoughts darted toward his daughter. Outwardly, he remained calm. "Go on."

"Has it never occurred to you to wonder how a prince of Kylock's standing managed to reach his eighteenth year without as much as one formal offer of betrothal?" Cravin didn't wait for an answer. "I'll tell you why, because Baralis, in his position as king's chancellor, managed to stop any proposals before they reached the ears of the king.

"The duke of Highwall has a daughter approaching her fifteenth summer. When she was but eight years old, he opened negotiations with the kingdoms for Kylock's hand. Baralis sent the girl a gift: a box of sugared delights. One week later she succumbed to brain-fever. One *month* later she couldn't remember her name. To this day she lives in a tiny room in the duke's castle, strapped to her bed to prevent her from injuring herself."

Maybor believed every word: Baralis had tried no less with Melliandra. "Did suspicion fall on Baralis?"

"There were whisperings, but Baralis silenced most of them by stating that he was still willing to go ahead with the betrothal, regardless of the girl's condition. Of course he knew the duke would never allow it, but it looked good all the same."

The stench of decomposing entrails seemed a fitting accompaniment to such talk. "What else have you heard?"

Cravin stood and contemplated for a moment; his tough and wiry body all angles beneath his robes. "I myself once entered into negotiations with Baralis. It was many years ago now. My eldest daughter, Fellina, was a match for Kylock in age. I sent a letter to the king, outlining my proposal. He never sent a reply. Baralis did. He was most gracious, saying that he had heard tell of my daughter's beauty and refinement; however, he said my letter had placed him in a difficult position as he had recently received a similar proposal from my great rival, Lord Gandrel. He pointed out that, while he favored Fellina's suit, he was barred from choosing between us, as the king didn't want to offend either party."

"Your daughter got off lightly," said Maybor, surprised at the emotion in his voice.

Cravin nodded grimly. "I am forever grateful for that. I learned a few years later that Gandrel had never considered marrying any of his daughters to Kylock. Baralis had invented the whole thing. He is a clever dog, he knew there was no way I could confirm Gandrel's proposal; at the time I hated the man with a passion and never spoke to him except in anger."

"Baralis kidnapped my daughter several months back," said Maybor. "I haven't seen her since."

Cravin did not look surprised. "Baralis will stop at nothing to get what he wants."

Maybor looked to either side of him, checking for ears that belonged to humans, not pigs. When he spoke, his voice was low and urgent. "What is it that he wants?"

"Power," murmured Cravin. "He wants to control the north. With Bren's armies at his disposal, he thinks he can dominate Annis and Highwall and Borc knows who else." He turned and looked Maybor straight in the eye. "As I said before, Baralis is a dangerous man."

Everything was starting to fall into place for Maybor. Why hadn't he thought of it himself? Baralis wanted to create a northern empire. The five-year border war with the Halcus fitted in nicely; he was merely softening the enemy up, so when the real war came he could hit them hard. "My son told me Kylock plans to invade Halcus once spring is fully here."

Cravin pulled back his lips to show a sharp-toothed smile. "Kylock has already invaded. I received word by pigeon yesterday."

Maybor hid his astonishment. "Aah. He decided to move fast, then."

"It would appear so," said Cravin. "Surprise was obviously his main consideration." A gust of wind caused him to draw his cloak close. "One thing's certain: the duke won't like it one little bit."

"Why can't he call the marriage off, then?" asked Maybor, wishing he too had brought a cloak.

"It's not that simple. The betrothal has gone too far now. He'll lose face by backing down, people will call him a coward. The best thing he can do is come up with a way of neutralizing the marriage."

"What d'you mean?"

"He should let the marriage go ahead as planned, but somehow—by either direct action or treaty—he should try and take the edge from the whole affair. At the moment the situation is fraught with risk: Annis and Highwall are nervous, the knights are having trouble in the south, and now Kylock's busy invading Halcus." Cravin shook his head. "The duke must to do two things: first, he needs to dissipate tension in the north; and secondly, he needs to put Baralis in his place."

Maybor couldn't argue with that. Despite the flies, foul smell, and cutting wind, he was beginning to enjoy himself. "Do you think he can pull it off?"

"I would never underestimate the duke," replied Cravin. "However, it's up to you and I to monitor matters carefully. If an opportunity presents itself, and in my experience one usually does, we must be there to seize the moment." A naked glance left Maybor with no doubt that the man was talking about treason.

Cravin reached in his cloak and pulled out a slip of parchment no bigger than the palm of his hand. He held it out to Maybor. "Take this, it is the address of a lodging of mine on the south side of the city. It's very discreet, no one knows it exists. If you ever need to meet anyone in private and don't want the eyes of the court upon you, feel free to use it as your own." Cravin began to move away. "The servants there always know how to contact me if you should ever have need." He bowed once and was gone in an instant.

Maybor tucked the parchment under his belt, waited a moment, and then began to trace Cravin's path back to the palace. The man's footsteps were stamped in blood, so his path was easy to follow.

Twenty

Melli followed Nessa into the stables. Long forgotten smells filled her senses: hay and dung and grease for the tack. The duke, who had seen fit to ignore her all of yesterday, had requested that she accompany him for a short ride. So here she was, dressed in a sturdy cloak with not a single frill to soften the eye, determined to pick the best mount she could find. Her father had kept stables in his estate in the Eastlands, and she knew from experience that nothing annoyed a horse owner more than when an inexperienced guest chose to ride his best mount. Melli knew that she was far from inexperienced, but the duke didn't, and he would be furious at her selection.

"I'll take that one," she said to the groom, indicating a fine chestnut stallion.

"But miss," said the groom, "the duke likes to ride Sparsis himself."

Melli turned to Nessa. "Did the duke express the wish that I should take any horse of my choice?"

Nessa nodded vigorously. Having spent a full day together, Nessa was now firmly in Melli's court.

The groom did not look happy, but complied with Melli's wishes. He saddled the horse, muttering words to the effect that it just wasn't decent for a woman to ride a stallion. He led the horse through to the courtyard and held his hand out for the mounting

Melli straddled the horse like a veteran. She settled herself in the saddle whilst her feet found the stirrups. Everything fit beautifully—the groom had a good eye. The horse she had ridden here was nothing compared to this powerful creature. She bent down and whispered gentle words of encouragement in his ear. They were going to be friends, she was sure of it.

"Where does His Grace intend to ride today?" she asked of the groom.

Seeing how well she sat the horse, the groom looked a little more respectful. "Well, miss, I can't be certain, but for short rides he likes to go to the meadow at the green side of the valley, behind the trees." He pointed to a place that looked to be no more than three leagues away.

"Very good. Tell His Grace that I shall meet him there." Melli pulled on the reins and turned her horse.

Both Nessa and the groom were openmouthed, but she gave neither of them time to protest. Her heels kicked against the stallion's flanks and she was off, trading cobblestones for grass in the swish of a horse's tail.

The wind was in her hair, fresh air was in her lungs, and a mighty beast lay between her thighs. It was wonderful. Melli felt free for the first time in many weeks. Even to be outside was a treat. The view was breathtaking. The lodge was situated on the curve of a slope that led down to a breathtaking valley. A lake lay at its center and trees, mostly firs, formed small groups around its edges like women at a dance. Ahead of her lay the mountains, terrible in their splendor, still white with winter's weeds.

The horse was nervous of its new rider and reacted skittishly to her commands, but Melli persisted in treating it gently, but firmly, and gradually, as they made their way across the valley, the stallion became settled.

It would be so easy to just ride away and never come back. Easy, yet dangerous. Melli valued her life too highly to risk galloping off into the mountains. Funny, but the idea of escape didn't appeal to her much at the moment. She was in no physical danger and the duke hadn't pressed her for any sexual favors, so she felt safe for the time being. And, if she were honest with herself, she was actually looking forward to the duke catching up with her. Melli couldn't wait to deal haughtily with his anger and then confound him by showing off her skills with a horse. He was such an arrogant man, practically begging to be taken down a peg.

Melli thought he would have requested her presence yesterday. All afternoon she had waited for his summons, hair dressed, pretty shoes pinching, and cheeks bright with the flush of fine wine. She was disappointed when no word came. Staying in her room was dull, and Nessa's company left a lot to be desired. The duke might be annoying, but at least he wasn't boring.

Her best policy concerning her mysterious parentage was, she decided, to stick to her original story, and no matter how hard the duke challenged her give nothing away. Stubbornness came naturally to Melli, so this course shouldn't prove too difficult. The duke wouldn't be able to trick, or catch her off guard, again.

Aware that her horse had not used a tenth of his potential, Melli urged him into a gallop. For an instant she was scared by the power. Then, a second later, she was thrilled by it. She brought her body down and gave him the reins. Ditches, streams, fallen logs, and boulders: her horse leapt them all with the grace of a demon. She could feel his sweat soaking her skirts. The ground was a blur and the distant trees were a target. She couldn't tell whose heart was beating faster: hers or her horse's.

The minute she pulled on the reins, Melli became aware of a sound behind her. Hooves were thundering at her back. It could only be the duke. She brought her horse to a halt and spun to meet him. Minutes passed as he drew close. His first words were: "Are you out of your mind! What were you thinking, taking my best stallion? It's a wonder it hasn't killed you."

Melli raised an eyebrow to an arch. "I didn't realize you had such protective instincts. Perhaps in a former life you were a shepherd." She turned her horse on a pinpoint and galloped off.

Unable to keep the smile from her face, Melli struck a path for the far trees. She heard the duke pursuing her, and after a minute he seemed to be gaining. "Come on, Sparsis," she whispered to her horse. "Time to show your owner your worth." A squeeze of thighs and a guiding pull on the reins and the course was altered enough to take in a filigree of tiny streams that were bent upon the lake. Horse and rider jumped them like gods. Then came one final leap. The stream rested in a depression and the breadth was hard to judge until they were on top of it. The bank on the other side was sharply sloped. The stallion cleared the water, and then slammed into the slope, shank first.

Melli was thrown forward. Almost in slow motion she saw the rocky bank approaching. She even knew which rock was hers. *Crack!* A sharp pain in her forehead, a sharper pain in her side, and then everything went black.

Jack felt a sudden pain in his forehead. He was holding a cup of water and lost his grip, sending it smashing to the floor.

Magra looked up. "Jack, are you all right?" There was genuine concern in her voice.

He wished she'd never spoken, for until her words had skimmed across his thoughts, he'd been seeing a vision of Melli. Gone now. Even as Magra got up from her chair, he was beginning to doubt it had happened.

Magra ignored the broken cup and took his hand. "Come on, Jack," she said. "Sit down by the fire for a while." The lines of her beautiful, haughty face were taut with worry. She led him to the bench and forced him to sit. Then she surprised him by kneeling down at his feet. Her cool hand still held his.

"Jack," she said softly, "you don't have to go through with it tonight." He started to protest, but she spoke over him. "No, hear me out. You can leave the cottage today. I have some gold set aside—not much, but enough to ease your journey. Please take it." She squeezed his hand tightly. "I would never forgive myself if anything happened to you."

Jack looked into the deep blue of her eyes. She was speaking the truth. It had been a long, long time since anyone had worried about him. He brought her hand to his lips and kissed it gently. Such smooth and fragile flesh. His mother would have been the same age, if she lived. "There's no need to worry about me," he said. "I'm going to be coming back. I promise you that."

"I expect you to keep that promise, Jack." Magra smiled, and for one instant she looked so like Tarissa it took his breath away. One final squeeze of his hand and she was up, brushing down her skirts and tut-tutting over the broken cup.

Tarissa came bursting into the room—Jack liked the fact that she wasn't one for discreet entrances. Seeing Magra picking up pottery fragments, she said, "What's been going on here? I only left to feed the chickens and when I get back, you two are busy destroying the place."

Jack and Magra laughed. The atmosphere in the cottage was so much lighter when Rovas wasn't around. Tarissa went for a cloth to soak up the water and Jack turned back to kneading the dough for the week's baking. They had no proper oven, so the freshly prepared dough would be taken to the town to be baked. It was nice to be here, all working around each other, exchanging jokes and small talk, holk warming on the fire, tallow burning with a smoky flame. It felt like home.

Jack was struck by a sudden deep hatred of Rovas. How could he have threatened to throw these two honest and hard-working women out of the house unless Tarissa did his bidding? He was a truly despicable man. Magra and Tarissa deserved better than someone who sought to control them by casting out a net of dependency and shared guilt.

Once finished with the kneading, Jack placed the loaves on a large wooden tray. With a sharp knife he slashed the top of each one and then covered them with a damp linen cloth.

Magra stepped forward. "If they're ready, I'll take them into town." She went to pick up the tray.

"But Rovas has taken the cart," said Jack. "You can hardly walk all that way on your own. I'll come with you."

"No, Jack. You can't risk going into town." It was Tarissa. "Mother will be all right. She'll find Rovas once she's there and he can bring her home."

"That's my plan," agreed Magra.

Jack realized that it *was* indeed a plan, drawn up by both women in advance to give him and Tarissa a chance to be alone. He took the linen cloth off the tray and removed half the loaves; he was not going to let Magra carry such a heavy weight all the way into town. She started to protest, but he stopped her. "I won't allow you out of the house, otherwise," he said. "Besides, I'm sure I can bake these into something on the fire. They might be a little flat, a little burnt, and a little tasteless, but if nothing else we can feed them to Rovas."

Everyone laughed. Magra picked up the newly lightened tray whilst Tarissa held the door for her. "Take care, Mother," she said, laying a kiss upon her cheek. Jack came and stood beside her, and both watched as the older woman walked up the muddy path and onto the muddy lane.

"Are you sure it's safe for her to go alone?" asked Jack as Tarissa closed the door.

"Really, Jack, you know Mother, she's a lot tougher than she looks. She might have been a delicate court beauty once, but that was over twenty years ago." Tarissa slipped her arm through his. "Come on, let's not waste a minute." She pulled him toward the fire.

Tarissa's words about her mother started Jack thinking about a subject he hadn't considered for some time. "Who is your father?" he asked.

Surprise flitted across Tarissa's face. "Why do you ask now?"

"Why not? Is it such a big secret?"

Tarissa sighed and turned her face toward the fire. "He was a very important person."

"Was?"

"He's dead now." Tarissa spun around. "Please, Jack, let's not spend today dragging up the past. I won't ask you any questions, so please don't ask me any." She took his face in her hands and kissed him full on the lips. "If we must talk about anything, let it be the future."

He kissed her back. Her saliva acted like a drug, taking his mind from its purpose. Nothing mattered anymore, only following the slope of her tongue to the softness behind her teeth.

They made love by the slow-burning fire. It was nothing like the first time; there was no terrible frenzy, no feeling that it was salve upon a wound. There was gentleness and touching—and wonder as he looked upon her form. When finally they fell apart, sweated skin resisting the separation, it was a feeling of tenderness, not relief, that united them.

Jack tilted Tarissa's chin and looked into her eyes. Tears welled at the corners. "What's the matter?" he asked, immediately thinking he'd done something wrong.

"Jack, I'm so worried. I might never see you again." As Tarissa spoke, a heavy tear slid down her cheek. "Promise me you won't do anything brave or daring. If it looks dangerous, just get out of there as fast as possible."

"I promise." His second today. Jack realized that Rovas' words were true: *"Magra and Tarissa would never forgive me if you didn't come back."* Surely then the smuggler could be trusted?

Jack had given Rovas' plan a lot of thought and there were still things that bothered him. "Did you ever help Rovas smuggle goods into the garrison?" he asked, trying to keep his tone light.

"Yes, I used to stand guard near the tunnel entrance, keeping watch for the patrol." Tarissa wiped the tears from her eyes. "Why do you ask?"

"That's how I'll make my escape. Did you ever enter the tunnel?"

"No, but I know it leads somewhere in the officers' quarters." Tarissa began to pull on her clothes. "You know there's a huge rock above the entrance?"

Jack nodded. He was pleased with what Tarissa said: it confirmed all that he had been told by Rovas.

"Will Rovas be there to help you out?" she asked.

"No," said Jack. "He said I could manage it on my own and that guards patrol the area regularly. So it would be too dangerous to wait around."

"For Rovas, maybe—that man couldn't hide in a blackened barn—but for me it would be easy. I used to do it all the time. I'd hide up a tree until I saw the rock moving, then I'd slide down and help push it out of the way. If the patrol was passing I'd hoot like an owl, so Rovas would know it was best to wait."

"You're not coming," said Jack. "It's too dangerous."

"Oh, yes I am. I won't even tell Rovas. I'll just be there to help with the rock. I'll find my own way back."

"No, you won't."

"Yes, I will, and you can't stop me." She was quite determined now.

Although Jack didn't like the idea, he couldn't help admiring Tarissa for her bravery. The thought that she was willing to risk her own safety for him was heartwarming. He grabbed hold of her arm and pulled her close. Tarissa squawked indignantly. She was in the middle of pulling on her drawers and landed in an unladylike heap in his lap. Jack burst out laughing; he couldn't stop himself. Tarissa slapped him, not at all gently, and scrambled to her feet. "Well, I'm coming and that's final. I'll have no man tell me what I can and can't do."

How could he prevent her? In some ways Tarissa was like Melli: stubborn to a fault. Part of Jack was pleased at her resolution. It was nice to think she would be waiting for him. "Well, it seems I have no choice but to agree."

Tarissa came and flung her arms around him.

"But," he said, disentangling himself and pushing her back so he could look directly in her eyes, "you must make me the same promise that I made you: no unnecessary daring, no bravery. First sign of danger and you're gone."

"I promise."

Jack held her arms tightly and wondered how he could strengthen the promise; it seemed too flimsy to guard the safety of one so precious. "Do you swear on your father's memory?"

Tarissa gave him a deep, unreadable look, and answered, "I do."

Tavalisk was eating otters. Sea otters, to be exact. Such adorable furry creatures and so tender when caught fresh from the womb. These ones had been caught by a master: no club marks to mar their fragile skulls. They must have been smothered, and carefully at that. The rocky coastline just north of Toolay was the only place these rare creatures existed. According to the men that caught them, their numbers grew less each passing year. The archbishop didn't believe a word; it was all a ploy to up the cost. Take these six beauties here: nearly a gold apiece at current market prices. It was nothing short of outrageous! Still, little was wasted. He intended to have a fine collar made from their pelts.

Oh, but they were succulent, though. All one had to do was hold a bone in the mouth and suck; the flesh came off more quickly than a cleric's robe in a brothel. All things considered, it was rather a strange-tasting meat: a little salty, a little fishy, a little piquant on the tongue. In fact, it wasn't really to his liking; but it *was* expensive. Sometimes that was all that counted.

There was a knock at the door and in walked Gamil. He was carrying a wax-sealed letter. "This has just arrived by fast messenger, Your Eminence. It's come all the way from Bren."

As Gamil leaned over him to hand him the letter, Tavalisk took hold of his assistant's robe and used it to wipe the grease from his hands. Gamil had little choice but to ignore the indignity.

"Aah," said Tavalisk breaking the seal. "It's from our friend Lord Maybor. My letter must have been forwarded to him in Bren." He raced through the spidery script. "The man writes like a blind monk. Hmm, he's still in our corner, though he is urging caution, he says—" Tavalisk read from the letter "'. . . there are ways to rid ourselves of the dark villain without opposing the match.' He's obviously afraid that if he comes out openly against the marriage, then his lands and position will be endangered, which of course they will. Kylock as sovereign could hardly let one of his subjects brazenly flout his wishes."

Tavalisk read on. "Maybor is basically asking me if there is any way I can use my influences to have Baralis killed: 'You are a great man, with contacts throughout the Known Lands, you must know someone in Bren who could do the deed.'" The archbishop broke into a high, tinkling laugh. "No. No, my dear Maybor. I'm not falling for that one. There'll be snow on the drylands before I do another man's dirty work for him."

"I don't understand, Your Eminence," said Gamil.

"I am surrounded by fools!" Although he sounded annoyed, Tavalisk was really rather pleased by the statement: rather fools than foxes. "Maybor is a self-serving coward. He probably has some personal vendetta against Baralis and thinks he can use me to settle it for him." The archbishop picked up an otter's rib and dipped it in sauce. He brought it to his lips, bit on it, and then began to wave it at Gamil as he spoke. "Now, I dislike Baralis as much as the next man, but the time isn't right to assassinate him yet. There are other factors to be taken into consideration first."

"Such as, Your Eminence?"

"The Knights of Valdis for one. Kill Baralis now and the pot will be taken off the boil; I'll lose my one chance of finally putting Tyren in his place." The archbishop was about to mention his plan to become head of the Church, but then thought better of it. He wasn't sure how much he could trust his aide. "Anyway, as a man of the cloth, it wouldn't be right for me to sanction murder." Was that a snort he heard from Gamil?

"So what does Your Eminence intend to do with Lord Maybor?"

Tavalisk ran his tongue along the bone then sucked upon the tip. "Lord Maybor will soon come to realize that he's involved in something more important than a mere petty rivalry. At such a time he will need the support of his friends. Write him a letter stating that when he finds the courage to follow his convictions, then I'll be ready with the gold to back them."

"Very good, Your Eminence. Is there anything else?"

"Yes, actually, there is. I've been wondering about our other friend, the knight. It's been a long time since I heard news of him. If memory serves me correctly, didn't the Old Man send out two of his cronies to track him down?"

"Yes, Your Eminence. I had the traitor interrogated in order to find out what the Old Man was up to, but he died on me."

Tavalisk paused in tearing a leg from the otter. "That was rather careless of you, Gamil. I wondered why you'd kept silent about the whole thing."

"I beg Your Eminence's apologies. I am not as skilled at these things as you are."

"Well, at least you recognize that fact. Go on." Off came the leg, tendons flapping in futile protest. Thigh meat was not as appetizing as rib.

"The last we heard about the knight, he was due to fight the duke's champion. I haven't been able to ascertain yet whether he won or lost, but by all accounts he was in pretty bad shape, so it's highly probable that the outcome was not favorable. If he's not already dead, then his days are surely numbered. The Old Man is not famous for his missions of mercy, and his two cronies would most certainly have arrived in Bren by now."

"Yes, I'm sure they have." Tavalisk had lost interest in the otters and pushed the platter aside. "Before you leave, Gamil, I wonder if you can do me one small favor."

"Certainly, Your Eminence."

"I'd be grateful if you could just run over to the market district for me. These sea otters are tender, but I think they might be off. Be so kind as to get me a refund. Tell the stallholder I intend to keep their pelts as punishment for selling shoddy goods. Obviously I'm willing to accept any further gifts he may feel the need to bestow upon me once the subject of informing the magistrates is mentioned."

Gamil bowed. "Your Eminence is master of the judicious threat."

Tawl had to get out of the palace. He needed to be alone to think, to walk the dark streets and look up at the stars. Feeling better than he had in days, he rose from his straw pallet. Tawl's first instinct was that of a knight after combat: mentally he checked every muscle, every tendon, every cell in his body for damage. Running through the procedure he'd learned at Valdis, he started at the heart and worked his way outward. Following the lines of the major arteries, his consciousness swept along with his blood.

Straight away he met a blockage. The blood vessels in his upper chest were damaged, some were blocked. Blayze's knife had severed them, the cauterizing iron had sealed them. There was muscle damage, too. He would need leeching to encourage the blood to flow through the tissue. Upward he traveled. His brain was swollen from the sleeping draughts. Envisioning the unnatural substances as debris, Tawl concentrated on sweeping them away with his blood. Next he went downward to his stomach. There was some minor internal bleeding: a legacy of either the hemlock or the fight. A gentle constriction of the blood vessels would give the lining a chance to heal. His kidney was recovering from a well-placed blow; there was a little swelling, but nothing that wouldn't mend on its own.

Finally, Tawl traveled to his limbs. A myriad of damaged veins and arteries caused him to switch his path like logs across a road. Blayze had given him a score of bruises, some barely registering, while others, like the one on his left shin, were surrounded by pools of yellowing blood. Tawl worked quickly, forcing blood through vessels that were threatening to close and drawing the flow away from ones that were too weak to bear the strain.

The last thing he came to were his circles. The burn was healing slowly. Skin was forming around the scab. Pink and shiny, fragile as a newborn babe, it was beginning to bridge the gap. It would be many months before his arm was fully recovered. There was nothing Tawl could do to quicken the process—even Valdis had its limits.

The monitoring complete, Tawl drew his mind from his body. A slight dizziness accompanied the shift. The doctors had done a good job. He'd be left with a few more scars but little permanent damage. A wiry smile crossed his lips; it was obviously going to take more than one man to kill him.

Nabber was nowhere to be seen. He was probably off somewhere looking for loot or trouble. He'd probably find it, too. Tawl smiled again, this time with real pleasure. There was no one like Nabber for getting himself into trouble.

A full ale skin lay resting upon the table. Tawl picked it up, unstoppered the cap, and began to pour the contents onto the fire. When the skin was half empty, he raised it to his lips and took a healthy swig. Never again would he lose himself to drink, but it wasn't in his nature to live like a saint. One mouthful was enough, though, and the rest of the ale he sent hissing to the flames.

It was time to deal with the past. Slipping his knife through his belt, Tawl made his way across the kitchens. A pretty maid showed him the way out and then hinted that she was free most evenings. He bowed deeply, tempted by her offer, yet declining it all the same. She was too young, too innocent, and he needed too much. He would strip her of all her illusions.

Outside the air was cold. The wind cut past his cheeks, clearing away any last traces of drowsiness. His chest pained him as he walked toward the gatehouse. The palace guards waved him through the gate. Shadows grew longer as he watched, and by the time he'd made his way across the square, they'd all merged into one and named themselves the night.

Bevlin was dead. To complete his quest now would be meaningless; *he* didn't know why the boy was important, or what he was fated to do. Tawl brushed his hair from his eyes. It wasn't that simple, but it would do for a start. He had to bring order to his life. He was no longer a knight, but he'd lived by Valdis' code for so long that it had made him who he was. Discipline and duty ran deep within his veins. The need to be worthy ran even deeper. *Es nil hesrl.* I am not worthy. They were the last words on every knight's lips, and doubtless he'd die with them on his own. Valdis would follow him to the grave.

Tawl lifted his bandaged arm. Surely there was some way to make amends for his mistakes. Not public amends—he was long past caring what other people thought—but personally, for himself. Forgiveness could never be his, so all he could hope for was a sense that his sins weren't committed in vain. The only thing he had to hold on to was his newly sworn oath to the duke. There at least was a chance to serve someone well; with honor, if he were blessed.

He had taken the oath entirely aware of what it meant. He wasn't drunk with liquor or punches, or lightheaded from loss of blood. He was stone cold sober. It marked the end of his knighthood and his quest, and knowing that he spoke it gravely. In a way it was little more than an official declaration of what he'd known since the night he'd murdered Bevlin: there was no going back. The oath was his way of severing all ties with the past.

Taking a turn-off, Tawl found himself in a narrow street lined by dark buildings. The full moon, which had shown itself earlier, was hidden behind chimneys and slates. A footfall, light as a landing bird, sounded in the distance behind him. Without conscious thought, Tawl's hand stole toward his knife. There were two of them. The breeze carried their odors and they disturbed more rats than one man alone.

Out came the blade, not a sound to mark its passing. Tawl slowed down and gave his pursuers chance to catch him. He counted to twelve and then turned around to meet them. He hoped they were well armed; it would be good to die fighting. Just as he leapt forward, a man's voice cried out:

"Here, Tawl! Leave it out. We didn't come all the way from Rorn to be murdered down a dark alley, did we, Clem?"

Clem shook his head. "No, Moth."

Tawl struggled to right himself. He couldn't believe it. What were two of the Old Man's cronies doing following him? An instant later he answered his own question: they'd come to Bren to kill him for Bevlin's murder. Only they didn't look very murderous.

"I see you finally got your hands on some nice weaponry," said Moth, eyeing his blade. "Course, Clem's got a better one, ain't you, Clem?"

Clem nodded enthusiastically.

"I see you're a little surprised to see us, my friend," continued Moth. "I must say we're a little surprised to be here. Never thought we'd get to see the beautiful brazen battlements of Bren, did we, Clem?"

"Not the brazen battlements. No, Moth."

Tawl didn't know how to react. Part of him wanted to clasp both men's arms and take them for a drink. Another part of him felt too ashamed to do anything but wait and discover their purpose. How much did the Old Man know?

"You're a difficult man to track down, my friend. If it wasn't for Clem here, we would never have found you."

"How was that, Moth?" asked Clem.

"Well, you were the one who insisted we take a walk in the full moon."

Clem smiled proudly. "That I did, Moth."

"So the credit's all yours, Clem."

"But you were the one who spotted him, Moth."

"You have a point there, Clem. I say we both did the Old Man proud."

"Why are you here?" demanded Tawl. He had the distinct feeling that, if left to their own devices, Moth and Clem could carry on like that all night. "Have you come to take me to the Old Man?"

"Not at all, my friend. You wouldn't be standing here if that was the plan. Would he, Clem?"

Moth had a point. Last time Tawl had encountered them he hadn't even heard them coming.

"We've got a letter to give you, ain't we, Clem?"

Tawl felt a pulse begin to beat on either side of his forehead. The smell of the abattoir caught in his nostrils. "Who is the letter from?"

Moth took off his cap and nudged Clem, who did likewise. "The letter is from the recent and most tragically deceased Bevlin."

Tawl couldn't look at either of them. There was a dry lump in his throat. "Why give it to me?"

"Because it's addressed to you, my friend," said Moth. "Just before the good man died, he sent a missive to the Old Man with a second letter inside it. Apparently he left instructions that—" He turned to his companion. "How did he put it, Clem?"

"That in the event of his death it should be forwarded to the knight, Moth."

"Beautifully done, Clem. No one can remember word for word like you."

Tawl felt sick. He'd come this far, sworn an oath that forever damned him, and had just found a measure of acceptance for his new fate. He didn't want to resurrect the past. There were too many memories that could drag him down. The only way he could cope was to keep it all behind him. "I don't want the letter."

Moth looked a little taken aback. "Well, we've got to deliver it, my friend. Will you do the honors, Clem?"

Clem searched in his tunic and pulled out a folded parchment. As dark as it was, Bevlin's seal could clearly be seen in the wax. It was the color of blood. Clem held it out for Tawl to take.

Despite everything, Tawl could not keep his hand from moving forward. His fingers itched to feel the smooth surface of the parchment. Just as he was about to take the letter, the moon rose over the chimneys. Full and large, it seemed to fill the sky, yet there was only one destination for its light: Tawl's arm. The bandage covering his circles glowed white in the moonlight. Instinctively Tawl pulled his arm away, the moonlight followed the move. He tilted his arm away from the moon, but somehow its light still caught the bandage. Under the linen lay the circles. Under the circles lay a man not worthy to bear them.

He was no longer a knight of Valdis. There *was* no quest. He didn't have the right to take the letter. He served the duke of Bren now, not Bevlin's memory.

Tawl pulled back his arm. "I can't take the letter. I'm sorry. If you'd found me four days earlier . . ." He couldn't finish the thought, let alone the words.

"But we came all this way," said Moth. "The Old Man won't be pleased, will he, Clem?"

"He'll be right mad, Moth."

"Look, me and Clem are going to walk away. We're going to leave the letter on the ground. When we're gone, you can take it and no one will ever know."

Tawl smiled at Moth and shook his head. "It's not as easy as that. I wish that it were."

"Me and Clem hate to see you upset, Tawl," said Moth. "Is there anything we can do to help—on the quiet, like, not a word to the Old Man?"

"No, nothing, but I thank you all the same." Tawl held out his arm and clasped both men's forearms in turn. "Please leave. Do whatever you have to with the letter."

Moth and Clem pulled aside for an instant and exchanged a few hurried words. "Clem wants to know if you need any coinage," said Moth.

"No, thank you, Clem." Their kindness was almost too much. He didn't deserve it.

A few more hurried words and then they both turned toward him. "Well," said Moth, "it looks like me and Clem will be on our way. We've decided that we're going to leave the letter anyway, haven't we, Clem? Can't go back with the thing. It wouldn't look good."

Clem nodded rather solemnly and placed the letter at Tawl's feet.

"Me and Clem wish you profit on your journey."

"And health at your hearth," said Clem.

"Nicely put, Clem," said Moth. The two backed away from Tawl as if he were a king. Shuffling backward they reached the end of the street, waved once in silent salute, and then were lost in the shadows of the city.

Tawl wanted to call them back. But he wouldn't. He wanted to read the letter. But he couldn't. He stood in the moonlight, a lonely figure without a cloak, and waited until he was ready. The letter shifted in the breeze, its corners lifting seductively. A trace of text could be seen for a moment; it was written in Bevlin's clumsy hand. Tawl knew he had to go: stay any longer and he would succumb to temptation and tear the letter open. His soul screamed to read it. Duty demanded he wouldn't: he was the duke's to command now. One oath broken was enough.

He turned and walked away.

Twenty-one

*N*abber watched from the shadows, hardly daring to breath. Every part of his still small body was intent upon willing Tawl to pick up the letter, but he didn't. The knight—for Tawl would never be anything except a knight to Nabber—walked away from the letter and never looked back. A very real pain constricted Nabber's heart and a very real tear fell down his cheek. Swift's words echoed in his ear: *"That's what you get for snooping where you're not wanted."*

How could he have let Tawl go out on his own, though? The knight was weak, injured, and obviously deranged: he'd poured a full skin of ale on the fire! A man like that needed watching, closely.

Nabber had spied on Tawl from the moment he got up from his pallet, eventually following him out of the palace. The castle guards had given him a bit of trouble; they didn't believe that he was a guest of the duke. Nabber snorted indignantly. He soon put them right, even had them apologizing and offering to share their supper. Round about now Nabber was wishing he'd taken them up on the offer: there was a hole the size of a decent pork pie in his stomach and it was getting bigger, and not at all quietly at that. There had been moments when Nabber thought his stomach had given the game away. It rumbled viciously while the two cronies had been talking to the knight.

Nabber knew they were from the Old Man before they even opened their mouths. Their menacing mismatched forms were a familiar sight on the streets of Rorn. No one messed with them. Quite a pair, by all accounts, their specialty being beating up reluctant shopkeepers. Nabber couldn't remember their names, but their faces were hard to forget.

When he'd first spotted them, he thought they were going to slice Tawl to ribbons. There had been one hair-raising instant when he felt sure he was going to have to jump in and save Tawl. Again. Wasn't to be, though. They'd come to talk to him. Seemed right friendly, they did. Nabber then decided they were going to kidnap the knight instead—particularly when the big one reached inside his tunic. But it wasn't a knife he wielded, it was a letter.

Nabber had quickly scuttled nearer. He wanted to catch what was being said. He was barely feet away, body pressed against a rotting timber, feet buried in a mound of . . . waste. Evil rats chewing at his toes, the smell of the abattoir on the breeze. It was just like home. He could hear everything. The letter was from Bevlin, and Tawl didn't want to look at it. Although the knight was adamant, Nabber felt sure that he would pick it up once the Old Man's cronies were gone. Only he didn't. Two minutes ago he'd walked away, leaving the letter unopened on the ground.

It wasn't right. There was no way that he, Nabber, friend of the great thieves and one-time disciple of Swift, was going to leave that letter there on the street for any milk maid or barrow-boy to pick up at their leisure. No. It was private property. And if Tawl didn't want it, then he certainly did.

A quick look left and then right, a sharp sniff of the air, and then he waded through the waste and onto the street. He went straight over to the letter and slipped it in his tunic. Strange, but in all his life Nabber had never really considered himself a thief; pocketing was more of a pastime than a crime, yet now, as he made his way back toward the palace with the letter resting against his chest, he felt for the first time that he'd taken something that wasn't his to take. He vowed he would never open it. The letter belonged to Tawl, and it was his duty to keep it for him.

As soon as Rovas dropped him off in the cart, Jack realized he had no idea how to carry a barrel of ale. Wider than a man, it wouldn't rest well on his shoulder, and it proved hard to get a decent grip if he held it at his chest. The sweat on his hands didn't help, either. He was scared. Talking about murdering Vanly was one thing, actually going through with it quite another. He was on the far side of town, and according to Rovas the garrison lay half a league to the south.

Jack lifted the barrel for the final time, dipping his head down and bringing it over his shoulder. If he kept his torso bowed forward, he could keep it balanced on his back. Rovas had filled it close to the brim. He could hear the ale sloshing away as he walked. The momentum of the fluid worked against him, slowing him down and causing his feet to hesitate as he stepped. He probably looked drunk.

After walking for five minutes he felt as if he needed a drink. His back strained with the weight and with the unnatural angle. The muscles in his arms were beginning to protest at being held over his head for so long, and he'd exuded enough sweat to fill a second barrel. The most annoying thing, however, was his hair: it had fallen down in a wet tangle over his face and now he couldn't see where he was going. Letting go of the ale was out of the question—if he put it down now he wasn't entirely sure he'd be able to pick it up again—so he was forced to walk watching his feet.

The night air was cool, but not cold, and the full moon illuminated every step. Not a good night for discreet getaways. Carrying the ale actually helped to calm Jack's nerves. On the journey here his throat felt so dry that he couldn't manage a word to Rovas, but now, forced to concentrate on bearing a load that weighed about as much as Tarissa, but was a lot more awkward to handle, his mind was firmly on the job in hand.

To lighten his mood, Jack began to whistle a tune. He knew it was a mistake as soon as he started, for the small low noise just made the night seem larger. He decided to carry on anyway, at least till he got to the chorus.

A cartload of people passed him; they were drunk and merry and laughed at his burden. Jack smiled and bowed his back further. He was close to the garrison now. Approaching from the north, he would come to the service entrance first. The road became muddy, and two people on foot walked past him. They paid the man with the barrel no heed. The dryness returned to Jack's throat as he fell under the moon-cast shadow of the fort.

The cartload of people were applying for entrance. There were two guards armed with spears and shortswords, just as Rovas said there would be. Everyone was laughing, guards included. A hamper was unloaded from the cart and the lid was taken off for inspection. The smell of roasted chicken hit Jack's nostrils. It made him sick. His stomach was too tight for food. After rummaging in the hamper and picking out a few morsels for themselves, the guards let the party through. They then turned their attentions to Jack.

"What you got there, boy?"

Jack swung the barrel down from his shoulders and placed it on the ground, tap up, in front of them. He brushed his hair back from his face and pointed at the barrel.

"What's the matter with you?" sneered the second guard. "Cat got your tongue?"

Jack's heart was beating so wildly, he was sure the guards would hear it. He shook his head violently, and then as an afterthought, bowed deeply to both men.

"He's dumb," said the first guard. "Look's a bit simple, too."

"Aye, he does that," agreed his companion. "His hair's right long, as well. Don't remember seeing anyone with hair as long as that in town before. Where you from, boy?"

Jack had no choice but to point toward the town.

"You're not going to get much out of him, Wesik. He's one arrow short of a full flight. Probably been employed by Ottley at the tavern. He's always on the lookout for cheap labor."

Jack nodded vigorously. He was tempted to back this gesture up with a simple smile, but opted for more nodding instead.

"You heard what happened at the tavern last week, Grimpley," said Wesik, the second guard. "A merchant got murdered in cold blood, throat slit and all. Who's to say it wasn't young long-hair here?"

"Leave it out, Wesik. This boy ain't no killer. The muscles in those arms were shaped by shifting barrels, not bodies."

Jack nodded again. He was getting tired of acting stupid. He would have liked to punch both men in the face—Wesik first.

"All right, all right. Have it your own way. What's in the barrel, boy? From the looks of that tap, it's Isro Amber." Jack nodded and Wesik continued. "Well, don't just stand there, pour us a cup."

Jack didn't have the slightest idea how to work the tap.

"Come on, come on. Quick about it."

As he reached toward the tap, Jack's hands were shaking uncontrollably. Under his breath he cursed Rovas for not showing him how to use it. The tap was tooled from brass and had a bolt, a lever, and a screw protruding from it. He opted for the lever first and then began to turn the screw. Both guards hovered over him, watching every move. Jack didn't realize how much he was sweating until he brushed his hand against his forehead: it came back soaking wet. With the screw loosened sufficiently to let the ale pass through the tap, Jack removed the bolt. Nothing.

"What you playing at, boy?" demanded Wesik.

Jack felt as if his heart was about to burst. Panicking, he started to pull, twist and flip indiscriminately, desperate to get the ale to flow.

Wesik swung his boot into the back of Jack's head. "Damn fool!"

Pain exploded in Jack's skull. He was sent forward against the barrel, chin catching against the metal tap.

"Leave the boy be, Wesik," said Grimpley, placing a restraining arm on his companion. "There's ladies coming."

Jack tasted blood in his mouth. Looking up, he saw three women approaching on foot.

"You armed, boy?" asked Wesik, eyes upon the women.

Jack shook his head.

Grimpley ran his spear point along Jack's tunic and down his legs, prodding every few inches to test for metal. "There's nothing on him."

Wesik crouched down beside Jack and grabbed the collar of his under-shirt. "Listen to me, boy," he said, his voice a slow, threatening drawl. "I'm going to give you fifteen minutes. If you're not out of here by then, I'm going to come looking for you." Slivers of chicken skin were caught between his teeth. He twisted Jack's collar. "Have you got that?"

Jack nodded.

"Good, now get yourself out of my sight."

Jack scrambled up, tilted the barrel a fraction, and heaved it toward his chest. It seemed twice as heavy as he remembered. His blood ran onto the wood. The guards let him through the gate and into the garrison. Wesik waited until he had cleared the steps and then said, "Fifteen minutes, boy, then I come looking."

Jack rounded the first corner he came to. He dropped the barrel on the floor, not caring how it landed. His head was reeling, his hands were shaking, and blood was spilling from his mouth. Fifteen minutes. He had no time to waste; he had to break open the barrel.

Footsteps followed by whispering voices. It was the three women at the gate. They walked past Jack as if he didn't exist. Looking around, he saw he was in a badly lit corner of the courtyard. In the distance, two men were playing dice against a wall. They were guards: spears rested in the dirt along with two flat ale skins. To the right was a large, well-lit build-ing; the shutters were open and it was full of people drinking and toasting. Probably the mess hall. A second, smaller structure leaned against it for support: the kitchens.

What to do next? Jack had read stories about heroes, and without exception they always knew what they were going to do and how they were going to do it. He didn't have a clue. Rovas had said it would be easy to find a bar or a pick to pry the barrel open, but Jack had no idea how he'd get his hands on anything like that. One of the guards' spears would do the job, but to try and take it from them would be madness. Maybe there would be something in the kitchens. He'd try there.

With the decision taken, Jack wasted no time. He rolled the ale barrel into the deep shadows of the corner and then slunk along the west wall until he came to the kitchen. The dicing guards never noticed his passing. Quickly he flitted around the side of the kitchen wall and through the narrow alleyway to the rear. Smells of roasting meat wafted from the doorway. The sound of laughing and singing came from the mess hall, and the sound of squabbling and shouting came from the kitchens.

Staying close to the wall and its concealing shadows, Jack inspected the kitchen courtyard. In the corner was a butchering block. His eyes searched for the gleam of an ax. A man in an apron stepped out from the doorway. Jack held his breath as he walked toward the very wall he was standing against. Sweat trickled down his back. The man came to halt about two horses' length from him. The moon picked that moment to disappear behind a cloud. Jack gave silent thanks to Borc. Lifting up his apron, the man fished around with the lower ties of his tunic and pulled out his manhood. He proceeded to piss against the wall. He hummed a tune whilst doing his business. Jack's right leg was beginning to cramp; he fought the desire to shift his weight onto his left side. He couldn't afford to move an inch.

The man finished relieving himself, looked at his manhood with pride, and then stuffed it back into his tunic. He paused a moment, as if he were listening for something, and then turned and walked back to the kitchens. Heaving a huge sigh of relief, Jack bent down to stretch his cramping muscle. The smell of urine met his nostrils.

He was running out of time. Dropping down on all fours, he began to crawl across the yard to the butcher's block. He couldn't see an ax from where he was, but there could still be something useful around the other side of the huge chunk of timber.

Jack crawled with a limp, his muscle still cramping. He knew he probably looked stupid, but that didn't matter: getting the barrel open as soon as possible was all that counted. The ground was muddy, yet it hadn't rained for several days. It was too dark to tell, but Jack guessed it was blood that soaked the ground around the block.

Luck was with him. At the back of the block was a meat hook. It wasn't as good as an ax, but it would do. Hooking it onto his belt, Jack crawled back to the kitchen wall.

Now came the dangerous part: he couldn't risk anyone seeing him, not now with mud and blood smeared across his tunic. The two guards had finished dicing. One was drinking from a third skin, the other was inspecting the point of his spear. Jack emerged from the alley and made for the wall. The moon appeared from behind the clouds. How long had he been? Five minutes? Ten? It was impossible to say. One thing was sure: he couldn't afford to wait for the moon to disappear again. Back brushing against the wall, Jack stepped sideways along its length. Everything was going well, till he stumbled against a tree root that had somehow forced its way under the wall. Both guards looked up. Jack froze. The guard with the spear began to walk toward the wall. Jack prayed he was hidden by the shadow. A voice called out. "Leave it, Bornis. It's only rats. Come and have a sup of ale before I finish the whole skin on my own." The guard hesitated a second and then returned to his companion.

Jack forced himself to count to a hundred before moving again. Time was getting crucial.

He reached the ale barrel with no further incidents. The corner was nice and dark, but just to make safe, Jack rolled the barrel into the recess behind the gate. No one could see him now—though the gate guards might hear him if he wasn't careful. Grasping the hook, he worked the tip between two of the planks. Why wouldn't his hands stop shaking? Slowly he began to crack the timber. Gently, gently, moving the hook back and forth, working it deeper into the join. There was a splintering sound and the hook became jammed in place. Jack grasped the handle firmly and swung it down against the barrel. *Crack!* The barrel opened. Ale gushed out at his feet. It was the most beautiful thing he'd ever smelled in his life.

Once the two timbers were cracked, it was easy to knock the rest of the wood inward. The metal hoops were no longer a problem. Jack pried the lid off the barrel, and as expected, there was a knife bundled in oilskin attached to its underside. Rovas had not lied. Unraveling the package, he dried the blade on his tunic and then tested it against his finger. It was so sharp he never felt it slice his skin.

Jack cupped his hands below the splintered timbers and caught a good measure of the foamy brew. He brought it to his face and didn't so much drink the ale as bathe in it. What little did find its way to his mouth tasted good. An idea occurred to him, and he lifted what was left of the barrel up above his shoulders and emptied it all down his chest. If anyone saw him now, he'd be just another beer-soaked fool.

Less than five minutes left. It was time to get down to business. What had Rovas said: the officers' quarters lay to the left of the service gate? Just as he was about to leave the shadows, Jack turned back and picked up the hook. It might come in handy.

The two gate guards were busy interrogating another visitor and they didn't see him dash by. Jack followed the wall until it turned east, all the time trying to remember Rovas' flour map. Ahead lay the covered arcade—just as the smuggler said. Sliding along the inside wall, Jack came to a supporting timber. Hunkering down, so his head would be lower than man height, he looked down the length of the arcade. Double doors. Two guards. Waiting for the watch to change was not an option: he was running out of time. What to do? What would heroes do? Silently slash both guards to ribbons?

Jack's legs were protesting at crouching down, so he decided to stand. As he did so, the butcher's hook that was looped over his belt caught on the material of his britches, causing them to tear all the way up to his waist. "Damn!" muttered Jack under his breath. He grabbed the meat hook and was just about to leave it on the ground beside him when he was distracted by voices. Looking out across the courtyard, through the wooden supports of the arcade, Jack spied a group of women and officers—seven or eight in all—and they were heading his way.

The hook was in his hand. There was only one thing to do. Keeping close to the beam and its shadow, Jack swung out. All his momentum was transferred to his right arm, and with one mighty heave, he sent the hook flying into the air: aiming straight for the officers and their ladies.

It was a silver streak across the sky. There was a dull thud, followed by a cry of pain. Then all hell broke loose. Women screamed in panic, men shouted for help. Guards came running from every direction. The hook had hit one of the officers in the back of the neck.

The guards at the double doors ran from their post toward the officers. Jack slipped out from the timber and ran through the shadows of the arcade. His heart was beating so hard he thought it would burst. The double doors were unlocked and he was through them in an instant. What had Rovas said? Stairs on the right. First door you come to.

Up the steps he dashed, the door was only a few feet away. Jack paused on the threshold to catch his breath. He pulled the knife from his tunic, brushed the hair from his eyes, lifted the door latch and burst into the room.

She was floating on clouds so high that she'd reached the place where the sky joined the heavens. A thin blue line and then nothing but white. Pain had long since gone. She could feel herself being pulled from her body. Not from the eyes, or the nose or the mouth, but from the side. She was escaping through a gap between her ribs.

Shadows hovered below, words and deeds merging into one. Earlier they were frantic: irons and needles flying like dog fur. Now they were quiet, the dog long dead.

Oil on her forehead, thyme leaf on her tongue, blood drip-dripping to a bowl.

"She's leaving us, Your Grace. Too much blood's been lost."

A hand hard with calluses gripped hers. "Melli. You must prepare your soul for God. Now is the time to lay your lies aside. Heaven only waits for those who are willing to speak the truth."

The thin blue line grew thinner. The white was so close it brushed against her cheek. Hot and cold, hard and soft, safe yet dangerous in one.

"Speak, child. Tell us who your family is. Lest your body rot waiting upon a father to bury it."

The clouds bore her upward to her mother. Words were difficult to form. The thyme on her tongue was as heavy as lead. "Tell Father I'm sorry."

"We can only tell him if we know who he is."

What was left of the blue line began to shimmer and fade. She knew she must speak before it went. "Maybor, Lord of the Eastlands, he is my father." The white was all about her; it stole into her body through the wound at her side. It began to force out what little substance was left.

"She must be saved at all cost. I don't care what you do: sorcery, devilry. *Just save her!*"

On the bed lay a man on top of a woman. Tears streaked down the woman's face. An imprint of a hand could clearly be seen on her cheek. Blood dripped from her mouth. "Help me," she sobbed.

Vanly sprang from the bed, pulling up his britches with one hand and reaching for his sword with the other. Jack lunged forward. His blade raked across Vanly's left hand. The man let his britches fall to the floor. Jack had time enough to thank Borc that the captain's undershirt was long enough to cover his vitals. He didn't fancy fighting a man whose tackle was on show. Vanly moved backward. He kicked off his britches, sending them flying toward Jack. Jack was forced to dodge them. This gave Vanly enough time to get a proper grip on his sword.

The captain leapt forward, blade in both hands, wielding it in the Halcus fashion. Jack jumped onto the bed. The woman screamed. Vanly's sword cut through the sheets. Scrambling over the woman, Jack sprang from the opposite side. Vanly was forced to turn to defend himself. His legs were crossed and his weight was distributed badly. Jack used this to his advantage, forcing Vanly further round by a series of quick thrusts to his left arm. Angry at being taunted, unable to wield his mighty sword because his feet weren't placed far enough apart, Vanly lashed out wildly. Using his sword as a knife was a terrible mistake. It was too heavy to be used thus. Jack dodged the blade and found enough space to slice his knife down the captain's side.

Shocked, Vanly stepped back. Beneath his oiled mustache, the captain's mouth was a thin line.

Jack knew his best tactic would be to crowd the man close, not giving him enough space to use his weapon. He leapt after him. Vanly tilted his sword up and Jack was forced to halt his attack; he wasn't quite ready to be impaled on the end of a Halcus blade.

Jack felt something against his foot: the end of Vanly's britches. Parrying his opponent, he noticed that both of the captain's feet were planted firmly on the other end. Jack bent down and tugged with all his might on the cloth. Vanly lost his footing and began to stumble backward. In came Jack, knife ready. The captain lost his two-handed grip on his sword, as he needed an arm to steady himself. It was all over. A sword of that size took two hands to wield. Jack lunged forward and stabbed the man in the heart. Vanly's blade clattered to the floor. Vanly himself followed after.

Jack had no time to relish his victory. Shouts could be heard coming from the direction of the stairs. He closed the door and turned to the woman. "Help me move the bed." She was too shocked to do anything but obey him. Wiping the tears from her eyes and the blood from her mouth, she came and stood beside him. Together they pushed against the oaken frame. It shifted with ease.

Underneath lay a raised square of floorboard: the trapdoor. Jack was so relieved he grabbed the woman and kissed her. "I'm sorry, I didn't mean to do that," he said, quickly realizing she was probably scared sick of all men.

She leaned forward and brushed the hair from his eyes. "It's all right. It doesn't matter," she said, trying to smile.

There was a loud knock at the door and a voice cried, "Captain! There's an intruder in the garrison. He's already brought one man down with a meat hook."

The woman took a deep breath and shouted: "Captain says he'll be with you in a minute. He's just finishing off his business."

The man grunted. "Best tell him to get a move on. This ain't no time to be wenching."

Jack and the woman listened as the man's footsteps moved away from the door. "Come on, then," she said. "Let's get this hatch open."

Jack nodded and they went to work on the trapdoor. It was heavy, but together they managed to lift it up. Peering down, Jack could see nothing but darkness. "Right," he said to the woman, "I'll lower myself first so I can gauge the drop. Then I'll stand below and catch you."

The woman shook her head. "I can't come with you."

"If you stay here, there's no telling what the guard might do."

"No," she said. "I've got to stay here. I can't go on the run like a criminal. I'll lose my livelihood. I'll tell the guards you overpowered me—if that's all right with you." The woman gave him a pleading look.

"You're taking a big risk. Come with me instead. I'll make sure you come to no harm."

She was firm. "No. You're wasting precious time. The guard will be back in a moment."

Jack had no choice but to leave her. Briefly, he toyed with the idea of knocking her out and slinging her body over his shoulder. No, he couldn't do that. She was too beautiful to hit over the head. He held his hand out and she took it, squeezing his palm.

"Luck be with you," she said.

"And with you also," he replied.

Taking a firm grip on the timber surrounding the entrance, Jack swung his feet into the blackness. Hanging by his arms, he couldn't feel the ground below him. The woman, whose name he would never know, gave him one last smile. He smiled back, silently counted *one, two, three,* and then let go of the wood.

Thud! He landed less than two seconds later. A sharp pain shot up both his legs and he fell onto his backside. Looking up, he saw the woman already beginning to draw the board over the top of the hole. The sight sobered him a little: they were both on their own now. Jack stood up and tested his legs; one ankle had been slightly twisted and both sets of muscles were sore. Above him a series of scrapes and bangs sounded and then he found himself in complete darkness. Time to get out of here.

The floor of the tunnel was boarded with rotting wood that cracked and splintered at every step. Its height matched his shoulders and he was forced to walk with his head bowed. His back, which had been through a lot earlier with the beer barrel, protested at every step. Hands held out in front of him, Jack scuttled along the length of the tunnel as quickly as he could manage. There was only one thing on his mind: Tarissa. She would be waiting for him at the other end.

The tunnel led downward for a while and then gradually leveled off. Never had Jack been in such complete darkness; his nose smelled earth and his feet felt wood, but there was nothing for his eyes to see. Splinters from the side braces stabbed at his hands. Stopping for a moment to catch his breath, Jack heard voices behind him. He looked back. A pale light appeared in the distance. Then he heard the unmistakable sound of dogs baying. It filled him with fear. He began to run as fast as he could. Faster and faster. They were gaining on him. His breath was like fire in his throat. The pain of a stitch ran across his belly. On and on he ran, not bothering to keep his hands out in front of him anymore.

Then all of a sudden he slammed into something solid. His entire body was jolted to the core. One of his wrists snapped back. He heard the sound of all his knuckles cracking at once. His knee smashed into the mass, while his chin took the last of the impact. Reeling with pain and dizziness, Jack scrambled on the floor of the passageway, groping for a way around the obstacle. The dogs were getting closer. He could now see individual torches, swaying with the movement of men.

The obstruction was solid, packed earth. Someone had blocked the tunnel. There was no way round. Jack clawed at the soil with his fingernails. He was trapped.

Trapped!

Then the dogs reached him. Panicking, Jack raised his arm for protection. One of the dogs tore at his arm, another went for his leg. The noise was deafening. Blood hungry, the dogs snarled and howled. Jack felt a pressure building in his head. He knew what it was and he welcomed it. A dog leapt at his face and he punched it down. The tension grew and grew, demanding release. He felt the sharp tang of sorcery on his tongue. The instant before he let go, something hard rammed against his chest. There was pain so terrible he couldn't bear it. Looking down, he saw the shaft of an arrow jutting from his tunic. It didn't look real. The dogs crowded about him and then he knew no more.

Twenty-two

No, Bodger, the quickest way to bed a woman isn't to tell her she's got a fine pair of melons."

"But Longtoad swears it works for him, Grift."

"Then Longtoad's women must all be stone deaf, for that sort of remark don't work on any wenches I know."

"What does, then, Grift?"

"Sophistication, Bodger. Sophistication. You go up to a wench, smile right nice and then say: *how's about me and you doing a spot o' rollickin'? I've had many women before and not one of them's complained.*"

"Hmm. I can see that might work, Grift."

"Never fails, Bodger. A woman likes a man to put his cards upon the table. It does you no harm to hint that your manhood's a fair size, too."

"Won't she be able to tell that already, Grift?"

"I should hope not, Bodger. Generally speaking, it's best not to pull it out until she's said yea or nay."

"No, Grift, I was talking about the whites of a man's eyes. Didn't you say that's how you can tell a man's size?"

"Oh, aye, I did indeed. It's gratifying that you remembered my wisdom, Bodger."

"I never forget a word you say. You've taught me everything I know." Bodger frowned and scratched his head. "Come to think of it, Grift, since I met you, I've had no success with women at all. They won't even look my way."

"Aah, Bodger, you've got much to learn. When they won't look your way, it's a sure sign that they're interested."

Bodger attempted a scathing look, failed miserably, and settled for a loud burp instead. "There's been a lot of coming and going in the palace these past two days, Grift. The duke's been dashing backward and forward from his hunting lodge, taking all kinds of doctors, priests, and supplies. I wonder what he's up to."

"Aye, it's mighty strange, Bodger. He took Bailor and his personal physicians with him yesterday, and now he's back again. The head groom says he was ordered to ready fresh mounts, so the duke's obviously intending to return to the lodge later."

"It must be something serious, Grift. I heard that it's a six-hour ride to the lodge."

"Aye, Bodger, a man like the duke doesn't ride twelve hours in one day unless it's a matter of life or death."

The sun slanted sharply across the room, fading the rich colors of the tapestries and sending a million motes of dust dancing into the air. Baralis was sitting up in his bed sipping on mulled holk. His hands ached as usual—even to stretch them around the cup was a strain—but apart from that one, solitary complaint he'd never felt better in his life.

The burns to his chest had completely disappeared. The only sign that anything had ever been wrong was a pale, raised line, which ringed his chest like the seam of a dress. He could feel where the sorcery had worked. Indeed, he could feel it still; its vestiges prompting old flesh to bond with new. The sensation was not unpleasant; a fertile burgeoning that tautened the skin and played upon the nerves like a fiddler, sending countless tiny impulses directly to his brain.

Three days he'd slept. Three perfect dreamless days where the only thing that he was aware of was the gentle hands of Crope. His servant was here now, stoking the fire as quietly as he could. He owed more than he could ever repay to the great hulking giant.

They met the year after he left the Great Plains. He had a purpose then and even knew his ultimate destination, the Four Kingdoms, but he wasn't ready to visit them yet. He needed to prepare, to learn, to plan. So first he went to Silbur.

Silbur, the shining jewel that sparkled at the center of the Known Lands. And that was exactly what it was: a jewel. A beautiful multihued city that had no purpose except for show. Religious councils met there, thousands made pilgrimage to visit the holy relics, He Who Is Most Holy sat upon his gilded throne, and every scholar who'd ever brought quill to parchment boasted about spending long hours on hard benches in its famous libraries. Silbur was a dead city, as much a relic as the bones and hair and teeth of long-dead saints and saviors that it depended upon for its income. There was no blood or flesh to the bone, no muscle to make it move. Great once, it had been unmatched in its arrogance and power. Towers were built tall to pierce the sky, walls were built low to scorn invaders. Silbur had no equal except for God.

The vision of its leaders had shaped the Known Lands. No one, they argued, should have more power than the Lord. Systematically, their armies tore apart the kingdoms and empires that made up the map of the civilized world. Emperors were evil, kings had commerce with the devil; the might of country took away from the might of God. They had to be broken. Bloody, terrible wars, the likes of which have never been seen before or since, ripped the continent asunder. Wars of Faith. A hundred years later only city-states remained. Silbur was mother to them all.

Gradually, as the century turned and religious power declined, great lords began to challenge the power of the Church. Harvell in the northwest had been the first to forge himself a new kingdom, Borso of Helch soon followed his neighbor's example, spending a lifetime claiming the land that became known as Halcus. Silbur, now weak, rotting from the inside, its leaders a series of weaklings and fanatics, could do nothing to stop them. Not that they'd ever been that interested in the north.

Now, two hundred years on, Bren sought the same recognition. The duke would have a kingdom where a city had been before. Baralis smiled into his cup of holk. There would be no sovereign in Bren, no king upon a throne. For the first time in four centuries the Known Lands would have an empire.

Another sip of the holk brought him back to the pale sunny mornings of Silbur. His first meal of the day was always a cup of holk and a pastry baked around a peach. He'd taken lodgings in the scholar's quarter and paid his way by scribing and healing. In many ways it was the best time of his life. Up every morning at dawn, a long walk down to the library, and then a whole day spent in study. He went unnoticed, one of thousands of black-robed scholars who came to read the ancient texts. Just another young man engaged in that most noble of pursuits: scholarship.

At nights he would go healing. Silbur did not tolerate sorcery under any guise. Practitioners were burnt at the stake. He had to be careful: discreet in his employment of potions, restrained in his use of magic. One night, returning home from a house where a young girl lay dying, Baralis came across a group of youths beating up a man. The victim was on the ground, whimpering as he was kicked continually by the youths. A thin man with a stick was directing the beating.

This was none of his business. Baralis lowered his eyes and stepped into the road to avoid coming any closer to the scene. The person on the ground cried out: *"Please stop. Me sorry, me sorry."* The thin man stepped forward and brought the stick cracking down upon his face.

"Shut up, you half-witted bastard," he said. "It's too late for mercy now."

Looking back, Baralis couldn't say what made him turn and face the men. The arrogant voice of the one with the stick? The pathetic plea from the victim? Or was it something else: the gentle push of fate?

Anyway, turn he did. Straightaway the beating stopped. "What are you looking at?" said the stick-man. "Bugger off, this isn't your concern."

Baralis knew better than to look afraid. "Leave him be," he said, looking at each man in turn, using his flint gray eyes as weapons. Two of the youths backed away—even then his voice had that effect on people.

"What will you do if we don't?"

Slowly, Baralis put down the sack containing his potions and scrolls, careful to pick a spot that was free of dirt. "I'll burn the hearts from your bodies and leave the skin untouched." It was said simply, with no boast—and that was what made the men afraid.

The two that had already backed away ran off. That left two others: the stick-man and his friend. One last kick to the victim's groin, and the friend was off. Baralis raised an eyebrow. "I think you'd better follow your little playmates. It wouldn't be wise to face me alone."

The stick-man's gaze met his. Slowly he sneered, then walked away.

From the ground came a small, soft voice. "Thank you, master. Thank you." The man stood up and Baralis couldn't believe his eyes: he was a giant, broad as a wagon, tall as a building.

"What's your name?" he asked.

"Crope, master." The man had been badly beaten, and not just once: his face was a mass of bruises and scars. He held his head low in a pathetic attempt to disguise his height.

"Come, follow me home, Crope," said Baralis. "Those wounds of yours need tending." And so the man had come to his chambers, and they'd been together ever since.

There was nothing Crope wouldn't do for him. An outcast from birth, he was ridiculed and hounded, blamed for everything from kidnapping to rape, from murder to thievery. Crope's only defense to accusations was simply to say he was sorry. Most of the time he didn't even know what he was saying sorry for. No one had ever shown him kindness. He lived in a world of fear, where his greatest concern was staying away from people who might pick on him: young boys, drunken men, fight-hungry soldiers. He only went out at night. Baralis had changed his life. He was his protector, his savior, his only friend.

Baralis stirred himself from his memories. He never liked to spend too long reminiscing. The future was what counted, not the past. "Crope," he called. "Has the young lady been asking about me?"

"The beautiful one with golden hair?"

"Yes, you fool. Catherine, the duke's daughter."

"She was here yesterday, master. She wants to come and see you as soon as you are well."

"Good. Good. I will see her next time she calls." Baralis put down his cup and rubbed his chin. He and Catherine had a lot to talk about: sorcery, sex, and treason. She owed him her life, and he wasn't a man to let such a precious debt go uncollected.

Maybor was busy teaching his dog to kill. He had taken a pillow, stuffed it with the shredded remains of Baralis' undershirt, tied it to a piece of rope, and hung it from the rafters at man height. He was now in the process of getting Shark to jump up to the place were Baralis' throat would be. The dog was learning fast. Maybor called the dog over, patted it rather warily, and gave it a huge chunk of bloody meat. "Good boy. Good boy." After a minute he stood up, went over to the pillow, set it swinging, and then backed away to a safe distance. "Kill, Shark! Kill!" he cried.

The dog leapt like a warrior, teeth drawn like knives. This time it went straight for the throat, and it didn't let go. Its grip was so great that it hung, suspended in the air from the pillow. Shark swayed back and forth, neck thrashing from side to side, feet kicking air, until the rope gave way. Dog and pillow came crashing to the ground. Even then Shark didn't let go. The dog worried away at the pillow until there was nothing left.

Maybor was distracted from this gratifying spectacle by a loud rap on his door. Who dared knock in such an arrogant manner? His question was answered immediately as the duke let himself in the room.

"Ah, Maybor, I'm glad I found you here." Looking around at the sight of feathers flying and linen shredded to ribbons, he said: "Training Shakindra, I see."

Maybor shrugged. "Personal protection, nothing more"

"Have you reason to need protection, Lord Maybor?"

"Probably less reason than you, Your Grace."

The duke laughed. "Well said, my friend. A man's power can be measured by the number of his enemies." He slapped his thigh and Shakindra came toward him. He bent down and stroked her ears. "Good girl. Good girl."

Maybor was glad of the chance to gather his thoughts. There was only one reason why the Hawk would come to his chambers: to discuss Kylock's invasion of Halcus. It wouldn't be right for him to broach the subject first: he had been told the news in confidence by Cravin. In reality, pigeons were only a day or two ahead of people, and he wouldn't be at all surprised if half of Bren knew about it by now. Still, playing ignorant suited him best at the moment. "To what do I owe this honor, Your Grace?"

The duke walked over to the table and poured two cups of wine. He handed the first one to Maybor, the second he left sitting untouched. "I was wondering if you would like to invite your family to Bren for the marriage ceremony."

Maybor nearly choked on his wine. It went down his throat, heading straight for his lungs. He coughed, he spluttered, he turned as red as a beet. Marriage! What was this? The duke was speaking as if the marriage between Kylock and Catherine was still going ahead. It made no sense. There was only one conclusion: no one had told him about the invasion.

The duke waited for Maybor to compose himself, his lips drawn together in a faint look of distaste.

"Are you aware, Your Grace," said Maybor, wiping wine from his chin, "that Kylock has invaded Halcus?"

The duke nodded. "Of course." He spoke in a manner that invited no questions.

Maybor was confused. Surely the duke would be furious over the news? The people of Bren would not like the idea of their precious heir being married to a king with a taste for blood. When the duke died, Catherine would rule Bren, and now, by invading Halcus, Kylock had shown that he was not the sort to sit passively by and let his wife rule alone. Indeed, the way things were progressing at the moment, it looked as if Bren might be destined to form one small part of Kylock's northern empire. Yet here was the duke, calmly making wedding plans. It made no sense.

"You never answered my question, Maybor," said the duke. "Will you bring your family to Bren?"

"My eldest son, Kedrac, is a great friend of the king. I'm sure Kylock would insist upon him attending the wedding." Maybor couldn't resist the exaggeration. Besides, if the marriage was going ahead, he needed to be seen to support it. Kylock would confiscate the lands of a traitor in an instant. Cravin was right, the best thing to do now would be to assassinate Baralis. The man wielded too much power and had too much influence over events. Once he was out of the way, the marriage would become less of a threat.

"And your daughter?"

Maybor was thrown off guard for the second time. "My daughter, Your Grace?"

"Yes, you do have a daughter, don't you?" said the duke. "What's her name, now?"

"Melliandra."

The duke spun around. "Aah, so she was probably called Melli as a child?" He didn't wait for an answer. "I heard that she is a beautiful girl. Do you happen to have a portrait?"

Stunned, Maybor nodded.

"Let me see it, then. If Melliandra attends the wedding, perhaps she can have the honor of waiting upon Catherine."

Maybor breathed a sigh of relief: so that was the duke's interest—seeing if his daughter was comely enough to be a lady-in-waiting to Catherine. Maybor dashed over to his desk. It would do him no harm to have Melli close to Catherine. In fact, the whole thing was perfect; when Melli was found she could take residence at the court of Bren. Not only could she befriend the woman who was destined to rule the most powerful city in the north, but also she would be a safe distance from any rumors that might cause her disgrace at Castle Harvell.

Unlocking his cedar-wood box, Maybor reached inside and pulled out his daughter's likeness. Carefully he cleaned it against his robe. The miniature was covered in fingerprints from constant handling: it was all he had to remember her by. He held it out. "Here is my daughter, Your Grace."

The duke took the portrait and held it so it caught the light from the window. He seemed pleased with what he saw. When he spoke it was quietly, more to himself than Maybor. "Oh, yes, yes," he said. "She is the one."

"So should I invite her to attend upon Catherine?"

The duke gave Maybor a shrewd look. "As you wish." He returned the portrait and then made his way to the door, his sword glinting with every step. "I hope that you and I can become friends, Lord Maybor," he said, pausing on the threshold. "I've known for some time that you have been opposed to the match of Catherine and Kylock, but let me assure you there will be nothing to worry about when it happens." With that he bowed curtly and left.

Maybor could only stare at the space that the man had occupied. He didn't have the slightest idea what the duke meant. In fact the whole visit was nothing short of bizarre: talk of friendship and families. A total disregard for Kylock's flagrant aggression. What did it all mean? Maybor poured himself a second cup of wine and sat down on his bed. Shark came and lay at his feet. Cravin's words from the other day came back to him. Perhaps the Hawk had come up with a way to neutralize the marriage.

When it came to being pests, spiders were second only to horses. Both creatures had an annoying tendency to leave things about that a man was likely to walk in. Now, spiderwebs might be less disgusting than horse dung, but they were definitely more creepy. Especially in the dark, when the only thing you could feel was their clammy threads brushing against your face, quickly followed by the scurry of tiny feet as a spider ran down your neck. Even now, Nabber could feel a handful of the eight-legged creatures busy spidering beneath his tunic. Unfortunately, nothing short of getting undressed would rid him of the pests, and he wasn't about to do that. No, sir. No one was going to catch him in his underwear down a secret passageway. He wasn't one of *those*.

The duke's palace was turning out to be most interesting. It was amazing where a little bit of reconnaissance could lead. No less amazing was the way people turned a blind eye to a boy wandering around on his own. Nabber supposed he didn't look like the dangerous cutthroat sort, which, while being a little disappointing, certainly came in handy. He simply didn't exist to the world of cooks, ash maids, and butchers. Guards occasionally gave him the once over, but generally after a little verbal dilly-dally, they left him well alone.

So here he was, down in the secret depths of the palace, keeping company with the foundations. Quite interesting, really, if you didn't count the spiders.

It had all happened by accident. Two days ago he'd been walking

along a harmless-looking corridor on his way to the nobles' quarters when
he was approached by two guards. These men had obviously been drinking and were looking for a little amusement. They questioned and taunted
him, and then began prodding his chest with their spears. Just before they
left, the smaller of the two had punched him hard in the chin. Nabber went
slamming into the wall. As the guards walked away, happy with the success of their bullying, Nabber became aware that something had happened
to the wall behind him. His shoulder blade had fallen against a tiny pro-
trusion in the stone. He didn't dare move until the guards were out of
sight. Only when their footsteps had faded into the distance did Nabber
feel safe to lift his weight off the wall. As soon as his shoulder came away
from the wall, a series of near silent clicks sounded within the stone. Nabber was torn between dual instincts: fear and curiosity. Curiosity won and
he stayed and watched the wall swing open.

Borc, did that passage smell when the wall moved back! The stench
of decaying rodents combined nicely with the strong reek of mold. It was
like being in Swift's hideout all over again—made him feel quite nostalgic for a moment. Of course, there was nothing to do but step into the
dark. The instant his feet landed on the inside stones, the wall fell back
into place. Nabber had to admit that it was a little scary to find himself in
total darkness. Rorn's alleyways by midnight were pleasantly shady compared to this. Still, Swift's words gave him comfort. *"There's nowhere as
profitable as the dark,"* he would say as he watched the sun set over the
city of Rorn. And so, with that maxim in mind, Nabber began to make his
way along the tunnel and into the depths of the duke's palace.

The past two days had proven very illuminating indeed. The possibilities for nefarious looting were almost unlimited. Swift would have wept
with joy. You could never tell where you'd come out: meat larders, nobles'
chambers, armories. There was even a tunnel that led outside to an open
sewer in the city. The whole palace was practically asking to be robbed!

Nabber quickly decided on his best course of action. He would stag-
ger along the passages, arms stretched out, spiders adangling, until he
came to places where the light seeped in through tiny hairline cracks in the
stone. Then he would step on all the surrounding flagstones until one gave
way and the wall opened up. He had to be careful, of course, for there was
a chance there would be people on the other side.

The first time he'd emerged from the tunnels he'd surprised a rather
noble-looking lady kneeling down to help a guard untie his britches. Nabber had tipped his cap respectfully and said, "If you're having trouble with

those ties, my lady, I always find that a little pig grease does the trick."
Well, the lady had run away screaming and the guard had just stood there
as if he were nailed to the floor. Nabber was back in the tunnel in no time,
lesson well learned: listen carefully before making an unexpected
entrance.

Some of the tunnels were too narrow for full-grown adults, and even
he'd had a little difficulty squeezing through them. Many of the lower
ones were waterlogged and more than a few were impassable, with water
levels reaching high above a man's head. Nabber supposed it was because
the palace was built on the shore of the great lake, and anything that lay
below water level had long since been flooded. Sometimes Nabber would
come across places that were well lit. Portcullises on the lake side let both
light and water in—probably built so that invaders couldn't swim under
the lake and into the castle. Rather clever, really. One of the portcullises
had nasty spikes which jutted out into the lake: one decent wave and a
diver would find himself impaled. Nabber was full of admiration for the
man who'd thought of that particular modification.

He'd been just about everywhere by now and was wondering whether
to share his newfound knowledge with Tawl. The tunnels would be perfect for slipping in and out of the palace unnoticed. Of course, the only
way he'd found so far was through the sewers, so a man wouldn't smell
too good at the end of it, but the benefits of a quick escape far outweighed
the hazards of a wall of sewage.

Nabber was worried about Tawl. The knight needed watching in case
he did anything irrational. Just as he seemed to be sobering up and coming to terms with his newly spoken oath, in stepped the Old Man's cronies.
They'd stirred up all the old memories, and with them the guilt. Trying to
get the knight to take a mysterious letter from the very man whose death
had caused all the madness in the first place: Bevlin. Tawl hadn't mentioned the incident and neither had Nabber. The letter, which was currently safe from water and sewage in the little room they shared just off the
kitchens, was on his mind constantly. There was no point in opening it; he
could only read a few words, so the message would have no meaning. But
it was more than that which stopped Nabber from breaking the seal.

Somehow it had become his solemn duty to bear the letter for Tawl
until he needed it. Nabber didn't doubt for an instant that a time would
come when Tawl would bitterly regret discarding the letter. His job was to
be there when he did.

Nabber made his way upward through the tunnels with remarkable ease. He was quite sure by now that he could see in the dark—and not a single carrot in his life! He was hoping to get Tawl to agree to move out of the castle. The guest-host relationship was wearing a bit thin, and Nabber was anxious to do some prospecting. Never since learning about the importance of contingency had his been so low. Not one gold piece, not half a weight of silver, not even a brass ring. A man could get nervous just thinking about it. He needed to be out there, or rather, back here, with no guest-host obligation to hold back his hand. Figuratively speaking, it wouldn't be pocketing, it would be thievery, but he judged himself ready for the promotion. Swift would be proud of him!

Now all he had to do was get Tawl to go along with his plan. There was no way he would leave the knight on his own; where the knight went so did he. Therefore, his only hope was to come up with a good reason why Tawl should move out of the castle. Nabber hadn't thought of one yet, but he was a great believer in thinking on his toes and he was quite sure one would come to him as soon as he saw the knight.

The quality of the darkness gradually changed and Nabber knew he was close to the entrance. Quite by accident he'd stumbled on one not far from the kitchens at all—in the chapel. This wasn't the same as the rest of the entrances, as it was hidden behind a wooden panel. It spiraled upward, ending in a single door. Whoever built the tunnels must have intended that it be cutoff from the other passages, as it was self-contained with no other entrances. Nabber had gained access by spotting a likely looking ventilation tunnel and managing to squeeze himself through it. Tempted by the look of the upper doorway, he followed his newly learned lesson and crouched down for a while to listen to what was on the other side. Guards, by the sound of it. Footsteps could be heard pacing back and forth at regular intervals, which meant that someone or something important must be on the other side. It didn't take a Silbur scholar to guess that there was trouble waiting behind the door, so Nabber backed quietly away.

Forcing his reluctant body through the ventilation tunnel, Nabber found himself right by the chapel entrance. He placed his ear against the wood. All quiet on the other side. One firm push and the wooden panel swung backward. As predicted, the chapel was empty. Nabber stepped out, replaced the panel, and took off his cap. If anyone came across him now he'd be just another boy praying for Borc's guidance.

He slipped out of the main chapel door and was just about to make a run for freedom when a voice piped up. "Hey, you, boy! What you doing in the chapel?"

It was a guard, but not a regular one, judging from his dress and his accent. Nabber smiled a little sadly and looked down at the floor. "Praying for the souls of my dearly departed family."

"Hmm," said the guard. "I didn't see you go in there. Did you see him go in there, Bodger?"

"Can't say that I did, Grift." A second guard emerged from behind a pillar. "Though I don't think we should bother the boy in his time of grief, Grift."

"You make me ashamed of myself, Bodger," said the first guard. "Go on, boy, get going. Here." He handed Nabber half a skin of ale. "Take this with you, it might ease your loss."

Nabber took the skin of ale and bowed to both men. "Thank you, gentlemen," he said. "My mother, Borc bless her soul, would weep to see such kindness from strangers. She always said that a man who would give away his ale one day, would give away his heart the next."

"Well spoken, my friend," said the older of the guards. "It's nice to see a young man who respects his mother's memory, ain't it, Bodger?"

The one called Bodger sniffled loudly. "Right nice, Grift." He blew his nose into the polishing cloth. "Right nice, indeed."

Nabber patted the man lightly on the shoulder and took his leave. He liked those two guards; they were a lot easier to get along with than the others he'd encountered around the palace. Bodger and Grift, eh? It wouldn't hurt him to befriend those two, especially as they guarded the nearest tunnel entrance to the kitchens.

A short walk brought him to the room he and Tawl shared. Not bothering to knock, he walked straight in. There was no sign of the knight. His weapons were gone. His pack was gone. A sinking feeling overcame Nabber. Tawl had taken off. Whirling around, Nabber took a more detailed scan of the room. Most of the knight's clothes still lay in a heap by his pallet, and various pots and pans were strewn across the floor. Even his bedroll had been hung above the fireplace so that the smoke would ward off the moths. Nabber rejoiced to see it. Tawl might be gone, but he was obviously planning on coming back.

Twenty-three

"Wake up, my dear. Wake up," came a voice, a little less distant than the last. Melli even thought she recognized it. Not a great friend, or a family member, but someone who cared nonetheless.

A part of her wanted to wake up, but it was such an effort. Her eyelids were as heavy as lead and she knew that the niggly, uncomfortable feeling in her side would show its teeth and turn to pain if she came around. At the moment she could experience the sensation without being aware of the hurt. It was better this way. If only the voice would leave her alone. But it kept on and on, by turns encouraging and cajoling, worried and then, if she moved a little, ecstatic. There was touching, too. Her hands were patted, her forehead was rubbed, her mouth was opened like a trap. Truth be known, she didn't move to give them encouragement, but to pull away from their prodding, prying hands. She wanted to be left alone.

It wasn't to be, though. The next assault was cool water; Melli felt it trickle along her hairline and then down her neck to her chest.

"Wake up, me dear. Everything's all right now."

This really was becoming too much. What would they do next? Hot oil? Magic potions? One thing was certain: they weren't going to give up. There was only one thing to do.

With a great effort Melli rallied the muscles about her eyes. Funny, she'd never even known they existed before. She supposed her eyes just flapped open and shut of their own accord. The muscles now seemed to be making up for nineteen years of anonymity. They were doing a good job of it, too. A delicate, needle-pulling pain accompanied the opening of her eyes.

"She's awake! She's awake!"

A blurry form slowly focused and a name, like a gift, came to match the likeness. "Bailor."

"She's lucid. She recognizes me."

The figure seemed rather excited about something. Other people crowded around, and Melli would not have been at all surprised if they'd burst out in applause. Her reflexes were tested, her pupils were stared into, fingers were held out for the count. Melli dutifully said, "two" or "three," but already she was getting a little bored. Life had been simpler when she was asleep. The final insult was when they began to force some foul-tasting liquid down her throat. She raised her arms in the air, slapping wildly, and shouted, *"Leave me alone!"*

That certainly seemed to have the desired effect. They all backed away, nodding and tutting and clucking like hens. Bailor ushered them out of the room and came to stand by her bedside. He squeezed her hand and said, "You are a very lucky lady, my dear. You nearly died the other day."

Melli decided Bailor could stay; his voice was kind and he wasn't looking at her as if she were a newly dissected specimen. Besides, if she was lucky she wanted to know about it. "What do you mean?"

"My dear, you fell off your horse. Don't you remember?"

It all came back to her: the horse, the mountains, the jump. She shuddered at the memory. How could she have been so stupid? There was no excuse for reckless riding. "What happened after I fell?"

"Well, that's what I want to ask you about," said Bailor very softly, kneeling down by her side. "You hit your head on a rock and knocked yourself clean out, but that wasn't what caused the most damage." He paused a second and squeezed her hand gently. "There was a knife inside your bodice and you fell right onto it. It went straight through your side. You almost bled to death."

Melli couldn't look into Bailor's eyes. The unspoken question—what was she doing with a concealed weapon?—lay heavily between them. It was ironic, really; for months she'd carried that knife with the sole intent of defending herself with it, and now it had nearly killed her. To make matters worse, Bailor and the duke probably thought she was an assassin. The strange thing was that she wasn't being treated like one. Surely it wasn't normal for a gaggle of physicians to tend to an assassin in a bed-chamber fit for a king? "Where is the duke?" she asked.

"Alas, my dear, His Grace had to leave early this morning. There are many things to see to at the palace. He should be back before nightfall, though. Yesterday he got here so late we didn't think he was coming at all." Bailor's face lit up as he spoke. "He is going to a great deal of trouble for you, my dear. Bringing physicians and medicines and maids. He insisted that I ride out here immediately, and only last night he turned up with a bodyguard for you. His Grace values you very highly, indeed."

"Why?" None of this made any sense. What was she to the duke? A possession, nothing more; a girl to dally with until he grew bored and moved on to the next. He might be attracted to her, but that could hardly explain all the trouble he had gone to.

Bailor stood up, joints creaking, and found himself a chair to sit on. Settling himself down, he turned his face away from the fire. His features were hidden in the shadow as he replied: "Melli, my dear, I think he's in love."

"With me?" This was preposterous, she hardly knew the man. Why, on the few occasions they'd met she'd done nothing but insult him!

"Yes, you. I've never seen His Grace so devoted to a woman. He's worn out a team of horses riding back and forth. He's even given up his bedchamber for you to stay in." Bailor leaned forward a little and his face caught the light. "Personally, my dear, I don't think he's ever met a woman who treats him as badly as you do. I think it sparked his interest. Most women just fall at his feet."

There was a small part of Melli that was quite pleased at what Bailor said. She did think of herself as less docile than most ladies of the court and it gratified her vanity to think that the duke had noticed this. The fact that he obviously appreciated a little backbone in a woman was further cause for pleasure. Melli chided herself; the bump on her head had obviously made her quite silly. The duke couldn't be interested in her, not a girl bought from a flesh-trader who had said she was a bastard. No. There must be more to this.

A worrying thought occurred to her. "Was I delirious at all?" Perhaps she had said something that she couldn't remember, something that might have given away who she was.

"No, my dear," said Bailor, making himself busy in the corner of the room. "This is the first time you've spoken in three days." He seemed uncomfortable with the subject, for he changed it abruptly. "By all accounts, His Grace was quite frantic. There was a moment on the first night when you'd lost so much blood that everyone thought you were going to die. Apparently the duke blasted the physicians, threatening to have them all killed if they didn't save you. You're very lucky, indeed."

Melli tried to sit up, but pain shot through her side.

"Easy, my dear. You've been stitched, so you'll be tender for a few days."

Feeling suddenly tired, Melli settled herself amongst the pillows. "So the duke will be here tonight?" she asked, more concerned with falling asleep than getting an answer.

"Most probably. He'd be here now if there hadn't been a spot of trouble in the west."

"Trouble?"

Bailor nodded. "Kylock invaded Halcus about a week back now and apparently he's smashed right through the border forces. The duke received a report today that said Kylock's now heading for Helch, slaughtering women and children along the way."

"I always thought the forces of Halcus and the kingdoms were evenly matched." Melli suddenly didn't feel sleepy anymore.

"Well, my dear, from what I've heard Kylock has brought in bands of mercenaries. He sends them ahead to torch villages and then moves his forces in to finish the job."

"Those are dirty tactics," said Melli. "King Lesketh would never have done anything like that."

Bailor smiled at her as if she were a child. "King Lesketh never won any wars."

That seemed rather a harsh statement coming from Bailor. Melli didn't believe it told the whole truth. "Why is Kylock killing women and children?"

"It creates terror. Word spreads that Kylock is ruthless and men become afraid for their families, so they surrender." Bailor sighed heavily. "The fact is it won't make any difference. Kylock will have them killed anyway."

"How can you be so sure?" Even though she asked the question, Melli already believed what Bailor said was true.

"He did it three days ago in the village of Shorthill, just east of the border. Two hundred women were given in payment to the mercenaries. They raped and then murdered them. Afterward they rounded up all the children in an enclosure and slaughtered them like cattle."

Melli felt a single shudder pass down her spine. For the first time she understood what she had known all her life: Kylock was evil. In the past she had called him cruel, brooding, and scornful, yet until now the full picture hadn't been clear. The warning signs were there, though. That was why she ran away from Castle Harvell in the first place; not because her father was making her do something against her will, but because the idea of marrying Kylock was loathsome to her. She'd had a lucky escape. Unlike the women and children of Shorthill.

Unwilling to think about the subject any longer, Melli said the first thing that came into her head. "What does the duke think of it all?"

Bailor brought his chair close and spoke in a low voice. "Well, that's the strange thing. His Grace looked very worried a few days ago; he wasn't at all happy about marrying his daughter to a king who looks set to conquer Halcus, but now he seems to have come to terms with it." Bailor shrugged, clearly puzzled. "When I spoke with him this morning he was almost cheerful. He was even making wedding plans."

"I don't understand," said Melli. "If the marriage goes ahead, then surely Kylock will end up ruling Bren when the duke dies."

"Well, judging from when I last saw the duke, that's no longer a concern." Seeing Melli yawn, Bailor stood. "Well, my dear, I must be on my way. You need to get some rest. I'll look in on you later." He made his way to the door. "If I send the physicians to examine you," he said, dark eyes twinkling merrily, "will you promise not to slap them this time?"

Melli smiled. "I promise."

"Master, the Lady Catherine is here to see you."

Baralis immediately stood up. He brushed down his robe and looked around his room. Everything was acceptable. "Show her in, Crope."

Two flickers of a candle later in walked Catherine of Bren. Baralis, who had long thought himself immune to beauty, took a sharp intake of breath. She was ravishing; her golden hair more glorious than any crown, her blue eyes more magnificent than any jewel. If he wasn't mistaken, she had made a special effort to look her best; the dress she wore was too fine by far for the light of day. Good. It was a sign of supplication.

"Well met, my lady," he said, bowing low. "May I offer you some refreshment? A little wine, perhaps?"

Catherine raised a beautifully arched eyebrow. "And will you be having one yourself, Lord Baralis? Or perhaps you're like my father—you will take a glass but not a drink."

Baralis inclined his head slightly and then walked over to the chestnut cabinet. He poured two cups of wine. Before offering the second cup to Catherine, he raised the first to his lips and drained it dry. "I am not your father, my lady."

Catherine took the second cup from him, her hand brushing against his wrist as she did so. "No, I can see that."

Baralis felt a little out of control. Catherine's nearness, together with the thick and heady wine of Bren, combined to make him a little lightheaded. He cautioned himself. Now was not the time to make mistakes. He turned his back on her. "Tell me, my lady. How safe is it to talk near walls?"

"You disappoint me, Lord Baralis. You are more like my father than I thought, for you match him in suspicion." She drew close to him again.

Her odor was distracting. She smelled like a child. "And you never answered my question," he said, refilling her cup. This time there was no mistaking the delicate pressure upon his wrist.

"If you mean secret passageways, Lord Baralis, then I'm aware of one or two."

Baralis concealed his excitement. "I expected as much. Are there any particularly interesting ones?"

"You mean is there one leading to my father's chamber?"

He was caught off guard by her frankness. Cursing the glass of wine that he had been forced to drink, Baralis said, "Would you tell me if such a passage existed?"

"Yes." Her blue eyes looked straight into his, and it was defiance that gave them their luster.

He began to realize that Catherine was dangerous. Her lover had been brutally murdered and her father had exalted the man who had done it. Revenge was what she wanted. He needed to know whether she sought it against her father or the knight. It was best to leave the subject of the passageway behind—it existed, there was little doubt about that, but now wasn't the time to press the matter. Better to let her think he had different priorities.

"Did Blayze know you could perform drawings?"

Catherine flinched at the mention of her lover. "Yes. But he won all his fights on his own. Never once did he ask for my help."

"I don't doubt it." Baralis judged it was time to remind Catherine of her debt. "For you would be dead by now if he had."

Catherine attempted to challenge his words with a disdainful gaze, but she couldn't quite keep the fear from her eyes.

Baralis continued, his voice low and alluring. "My lady, sorcery is a dangerous weapon. One should never wield it lightly."

"Lightly, Lord Baralis!" said Catherine, as quick as a whip. "I never wielded it lightly. Blayze's life was in danger, I had no choice."

"You were a fool! If I hadn't intervened there would be no skin on that pretty chest of yours. I took the impact for you."

"You look fine to me."

Baralis grasped the fabric of his robe and ripped it apart. The silk tore like parchment, parting to reveal his chest beneath.

A tiny noise escaped Catherine's lips and her hand fluttered to her chest. Slowly, she shook her head. "No, no."

"Yes, my sweet Catherine," said Baralis, purposely dropping her title. "This is what your drawing did to me."

His words had the desired effect. Catherine turned as pale as a sheet. She drained her cup and went to sit down on the bed. "I had no idea. No idea at all."

Baralis drew the silk over his skin, covering the seams where old flesh met new. "Little girls shouldn't play with fire."

Catherine was clearly nervous now. Her thumb was in her mouth as she chewed upon the nail. "Will you tell my father?"

This was what he had been waiting for. "No. It will be our little secret."

"And what do you expect in return?"

"Friendship, my sweet Catherine. Nothing more." Baralis spoke like a suitor, using his voice to coax and caress. "You and I could do much for each other. We have the same plans and we want the same things. There is nothing we couldn't do together." He leaned forward and ran his hand down the perfect smoothness of her cheek. Catherine's first instinct was to shy away, but after a moment's hesitation she seemed to accept the touch, even tilting her head forward as he withdrew.

"What do you mean when you say we have the same plans?"

Baralis knew he had her. All he had to do was say what she wanted to hear. "We both want to see the knight dead." Even as he said it, he realized it had to be so. The drawing that had smashed into him on the night of the fight had told him much about the man who had repelled it. The knight was dangerous; powerful people stood behind him. He was meant to become the duke's champion. It wasn't just a lucky win: fate had led the dance. Where she might lead was hard to tell, but she never picked partners lightly. Tomorrow he would know more.

For today, though, his priority was Catherine. She had to leave this chamber firmly on his side. "We should help each other," he said.

"And what's in it for you, Lord Baralis?"

How much to say? It wouldn't be wise to give his ultimate plan away. Catherine probably hated her father at the moment, but would she want him dead? Baralis found the strength of family ties hard to judge, and so tended toward caution in such affairs. "I want the marriage to go smoothly."

"Is that all?" There was a shrewd look on Catherine's beautiful face.

"*All*, my sweet Catherine. The greatest union in the history of the Known Lands should not be dismissed so casually." Baralis made his voice ring like a fanfare. "You will be ruler of the vast territories of the north. Men and armies will wait upon your bidding. Jewels and riches will be yours beyond compare. More than a queen, you will be an empress."

Two bright bursts of red shone high on Catherine's cheeks. Her soft lips trembled and then hardened to bone. "An empress?"

She was his. He had judged right: she craved glory as much as her father. The ruling house of Bren was as ravenous as its emblem, the hawk. Ambition ran in the blood: that and lechery. The maiden's belt that Catherine wore was not for show. Too many of Bren's daughters had shamed themselves with lust. They were like cats in heat. Even now she sat there, legs a fist too far apart for decency, bodice cut a finger too low for good taste. Baralis turned his back on her; he could not afford to let her beauty distract him.

"You will surpass your father in the breadth of your vision. He sees a kingdom, *you* will survey an empire. Your name will move the lips of generations. Catherine, Empress of the North, will be remembered throughout history. Your deeds will be spoken of long after your father's name has been forgotten." Baralis wheeled around to face her once more. "By helping me, you help yourself."

"What would you have me do?"

As Catherine said that one, delicious sentence, Baralis felt the tension drain from his body. He walked over to the cabinet and poured himself a half cup of wine. Only when he had drunk its measure did he speak. "To start with, I need to know exactly what your father is up to at all times. Who he meets with, where he goes, what intelligences he receives, even what he's thinking. At a later date I may need to know about the passageway to his chambers; the knight will be spending much time there and it will make for a convenient assassination. Lastly, I need you to reinforce to your father how strongly you feel about the marriage. Tell him you have been out in the city and have met with nothing but encouragement from your people. Perhaps you might throw a tantrum and threaten to throw yourself off the battlements if your father looks set to forbid the marriage. Use your own judgment."

Catherine nodded obediently at everything he said.

Baralis noted the familiar light of intrigue upon her face and continued. "Now, before you go, tell me what you know about Kylock's invasion of Halcus."

She spoke breathlessly, like a little girl eager to please. Baralis listened to what she had to say. He was worried about the content, but more than happy with the delivery.

Cold water was thrown against Jack's face. The bucket followed after. "Wake up, you kingdoms' bastard."

Jack opened his left eye—the right one refused to do his bidding—and looked at his surroundings. At first he thought he'd gone to hell, for everything was tinged as red as the devil. A second later he realized he was seeing everything threw a crimson haze. His good eye was filled with blood. Which was a little unfortunate as it was the only one he had working at the moment. Still, one red eye was better than none.

The man who'd thrown the bucket looked about as mean as Frallit on a feast day. He was the same color, too. However, the master baker managed to look red about the jowls regardless of bloody eyes.

"What you smirking at, boy?" A quick kick to the kidneys added force to the question.

Jack tried hard to change his facial expression. It wasn't easy. His jaw refused to do whatever it normally did and his lips proved too thick to move.

"Don't you be playing me for a fool, boy. 'Cos I'll wipe that smirk right off your face." The man slapped Jack hard against the cheek and sent him reeling backward.

Jack felt a single knifepoint of pain in his chest and then the floodgates opened. Every muscle, every bone, every cell of his body cried out in protest. Four limbs throbbed with separate hurts. Back and belly were afire, and he felt as if there was a huge crack running down the middle of his skull. There was so much pain, in fact, that after the initial shock of discovery, it all blended into one, canceled itself out, and then settled upon the original piercing spot in his chest as its sole representative.

"Not smirking now, eh?" prompted the guard.

Jack's thoughts were clouded by pain. He wasn't sure how to react. By turns he tried nodding and scowling. Luckily, nodding came easier and the guard appeared to back off a little. Feeling relieved but decidedly unheroic, Jack breathed a sigh of relief. Another mistake, as his chest protested strongly at the exertion. A sickening warning pain swelled up from his lungs. Blood came with it. Leaning forward, he spat a froth of saliva and blood onto the ground.

"I wouldn't be worried about that, boy," said the guard. "In my experience, hanging is the greatest of healers. Better than any physician for curing the ailments."

Jack was getting heartily sick of the guard. He scanned his brain for a suitable insult, could only come up with, "you Halcus sheep-lover," but decided to use it anyway.

Crack! A well-placed boot smashed into his chin. Another followed straight after. And then another.

"Here, Gleeless! Leave the boy alone," came a second voice. "The hanging's not for a week yet, and there's no pleasure in putting a noose around a corpse."

Gleeless grunted, gave one final kick to Jack's side, and then followed his friend from the cell. There was a clink of metal, a turn of key, and then a patter of hard feet on even harder stone.

Jack now knew better than to sigh in relief. Lying on the floor, looking up at the low, barreled ceiling, he tried to relax all his smarting muscles. He could deal with everything, even the new blows from the guard, except for the pain in his chest. It was like a whirlpool in his center, drawing in his strength and his awareness, and he had to fight it all the way. He had a distant memory of a jutting arrow and dogs with blades for teeth. No, he didn't want to think about that. He had to focus on something, though, to keep his mind from the gaping, swirling trap that was sculpted from pain in his chest. He could lift up his head and take a proper look at his body, but he had a feeling he wouldn't like what he saw, so he dismissed that idea on the grounds of his own squeamishness.

There was one thing left for his mind to grasp at. One thing that would distract his thoughts from the arrow wound to his chest: Tarissa. She would have been waiting for him in the woods that night. Hours and hours alone in the dark and he hadn't come through for her. Jack thumped the ground with his fist. He had let her down. Thinking about it was torture. At what point had she given up on him? Midnight? Dawn? He could see her now: chestnut curls escaping from her hood, face tight with worry, hand upon her knife. She would have stayed till dawn, he was sure of it.

What must she be thinking? That he was captured, dead, or, worst of all, that he had just taken off and left her once the job had been done.

This was Rovas' doing. The tunnel was blocked and he'd walked straight into a trap. The smuggler had no use for him now that Vanly was dead. It was so much easier to let the soldiers have him. This way Tarissa and Magra would think that he had been captured, not betrayed. Again and again, Jack brought his fist down on the stone. How could he have been so stupid! Rovas had led him forward, laughing all the way. It was the perfect plan: get someone else to do your dirty work and then have them hanged for it.

Right now Rovas was probably comforting Tarissa, his hands resting a little too low around her waist, his mouth a little too close to her ear.

Jack felt pressure building within his head; the picture of Rovas touching Tarissa was unbearable. A sharp tang in his mouth and then the cell began to shake. A stone came hurtling down from the barreled ceiling and crashed right by his feet. It acted like a slap in the face, shocking and sobering in one. He worked quickly to control himself, imagining the sorcery like bile that had to be swallowed. He took it back into his gut and forced it to stay down. Blood coursed from his nose as the pressure in his head sought release. He felt a warm trickle from his ear a moment later.

"What in Borc's name was that?" shouted someone.

Jack was shaking from head to foot. The sorcery, the falling stone, and the image of Rovas and Tarissa together was too much for him. He wanted to cry, only heroes didn't do things like that, so it was a point of honor that he wouldn't either. Besides, the way his face was at the moment, crying would only bring him more pain.

He felt so weak, so out of control. For the first time his mind had shown him what he had unconsciously known since his first week at the smuggler's cottage: Rovas wanted Tarissa. He was in love with her and would let no one else have her. It explained so much. That was why Magra had pushed them together; not because she wanted to see him and Tarissa become lovers, but because the alternative was so much worse. She couldn't let Rovas take her daughter. The man had been like a father to Tarissa for nearly twenty years, his desire for her was almost incestuous. Magra, a noblewoman of the highest order, would rather see Tarissa with a baker's boy than the man who had once been her lover and second parent to her daughter.

Jack's head was spinning. Tarissa had to be saved from Rovas. It wouldn't be long before the smuggler came up with another heinous scheme to bind her more closely to him. He would stop at nothing. Murder, blackmail, coercion—anything to keep control.

Jack pounded his fist against the stone floor. Rovas wanted Tarissa. Why hadn't he admitted it to himself sooner? If he had he wouldn't be here now, locked in a Halcus dungeon whilst Rovas offered a wide shoulder for the woman to cry on. He'd been so easily fooled. He should have checked the tunnel out before he went ahead with the plan. Jack did not doubt for one moment that the tunnel had been blocked off long ago—and that Rovas was well aware of it. The smuggler had knowingly sent him to his death.

Jack cursed his own stupidity. He'd been as pliable as newly kneaded dough. Not anymore, though. A part of Jack hardened as he lay on the floor of the Halcus cell. For too long now he had allowed himself to be domineered and manipulated by others. Frallit bullied him, Baralis beat him, and Rovas had betrayed him. It was time he took his life into his own hands. No longer would he let himself be led like cattle to pasture. From now on the future would be his.

There was one thing that was his alone, one advantage that he had tried to deny and ignore for too long. Sorcery was in his blood. It was making him shake now; it had made the stone break free from the ceiling. Already he had moved buildings and people and changed the way things were. What else could he do? At the moment it was a product of rage, called up in anger, dormant for months at a time; he needed to control it. If he could command the power properly, no one would dare take advantage of him again.

Jack clenched his fists hard. Rovas had sent him running into a wall of dirt and he wasn't going to get away with it. The guard said that the hanging was a week off. Good. That would give him plenty of time to plan his escape. He needed a few days to regain his strength. Right now he doubted if he could stand, let alone make a run for it or snatch a blade. More importantly than that, he needed the chance to practice using his power. He would master the sorcery inside.

Ignoring the protests of a bevy of muscles, Jack pulled himself up to a sitting position. The wound in his chest reasserted its presence by racking his body with a deep and stabbing pain. Jack fought against it, willing away the hurt. He had more important things on his mind. The stone by his feet seemed the natural place to start. He was going to make it move. Clearing his thoughts of all matters except the stone, Jack began to concentrate upon its center. Slowly, he forced his will against the surface, imagining he was pushing it with his mind. Nothing. No flutter in his stomach, no pressure in his head. He tried again, this time envisioning

himself entering the stone and shifting it from within. Not a single movement, no matter how hard he concentrated.

Disappointed, but not really surprised, Jack shifted his position. He
knew what he had to do next. He flashed an image up in his mind: a picture of Rovas comforting Tarissa, his large red hands resting gently upon
her back as he leaned forward to whisper lies in her ear. It was all the help
Jack needed. Instantly, he felt his saliva thicken with sorcery, felt his brain
pressing against his skull. There was a brief instant where he worked to
focus the energy, and then the stone shattered into a thousand pieces. Fragments of stone shot against his body like arrows and a halo of dust blew
up from the floor.

The dust settled to reveal a small mound of debris at the center. Jack
felt sickened, not triumphant. Tired to the point of collapse, he lay down
again on the ground. The shivering, which had never quite stopped from
the first time, suddenly became much worse. Raising his knees to his
chest, he curled up in a ball to keep warm. Weakness swept over his body
like a cool breeze, and it wasn't long before he fell into a fitful sleep, head
resting close to what remained of the stone.

Twenty-four

*T*awl was worried about Nabber because he knew Nabber would be worried about him. He knew he should not have left without a word to the young pocket, but he'd been given little choice in the matter. One minute he was sitting in his room, greasing his blade, and the next in walked the duke requesting that he accompany him on a trip to the mountains. He couldn't refuse. He was oathbound to obey the duke at all times. Of course, Nabber was nowhere to be found—only Borc himself knew what that one got up to during daylight hours—and time was of the essence. A team of horses was waiting in the courtyard and the duke was not a patient man. A note was of little use, for the pocket couldn't read; the only thing he could do was to leave behind as many of his belongings as possible, that way Nabber could be certain he was intending to return.

Nabber was a bright boy, too bright by far for his age, and Tawl had little doubt that his resourcefulness would stretch as far as finding out where he had gone. Yet he would be worried all the same. Tawl smiled as he thought of the boy. Nabber considered himself to be his personal nursemaid; tending his ailments, watering his ale, and monitoring his every move. Like a pesky fly, no amount of swiping could make him go away. With loyalty like that he would make a fine knight—as long as they kept him away from the gold!

It was a good feeling to know that somewhere someone would be thinking of him. Nabber had saved his life, walked by his side for hundreds of leagues, and never once given up on him. Tawl didn't know what he'd done to deserve such friendship, but he was glad with all his heart that he'd met Nabber that fateful day when the *Fishy Few* landed back in Rorn. He had sworn an oath to the duke and that would always come first, but he owed a great debt to Nabber and he would be there if the boy ever needed him.

The problem was, whilst he was in the mountains watching over the duke's latest dalliance, Nabber was probably getting himself into all sorts of mischief in Bren. The boy had a genius for trouble. He'd probably be all right, though: he was resilient as well as resourceful.

Tawl stood up and stretched his aching muscles. All night spent on a hard bench had done them no good. Still, it had been a long time since his biggest complaint was sore muscles, and a wooden bench in a fine lodge was better than a blanket on the ground. He was healing quickly: it was always the way; no matter how much he misused his body, it never let him down. That at least he could be thankful for.

Two physicians came to the door. Tawl recognized them, so he let them pass. He wondered what was so special about the woman inside the duke's chamber. Doctors, maids, dressmakers, and priests: they had all been in to see her. "Watch over her," the duke had said, not mentioning why, or for how long. Tawl never questioned him once during the six-hour ride. As a knight he had learned to respect orders and now, no longer a knight, orders were all that he had. They gave structure, if not meaning, to his life. The duke was a worthy leader, a military man who had fought in his own campaigns. To serve him was not such a bad fate. Better than spending his days drinking himself senseless and his nights fighting in the pits.

A serving woman came up to him with a tray of food and drink. She handed it over and then waited for him to take a taste. They had gone to a lot of trouble for him in the kitchens: fine meats and cheeses and a pretty lady to bring them. He smiled his thanks and the woman smiled back a proposition. Wide hips sent her skirt flaring, and fine shoulders challenged the seams of her dress. "I'll be in the kitchens if you need anything more, sir," she said.

He had gone without lovemaking for too long. Now that his blood was free of ale and his body free from pain, he felt the familiar need for passion, the desire to lose himself in the curves and folds of a woman's body, and perhaps, if he was lucky, forget his demons for a while. He spoke gently, "My lady, I would see you later if I may." Taking her hand, he brought it to his lips. It smelled of butter and parsley.

"I will be waiting," she said. Bowing deeply, she withdrew, hips swaying like only an older woman's could, confident in the power of her charms. Tawl watched her walk down the long corridor, admiring her all the way. A figure crossed the woman's path and she dropped to the floor in a low curtsy. It could only be the duke. Tawl stood and waited for him to approach.

"Well met, my friend," said the duke, clasping his hand. "When I said you were to watch over the lady, I didn't expect you to wait outside her door."

Tawl returned the handclasp firmly and managed a wry smile. "Your Grace should know that I take my orders seriously. Though I might have murdered the first man I saw with a cushion—this bench is harder than stone."

The duke grinned, but when he spoke his words were serious: "Tawl, I didn't bring you here as a guard. I brought you here because I need someone I can trust." Gray eyes regarded him coolly. "I think I can trust you."

Tawl met the gaze full on. "I will not break my oath."

"I know." The duke rested his hand on the carved door. "Inside here is a lady who will soon find herself in a very dangerous position. People will want to murder her. I will tell you more later when everything has been finalized, but one thing is certain: she must be kept safe at all costs. Guards are of little use except for show. Men with spears will not stop a determined assassin. I need a man with initiative, someone who will be alert day and night and who won't flinch at handling a sudden threat."

The duke paused for a moment, assessing the effect his words were having on Tawl. "When I watched you that night in the pit, I saw a man who was determined to win, no matter what the cost. I also learned that you were a knight, so your skills and loyalty are beyond question. I think you will protect the lady with your life."

"I will."

"I am well satisfied," said the duke. He turned away from Tawl and ran his hand over the carving of the hawk on the door, fingers feeling out the talons. "Of course, protection takes many forms."

Tawl felt a shift in the mood of the conversation, yet said nothing, preferring to let the duke speak on.

"There will be many people who will want to talk to the lady. People who will try and fill her head with lies, or manipulate her thoughts. She must be kept away from such influences. I want her totally isolated from the goings-on of the court. No one must see her without my permission, and she must be told nothing of politics or matters of state. She needs to be monitored closely at all times."

Tawl didn't like the sound of this. "So you would have me the lady's keeper?"

"No," said the duke quickly, "I would have you her friend."

"I choose my own friends, Your Grace."

"Then it is only fitting that you meet the lady in question." The duke pushed against the door and beckoned him forward.

They walked through a large dining room and then into a dimly lit bedchamber. A thin, dark-haired girl sat up in the bed. Her eyes were large and dark, and her chin was as blunt as a spade.

"Tawl," said the duke, "may I present the Lady Melliandra."

Melli was not in a good mood. She was heartily sick of being prodded and poked, and force-fed curds and whey. Her father had been right to hate physicians; not content with a patient being sick, they had to make them miserable as well. She wanted a leg of beef—a whole one, barely roasted—a jug of decent claret, and a chamberpot that didn't cut into her bottom like a knife.

Another thing she didn't like was the constant comings and goings. Ever since she came around yesterday, people had walked into her room as if the door, and the custom of knocking upon it, simply didn't exist. Physicians physicianed her, priests prayed for her, and dressmakers measured her: all united in their total disregard for her privacy. To top it all off, no one would answer her questions. No matter what she asked, they just smiled and nodded and said, "We'll see." She had just worked herself up into a satisfying fit of self-righteous anger when in walked the duke.

There was someone with him, a tall golden-haired man who looked like he'd stepped straight from a legend.

"Melliandra," said the duke, "I would like you to meet my new champion, Tawl of the Lowlands."

The man bowed graciously, his back broadening to a curve. "My lady."

Melli wasn't sure how to react. This stranger before her didn't deserve to be the target of her wrath. As he straightened up, she noticed there was a bandage around his chest and a second one around his arm. His blue eyes met hers and what she saw there destroyed her anger instantly. "I am pleased to meet you, Tawl," she said.

"What's this, Melliandra? Has the fall from the horse knocked the ire from your tongue?" The duke smiled. He made his way over to the window, drew back curtains and shutters, and then turned to look at her. "You have lost color and weight."

"And you, sir, have lost none of your ability to insult a lady." Something was niggling at Melli. She couldn't remember having told anyone at Bren her real name, yet for the past day everyone had been calling her Melliandra, and "Lady," at that! Perhaps Bailor was telling the truth about the duke being in love, for people were treating her with new respect since the accident. A touch of pride settled itself in Melli's brow. It was only fitting that a man such as the duke should see her true worth, after all she was the daughter of the greatest lord in the kingdoms. Obviously her breeding showed through her present disguise.

"Leave us now, Tawl," said the duke. "Go and take some rest. I will talk with you later."

The golden-haired man bowed a second time and made his way from the room. Melli noticed that he didn't make a sound as he walked. As soon as the door was closed, she said, "Why was it so important that I meet your champion? Is he one more person to watch over me?"

"You flatter yourself, Melliandra," said the duke, coming to sit on the bed. "But not without reason. Yes, I would have him look after you." His lean, dark face was unreadable, his eyes bright like a hawk's. "When I value something highly, I make sure I keep it safe."

"So you value me highly?" Melli felt a little nervous at the sudden change in the conversation. The duke was so close she could smell him.

"I do." He took her hand and brought it to his lips.

His touch was rough, pleasing. Unnerved, she pulled away. "Why this sudden change of heart? Last time we spoke I remember no such consideration."

"When I was told you might die, I realized I didn't want to lose you." The duke spoke smoothly, but the words didn't quite fit the man.

"Me, an illegitimate daughter of an impoverished lord?"

Abruptly, the duke stood up. For the first time Melli noticed he wasn't wearing his sword. Strange, she had never seen him without it before. It made her a little wary.

"Melliandra, since my wife died twelve years ago, I have kept women from my life. Yes, I took comfort—I would hardly be a man if I did not, but I only sought pleasure, not company." The duke turned to face her. "Until now. You have not been out of my thoughts since the day we met. Your pride and wit are matchless; you infuriate and beguile all in one. My wife was the last woman who challenged me so, and I had long forgotten what it was like to be with a woman who was my equal."

Melli was reeling. The last thing she had expected was such a magnificent declaration. *My equal*, he said. For the first time in her life, Melli knew what it was like to be valued for herself, not for her title, or her beauty, or the greatness of her father's wealth. But for what was inside. For what formed her words and shaped her actions and made her who she was. This man before her wasn't wooing Maybor's daughter, he was wooing a girl with no money and no prospects, yet he was treating her like a peer. Melli was thrilled.

The duke stood, waiting upon her response.

She was unsure what to say. Quickly she tested a few sentences in her head, but nothing seemed right. "You have caught me by surprise, Your Grace."

"I am not displeased." The duke smiled sharply, skin stretching over the hook of his nose. "But I am concerned lest I tire you. The physicians advise me you need rest."

"I feel fine." Melli was reluctant to let him go. "Though I'm worried about the horse. What became of him?"

"He is dead. He died by my own hand: a lame horse is no use to me."

Melli felt ashamed. Her pride, which moments earlier the duke had praised her for, had been the cause of the horse's death. "I am sorry," she said.

The duke nodded gently. Reaching into his tunic, he pulled out a package wrapped in silk. "I have something I would give you."

It was the pig farmer's knife, she was sure of it. With trembling hands she took the bundle from him.

"Open it."

Melli unraveled the silk and something heavy glinted and then fell onto the bed. It was a knife, but not hers: an exquisitely carved blade worked in silver and gold, with rubies and sapphires studding the hilt. It was the most beautiful thing she had ever seen.

"Do you like it? I thought perhaps you would need a new one, seeing as you bent the last one out of shape."

Melli searched for warning in his voice, but could find only irony. She took the knife in her hand and it fit like a glove. The jewels danced with the sun, sending colors flying like sparks.

"It is a lady's blade, wrought five hundred years ago for a beautiful empress in the Far South. 'Tis rumored she only wielded it once, to kill her husband's mistress." The duke began to make his way to the door. "Tomorrow I will bring you a scabbard, then you will have no excuse for keeping it close to your chest." One quick shrewd look, one curt soldierly bow, and he was off, leaving the room larger by his absence.

Melli drew the knife across the bedsheets, slicing them clean apart. She was confused, excited, disappointed that he'd gone.

Garon, Duke of Bren, known as the Hawk by his enemies, walked down the long corridor and into the small chambers that were temporarily his own. He was anxious for his sword. He missed its reassuring weight around his waist and the coolness of the blade down his thigh. A newly purchased maiden waited in a state of undress. He had requested her presence earlier and now found he had no taste for lovemaking. He dismissed the girl with a single wave of his arm. She scurried away like a rat, a tiny cry of disappointment escaping from her lips. The duke barely heard it.

His visit with Melliandra had gone well. Very well. The unusual thing was, that at some point during his seduction, he had actually begun to believe what he said. She *had* captured his interest: her tongue was quick and her spirit was lively. She was an exceptional woman indeed.

He poured himself a half cup of wine and, after checking to ensure that his manservant was not in the room, he drank it. The idea of giving Melliandra a jeweled dagger had been inspired. He must remember to thank Bailor for the suggestion. The head of his household was a perceptive man. He had guessed that broaches and earrings would not have caught the lady's interest. And he was right: Lord Maybor's daughter could have any adornment she chose and a few trinkets more would fail to impress. Of course, the question was what she was doing with a knife stuffed down her bodice in the first place. The duke was inclined to look upon it kindly, perhaps even admiringly. She was a lady prepared to actively defend her honor.

He rubbed his hands across his chin. The beginnings of stubble caught the rough skin on his fingers. It was almost time for his second shave of the day. The duke went over to the table, picked up his sword, and hooked it on its loop. No scabbard for him; he liked his blade naked. Not only was it more threatening, but it also forced him to think before he made a move. The need to prevent a gash to leg or hand kept his reflexes well honed.

As he rubbed a soft cloth across the blade, his thoughts were with Melliandra. A beautiful new wife was just what he needed. And a bouncing baby boy for his heir.

He would marry Melliandra and she would provide him with an heir. It was a brilliant plan. Perfect in every way. At this point in time Catherine was committed to marrying Kylock; the betrothal had been settled by proxy, so it was as good as set in stone. The problem—and Lord Baralis knew this very well, though he wasn't about to admit it—was that Kylock seemed set to conquer Halcus. This would not only make Annis and Highwall very nervous, but it would eventually lead to war. The crux of the matter was that Catherine was his only child, so on his death Bren's leadership would pass to her, and by implication her husband as well. The duke did not like this fact one little bit. It had kept him awake at nights, especially after he received news of Kylock's successful invasion of Halcus.

To back down from the marriage at this point would be disastrous. It could lead to another war in itself, as the kingdoms would take it as a grievous insult. To make matters worse, there was currently some rumor that Catherine's wedding dress had been seized and then burned by a coalition of southern forces. So now it was almost a matter of pride that the wedding go ahead; he wouldn't let the southerners think they had intimidated him into backing down. The duke drew the polishing cloth taut against the blade. The Hawk backed down for no one.

The whole situation was too dangerous. His alliance with Tyren and the knighthood had long worried the south, but they had been content to leave matters well alone until the announcement of the union between Bren and the kingdoms. He knew what everyone was frightened of: the emergence of a single power that encompassed the north. Anchored by the kingdoms in the west and Bren in the east, it would be an empire the likes of which had not been seen in centuries. That was what Kylock and Baralis wanted. Oh, Baralis was ever the diplomat, denying and then minimizing the threat, but he had his eye on the prize, and a very clever and calculating eye it was. The duke began to pace around the room. By taking a wife himself and fathering a legitimate male heir, he would confound the plans of Baralis and Kylock, diffuse the growing tension in the north, and still appear resolute to the south.

It was nothing short of magnificent. By fathering a son, Catherine would no longer be his heir, so the union between her and Kylock would not be seen as a threatening coupling of might, but rather a traditional royal marriage sealed with bonds of friendship and trade. The wedding would no longer have a sting.

Let Kylock do what he would with Halcus; as soon as Melliandra was with child, it would not be Bren's concern. He would go to Annis and Highwall and promise neutrality. That would ensure the war didn't escalate, for there was no way the kingdoms could take on the might of Highwall alone. Even now, that city with the infamous granite battlements was preparing for war. The duke received daily reports from Highwall, and its leaders were taking the situation seriously. Just last week they passed a law stating that every man must practice archery for twenty hours a week, and that a fifth of all income was to be contributed for defense.

The duke sat down at his desk. In the half hour he'd been away, more reports had arrived. Briefly he read one. Kylock had taken the town of Nolton, a strategic gain, for it lay halfway between the border and the capital, Helch. Five thousand women had been slaughtered in its sacking. There was no death count given for the men. Brushing his hands over his shortly cropped hair, the duke wondered exactly what Kylock was up to. Killing women was simply uncalled for. The duke was a military man; he'd taken many towns and villages over the past twenty years and never once had he ordered women killed. Of course, it was a hazard of war that some would die and many be raped, but there was no benefit to be gained by actively pursuing them. In fact, killing of innocents usually had the effect of hardening enemy resolve.

Whatever his motives, Kylock was certainly doing something right. He'd cut through the Halcus defense as easily as if it were butter. He was actively recruiting mercenaries, too. Four days ago a whole battalion of them had crossed through the Bren pass on the way to the front. The duke stood up again; he was restless. He needed to be in the city. Events had to be monitored closely and he felt cut off here in the hunting lodge.

The ironic thing was that his plans required that he be here. Melliandra couldn't be moved at the moment, and he needed to woo her fast. The marriage had to be announced before everything got out of hand. And judging by the rate Kylock was thundering through Halcus, that wouldn't be long at all.

Melliandra's safety was another consideration. As soon as Baralis learned of his imminent marriage, he would be furious. It would be a bludgeon to his plans. His first instinct would be to murder the bride-to-be, or the groom. The duke was not worried about himself, but Melliandra would need watching day and night. He was already happier knowing that Tawl would be guarding her. He had a good feeling about the knight. A man like that would lay down his life to protect a lady. Still it wasn't wise to underestimate Baralis. He was a silken viper with poison on his tongue. He craved power on the grandest of scales and was not the sort to sit and watch quietly whilst it was stolen from under his nose.

Things would have been so different if old King Lesketh hadn't taken it into his head to drop dead before the marriage had taken place. It was a blessing, really, for it had given the duke a chance to realize he was making a huge mistake. Kylock did not want a bride, he wanted Bren.

Sitting himself down in front of a small silver mirror, the duke took out his knife and began to shave. He enjoyed the twice-daily ritual. He would let no manservant with soap or pig lard near him. He preferred to shave dry and alone. The blade was so sharp it cut without pressure, skimming over his flesh like a calm-water skiff. Not once in ten years had he drawn blood.

He would stay here tonight and depart at midmorning. That should give him at least one more chance to talk with Melliandra. He had to be so careful with the girl. Bailor was right: she was playing a game of her own. A game called: "I can do fine without my father's name or wealth." She had to be flattered, but not in the traditional way; poetry and compliments would have little effect. What he had said earlier about equal partners seemed to please her, so he would give her more of that. His long-dead shrew of a wife had finally come in useful, too, adding a pleasing air of tragedy to the whole proceedings. Well, in a way, their relationship had been tragic: she had certainly done her best to put him off marriage for life.

The duke nearly ruined his ten-year record by smiling at a crucial moment. His hands were quick, though, and the skin remained unbroken.

Yes, Melliandra would need a quick but subtle courtship. He would not reveal to her what he knew of her identity, best to let her think he was in love with Luff's bastard daughter, that way she would be wanted for herself alone. He supposed he could marry any one of a number of women at court, but he hadn't avoided a second marriage for twelve years to jump quickly into a wedding with politics as his only motive: Melliandra *was* the only woman who had had engaged the interest of his mind as well as his loins. Besides, by taking a girl from Castle Harvell for his bride, he just might retain the goodwill of the kingdoms.

Of course, he would never have dreamed of marrying her if she hadn't been Maybor's daughter. As it was, it had all worked out beautifully; he would gain a powerful friend in Lord Maybor, neutralize the marriage of Catherine and Kylock, and nip the threat of an empire in the bud. Perhaps as a dowry he would ask for the stretch of land west of the River Nestor. That would please his people greatly, as eight hundred years before the same ground had belonged to the king who ruled Bren's territories. It would be most satisfying, not to mention profitable, to have it back within the fold.

Shaving finished, he rapped the knife against the table to clean it. The amount of hair that fell from the blade was barely visible; another man would not have bothered for such a tiny crop. The duke did because he knew that discipline and ritual mattered.

Baralis brought a fingertip to his lips and tasted the bead of honey upon it. A sweet stinging that owed little to the bee. In the background, Crope moved a sturdy chair close to the fire and then raked the coals to make them dance. This time when he left his body behind he would not come back to find it as cold as a stone.

Blood still flowed from a finger that looked bloodless, coming to the surface like a glossy red jewel. The cup captured its measure and a drawing made it move. Baralis' brow furrowed in anticipation of the burn. Across his forehead he made the line of the horizon, and then bent low to inhale the drug that would send his mind above it. His lungs fought the poison all the way. Immediately he grew lighter. Too light to be held by a heavy body, too restless to be bound by four walls. Up and up he rose, making for the highest point, the clank of earthly chains in his ear.

The heavens had no power to tempt him tonight. They were a woman whose charms had long faded.

East and south he traveled across the darkening sky, over the listless land and then above the skittish sea. They knew he was coming and sent out a beacon, yet he would have found his way regardless of guidance. Larn glowed like a pearl in the dark.

A chamber awaited, four men around a stone table. Eyes closed, minds ready for the meet.

"Welcome, Baralis," came the first voice that was not really a voice at all, more a sliver of pure thought. "We are glad you are here. What do you want from us?"

Baralis styled himself a trace of a body and cast it to the wall like a shadow. There was tension in the room: Larn had its own agenda, its high priests were afraid. *He* would speak for now, though. It was up to them to say if their paths would cross in purpose.

"You have an interest in a knight named Tawl. I would know what it is." Baralis felt a collective indrawing of breath.

"He came here for a seering. We showed him the way."

"What way was that?"

"To the kingdoms."

Now it was Baralis' turn to inhale deeply, only he had no body nor breath to breathe. His shadow wavered. "What did he seek?"

"A boy."

"Why?"

His question was met with silence. A candle guttered and the flame died away. A stream of liquid wax shot down its length and ran onto the hand of one of the four. The man didn't flinch. Baralis grew impatient. He knew they were communicating amongst themselves, intriguing, calculating, deciding the risks. Something was worrying them and, if he wasn't mistaken, they were about to ask for his help.

Finally a voice spoke up. "It might have been an error to give the seering. Since the knight left us many of our seers have been tormented by dreams; they see our temple collapsing and the seering stones sundered. We feel the knight may hold our fate in his hands."

"And where does the wiseman Bevlin fit in?"

"His life wish was to raze our temple to the ground."

"Was?"

"He is dead now."

Baralis kept his surprise well hidden. There was little point in asking how the wiseman died: Larn had a way with murder. "So the knight was his disciple?"

"Perhaps. What is your interest in him?"

"He is now the duke of Bren's champion. His fate lingers like an aftertaste on my tongue."

"And does he still seek the boy?"

For an instant Baralis' mind alighted upon something remembered in the distant past: a nursery rhyme that spoke of three bloods. Just as he grasped it, it was gone. The incident unsettled him; it was like a warning. The knight and the mysterious boy: they both had some bearing on the future. *His* future. So what was their connection to Larn? The very fact that the high priests were worried was alarming enough. With power and resources such as theirs, it took a strong threat to cause them anything more than a moment's distress. Baralis had the feeling that everything was connected: the marriage, the empire, the knight and Larn, but a common thread eluded him.

"Why do you ask about the boy?"

"We would like to make sure that the knight never finds him. If you can help us with this, then we will be prepared to help you."

"How?"

"We know your plans, Baralis. We knew what you were born to do. Even before your mother's womb took the seed, we were aware of what you would be. Our fate is connected with yours. As you rise, so do we."

Although he was hearing this for the first time, the words seemed familiar; they played upon his eardrums like a well-remembered song. Fate hadn't chosen him to let him dance alone. Powerful allies were needed to ensure his success. He would like to question the priests further, but he had the feeling that Larn couldn't see the complete picture, either. He would only get riddles for answers. No matter. He could find things out on his own.

"If you wish I can keep an eye on the knight," he said. "And if he makes a move to leave the city, I will stop him before he reaches the walls."

"What do you ask in return?"

"Knowledge of your seerings. A great war will soon be upon us, and I would like all the advantages of foretelling on my side."

"Our seers seldom give facts, Baralis. Only guidance."

"I need no lessons from you, high priest."

"So be it. We will feed you whatever information we deem necessary."

Already the games had started. Men of their kind loved nothing better than to mince and parry words. "I hope my diet will not be found wanting meat."

"Seeing that you are such a cynical man, Baralis, we will give you a sample of our fare to seal the pact."

"Go on." Baralis felt himself weakening. He had been here too long and traveled too far. His shadow rippled and thinned away. Then the contractions started. Over hundreds of leagues his body began to exert its powers, sucking him back with all the pull of the grave.

"Two days ago one of our seers spoke of you. He said that for now your greatest threat is a girl with a knife at her side. Is that meat enough for your plate?"

Baralis gave in to the unbearable pressure of body, the power of the physical world. The pull created a vacuum and he had no choice but to fill the void. He bade the priests farewell, yet already he had diminished in their thoughts. They sent him one final reminder: "Watch the knight for us." He scarcely heard it. A great rush filled his ears as he was forced from the temple.

The sea salt had taste and the bird droppings stank of vinegar, and then the acceleration started and he knew nothing more.

Twenty-five

Jack was kicked awake. Without conscious thought he retaliated; hand thrusting out to catch his attacker's ankle.

"You kingdoms' bastard," came a familiar voice, quickly followed by a familiar sensation as Gleeless the guard kicked him once more for his impudence.

Jack hardly cared about the impact of the kicking—at some point yesterday pain had lost its power over him and he now existed in a state of fevered calm—but he did take offense at the *insult* of the kick. Gleeless needed to be taught a few jail-side manners. Now if only he could pick himself off the floor, he'd be the man to do it. At the moment, though, his left arm seemed to be the only part of him that was functioning properly, whilst *all* of Gleeless' limbs appeared to be in working order—though he did favor his right leg—and odds of four to one were a little discouraging, to say the least.

Gleeless backed away and returned a moment later with a cup of ale and a bowl of eels. Jack's stomach turned at the sight of them. In Baralis' books the heroes were always given stale bread and water, but since he'd been here they'd fed him nothing but eels. The Halcus knew how to use food as a weapon. A spinning sensation rounded up his thoughts like cattle and Jack's head became heavy with the load. He drifted to a world where sausages held knives and hams aimed crossbows at cheese.

When he came to next, the grease on the eels had congealed. The light from the arrow loops had shifted across the cell floor and was now highlighting a trail of beetles that were making their way to the bowl. Jack pushed the eels in their direction; they were welcome to them. The ale was his, though. He found it hard to pick up the cup, his hands were never quite where they should be, and they were trembling so much that getting a firm grip was nearly impossible. To make matters worse, every few seconds *two* cups would appear, and he was never quite sure which one to go for. Rolling onto his stomach, he brought his head down toward the cup; his vision betrayed him again and another appeared by its side. He had the bright idea of aiming his mouth in the middle of the two cups. It worked. The ale was warm and there was something unpleasant floating in it, but he lapped it up like a dog. As he drank he noticed a tapping noise, and it took him a few seconds to realize that it was the sound of sweat dripping from his brow into the cup.

The eels were now alive with beetles. The eels moved more lethargically in death, borne on the current of a hundred hungry mandibles chomping away at their flesh. The sight of it sickened Jack. He rose up from his cup and began to concentrate on the bowl. He was getting better at summoning sorcery. Imagining his stomach was a skin of water, he squeezed upon the muscles, forcing the fluid to rise. At the same time he distilled his thoughts, losing all but one: the desire to destroy the bowl. The kindling was in place, but he still needed a spark to make it catch. Jack flashed an image of Rovas through his mind, a picture of the smuggler leaning forward to whisper words of comfort in Tarissa's ear. So close he left saliva on the lobe. The sorcery rushed through his body to his mouth. He felt it alight upon his tongue and an instant later the bowl of eels exploded outward.

Beetles and parts of beetles rained down upon his body. Eels and their gravy were thrown against his skin, and shards of pottery punctured his shaking flesh. A wave of nausea rose up in him and he was helpless to stop it. Leaning forward, he lost the contents of his stomach into the rushes. It wasn't the insects, or eels, or sorcery that made him sick, it was how low he had to stoop to call the power from within. He was ashamed of using Tarissa as his catalyst. In Castle Harvell there had been a plain-looking laundress called Marnie. One day she had invited him to the small dark room where she kept her stocks of lye and fuller's earth. She placed her firm fleshy hand upon his arm and brought her thin lips forward to meet his. He hadn't wanted to kiss her, but in his mind he conjured up an image of Findra the table maid and superimposed it over Marnie's face. Feeling an instant flare of excitement, he kissed her and fondled her heavily muscled breasts. Afterward he felt remorse. Not only had he used Marnie, but Findra as well. Although he never went near the laundry again, he never forgot his guilt. Even now, the smell of freshly laundered clothes was enough to make him redden with shame.

He had used Tarissa's image as surely as he'd used Findra's.

Jack felt his consciousness slipping away. He fought the sensation; he didn't want to lose any more hours to fevered fancy. He brushed the refuse from his skin, careful not to look at his arms. Over the past two days he had become adept at not *seeing* his body. The sight was too appalling. Tooth marks bloated by pus had caught his eye once, and he was determined it wouldn't happen again.

The only thing that caused him any real discomfort was the arrow wound in his chest. Situated high up by his right shoulder, Jack could feel it pulling at the surrounding flesh. The arrowhead had been removed—by whom he'd never know, certainly not Gleeless—but apart from that nothing had been done. No hot iron, no stitches or ointments had been used, and his tunic was attached firmly to the wound. Jack had come to the conclusion that if he were to pull his tunic away from the newly forming scab, he would probably bleed to death.

Jack began to lose himself in the thickness of his thoughts. Marnie the laundress appeared before him, demanding that he take off his tunic so that she could wash it. Master Frallit was behind her, scolding him for getting pus in the dough, and Grift filled Bodger's glass with beetle-colored ale, whilst telling him why washer women were better in bed.

"You lazy, good for nothing villain." And then:

"Come on you foul-smelling vermin, get up on your feet and show some respect."

It took the impact of several kicks to convince Jack that the voice wasn't part of his dream, as the words seemed to fit right in with the rest of the content.

He opened his eyes just in time to see Gleeless swinging a bucket, the contents of which ended up in his face. "Thought that would wake you," said Gleeless, nodding like a surgeon in mid-diagnosis. "Got a little friend here for you." He made a beckoning gesture with his hand and in walked a second guard, pushing a man before him. "He's from your homeland, so you two should get on just fine." Gleeless turned to the man. "What's your name again, mate?"

"Bringe," said the man.

The man was in a bad way. His nose was broken, both eyes were ringed with black bruises, and his wrists bore the unmistakable mark of the rope. He had been tied to a barrel and then beaten.

"Now, Bringe here is going to be spending the night with you," said Gleeless, making his way to the cell door with the second guard. "Don't forget to ask him his opinion on Halcus torture, 'cos this time tomorrow the chief persecutor will be coming for you, and it might be helpful to know in advance just how mean he can get if he's crossed." Gleeless smiled rather amiably and then turned and closed the door.

Tavalisk ran a pudgy hand over the pale and gelatinous substance, picked a likely spot for testing, and then stabbed his finger into the flesh. Perfect. The tripe was as soft and welcoming as a young boy's thighs. The substance quivered as if it were alive, its oyster-colored flesh giving off the subtle aroma of bile. Countless tiny glands roughened the surface, providing the only variation to the bland and bloodless gut. Tripe: the stomach lining of the pig. Not a great delicacy in anyone's opinion, but delicious all the same. Nothing could match it for texture and taste, nothing was quite as teasing on the tongue. Most men would make the mistake of boiling it with salt and onions, but Tavalisk knew differently. It required a delicate poaching in pork broth and vinegar; only then would it reveal its true complexity of flavor. Done right, and one could almost taste every separate meal that had ever been eaten by the pig.

He cut himself a portion, marveling at the ease with which it took the knife. Just as he brought flesh to lips, a knock sounded on the door. The archbishop tutted angrily and cried, "Enter," in such a way that the word was transformed into an insult and a warning.

"I trust Your Eminence is well today?" said Gamil, walking into the room.

"I was feeling quite well until about ten seconds ago, Gamil, then for some reason my spirits took a sharp turn for the worst."

Gamil carried on as if Tavalisk hadn't spoken. "I have news of Kylock's invasion, Your Eminence. Apparently he's sweeping through western Halcus like a brushfire. The man is a demon, ordering the killing of women and children, slaughtering cattle, and constructing dams to flood the fields. Not to mention the fact that he's burning every hayloft and chicken coop in sight. The newly crowned king seems intent on bringing Halcus to its knees."

"Hmm." The archbishop nibbled daintily on his tripe. "Kylock is turning out to be quite an interesting character. I must say, I wholly agree with his decision to murder the women of Halcus—they're an ugly and shrewish bunch, the lot of them!"

"But isn't Your Eminence worried about the consequences? If Kylock reaches Helch, then the whole of the north will turn into one huge battle-field."

"Now, now, Gamil," said Tavalisk, waving a tripe-tipped fork in his aide's direction. "There's no need to panic. A battlefield in the north is nothing to lose sleep over. It's the south that matters to us. The secret is to keep the south *interested* in the war without actively involving them in it." Tavalisk threw some tripe to his cat and the creature greedily snapped it up. "Marls and Toolay would up timbers and run at the first sight of a sol-dier brandishing a halberd, and I intend to use their fear to my advantage."

"How, Your Eminence?"

"Simple, Gamil. I will convince them that the only way they can stop the war from spreading south is to make sure that Baralis and Kylock are firmly thwarted in the north. Of course that will take resources: arma-ments, finances, mercenaries, supplies . . ." The archbishop made a sweeping gesture with his arms. "And the southern cities are the ones who should supply them. Not to mention the fact that they can finally rid them-selves of those pesky self-righteous knights."

"Talking of the knights, Your Eminence, Tyren and the duke of Bren have entered into an agreement where both parties now guard cargo trains from the south to the north. I think it was the rumor of the seized wedding dress that did it. The duke of Bren can hardly sit back and let his cargoes be publicly seized by the four-city force. It's too humiliating. So now when we attack the knights, we're as good as attacking Bren, as well."

"Isn't the buildup to a world war beautiful to behold, Gamil?" Tavalisk threw a second piece of tripe to his cat. This time he flung the morsel high up, so it landed atop a tapestry that was hanging from the wall. That would challenge the beast. "An insult here, a few slaughtered cattle there, and the next thing one knows, people are lining up on oppo-site sides, knives drawn, ready for a fight. It's quite thrilling, really."

The cat, who had been eyeing the out-of-reach tripe for a few moments, finally decided to make its move. It jumped up, claws extend-ed to catch at the cloth. The tapestry, which was suspended by a chain from the wall, began to swing from side to side erratically. The cat clung onto it, four limbs spread-eagled against the likeness of Kesmont's horse. The tripe worked its way loose and fell to the floor with a dull slapping sound. The cat tried to jump after it, but one of its claws was caught up in the fabric and it hurtled downward only to find itself suspended from the tapestry by its hind paw.

Gamil made to free the trapped creature.

"No, don't help it, Gamil," said the archbishop. "Even dumb animals must learn the price of greed."

The cat squawked loudly and began to thrash wildly against the wall.

"But Your Eminence, it will hurt itself."

"It should have thought of that sooner. Now, anything else?"

Gamil was forced to speak over the sound of the cat screeching. "Two more things, Your Eminence. First, the knight has become the duke of Bren's champion, and second, the Old Man's cronies are on the way back home."

There was a loud crash as cat and tapestry went careening to the floor. Tavalisk ignored the noise. "So they didn't manage to murder the knight?"

"No, Your Eminence. They never tried to. They were there to deliver a letter, not a knife."

Tavalisk paused in mid-chew. "It would be most interesting to know the contents of that letter, Gamil." The archbishop sighed daintily. "We must continue to have the knight watched closely, you never know what we might discover. Now if there's nothing more, kindly take your leave."

"Certainly, Your Eminence," said Gamil, walking to the door.

"Just before you go, Gamil, I wonder if you could do me a small favor."

"Take your cat to the physician to see if he can stop the bleeding?"

"Well done, Gamil. I see you've reached the point where you can anticipate my needs."

Bringe was not a happy man. Everything had gone downhill since he hacked Maybor's orchards. Baralis had paid him his fee promptly—nineteen pieces of the king's own gold—so he had nothing to complain about there. Unfortunately, a few days later his wife had decided it was high time to give the brewing vat its once yearly clean. So, while he was out at the local inn sharing a cup of tavern-keeper's best with the full-thighed Gerty, his rat-faced wife was busy discovering his hidden stash under the brewing vat, wrapped in linen, and packed with grease to stop the coins from clinking together.

By the time he'd returned from the inn she was gone. A few decent slaps to Gerty revealed that she and his wife had an aunt in Highwall. A few decent kicks to the bailiff revealed that his wife was last seen paying two golds for the protection of a merchant train that was heading east. Bringe started after her, the now miserable and wailing Gerty in tow. Four days later he caught up with the train. His wife set the guards on him. Whilst he was being shot at, Gerty was busy ingratiating herself with her older sister. When the merchant train pulled away, he found himself alone.

He continued drifting east, robbing food and money to live. His plan was to catch up his wife and Gerty in Highwall, but the Halcus put a stop to that. Two weeks back he was picked up by them as an enemy spy. Kylock's invasion had sent them into a mad frenzy, seeking out any men from the kingdoms to torture and burn.

So here he was, stuck in a Halcus prison cell, his face a match for a squashed pumpkin, being stared at by some fever-crazy wild man. "Don't come near me, longhair," he warned. No one was going to give him a dose of the ghones. Or anything else contagious, for that matter.

As Bringe became accustomed to the dimness, he realized that the stranger was younger than he first thought. He was in a bad way. Down both of his arms were a series of sores that looked as if they might be bite marks, and he was shaking from head to foot. Bringe spat in distaste. "What you in here for, boy?"

The stranger sat in a heap of dirty rushes. A trickle of blood ran down his neck where the guard had kicked him. "I murdered a man," he said.

Murder? The boy went up in Bringe's opinion. "I'm in here under suspicion of murder myself. A merchant was killed in the tavern a couple of weeks back and everyone swore it was a foreigner who did it. When they couldn't pin that one on me, they got me for spying instead." This wasn't entirely true, but it made him sound more important than admitting he was one of hundreds who'd been rounded up for no other reason than they happened to hail from the kingdoms. The part about the tavern murder was true, but it was his last cell mate who was charged with the murder, not himself.

"What's your name, boy?"

"Jack."

Bringe didn't like the look of Jack one bit. His skin had a sickly look to it and his eyes were bright with madness. "People call me Bringe." That statement met with no response, so he soldiered on. "From the kingdoms, eh? Whereabouts?"

"Castle Harvell."

"I'm from the Eastlands myself. You know, near Lord Maybor's estate."

At the mention of Lord Maybor, the boy turned white. He shifted himself to his knees and asked, "Did you know his daughter, Melliandra?"

Bringe had seen her ride past his cottage once or twice in her brother's company. An uppity-looking wench if ever he saw one. "Yes, I knew her well. Course she spends most of her time at court now."

"She was beautiful, wasn't she?" The boy looked to Bringe for confirmation.

"Aye, breasts as firm as walnuts. She's the type that's hairy down below, too."

The boy struggled to pull himself onto his feet. A kennel's worth of bites had torn his britches to shreds, and his legs were shaking like aspic. Once upright, he came tottering toward Bringe, sweat dripping from his chin and a manic look in his eye. Too late, Bringe realized that the boy meant to hit him. The boy's fist landed firmly on his newly broken nose. A sickening crunch was followed by the quick flare of pain. A second later, the boy reeled backward and collapsed onto the floor.

Bringe brought his hand to his nose to stop the bleeding, contemplated beating the boy, decided it would only get him into more trouble, and settled for a swift kick to the abdomen instead. The boy groaned and spit blood from his mouth. In a way Bringe respected him; a man who defended a woman's honor was not all bad. It was the women themselves who were vicious money-grabbing mares.

"Come on, Jack," said Bringe, offering the boy a hand. "Let's not fall out over a woman."

The boy refused his help, dragged himself into a sitting position, and proceeded to scowl at him.

"Of course you've got to give kingdoms' women their fair due," said Bringe, entering into one of his favorite subjects. "No one can match them when it comes to thighs. Halcus women are too skinny, Highwall women are too muscley, and Annis women are so tall that you wonder if it's a thigh or a tree that you're grabbing." Bringe met with no response, but decided to continue on regardless.

"Everyone knows that kingdoms women are the best. That's what the tavern murder was all about. The captain here, I forget his name, sold a kingdoms girl to a flesh-trader. By all accounts he made a fortune. A couple of weeks later a man turns up asking about her. 'Tis rumored he was her betrothed. Anyway, the next day the merchant that he questioned is found dead. Throat slit down a dark alley."

"Was the captain named Vanly?" asked the boy.

Bringe nodded. "That's him."

"How long ago did this happen?" The boy's demeanor changed. He was lucid, sharp, his whole body leaning forward in anticipation of the answer.

"I think the girl was sold a couple of months back now. During the wintertime. Apparently Vanly found her in a chicken coop."

"What was the girl's name?"

Bringe scratched his head and tried to remember what his cell mate had told him. "Something beginning with *M*, like Minnie or Melda."

"Was it Melli?"

"Er, I'm not sure."

"Think. *Think!*"

Bringe was beginning to feel a little nervous. The boy looked set to explode. "Melli, you say. It *does* sound familiar."

"And this girl was sold to a flesh-trader?"

"Aye, that much is common knowledge. For weeks afterward that was all the town's people could talk about: the killing Vanly made on the deal." Bringe's eyes flicked nervously to his companion. One look at the boy's face and a primal instinct warned him to back away. He didn't know what he was dealing with, but one thing was certain: the boy was dangerous.

It was a sham. Tarissa, Magra, Rovas; they'd all played him for a fool. Right now they were probably sitting round the fire, laughing away at how stupid he'd been.

All the time that he'd stayed in the cottage, Melli had been alive.

How could Tarissa do it? How could she have loved him and kissed him and lied through her teeth? He felt crushed by the weight of her lies.

A slow pressure began to build within him. He hardly noticed the push.

Where did the lies end? Did Tarissa really hate Rovas? Or had that been just another acting feat?

The pressure built steadily, rising upward to meet his thoughts.

Tarissa said *she* was the one who was supposed to kill Vanly.

She said that Melli was dead.

His head pounded in time to the list of her deceptions.

She said she would come with him to Annis.

She said she loved him.

She said she would wait for him.

LIES. LIES. LIES.

He couldn't bear the pain.

The pressure turned to fire in his blood. It burnt a trail along his tongue and crackled forth like a whip. Jack felt the rush of sorcery. Glorious, terrible, uncontrollable, it fed off his thoughts like fuel and ate away at his soul.

She had betrayed him.

The air shimmered then thickened around him. The building began to shake. Stones and masonry came crashing to the floor. The earth jolted beneath his feet. It began to rock back and forth, the stones churning themselves to mud. The bars on the cell door buckled and the frame fell away from the wall. A warm wind carried the stench of metal around the cell. The power that tore through his body terrified and entranced him. Without stopping to think, he made his way through the opening and up into the garrison.

He heard the sound of screams through a filter of fire. People were rushing back and forth, blood marking each body like a cattle brand. All around him destruction reigned; walls collapsed as he passed, metals spat sparks, and timbers burst into flames. The ground erupted into hills of dirt and stone, sending rocks blasting through the air. Barrels exploded outward; their contents thrown hissing into the blaze.

She had betrayed him.

Sorcery danced around him like lightning.

He passed through the chaos untouched. Enthralled and helpless to stop himself, he walked through the garrison like the phantom of death.

The timber roof of the main building caught light. It flared like kindling, turning the twilight into midday with its brightness. Dark, ash-heavy smoke soon rivaled the light, screening and choking and turning the courtyard into an abyss. The huge crossbeam that supported the roof came crashing down to the floor, crushing two guards and casting sparking splinters to the breeze. The outbuildings were soon engulfed, followed by the stables and the gatehouse.

Horses and pigs squealed. Men dashed across his path, clothes on fire, terror on their faces, and screams on their lips. On Jack walked, sorcery crackling with every step.

The entrance came into sight. The portcullis was up and the postern gate was alight. Jack stopped and watched it burn. Air rushed past him, blowing hot and fast, sending his hair streaming behind him. Up in the guard tower he spied a young guard trapped by the flames, deciding whether to jump or be burned. Jack saw fear on his smoke-blackened face. The flames came closer, licking at his heels. The man made the sign of

Borc's sword and jumped. The dull thud of his landing acted like cold water to Jack. He forced himself to look at the guard's body. Blood seeped treacle-slow from a gash in his head. His right leg bent outward at an unnatural angle, and his fingers twitched as if he were strumming a lute.

Jack knew he had to stop. This man didn't deserve to die. He had jumped to near-certain death, yet his courage would be in vain if the sorcery didn't end.

He reached down into himself. Down toward the source. It was like swimming against a tide of light. Fast and furious the power raged. Belly-strong and sharp-minded, it fought him all the way. The part of Jack that was still rational realized that power couldn't exist without the pain of betrayal. Violent emotion was its lifeblood. He tried to put Tarissa from his mind. Deeper and deeper, he went, through layers of tissue alive and ringing with sorcery. Thrusting his thoughts into the source, as surely as thrusting his hand into the fire, Jack struggled to cut off the flow.

His mind was seared, and like a piece of meat, the juices were sealed within. He couldn't release the pain. Afraid and trembling, he opened his mouth and screamed:

"No!"

The sound had a force of its own. It acted like a dagger, piercing the madness with the cool gleam of steel. Jack's will rose up in its wake, pushing the sorcery back down to the blood. There was one unbearable moment when his body felt torn in two, and then everything coalesced, rearranging itself into a different but complete form. A wave of suction ripped through his tissue, robbing the strength from his muscles. It left Jack limp.

Suddenly he couldn't stand, or raise an arm, or even blink an eyelid. He slumped onto the ground. Feet away from the guard who had jumped from the battlements, Jack gathered his last remaining store of strength and reached out toward the man's twitching hand. Pain clawed down his spine and his arm felt as if it were buried under a mountain of earth. Still he pushed on, becoming obsessed with the desire to touch the guard. It was the only thing that counted in the fiery hell that had become the night. Inch by inch he dragged his arm across the dirt until he could move no more. A finger's length divided them. The guard, as if aware of Jack's efforts, opened his eyes. They were a clear and peaceful blue.

Slowly, his whole body quivering with spasms, pain flaring to cloud his bright eyes, the guard reached out to meet Jack's hand. Jack felt rough fingers touching his and his heart thrilled with joy. Tarissa was gone. The pain was gone. He and the guard, lying side by side on the scorched earth, were the only things that mattered.

Sure that the power had been withdrawn, Baralis stepped out of his bed. He was irritated to see that he was shaking. Donning a fine ermine robe, he made his way to the fire. His hands ached badly tonight. As always there was a jug of holk resting amongst the embers. Pouring himself a brimming cup, he downed the warm and spicy liquid in one swallow. Only when the holk had worked its trade upon his hands, did he feel calm enough to think about what he had just experienced.

Tonight, somewhere in the Known Lands, someone had performed a drawing that defied all reason.

Woken up from an early, fitful sleep, Baralis felt the first wave of the most powerful sorcery he had ever encountered. Terrifying in its strength, it sent spasms racing down his spine, spiking his very soul. There seemed no end to it. On and on the power flowed. First for seconds, then for minutes, then for *hours*. Never before had he felt anything to match it. Even now the very substance of the air crackled with the aftermath. Half the city of Bren had probably awakened in their beds. Few would know why.

Baralis was afraid. The person who had done this was powerful beyond telling.

Gathering his strength, he sent out his perception. Already weak from his journey to Larn the day before, he could do little but test the essence of the sorcery. Like a man holding a wet finger to the wind, he could tell from which direction the aftermath came: west. But, if he wasn't mistaken, not as far west as the kingdoms. Which meant Halcus or Annis or Highwall. A terrible thought occurred to him: could it be Kylock, suddenly free from the tyranny of drugs? Baralis' heart quickened at the thought. Quickly he *tasted* the air around him. The sorcery played upon his tongue with a familiar tune. Not Kylock. No. Someone else. Someone whom he had encountered before. Someone who had copied Tavalisk's library word for word.

The baker's boy.

Risking sanity, and with no help from his potions, Baralis' drew the aftermath into his mind. Such lightness, such pain, such flickering flames. And then the clear blue eyes of a man close to death. It was all there, written upon the ether in a foreign tongue. There was little he could make sense of and no time for translation. One thing was certain, though: Jack *was* responsible for the drawing. He had not been mistaken. All sorcery had its own unique signature, and once Baralis perceived an individual's pattern, he never forgot it. This was the third time now that the baker's boy had signed his name across a drawing.

He exhaled deeply, eager to be free of the alien force. It left him, but not willingly. He felt it clawing away at the fiber of his brain, trying to restructure his mind to mimic that from which it came. Baralis was too much the master to let it gain a footing. No one's aftermath was going to make a madman out of *him*.

Still, there was a price to pay. He was overcome with a terrible, draining weakness. No longer possessing strength enough to return to his bed, Baralis sat by the fire and sipped his holk. He knew he needed to sleep, to recuperate like an invalid, but his thoughts raced ahead, leaving his body to fend for itself.

What was the purpose behind Jack's power? Such a gift—for talent on such a scale could be neither taught nor inherited—was not given without purpose. Baralis searched his mind, looking for connections and prophecies and patterns in the dance. Something began to niggle away at him. Something heard the day before at the table of Larn's high priests, when they had spoken about the knight:

"He came here for a seering, we showed him the way."

"What way was that?"

"To the kingdoms."

The boy the knight was looking for came from the kingdoms. The hairs prickled on the back of Baralis' neck. It was Jack, the baker's boy. He knew it without a doubt. Larn lived in fear of his former scribe.

What did it mean? And, more importantly, how did it affect him? Baralis warmed his hands upon the holk jug as he tried to make sense of this latest development. The boy was important; he had great powers, the wiseman Bevlin had sent a knight to search for him, and Larn didn't want him found. What was it the priests had said before he left?

"Our fate is connected with yours. As you rise, so do we."

Then if the boy was a threat to Larn, he was a threat to him, as well. In a way Baralis already knew this. He had known it all those months ago when eight score of burnt loaves had been transmuted into dough. Jack was a thorn in his side then, and it seemed he still was now. He should have killed him when he had the chance.

The key to this mystery was the wiseman Bevlin; he alone knew the true purpose of the boy. Only he was dead, very probably due to the efforts of Larn, and his secrets had gone with him to the grave.

Or had they? The base of the jug had been in the fire and Baralis spotted ash on his fingers. Absently, he rubbed the silvery powder away. The wiseman himself might have turned to dust, but his books and his records would still remain. Yes, that was it. Tomorrow he would look into procuring Bevlin's possessions. A man like that was bound to have consigned his thoughts to parchment. All he had to do was locate who currently held them and make him an offer he couldn't refuse.

With a plan decided upon, Baralis felt in control once more. He would get to the bottom of this. The baker's boy might have great ability, but experience and cunning always won in the end.

Jack woke up with a start. He was cold and his clothes were soaking wet. People were close, shouting, dashing, and carrying bundles through the dark. There was a brief blissful moment of confusion, and then he remembered all the horror of the night. The guard! What had become of the guard who had jumped? Jack looked around. He was lying in exactly the same place as before and the guard was at his side. How long had he been out? Minutes? Hours? It was impossible to say. Yet the gatehouse was now reduced to charred and smoking rubble, and the rest of the garrison seemed to have met a similar fate. Flames still flickered here and there, sparring with timbers and outbuildings, but they lacked the fierce frenzy of before.

He knew he had to get up. It wouldn't be long before the people who were busy hurrying to and fro decided that the two men lying at the side of the gate needed moving. He moved his arms close to his body in preparation to push himself up. His muscles screamed with pure pain. A hard ball of sickness welled up in his throat, and bringing it up nearly choked him. Retching hard, he spat out a dry lump of something pink-colored. Jack quickly covered it with dirt. He didn't want to know what it was.

Trying to stand up again, he shifted his weight to his arms. This time he was determined to ignore the pain. Everything was going well until it was his legs' turn to play their part; they shook violently for a moment and then buckled, sending him crashing back down to the ground. He landed badly. His shoulder hit first, sending a sharp spasm straight to the arrow wound on his chest. "Damn!" he cursed, frustrated by his weakness. He took a deep breath and began again. Humming a tune, he struggled to his feet. He swayed like before, but countered his legs' desire to crumble, by refusing to let them bend at the knee. After a few seconds of standing soldier-straight, his blood started flowing downward, and gradually Jack began to feel a little stronger.

Someone approached him. "You all right, friend? Do you need a hand?"

Jack looked at the stranger blankly. There was no accusation on his face, only concern. The man didn't know who he was. Jack knew better than to speak, so nodded instead, making a small patting gesture at his throat, as if the fire had rendered it raw.

"How about the other fellow?"

Not once during the time he had been trying to stand had Jack seen the guard move. He raised his arms in a pulling gesture and the man came closer to give him a hand with the body. "I don't believe I've met you before, my friend," he said, as he grabbed the guard's shoulders. "Though with all that dirt on your face, you could be my wife and I'd hardly know it." The man smiled broadly, showing intricately crooked teeth and a fat red tongue. "Come on, lad. Look lively, grab those feet. My name's Dilburt, by the way."

Jack bent down and took hold of the guard's ankles. He almost couldn't believe what he felt: the flesh was warm. Not cold, not cool, but warm. He was alive. Jack felt a wave of simple joy ripple through his body. Buoying, invigorating, it chased away the pain.

"What you so happy about, lad?" asked the man, not unkindly. "Has all the soot gone to your head? Or are you relived that this guy's feet don't smell as bad as you thought?" Not waiting for an answer, Dilburt counted: "One, two, three," and together they hoisted the guard into the air. "Through here, lad," he said, tilting his head toward the gate. "A camp's been set up for the sick."

Bearing the guard's body was a duty to Jack. His muscles ached, his head spun, and although the stranger took the greater part of the weight, the strain on his shoulder caused an inferno of pain.

Two minutes later they came upon a makeshift camp. Campfires and tents had been hastily built, and pallets and bedrolls lined the ground. People had collected in large groups, and if anything the mood was festive; cups topped with froth caught the firelight and the smell of roasting meat filled the air. Somewhere, a woman with a fine voice was singing a song that was anything but sad, and all around people were chattering in high, excited voices about what had happened that night.

Jack did not want to join the throng. He stopped in his tracks, causing Dilburt to come to a halt. "What's the matter, lad? Tired?" he asked. "Only a bit of a way to go now. The sick are being tended on the other side, close to the wall."

There seemed little choice but to follow the stranger. Somehow the guard had become his responsibility, and Jack felt it wouldn't be right to leave him until he was sure that the man was getting the help he needed. It was the least he could do. Lowering his head, he stepped forward.

"Good, lad," said Dilburt, adjusting his grip on the guard's body, taking even more of the burden upon himself.

At that moment Jack wished he could speak. He would like to have thanked the crooked-toothed man who had helped him and the guard without question. Instead he smiled softly.

The stranger seemed to understand. "Eh, lad," he said, "on nights like this, a fellow can't count himself a man unless he's willing to do his part."

No heads turned as they passed through the crowds. People seemed strangely excited, like they did at Castle Harvell on the eve of a big feast. There was a sheen on many a man's brow and a blush on the bosoms of women who had loosened their laces for the sake of their health. Snatches of conversation reached Jack's ears:

"It was an earthquake, I'm sure of it. Just two days ago the jailers reported feeling a tremor beneath the cells."

"Kingdoms spies did it. They doused all the timbers in oil and set fire to them with flaming arrows."

"The kingdoms dug a mine beneath the garrison and set it alight, that's what caused the earth to shake."

"I heard one man walked through the flames untouched, like an angel."

"It was the devil."

"It was Kylock."

"The two are one in the same."

Jack was glad when they reached the sick tent. He'd had his fill of rumors. Several rows of soot-blackened, groaning men were laid out neatly like cards. The sound of hacking and spitting filled the air.

"Dead or alive?" came the curt, efficient voice of a self-important physician.

"Alive—until you get your hands on him," piped up Dilburt.

Jack had to bite his tongue to stop himself from laughing. He was liking his co-bearer more and more by the minute.

"Over there, then," said the doctor, indicating a clean, linen-covered pallet. Once they had laid the guard down, he turned to Jack. "You look like you're in a bad way under all that soot. Wait over there by the stoop and I'll take a look at you when I've got a minute." He appraised Jack coolly, his eyes taking in the chest wound and the sores running down his arms.

Jack began to feel nervous. He wondered how many of his injuries the soot had covered, but he couldn't risk glancing down to check. He looked to Dilburt for help.

"If I were you, lad," he said, "I wouldn't let him near me with a maypole. You're alive and you're standing and Borc willing you'll live through the night. A man couldn't hope for more." He came forward and put his arm around Jack's shoulders. "Come on, lad. Let's not waste this good man's time any longer. If left too long his patients might start getting better on their own, and we all know there'd be hell to pay if that happened." He smiled a gloriously disarming smile, winked at the physician, and began to steer Jack away from the camp.

Jack pulled away for an instant. He had to say farewell to the guard. Dilburt made a slight nodding movement of his head. "Very commendable of you, lad. I'll wait over here till you've done."

What was it about this man? Dilburt seemed able to read his thoughts as easily as others heard his words. Jack watched a moment as he backed a discreet distance away, bald patch shining in the moonlight like the bottom of a cup raised in drink. Walking back to the guard, Jack rested his hand lightly on the man's arms. Sweat gleamed on the guard's brow and his whole body was shaking. His right leg fell to one side, and above his knee the skin was white and strained where a splintered bone pressed against the flesh.

"I'm sorry," whispered Jack.

The guard's eyes opened. He looked at Jack for a moment, a world of compassion in his clear blue eyes, and said simply, "I know."

Jack squeezed his arm, probably too tightly, for his heart felt heavy, and physical things became difficult to judge. "Rest easy tonight, my friend," he said softly, and then turned and walked away.

Dilburt came to meet him, offering an arm on which to rest his weight. For the third time that night, the crooked-toothed man read his thoughts, for he didn't say a word, merely guided Jack away from the camp.

Half an hour later, too exhausted for words or thought, Jack and Dilburt approached a small, neatly timbered building. By this time Dilburt was all but carrying him. "Here we are, lad," he said. "Home sweet home." Dawn was breaking, and the sun's first rays framed the neatly timbered cottage like a halo.

A woman with a face as large and smooth as a round of cheese came out to greet them. "Husband!" she cried. "What are you doing mooning around outside with a sick man on your arm? Come in this instant and let me tend him." She clucked like an angry hen, coming forward to take Jack's other arm. "Really! Dilburt Wadwell! I always said you had tallow for brains, and I've been proven right tonight—for the fire has surely melted them."

Jack felt himself pressed against the considerable bounty of Mrs. Wadwell's chest. She smelled wonderfully familiar: yeasty, buttery, good enough to bake. Leading him through a doorway so low that all of them had to bow to pass, she led him into a warm bright kitchen. The rushes were so fresh they crackled underfoot.

All this time, Mrs. Wadwell kept up a good-humored tirade at her husband. "Dilburt, don't just stand there as if you're waiting for Borc's second coming. Pour the lad a mug of holk—and not one of your skimpy half measures, if you please. I don't want to see the rim of the cup." Firm hands forced Jack down upon a cushioned seat. "And while you're at it, bring me a bowl and some water. This boy's in need of a good wash."

Dilburt caught Jack's eye and smiled ruefully. "Aye, my wife would have made a fine general if she'd been born a man."

"Enough of your chatter, husband," said Mrs. Wadwell, seeming anything but displeased. "This lad is suffering for want of my holk." She rested a heavy hand upon Jack's forehead, felt the heat from his skin, and then rolled up the sleeves of her dress. "I can see I'll be here all morning."

Jack leaned back in the comfortable chair and was content to let her tend him. Her touch was efficient, if a little rough, and her enthusiasm was boundless. A quarter-candle later she had given him a shave, cleaned all his "decent parts," rubbed salve into his various dog bites, and applied a cold compress to his forehead. Lastly, Mrs. Wadwell came to the arrow wound in his upper chest. Whilst washing him, her damp cloth had skirted around the mass of clotted and scabbing blood. Now she gave it her full attention.

"Husband, put down the compress and bring me the best of the summer wine," she said.

Dilburt promptly made his way to the far side of the cottage. Mrs. Wadwell took this opportunity to whisper in Jack's ear, "I suspect that under all that blood, I'll find a very nasty arrow wound."

Jack opened his mouth to make some excuse, realized he couldn't talk because his accent would give him away, and so was forced to settle for shrugging his shoulders.

Mrs. Wadwell leaned very close. Her huge bosom brushed against his face. "I'm glad you're not going to try my patience with a lie, lad. For it would only upset my Dilburt. He's a kind-hearted man, can't see anyone sick without bringing him home. He's got it into his head that I can care for folks better than any doctor, and if I do say so myself, he's right." She patted Jack's arm. "Anyway, the point is this: if my husband's content not to ask questions, then so am I. Oh, I know very well what caused the wounds on your arms and legs—though I doubt if my Dilburt does. But I trust his instincts. He's never brought anyone bad to this house since I've known him, and I don't think he's started with you."

Jack felt he had to risk speaking. "Thank you," he said.

Mrs. Wadwell made a clucking noise. "You have my Dilburt to thank, lad, not me."

Dilburt returned with a jug of wine. He broke the waxed seal and proceeded to fill three cups with the deep, red liquid.

"No, husband, the wine's for cleaning this lad's wound, not for drinking."

"That may be so, woman, but I think it's about time we all had a drink."

Surprisingly, Mrs. Wadwell didn't argue with her husband. She took her cup with good grace and passed the other over to Jack.

"I think I will propose a toast, wife," said Dilburt.

"I think you should, husband," said Mrs. Wadwell, nodding her large head judiciously.

Dilburt raised his glass. "To a long night, a bright fire, and friends well met in need."

"Nicely said, husband." Mrs. Wadwell downed her wine in one draft, burping splendidly when she'd finished. "Now help me get this boy onto the bed. Once I've cleaned and dressed that chest wound, I'll be sending him straight to sleep."

Twenty-six

No, I'd have to disagree with you there, Bodger. I think that when the time comes for Nabber here to do his first spot of rollickin', his best bet is to go for an older woman. Not a young slip of a girl with no meat on her bones and no hair on her upper lip."

"Just how old should this woman be, Grift?" asked Nabber, a picture of an old woman with a mustache flashing through his mind.

"Old enough to know what she's doing in the dark, Nabber."

"I didn't know women's eyesight improved with age, Grift," said Bodger.

"It doesn't, Bodger. But their ability to please a man does. Right grateful, too, they are."

"Grateful for what?" asked Nabber.

"A spot of male company. Mark my words, young Nabber, an older woman is not only the most experienced between the sheets, but she'll be willing to wash them for you afterward."

"I wouldn't let an older woman do that for me, Grift," said Bodger. "Clean sheets set my scroff sores running."

Whilst Grift told Bodger the best way to dry up scroff sores, Nabber busily downed more ale. Even though it was early and dawn's chill was still hanging in the air, he was feeling slightly tipsy. Over the past few days he had become friendly with the two guards who were stationed outside the chapel and had taken to sharing a few drinks with them on his way to and from the secret passageway. At this point, Bodger and Grift thought that he was a boy so devoted to his mother's memory that he spent all his spare time in seclusion praying for her in the chapel. He felt a little guilty about that, but with Tawl gone he had little to do, and the secret passageways were his only diversion. That and downing good ale and bad advice from Bodger and Grift. A woman with hair on her upper lip, indeed!

"Did you feel the air last night, Grift?" asked Bodger.

"Aye. Woke me up, it did, Bodger. I was having a nice dream about being back at Castle Harvell. Everyone was there in the kitchens going about their business, when our old friend Jack the baker's boy set the place alight. The whole building went up in flames. Horrible it was. The next thing I know, I'm wide awake and the air is so thick it's crawling across my skin like a plague of centipedes."

"I wouldn't repeat that story to anyone else if I were you, my friend," came a softly sinister voice.

Nabber and Bodger and Grift all looked around to see who it belonged to. Standing in the shadows was a tall dark man dressed in black silk. The two guards immediately stood up and brushed down their clothes.

"Lord Baralis, this is an unexpected pleasure," said Grift, hastily throwing a cloth over the ale skin.

"Don't worry gentlemen, I haven't come to check up on you, or to reclaim my debt—though a little reminder of your obligation will do no harm." He smiled coldly, thin lips stretching over glinting teeth. "No. My business is not with you, but rather your young companion: Nabber, if I'm not mistaken."

Nabber had the distinct feeling that this man before him was seldom mistaken about anything. "That's me, what do you want?"

"Privacy."

Up until that point, Nabber thought that Bodger and Grift were incapable of fast movement; they seemed to exist in a lazy, semi-drunken haze where their bottoms never left their chairs. Borc, was he wrong! At the word *privacy* they scooted out of the chapel so fast they could have won a race.

The man in black waited until the door was firmly closed, and then moved toward the altar. Coming to rest in front of the central panel, which marked the entrance to the secret passageway, he spun round and said, "You are a friend of the knight's, are you not?"

Lord Baralis was no longer in the shadows, yet the darkness clung to him like a fragrance. It was difficult for Nabber to tell exactly what he looked like—except for his eyes. They glittered with the cold light of a predator.

"And if I am?"

"Don't mince words with me, boy, for it will be to your disadvantage if you do." Lord Baralis seemed to check himself; he rubbed his hands together and stepped forward a little. "However, it will be to your *advantage* to answer me promptly and with the truth."

Nabber caught a whiff of the sweet smell of loot. "The knight and I are old friends. Go back a long way, we do."

"Aah." Lord Baralis issued a smile as smooth as his voice. "You're a sensible boy, I see."

"The most sensible in Rorn."

"Is that where you met the knight—Rorn?"

Nabber rubbed his chin. "Just about how advantageous would it be for me to tell you that?" He couldn't see that disclosing the information would do Tawl any harm. So why not make a little loot? It was nobody's secret.

"Answer all my questions today and I will give you ten golds."

"Done! If you have the money about your person."

Lord Baralis reached inside his robe and brought out a velvet purse. Without pausing to measure coinage, he offered it out for Nabber to take. "This should be sufficient."

Nabber took the purse. His first instinct was to count the loot, but he remembered the way Swift handled himself in similar situations, and so he quietly slipped the purse into his tunic. Of course the minute Swift was alone he'd tally the money with the skill of a professional lender. And if he found it wanting, he would quickly dispatch a man to break the offender's fingers. Somehow Nabber doubted if he'd be doing the same with Lord Baralis.

"So, how long have you known the knight?"

"Long enough to call him a friend." Nabber thought Lord Baralis would take him to task on the vagueness of his answer, but he let it pass.

"Has he been looking for the boy since you met him?"

"Way before then." Only after he spoke did Nabber begin to wonder how Lord Baralis knew about Tawl's quest.

"Did you ever go with him to meet the wiseman, Bevlin?" After each question Lord Baralis moved a few steps closer. He was now only an arm's length away from Nabber. His breath smelled sharp and sweet.

The purse in Nabber's tunic began to feel heavy, like a burden. "I met Bevlin once. Nice man he was, cured me of the northern shivers."

"Where is his house?"

"Less than three weeks ride east of here."

"Do you know if he had any relatives or acquaintances who would currently be in possession of his belongings?" Lord Baralis' eyes narrowed. "I know he's dead, of course."

The purse now became hot as well as heavy. "Can't help you there, my friend."

"Do you think there's a chance his possessions might still be in his house?"

Nabber had buried Bevlin. He'd dug a shallow grave and then dragged the wiseman's body out of the cottage to the plot that lay under the sill. He scrubbed the blood from the floor, dampened the fire, threw out all the goods that were perishable, let the hens free from the coop and the pig free from the sty, sealed all the shutters, and locked and bolted the door. "Yes," he said. "There's a chance Bevlin's things are still where he left them." Nabber thought for a moment and then added, "Why do you want to know?"

"He and I were involved in the same type of scholarly research. We shared a passion for crawling insects. Bevlin had an unrivaled collection of books on the subject, and I worry that if they were to fall into the wrong hands they might be treated badly." Lord Baralis made a small, self-deprecating gesture. "Only experts like myself would fully appreciate their value." He looked Nabber straight in the eye. "Now, can you remember exactly how to get to his house?"

Insects? He looked the sort. "Yes."

"Draw me a map," Lord Baralis' voice was as thick and tempting as honey, "and I will make it worth your while. Accompany my servant on the journey and I will make you a rich man."

Tempting though the offer was, Nabber had no intention of agreeing to it. Not only did he feel honor-bound to wait for Tawl's return, but more importantly, a long journey meant the one thing he hated most in the world: horses. No one was going to get him on one of those ugly, bad-tempered, flea-ridden things unless it was a matter of life and death. There was a problem with accepting the first offer, though: he couldn't write, let alone draw a map. "I could *tell* you exactly how to get there, but I'll do no drawing—my hand, you know, injured it in a boating accident."

"Hmm." Lord Baralis spread the sound over two skeptical syllables. "Very well. Tell me now and I will have your payment delivered to you within the hour."

Nabber didn't feel it would be a wise move to question the man's integrity. The loot would come. He had an instinct about such things. He took a deep breath. "Well, you ride east as far as . . ."

Tarissa was laughing at him. Her jaw was wide, her curls were bouncing, and her head rocked back and forth. So long and hard she laughed that the strings of her bodice gave way and her breasts spilled out over the fabric. A rough hand reached out and tucked them back in, the fingers lingering long over the milky white flesh.

Rovas! he screamed. *Rovas!*

"Ssh, lad. Ssh. Everything's all right now."

Jack found himself looking up into the smooth, round face of Mrs. Wadwell.

"It was a bad dream, that's all. No need to worry."

Her voice had a calming effect upon him, and the line between sleeping and waking drew itself anew. His muscles relaxed and he slumped back down against the sheet. It was wet with sweat.

Mrs. Wadwell stood up and busied herself around the room, opening shutters, stoking the fire, and pouring some broth into a bowl. "Sit up, lad," she said, "and drink this." She handed him the bowl and didn't blink until the spoon was at his lips. "That's a good lad."

The last thing Jack thought he wanted was broth, but as soon as the spicy liquid met his tongue, he was overcome with a ravenous hunger. He had hardly eaten in a week, and it was as if his body was determined to secure some nourishment despite his brain's reluctance. Mrs. Wadwell nodded approvingly and fetched him some more food: another bowl of broth, a full crusty loaf, a wedge of cheese that would have stopped open a door, and a cold roast chicken that looked like it had been hit by one.

"I pressed it whilst it roasted," said Mrs. Wadwell, seeing Jack eyeing the flat chicken suspiciously. "If you squash a bird in the oven with decent size weights, it forces the juices into the meat. Turns right tender, it does."

"Aye, lad, no one roasts a bird like my wife." Dilburt came toward the bed, the smile on his face bright with undisguised pride. He patted Mrs. Wadwell affectionately on her bottom. "You won't find a finer woman anywhere."

"You soft old coot," she replied, winking at Jack. "Go and cut me some wood. If the fire burns any lower, I won't be able to warm the chickens let alone roast them."

Dilburt obediently left the cottage. Mrs. Wadwell straightened Jack's bed, made sure all the food was within reach, and then followed her husband outside, muttering something about not chopping the green ones.

Jack wasted no time; he tore into the food the moment the door banged shut. It was the most delicious meal he had eaten in his entire life. The bread was chewy and tasted of nuts, the cheese was cream-heavy and bright with herbs, and the flat chicken was so tender it fell off the bone. With each bite the memory of eels and their gravy receded into the distance.

The memory of last night was not so easy to eat away. The more full his belly became, the more freedom his thoughts seemed to have to soar where they pleased. Everything came back to him in terrifying detail: the fire, the sparks, the creaking of timbers, and the low rumble of moving earth. The screams were the worst thing. The terrified screams of people burning, or choking, or just plain afraid. Suddenly the room filled with the sound of their screams. It was a visible force, whipping the air round like a whirlwind. The food turned to ashes in his mouth and he brought his hands up to his ears, desperate to stop the sound.

He had done this! People were dead because of him. The fault was his and his alone. Tarissa and Rovas had played him for a fool, lying about Melli's death, lying about the tunnel, lying about how much they cared. Yet rather than take his anger out on them, he had turned it toward innocent people instead.

The screams died away, as if content for a while that he had acknowledged his guilt.

He needed to make sure something like this never happened again. The power within him was too dangerous to be used in anger. It caused him to lash out uncontrollably, making itself his master. He had been right in the Halcus cell to try and force the sorcery to do his bidding, but he had come nowhere near success. He doubted if he could on his own. Who was there to help him, though? Even a powerful man like Baralis was forced to keep his powers hidden. The world condemned sorcery. People who used it were branded as demons and burned at the stake. And after last night he knew why.

Was that all that sorcery was good for? he wondered. Destruction?

Jack swung his feet onto the floor and tested the strength of his legs. Hardly good enough for standing, but he needed to relieve himself badly and he wasn't about to take a pot to his bed like an invalid. He'd rather fall on his face trying to make it outside. Taking a deep breath, he transferred his weight to his legs, groaning like an old man as he hauled himself up. Nausea fluttered around his belly and he was forced to swallow hard to keep it down. A grim smile stretched his lips. He didn't fancy seeing the pressed chicken again; it hadn't looked too appetizing the first time around, no matter how good it had tasted.

Once his legs felt sure enough to take his weight, he risked stepping forward. Muscles in his chest, his abdomen, his behind, and his legs protested violently, and then finding their cries ignored, they set to quivering like eels in jelly. Finding the quivering ignored, they actually shaped up and did his bidding. Jack knew that his muscles were unhappy, but plodded on regardless.

Opening the door, he discovered a bright beautiful day scented with the full promise of spring. Flowers bloomed on either side of the door and flies, lazy after a morning's work, sunned themselves on the broad green leaves. At the far end of the garden Mr. and Mrs. Wadwell were deep in conversation with a small dark man. As soon as Dilburt saw Jack emerge from the cottage, he practically pushed the man away, diverting his attention by leading him down the muddy lane. Mrs. Wadwell came rushing forward, a plump finger on an even plumper lip. "Inside, lad, inside," she hissed.

Jack obeyed her immediately. Not content with closing the door, she took the precaution of bolting it. "In bed now, this instant. I'll bring you a pot if need made you stray."

Too embarrassed to say anything, Jack merely nodded.

"Now, lad, if anyone should happen to come here, you're Dilburt's sick nephew from Todlowly." Mrs. Wadwell thought for a second. "And the ague has taken your voice."

So she knew he was from the kingdoms. In that case, he might as well speak freely. "Who was that man in the garden?" he asked.

"A friend of Dilburt's from the garrison." Mrs. Wadwell handed him the largest chamberpot he'd ever seen in his life. The sides were painted with waterfalls. "My sister makes them herself," she said.

He took it from her and placed it on the floor. Relieving himself would have to wait. "Do they know anything more about how the fire started?"

Mrs. Wadwell wasted no words. "A prisoner did it. A man from the kingdoms with chestnut hair and an arrow wound in his chest."

"I'll go now," said Jack.

A heavy hand clamped down on his shoulder. "You're in no fit state to go anywhere, lad. At least stay another night until you're strong enough to leave." Courage gleamed softly in the darkness of her eyes, and the lines of her jaw suggested a formidable depth of determination.

Jack was overwhelmed by her offer. Here he was a stranger, an enemy and a murderer, yet she was prepared to put herself at risk by harboring him. He couldn't let her. "No, I must go," he said. "I owe you and Dilburt too much as it is." He took her hand and kissed it gently. "Though I thank you from my heart for your kindness."

Mrs. Wadwell snorted dismissively. "Dilburt's never wrong about anyone. If he says you're all right, then it's good enough for me." She smiled, a little sadly, and ruffled his hair. "Well, if you're set on going, then you might as well know the worst. The whole county is teeming with soldiers who are looking for you. Every man, woman, and child is on the alert and your description has been circulated far and wide. In a day's time you won't be able to show your face within a fifty-league radius of the garrison. A week from now there'll be nowhere you can hide."

"What do they know about me?"

"Apparently, the prisoner who you shared a cell with told them that you were a plant, sent here by King Kylock on a special mission to infiltrate and destroy the garrison." Mrs. Wadwell gave him a hard look. "He also said you were a mighty sorcerer who had the elements at your command."

"Do they believe him?"

"You know folks, never want to believe anything that smacks of sorcery, so they've come up with all sorts of theories to explain the fire and the explosions. Still, people talk, and what can't be said freely in public is whispered soft and long in private."

Jack opened his mouth to speak.

"Nay, lad," she said quickly, "I don't **want** to know the truth. I look at you and I see a young man who's ill **and** confused, nothing more." She smiled brightly. "Let's leave it at that, eh?"

A soft tapping at the door stopped Jack from giving his thanks. There was a tense moment whilst Mrs. Wadwell drew back the bolt, but Dilburt stood there alone.

"Did he see the lad?" she asked.

"He did, but I told him what you said and he seemed happy enough." They exchanged a brief, telling glance, and then Dilburt said, "I'm sorry lad, but I think it's better that you go. If it was me alone, you could stay here until they knocked down the door. But, the wife . . ." Slowly, he shook his head. "I'd be a broken man if anything should happen to her."

Jack nodded. "I know, Dilburt. Your wife is the bravest woman in all of Halcus, and I would not see her harmed for the world." As he spoke, he realized he meant every word he said.

Dilburt came and put his arm around, Jack. "You're a good lad, truly you are. I'm glad I brought you home."

A noise escaped Mrs. Wadwell's throat that sounded suspiciously like a sob. From her sleeve she pulled out a handkerchief the size of a small tablecloth and blew into it loudly. Having finished this, she turned to Dilburt. "Well, what are you waiting around for, husband? If the lad's going, you need to get him some supplies."

Dilburt smiled ruefully at Jack and then busied himself about the cottage, wrapping cheeses and meats, filling skins with wine, and pulling clothes from a trunk.

Mrs. Wadwell slapped her broad hand on Jack's forehead. "Still some fever there," she pronounced. "I'll have to give you some medicine." Pulling a silver flask from her tunic, she urged him to drink, "down to the last drop."

Jack had only tasted brandy once before in his life. Master Frallit had been given a bottle one Winter's Eve by the poulterer's widow—an amorous lady who had her eye on a quick second marriage—and he promptly hid it amidst the flour sacks. Jack found it there the next morning, and by the time that Master Frallit discovered him, half of the brandy was gone. He was so drunk that he never felt the beating. Which was, he now realized, a sign of good medicine. Anything that could numb the sensation of Frallit in full frenzy must be very powerful indeed.

Whilst he drank the brandy, Mrs. Wadwell inspected his various cuts and bruises. Every now and then she would shake her head and make soft clucking noises. She redressed his shoulder wound and rubbed his legs and arms down with the last of the good wine. When she was finished, Dilburt stepped forward with several choices of clothes for him to wear.

Mrs. Wadwell became a military commander, choosing the clothes that would best blend in with the surrounding countryside. Unfortunately, size and fit were not on her mind. The brown tunic she chose was so long that it prompted the appearance of the large scissors—Jack was beginning to realize that everything in the Wadwell home was done on a grand scale—and a good length of fabric was cut from the bottom. The breeches presented a similar problem, but a length of rope so thick it could have docked a ship was quickly tied about his waist to keep them up.

By the time they had finished with him, Jack was loaded up like a packhorse and armed to the teeth. Three knives of deadly sharpness and varying size were concealed about his person, together with a bag full of small caltraps that could bring a charging horse to a halt. The fact that Dilburt had a supply of siege foils in his house did not surprise Jack in the least: the Wadwells were a couple who liked to plan ahead.

Mrs. Wadwell leaned forward and planted her plump lips on Jack's cheek. Her massive bosom was squashed against his chest. "Farewell, lad, I'll be sorry to see you go." One firm bone-crushing squeeze and then she backed away, instantly changing from earth mother to general. "Now, when you leave, go by way of the back woods. Keep under cover whenever possible. Spring's come early so there's enough foliage to cast some decent shadows. After about half a league of heading due south, you'll come to a brook, follow it upstream for about . . ." She paused, considering. "How far would you say, husband?"

"No more than four leagues, wife."

"Right you are. After four leagues, you'll come to a fork, follow the stream that leads up into the hills—you should be facing northeast by this time—and from there you should be able to make your own way. The woods are pretty much deserted, but keep your eye out for poachers, just in case."

Jack obediently nodded to all the instructions. The brandy had set his blood afire and the weight of all the food and supplies was making it difficult for him to stand. He didn't have the heart to tell them they had given him too much to bear. He would have to lose some bundles later, when he was alone. Which was sad, because he valued their gifts. His legs would have it no other way, though. He knew they would give way if he asked too much of them; they were already trembling now, just standing with the weight.

Dilburt took his hand and clasped it firmly. "Take care, lad. And remember my wife's directions, no one knows the country round here like she does."

They led him to the door, checked that no one was outside, and then let him through. As they accompanied him to the back of the cottage, Jack noticed they were arm in arm. The sight of such casual, everyday affection affected him deeply. He had imagined such moments with Tarissa: moments where they linked arms without conscious thought, or where they exchanged kisses as easily as smiles. All gone now. He was alone, his dreams shattered like glass, leaving splinters to pierce his soul. How could she have done it? How could she have betrayed him so completely?

There was no anger now, only sadness and, as Mrs. Wadwell had wisely guessed, confusion. Tarissa said that she loved him, and everyone, even Bodger and Grift, had told him it was wrong to hurt the one you love.

So it was a lie. And amongst a catalog of falsehoods and deceit, it was still the one that hurt the most.

"There you go, lad," said Mrs. Wadwell, breaking into his thoughts. "The woods are over yonder. They're quite a walk, but you'll be all right once you reach those first set of trees." She smiled at him kindly, her large face almost completely free of wrinkles.

They had already said their good-byes, so the only thing left was to give his thanks. He turned to face the couple who were his enemies. Halcus was now at war with the kingdoms, yet these two people before him had shown him more kindness in the last day than anyone at home ever had. With the possible exception of an old lady pig farmer who lived just off Harvell's eastern road. Certainly they proved to him that the Halcus were not the arrogant, godless people that everyone in the kingdoms believed them to be. The idea of war suddenly seemed appalling to Jack. It was easy to hate a country, yet hard to hate its people once you knew them. Mr. and Mrs. Wadwell were happy, good-hearted folks, and they didn't deserve to be brought to their knees by Kylock.

A deep weariness came over him, settling on his shoulders like an extra burden. For some reason that he couldn't explain, he felt responsible for everything, not just the destruction of the garrison, not only the fate of the couple in front of him, but more. Much more.

"Well," he said softly. "I'll be on my way."

"Aye, lad," murmured Dilburt.

"I want to thank you both for everything you have done for me. I'll never forget your kindness." Jack looked first at Dilburt and then his wife. "Never."

Mrs. Wadwell's large handkerchief put in an appearance as the lady herself dabbed it around her eyes. "Go now, lad," she said. "I'll watch you till you're safely to the trees."

Jack smiled briefly, sent a quick prayer to Borc to strengthen his step, and began the long walk to the woods.

Twenty-seven

Melli was beginning to wish that she'd never called for a mirror, as the face reflected in it was surely not her own. Who was this girl with the deathly pallor and eyes as large as pancakes?

"Nessa," she called. "Bring me some wine, as strong as it comes." The duke would be here any minute and she would have some color in her cheeks by the time he arrived even if she had to drink herself silly to do so.

Melli put down the mirror and took up a small silver vial containing fragrance. She dabbed it on her bosom and neck, sprinkled a little on the surrounding sheets, and finished by letting a single glistening drop fall upon her tongue. The bitter taste made her wince.

While she wondered if it would be better for the duke to find her in bed, or on the bench by the window, Nessa returned with the wine. "His Grace is on his way, miss," she cried. "He'll be here in a moment."

"Well, hurry with the wine, girl," snapped Melli. A second after the cup was placed in her hand, it was pressing against her lips. She drank all the wine except for the last drop, which, in a sudden burst of inspiration, she scooped up onto her fingertips and proceeded to rub into both of her cheeks. She knew she was behaving like an expectant courtesan, and at any other time, with any other man, she would never have deigned to primp and preen, but over the past few days she had found herself becoming more and more attracted to the duke, and she now found herself rather anxious to look pleasing for him.

The trouble was she didn't know how to. All her life she had paid little or no attention to her appearance. From as early as she could remember she had been hailed as a natural beauty; years of hearing this had caused her to scorn all the usual range of feminine embellishments. Powders, perfumes, and plucked eyebrows were mysteries to Melli. As were colored waxes, greased soot, and rouge.

The door opened and in walked the duke. The first thing he did was sniff the air. Melli instantly realized she had overdone the perfume and quickly threw the heavily scented coverlet from her bed.

"You smell like a cheap tavern wench," he said.

Melli felt the heat come to her cheeks. She shot a venom-filled glance at Nessa: it was the servant girl's perfume she was wearing. Unable to think of a suitably withering retort to the duke's insult, she settled for haughtily dismissing her maid. "Do not stand around gawking, girl. Leave us. And take this coverlet with you—I insist you wash it yourself. That should teach you not to spill perfume again."

The duke waited until Nessa had left the room before he crossed over to Melli's bed. He took her hand and placed a brief kiss upon her wrist. His lips were cool and dry. "I have another gift for you," he said, pulling a silk-wrapped object from his tunic.

There was a small part of Melli that found the duke's behavior rather perfunctory; it was as if he were performing a military maneuver: first the kiss, then the gift, then a little verbal sparring. The exact same scenario had been acted out the day before, when he had given her a scabbard in which to keep her knife. She turned over the package in her hand and wondered if her misgivings were grounded in good sense, or merely the folly of an idle mind. After all, she had been cooped up here on her own for five days now.

"Open it," he commanded.

Melli unwrapped the silk to find a large glove inside. The leather was thick and brightly painted with scrolls and flourishes. "A falconer's glove?" she asked.

"Yes," said the duke, "and the falcon to go with it." He clapped his hands together sharply, and a man entered the room. Upon his arm he carried a large, silent bird that wore a hood.

"A gerfalcon," said Melli, unable to keep the wonder from her voice.

"Aye, miss," replied the falconer coming forward. "And a lady, too."

Melli knew that female gerfalcons were considered the most precious of all the hunting birds. "It is truly beautiful," she said.

The duke smiled at her softly. "Put on the glove."

Feeling a little nervous, Melli slipped on the glove. Her father's eastern estate boasted a mews, but in the kingdoms falconry was an exclusively male sport and so she had never handled a hawk before.

"I scented the glove, miss, so it will smell just like home." The falconer brought his arm on a level with hers, tapped gently on the bird's belly, and then drew his arm down. At the same time the duke took the underside of Melli's arm and moved it forward. The gerfalcon took the cue and stepped neatly onto Melli's glove. The bells strapped to the bird's feet tinkled brightly.

What struck Melli first was the sheer weight of the thing. The creature was dense and solid. The duke still held her arm near the elbow, and she was grateful for the support. She felt the bird's talons grasping at her wrist through the leather, and she became a little afraid.

"Easy, miss," said the falconer. "Don't fret, my beauty won't hurt you." He stroked the bird's belly and whispered words of tender encouragement.

Melli felt the duke holding her arm firm, stopping it from shaking. On his prompting she risked raising her other hand to touch the bird. The speckled feathers of its breast were soft beyond telling. It was a joy to feel the warm down beneath her fingertips. The creature's heart was beating faster than her own. Growing more confident, she moved her arm nearer her face. The gerfalcon shifted for a moment, resettling its wings and then gripped her wrist anew. This time Melli enjoyed the feeling.

The falconer smiled at her. "You're a natural, miss. I've never seen my beauty calmer."

Even though she knew the man was flattering her, Melli couldn't help but feel pleased. "What's her name?"

"Well, miss, a hawk has two names. The first is given when she's just a chick, newly taken from the nest. The second is given the day she's ready for her master's wrist."

"And is she ready?" asked Melli.

The falconer nodded. "She brought down a crane for me, just two days past. You should have seen her fly, miss. Sweet and as sure as an angel, she was."

"So, Melliandra," said the duke, "she needs a second name."

Melli caught the offer of his words. "You want me to name her?"

"She is yours, you must call her what you will."

"But I know nothing about falconry. I couldn't possibly take her."

"Once you are well enough," said the duke, "we will ride down to the valley with our birds upon our wrists, and I will teach you everything you need to know." He reached out and stroked the bird's breast; as he did so, his fingers brushed against Melli's. "Name her now and claim her as your own."

Melli was thrilled beyond words. This magnificent creature would soar upon her bidding. "I name her Aravella." Tears prickled, fast and unexpected. After all these years she was still moved by the sound of her mother's name.

"Beautiful, miss. Beautiful," said the falconer.

"A name worthy of greatness," said the duke.

Melli looked up from the hawk and found herself staring into the duke's eyes. She was overcome with feelings of sadness and joy. "Thank you," she said. "In all my life, I have never received anything as precious as this."

"I would give you everything I own," he said, "if you would only be my wife."

Baralis was walking across one of the many deserted courtyards of the duke's palace. He had just paid a man to travel to Bevlin's cottage and tear the place apart, and was about to calculate how long it would be before he was in possession of the wiseman's library when a sharp pain stabbed at his chest. The sensation was so sudden and so violent, it stopped him in his tracks.

Closing his eyes, he sought out the blackness of self-awareness. His heart raced ahead of his thoughts; beating wildly it conveyed a silent warning in the rhythm of the blood. Words barely remembered amid so much else that had been said in Larn flashed across his mind like lightning:

"Two days ago one of our seers spoke of you. He said that for now your greatest threat is a girl with a knife at her side."

Struggling to keep his feet, Baralis looked around the courtyard. A sandstone bench resting under a leafy trellis gave him something to aim for. By the time he made it there, he had calmed himself. A body heavy with the weight of foretelling slumped against the stone. Only it wasn't foretelling, exactly—the seers of Larn had done that already—but more a sign that it was coming to pass. Somewhere, right now, someone's fate was in the balance, and the racing of his heart meant the outcome would surely affect him directly.

As he rubbed the sweat from his brow, he racked his brain trying to imagine who the girl with the knife could possibly be.

"Easy, boy. Easy," whispered Maybor, running a hand over his dog's bristling snout. Shark growled deep in her throat, a chilling sound that told of deadly intent. She had caught a whiff of the enemy and her hackles rose to the scent. All the baiting had paid off. Eager to attack the man sitting alone in the distance, she strained against the leash like the killer she was. "Good boy. Good boy."

Maybor had recently discovered that the combination of fine clothes on his back and a fine animal at his side turned heads, especially women's. With this in mind he had taken to walking through the palace grounds each day, leading Shark on a fine leather leash. He enjoyed the admiring looks from the ladies and the envious glares from the lords. This afternoon, however, he had spotted something more interesting than a blushing maiden: Baralis secretly engaging the services of a journeyman. A messenger, judging from the leanness of his horse.

The meeting was near the stables. When Maybor had first come upon them, he had toyed with the idea of setting Shark loose. But there were too many stablemen around, any one of whom might have spotted him nearby. More importantly, one of them might have stepped in to save Baralis and taken an ax to the dog. Maybor was growing rather fond of Shark and hated the idea that she might get hurt. So he had stayed where he was, watching the two talk from a discreet and shady distance. He wasn't in the least bit surprised when the meeting ended with the journeyman receiving a heavy purse; money was the only way Baralis could ever get a man to do his bidding. As he watched, the two parted and Baralis began to make his way back to the palace.

Never one to take traditional routes, Baralis slipped down alleyways and slid under bridges, taking a path less peopled than any normal man might choose. Feeling rather pleased with himself, Maybor trailed him all the way. Shark stalked her prey well, never once letting Baralis from her sight. Eventually they had come to a fair-sized courtyard. Deserted at this time of year, it was probably a haven for romance in high summer. Trees and shrubs were beginning to show their green, and flower beds were hoed and ready for planting.

Maybor was just about to follow Baralis across when the man suddenly doubled up on the spot. He clutched at his chest and then turned an unpleasant shade of puce. Maybor immediately sent a prayer to Borc, thanking him for sending a seizure to his enemy. Unfortunately, Baralis seemed to recover. He stumbled over to a bench and sat whilst he caught his breath.

Shark's head was moving from side to side, and when Maybor looked down he saw that she was wearing away at the leash. She chewed with chilling determination. Time and time again, she had ripped apart bags filled with the remains of Baralis' undershirt. The man's scent was burned upon her soul. Now the time had come to strike her prey.

"Easy, boy. Easy."

Maybor looked quickly through the bushes to the place where Baralis was sitting. Deep in thought, the man didn't look as if he'd be moving for some time. Maybor then whirled around and searched the surrounding masonry. Aha! Just the thing. Near the bottom of the wall was some fancy stonework: cherubs aimed bows at demons, whilst nymphs frolicked with lions. The arm of one of the cherubs was styled in relief, jutting out from the wall at an angle, its elbow forming a shape that was as good a loop. Maybor threaded Shark's leash through the stone and tied a fine soldier's knot in the leather.

Shark growled with anger and began to pull against the leash. Her whole body thrashed violently from side to side, but knot and stonework held.

Maybor was careful to pick his distance before kneeling down by the dog, making sure that he was at least a leash-length away. Shark had worked herself up to an eye-bulging, muzzle-frothing frenzy. "Ssh. Easy now." The dog calmed a little. "That's a good boy." Maybor risked bending forward a little. He took a deep breath and then hissed: *"Kill, Shark, kill!"*

The words had a profound effect on the dog. Her ears pricked up, her hackles rose, and she began to chew with terrible intensity upon the leash. Her teeth tore at the leather as if it were silk.

Maybor knew the time had come for him to make a quick exit. In less than two minutes, Shark would be free, and he couldn't risk being here when she ripped out Baralis' throat. He paused a second to admire the deadly slant of the creature's teeth, briefly imagined them covered with blood, and then cut a hasty path toward the stables.

The duke had commanded the falconer to leave with the hawk. Melli was hardly aware of the man taking the bird from her wrist. Her head was reeling. *Marry!* She couldn't believe her ears. Had the duke lost his senses? She risked a quick look at his face. Gray eyes met hers without a blink.

"You think I jest, Melliandra?" His voice was as serious as his expression.

The door closed with a discreet sweep and click. The falconer leaving with his bird.

Melli stood up and walked over to the window. She needed time to think. However, the duke appeared to have a different plan, for she heard his footsteps behind her, and then felt the weight of his hand on her shoulder. His grip was firm. Firm enough to draw her round.

"Melliandra," he said, "I am not a man who speaks lightly. I told you the other day how I felt about you. Could you not guess at that time that I would want to marry you?" His hand slid down the length of her arm and caught at her fingers.

His palm was dry, she noticed. "You purchased me as if I were a sack of grain, and now you want to marry me?" It didn't make sense. The duke was a proud man, yet here he was proposing marriage to a girl he believed to be illegitimate. Such a union would only bring him shame. Unless, of course, he was too in love to care. Melli's pride rose up like a lid over a boiling pot. Why wouldn't he be in love with her? Many others had been before. Castle Harvell was full of men who had fallen at her feet—though she was quite sharp enough to know that it was her father's money, as much as her own personal charms, that sped the bending of their knees.

Unlike the vain and pimply noblemen of the kingdoms, the duke knew nothing of her family or wealth, yet he still wanted to marry her. Surely that must count for something?

Melli returned the pressure of his hand.

The duke took the gesture as his cue. "Melli, if you agree to marry me, I swear that you will not be just a bedmate. We will play, hunt, and politic together. You will be by my side, but not as my lover or my wife, but as my equal." He grabbed hold of her other hand. "Imagine it, Melliandra: you and I, the duke and duchess of Bren, walking arm and arm through our palace, talking policy and power one moment, and love and life the next."

Strange, thought Melli, the words themselves were tantalizing, but they were spoken with little emotion, like an actor running through his lines for the first time. Still, the duke was a dispassionate man, and by his own admission, he had gone many years without strong feelings toward any woman except his wife. Perhaps the combination of natural reticence, combined with old-fashioned nervousness, made him speak the way he did. "And what about my past?" she asked, desperate to give herself time to think. "Many would scorn me because of it."

"If anyone dared to scorn you, Melliandra, I swear I would kill them." There was emotion in his voice this time: the huskiness of threat and the tremble of anger. "I will not tolerate a single word spoken in mockery or contempt."

Melli's heart thrilled at the sheer power of the duke. He *would* kill anyone, she didn't doubt it for an instant. It was pleasing to think that such a man would be actively defending her honor. Not wanting to betray her thoughts, Melli pulled away. She threw a question to test him. "How do I know you speak the truth about involving me in affairs of state? It could be a ploy to tempt me into agreement."

The duke walked over to the sideboard and tested the jug for wine; finding it empty, he spun around to face Melli. His sword sent light flashing across her face. "You're not the type of woman to sit quietly and embroider all day," he said, a dry smile lifting the corner of his mouth. "Gardening, gossip, and housewifery are not pursuits that will engage your interest. Indeed, that is what I love about you—you're spirited, you're independent, and you're not afraid to speak your mind." His smile was full now and bright with admiration. "You could certainly teach the ladies of Bren a thing or two."

"Not how to put on cosmetics, that's for sure."

The duke laughed. "I had wondered what those marks on your cheeks were."

"One of your vintage reds," she said, secretly hoping that she didn't look too embarrassing.

"I would stick to drinking it next time."

"*Hmph!*" Melli picked up a pillow from the bed and threw it at him. The duke's sword was out in an instant. The pillow never reached him. The blade sheared it in two, sending goosedown flying into the air like snowdrops. He looked magnificent standing there, sword held aloft, muscles tensed, skin dark against a flurry of white feathers. Slowly, he looked toward her and smiled. "You'll have to be faster next time."

"No. I think I'll just blunt the edge of your sword when you're not looking."

"I like a woman who can think on her feet."

"I like a man who looks good covered in goosedown." They both laughed merrily. The sound of shared laughter acted like a charm upon the room, changing the atmosphere, making it lighter, less serious and, as the sun broke free from distant clouds, bringing sunshine to accompany the joy.

The duke put down his sword and walked toward Melli. She was sitting on the edge of the bed. He came and knelt by her feet. "Agree to marry me now, Melliandra, or as Borc is my witness, I will lock you up in here until you do."

"And will you make me pick up the feathers one by one?"

"With tweezers, no less."

Melli took a moment to look at the duke. He was a handsome man; the lines of his face told of experience and the hook of his nose told of power unchallenged. She liked the way he dressed—plainly, like a soldier—and she liked the way he carried himself—turning every movement into a simple statement of pride. Unlike Kylock, he laughed and had a sense of humor, and although Melli was sure that he could be cold and calculating, she was also sure he would never be cruel. And in that respect, he was a world apart from Kylock.

"What say you, Melliandra?" The duke's voice was soft.

Melli reached out and brushed the goosedown from his shoulders. The muscle beneath her fingertips was hard as stone. "I agree to marry you, Garon, duke of Bren. I am willing to become your wife."

It was time to leave this place. His heart had recovered from the shock of foretelling, and the wind that blew across the courtyard cut straight to the bone. Under his robe, his hands were curled up like nestling birds; he would need to bring drug to lip before they could be straightened once more.

Just as he tensed his muscles to raise himself from the bench, Baralis felt a sharp pain in his chest. His heart stopped dead. A dull ache raced up his left arm. Even as panic gripped his soul, he knew a second telling was its cause. Stronger than before, much stronger, it overrode all communication from eyes and brain. A vision filled the void of a not-beating heart.

Seen in his belly as much as his head, it was a girl with dark hair. Her lips shaped words that he could not hear, and the man whom she spoke to was a shadow without form. Baralis felt a stirring in mind and groin. He knew this woman. He had seen her naked, emerging from her bath, candlelight resting on the welts on her back. It was Maybor's daughter. Melliandra.

The second her name came to him, the vision was sucked back to his heart. The jolt coursed down his spine like lightning. The beat began again, shocking, sickening, sending his whole body scrambling to fall in time. Baralis' lungs contracted violently and the air from the vision was expelled from his lungs; he tasted cheap perfume and expensive wine as it raced along his tongue.

Out of time, out of strength, and outside of rational thought, Baralis opened his eyes. A dark blur raced toward him. Paws hardly touching stone, it hurtled forward, muzzle drawn back to reveal an armory of teeth. A low growl sounding deep in its throat. Froth foaming at its jaw. It meant to kill him.

Instinct and split seconds were all that he had. With a brain reeling like a spindle on a wheel, he could barely think, let alone react. Deep inside he found a resource more primitive and more deadly than thought: the will to survive. A whiff of dog and a glint of teeth were enough to set it in motion. The animal barreled ahead, fur flying, mere feet away now. A hand shot out from Baralis' robe. He hardly believed it was his own. With neither time nor consciousness to form a drawing, something came half-remembered from the plains. A right of passage from boy to hunter. Without weapon or warning, but with alcohol high in their blood, they stopped a charging boar in its tracks.

Hand held out to command the beast, sight trained on a spot between its eyes. A thick band of instinct rising up from the gut, and the mastery of willpower forced upon the beast.

Baralis felt the air push against his face. Saw the black and pink of its gums. Eyes bright with savagery met his. Words and thoughts were obsolete, *purpose* was what counted. Wills clashed a half-second before bodies met. Eye to eye, Baralis bludgeoned the beast with his will.

No stronger force existed in the universe in that instant. The dog responded as if whipped. Strength drained from its body and purpose drained from its soul. Momentum carried it forward to Baralis' throat. Muzzle closed, snout down, it slammed into him like dead weight. He was thrown backward toward the ground, the dog landing on top of him.

Baralis blacked out.

Wet and warm, something brushed against his face. Heart racing like a stallion on the chase, body shaking like a long-hunted fox, he forced thought and eyesight into focus. He was lying on his back looking up into a late afternoon sky. The dog was by his side, licking his face. Blood was still wet around its mouth, and it was standing with one front paw drawn up, as if injured.

The creature wagged its tail when it saw him move and doubled its licking efforts. Baralis caught the stench of foul play upon its breath. Strangely, he found himself warming to the beast. Lifting up a hand too gnarled to show to ladies, he stroked the dog's ears. "No harm done, my pretty lady," he said.

Two men waited in the antechamber. One had been known to the duke for twenty years, the other for twenty days, yet he trusted them both the same.

First he spoke with Bailor. Taking him to one side, he spoke for his ears alone. "Your speech worked well, my friend. The lady has agreed."

Bailor's smile was triumphant, yet his words were uncharacteristical-ly modest. "More your delivery than my speech, Your Grace."

The duke glanced at the second man. Tawl's eyes were averted and he was busy putting edge to sword. The duke risked a short laugh. "I was as wooden as the floor I stood on, but the lady seemed not to mind."

"And the gift?"

The head of his household was anxious for praise. In this instance, the duke didn't mind giving it. "An excellent suggestion, Bailor. She loved it. Her eyes sparkled like sapphires when the falconer handed her the bird." The duke paused for a moment, considering Melliandra's face. "She will be good with the falcon, I know it. She has more spirit than a score of trained huntsmen. A remarkable woman, indeed."

"She is that, Your Grace."

The duke noticed Bailor's eyes settling on his shoulders. "Threw a pillow at me, she did," he said, brushing away the last of the goose-down. "I've never met a more infuriating wench." The memory of her soft, hesitant kisses played upon his mind. It had been many, many years since any woman had excited him so. More than her beauty, it was her peculiar mixture of confidence and innocence that set his blood on fire. Without a doubt he would marry her soon. He would not wait untold months for the marriage bed; he was too old and his plans too pressing for the indulgence of a long betrothal. He could have taken her then and there—she had been willing enough—but no, he would not risk a begetting before their wedding day. When Melliandra was with child, people would keep careful count of the moons, looking for the slightest excuse to shout "illegitimate!" The duke shook his head. He would not give them a single arrow of doubt to shoot from their suspi-cious bows.

Besides, he liked the idea of waiting. It was a novel experience for him, and one that would surely heighten the joy of their first union when it finally came. He would take no substitute to warm his bed in the mean-time. All other women seemed like pale imitations compared to her.

"Bailor," he said, "go to Melliandra now. You are the closest thing she has to a friend. If she is having any doubts, reassure her. See that she gets anything she wants. Tell her I will be back later to take her for a short walk in the gardens. She must feel as cooped up as a hawk during training, stuck in that bedchamber all day. Get Shivral to play his harp whilst we walk, and have some refreshments waiting in the arbor. Fruit punch and sugared fancies, you know the sort of thing."

"Yes, Your Grace." Bailor hesitated for a second. "Though perhaps if I might make a suggestion?"

"Go ahead."

"Bring strong wine and meat instead. The lady's tastes differ greatly from the hothouse flowers at court."

The duke rubbed his chin. "Do it."

Bailor bowed and began to make his way to the adjoining door.

The duke pulled him back, for the first time speaking in a voice meant for two, "Find out from the physicians when the lady will be fit for the ride to Bren."

Bailor nodded and then left the room.

Turning to face the second man, the duke said, "Tawl, can I trust you to keep a confidence?" More statement than question, he didn't wait for the knight to reply. "The lady who you have been charged with guarding has just agreed to become my wife."

Tawl bowed simply. "I wish you joy, Your Grace."

The duke had known thousands upon thousands of men in his time, some bad, some good, most a mixture of the two, and he had developed the ability to quickly judge a man, to see where his strengths and weaknesses lay. To know what drove him forward. Somehow, despite all his experience, Tawl eluded him. Oh, there was a lot to see: the knight was entirely trustworthy, loyal, and probably gallant to a fault, but his motives were hard to pin down. Unlike Blayze he had no interest in the trappings of glory. Fine clothes and a purse full of gold meant nothing to the knight.

Nor, would it seem, did the chance to be close to greatness. The court at Bren was filled to the beams with men and women who hoped for power and influence by ingratiating themselves with either the Hawk or his daughter. Bailor was one of the few who had found success with this all too common ploy. Instinct told the duke that Tawl wanted none of it, which, although making him an enigma, also made him a man whom he would gladly entrust with the safety of his most precious possession: Melliandra.

The duke glanced quickly at the knight. Tall, imposing, built like a warrior, but with the manners and bearing to match any man at court. He was the perfect person to keep watch on his bride-to-be: honorable, loyal, and deadly with a blade.

"So, Tawl," said the duke heavily, "you now understand why the lady is in great danger."

Tawl nodded. "Yes. Though greater danger awaits her at court."

"I know. It is a risk I must take."

"I suggest that you and the lady travel in separate parties to Bren. I will travel with Melliandra, but I don't want to be weighed down with a battalion of guards. I want to be light on my feet in case of danger."

The duke nodded. The advice was sound. "You are in charge of her safety."

"Who else knows of the engagement?"

"Bailor." He thought for a moment. "And the falconer was there when I asked for her hand."

"That was a mistake."

The duke smiled. "I know, Tawl, but when the moment is right . . ." He shrugged.

"Good sense goes out the window." Tawl's raised an amused eyebrow and both men laughed. "Have Bailor speak with the falconer as soon as possible. Find out all the people he has come in contact with since he left the lady's chamber. Have them all confined here, in the lodge, under sun and moon watch until the official announcement is made."

The duke nodded. "Anything else?"

"Once the lady arrives in Bren, I personally want to examine her chambers before she takes residence. All her guards and servants are to report to me, and her food is to come directly from your personal cook. You do have a tester?"

"Yes."

"Good. For the ride back she must have your gentlest mount. After her fall she will be horse shy."

"What about speed?"

"I will take her on my own if need arises."

The knight was good. Very good. It was far better to have Melliandra riding at his back in an emergency than having to fend for herself. The duke felt well pleased with his decision to have Tawl guard her. Already his mind was more at ease. "Do you need anything special for the ride?"

"A boy's breastplate for the lady, and for myself a bow and a quiver of barbed arrows. I have swords and knives enough of my own."

"So I noticed," said the duke, motioning to the green felt cloth that was spread out on the floor. Resting upon it was enough polished steel to defend an entire garrison.

Tawl smiled almost sheepishly.

The duke was beginning to like him even more. "Oh, and one more thing before I go. I want you to befriend the lady. She knows no one in Bren except Bailor and me, and she must yearn for extra company."

"What about your daughter, Catherine?"

The duke drew in his breath: what *about* Catherine? His daughter would be furious once she learned he intended to wed. Not only was he stealing her glory, but also—if Melliandra was to give birth to a boy—her inheritance as well. Catherine was unpredictable at the best of times. It was better for the moment if he kept the news from her. He already had enough on his hands at the moment, and he had neither the time nor the inclination to deal with one of his daughter's childish tantrums. "I don't want my daughter to know anything about the marriage until I make the official announcement."

"As you say."

"I think that's everything. Bailor is yours to command, as are all my staff. Make sure he informs you when it is safe for the lady to travel." The duke made his way to the door. "Tawl," he said, as he paused on the threshold, "I feel better knowing that Melliandra is in your care."

The knight inclined his head. "I will defend her with my life."

Twenty-eight

Jack ate a small breakfast of pork and damp drybread as he counted his mistakes. Yesterday, an hour after entering the woods, he had discarded at least half of the supplies given to him by Mrs. Wadwell. Mistake number one was leaving the cumbersome oiled cloak behind. The skies had been a beautiful, cloudless blue the day before and he reasoned to himself that, as it was spring, they were bound to stay that way. Wrong. The downpour had begun in the middle of the night. Raindrops as hard as pebbles had woken him from his sleep. Scrambling in the dark, over ground rapidly turning to mud, he was soaked to the skin before he found shelter.

Mistake number two had been transferring the items that he needed from the heavy leather bag to the lighter cloth sack, for his supplies were now as wet as himself. So he was now reduced to eating damp drybread: contrary to popular belief, it *didn't* benefit from a soaking.

Mistake number three was *where* he had left his supplies: out in the open where anyone could spot them. Yesterday it hadn't seemed important: they were dead weight that needed to be dropped as soon as possible. Today they were signposts that could point to who he was, where he was going, and most importantly of all, the identity of the people who had helped him on his way. Large was the Wadwell's trademark, and if he had learned that spending less than one day with them, then everyone in the surrounding countryside was bound to know it, too. One look at the size of the ointment jar, the length of the bandages, and the diameter of the cheese would be enough to seal their fates.

How could he have been so stupid? Jack threw the drybread on the ground. It landed soundlessly, cradled by a bed of wet leaves. He had to learn to think before he acted. Standing up, he kicked at the bed of leaves, sending them flying into the air. Green and newly budded, stripped from the tree by cutting rain, they slumped heavily back to earth. Sometimes even thinking was dangerous.

Strangely enough, his fever had actually subsided. Jack felt more clear-headed than he had in weeks. The gentleness of nature seemed to act like a salve. Raindrops gathering mass on the underside of branches flashed with simple brilliance when plump enough to fall. The many greens of spring were soft on the eye and even softer underfoot. Everywhere the sound of water dripping, running, and pooling could be heard. It competed with the calls of small animals and birds. Most of all it was the smell. Fresh and old in one, the scent of new leaves and ancient earth mixing in mist-damp air. Jack's lungs were full of it, his blood ran with it, and gently it pushed against the outside of his skin.

Muscles that a day before had been tense and sore were now relaxed and merely tender. Dog bites had flattened and dried, and wounds had lost their fester. Even the gash in his chest felt better, the pain not so biting, the terrible itch of knitting flesh and bones now no more than a simple irritation.

How much was nature's work and how much Mrs. Wadwell's was impossible to tell. At the end of the day, Jack supposed, looking over the expanse of tangled woodland, it was all one and the same.

Time to be on his way. The sack, which he swung over his left shoulder, was so saturated with water, it dripped. Pork, drybread, nuts, fresh clothing, a few good knives, and his bedroll were all contained, wetly, within. In fact the whole thing was now almost twice as heavy as before. Jack smiled grimly. No doubt about it, he was not cut out for adventures. Any self-respecting hero would have known rain was on its way, built a suitable shelter in a matter of hours, and buried the remaining supplies in an unmarked grave. Instead, here he was, shoes squelching with every step, hair plastered to his skull, and body weighted down with a sack full of little else but water.

Jack looked up past the branches to the sky. An unremarkable gray met his eyes. It was impossible to tell which way the light came from. *"Head east and then northeast,"* Mrs. Wadwell had said. *"Follow the brook upstream."* Well, he'd found the brook; it was behind the group of hazel and hawthorn bushes that he was heading toward, but judging from the noise, it was no longer a bubbling woodland brook but rather a raging torrent of purposeful water. Now all that remained was to follow its path *down*stream.

He wasn't ready to leave Halcus and the garrison town just yet. He had business to attend to with certain people in a certain well-appointed cottage which, as best as he could gauge, lay several leagues to the west.

A few hours later Jack fell under the shadow of the garrison. Rain diluted the sweat on his forehead, sending it streaming off the end of his nose and down his neck into his tunic. He judged he was near the place where the tunnel had ended before someone had sealed it up with dirt and stone. The place where Tarissa said she would wait for him. The place where he had been betrayed.

Jack knew better than to pursue such thoughts. Too dangerous by far, especially here, with the blackened walls of the garrison looming high in the distance. It was neither the time nor the setting for a second disaster. So he buried his hurt deep, binding it away from the light of his thoughts, afraid that even as little as recalling the curve of Tarissa's cheek, or the sheen of her chestnut hair, might spark the fire within.

The woods in these parts were patrolled. Rovas had told him that, and his own observations confirmed it. Footprints freshly embedded in the mud and wads of snatch spat to either side of the path told of guards passing not long ago. Less than two days after the fire, they were bound to be on the alert. Jack slipped from the path and into the bushes. Thorns tore at his britches and barbed branches caught at his sack. His chest was aching badly now; the long walk and the weight of the supplies had finally taken their toll. A mouthful of brandy might help. If he remembered rightly, there was a pewter flask in his sack, and he was pretty sure that Mrs. Wadwell would have filled it with some of the pale gold liqueur. Ducking down amongst the undergrowth, he hunkered in the dirt to search through his belongings.

The second his bottom landed in the mud, footfalls sounded. Twigs crackled underfoot. The drizzling rain cut visibility down by half. Voices, muffled, distant, filtered through the mist.

Jack drew in a deep breath and settled lower in the bushes. Slowly, he reached for his sack. "Mistake number four," he whispered to himself: not carrying a knife at his waist. His hand felt for the sharpness of blade. Under pork and flask, resting at the bottom in a porridge of drybread and rainwater, his hand closed around a wooden shaft. He drew it out a finger's breadth at a time, careful not to disturb the surrounding contents.

The voices drew nearer. Casual talk at first: complaints about the rain and their superior officer. Jack dared not look out from the bush. He wiped the knife against a branch, scraping wet lumps of drybread from the blade. The handle wasn't important.

He knew the moment the voices died away that his tracks had been found. The guards were playing it shrewdly, not giving him the chance to escape by raising the alarm. Picturing them following the tracks to the bushes, Jack raised himself onto the balls of his feet, still crouching, yet ready to pounce.

To the right, the bushes began to rustle. Sharp whispers were exchanged. Steel slithered against leather. Jack tensed his muscles.

"Who goes there?" came a voice, nearer than he had expected.

Jack sprang up from the bushes. Two guards faced him, swords drawn. For an instant their faces registered fear. A second later they were upon him. The first man sprang forward, whilst the second took the flank.

Up came his knife, more a probe than an attack. Rovas' advice played like a commentary in Jack's ear: *"Never panic. Remember, the other man is always at least as scared as you."* Nothing about two men, thought Jack. Or was there? Divide and separate seemed to fit the bill.

Stepping forward, his foot brushed against the sack. His mind grasped a possibility. Almost before the idea formed in his head, he had done it. Jack kicked the sack with all his might, sending it flying into the chest of the first man. Not pausing for an instant he sidestepped to face the second guard. Tiny drops of rain rested atop his oiled mustache.

Rovas was in Jack's ear. *"Do anything to throw your opponent off guard: dance, laugh, cry. Anything."* An earth-shattering primal scream sounded, and it took Jack a moment to realize that he, himself, had made the noise.

Leaping on the second man, Jack brought him to the ground. His knife was embedded in the man's sword arm before he knew it. Blood gurgled onto the mud. The man flailed his sword and tried to knee him in the vitals. Jack sprang up to avoid the knee. Landing straight down again, knife carrying the momentum of his entire body, he stabbed the man in the heart.

Whip-quick he was on his feet. The entire contents of the sack were strewn over the bushes. Nervous, circling, the first guard kept his distance. *"Feign a weakness to encourage a careful man to attack."* Blood from the dead guard ran down Jack's side. He stumbled to the left as if injured, righted himself, and then came forward, favoring the opposite side. The gleam of weakness perceived flashed in the guard's eye.

Ignoring the pain in his shoulder, Jack concentrated on watching the line of the guard's body. He was about to attack to the left, he was sure of it. The instant the guard made his move he was ready. The man's sword jabbed straight for the bloodstain. Jack spun toward it, left fist clenched, and punched the hand that held the hilt. How he managed it, he would never know. It was perfect timing and placement. He hit the hand with such force that the man lost his grip on the blade.

"Never pause to admire your handiwork, no matter how brilliant the move." Jack lunged forward. The guard ducked, hand scraping in the mud in search of his sword. Thrown off balance for an instant, Jack looked up to see a thin streak of light heading toward him. The guard had thrown the blade. Launching himself into the air, Jack leapt to the side. He felt the graze of metal on his shin bone, and then pain exploded in his chest as he landed, shoulder first, in the mud.

The guard was on him before he knew it. No longer with sword, he was brandishing a large wet rock. Heaving it high above his head, he made ready to slam it into Jack's face. *"When you've been grounded by a foe, always go for his knees."* Jack's leg shot out, he didn't get the knee, but he got the shin. The guard stumbled backward, attempting to regain his footing. Holding the knife in front of him, Jack tried to stand. Just as he gathered momentum, his foot slipped and he was sent hurtling toward the guard. The man's groin was on a level with his knife.

Jack cringed as the blade went in; he had planned to get him in the chest. The guard screamed and screamed again. Blood welled over his thighs, soaking his britches. The rock fell from his hands and landed harmlessly by his side. Standing now, Jack aimed his knife with care. Straight for the heart this time, a nice clean blow. The second the knife was out, the guard slumped to the ground.

Pain throbbing in his chest, shaking from head to foot, and dangerously close to panicking, Jack began to run. He had to get away. Two men dead: their screams sounding in his ears, their blood on his clothes— Rovas had done a fine job.

Not stopping to pick up the strewn supplies, he fled from the fight scene. Racing through mud and brambles, jumping over logs and branches, he ran until the pain was too much. A sticky warmth close to the top of his tunic told him that the arrow wound had reopened. Slipping the knife into the rope that formed his belt, Jack pressed hard against the wound with his free hand. He counted to a hundred ten times before he let his hand down. The bleeding had stopped. The fabric of the tunic was stuck to his chest. Grimacing, he let it be.

He walked slowly now, every step a concentrated effort of muscle and willpower. Without realizing it, he had drawn nearer to the garrison. Through thinning trees he spotted the gray stone walls. Ahead lay the road and the main gate. The gatehouse no longer had roof or timbers. The top layers of stone had toppled to the ground. They lay in a blackened heap surrounded by soot. Something bright caught Jack's eye. At first he thought it was a flag. Drawing nearer, he made out the freshly logged lines of a gibbet. A man in a red coat swung from its upper beam. Slowly the rope turned in the wind, and even from a distance, Jack recognized the face of his short-lived cell mate, Bringe. The man had lied himself into a hanging.

Jack had little sympathy for him.

A sharp blast of air buffeted his body, chilling him to the bone. Turning away from the garrison, Jack spied two hills on the horizon. Lit by sunlight escaping from a break in the clouds, they looked strangely familiar. He stood and stared at them for a moment before realizing that for months he had looked at them from the *other* side. Rovas' cottage lay nestled in the valley behind.

Checking that the road was clear, Jack sprang across it, quickly making for the shelter of the woods. He walked for hours.

The rain stopped, the temperature dropped, and the woods thinned to a single line of trees; Jack hardly noticed. He had his sights set on the joining point between the two distant hills, and reaching it was all that mattered.

Tavalisk regarded the artichokes carefully. The look of them was the thing. It told one all one needed to know about the softness of the yellow flesh within. The broad flat bottom must sit with a certain indolence upon the platter. Like an aging whore, it must be ready to yield. The thorny leaves at the top of the bud should look like the devoted at the confessional; their desire to reveal their secrets so great that one could see them, ripe, upon their lips.

The archbishop raised a choosing hand above the platter. They all looked so good that he was about to resort to *one posy, two posy,* when in walked Gamil.

"No knock!" Tavalisk's voice was high with anger.

"Such news, Your Eminence." His aide was short of breath.

"There is no news, Gamil, that is so important it warrants an invasion of my privacy. No news at all." Tavalisk turned back to his artichokes. "Now kindly wait until I bid you speak."

The archbishop grabbed at the nearest specimen. Testily he plucked at the outer leaves, casting them aside. He would not deign to scrape them between his teeth like a poor man. He was only interested in the heart. For good measure, he threw a few Gamil's way, making sure that they were good and greasy first. Warm olive oil was near impossible to remove from silk.

The heart emerged, urine yellow, glistening like a jewel. Tavalisk dropped it upon his tongue, where it came as close to melting as any vegetable ever could. "I think you'd better go ahead and speak, Gamil," he said, picking a second artichoke from the platter, "for holding your peace ill suits you. You look like a Marls sausage—badly stuffed and lacking in meat." In truth, Tavalisk was rather eager to hear the news, but it wouldn't do to betray that fact to his aide.

"Our four-city force intercepted a messenger heading to Valdis. He was carrying a note addressed to Tyren himself."

"Who was it from? The duke of Bren? Baralis?"

"It was neither signed nor sealed, Your Eminence, but the messenger spoke with a kingdoms' accent and his livery was crested in gold."

"Give me the letter." In his excitement, Tavalisk actually wiped his hands on his own robe.

Gamil pulled a roll of parchment from his scribing bag and handed it to the archbishop.

After several moments of study, Tavalisk put it down on his desk. "You realize that this letter is from Kylock?"

"I thought as much, Your Eminence."

"From what I can gather, he has entered into an agreement with Valdis. Tyren is sending knights to Halcus to fight on his behalf, and in return Kylock is promising the knighthood exclusive rights to northeastern trade and a cut in the spoils of war."

"I think the deal has already been struck, Your Eminence. Just this morning I received a report from Camlee, telling of forty score of knights passing through on their way up north."

"And our four-city force let them pass?"

"We had little choice, Your Eminence. Our forces were spread out and there were too many to attack."

"Hmm." Tavalisk began plucking at a third artichoke. "Were they well armed?"

Gamil nodded. "War horses, full armor, steeled to the hilt."

"So by the looks of things they were heading for a battle?"

"It would appear so, Your Eminence."

Reaching the heart, Tavalisk pounded it to a pulp with his fist. "It seems that the newly crowned king is full of surprises. First the invasion and now a secret treaty with Tyren. Young Kylock is turning out to be quite the dark horse."

"What does Your Eminence intend to do about this?"

"Well," said Tavalisk, scraping the pulp from his hand, "making the document public will do little good. It's not signed, so therefore it's worthless—Kylock will simply deny he ever sent it." He poured himself a glass of wine. "However, it would be interesting to see the letter fall into the duke of Bren's hands. I'm willing to make a bet he knows nothing of this alliance, and once he learns of it . . ." Tavalisk shook his head ". . . who knows what he'll do."

"It certainly puts him in a difficult position, Your Eminence. He is a well-known supporter of the knighthood and everyone will come to the conclusion he asked Tyren to help Kylock."

"Undoubtedly you are right, Gamil. When this news comes to light, the duke of Bren will look like he's secretly working to bring Halcus to its knees." Tavalisk took a long gulp of wine. He was beginning to feel rather excited. "Annis and Highwall won't like this one bit. They'll take it as proof that the duke is planning a grand northern empire: Bren, the kingdoms, Halcus. It's only a matter of time before their names will be added to the list."

"Annis and Highwall are no longer arming in secret, Your Eminence. They have both taken to parading their soldiers in the city streets for all and sundry to see. Just last week we intercepted a cargo bound for Highwall: eight covered wagons stocked with resin, sulfur, and quicklime."

The archbishop smiled. "The stuff of siege warfare," he said. "How interesting. I hope we let them pass?"

"Only after sufficient toll had been taken, Your Eminence."

"Toll?" The archbishop raised his glass to his lips only to find it empty. Had he drunk that much already?

"A wagon's worth of the three. In the correct proportions, no less. The merchant seemed not to mind. He said more was on its way."

"Is it indeed? Highwall seems intent on stocking up for a war." Tavalisk ran his finger over the rim of the glass. "Mind you they have good reason to be, trapped as they are between Halcus and Bren."

"If this letter were signed, Your Eminence, it would be enough to start a major war."

"Oh, one will start anyway, Gamil. With Tyren's help, Kylock will make it through to the capital. The knighthood have had men in Helch for over five years now—supposedly negotiating peace, if I remember correctly. Anyway, after all that time they are bound to know the castle's defenses like the backs of their hands. And Tyren will certainly be feeding Kylock information along with manpower." Tavalisk's hand slipped on the glass and it fell to the tiled floor, smashing soundly.

Without a word of encouragement, Gamil came forward, knelt down, and began to pick up the glass around the archbishop's feet. The sight of Gamil's arched back was too tempting for Tavalisk to resist, and he raised his feet up off the ground and brought them to rest on his aide's back. "All things considered, young Kylock has made a very shrewd move, bedding down with Tyren. On the other hand, of course, Tyren himself may not have been so shrewd. He's got himself involved with a cause that is anything but noble: women and children being slaughtered, towns being razed to the ground. At some point the knights are going to question the integrity of their leader."

"But the knights are sworn to obey Tyren, Your Eminence," said the footstool. Gamil was forced to stay, kneeling down like a dog, until the archbishop removed his feet. "It's one of the founding principles of Valdis."

"If I needed a lesson in history, Gamil, I would call a scholar, not a servant." The archbishop dug his heels into Gamil's back. "Tyren has made mercenaries out of his knights, selling their services first to Bren and now to the kingdoms." Tavalisk shook his head. "Founding principles aside, there'll be people in Valdis who aren't happy with the way things are going, and it won't be long before they make their displeasure known. No one makes more noise than the morally self-righteous."

"Perhaps Kylock has promised them converts, Your Eminence."

The archbishop took his feet from his aide's back. Gamil had actually said something intelligent. "You mean: 'Fight for us and if we win, we'll all follow Valdis' fanaticism'?"

Gamil nodded and stood up. "Fanaticism is a strong word, though, Your Eminence. Valdis' beliefs are, for the most part, almost identical to ours. They are just more zealous, that's all."

"Really, Gamil, theology *and* history in one day. I think you missed your calling."

"I confess, Your Eminence, that scholarship has always interested me."

"No, not a scholar, Gamil. I was thinking more of a town crier, as they're famous for shouting out news that everyone already knows." Tavalisk smiled sweetly at his aide. "Time you were on your way, Gamil.

Try and find out if there's any truth in the theory that Tyren is angling for religious control in the north. And send the letter on to the duke of Bren. Use your swiftest messenger. No, on second thoughts, tie it to a bird. Speed is of the essence."

"A dove will not be large enough, Your Eminence."

The archbishop sighed heavily. "I will follow you down later and put a compulsion on an eagle. It will ruin me for this evening, though. I'll be far too tired to bless the seven sacred strangers."

"Perhaps you could just bless two or three of them, instead."

Gamil was becoming a little impertinent. The ritual of the seven sacred strangers had been performed in Rorn for hundreds of years. Once a year the city gates were closed from midday to midnight. When they were opened, the first seven foreigners to pass through them were blessed by the archbishop, bathed in holy water by nubile virgins, and then given seven gold pieces by the doddering old duke himself. It was more of a commercial than a religious ritual, as it was designed to promote Rorn as a city that welcomed foreign trade and foreign money.

Widely popular—probably due to the presence of the wet and scantily clad virgins—it was looked forward to for months. Every child ate seven cherries, every man drank seven glasses of wine, and every woman had seven bracelets jangling about her wrist. For Gamil to suggest that he should bless only two or three strangers was nothing short of blasphemy.

"Pay the old crow in the kitchens to put the compulsion on the bird, Gamil. I will not be doing it myself." Public ceremonies were too important to miss, particularly now, when he needed the support of the masses more than ever. If war was coming, the people of Rorn must trust him enough to let him take the lead. Besides, using sorcery was always a risk: one could never tell when one's drawing was being monitored. All in all, it was far better to have someone else do the job: the blame could be more easily shifted that way.

"Is there anything else, Your Eminence?"

The archbishop regarded his aide coolly. "Since you have treated me to so many lessons today, Gamil, I think it's time I taught you one in return. It's called the lesson of the presumptuous servant."

Jack was learning the art of blocking everything out. He was aware of the sensations of pain, exhaustion, hunger, and thirst, but only dimly, as if he was experiencing them in a dream. In fact he felt almost drunk. But not in a light-headed, dizzy sort of way, more a heavy-headed, heavy-footed sort of way. The sensation reminded him of the times he'd been caught drinking by Master Frallit. Too much ale followed by a sound thrashing and an earful of insults did strange things to a boy's mind. Not to mention his body.

Jack smiled to himself. He felt almost nostalgic about those beatings now. Castle Harvell existed in his memory as a safe and cherished haven where worries were purely childish and life was simple if a little dull.

Right about now dull seemed pretty appealing. The rain had started up again, lashing through the air in sharp, angry sheets. The wind whipped low around his ankles like a small and pesky dog, and the air was cold as spring could make it. A night for firesides, not adventures.

Jack had been walking for hours now. The two hills, for so long in front of him, were now casting shadows on his back. The ground under-foot was beginning to level off and, without recognizing as much as a bush or a tree, he knew he was drawing closer to the cottage.

It was dark. The trees, the hills, the clouds, and the rain all threw their pennies into the pit. He could see his feet beneath him, spot trees before he walked into them, but everything else was lost in darkness. Step after step he took blindly. Singing helped. Frallit had taught him many baking songs; some were bawdy ballads of master bakers slipping love potions into their pies, a few were actual recipes—the rhyme making them easier to remember—and others were slow, methodical tunes designed to knead bread by. Jack liked the kneading songs the best. Singing them now, whilst he was alone and in the dark, helped to keep his spirits up. They acted like a talisman, carrying with them all the good memories of the past.

> *I bake a little slowly, 'cos I'm not a clever man*
> *I knead all morning and I sleep when I can*
> *I'm up all night to keep the oven hot*
> *But I always pause once a day*
> *No matter what my masters say*
> *And count my blessings for what I've got.*

Jack's steps matched the meter of the words, just as his hands once had. After ten verses, even the toughest dough would bake up to a fine crust. After eleven verses, Jack was usually overcome by a fit of yawning: it wasn't the most lively of songs. But it was simple and honest, and love of baking was written into every line. For the moment it was just what he needed: something familiar and methodical to keep his mind from the pain and his feet stepping one in front of the other.

Abruptly the ground dipped under him. He threw out his leg to catch the firmness of earth. His foot encountered the wet slipperiness of mud and slid downward, throwing his body off balance. Grasping in the dark, he found nothing to break his fall. Roots and twigs tore at his legs and the mud carried him down the slope, sending him into the darkness beneath. A thorned branch slashed against his cheek. His knee crashed against something hard and jagged. Feet scrambling in the mud, he hurtled forward. Something white glimmered ahead. *Rocks!* was the last thought he had.

Twenty-nine

*T*he rain *stopping* was what woke him. The constant pitter-patter was an accompaniment to his dream, and when it no longer beat against his cheek, the dream turned nasty, presenting him with a sudden, sharp drop. His body jerked convulsively and his eyes opened. Jack was looking at the sky. Gray, cloudy, close to the ground, it spoke of more rain to come.

He was lying on a bed of mud-covered rocks. His arms and legs were as stiff as broom handles. Raising up his hand, he cautiously felt the back of his head, near his neck. *"Aagh!"* Something large and tender as a plover's egg did not want to be touched. Gingerly, he felt around the lump. His hair was stiff and matted. It could be dried mud, he thought, but more likely it was blood. Bringing his hand forward, he grazed his fingers against his cheek. A neat line of scabbed flesh rose above his skin, two days worth of stubble surrounding it like thorns.

Jack sat up. Water, which had been pooling in the dip of his belly, ran down his thighs and onto the rocks. He now knew the meaning of being soaked to the bone. His clothes were plastered against his body, his fingers were swollen like sausages, and his feet were swimming in his shoes. As if the action of sitting up had forced his senses into action, Jack felt suddenly cold. He began to shiver, and try as he might he couldn't seem to stop himself.

He had to get his blood pumping. Bracing his body, he forced himself to his feet. A wave of dizziness threatened to bring him straight down again, but Jack refused to give in to it.

Whereas sitting up had made him realize how cold he was, standing up made him feel the pain. Chest, head, legs, knees, all ached with vicious delight. Jack had once heard a physician say that it was impossible to feel more than one source of pain at any given time. The man was a fool.

A peculiar dryness tickled at his throat, and when he recognized what it was he burst out laughing. He was thirsty! Here, surrounded by dripping rainwater, damp air, and wet clothes, with the rain newly stopped and more on its way, he was actually feeling thirsty. It was really quite ridiculous.

When the sound of his laughter died away, another sound took its place: water running then splashing against rocks. It was so loud, he wondered why he hadn't noticed it before. It seemed his senses were coming alive in stages and hearing was obviously last on the list. Directly ahead lay a thick copse of trees. Turning around he noticed that the rocks to the far left were bubbling with falling water. He scrambled over toward them, feet slipping in the mud. A large boulder blocked his path to the water and he was forced to clamber over it.

What he saw on the other side made him stop dead.

It was the pool where Tarissa had taken him the day she said she loved him. The rocks, the waterfall, the glade. Destroyed by two days of torrential rain. The once clear water was brown with mud, clotted with twigs and leaves, and dead birds and vermin floated in it. The waterfall spilled more of the foul matter into the pool and sent what was already there churning around in spirals. The water stank. Gone were the daffodils; flattened and decaying, their remains were strewn across the ground. The rain had stripped the leaf buds from the willows, and the trees hung bare above the pool like skeletons.

Grass was trampled and thick with oozing mud. Worms and centipedes and other creatures of the soil lay glistening, struggling to right themselves, forced to the surface by the rain-soaked earth. They were everywhere he looked.

Jack's mind flashed back to that one perfect day—the best of his life—when they sat by the pool and he'd washed Tarissa's feet. She was so beautiful, so full of life, so much cleverer than he. That was the day she'd agreed to come away with him to Annis. Flinging her high atop his shoulders, he'd given her little choice. Jack smiled, remembering how hard she had kicked and screamed. There was no one like her. No one at all.

His memory receded and he was left looking at the wreckage of a once flawless scene. How could she have done it to him? Smiled and led him on, and said she loved him, and made love to him. And all the time, behind each word, each kiss, each tender look, there lay a snarl of lies.

Melli was alive, and all three of them—Tarissa, Rovas, and Magra—had told him she was dead. They had kept him in the cottage, carefully steering his hate, like cattlemen with their sticks, toward the man they said had killed her. Like a fool, he had committed the murder for them.

The strength drained from Jack's legs and he collapsed down upon the rocks. He stayed there, water splashing against his shoulders, head bowed down toward his chest, until the shivering became so intense that he was forced to move on.

Melli was just about to start on her second plate of eggs and bacon when a knock sounded upon the bedchamber door. "I'm dressing, come back later," she called.

A second knock came, followed by a man's voice. "I imagine dressing must be difficult without a dress, my lady."

The voice was half-familiar, the tone was mocking. Whoever it was must know that she had no clothes in her bedchamber, only various nightgowns. Interest piqued, she put down her knife and spoon. "Who is it?"

"Tawl, duke's champion."

So, it was the man who was charged with protecting her. For days now she had been aware of his presence on the other side of the door. Sometimes when it opened, she would catch sight of him, always sitting on the floor, mending his clothes, or polishing his weapons, eyes gallantly averted lest he catch a glimpse of a lady undressed.

"Enter," she said.

The door opened and in walked Tawl. Dressed plainly, his clothes were a poor disguise for the body beneath.

"You are alone?" he asked, scanning the room.

"Surely you must know that already, seeing as you monitor the door like my keeper." Melli picked up a slice of bacon with her fingers and slipped it between her lips.

Tawl shrugged. "I watch the physicians come and go."

"And how do they look once they leave?" Melli was feeling a little mischievous.

"Relieved," said Tawl dryly.

Melli laughed. "What brings you here? I thought you were supposed to watch me from a distance?"

"I've come to take you to Bren."

"What?" Melli was taken by surprise. "I thought the physicians said I wouldn't be fit to travel for another day or two yet."

"They did."

"But—"

"I'm going to take you now," Tawl said, "regardless of what the physicians say."

Melli was rather pleased; she was getting a little bored of being cooped up in her bedchamber like a rescued damsel. "Does the duke know of this?"

"He left for Bren earlier this morning. I told him, and only him, that you would join him there tonight." Tawl came closer to the bed where Melli sat, cross-legged, with a plate of food in front of her. "Open your nightdress."

Melli stared at him.

"I want to take a look at your knife wound."

"How dare you suggest such a thing!" Melli was indignant. "Leave me this instant, or I will be forced to call the guards."

Tawl didn't move. "Lady," he said, his voice betraying a measure of impatience, "I have no desire to see you naked, but I do need to see your wound to check for myself if you're ready to travel. In my experience physicians tend to be overly cautious, but I'd like to make certain before I put you on a horse." He folded his arms with infuriating calmness. "Now, either lift up your gown and show me your side, or sit there and shout for the guards until you're blue in the face. For as far as I'm aware, there's not one of them within earshot."

Realizing her mouth was agape, Melli abruptly closed it. Bursting with anger, she could think of nothing to say. She glared at the man, muttered a few choice curses under her breath, and rolled onto her side. In her haste to get the matter over and done with, she ripped the ribbons from the seams. With a great show of indignant modesty, she pulled back barely enough of the gown to reveal the bandaged wound that lay just beneath her rib cage. "Go ahead," she said. "Make your examination."

Tawl came forward. Before he touched her, he blew on his hands to warm them. Melli strained her neck to see what he would do. A quick flash of silver streaked through the air. Only when she felt the bandage fall away from her skin did she realize he had drawn a knife. His touch was gentle, but firm. He placed one hand upon her rib cage and another below the wound. Slowly he pressed against her flesh, testing muscle first and then probing deeper, feeling for her organs. His expression was serious. Melli noticed how finely his lips were shaped. He made a small noise in the back of his throat and then ran his thumb along the wound. A second later she felt his thumbs to either side of the injury.

He stood up. "Wait here," he said.

She watched him walk into the next room and rummage around in a leather saddlebag. When he returned he was carrying a small blue jar. Uncorking the top and dipping in his fingers, he scooped out something that looked suspiciously like axle grease. Seeing her expression, Tawl smiled. "I make it myself," he said. He warmed it between his fingers and then slapped it onto her skin. "The wound is healing cleanly, but there's a lot of stiffness in the muscle beneath. There's little chance the cut will reopen during the ride, but your side will give you some trouble." He massaged the grease into her flesh, working it down to her muscles.

"So how did you learn all this? Were you one of those physicians who got sick of blood and guts and decided to turn to a peaceful life of fighting instead?" Melli was beginning to feel a little contrite. She was also quite enjoying the sensation of Tawl's large hands pushing against her belly.

He ignored her attempt at humor. "No. When you're on your own a lot you pick up things here and there." He shrugged. "You learn how to patch things up until you make it to the nearest town."

It wasn't the answer she had expected. She was about to question him further, when he tapped her on the ribs.

"Lift up a moment," he said. "I need to retie the bandage."

She did as she was told. She felt his capable hands cupping the small of her back and threading the bandage beneath. He tied it more firmly than the physicians, and a fraction lower, too. He finished the job by tying the strangest knot she'd ever seen around her waist. With almost touching delicacy, he trimmed off the frayed ends and then flattened it out so it wouldn't press against her.

"That's the best I can do," he said, gathering either side of her gown and bringing them together. "I'll leave you now and send in your maid to help you dress. Wear a loose wool skirt and under no circumstances put on a corset. I'll be coming back later with a breastplate. I'll make sure it's well padded around the sides."

"Armor?" Melli was genuinely shocked.

Tawl nodded. "Your life is in danger. There are those who would stop at nothing to prevent the duke from getting married again."

Feeling rather stupid, she asked why. Prepared for a typically condescending male answer, where the facts were laid out in simplistic terms that females could easily understand, she was surprised at his forthrightness.

"The timing for one thing. Catherine and Kylock are due to be married soon, and both parties think that *their* wedding will be the most important event of the decade." Tawl cleaned the grease from his fingers with the remains of the bandage. "I don't think either of them are going to be very pleased at being upstaged by you and the duke. In fact, most of the population of the Four Kingdoms are going to be mad as hell. At the moment they believe their king is marrying the sole heir to Bren."

"My marriage won't affect Catherine's status."

"It will if you have a child, and it's a boy."

Melli felt a nervous flutter in her stomach. What had she gotten herself into? She was marrying a man she barely knew and who, in turn, knew nothing of her. Grabbing at the seams of her nightdress, she twisted the fabric between her fingers. He didn't know she was Maybor's daughter. How would the news affect him? Would he be angry at being deceived, or pleased that she was, after all, well bred and well dowered? Her social position seemed to mean little to him. Indeed, that was one of the things that most attracted her to him: the fact that he judged a woman by her character, and not her family or wealth. And then there was his power. She couldn't imagine herself with a man who was not her equal. She needed someone strong, someone others would look up to.

The duke was the most powerful man in the north. Single-handed, he had turned a city into a kingdom. It would only be a matter of time before he named himself a king. Melli released her grip on her nightgown. Her hands were damp with sweat. Perhaps her father would get his wish after all: she might one day be a queen.

The strange thing was, the title itself didn't interest her. What was the use of being a queen if all one did was wear fine clothes and a crown? No, she wanted real power, the kind the duke had promised her. She wanted to be able to make decisions and influence events, to be a *partner*, not a possession. There was too much of Maybor in her to play the role of a passive spouse. The duke sensed this about her, and more than accept it, he welcomed it. He wanted her by his side both in bed *and* the council chamber. He could have a thousand beautiful, submissive women, but he had chosen her instead. And that, more than anything else, was the reason she had agreed to marry him.

She knew nothing about him, didn't even know his age, and now it seemed, after listening to what Tawl said, she couldn't even be sure of his motives. Was he marrying her to have a child? Surely not; there were many women at his court who would be more suitable mothers to a potential heir than herself. The duke believed she was illegitimate, and that was hardly the sort of legacy he would want to pass down to his son. Melli shook her head from side to side; she didn't believe it. Even his gifts—the knife, the scabbard, and the hawk—spoke of a man who was thinking of adventure and excitement, not domestic bliss.

Tawl brought her back to the present. "I will return within the hour, my lady," he said gently, seeming to sense that her thoughts had taken her far away.

She nodded. "So be it."

He bowed, his golden hair almost sweeping the floor as his back broadened to a curve. Turning from her, he left the room without a sound.

Melli took a deep breath the moment the door was closed. So she would be with the duke this evening in Bren. She had left the city as a servant and would return as its mistress. It seemed too unbelievable an irony to be dismissed as mere chance.

A log on the fire suddenly flared up, casting sparks and flames from the hearth. *"Where I come from we call people like her thieves. Their fates are so strong they bend others into their service. And what they can't bend they steal."* Alysha's words rose up with the smoke. Had the flesh-trader's assistant been right all those weeks ago? Was it her fate to be married to the duke? And if it was, had everything she'd done and everyone she had come in contact with led her to this? The Halcus captain, Fiscel, Bailor, perhaps even Jack and her father: had she used them all to bring herself to this point?

Melli made no move to stamp out the sparks on the rug. She knew not one of them would catch.

If she was to believe what Tawl said, then her marriage to the duke would have a profound effect on the future of the north.

"My lady," came a voice. It was her maid, Nessa. "Are you all right? You look a little pale."

Melli was glad of the interruption; her thoughts were taking her to a dangerous place, one where the landscape was preordained and where people were little more than accessories of fate.

She made an effort to be bright. "I'm fine, Nessa. Don't just stand there gawking, hurry up and help me dress. I'm leaving for Bren in less than an hour."

The maid came forward and began to brush out her hair. "Why miss, you're shaking like a leaf. Are you worried about the journey?"

Melli shook her head. She sat back a little and tried to relax. It wasn't the journey to Bren she was worried about—no harm would come to her, she was sure of that—it was what she would have to do once she got there.

The duke must be told who she was. The lie about her being illegitimate had gone on for too long. He had to know the truth. The stakes were higher than she had thought: politics, power, succession, and even war were all caught up in the match. Melli sighed heavily. It was time the duke learned that his future wife was the daughter of the richest and most influential lord in the kingdoms.

Jack lay flat on the ground. His legs and stomach were mired deep in the mud. It had been drizzling steadily for the last hour and he was soaked from head to foot. He barely registered the cold and the rain. He was watching Rovas' cottage.

The heavy clouds had forced the night's hand, making it come earlier than spring usually allowed. Lanterns had been lit in the cottage; Jack could see their warm glow escaping through knotholes in the shutters. The fire was burning well, too, as hearty puffs of smoke came bellowing from the chimney. All in all it was a heartwarming sight. A cozy home where ivy formed a living frame around the door and where the whitewash shone a welcome for its master.

Jack spat out a mouthful of bile. He swung his head around and scanned the road to the left. Still no sign of Rovas.

How long he'd been lying here was hard to tell; certainly long enough for midday to turn to dusk. After he'd left the waterfall, he had come straight here. The nearer he got, the lower he stooped, until in the end he was crawling on all fours like a dog. He didn't want them to see him. Through all his dealings with the three in the cottage, they had been the ones with all the advantages. It was they who trapped and manipulated. They who watched and monitored him like an insect under glass. Now it was time he had the upper hand.

There was power to be gained by being an observer. Jack felt the thrill of the spy as he lay and watched the cottage from the darkness; it gave him a feeling of control. Things would move at his pace, when he was good and ready. When Rovas had returned from market, and when everyone was in their place. The element of surprise would be his.

Jack's ears caught the sound of something rattling in the distance. After a few moments, Rovas' cart lurched into view. The man himself sat on top of it, a heavy cloth pulled over his back to keep out the rain. Even before he had jumped down from his seat, the door opened. Jack caught his breath. It was Tarissa.

For hours he had known that she was in the cottage. Once or twice, before the shutters had been closed, he had spotted her silhouette against the oilcloth. Yet seeing her now, in the flesh, was still a shock. Close enough to see unfamiliar lines of worry on her face, yet not so close he could hear her speak, she took the cloth from Rovas' back and then let him through. As the door closed behind them, Jack saw her hand steal up to test the temperature of his forehead. The sight of that small intimate gesture, so casually offered and accepted, caused the last vestiges of softness to harden within Jack's heart. They were in league with each other, there was no doubt about it. The two of them had plotted everything out right from the start. Tarissa had just pretended to love him, just as she had pretended to hate Rovas.

Jack scrambled to his feet. His legs had been so long without weight that they buckled under him and he fell back down to the ground. *"Damn!"* he hissed. He was sick of being weak, angry at his body for failing him, tired of existing in a world where he had to run or hide. Rovas had a lot to answer for.

This time when he stood, his legs stayed firm. As he walked toward the cottage they became firmer. Firm enough to kick down the door.

Crack!

Pain shot down his side and through his shoulder. The door hinges splintered and gave way. He heard Tarissa and Magra scream. A second kick and the door fell inward. The first person he saw was Rovas. He had a carving knife in his hand. Behind him were the two women.

"Jack!" cried Tarissa, lunging forward.

Rovas elbowed her back. "Stay where you are."

Tarissa thumped him hard in the back. The sudden burst of strength caught the smuggler off guard, and she managed to dodge round him. Arms outstretched, she ran toward Jack.

She looked so frantic he almost gave in to her. But he didn't. He turned to the side. "Don't come near me, Tarissa."

She came anyway. The same hand, which moments earlier had reached out to touch Rovas, now reached out toward him. "You're soaked through and hurt." Turning to Magra, she said, "Mother, put some water to boil."

"Don't bother, Magra," said Jack. "I won't be staying long."

Tarissa laid her hand upon his arm.

Jack pulled away. "Tarissa, go outside and take Magra with you."

"But Jack—"

"I said go!"

The force of his words were so great they made her flinch. He saw her look toward her mother. Magra nodded faintly. Both women made their way to where the door once stood. As Magra stepped past him, she whispered something low, meant for his ears alone, "It's not what you think, Jack."

He heard, but did not acknowledge her with either look or gesture. His eyes were on Rovas. The smuggler was standing comfortably, even cockily, resting one arm against the hearth whilst the other held the blade at his side. Despite his air of nonchalance, Jack noticed his knuckles were white above the hilt.

Behind him he heard the two women leave the cottage. He waited a moment to give them time to walk away a little and then said, "So, Rovas. What's your life worth to you?"

Rovas smiled his old, familiar charming smile. "Lad, I tell you now, my life's not yours for the taking."

"Isn't it?" Jack was surprised at how cold he sounded. He stepped forward, hands by his side.

"What you gonna do, lad?" Rovas' voice was rising to a taunt. "Make me burst into flames?"

Jack was across the room in one leap. Knife still at his waist, he lunged for Rovas' throat with bare hands. The smuggler raised a fisted hand from the hearth and smashed it right into Jack's arrow wound.

Pain exploded in his chest. Tears filled his eyes. He went reeling backward, arms flailing, searching for something to break his fall. His flank caught the corner of the table. The point stabbed into his kidneys. The extra pain focused his reflexes and he shot his arm around to steady himself against the table edge.

Even as he righted himself, Jack felt the flare of sorcery in his gut. His skull seemed to contract around his brain, forming a tight band of pressure round his thoughts. *No. No,* he willed himself. He was going to deal with Rovas alone. Quickly, desperate to do something physical, Jack grabbed at a bowl that was resting on the table. Heavy, filled with cooling chicken broth, he threw it straight into Rovas' face.

The smell of chicken and onions filled the air. The broth splashed over Rovas' chin and shoulders. He brought his arm up to stop the bowl from crashing into his face. It went flying into the hearth, smashing against the stone.

Jack tasted something salty and metallic in his mouth. It was blood. Sorcery was choking in his throat, and his desire to keep it back was so strong that he had bitten straight through his tongue. He clamped his lips tightly together, afraid of letting even a breath of power out through his mouth.

Rovas wiped his face on his sleeve. With knife held out in front of him, he stepped forward and then to the side, effectively cutting off the entire area surrounding the hearth. Jack realized what he was doing: he was trying to claim as much of the available space as possible for his own. It was a form of intimidation, designed to make one's opponent feel cornered. Rovas rocked on the balls of his feet, his legs slightly bent at the knee. "Come on, then, Jack," he said. "Let's see if you're good enough to beat your teacher."

Talking was a distraction. Jack didn't listen. He didn't speak. He didn't even breathe.

He leapt forward and down, slashing at Rovas' thighs with a blade he was hardly aware that he'd drawn. The smuggler was forced to bend low to guard himself, awkwardly arching his back. Jack felt the rake of Rovas' knife against his shoulders. He welcomed the feeling. Anything real, any sensation, any action—even pain—was a welcome distraction to sorcery. Jack shot up from his squatting position. Raising his elbow above his head, he caught Rovas hard on the chin. The smuggler countered by trying to knee him in the groin. Jack was all reflexes. He jumped back, just enough to protect his vitals, whilst his knife came up to slash at Rovas' leg.

His mouth was full of blood, his lungs were bursting with spent air, and his belly was bloated with sorcery. Still he didn't breathe. Keeping everything inside was the only way to retain control.

The pressure in his head made him wild. Again he leapt forward, desperation his only guide. Rovas was ready this time. He stepped back, Jack saw him reach behind, and a second later something bright and coppery streaked across the space between them.

In that fraction of an instant, Jack focused his thoughts. Not on Rovas, but on the object he held. He opened his mouth and let a wisp of sorcery out.

"*Aagh!*" screamed Rovas. The heavy copper pot dropped out of his hands and onto the floor. It landed—hissing and spluttering—in a pool of chicken broth. Jack caught a glimpse of Rovas' palm: it was seared like a piece of meat.

Jack was shaking. He felt the warm trickle of blood down his chin. The power had lost its push and he felt free to breathe once more. There was a part of him that felt triumphant: somehow he had mastered the sorcery, managing to let out just enough to do what was needed.

Rovas' left hand lay limply by his side. The knife was in his right.

"You're not a man," he hissed, drawing circles in the air with his blade, "you're a freak of nature."

Filling his lungs with new air, Jack threw all his weight into his free arm and punched Rovas in the face. The smuggler's blade caught him as he drew back. Jack was hardly aware of it. He felt strong, powerful, in charge. And it was time to make Rovas pay.

Jack took over the fight. He knew Rovas' moves before he made them, anticipated his defenses and countered his attacks. As soon as a weakness was spotted, it was exploited. At the first hint of an advantage, Jack was there nipping it in the bud. He allowed Rovas neither time, nor space, nor opportunity. He was younger, faster, and fitter, and he wore the man down.

Before he knew it, Rovas was on the floor and Jack's hands were at his throat. Both knives were long gone. Jack squeezed the red and fleshy neck, his fingers pressing against the windpipe. Rovas' eyes were wet and bulging, and blood trickled from his nose and temples. As Jack bore down on him, his tongue began to protrude from his lips. A choking noise gurgled at the back of his throat. Jack pressed harder. He could now feel the curve of the windpipe, and forcing it closed was all that mattered. The smuggler's face began to take on a bluish tinge. The choking noise faded away, replaced by a weak hiss. Jack's thumbs were knuckle-deep in Rovas' throat. His mind was playing pictures of the garrison alight with flames, of the escape tunnel ending in a dirt wall, and of Tarissa reaching up to feel the temperature of Rovas' forehead. Laughter, cruel and taunting, sounded in his ears. His thumbs dug deeper.

"Stop! Stop!"

Jack felt someone tugging at his arm. He lashed out blindly. He heard the skitter of pots and pans, followed by a dull thud as someone slammed against the wall. Glancing up, he saw Tarissa lying in a crumpled heap on the floor. Before he had time to react, something hard slammed into his jaw. The force of the blow sent him reeling. He fell sideways, losing his grip on Rovas' neck. Struggling to his feet, he whipped around and was presented with the sight of Magra brandishing the same copper pot that had been used against him earlier. She had drawn it back for a second blow.

"Get away from him," she cried. "Or as Borc is my witness, I swear I will kill you."

Jack stepped away from Rovas' body. His vision was blurred and his jaw felt as if it had been smashed with a hammer. Behind him he heard Tarissa getting to her feet.

Magra placed the pot on the table. She went over to Rovas and knelt by his side. Putting her ear to his mouth, she listened for the sound of breathing. Her fine features were taut with worry. She looked ten years older than when Jack had seen her last. After a moment, she straightened up. "He's alive," she said. Her voice was oddly unemotional. Sighing heavily, she stood up. "Fetch me some water, Tarissa, and a little soured wine."

"No, Mother." Tarissa stepped forward and shook her head. "I'm going to see to Jack."

The two women looked at each other. After a moment Magra shrugged. "Do whatever you have to." She turned and walked toward the larder.

"Jack," said Tarissa softly. "Are you all right? You're covered in blood." She raised her hand nervously, afraid to touch him, yet wanting to all the same.

"I'm fine." Jack stepped away from her. He was confused and tired, drained of all strength and emotion.

"We were so worried about you," said Tarissa quickly. Her eyes were bright with tears. "Rovas has been staking out the garrison. When you didn't turn up that night I didn't know what to think. I couldn't sleep or eat."

"You should be on the stage, Tarissa."

"What do you mean?"

Jack spoke quietly; he was too exhausted for anger. "You know very well what I mean. The tunnel was blocked. You and Rovas sent me running into a dirt wall."

Tarissa's mouth fell open. "But Jack—"

"No," he raised his hand, "I don't want to hear any more lies."

"I'm not lying." Tarissa's spirit was returning. Her cheeks were red and blotched. "Every day since you left we've been out looking for you. As soon as I learned you were captured, I begged Rovas to try and rescue you."

"Didn't do it though, did he?" Jack's voice was sharp.

"No. It was too risky. We were going to leave it until the day they took you for questioning."

Jack shook his head. "Look, Tarissa, I don't care what you say. Rovas wanted me dead. He sent me into the garrison knowing the tunnel was blocked." He hung his head down; looking at Tarissa only confused him further. He didn't know what to believe.

"I didn't know the tunnel was blocked." There was an edge to her voice now. "I waited all night for you. It was morning before I left the tunnel entrance."

In the background Magra tended to Rovas. The smuggler was regaining consciousness. His coughing and spluttering was a sign to Jack to move on. He hadn't achieved anything by coming here. It had been a mistake. Better to go now and never return.

Jack glanced around the room looking for his knife. He spotted it lying underneath the table. Bending down to retrieve it, he said softly, "I know you lied about Melli being killed. I need to know what became of her." Hearing Tarissa's sudden intake of breath, he braced himself for another lie.

"I'm sorry, Jack," she said, her small pink lips quivering. "The whole thing was set in motion before we even knew you. After that it was too late."

"*Set in motion,*" repeated Jack, anger flaring fast. "You mean when you and Rovas deliberately set out to lure me into acting as your personal assassin."

"It wasn't like that." Large tears rolled down Tarissa's cheeks.

His hand enclosed around the knife's hilt and he stood up. "I don't care anymore. Just tell me what happened to Melli."

Tarissa wiped her face. "She was sold to a flesh-trader called Fiscel. He took her east toward Bren."

"Was that where he was going to sell her?"

"I don't know. He might have headed south once he crossed the mountains."

"That's all you know?"

"Yes."

Jack looked into the hazel of her eyes. He was sure she was speaking the truth. "Put some supplies in a bag for me: food, water, clothing, you know the sort of thing."

"You're not going?" Tarissa looked horrified. "You're wet and you're bleeding. You can't go."

"Watch me." Jack made his voice harsh—he was afraid of giving in to her. Stepping over the door, he made his way outside into the cool night air.

Tarissa followed him. "Take me with you," she said.

Jack shook his head. "No."

She grabbed hold of his hand. "Please, Jack. Please. I'm sorry about the lies. I never wanted to hurt you. I tried to tell you about Melli that day by the pool."

"It's too late, Tarissa." He pulled his hand free. "Get back inside. Don't bother with the supplies."

She fell down to her knees and clutched at his britches. "Jack, don't leave me. Please, I beg you." Her voice was high, almost hysterical. "Take me with you. There's nothing for me here. I hate Rovas."

"Stop lying, Tarissa." Gently he pried her fingers away from the fabric. The temptation to bend down and take her into his arms was so great that he had to turn his back on her.

"Please, Jack," she said, kneeling forward on the wet ground. "I'm sorry. I'm sorry."

"I can never trust you again, Tarissa. Never." He cursed his voice for breaking. He couldn't look back now—if he did she might see the tears in his eyes. He began to walk away.

"Where are you going?" she cried. Her voice sounded small and frightened.

"East," he said softly.

The wind picked up, brushing his hair into his face and carrying the sound of Tarissa's sobbing straight to his ears. He didn't stop. He carried on walking, step after step taking him further away from the woman he loved.

Thirty

*I*t was a beautiful morning in Bren. The rain that had dogged the city for seven full days had finally stopped and everything—the sky, the streets, the buildings, and even the people—was brighter because of it. The sun shone gold, giving out the first real warmth of the year, and the fragrance of mountain flowers was carried on the breeze. Women dressed more boldly than they had in months, walking the streets with hips that held messages in their sway. Men leaned out of windows to watch them pass, puffing out their chests and whistling like songbirds. Spring had come to the city by the lake, late as usual, but glorious nonetheless.

Madame Thornypurse ordered the maid to open the shutters. As a rule she didn't like fresh air—it caused the rat oil to evaporate faster—but it *was* spring, and as a businesswoman and a lady of the world, it was her job to make the proper seasonal adjustments. Men's fancies turned to lust in spring, and nothing, absolutely nothing, was as good at attracting that fancy as a house full of whores.

Just this week she had taken on three new girls, each and every one of them good and plump, with bellies as round as cheeses and thighs as wide as milk churns. Not a beauty amongst them. That didn't matter; crooked teeth, a few pockmarks, and a sallow complexion could either be hidden, disguised, or overlooked. A pancake for a bottom, however, was a flaw far too serious to ignore. Men needed a good handful down there.

"Sister, dear," came a voice from behind, "might I offer a humble suggestion?"

Madame Thornypurse turned to face her sister, Mistress Greal. Two weeks ago, about the time her beloved Corsella went missing, Mistress Greal had arrived from the kingdoms. Sadly, she had lost her looks. Two of her front teeth were missing, and her left wrist was curiously misshapen. Ringed with broken bones, it looked as if she were wearing a strange, primitive bracelet. Madame Thornypurse would have liked to question Mistress Greal about the mishaps and her reasons for leaving Duvitt, but she was a little afraid of her older sister and so tactfully held her tongue.

"Yes, dearest sister. I treasure your advice as if it were Tyro gold."

"Get those lazy good for nothing girls off their buttocks and make them stand by the windows. At the moment the only thing they're liable to catch is a cold."

Madame Thornypurse nodded. Her sister's suggestion was, rather annoyingly, a good one. She clapped her hands. "Girls! Girls! Go to the windows and call to every man who passes."

"And pull your dresses down low, so they can see your wares," added Mistress Greal sharply.

The girls moaned and scowled and adjusted their ruffles downward. They went over to the windows, casting resentful glances toward Mistress Greal as they settled themselves against the sills. Madame Thornypurse had noticed that none of the girls liked her sister very much, but they always obeyed her.

"May I be so bold as to make another suggestion, sister dear?"

"Certainly, dearest sister."

Mistress Greal came forward and laid her good hand upon her sister's arm. "We need to invest in a great beauty."

"We do?" Madame Thornypurse admired her sister greatly, yet she couldn't help feeling a touch of peevishness. It seemed that Mistress Greal was intent on running her business. In just over two weeks she had taken over the ordering of food and drink, started supervising the maids, and now, it seemed, she dared to challenge her choice of girls!

"Yes, sister dear. The last girls you acquired are all a little, how should I put it . . . ?" Mistress Greal's thin nose went into the air like a dairyman sniffing for mold. "Ugly."

"Ugly?" Madame Thornypurse spat out the word.

Mistress Greal's good hand squeezed like a vise. "Don't take on, sister dear. I meant no offense. They're all as plump as sausages and I'm sure you got them cheap, but we need one girl, just one, whose beauty is so compelling that tales of it travel throughout the city. The beauty of that one girl will draw men here by the dozens."

"But a single girl can only service four men in one night."

"Aha! There you have it." Mistress Greal's crooked finger poked against the flesh of her sister's arm. "Most of the men will have to settle for the other girls instead."

"But won't they just leave?"

"Not after two glasses of my Duvitt special brew, they won't." Mistress Greal smiled thinly, lips pressed together to hide her stretch of toothless gum. "Once men have had a few, one woman begins to look much like another. We'll snuff out most of the candles, block off the chimney to increase the smoke, and serve them the strong stuff. They won't be able to see their hands in front of their faces, let alone tell the difference between a filly and a mare." Mistress Greal was triumphant. "The secret, sister dear, is to get them here in the first place."

Madame Thornypurse tried to find flaws in her sister's reasoning, but came up blank. "It does sound rather profitable."

"It's the oldest business practice in the Known Lands, sister dear: bait and switch."

"Bait and switch?"

Mistress Greal nodded. "In your own small way you were doing it before Corsella went missing. My niece was quite beautiful enough to attract men from far and wide."

Madame Thornypurse was torn between indignation over the phrase *your own small way* and pride at having her beloved daughter complimented. Pride won. "She takes after me, you know. Everyone says so."

"Beauty runs in our family, sister dear." Mistress Greal's hand rose to her bony breast. "It breaks my heart that I haven't been able to see my precious niece. Do the bailiffs have any idea what has become of her?"

Madame Thornypurse sighed heavily. "No, they say she will turn up sooner or later. I pray to Borc each night to keep her safe."

"Sister dear, come and lie down," said Mistress Greal. "I can see you're upset. I'll have the maid send in a drop of brandy."

"You loved Corsella, didn't you, dearest sister? You sent her all those gifts: the necklaces, the bracelets . . ."

"She was like a daughter to me, sister dear. When you were ill with the pox that time, I looked after her as if she were my own." Mistress Greal pulled herself up to her full height. "If any man has harmed as much as a hair on her head, I swear I will see him in hell for it."

On hearing her sister's words, Madame Thornypurse felt a warm glow in her heart. Mistress Greal might be many things—overbearing, bossy, and shrill to name but a few—but she was, above all, a woman of her word.

A sudden distraction caused both women to turn toward the windows. The girls were shouting and cheering. One of them, a sweet-looking girl with a harelip, turned around. "We've got one, madame. He's on his way in right now."

Madame Thornypurse rubbed her hands together. "And so early in the day, too." She nodded graciously to her sister. "Wise as ever, Mistress Greal."

Mistress Greal inclined her head like a queen. "You know me, Madame Thornypurse: anything to improve business."

Both women went for the door. Due to Madame Thornypurse's sore foot, Mistress Greal got there first. She swung open the door. A man, lean and travel-weary, waited on the other side. "Good morning, kind sir," she said. "Are you looking for a little comfort?"

"That, some decent food, and a bed for the night, if you've got one." The man spat out a wad of snatch and ground it into the step with the heel of his boot.

"Come in, come in," said Madame Thornypurse, pushing her sister out of the way. "Hot food, a warm bed, and the comeliest girls in Bren await you."

"After you've put down a small deposit first, of course," added Mistress Greal.

The man pulled out his purse and pressed a gold coin into her palm. "Now, woman," he said, "run along and fetch me some ale."

Mistress Greal had little choice but to do his bidding. Off she went, her skirts swishing violently in protest.

Madame Thornypurse turned toward the man; she linked her arm around his and smiled coquettishly—*she* at least had all her front teeth. Leading him into the room, she said, "So, handsome sir, what do they call you at home?"

"Traff. They call me Traff." The man was busy eyeing up the girls.

"And what line of work are you in, Traff?" Madame Thornypurse beckoned over her two best: Dolly and Moxie. The girls came quickly, giggling and jiggling, just as they'd been taught.

The man reached out a hand to squeeze Moxie's breast. "I'm a mercenary."

Madame Thornypurse was well pleased. His kind always had cash, or the means to get it. "So, what brings you to our fair city?" She disengaged herself from his arm, freeing it up for Dolly. If she was lucky, he'd pay for both of them.

Traff's mouth twisted to a bitter smile. "I've come to find my betrothed," he said.

Tawl knocked softly and then let himself in. Melli was standing in the middle of the room, legs apart, arms out, brandishing her silver blade at an imaginary foe. The instant she saw him she blushed and dropped her arms to her sides.

"You might have knocked," she said.

"I did. *You* might have listened."

Tawl could see her deciding whether to frown or smile. Over the past few days he had learned that Melli's emotions were always written openly on her face. Fear, joy, pain, anger, and most commonly, indignation, could be seen flashing regularly across her eyes, bending the curve of her lips, and raising the furrows on her brow. Even her skin tone changed. She could never hide a thing.

"Well, knock louder next time," she said, settling for half a frown.

Tawl bowed in acknowledgment of the reprimand. He came over to her and laid his hands on her shoulders. "When you have a real opponent to wield your blade at, don't stand so rigidly, bend your knees a little." He pressed her down to the right position, tilting her back and raising her arms. "This way there'll be less chance of being thrown off balance." His hand closed around her fingers as he felt how she held the knife. Gently, he adjusted her grip to the correct position. "Your wrist, on the other hand, should never be bent. Or all the strength in your shoulders and flank will go to waste." Demonstrating his point, he ran his fingers along the muscles in her side and shoulders. "If you bend your wrist, you break the line, and the only muscle you'll be left with is your forearm. You try and stab a man like that and at best you'll strain your wrist, at worst you'll break it."

All the time he was speaking, Tawl was acutely aware of Melli's nearness. She smelled fresh and clean. Her dark hair shone brilliantly and her skin was so smooth it was like touching sun-warmed marble. She had been in the duke's palace for four days now, and her appearance changed everytime he saw her. She was growing stronger and plumper, the dark circles around her eyes had disappeared, and there was color in her cheeks. Gone was the thin, pale girl he had first set eyes on. In her place was a woman, strong and vibrant, with a mind and will of her own.

He was beginning to realize what the duke saw in her.

The precautions for the ride had proven unnecessary. Tawl was almost certain that the falconer had spoken to no one before he was confined, and therefore tales of the proposal had no chance to spread. The only danger during the journey had been the incessant rain. The ground quickly became slippery and waterlogged, and the horses had to be prodded into making every step. Fearing for Melli's health, he had stripped off his outer cloak and wrapped it around her. Looking back sometime later, he had caught a glimpse of her face. She looked ill: skin gray and shiny, lips drawn together in pain. Lifting her from her own horse, he had put her on the back of his. The ride had taken nine hours, where normally it took six, and Melli spent most of it resting against his back, hands clinging around his waist, silent all the way.

The duke had come down to the stables to greet them when they arrived. By this time they had both dismounted, and Melli never mentioned the fact that she had ridden most of the way at Tawl's back. Neither did he. Tawl saw the way that the duke looked at his bride-to-be, and although the man had encouraged him to become friends with Melli, he doubted if he would be pleased to learn that for nearly half a day they had sat so close to each other that even the rain couldn't come between them.

For Tawl the journey had been a time to think. Brought up in the marshlands, he loved the rain. He grew up to the sound of it falling. The taste, smell, and touch of it brought back memories older than the woman he rode with. His earliest recollection was lying in his cradle, listening to the slow drip of water as it leaked through the thatch. His mother never bothered having the roof repaired, she said there was never enough money to pay the thatcher, but Tawl suspected she liked to watch the raindrops as much as he. After the rain had stopped was the best of all. His mother would gather all the water from the waiting pots and pans, put it into her best copper pot, add various herbs and spices, and then warm it over a gentle flame. Nothing in his life had ever tasted better than his mother's rainwater holk.

Tawl's thoughts drifted from childhood to knighthood, from his quest to his oath, from his past to his present. There was much he left untouched. Some things were still too painful to think about. Some things would *always* be too painful to think about.

He had found a certain peace within himself on the journey in the rain. He had a purpose here in Bren, and a sworn oath to bind him to it. Loyalty was in his blood: he needed someone or something to give his life to. It had always been that way. Ever since his mother had made him swear to look after his sisters, he had existed to serve others. It was what he was born for.

Now that his ties to the knighthood had been broken, fealty to the duke had taken its place. The quest was in the past—he had accepted that now. It was far better to put the failure behind him than relive it every night in the pits.

The one thing that dragged him back was the letter. It plagued his dreams and shadowed his days. He would never know what Bevlin wanted to say to him. The wiseman's words were gone forever, the paper rotting in a roadside along with the slops and the dirt. With all his heart, he wished he could have taken it from Moth and Clem. If only they had found him earlier, before he'd sworn himself to the duke, things would have been different.

Loyalty had its price, and it always closed more doors than it opened. The wiseman's quest was one of those closed doors. It had to be. Tawl knew himself too well: if he had taken that letter from Moth and Clem and read it there, down the darkened alleyway with the stench of the abattoir filling his lungs and the scurry of rats as accompaniment to the text, he would never have returned to the palace. No matter what the letter said, what promises it held, what explanations it gave, or what favors it asked, he would have been bound by them. Once he knew the contents, the city of Bren would not have been able to hold him.

Which would have meant two oaths broken, not one.

Good work could be done here. His presence was of value. The Known Lands were dissolving into a whirlpool in front of his very eyes. Forces were coming together, and as they vied with each other for mastery, they formed a current so strong that they sucked others in with it. At best the whirlpool promised the redistribution of power in the north, at worst war and destruction. One thing was certain: Bren was at its center.

And Melli, proud and beautiful and with secrets to hide, was about to become the eye of the storm. The danger to her life was real, especially once the engagement was officially announced. There would be those who wanted her dead. Catherine, the duke's daughter, was one of them; Kylock's chancellor, Baralis, was another. Not to mention a court full of nobles; bound together by generations of petty rivalries, they would not look kindly on their duke marrying an outsider instead of one of their own.

Another factor was the lady herself. Melli was not who she said she was. Her accent placed her from the kingdoms, and her bearing placed her in the nobility. Tawl could not believe she was an illegitimate daughter of a minor lord. She was too nonchalant about being in a palace, too comfortable with luxury and command to be a naive member of the country gentry.

Well, if she was lying it wasn't his concern. *Protecting* her was. Melli was his responsibility, and guarding her had become the most important thing in his life. For over a week now, he had watched her day and night, afraid to leave her door for even an instant in case he returned to find her gone. *She* would not end up dead in his absence like his sisters. He would never make that same mistake again, and protecting Melli was his one chance to prove that to himself. Keeping her safe would never make up for his sisters' deaths, but perhaps, just perhaps, it might prevent them from being in vain. The past could not be changed, but it could be learned from. And that, Tawl had realized long ago, was the best he could ever hope for.

The door opened and in walked the duke. Tawl had his hand on Melli's hand and his arm around her waist.

Melli pulled away. "I've had enough of your self-defense lessons for one day, Tawl," she said, her voice conveying boredom and irritability in equal amounts. Turning to the duke, she added, "A woman can only take so much thrust and parry before she gets battle weary and needs to eat."

Tawl could not help admiring her quick wittedness. She had turned a potentially embarrassing situation into something perfectly innocent. Both of them had been enjoying the lesson in knifeplay, and they had, without realizing it, moved closer together, so that their bodies now stood only a finger's length apart. Tawl chided himself for his stupidity. He should have known better than to draw Melli into a position that could have compromised her honor. As a knight he had been trained to protect a lady's reputation at all cost.

Hearing her words and tone, however, the duke seemed satisfied; his expression visibly relaxed. He walked over to Melli and kissed her lightly on the cheek. "So, Melliandra, you have been learning the art of self-defense?"

"Tawl insisted upon it. He says it's no use me having a blade if I cannot handle it properly."

The duke nodded and looked at Tawl. "You are right, my friend. I am glad you thought to teach her." There was genuine gratitude in his voice. "If anything happened, and you or I weren't around, I would feel better knowing that Melliandra could at least put up a fight."

Tawl wanted to say that he would always be by Melli's side, but he judged it prudent to hold his tongue. Instead, he bowed and said, "Your future wife will make a fine swordswoman. Now, if you will excuse me, I will leave you alone."

The duke put out a restraining arm. "I would like you to stay a few minutes, Tawl. I have just received something you might be interested in seeing." From his tunic, he pulled out a roll of paper. It was damp and watermarked; the ink had run and it was badly creased. He handed it to Tawl. "Take a look, see what you think."

Tawl took the letter. Still wet around the edges, it threatened to fall apart in his hands. Addressed to Tyren, it was a point by point account of a proposed treaty between Valdis and the Four Kingdoms. In return for the knighthood agreeing to fight with the kingdoms against the Halcus, they would be given exclusive rights to trade routes in the northwest and a cut in the spoils of war. Tawl handed the letter back. "How do you know it's genuine?"

"I don't." The duke gave the letter to Melli. "It came this morning on the leg of an eagle. It's my guess that the archbishop of Rorn sent it. He has men throughout the Known Lands—mostly clergy—who act as his spies and informants. He makes it his business to know what's happening before anyone else does."

Tawl changed the subject. He had no love for the archbishop of Rorn. "Do you monitor the passes?"

"Yes. That's what I'm worried about. For ten days now I've been hearing reports of knights on the move."

"West?"

The duke nodded. "Fully armed, mounted on warhorses, trailing enough mules to supply a siege."

"Then the letter is probably genuine." Tawl had a strong desire to have a drink. It seemed that everytime he managed to make some order out of his life, something came along to tear away at what he'd built. Oh, he'd heard all the rumors about Tyren being corrupt, but he could never quite bring himself to believe them. Until now. The letter was proof that the man was using Valdis to fulfill his own personal agenda. He had made mercenaries out of the knights.

Tawl felt a deep sense of loss. For so long the knighthood was all that he had: it was his family, his religion, his life. Hearing of its decline filled him with bitter sadness. He had believed in the ideal. He still did. If he had been free to go back, he would. But it was too late. Valdis was another closed door.

"What do you know about Tyren?" asked the duke. He walked over to the side table by the wall and poured three glasses of wine of varying measure. The fullest he gave to Melliandra, the emptiest he kept for himself.

Tawl took a sip of the wine. He would have preferred ale. "Tyren was the first person I knew at Valdis; he recruited me before he was made leader. I always counted him a friend."

"And now?"

"He is still a friend." Old loyalties had a power all of their own. Tawl could not bring himself to say a word against Tyren.

The duke gave him a hard, appraising look. Finally, he said, "He is a friend of mine, also."

"I heard he sent knights to fight in your southeastern campaigns."

"He did. And I admit I promised him the right to safeguard Bren's trade, but never once did I sanction unnecessary bloodshed or pillage. Most towns surrender peacefully." The duke brought the wine to his lips but did not drink. "When the south was busy persecuting the knights, I offered them safe haven. Bren and Valdis have been allies for many years now."

"Perhaps Tyren thinks you still are. After all, he is fighting for the man who will soon marry your daughter." Tawl sighed heavily. He did not like politics. To him diplomacy was just an excuse to lie and deceive, and treaties were nothing more than a catalog of greed and compromises.

"If you're right," said Melli, cutting straight to the heart of the matter, "why then didn't he inform the duke of his intentions?"

Tawl knew the answer to that, and he suspected the duke did, too: Tyren wanted to be on the winning side, and at this point in time it looked as if Kylock was set to dominate the north. The leader of the knights was hoping to benefit from Kylock's success. Why bother consulting with the duke, when the man who would one day take his place was so much more accommodating and ambitious?

Only now Kylock might not take the duke's place. The three people in this room and the falconer knew that a marriage would soon be announced that threatened to take the title of Bren away from Catherine and her husband. All Melli needed to do was beget a male child and the balance of power would change in the north. It would shift eastward, back toward Bren. Tawl was more worried than ever about Melli's safety. He was now forced to add Tyren and his fellow knights onto the growing list of her potential assassins.

"May I speak plainly, Your Grace?" he asked.

"Certainly."

"Make the betrothal announcement soon, and arrange the marriage quickly thereafter." Tawl was about to say more, giving the reasons behind his advice, but the duke forestalled him with a warning glance.

"I agree entirely, my friend. With a lady as beautiful as this," he paused and smiled at Melli, "it's hard for a man to wait."

Tawl bowed in acknowledgment of the reprimand. The duke obviously wanted to keep Melli in the dark about the politics surrounding the wedding. The truth was he needed to marry her quickly before events on the far side of the mountains got out of hand.

Suddenly feeling rather weary, Tawl asked if he could take his leave. He did not want to stay and witness the duke's deception. Putting his wineglass down, he was surprised to see that it was almost full. The desire to drink had thankfully passed. He smiled to himself. If it had been ale, things might have been different.

As he made his way across the room, he tried to catch Melli's eye, but she purposely avoided him. He wondered if she realized how much the duke underestimated her.

The second the door was closed, Melli turned to the duke. "So you are hoping to marry me quickly?" She strode into the middle of the room, centering herself on the green and scarlet rug that rested idly against the stone. As always when she was nervous, her instincts were to go on the attack.

The duke put his glass down and stepped toward her.

Melli had turned the rug into her own territory and she did not want him intruding upon it. She raised her hand. "Come no further, Your Grace. Lest you bring the truth in your wake."

He did not seem pleased, but he stayed where he was. "Do not let what Tawl spoke of concern you," he said, his voice edged with impatience. "I had planned to marry you quickly before today." His gray eyes met hers without blinking. He stood straight, his sword ran gleaming along his side. His deep blue cloak cast a cold hue upon a face already lacking in blood. "I see no reason to change my design."

Melli felt afraid. For the first time since she had met him, she realized how powerful he was. On his word armies would move. All along she had known what he was, but until now she had not seen the force behind the man. She got the distinct feeling he would marry her now, even if he had to drag her unwilling and unconscious body to the altar.

It was time to tell him who she was. For too long she had put it off:

this was the fifth day she had spent in the palace since returning from the lodge, and now, perversely, when she felt at her weakest, it seemed the right moment to do it. Determined to be in control of the situation, Melli made the duke wait whilst she retrieved her wine from the chest. With slowness just short of insolence, she made her way back to the center of the rug. Curbing her desire to down the wine in one swallow, she took a single, taunting sip. "What *would* give you reason to change your design?"

The duke's face was unreadable. His hand came to rest on the hilt of his sword. "When you come to know me better, Melliandra, you will learn that I am not the sort of man who enjoys playing games. Now speak your piece before I lose my temper."

This was not the cue Melli was hoping for, but she had a lifetime of experience dealing with people quick to anger—that was the one defining trait of the Maybor men—and she refused to let him intimidate her. "Very well," she said. "Let me tell you this: I am not who you think I am."

Was that a smile that flitted across the duke's face? Just as quickly it was gone. "Go on," he said.

"My father is not Lord Luff, and I am nobody's illegitimate daughter." As she spoke, Melli was aware of a measure of pride entering into her voice. "My family holds power in the kingdoms second only to Kylock. My father is Maybor, Lord of the Eastlands."

She didn't know what reaction to expect from the duke—disbelief, disappointment, rage—but she had expected *something*. However, the duke remained composed, even to the point of pausing to take a drink from his glass. Wiping his lips with his fist, he said, "And how did you end up here?"

Melli had already prepared her story. "I had an argument with my father and I ran away from home. I had just seen the error of my ways, and was about to return to the court, when I was kidnapped by Fiscel the flesh-trader." Her words sounded a little stilted, so she added with venom, "What does it matter to you, anyway? You are not my keeper."

"But I am the man you agreed to marry."

The duke turned his back on her. Melli seized the opportunity to take a hearty gulp of wine. She was amazed the duke was taking the news so calmly.

Spinning round to face her, he said, "I cannot say that what you have disclosed surprises me. All the time I have known you, I have never once seen a sign of the humility that is so often the birthright of the illegitimate.

Instead, I see a woman who is used to wealth and power. I do not doubt that you are Maybor's daughter."

"And does it affect your opinion of me?"

"No. I asked *you* to marry me—not your family."

"Are you angry?"

"No. You lied to protect your family's good name, and later you were trapped by that lie. I hope one day to inspire such magnificent devotion."

Melli could hardly believe what she was hearing. The duke was actually making excuses for her! And noble ones, at that. There was only one possible explanation: he must truly love her.

The duke came toward her and this time Melli let him set foot on her rug. He took the glass from her hand and threw it toward the grate, where it smashed loudly, sending wine and splinters spilling onto the stone. Clasping hold of her hand, he bent down on one knee. "Listen to me, Melliandra," he said. "I want you, and only you. I make no decisions lightly and it would take more than a few falsehoods to make me change my mind. My first wife and I were betrothed at birth, so you are the only woman I have ever asked to marry me. And now that you have agreed, I am anxious that the wedding be soon." He looked her straight in the eye. "I may be a forgiving man, but I am not a patient one."

Melli was experiencing a confusion of emotions: pleasure, pride, astonishment. Nothing the duke had done impressed her more than the casual way he dismissed her family as unimportant. It made no difference to him whether she was rich or poor, highborn or illegitimate. This man, who wielded power as casually as others wielded blades, wanted her for his wife. She came and knelt beside him. Raising his hand to her lips, she said, "I will marry you as soon as you wish."

Taking her in his arms, he kissed her full on the mouth. His lips were devoid of softness, and she found herself pressing against the hardness of his teeth. Abruptly, he pulled away.

"I must go. Arrangements need to be made. I think we will announce our marriage at the Feast of First Sowing." Standing up, he began to pace the room. "Then with the Church's blessing we can be married within a month."

Melli stayed where she was, his saliva slowly drying on her lips. She was disappointed that he had left her side. Something inside of her had been stirred by his nearness and she felt cheated by his withdrawal.

"I will send Bailor to you," he said. "You and he can make whatever arrangements you wish—clothes, jewels, settlements. I will leave that all to you."

"Can I inform my family?"

Again, another smile. "I don't think that's necessary just yet."

"Am I now free to move about the palace as I please?"

"No. Until the announcement has been made you will see only Bailor, Tawl, your maid, and myself." Perhaps realizing he had spoken harshly, he added, "You must be patient a little longer, my love. Things will be different after First Sowing."

Melli ran her fingers along the weft of the rug. From a distance the design had looked like flowers, yet now, looking closely, she saw that they weren't flowers at all, rather cleverly woven chains.

"Keep me locked up here too long," she said, "and you run the risk that I might escape." There was little jest in her words. Somehow, from a moment of pure elation, things had rapidly slid backward into doubt. Why did he insist on keeping her away from his court? And why did he want to marry her so quickly? She believed that he loved her, but he seemed too calculating a man to be swept away by adolescent eagerness. Indeed, the manner in which he was pacing around the room whilst thinking out loud gave the impression he was planning a military campaign, not a wedding.

"I promise you won't have to wait much longer," he said, coming toward her for what she knew would be a farewell kiss.

"Tell me something before you go," she said. "Will the fact that I'm from the kingdoms have any effect on the marriage between your daughter and Kylock?"

The duke gave her a long, appraising look. "The marriage will go ahead as planned."

That was not what she asked, and he knew it. Before she could challenge him further, he was opening the door. "I must go. I have a meeting to attend. Tomorrow I will arrange to have Bailor take you to the treasury and you can choose a ring." He bowed formally and then left the room.

Melli fell backward onto the rug. The meeting had left her dissatisfied. She suspected that she had been expertly manipulated, yet she couldn't put her finger on exactly how. After all, the duke had forgiven her for all her lies and obviously did not care whether she was a noblewoman or a bastard. Taking a deep breath, she stood up. She was probably reading too much into everything. The duke loved her, he wanted to marry her, and if he had to wed her sooner for political reasons, then that was hardly an unforgivable sin. She could not blame him for acting like the leader he was.

Crossing over to the bed, she felt something warm and sticky trickle down the back of her arm. Reaching up to touch it, she knew what it was before she saw it: blood. She had cut herself on a sliver of glass.

Baralis knew it was unwise to take even a half measure of his painkilling drug, but he took it all the same. He had a meeting with the duke—his first in several weeks—and he needed to be clear-headed. Of late the scar ringing his chest had troubled him greatly, and he had now reached the point where pain clouded judgment every bit as much as drugs.

The bitter taste suited both his palate and his mood, and he swallowed the powder dry. Things were not going well. The duke had been avoiding him for too long, canceling meetings, running off to his hunting lodge in the mountains, and declining all requests for an audience. Delay tactics. The man did not want to be pinned down on a date for the wedding of Kylock and Catherine. Now, with events coming to a head in Halcus, and Kylock busy striking side deals with the knighthood, it looked likely that the duke might back out of the match altogether. Or at least try to.

Baralis idly stroked the fur of Maybor's dog. She was his creature now. She lay by his feet, luxuriating in the warmth of the fire, snoring faintly and smelling of her last meal. Crope liked to spoil her, giving her the tenderest sweetmeats and the bloodiest livers, warming them first between his hands until they were the temperature of living flesh. Baralis smiled to himself. He might control the dog's will, but her heart and her stomach belonged to Crope.

He knew it was time to leave—the duke would not like to be kept waiting—but he felt disinclined to rush to His Grace's summons like a paid lackey, or an overzealous merchant. It was time the duke realized that the king's chancellor was not a man to be toyed with. Besides, he felt weary to the bone. He had just come from talking to the duke's handler, and at first the man had been unwilling to admit that he had read the message which came tied to the bird. The compulsion which followed, whilst successfully loosening the handler's tongue, had drained Baralis of all his strength.

It was worth it, though. He now knew exactly what Kylock was up to with Tyren. The only problem was that so did the duke. That was what made Baralis nervous: the summons to the meeting had come only hours after the eagle had landed.

An ensorcelled bird was like a woman who wore too much fragrance: her arrival could be sensed before she was seen, and her presence lingered long after she was gone. Baralis knew the moment the eagle touched down in the palace dovecote. He waited an hour to allow time for the message to be passed on, and then he paid the handler a visit. Normally he wouldn't bother with such petty investigations, but ever since the day in the courtyard, when he had experienced an extreme sensation of foreboding, he was reluctant to let even the smallest incident go unquestioned.

Something was not going to plan. Every stretch of scarred flesh on his body pulled and tingled a warning. The only thing he knew for certain was that a girl was involved, Larn had told him that much. His own vision had confirmed who it was. Baralis began to massage his pained hands. He could think of no reason why the dark and lovely Melliandra would be a threat to him. She was a disgraced runaway, nothing more. It made no sense.

Even without a prophecy on his back, he knew that events did not bode well. Kylock was bringing the Halcus to their knees. That one simple fact was sending shock waves to the four corners of the Known Lands. All eyes were turned to the north and there was now no mistaking what they saw: an empire in the making. There was little doubt in Baralis' mind that the duke was currently planning ways to limit Bren's involvement. After reading Kylock's letter of this morning, his need was more pressing than ever.

Baralis stood up. The dog went to follow him, but he waved her back down. Things would have been different if only Kylock had waited to show his teeth. The boy was turning out to be a military genius—winning a war that had long gone stagnant—but he had acted too soon. The marriage should have been consummated before as much as a single soldier crossed the River Nestor. If *he* had been in the kingdoms, not stuck here in Bren waiting upon a duke conspicuous by his absence, he could have controlled the pace and order of events. The new king might have talent on the battlefield, but he was too young and inexperienced for the subtleties of politics.

As Baralis made his way along the tall stone corridors to the duke's chambers, his step was heavy. He could not guess why the Hawk had called the meeting, but he was shrewd enough to know that the man was up to no good.

He was greeted by a guard who was expecting him. Shown through to a private staircase, he climbed up the short flight of stairs toward a heavy bronze door.

The door swung open. "Ah, Lord Baralis. I was wondering what had become of you." The duke beckoned him in. "I thought perhaps my messenger had failed to find you."

Baralis made no attempt to fill the ensuing silence with excuses. Let His Grace think whatever he wanted.

The duke was standing in the middle of a large reception room. He beckoned Baralis to sit.

"I will stand, if you don't mind, Your Grace."

The duke shrugged. "As you please." He walked over to the window and pulled back the metal shutters. "It is a fine day, is it not, Lord Baralis?"

"Yes. If you speak purely of the weather." Baralis strolled over to the duke's desk. It was covered with maps and charts. He recognized the shape of the kingdoms amongst them.

"I speak of all things, Lord Baralis." The duke was smiling, his eyes skimming the lake. "*Everything* is fine today."

Baralis did not like the way the man sounded. "Perhaps you should tell me what you're so pleased about, Your Grace. I for one see nothing to inspire such satisfaction."

"You're a little sour for a man who is about to receive good news."

"Most things turn sour when they have been kept waiting too long."

The Hawk spun around. "Then I shall make you wait no longer. You know why I have summoned you here?"

"I know why you have failed to summon me *before* now."

"I admit I have been somewhat slow in setting a firm date for my daughter's marriage, but I intend to rectify that, here, today." The duke stepped forward. "Tell me, Lord Baralis, does two months hence seem fair warning to you?"

This was the last thing Baralis had expected. He had come to the meeting with the belief that the duke would delay him further, either that or attempt to back out of the match completely. He hid his surprise. "Two months will take us into summer. That appears to be satisfactory. I will, of course, require written proof of your intent." Baralis expected the duke to balk at his request, but the man merely nodded.

"You will have it within a week. I will set my scribes scribing and my lawyers lawyering. Do you need anything else?"

Suspicion replaced surprise. The duke was being too accommodating. "Might I ask Your Grace what has brought on his sudden urge to name the day?"

"Certainly, Lord Baralis. Catherine came to me yesterday and begged me to set a date." The duke smiled smoothly. "What father can refuse a daughter's plea?"

He was lying, Baralis was sure of it. "How strange she never thought to plead before now."

"Come now, Baralis. I would have thought you've had enough experience with women to know that the one thing they are is unpredictable." The duke was looking rather pleased with himself.

"When exactly did you become so indulgent over women?"

The acid-toned question had a marked effect on the duke. His smile petered to a thin line and his brows came down to meet his nose. He cut abruptly across the room. "I have more important things to do with my time than trade barbs with you, Lord Baralis. I have said my piece, now make your arrangements."

Baralis was not so easily dismissed. "When can I make the official announcement?"

"*I* will make the official announcement, Lord Baralis. The Feast of First Sowing is in four nights time; I shall do it then."

"That will leave me no time to consult with the king."

"I can always put it off, if you wish."

Baralis did not like this one little bit, but as the duke was well aware, an announcement without royal clearance was better than no announcement at all. "That will not be necessary. First Sowing is fine."

"I thought that would be agreeable to you." The duke gave Baralis a shrewd look. "You may go now. I trust you will be discreet until I make my decision public." He turned his back and began to look over the contents of his desk.

Baralis had no choice but to bow and leave.

Thirty-one

*M*aybor thought he was going mad. He had heard it happened to people who did not eat enough meat, but each month he personally ate enough pork and venison to supply an entire village for a year. So he couldn't understand it. Now, if it had been fish, it would have been a different matter altogether. Fish was the food of women and priests and he never, ever, ate it unless it was well stuffed with meat.

The thing that was fueling his fancy was that on two occasions over the past few days he could swear he'd seen his daughter wandering around the palace. Just this morning, less than an hour ago, he had been making his way—discreetly, of course—from a certain lady's chamber. Hearing footsteps, he'd looked around to see a girl walking in the distance. The sight of the tall slim figure with dark hair falling to her waist set his heart aflutter. It looked like Melliandra. A golden-haired man walked behind her. Forgetting discretion, Maybor followed the two, hoping to catch a glimpse of the girl's face. They walked down a series of corridors and stairs, and finally disappeared behind a heavy bronze door. The girl never turned around once.

The moment she disappeared, Maybor began to doubt that she was his daughter at all. Probably just some young noblewoman who happened to share Melliandra's height and coloring. He tried to dismiss the incident as folly, but it played on his mind. Twice he had seen the mysterious girl and each time he could have sworn she was his daughter. Which, in Maybor's reckoning, made him either a madman or a fool.

Melliandra could be anywhere in the north. He had written to his son

Kedrac asking him to offer a reward to any man who found her, but so far no one had come forward. Maybor rubbed his jowls. If only he was there himself. He would personally see to it that his daughter was found. If nothing else, he was a man who could make things happen.

Though only in the kingdoms. And that was, as he saw it, the real reason behind his madness: he was sick of being stuck in a city where he wielded no real power and where no one realized just how wealthy and influential he was. It was enough to drive Borc himself insane! Indeed, if he remembered his scriptures correctly, toward the end Borc *was* overcome with visions of his long lost family. Perhaps he had stayed too long in Bren, as well!

"More meat, Prisk," he called to his manservant. Thinking for a moment, he added, "And bring me some fish, too—a meaty one, mind, not a fishy one." A man could never be too careful in matters concerning his sanity.

Prisk, a skinny man with a birthmark the size of a cucumber running across his face, stood his ground and coughed, which was his way of letting his master know that he had something to say to him.

"What is it, Prisk?" barked Maybor. "Speak. Don't stand there coughing like a man with the 'tubes."

"A message from the duke, my lord. He requests a brief meeting with you in the privacy of his chambers."

Maybor rose up and slapped the man in the face. "How dare you not tell me before now?" He turned his back on the stunned servant. "Fetch me my cloak, the red one lined with ermine. And cut me a lemon for my breath."

Minutes later, Maybor was striding through the palace looking like a king. Later perhaps, after he had seen the duke, he might pay a visit to his ladyfriend; it would be a shame for such magnificence to go to waste.

As he passed through the great hall, he spotted someone he hadn't seen for several days: Baralis. The man was walking along with Shark at his side. When he saw Maybor, he changed his course. The dog followed him like a shadow.

"Good morning, Lord Maybor," said Baralis, his voice rich with contempt. "Attending a coronation, are we?" His eyes swept across Maybor's cloak.

Shark growled right on cue. Maybor could hardly believe that Shark, *his* Shark, was growling at him. A quick scan around was enough to ensure him that there were too many people present for Baralis to get up to any funny stuff. "What have you done with my dog?" he demanded.

"*My* dog, now, I think," corrected Baralis. He stroked the dog's ears lovingly. "I have quite a way with animals, you know."

Maybor wanted to draw his sword and hack the man's head off. He had loved that dog! True, he had always been a little afraid of it, but he had grown very fond of it toward the end. And to watch it rubbing up against Baralis' leg, like a she-cat in heat, was more than he could stand. "You have bewitched it," he hissed.

"And you, Lord Maybor," said Baralis with irritating calmness, "trained it to kill me."

"Prove it."

Baralis smiled softly. "The fact that the attempt failed is proof enough for me."

"You think you're so clever, don't you, Baralis? But it won't be long before you're sent back to the kingdoms with your tail between your legs. The duke has no intention of marrying his daughter to Kylock." Maybor was quite sure of what he said; after all, the duke had been dragging his heels over naming a date for weeks. Now, with Kylock rapidly closing in on the Halcus capital, he was less likely to agree to the match than ever.

Baralis actually laughed. "Oh, Lord Maybor, you are woefully misinformed. Particularly for a man whose title is king's envoy." Baralis brought his hand to his chin, as if deep in thought. "But then, you are envoy to a *dead* king. Lesketh did spend the best part of winter in his grave."

Maybor was rapidly losing his temper. He spoke between gritted teeth, spittle escaping with his words. "What is your point, Baralis?"

"My point, Lord Maybor, is that the duke and I have already decided upon a date for the wedding. If you weren't so busy training dogs and dressing up like royalty, then you might have discovered that for yourself."

"How dare you!"

Baralis swooped close. "No. How dare *you*, Lord Maybor? Any more attempts on my life like the last one, and I will smite you down where you stand." He pulled away, eyes flashing with hatred. "And after our last little encounter in this hall, you know that is no idle threat."

Both men stood glaring at each other for a moment.

Baralis finally turned away. Tapping Shark gently on her neck, he said, "Come my precious, let us leave this place. Your old master has things to do—like acquaint himself with current events, for one thing." He inclined his head to Maybor and then cut a path toward the kitchens. Shark matched him step for step.

Maybor watched them go. He hated Baralis with a loathing so deep he felt it in his bones and in his blood. The man was a demon.

Smoothing down his robe, Maybor looked around the hall. No one was close enough to have heard what was said. A young maid with a milk yoke across her shoulders, and a pleasing plumpness about her waist, caught his eye and smiled. He turned away. He had too much on his mind for even the briefest of flirtations. For one thing, he was late for the duke. Though he now felt less inclined to be prompt than he had five minutes ago. If what Baralis had said was true, then he and the duke had decided upon the wedding date and the arrangements without once consulting him. It was an outrage! As king's envoy he should have been party to all meetings concerning the match. Maybor flew up the stairs. He would have a few choice words to say to His Grace. Madman he might be, but he was nobody's fool.

Arriving at the entrance to the duke's chamber, Maybor was greeted by a plainly dressed guard. The man waved him through to a discreet flight of stairs. Maybor could not help but appreciate the arrangement, as the staircase meant the duke's chamber was actually on a separate, higher level than the entrance. Good for both security *and* privacy. When he finally got out of this Borc-forsaken city, he would have something similar built in his Eastlands estate.

The door at the top was heavy and imposing, and as it was unguarded, Maybor opened it for himself. He found himself in a large reception room. The duke, who had been standing by his desk studying various papers, came forward to meet him.

"Aah, Lord Maybor. I am gratified that you could come on such short notice." He threw a glance back to his desk. "And I am well pleased that you came when you did; you have saved me from certain boredom. I enjoy reading contracts about as much as I enjoy having leeches pulled." The duke grasped his hand firmly. "Well met, friend. Sit and I will pour us some wine. You have a taste for lobanfern red I believe?" Not waiting for an answer, he turned and started pouring wine into cups.

Maybor was thrown a little off balance. First of all, he had expected to be met by a second set of guards, not the duke himself, and second, he couldn't understand why the man had greeted him as if he were a long lost friend.

"There you are, Maybor," said the duke handing him a brimming cup. "I think a toast is in order, don't you?"

"It depends upon what we're toasting."

The duke smiled and raised his cup toward Maybor's. "Let us toast to the future. For it looks better today than it has in many weeks."

Maybor pulled his cup away. "So it is true that you have set a date for the wedding?"

The duke just managed to save his wine from spilling onto the floor. "Who told you this?" he demanded.

"Baralis."

"When?"

Maybor did not like answering questions like a common servant. "That's not important. I want to know exactly when you and he came to this agreement."

"Baralis and I came to no agreement. I merely informed him of my intentions. He had no say in the matter."

Maybor grunted. It was just like Baralis to exaggerate the part he played in events. "Why was I not informed at the same time as he?"

"I brought him here late last night with the lawyers and scribes. I wanted to see you alone, by myself, today." The duke took a sip of his wine. His hawked nose rested against the rim of the cup. "Tell me, Lord Maybor, am I right in supposing that you have been somewhat reluctant in your support of the match?"

Maybor did not like to mince words. "I don't trust Baralis one little bit. The man is too ambitious for his own good. I think he's trying to place Kylock in a position where he can take over the entire north—including Bren. And frankly, Your Grace, I'm surprised that you're about to sit back and let him." Maybor finished his speech by downing the lobanfern in one. With a certain amount of satisfaction, he slammed the empty cup on the table.

The duke did not seem at all surprised by his outburst. He stood very still, one hand on his cup, the other resting against the hilt of his sword, and said quietly, "Lord Maybor, when you get to know me better, you will come to realize that I *never* sit back."

Maybor was impressed by the duke's tone, but he didn't want him to know it. "None of this will be my concern much longer, Your Grace. Sit back or forward—do whatever you will. My job is done here and I shall be returning to the kingdoms as soon as arrangements can be made." Although he was speaking for dramatic effect, the idea of going home appealed greatly to Maybor. It would be good to sleep in his own bed, to eat good plain kingdoms food, and to be amongst people who respected him.

"I wouldn't go just yet, if I were you, Lord Maybor."

There was something strange about the duke's voice. "What do you mean?" asked Maybor.

"I mean, my friend, that you should at least stay until the Feast of First Sowing. That is when I intend to make the official wedding announcement." The Hawk was smiling slyly.

"I will stay, if that is an official request."

"No, stay for a different reason."

"What reason?"

"Stay because you might be pleasantly surprised by what you hear and who you meet."

"I have no love of riddles, Your Grace." Maybor was becoming a little impatient.

"Neither do I, my friend. So I will say this much: stay until the Feast of First Sowing, and you will finally see your fellow envoy put in his place." The duke crossed over to the door and opened it. "Now, if you will excuse me, I have to visit the bride-to-be herself."

Maybor followed him out of the door. Together they walked down the staircase and through to the main entrance. When they reached the outer door, the duke turned and put his hand on Maybor's arm.

"Before you go," he said, "let me give you some advice."

Advice? Maybor did not like the sound of this. "Go on."

"The Feast of First Sowing may provide a few shocks to those sitting around the table, but I would suggest that you, my friend, try to conceal your surprise. It would please me greatly if I knew I could count on your . . . " the duke searched for the appropriate word ". . . composure."

Maybor stepped away. He would not agree to something blindly. "I will make you no promises, Your Grace."

Strangely, the duke seemed satisfied with this. "As you wish." He inclined his head and began to walk down the long corridor in the direction of the ladies' quarters.

Maybor headed in the opposite direction, his step lighter than when he had come. He didn't know what to make of the meeting, but it would certainly do no harm to stay put for a few days to discover what the duke was up to. Anything that promised the unraveling of Baralis' plans was well worth waiting for.

"Well, you're right and you're wrong, Bodger," said Grift. "It *is* true that ale makes a man randy and then hinders his performance, but really it all depends on the *amount* of ale he drinks."

"You mean the more he drinks the less impressive his performance gets?"

"Aye, pretty much so, Bodger. However, a little known fact is that eventually, if a man drinks enough ale—say, twenty skins full—he passes through the drunken stage and emerges on the other side as a rollickin' god of a stallion."

"A rollickin' god of a stallion, Grift?"

"Aye, Bodger. You've heard that if men on the battlefield go long enough without washing then they actually get clean again on their own?"

"Aye, Grift."

"Well, it's exactly the same for ale. Drink enough of it and a man will eventually end up as sober as a bailiff and randy as an owl. The trouble with most men, Bodger, is that they just don't have the staying power to see it through. They haven't got the guts for it."

"What about you, Grift? Have you ever reached the rollickin' stallion stage?"

"What d'you think put the smile on Widow Harpit's face last Winter's Eve, Bodger?"

Bodger thought for a moment, nodded, poured himself a cup of ale, drank it, and then poured himself another one.

"Easy does it, Bodger. Timing is everything."

Bodger downed the second cup and poured himself a third. "I think I'll be arranging to see Tessa the ash maid tonight."

"You can do better than an ash maid, Bodger. Lowest of the low, they are. You don't want to rollick beneath yourself."

"Ash maids can't be beneath me, Grift. I remember you once said that the most refined girl in all the kitchens was none other than an ash maid. Jack's mother, I think she was."

"Aye, Bodger, I did at that. Lucy was her name." Grift smiled tenderly. "A beautiful girl. Clever, too. Of course, she wasn't always an ash maid—that's the difference here."

"What was she before, then?"

"A chambermaid, Bodger. She used to spend all her time upstairs in the nobles' quarters. Then, once she got pregnant, she sort of hid herself down in the kitchens. She took the lowliest job she could get: tending the great cooking fire, and never once set foot in the nobles' quarters again."

"That seems a bit odd, Grift."

"Perhaps she wanted to hide her shame, Bodger. She never did say who the father was."

The two men drank in silence for a while. They both felt the need to show a little respect for the dead.

Tawl was on his way back to Melli's chamber when he heard the sound of footsteps behind him. They seemed to have come from nowhere. Instinctively his hand felt for his sword. Spinning around, Tawl drew his weapon and turned to face his attacker.

"Don't hurt me. It's me, Nabber."

Angry, poised to strike, sword quivering in his fist, Tawl thundered at Nabber: *"What in Borc's name are you doing here?"*

Nabber shrugged sheepishly.

"Never do that again," hissed Tawl, shocked at how close he had come to hurting the boy. "You could have got yourself killed." He resheathed his sword.

Nabber risked a smile. "Sorry, Tawl. Just thought I'd test your reflexes, that's all. You're a bit jittery, if you don't mind me saying so."

Tawl had to turn away to hide a smile. It was impossible to stay mad at the boy. Looking back in the direction that Nabber had come from, he couldn't work out why he hadn't heard him coming sooner. The corridor was long and straight. "How did you manage to sneak up on me?" he asked.

"Don't insult me with a question like that, Tawl. I'm a pocket, ain't I? Stealth is my trade."

"Well, stealthily return the way you came."

"Can't I stay with you for a while? Ever since you got back to the palace, I've hardly seen you. Seems to me that you're dropping your old friends now you've got a high and mighty lady to look after." Nabber pulled himself up to his full height. "Well, let no one say that I ever stuck around where I wasn't wanted. I'm heading back to the streets." He began to walk away.

Tawl reached out and caught Nabber's sleeve. He felt very protective toward the boy and did not want him returning to a life on the streets. True, Nabber could be bluffing, but he didn't want to risk it. "All right, you can come and sit outside the lady's chamber with me. But you've got to promise to be good and not take any valuables."

Nabber smiled broadly. "I'll treat them as if they were my own."

"Hmm, that's what I'm worried about."

The two of them walked to the ladies' quarters. Nabber told Tawl about his two new friends—Bodger and Grift—and then the conversation turned to Baralis.

"I tell you this, Tawl," said Nabber. "That Baralis is one scary devil. Just the sound of his voice alone is enough to send a man's knees aquivering."

Tawl had heard Baralis' name mentioned several times by the duke. He'd even seen him once or twice around the palace. Tall, dark, dressed in black, people always moved out of the way to let him pass. As soon as the announcement of the duke's marriage was made, Baralis was one man Tawl intended to watch closely. As envoy to the kingdoms, he would ill like Kylock being robbed of exactly what he had come here to secure in the first place: Bren's ascendancy.

Tawl was so busy with thoughts of potential threats to Melli that something important almost slipped his mind. Almost. Just as they turned in to Melli's reception chamber, Tawl pulled Nabber back by catching hold of his tunic. "How come you have spoken to Baralis?" he asked.

With a great show of dignity, Nabber freed himself from the grip. His hand came to rest on his chest like an actor about to speak from the heart, and he said, "You know me, Tawl. Powerful people flock to me. I can't do anything about it."

Tawl winked at the two guards flanking the door. He then grabbed hold of Nabber's ear, twisted it sharply, and proceeded to march the boy into the chamber. Only when the door was firmly closed behind him did he loosen his grip a little. "Now, Nabber," he said, pleasantly. "You have two choices: one, you can either tell me the truth—in which case I will only hurt you slightly; or two, you can lie to me and I'll tear your ear off." Tawl demonstrated his ability to do this by tugging firmly on the ear. Nabber howled. "Now, which will it be?"

Nabber tried to wriggle free, but Tawl just pinched harder on his ear. "All right, all right," the pocket said. "Let me go and I'll tell you what happened."

Tawl shook his head. "I'm not going to release you until I hear the truth."

"You're a cruel man, Tawl." Nabber's face was turning an unpleasant red. He took a deep breath. "Baralis was asking me questions about Bevlin."

Bevlin? This was the last thing Tawl had expected. He let go of Nabber's ear. Suddenly he didn't feel like playing games. "Tell me exactly what happened."

Nabber brushed his tunic down and rubbed his ear. "He came down to the chapel when I was with Bodger and Grift. He asked me a lot of questions. You know, about where the wiseman lived, about his books. About you."

"What did you tell him?" Tawl's voice was grim. He didn't like the sound of this one little bit. Why would Baralis be interested in him? It didn't make any sense.

"Only things that were common knowledge, Tawl. I swear it. I told him where Bevlin's cottage was, how long I'd known you, that sort of thing. He already knew about the quest—"

Tawl interrupted him. "He knew I was looking for a boy?"

Nabber nodded. "Swift's honor, he did."

"And why was he interested in Bevlin's cottage?"

"He was after his books. Apparently both men shared a love for crawling insects."

Tawl's gut sent him a warning; it tightened, forcing bile into his throat. Baralis wanted Bevlin's books. But why? Insects were a poor excuse. As he tried to work out what Baralis could want, another thought flashed across his mind, blocking all others in its wake.

"If he goes to the cottage, what will he find?" The last time he'd seen the place there was blood spread across the floor and a dead man in the middle of it.

Nabber immediately understood the question. "He'll find a nice clean home with everything in order."

"And the body?"

"I buried it."

Tawl looked deep into Nabber's brown eyes. The young pocket never ceased to amaze him. He had taken care of everything. When he himself had ridden away in a tortured, cowardly frenzy, Nabber had stayed behind and dealt with the body and the blood. Tawl felt ashamed of himself. He also felt a great respect for Nabber. "Thank you," he said.

"I was just doing what Swift taught me—looking out for my friends."

Tawl held his hand out and Nabber took it. "You're the only friend I have," he said, clasping the boy's arm firmly.

"I'm the only one you'll ever need."

The door opened and in walked the duke. Seeing Nabber, he assumed he was a servant. "Leave us, boy. I would speak to my champion alone."

"It was dark the night of the fight, Your Grace," said Tawl, preventing Nabber from leaving by placing a restraining hand on his shoulder, "so I will forgive you for not recognizing my second: Nabber of Rorn." He pushed the boy forward.

Nabber flushed with pride. He executed a rather impressive bow. "Your Grace."

The duke inclined his head graciously. "Please except my apologies. Rorn, eh? Happen to know the archbishop, do you?"

"He's a slippery blighter, I can tell you that much."

The duke laughed. "You can come and work for me anytime, Nabber. I wish more of my counselors would put things as succinctly as you do."

Nabber was beaming from ear to sore ear. "Anytime you need a spot of advice, Your Grace, just look me up. Tawl always knows were to find me." He bowed again. "Now, I must be off. Commerce calls."

Tawl and the duke watched him go.

"A remarkable boy," said the duke once Nabber had left the room.

"In more ways than one," replied Tawl. He made up his mind that he wasn't going to question Nabber any further about Baralis. He had the strong suspicion that the boy had probably sold the man information, but that was Nabber's way. It was what made him who he was, and he could hardly be blamed for it. Besides, it sounded as if Baralis had another source of information. Someone else had told him about the search for the boy. Tawl scanned his memory for those who knew about the quest. The archbishop of Rorn. Tyren. Larn.

"Tawl." The duke interrupted his thoughts. "Are you all right? You look like a man whose thoughts are far from his body."

Very far. Hundreds of leagues to the south, across a stretch of treacherous ocean, on the cursed island of Larn. The place of his undoing. Were the powers that be still working against him? Were they not content with all that they had done?

Tawl pulled himself back. "I'm a little tired, Your Grace. Nothing more."

"You have been spending too much time guarding my lady," said the duke.

"Do you wish to speak with me?"

"Yes. Briefly." The duke motioned toward the far door. "Is Melliandra in her bedchamber?" When Tawl nodded, he lowered his voice. "In two nights time, on the Feast of First Sowing, I will make my wedding announcement. I'm counting on you to monitor the events at the table. I will have my hands full fending off verbal attacks. I need you to keep an eye on people. Note their reactions—especially Lord Baralis'—and be ready to pull Melliandra out of there if anything should happen."

"I will be there," said Tawl.

The duke nodded. "Good. Do you want to sit at the table next to Melliandra, or would you prefer a more discreet vantage point?"

"I would rather be concealed."

"As you wish. Arrange whatever is necessary." The duke looked grim. "That's all for now. I mustn't keep my bride-to-be waiting." He walked over to the connecting door. "Remember, Tawl, I'm counting on you to tell me who my enemies are."

Darkness had fallen and it was time to look for shelter. The land he was walking across was plowed and ready for sowing, so that meant that there was probably a farm nearby. Farms boasted outbuildings and chicken coops and barns: places where a man could rest undisturbed for the night. Provided, of course, he was prepared to leave before dawn. Farmers woke earlier than priests.

Jack scanned the horizon. Which way to turn? Since leaving Rovas' cottage, his instincts had pointed him to the east. Why should he change his course now? Tired, hungry, cold and alone, he carried on walking straight ahead.

The last time he had eaten was two days back. Almost crazy with hunger, he had risked nearing a farmhouse in daylight. The chicken coop was farthest away from the main building, so he headed there. He managed to crack open and eat half a dozen eggs before the dogs were set on him. With yolk dripping down his chin and a few more eggs stuffed down his tunic, he made a run for it. He had escaped unharmed, though sadly he couldn't say the same for the eggs. Not only had the shells cracked open, but the yolk had somehow gotten down his britches. A few hours later, the smell was enough to put him off eggs for life.

In the end he'd finally thrown himself, fully clothed, into a stream. Having lived through the rains of a week ago, he was not only accustomed to being soaked to the skin, but he'd also built up a certain immunity to it. It would take more than a quick dip in the stream to kill him—even if it *did* take his clothes a full day to dry.

Sometimes Jack just wanted to laugh. Here he was: one-time baker's boy and scribe to Baralis, fleeing across eastern Halcus being pursued by the enemy, nothing to his name except the clothes on his back and the knife at his waist, and with a body bearing so many wounds that he had to keep checking to see if any had reopened and started to bleed. This was definitely not how adventures in books went. He should be famous by now, rich and accomplished, a band of ardent followers in tow, and royalty waiting upon his every word. He should have the girl of his dreams, too.

Sometimes Jack just wanted to cry. When he thought of Tarissa, of leaving her kneeling in the rain outside Rovas' cottage, her saying that she was sorry and pleading to come along with him, he wondered if he'd done the right thing. Those were the worst times of all. The times when it was hardest to carry on. The times when he had to physically stop himself from turning around and running back to her door. Once, just once, he'd given in to the impulse.

It was late at night—always the worst time for people alone—and he couldn't sleep. No matter what he tried, he could not get Tarissa off his mind. And then, as the moon began to dip toward the west, he reached a point where he no longer wanted to. He wanted to see her, touch her, put his arms around her, and whisper softly that everything would be all right. He headed back there and then, not bothering to wait until dawn. Hours he walked, retracing steps he'd already taken, walking paths he'd already walked. The darkness was his ally and the shadows were his friends. They led him on through the night, making him feel so small and insignificant that he questioned his own judgment. Who was he to condemn another? Who was he to walk away from someone, when he himself was guilty of so much? In a world made large by the glimmering of distant stars, Jack began to feel that nothing he said or did was important. To be alone was frightening, and he needed someone else to make up for all that he was not. He needed Tarissa.

The sunrise changed everything.

Pale and majestic, the morning sun rose above the hilltops. Its gentle rays searched out uncertainties just as surely as shadows and made them both disappear with a speed unique to light. As the rays from the sun strengthened, so did Jack's willpower. As the sun rose higher, Jack's steps became slower. The world had boundaries again: hills and streams, forests and mountains. It was smaller, less intimidating: a place where one man could make a difference. Resolution returned to him. Tarissa had betrayed him. He didn't need her; better to be alone than with someone he couldn't trust.

Stopping by a stream, he brought water to his lips. He could feel the sun on his back, warming, encouraging, beckoning him to turn around. He had already said his farewells and come so far, it was pure foolishness to return. Standing up, Jack spun around and began once more to walk east, toward the sun.

As the day went on the sun slowly arced across the sky. Eventually, when it reached the point where it was shining from behind him, the very nature of its rays changed: no longer did they beckon, they pushed.

In the distance, Jack spotted a pinpoint of light. A farmhouse. His heart thrilled at the sight of it. If he was lucky he'd have shelter tonight.

Making his way toward it, he took stock of his body. The gash Rovas had given him on his forearm was healing nicely. Running his fingers down the scab, he could detect no wetness or swelling. Good. His kidneys had pained him on and off for the past few days—the table corner had delivered quite a punch—but for now there was just a bearable dull ache. Bringing his hand up he felt his lip: it was still as big as a barmcake. Magra had wielded the copper pot like a prizefighter, catching both his jaw and his lip in one well-placed blow. Jack dreaded to think what his face looked like: bruises, swelling cuts, and a week's worth of beard on his chin. He had taken to tactically avoiding still water in order to postpone the shock of seeing himself. He always drank from moving streams.

All the old injuries to his arms and legs—the dog bites and other wounds he'd received from various exchanges at the garrison—were in the process of changing from scabs to scars, and so they no longer bothered him. However, the one thing that did cause him trouble was his upper chest on his right side, where the Halcus arrow had hit. Mrs. Wadwell had tended the wound, and it would probably have been all right by now if only Rovas hadn't landed a punch squarely in its center. Jack found he had to be careful with it. He could never put too much pressure on his right arm, nor bear any weight on his right shoulder. All he had to do was slip his hand in his tunic to know that the wound was infected. Bloated, sometimes weeping after a long day's walk, it looked about as bad as it smelled. Purple veins ran close to the surface, and it was now ringed, courtesy of Rovas, by a yellowy green bruise.

It throbbed as he approached the farmhouse. Later, before he slept, he would have to slice it open to let out the pus. He tried to keep it clean and always bathed it once a day, but he needed wine, not water, to do the job properly. That or a cauterizing iron.

Jack stooped down in the bushes. There was now only a small meadow between him and the farmhouse. This was a dairy farm. He listened for the sound of dogs or geese. He heard nothing but the gentle lowing of cattle and their young. He risked moving forward. The cattle picked up his scent, but after a few warning sounds they settled down. He was not a fox, and they knew it. Quickly he cut across the meadow. Stepping in cow pats wasn't pleasant, but it was useful; it made him smell familiar if there happened to be any geese or poultry around. He made his way around to the back of the building. There was a large pigpen, which he stayed well clear of, a barn and a dairyshed. He made for the dairyshed. If he was lucky, there would be cheese, cream, and buttermilk.

His stomach grumbled loudly at the thought of food. Jack whispered gently to it, as if it were a small animal. "Not long now," he said.

The door to the dairyshed was held closed by a rusty latch. It lifted easily. In he went, plunging from moonlight into darkness. For a few minutes he stood still, waiting for his eyes to grow accustomed to the dark. His nose, however, needed no such luxury. It told him food was around, most precisely cheese.

Hunger did strange things to a man. Jack didn't feel in the slightest bit guilty about eating whatever he could find. If he had money, he would have left it. But he didn't, so he would take what he wanted anyway. He needed to survive, and if he had to steal to do so, then so be it. The one thing that he'd learned since leaving Castle Harvell was that the world wasn't a fair place. The farmer who woke in the morning to discover half a cheese missing should count himself lucky. A lot worse could happen to a man.

Too many things had happened to Jack over the past months for him to remain naive. When he'd left the kingdoms, he was little more than a boy. Trusting and innocent, he had taken everyone at their word. Not anymore, though. It would be a long time before anyone fooled him again. Still, in some ways he'd been lucky. Even amidst all the fire and chaos at the garrison he had been treated with kindness. Dilburt and Mrs. Wadwell had saved him in more ways than one that night. They had shown him what goodness people were capable of. With generous hearts they had taken him in and cared for him. They asked no questions, nor for anything in return. Jack would remember that always.

No, the world wasn't a fair place, but it wasn't a bad one, either.

Once his eyes could make out variations in the darkness, Jack set to work looking for whatever food he could find. The cheeses were on a shelf and he brought one of them down. With steady hands he unwrapped the linen cloth. He resisted the urge to bite straight into it and cut himself a fair-sized wedge, instead. His wound would have to wait until tomorrow now; he couldn't risk slicing it with a dirty knife.

The cheese was well worth the sacrifice. It was delicious: sharp, crumbly, and dry. Further investigation uncovered a large jug of buttermilk. He sat down on the rush-covered floor and ate and drank himself sick. Cheese and buttermilk, while fine on their own, did not make the best combination. Too rich and creamy by far.

With a stomach now grumbling from overindulgence, Jack curled up in a ball and covered himself with rushes. Closing his eyes, he settled down and listened for rats. He could never sleep without first being sure that there were none of the evil glassy-eyed rodents around. He hated rats.

He was almost disappointed when there was nothing to hear but the creak of the woodwork and the sound of the breeze whistling through the cracks. An absence of scurrying noises meant that he was free to sleep. Nowadays he was almost more afraid of sleep than he was of rats. His dreams gave him no peace. Tarissa was always in them, crying and pleading one minute, laughing slyly the next. The garrison burned anew each night, and sometimes she burned along with it. Rats might make his flesh crawl, but they never left him feeling guilty and confused.

Before he knew it, his eyelids had grown heavy, and sleep gently eased her way in. Perhaps it was the unique combination of cheese and buttermilk, perhaps not, but for the first time in many weeks he didn't dream of Tarissa. He dreamed of Melli. Her pale and beautiful face kept him company through the night.

Thirty-two

Smoke rose from a forest of candles. A field of wildflowers rested in silver bowls. A mine's worth of silver graced the finest linen and a mountain's worth of crystal caught the light. A rainbow of colors decked the walls, whilst a meadow of fragrant grasses graced the floor. It was the Feast of First Sowing in Bren, and the duke's palace was dressed in its springtime best.

Long tables spanned the length of the great hall. Swans swam across the tabletops, their brilliant white feathers masking cooked birds beneath. Boar's heads stuffed with songbirds rested upon exquisite tapestries of blue and gold, and newly birthed calves were impaled upon spits.

The lords and ladies who sat around the tables were the most influential people in Bren. Their clothes were made from the finest materials, but the colors were strangely subdued: dark grays, deep greens, and black. The women made up for the plainness of their dresses by wearing their grandest jewels. Diamonds and rubies flashed in the candlelight, and precious metals tinkled with each raised cup.

The duke surveyed the hall. The court was apprehensive tonight. Men and women alike were drinking heavily, yet eating barely anything at all. Lord Cravin caught his eye. He was an ambitious and powerful man who had long been opposed to the match of Catherine and Kylock. The duke inclined his head toward him. Cravin would be pleasantly surprised this evening. Lord Maybor, who was sitting nearby, spotted the exchange. The duke raised his cup to him. Maybor, red of face and dressed more magnificently than anyone else around the table, mirrored his gesture. The duke actually had to stop himself from laughing. The man had no inkling that this night would change his life.

He glanced quickly to the small door that stood to the side of the main table. Behind its wooden panels waited the lady who would alter the course of history: Melliandra, his bride-to-be. She had no idea her father was here. He could see her now, downing a little more wine than was good for her and scolding her servant for listening at the door, whilst she herself did the same. It wouldn't be long now before he brought her out.

Shifting his gaze from the door, back to the table, something caught his eye that gave him cause to be wary: Baralis was sitting next to Catherine. That in itself was a blatant disregard of his wishes, but what was more alarming, however, was the way the girl leaned over the man, feeding him meats and sweet breads, her breasts brushing against his arm. Any other time the duke would not have tolerated such behavior. He would simply have pulled Catherine from the table and sent her to bed. She had obviously been drinking, for nothing else could explain her immodest behavior. Even as he watched, Baralis placed a restraining hand upon Catherine's arm and moved his chair a little way back from hers. The duke was pleased, but not surprised. Baralis was not a stupid man.

But he would soon be an angry one.

And Catherine? How would she react? She would not be pleased, that much was certain. The duke shrugged. Temper tantrums of young girls were easily dealt with.

It was time. Eating had stopped, and drinking had reached the point where people no longer bothered to hide the quantities they drank. The duke brought down his cup, banging it loudly on the table. All eyes turned toward the noise. He stood up, and a hush descended upon the room.

Maybor had been waiting for this all night. He'd barely tasted the seven pheasants, the haunch of venison, and the two jugs of lobanfern red which he had consumed. His mind was on what the duke was going to do to Baralis. It was high time that villainous demon was dealt with once and for all. Of course, the puzzling thing was that Baralis would finally be getting his way tonight: Kylock would wed Catherine. Indeed, His Grace was in the process of making the announcement now. Maybor sat back in his chair, his cup resting upon his knee, and listened to what the duke was saying.

"My lords and ladies," he said, speaking in a strong and ringing voice, "I have chosen the Feast of First Sowing to make two important announcements. As you know, First Sowing is traditionally a time when we pray for healthy crops and high yields from the seeds which we have newly sown. I hope for the same bountiful harvest from the two seeds I sow tonight."

The duke paused. A wave of nervous chatter and coughing rose up to fill the silence. People shifted restlessly in their seats. Maybor noticed many a person using the short break to bring wine cups to their lips. All was silence when the duke spoke again.

"Firstly, I must inform you of my decision to go ahead with the marriage of Catherine and Kylock—"

The duke was cut off in midsentence by the noise of the crowd. A wave of something close to panic spread fast across the room. Breath was sharply inhaled, eyebrows were raised, and expressions of disbelief were on everyone's lips. Maybor glanced toward Lord Cravin: the man's expression was grim. Baralis and Catherine, on the other hand, looked as smug as a pair of newlyweds. Maybor began to feel a little wary. What if the duke had been leading him astray? Promising something that would upset Baralis, just to keep him quiet?

The duke did not look pleased. The skin was drawn tight across the bridge of his nose and his lips were drawn into a whip of a line. He rapped his cup on the table. *"Silence!"* he boomed.

Every single member of the court froze on the spot. Cups were suspended in midair, tongues were caught in mid-flap.

Satisfied, the duke continued. "Not only have I decided to go ahead with the match, but I have also set a date. Two months from tonight, my beloved daughter Catherine will wed King Kylock."

The crowd lost control once more. The hall was filled with the hiss of dissatisfied whisperings. It was a testament to the duke's power that no one dared speak out loud.

Abruptly, Lord Cravin stood up. He bowed to the duke. "I request Your Grace's permission to leave the table," he said, pronouncing every word precisely.

"Request denied, Lord Cravin. You will sit and hear my second announcement like everybody else."

Humiliated, Lord Cravin shot a look filled with pure malice toward the duke.

Maybor fancied he saw a spark of amusement twinkle in the duke's eye. The court, seeing how sharply Lord Cravin was dealt with, grew more subdued.

The duke beckoned his daughter to stand. Catherine did as she was bidden, her pearls resting like raindrops against her dress. Borc, but she was beautiful! thought Maybor. Her pale and heavy hair was piled high atop her head. Combs and pins didn't quite succeed in keeping all the locks in place, and several golden curls fell like jewels around her face.

"To my daughter, Catherine," said the duke, raising his cup high. "Who, even before the crops begin to ripen in the field, will become queen of the Four Kingdoms."

Maybor choked on his wine. *Queen of the Four Kingdoms.* Melliandra should be the woman who bore that title. *His* daughter should have been queen. In all the plotting and politicking surrounding Catherine's inheritance, somehow the fact that the duke's daughter would be made queen of the kingdoms had gone unnoticed. Even by himself. Maybor suddenly felt very tired. The crowd cheered halfheartedly. With Kylock rapidly approaching the Halcus capital, things looked very different than when they had first enthusiastically accepted the betrothal.

The duke waved Catherine down. "Now," he said. "I come to my second announcement. I have been a long time unmarried. It is over ten years since my beloved wife died, and I think now is the time for me to take another wife."

The crowd was stunned. No one spoke. No one moved.

Maybor leaned forward in his chair. He had an idea of what the duke was up to: he was attempting to supplant Catherine as his heir by producing a legitimate male child to take her place.

The duke continued. "I have recently met a lady of high birth. A beautiful young woman who has agreed to be my wife. I know this will come as a surprise to most of you here, but I intend to marry her within the month."

With the noise of the crowd sounding in his ears, Maybor turned to look at Baralis. The man was as pale as a corpse. This was coming as a rather nasty surprise. Maybor smiled softly. The great lord's plans were about to go sadly awry.

Melli was growing impatient. She had paced the length of the antechamber so many times now that she could swear her feet had worn a path in the stone. "Nessa, what d'you hear now?"

"Well, m'lady," said the small and dumpy girl. "I think His Grace looks set to introduce you."

"Out of my way." Melli pushed Nessa away from the door and put her own ear to the wood. The crowd, which had been so vocal only minutes earlier, was now ominously quiet. Melli stepped away when she realized the duke was speaking. For some reason, she didn't want to hear what he said about her. "Pour me another glass of wine," she ordered. Nessa swiftly obliged. Melli's hands were shaking so much that she was forced to drink the wine leaning forward, with her neck stretched out, to avoid any spilling on her dress.

Just as she brought the cup to her lips, three knocks sounded upon the door. The signal for her to make her entrance. Thrusting the cup into Nessa's waiting hand, Melli smoothed down her dress. "Do I look all right?" The maid nodded, but Melli barely noticed. The door opened up in front of her and she was blinded by light and smoke.

Melli heard the sound of a thousand bated breaths. She froze, unable to move a limb. A trickle of perspiration ran down her cheek. Never in her life had she been so afraid. She felt a strong desire to turn around and run away, all the way back to the kingdoms and the safety of her father's arms. What had she gotten herself into? A hostile court awaited her, ready to criticize and condemn.

Then, just as her eyes grew accustomed to the light, the duke was by her side. His arm was upon hers, lending her strength. His lips gently brushed against her lips. "Come, my love," he said. "Come and meet your courtiers. I promise I will not leave your side." Never had she heard him speak so tenderly. His voice was both a caress and a comfort. He looked into her eyes. "Your beauty makes me very proud tonight." Guiding her from the shadows, he led her into the great hall at Bren.

"This, lords and ladies," he said, walking her toward the main table, "is Melliandra of the Eastlands, daughter of Lord Maybor, and the woman who will soon become my wife."

Maybor dropped his cup. It was Melliandra. *His* Melliandra. All these months of not seeing her, and now she had turned up here. He stood up. In three mighty leaps he was beside her. A second later she was in his arms. Tears were streaming down his cheeks. He didn't give a damn if anyone saw them. He ran his hands along her hair; it was as soft as he remembered. She was so small, so frail. He didn't want to let her go.

"Melli, Melli," he whispered. "My sweet Melli. I never thought I'd see you again." She was shaking like a newborn. He felt something wet on his neck, and realized that she was crying, too. Maybor pulled away, wiping the tears from his eyes with his fist. His daughter was ten times more beautiful than he remembered.

"Father, I'm sorry," she said quietly, for his ears alone.

Maybor took up the corner of his robe and gently rubbed the tears from her cheek. "Hush, little one. Now is not the time for regrets. We are a family again, and the time has come for us to act like one."

Catching hold of Melli's hand, he turned to face the duke and his court. A performance was called for now. A good one. Not only did he need to make these people think that he had known about the wedding all along, but he also had to impress them. Three days back, the duke had asked if he could rely on his composure. Tonight, he would prove that he could be more than composed—he would actually seal the pact.

Maybor cleared his throat. He looked around the great hall, meeting every eye that was focused upon him. When he spoke, he did so slowly, giving proper weight to every word. "I am more than pleased to give my only daughter, Melliandra, in marriage to Bren. I choose the word Bren carefully for I am well aware that Melliandra will wed more than just the duke; she will wed the city itself. I can never hope to repay such an overwhelming honor, but as a father it is my duty to try. I have humbly offered the duke one-third of my eastern holdings and one quarter of my wealth. He has cordially accepted, and the contracts have been drawn." There. Let no one say that Maybor could not think on his feet.

He quickly looked toward the duke. The man nodded his approval. Hastily grabbing a cup from the table, Maybor came to stand between the duke and Melliandra. "A toast," he cried, uniting the two lovers' hands. "A toast to a glorious match between two of the oldest families in the north. May the might of Bren and the Eastlands forever be united."

As Maybor drew his cup to his lip, something dark in the corner of his vision caught his attention. It was Baralis. He looked ready for murder.

Tawl watched as the crowd went into a frenzy over the toast. They hardly knew what to make of the marriage, but somehow Lord Maybor had managed to whip up support. Who could not be moved by the sight of a man weeping in happiness at the announcement of his daughter's marriage? The worldly and cynical court had been touched by such a spontaneous show of paternal affection. Particularly when the man in question had gone on to compose himself and then give a gracious speech. Tawl smiled, his lips brushing against the thick satin curtain. He could certainly see where Melli got her spirit from.

Tawl could see nearly everyone in the room from his position at the side of the head table. He was concealed in the passageway that connected the great hall to the kitchens. Normally it was used by servants carrying hot food to the tables, but tonight Tawl had turned it into his own personal den. He had arranged to have a thickly lined curtain hung from the entrance and had forbidden anyone in the kitchens to set foot in the passage during the feast. It was the ideal place to keep a discreet eye on what was going on, and if matters came to a head, it would also provide the means for a quick escape. He could have Melli out of the hall and into the kitchens in less than a minute.

He didn't think it would come to that, though. Not tonight. But it would come soon. He pressed his eye against the slit and searched out Baralis' face. The man was not even bothering to keep up appearances. Whilst the people of the court were at least putting on a *show* of goodwill for the newly betrothed couple, Baralis was sitting there, lips drawn to a thin line, eyes dark with hatred, stabbing away at the tabletop with the point of his eating knife.

Tawl's gaze traveled to the girl sitting to the right of Baralis: the exquisite Catherine of Bren. Appearances could be so deceptive. She looked like a chaste virgin: she was not. She looked like a sweet angel: she was not. She looked like the sort of girl who would never harm a fly: most definitely, she was not. Even now, Tawl could remember the venom in her voice the day she had sworn to see him dead. Unpredictable, dangerous, and a consummate actress, the duke's daughter was not what she seemed.

Just as the cheering died down, Catherine stood up. Tawl saw how pale her face was and how her hand shook as she grasped the back of the chair. His fingers encircled his blade.

"I would like to propose my own toast," she said, her voice high with emotion. "A toast to my father. A man who would rather make a fool of himself by marrying a woman half of his age than let his daughter keep her rightful place." With that, she swept her arm across the table, sending plates and cups flying.

Two unarmed guards, whom Tawl had briefed earlier for just such a situation, came to lead her away. She fought them off. "This marriage is a farce," she cried, wrestling free of the first guard's grip. Her body became stiff and her eyes began to cloud over. Her cheeks began to fill out as if she were holding her breath. The hand that held the chair shook violently. The very air surrounding her seemed to thicken. All of a sudden she composed herself.

Tawl, from his position at the far side of Catherine, saw the reason why. Baralis had caught and squeezed her hand, then whispered three words in her ear.

The effect the words had on Catherine was dramatic. With great dignity, she pulled away from the guards. "Unhand me," she said. "You forget who I am." A withering gaze completed the reproof. Both men fell back immediately, not even pausing to check with the duke. Head held high, back straight as a spear, Catherine made her way across the hall. She exited through a side door.

When she was gone, the court began to whisper uneasily.

Behind the curtain, Tawl was nervous. His palm was wet around the knife. He had taken a risk not coming forward the moment Catherine stood up. He had no wish to humiliate her by leaping out of nowhere, brandishing his knife in her face. The duke would not have approved. It would have looked as if he didn't trust his own daughter. So he had stayed put, prepared to show himself only if Catherine made a move toward Melli. Yet now, thinking about it, Tawl wasn't sure that she hadn't.

Quickly he looked over to Melli. She was sitting down. The duke was on one side of her, Maybor on the other. She looked tired and a little shaky. As he watched, her father poured her a cup of red wine. With little ceremony, she raised it to her lips and downed it in one. Tawl smiled. Melli was her usual self.

Still, he had the nagging feeling that something had nearly happened here. Something had passed between Catherine and Baralis. A communication, a warning. And by the looks of it, it had been promptly heeded. In the space of a few seconds, Catherine had changed from a woman about to fall into an anger-driven trance to a self-possessed lady of the court. What had Baralis said to her to bring about such a change? And what would have happened if he had said nothing at all?

Tawl's mind traveled back five years to the very first time he'd met Bevlin. That evening was the only time the wiseman had ever spoken openly about sorcery to him. *"Yes, there are those who still practice,"* he had said, *"most think it would be better if they didn't."* Was Catherine one of those? Was Baralis? The night he fought the duke's champion, he had felt something working against him, weakening his will, sapping his strength. Catherine had been Blayze's lover. Had she used sorcery to aide his cause that night?

Tawl ran his fingers through his hair. He couldn't be sure. All he had to go on was a dangerously blank look in Catherine's eye and his own intuition. It should have been enough, though. Tawl was appalled at himself—ignorance was no excuse. He should have gotten Melli out of there. To hell with humiliating Catherine!

He brought his eye close to the slit once more. Melli was sitting at the head of the table. She was putting on an excellent show: eating, drinking, laughing, flirting with Lord Cravin whilst playfully reprimanding the duke about the lack of hot food. She was very brave and very strong. After such an unpleasant incident, most women would have run crying to their rooms. Not Melli. It would take more than bitter words to crush her spirit. Tawl noticed that her left hand was absent from view. Following the line of her arm down, he saw that under the table she was grasping a very tight hold of her father's hand. Her knuckles were white with the strain. Tawl became very still looking at the sight of Melli's small pale hand. He would never forgive himself if anything happened to her.

As he withdrew from the curtain, he noticed that Baralis was no longer in his seat. He hadn't even seen him leave. Yet he could guess where he was headed. Satisfied that Melli would be safe for a while, Tawl stole down along the corridor. Cutting through the kitchens to the main gallery, he worked his way back toward the hall. As he drew close to the main door, he noticed the black-robed figure of Baralis heading off in the distance. Tawl followed him. The man knew the palace like the back of his hand. Taking turnings Tawl had never noticed, climbing staircases that were hidden by either curtains or shadows. Eventually they came to part of the palace Tawl recognized: the ladies' quarters. He watched from a stone recess as Baralis approached a set of bronze-covered double doors. He did not have to knock. The doors swung back and Catherine stood waiting. Hair loose and wearing a gown that revealed her naked shoulders, she beckoned Baralis to enter.

Tawl turned as the door closed behind them. With a heavy step, he made his way back to the great hall. In the morning, when the duke summoned him to give his account of the evening, what should he say? He took a deep breath and was slow to let it out. How could he tell the duke that his greatest enemy might turn out to be his own daughter?

Thirty-three

*F*or two days now, Jack had been walking across land that was both more populated and less flat. He was not happy about either. Walking downhill was fine; sometimes he even broke into a run, but uphill . . . Jack shook his head. Uphill was an entirely different matter. His thighs were sore, his knees were playing up, even his ankles were acting strangely, refusing to allow his feet to pivot properly, causing him pain with every step. If *he* were ever called upon to design a world, it would be downhill all the way.

Jack's main problem, however, was people. He just couldn't seem to avoid them any longer. The roads were packed with them, the fields were full of them, and the woods had grown so sparse that he was now forced to dash from tree to tree like a spider in search of shade. The one certain way to attract attention, Jack had discovered, was to run across fields in search of cover. He had been chased by two farmers with pitchforks, one dog, and an entire flock of geese. The geese were the worst, honking loudly and taking vicious pecks at his vitals. He'd rather be attacked by a dog any day.

Hearing a cart rattling by, Jack dived to the ground. He was just off a large road that was hedged on either side by bushes and bracken. Instead of carrying on, the cart lurched to a slow stop. Jack drew in his breath. Had the driver spotted him? Body flat against the ground, Jack lay as still as he could manage. He heard the soft pad of feet in the dirt, and then the bushes next to him began to move. They continued to rustle for some time. Jack assumed that the driver was relieving himself and so decided to stay put. Just when the rustling stopped, and he felt safe to release his breath, the bushes parted and a man stepped through. He had a basket in one hand and a scythe in the other. Seeing Jack, he stopped in his tracks.

Up came the scythe. "Young man," he said, in a pleasant, lilting voice, "if your intention is to rob me, I warn you now that I have nothing but herbs in my basket. And nothing but mushrooms in my cart." He smiled brightly. "Poisonous ones, at that."

Stunned, Jack stayed exactly where he was. The scythe was just about the deadliest-looking thing he had ever seen.

The man noted what he was looking at. "For the herbs, you know."

Jack decided to speak. "Sir, I am sorry to catch you unawares. I didn't mean to frighten you." He tried to keep his words muffled to disguise where he came from.

The man smiled more broadly than ever. He was of middle height and had shoulder-length gray hair. Not exactly old, yet past middle age. With a casual gesture, he hooked the scythe onto his belt. "First of all young man, you did not surprise me in the least; secondly, as I've been aware of your presence since before I stopped my cart, you most definitely did not catch me unawares."

Jack risked sitting up. He brushed the dirt from his face and chest. "You saw me duck into the bushes?"

The man raised his hand to his clean-shaven chin. "You could say that." From his chin, his hand sprang forward. "I'm Stillfox, pleased to meet you."

Gingerly, Jack took the proffered hand. With a grip as firm as a man half his age, he heaved Jack off the ground.

"Find any interesting herbs while you were down there?" Stillfox asked, eyes twinkling.

Jack shrugged.

He lifted his hand up and examined his palm. "Of course you didn't. What would a lad from the kingdoms know about Annis herbs, eh?"

Jack pulled back his hand.

Stillfox laughed. "Don't worry, I'm not a fortune-teller. Your palm didn't tell me that, your accent did."

Feeling very foolish, Jack mumbled his apologies. Too many things had happened for him to take in at once. He could hardly believe he was in Annis, for one thing. Oh, he'd seen the mountains looming up on the horizon for days now, but he'd paid them little heed, thinking they were impossibly far away in the distance. For the past two days the clouds had been so thick that he hadn't seen the mountains at all. Had he really come that far? Or was it far at all? All the time he'd stayed in Rovas' cottage, he had no idea where it lay in relation to the rest of Halcus. He had been close to the border for months and not even known it; yet another thing Tarissa had kept from him.

It made sense now: the garrison was situated where it was—in what he had assumed to be the middle of nowhere—to protect the Halcus-Annis border. Even Rovas' smuggling business would benefit from closeness to the great trading center. "How far are we from the city?" he asked.

Stillfox was busy searching his basket. He didn't look up. "Annis is twelve leagues to the east. A good morning's ride, or a full day's walk." Pulling out some rather dry-looking pieces of bark, he cried, "Aha! I knew I had some."

"Some what?"

"Willow bark for your fever, and witch hazel to clean out your wound."

Jack's hand stole to his chest. "But—"

"I can smell the fester," said Stillfox, answering his question before he had even asked it. "It needs seeing to, lad. It's a wonder you've got this far."

"You don't know how far I've come." Jack was surprised by the sharpness of his tone. His thoughts were on the garrison. He had to be careful; he didn't want this man knowing where he'd come from. Everyone in Annis must have heard about the fire by now.

Stillfox smiled briskly. "Perhaps not, but I do know where you're going."

Jack looked directly into his eyes. He was older than he'd first thought. There were thick bands of black around the blue of his irises. "Where am I going?" he asked.

Stillfox blinked once. "Home with me."

It wasn't the answer he expected. "Why?"

"You will not come unless I tell you?"

"No."

Nodding heavily, he said, "Very well. From the moment I put my cart on the road this morning, I sensed your trail in the air. I simply urged my horse forward and followed it here."

"What trail?" Even as he asked, Jack knew he wouldn't like the answer.

"Sorcery, lad." Gone was the brightness from Stillfox's face. "You are carrying the vestiges of your last drawing along with you."

Jack knew the color drained from his face, but could do nothing to stop it. He began to move forward. "I don't know what you're talking about. It's time I moved on."

Stillfox caught his arm. His grip was not gentle. "Don't be a fool, lad. You need help, and I'm offering to give it. It would be most unwise to turn me down." The lilting tones had been replaced by a low and forceful voice.

Jack pulled himself free. "And who are you to decide what's wise and unwise?"

Stillfox gave Jack a hard look. "I'm someone who knows that Annis is crawling with Halcus soldiers who are busy looking for the man who burned down their garrison."

Rovas had told them where he was headed! Jack kicked at the dirt. Tarissa had asked him where he was going, and he'd replied east. She could have guessed he would head to the very place where they had planned to go together. Jack wondered how long it had taken her to decide to tell Rovas. Obviously not very long, for the Halcus were now ahead of him.

Jack glanced sideways at Stillfox. How could he be sure this man spoke the truth? And what exactly did he know about the garrison? "I have nothing to fear from the Halcus," he said.

"They have posted descriptions of the man they're after all over the city. Tall, brown haired, speaks with a kingdoms accent." Stillfox gave Jack a hard look. "Annis and Halcus are very friendly at the moment— seems they'll soon be fighting on the same side—and there's nothing Annis wouldn't do to help her would-be ally. Nothing would delight her more than turning over a notorious war criminal."

"*War criminal?*" Jack didn't even bother to keep the surprise from his voice.

Stillfox nodded. "Kylock has just reached Helch. The garrison that was destroyed was due to send troops and supplies to aid the capital. But because all the provisions were burned and so many men were injured, the transfer never went ahead. Some are saying it was that one inspired act of sabotage that gave Kylock the edge. I don't know if that's true or not, but one thing's certain: Helch will be surrendering soon. Very soon."

Jack's blood ran cold. Was there no end to his crimes? A deep pit opened up in his thoughts, but he refused to look into it. Lined with his own guilt, it threatened to take him downward to prophecy and torment. He would not go there. He spoke to distract his thoughts, and then found he had not distracted them at all, rather refined them. "Kylock will win the war." Intended as a question, it turned to a statement upon his lips.

Stillfox's hand came back down upon his arm. "Come with me. I swear no harm will befall you whilst you stay under my roof."

There seemed to be more than pressure in the old man's grip. Jack drew strength and calmness from it. The pit closed and he was no longer afraid, just confused. "Why would you help me?" he asked.

Even as he answered, Stillfox began to guide him toward the road. "I help you because I recognize my own." The lilt returned to the man's voice, and Jack wondered for an instant if it was to disguise the trace of ambiguity in his words.

"Ssh!" hissed Stillfox, before he could speak. There were riders on the road, and they crouched down in the bushes until they had passed. Once the road was clear, Stillfox urged him forward. Heading for the back of the cart, he pulled up the oil cloth. "Under here. Quick." Jack slid under the oil cloth. The cart smelled of mold. Stillfox tucked him in and then made his way to the front. Taking up the reins, he whispered, "Feel free to eat the mushrooms. I was lying when I said they were poisonous."

Tawl watched as the duke approached. His Grace had originally wanted to meet in Melli's chambers, but Tawl did not want to risk Melli overhearing what he had to say. So they had arranged to meet here, in the ladies' courtyard.

"Well met, friend," said the duke, coming forward to clasp his hand. "Last night went well, did it not?"

"Mel—" Tawl stopped himself. "Your lady conducted herself with strength and grace."

The duke nodded. "She was magnificent, wasn't she?" He paused a moment, obviously well pleased. "Her father was brilliant, too. He won more hearts by dashing over to his daughter and weeping, than he could ever have done by giving away his gold. I couldn't have planned it better."

For some reason, what the duke said annoyed Tawl. "Have you heard the news from Helch yet?" he asked, deliberately changing the subject.

"No. I've been spending all morning seeing lord after relieved lord. Last night's announcement has certainly made the court rest easier in their beds."

"Kylock has broken Helch's defenses. He's made it inside the city, and now there're only the castle walls between him and certain victory."

The duke drew a quick breath. His hand fell to his sword. *"Damn him! When did this happen?"*

"Two days back."

"Castle Helch is a mighty fortress. A decent army could defend it for months."

"You forget that Kylock has inside knowledge. The knights have been feeding him information about Helch's defenses. That's probably how he managed to break through the city walls so fast."

The duke grunted. "This is ill news indeed." He turned his back on Tawl and began to pace around the courtyard. After a few moments, he spun around. "The sooner I marry Melliandra, the better. I told the court I intended to marry her within a month, but I can't risk waiting that long. I must disassociate both Bren and myself from what Kylock is doing to Helch. The moment that city falls, Highwall and Annis will be up in arms, and if they think, even for one instant, that Kylock will one day rule this city, they won't hesitate to move against us."

"By tonight they will all know of your intentions to marry."

"Intentions are no longer enough. Right now I need Melliandra wedded and pregnant. Only then will Bren be safe."

Tawl knew the duke was right. He didn't like the way he spoke of Melli, though. "The lady herself may be in danger."

"What d'you mean?"

"I think Lord Baralis will make an attempt on Melliandra's life in the next few days. Last night I watched him at the banquet. He did not look pleased." As he spoke, Tawl wondered what, if anything, he should say about Catherine. "I have reason to believe he might try an attempt on her life." He found he couldn't bring himself to tell the duke that his daughter could be plotting against him. He hurried on, not giving the man a chance to question his reasoning. "So the quicker you marry the lady, the better. It will be a lot easier to keep her safe once she takes up residence in your chambers."

"Yes." The duke nodded slowly. "Just this morning I received the blessing from the clergy. They have no objection, so I am free to marry her when I choose. Of course everyone will expect me to wait a couple of weeks."

"It would be better if the marriage ceremony was a discreet one," said Tawl.

"You are right." The duke pulled his sword from his belt. He began to inspect the blade, holding it up to catch the sunlight. "Perhaps it would be better if we kept the ceremony secret and only announced it the following day, by which time it would be too late for anyone's objections." Finding the blade sound, he slipped it back in its loop. "And there will be nothing that Lord Baralis or the court can do about it."

Although Tawl knew it was for the best, there was a part of him that didn't want the wedding to go ahead too soon. Perhaps not even at all. He had started to care about Melli, and it angered him to see how casually the duke manipulated her for his own political ends. Tawl had no choice but to keep these feelings well hidden; his first loyalty was to the duke.

"Can any legitimate objections be raised to a secret wedding?"

"Not if all the proper clergy, the archbishop, and enough respected witnesses are in place," replied the duke. "My great-grandfather wed a girl in secret. She was a lowly lord's daughter and he, by that time, was well into his dotage. Everyone protested. The whole city was up in arms for months, but no one could annul the marriage because it was done with the Church's blessing."

"So there is a precedent?"

"Yes." The duke smiled thinly. "Just to make sure of legitimacy, I will order Catherine to attend."

This was the last thing Tawl wanted. The moment Catherine knew about the wedding, she would go running to Baralis. Tawl chose his words carefully. "Your daughter was very upset last night. She might do something irrational."

The duke made a dismissive gesture with his arm. "Do not be worried about her girlish tantrum. It was nothing—hurt pride, that's all. It was to be her evening and I stole her thunder." He turned his back on Tawl. "I can hardly blame her, really."

"So you intend to tell her of your marriage plans?"

"The moment I have finalized them. Last night proved that I have already kept too much from my daughter. If I include her in the ceremony, she will no longer feel left out."

Tawl kept his face impassive. "Very well. When will the marriage go ahead?"

"I will arrange it for two days hence." The duke was thinking out loud. "Yes. That should give the old archbishop plenty of time to dust off his robes. The ceremony can be held in the ladies' chapel here, in the palace."

"The one belowstairs?"

"No. That is for the servants' use. The ladies' chapel is more fitting, and more discreet."

Tawl nodded. The servants' chapel was too public a place. Anyone could smuggle themselves in there; it was guarded by two men who were half drunk all the time. "I will see to the security. Tell no one today except the archbishop. Inform everyone else the morning of the wedding." Tawl's thoughts were on Catherine.

"Very well." Now that the decision was made, the duke looked eager to be off. "I will go to the archbishop first, then to Melliandra, then to Catherine."

"But—"

"No, Tawl," interrupted the duke, "I cannot tell my daughter of my wedding only a few hours before it's due to go ahead. It will look as if I don't trust her." The hard look he gave Tawl put an end to the subject. "Now, I will send Bailor to you, and you can coordinate everything with him. There must be flowers and so forth in the chapel. I do not want Melliandra disappointed in any way."

Tawl bowed. "I will make sure that everything is in place."

"Good. I will be counting on you." With that the duke turned on his heel and walked off across the courtyard.

Tawl stood where he was for some time. The midday sun shone down upon his back, casting a small but dark shadow in front of him.

Crope hurried down the market streets. He hated being out in the daylight, especially when the sun was shining. People would stare, men would laugh, and children would throws sticks and stones. He had tried keeping his hood up, but on a bright warm day like this, it just drew more attention to himself. He looked like an executioner. If only the people weren't there, then he could spend as long as he wanted looking at all the animals in cages: the partridges, the piglets, the owls. As it was, he barely risked slowing down at all—except for the owls—for he was afraid the stallholders would curse him for scaring away paying customers. He'd been cursed a lot in the past for that.

Still, he had his comforts. In a small pouch in the side of his cloak nestled a large rat. Big Tom, as Crope liked to call it, went everywhere with him. Big Tom had been one of his master's 'speriments, and had been born one leg short of a foursome. His master had ordered the creature to be drowned, but Crope didn't have the heart to do it. Big Tom's beady little eyes reminded him of his mother's. He limped good, too. So, for the past few months, Big Tom had been living with him; he couldn't risk his master finding out he had disobeyed an order. Crope shook his head vigorously. He wouldn't want *that* to happen.

As Crope made his way to the herb stall, trying hard to remember his master's exact directions, his hand stole into his tunic, feeling for the reassuring weight of his second comfort: his painted box. Just to touch it made him feel better. It was his oldest and most precious possession, given to him by a beautiful lady many years before. The lady had been his friend. They had shared a love of animals, especially birds. Painted on the box were her favorites: seagulls. She said they reminded her of home.

Crope was disturbed from his memories by someone rudely pushing past him. "Out of my way, you lumbering simpleton," cried a small, bad-smelling man who was carrying bolts of cloth in one hand and clutching pins and scissors in the other. Obviously a tailor. Before Crope had time to say he was sorry, the tailor was gone. Crope watched him dive in and out of the crowds and found some satisfaction in the fact that *he* was not the only one who the tailor pushed aside. Women, old men, and stallholders were all shoved out of the way. Then, as Crope looked on, the tailor made the mistake of picking on the wrong person. He elbowed a tall, dark man, and instead of moving out of the way, the man turned around and punched him in the face. Bolts of cloth and pins went flying. The tailor fell to the ground. The man kicked him once while he was down, spat on him, and then carried on walking, oblivious to the hostile glare of the crowds.

Crope's heart was racing. He recognized the man: it was Traff, his master's mercenary. As he watched, Traff slipped into the crowds. After a moment Crope followed him.

Feeling rather excited, Crope stroked Big Tom. "Master will be pleased," he whispered to the rat, as he started trailing Traff across the city.

"I am very pleased, Crope," said Baralis. "You have done well."

Crope beamed. "I spotted him with my own eyes, master."

"Where did he end up?"

"A right nice place, master. There were ladies leaning out from the windows."

"Hmm, a brothel. Was it in Brotheling Street?" Seeing Crope's blank expression, Baralis tried again. "Were there lots of other places nearby with ladies leaning from windows?"

Crope nodded vigorously. "Yes, master. Beautiful ladies—a whole street of them."

"And did Traff spot you following him?"

"No, master, but he might have heard the lady shoo me away."

"What lady?"

"The lady with no front teeth. She spotted me outside the house and told me to . . ." Crope searched for the exact words ". . . bugger off back to the cave that I'd come from."

Baralis waved his hands. "Enough. Go now." He waited until his servant had lurched out of the room and then took a deep breath. Crope had just found someone who could turn out to be very useful. Very useful, indeed.

The painkilling drug, which he had been about to take when Crope returned, lay ready on his desk. Baralis picked up the vial and threw it on the fire. It burned with a pure white light. He wouldn't have need for it now.

A soft knock came at his door. He knew who it was before the last rap sounded. Flinging back the door, he said, "Catherine, I warned you not to come here." His voice was not gentle. He checked to either side of the passageway before letting her inside his chamber.

She noticed his precautions. "I am not a fool, Lord Baralis," she said. "Do you think I would come here without checking to see if I was followed first?" The color of her cheeks was high. She had been drinking.

Closing the door, Baralis crossed over to his desk and poured her a glass of wine. It suited him to have her drink a little more. He handed her the glass. As he did so, he traced the line of her wrist with his fingers. Making his voice as rich and seductive as the wine he had just poured, he said, "Forgive me for speaking so sharply, my sweet Catherine. I was worried for you, nothing more."

He could see her deciding how to react to his words. Her pink lips trembled, then softened. "Would that my father showed me similar consideration."

Baralis' smile was tender. She was nothing but a child playing a grown-up game. Catching hold of her hand, he led her to the bed and bid her sit. As she settled herself down, he reached out and touched her golden hair. A calculated gesture, nothing more. "Drink up, my sweet Catherine," he said softly. "And then tell me why you have come."

The wine was still wet upon her tongue as she said, "Father is marrying that woman in secret. Two days from now."

"He told you this?" Baralis did not allow himself as much as a flicker of surprise.

"Yes. He wants me to stand by his bride's side at the ceremony. He hopes that we can become friends." Catherine's voice became shrill.

"Friends! How dare he? After taking the very birthright from under me, he expects me to be friends with the woman who is responsible for it."

Baralis barely heard what Catherine said. His mind was racing ahead. The deed would have to be done sooner than he thought. As soon as possible. The duke had to be murdered. Kylock must have Bren. For decades he had planned, and nothing, not now, not ever, would be allowed to stand in his way. The north would be his.

Crossing the room, Baralis went and stood by the fire. Once he had warmed himself enough, he spun around to face Catherine. "What is the best way to get to your father?"

Catherine hesitated for a second. "There is a secret passageway leading up to his chambers from the servants' chapel. There is only one guard set to watch it. Father uses it to smuggle low-born women into his bedroom. The entrance is behind the middle panel at the back of the altar."

Baralis missed neither the hesitation, nor its meaning: Catherine was not as reckless about this as she was pretending to be. There was still a part of her that owed loyalty to her father. Baralis realized he would have to change his approach. He could not run the risk of Catherine doing something irrational—like running to the duke. She was dangerously unstable—last night had proven that: as the guards were leading her from the table, she had actually attempted a drawing. There, in the great hall, with all of Bren's court looking on, Catherine had tried to use sorcery against Melliandra. He had blocked her, of course. The foolish girl had no idea of self-restraint. If she had been caught using sorcery, her father would have had no choice but to disinherit her on the spot. Sorcery was not tolerated in the north.

Yes, thought Baralis, he would have to be careful what he said to Catherine. The girl could not be relied upon.

"It is not your father who I am interested in, it is his wife. Once they are wed, Melliandra will not leave his side. The duke's weak points will become hers."

"I want that woman dead." There was no hesitation in Catherine's voice now. "Her and her precious protector, the duke's champion."

Baralis came and sat beside her. He took her hand in his. "Have no fear, my sweet Catherine, I will take care of both of them for you."

"And my father?"

"I have no quarrel with him," lied Baralis. "He will be left well alone."

Relief flashed across Catherine's face. She worked quickly to conceal it. "Once that woman is out of the way, Father will come to his senses."

She was wrong, very wrong. If only Melliandra were murdered, the duke could go on and wed another woman, have another child, and Catherine's inheritance would be threatened once more. Baralis could not allow that to happen. What was Catherine's would soon be Kylock's. And what was Kylock's was *his*.

"Go now, my sweet Catherine. I will arrange everything." He pulled her up off the bed. "You need not concern yourself with the details."

"Will you do the deed yourself?" she asked as he guided her toward the door.

"No. I have someone in mind who will do it for me." Baralis rested his hand on the door latch. A certain mercenary named Traff would do the deed.

"And will you use the secret passage?"

Baralis brought his finger to his lips. Catherine was asking too many questions. Opening the door, he checked that no one was in sight. Just before he let her go, he placed a kiss upon her lips. Catherine leaned forward to meet him. He pulled away before the kiss had a chance to become anything further. "Trust me," he whispered, just before he closed the door.

Thirty-four

Jack was dreaming about Melli again. Somehow she had stolen into his old recurring dream about the city with high battlements. She was trapped behind the walls, unable to escape. In the distance he heard a noise: a shouting, angry mob. Only when the noise grew louder did he realize it was not part of his dream. He opened his eyes. He was in a small store-room that had been hastily adapted for sleep. There were no windows, so it was dark. Panicking slightly, Jack stood up. His head brushed against something—drying herbs from the smell of them. Back bent to avoid them, he made his way toward the door.

Stillfox was leaning out of a window. As soon as heard Jack enter the room, he drew back the shutters. "Gave me quite a shock there, lad," he said, patting the area of his chest where his heart lay.

"I'm sorry. I came to find out what the noise was."

"Helch has just surrendered to Kylock. He gave them little choice. He burned the entire city. Only the castle remains intact. All of Annis is up in arms about it. People have taken to the streets in protest. . . ."

Stillfox carried on, but Jack was no longer listening. He stood very still as the world went black around him. This time he didn't fight it. Kylock had taken Helch. The war had just begun.

Baralis glided through the streets of Bren, his feet barely touching the filth. It was early morning, and the rising sun cast his shadow long before him. As he approached Brotheling Street, he slowed his pace. He spied an old man rummaging amidst the refuse in an open drain. He would do.

"You," he said, approaching the man. "Which of these brothels is kept by a woman with no front teeth?" To ensure his question was answered promptly, Baralis drew the slightest of compulsions around his words. Time was of the essence today.

The old man opened a mouth ringed with sores. "Madame Thornypurse has a sister with no front teeth. Her place is the red-shuttered building to the left." The man looked confused, as if he barely comprehended what he was saying, or why.

Baralis inclined his head to the man. He contemplated throwing him a coin in payment, then thought better of it. Why waste money paying for something that had already been freely given? He turned on his heel and headed toward the building which the old man had described.

He knocked loudly upon the door. A few moments later a woman answered. Seeing him, the ridiculous creature made a great show of primping her hair and smoothing down her dress. "Yes, handsome sir, can I help you?"

She had all her teeth, though crooked and yellow as they were, they did her no favors. "Who am I speaking to?" he demanded.

The woman curtsied like a blushing maiden. "Madame Thornypurse, proprietor of this fine establishment."

"Have you a man named Traff staying here?" Baralis caught the unmistakable odor of dead rats in his nostrils.

The woman's hand fluttered to her chest. She was just about to speak when a second woman pushed her aside.

"We never divulge the names of our customers," she said. It was the woman with no front teeth.

Baralis, recognizing an opening for bribery, pulled a gold coin from his cloak. "I have important business to discuss with Traff," he said, pressing the cool coin into the waiting palm of the woman with no front teeth.

"Come inside, noble sir," she said. "I will bring Traff to you."

He was led into a large, untidy room where several young girls lay sleeping on the floor. "Do you have anywhere less public where we can talk?"

"Of course," said the woman who smelled of dead rats.

"Though it will cost you extra," added the woman with no front teeth.

Another gold coin changed hands and Baralis was ushered into a small, dimly lit room near the back of the building. There was one window in the room and the shutter was firmly closed.

The door opened and in walked Traff. The mercenary made a point of chewing on his snatch for a moment before spitting it out and speaking. "What do you want, Baralis?" He pulled his hand knife from his belt and began to clean the dirt from under his nails with the blade.

Baralis regarded the mercenary coolly. Traff did not look in a good way. His hair was greasy, his clothes were dirty, and he now boasted a short beard. Flakes of snatch nestled within the bristles. The dirt he cleaned from his fingertips was the color of dried blood. "Been in a fight?"

Traff looked up. "None that I've lost."

The mercenary was as insolent as ever. Baralis decided to get straight to the point. "Have you heard that the duke is to marry Maybor's daughter?"

Traff flung his knife across the room. It flew past Baralis and landed embedded in the wall. *"No one will marry Melli,"* he said.

Baralis had a defensive drawing ready upon his lips, but on hearing Traff's words he breathed it back into his lungs. He didn't know what caused the mercenary's anger, but he could use it. "My thoughts exactly, my friend," murmured Baralis. "I don't want Melliandra wed, either."

"Why?" Traff was suddenly more interested.

"Because I want Bren to remain Catherine's. If Melliandra weds the duke and then gives birth to a male child, Catherine will no longer inherit her father's title." The truth suited Baralis for the moment.

"What are you planning to do?"

"I plan to murder the duke." Baralis took a guess at Traff's motives. "As for Melliandra, you can do what you want with her."

Traff licked his lips. "How do you plan to do this?"

Baralis permitted himself a tiny smile of self-congratulation. It seemed as if he'd guessed right: Traff was enamored of Maybor's daughter. It had probably happened when the mercenary had been sent out to capture her. Baralis began to feel more confident. Fate was once again on his side.

He took a short breath and looked Traff straight in the eye. "I want you to help me. The wedding will take place in private tomorrow. When the couple returns to their chambers after the ceremony, I want you and your knife to pay them a visit. I know of a secret passageway leading from the servants' chapel to the duke's quarters. You will use that to gain entry." Baralis paused briefly as he reshaped his plans to meet with Traff's needs. The mercenary wanted Melliandra for his own. So, if Traff was going to run away with her, then the newly wed couple must not—under any circumstances—be allowed to consummate the marriage. Baralis could not risk Melliandra popping up a few months later, claiming to be carrying the duke's child. "You must be waiting for them the moment they return from the chapel."

Traff gave Baralis a long, hard look. "How do I know I can trust you?"

"You can't. The only thing you can be certain of is that I will be waiting by the entrance to the passageway to make sure you have done the job. From the kitchens, it will be easy for you and Melliandra to make your escape. I will make all the necessary arrangements." Baralis stepped forward and rested his hand on Traff's arm. "I won't ask what you want with the girl. That's not my concern."

Traff drew back from the touch. "Will there be any guards in the duke's chamber?"

"Just one. I will make sure he receives a little something in his ale to slow him down." Poisoning guards was easy: no one tasted their food.

"I want five hundred golds in my possession by the end of the day."

"Done." Baralis moved toward the door. "Crope will see to it. Be waiting on the east side of the palace, close to the servants' entrance tomorrow at sundown. I will come for you." Just as he was about to leave, Traff surprised him by asking:

"Is Melli in love with the duke?"

Baralis recognized the glint of obsession in the mercenary's eye. He was not displeased. "No. Her father is forcing her into it."

As he had hoped, Traff was pleased with the answer. The mercenary smiled thinly. "I guessed as much. I will be there tomorrow."

"Good. Do not be late." Baralis turned and left the room. The woman who smelled of dead rats rushed to greet him, but he shook her off. He found his own way out.

Baralis was in a good mood as he traveled back to the palace. The meeting with Traff had gone better than he could possibly have imagined. The fact that the mercenary was infatuated with Maybor's daughter made everything easy. Traff had jumped at the chance to murder the duke. Events were moving in his favor once more. Picking up his pace, Baralis rushed across the city. He had much to do today; there was gold to be procured, poison to be made, and guards to be reminded of their obligations.

Mistress Greal was shin-deep in sewage. She barely smelled it. She was busy extracting a large splinter from her cheek. With her good hand, she gripped at the wooden tip and then pulled as hard as she could. The pain was excruciating. The splinter had gone deep, and as it came out, it brought blood welling to the surface. Mistress Greal counted herself quite fortunate; a finger's breadth higher and it could have been her eye. She made no attempt to stop the bleeding. What was a little blood compared to what she had just heard?

Pressing her ear against a certain wood shutter had been the cause of her injury. Curiosity was what brought her outside in the first place.

As soon as the dark nobleman came to the door, she knew he was from the Four Kingdoms. When he asked to see the mercenary, her interest was piqued. While her sister went off to fetch Traff, Mistress Greal made her way outside. She waded through the filth at the side of the building to the back wall. Once there she positioned herself close to the window and listened to the conversation between man and mercenary. Her surprise at finding out that the mysterious nobleman was none other than Lord Baralis, king's chancellor, was quickly overwhelmed by the greater surprise of hearing what he planned to do.

Mistress Greal had been listening at doors, windows, walls, floorboards, and screens all her life. It was amazing what a poor spinster woman could pick up if she had sharp ears and a good nose for intrigue. Mistress Greal had both. As a matter of habit, she routinely eavesdropped on her girls, her customers, her rivals, and most recently her sister, Madame Thornypurse. She'd heard casual gossip, lots of petty arguments, more than a few useful business tips, and many unpleasant remarks about herself. But never once in all the years she'd spent pointing her batlike ears where they had not been invited had she come across anything to match the scale of what she'd just heard.

A plot to assassinate the duke of Bren! It was a blackmailer's dream. Mistress Greal stood amidst the warm and stinking sewage and contemplated what to do next. Should she act now and prevent the murder from going ahead? Or should she bide her time until the deed was done and only then make her move? Raising her hand to her face, Mistress Greal rubbed a finger across her lips. She felt the all too familiar concavity that marked the absence of teeth. Teeth that had been knocked out by Lord Maybor. The very man who was father of the bride.

Mistress Greal's small eyes narrowed to slits. She would let the murder go ahead. Lord Maybor would suffer more that way; he would lose both his daughter, and his chance to be related by marriage to the duke. Yes, she would keep her little secret until the harm had been done. Not only was there more satisfaction to be gained that way, but also more money: everyone knew it was more profitable to be a blackmailer than an informant. Feeling rather pleased with herself, Mistress Greal headed back toward the brothel, wading slowly through the filth.

"There, boy," said Stillfox, handing him a peculiar wooden cup. "Drink some of the lacus; it will help to bring you round."

Jack's world gradually began to expand outward once more. His field of vision, which upon hearing that Helch had surrendered to Kylock had narrowed to a darkened pinpoint, now enlarged enough for him to see the cup and the hand that held it. The drink's strong but fragrant odor seemed to act like a charm, dispelling the reek of slowly decaying corpses from his nostrils and his thoughts.

He had been there! To the Halcus capital. He had stood amidst the carnage that Kylock had created. There, and so many other places, whether in the future or the past, he did not know. He had seen the truth of war. It was not the sum of glorious fights and flashing blades and men bound by honor. It was bloody, dirty, and disorganized. Flies, fever, infection, mud, tainted water, and starvation. Victory came to the most ruthless, not the bravest. Jack had seen the bodies of young children, their mothers raped and mutilated by their sides; he had seen young men bleeding to death from the groin, their manhood and testicles hacked off; he had seen old women wandering aimlessly through a city whose streets were red with blood. Jack had seen enough to know that Kylock was the most ruthless of all.

Yet what difference did it make to him? He had no part in anything.

Feeling weary and confused, Jack brought the cup to his lips. The silvery fluid reached out to meet his tongue. It tasted sharp and pungent, strange and yet familiar in one. He felt its progress as it slipped down his throat and nudged itself into his belly. Once there it grew heavy like a many-course feast.

"Don't fight it, Jack," said Stillfox. "It wants to make you sleep."

"Why?"

"The lacus likes to work on a slumbering body and a still mind." Stillfox ran his hand over his cleanly shaven chin. His expression was serious. "Drink up lad, you are very weak."

Jack drained the cup dry. There was something about the liquid that caused it to tingle against his gums. It left a metallic aftertaste in his mouth. "Is there sorcery within the drink?" he asked.

Stillfox nodded, a faint smile gracing his pale lips. "Not my doing, though. We have the nomads of the Great Plains to thank for that." He stood up and began to busy himself about the cottage, hanging herbs and putting pots on to boil.

Jack yawned. He could still hear the sound of shouting from outside. "How long was I . . ."

"Entranced?" Stillfox looked up; he was pulverizing bark with a pestle. "For the best part of an hour, I would say. You completely withdrew into yourself. Your eyes were open, but they were not seeing what was before them. Your skin became cold and the color left your cheeks. You were no longer in my home." The man who was almost, but not quite, old gave Jack a questioning look.

Jack wondered how much to tell him. Who was he? Could he trust him? Since arriving in the herbalist's cottage the day before, Stillfox had said very little. He had been too busy to talk: tending wounds, making medicines, cooking food, and seeing to his herbs. Jack appreciated the silence. Stillfox had asked no questions, and he was grateful for that. Normally Jack would have trusted the man completely, judging his intentions by the kindness of his actions. Things were different now. His time at Rovas' cottage had taught him that appearances could be deceptive, and that even a smiling face could be a treacherous one.

"What did you mean when you said you recognized one of your own?" As Jack spoke, he realized how tired he was feeling. The lacus nestled in his belly, slowing his blood and thickening his thoughts. He fought against it, in defiance of Stillfox's advice.

"I am a sorcerer like you," said Stillfox.

Jack had quickly learned that the herbalist had two voices: a lilting country voice which he spoke with most of the time, and a strong plainspeaking voice which he only used when the conversation took a serious turn. It was the second voice he spoke with now.

"I am a modest practitioner. Occasionally I enhance the healing properties of my herbs, but not often. Sometimes I communicate with wisemen far away, and once in a while I am forced to draw in self-defense." Stillfox shrugged. "I am not a powerful man like you."

Jack felt the quick flare of anger. "I'm not powerful, and I'm not a sorcerer." He squeezed the wooden cup between his hands, determined to ruin its perfect smoothness.

"Don't make a liar of yourself, Jack. You know I speak the truth." Stillfox's voice had a matching edge of anger. "The longer you insist on denying what you are, the more damage you will do. Look what happened at the garrison. You were out of control. You didn't have the slightest idea how to stop what you started. Sheer desperation—nothing more—put an end to the destruction." The herbalist was trembling. "You're dangerous and it's time you learned how to control yourself."

Jack felt the cup break in his hand. "What makes you think you know so much?"

"I felt it. I felt the blind unfocused rage. I felt wave after ceaseless wave of drawing." Stillfox's hand was up and pointing. "Don't flatter yourself, Jack. You might be strong, but you have no skill whatsoever. What you did at the garrison was unforgivable. You let your emotions form the drawing: the most foolish thing any sorcerer could do. You acted like a spoiled child—making others pay for your pain. Your power is matched only by your ignorance.

"And that's why I brought you here, Jack. Not because I'm in the habit of helping road-weary travelers, but because you're a danger to those around you, and it's about time someone took you in hand."

Jack was aware that Stillfox was looking at him, but he couldn't meet the herbalist's eyes. He looked down at the broken cup instead. He was no longer angry; he was ashamed. Everything Stillfox had said was true.

"I never meant to hurt anyone."

Stillfox was beside him in an instant, his arm coming to rest on Jack's shoulder. "I know, lad. I know." The herbalist's voice was soft and lilting once more. "I'm sorry I spoke harshly—"

"No, don't be," said Jack. "I deserved it. You're right, I am dangerous." He let the pieces of cup fall to the floor. It was time to place his trust in someone. He took a deep breath. "I need help. I don't know what's happening to me, or why I've got these powers. I feel as if I'm supposed to do something, only I don't know what it is."

Stillfox nodded gently. "What did you see before?"

"I saw Helch as clearly as if I were there. The blood, the flies, the bodies." Jack shuddered, remembering. "It was like a warning."

"And has anything like this happened before?"

"Yes. There have been other times in the past few months." Jack made a small, helpless gesture with his hand. "Whenever the war is mentioned, my stomach knots up, and I get an overwhelming urge to take off and be part of it."

"To go to Helch?"

"No. To Bren." Jack met Stillfox's gaze. "I think I've known all along that Kylock would win the war with the Halcus."

"He hasn't won yet," said Stillfox. "The capital may have fallen, but all of eastern Halcus is free. It could take Kylock weeks, even months, before the entire country surrenders."

"What happens when it does?" Jack thought he already knew the answer, yet he wanted to hear it from Stillfox, from a man who lived in Annis.

"The north will turn into a battlefield. No one will be willing to stand around and watch Kylock build himself an empire. The fact that he's made it to Helch has caught everyone by surprise. It's nothing short of miraculous, and Highwall and Annis are both terrified that they could become victims of a similar miracle." Stillfox was back pounding at the bark with his pestle. "Kylock will soon have Bren on one side of the mountains and Halcus on the other. And it won't be long before he turns his gaze on the powers in between."

"How soon will this happen?" asked Jack.

"I can't say. It depends on Kylock. Annis and Highwall are waiting to see what he'll do next."

Jack suddenly felt very tired. The lacus was reasserting itself. He stifled a yawn. It wouldn't be long now before he fell asleep. "What has all this to do with me, though? I'm from the kingdoms. I should be glad that Kylock looks set to forge an empire."

"I think you already know the answer to that, Jack," said Stillfox softly. "You have a part to play in what is to come."

"But why—"

"It doesn't matter why. That's not important. It's *how* that counts. What happened at the garrison proves that you are somehow involved in the war. Without knowing it you actually aided Kylock's cause." Stillfox spoke quickly and in earnest. "What you need to do now is gain some measure of control over your powers so that nothing like that happens again. Next time you form a drawing you should know exactly what you're doing, and what the consequences are going to be. I can't tell you what your role will be—that's for you to find out on your own—but I *can* prevent you from making further mistakes. You need to be taught how to master what you have inside. That much I can do."

Jack looked into Stillfox's blue eyes. "Why would you do this for me?"

"Perhaps I, too, have a role. Perhaps I am meant to teach you."

"No, Bodger, if you want to get a girl randy, you don't give her oysters."

"Why not, Grift?"

"Because you can never be too sure with oysters, Bodger. They're more likely to give a wench a nasty rash around the vitals than get her feeling randy."

"Really, Grift?"

"Aye, Bodger. That's if she doesn't choke on 'em first."

"What food does get the women going, then, Grift?"

"Bread pudding, Bodger."

"Bread pudding, Grift?"

"Aye, Bodger. The strongest aphrodisiac known to man. There's not a wench alive who won't be willing to lie flat on her back after two servings of good and thick bread pudding. It takes the fight right out of a girl."

"So it doesn't exactly make a wench randy, then, Grift. It just sort of wears them out."

"Exactly, Bodger. That's the best a man like you can hope for." Grift took a swig of his ale. "Mind they don't eat it with sauce, though."

"Why's that, Grift?"

"Sauce makes wenches uppity, Bodger. Start demanding satisfaction, they do."

"Ah, gentlemen, as talkative as ever, I see."

Bodger and Grift both swung around at the sound of the smooth, mocking voice.

Baralis was standing by the entrance to the chapel. He had managed to open the door and step inside without being heard. "You are alone?" he asked as he closed the door.

Grift nodded. "Aye, sir." By his foot lay an empty jug of ale, and he silently nudged it under the pew. He didn't want Baralis knowing how much they had been drinking

"Good. Then I will get straight to the point. You do recall that you owe me a debt of gratitude?" Baralis didn't wait for a reply. "I could have had both of you whipped for the insolence of your tongues." A tiny smile graced his lips. "And still could, if I chose."

"We're most sorry about what we said on the journey here, Lord Baralis," said Bodger. "We meant no offense."

Grift placed a silencing hand on Bodger's arm. *He* would deal with this. "What do you want from us, Lord Baralis?" The man was not after apologies. He had come to strike a deal.

Baralis approached the two guards. He lifted his nose up and sniffed at the air. "Ale to wash down the gossip, eh?"

"Just half a jug—"

Grift stopped Bodger in midsentence by a swift kick to the shin.

"What's it to you?" he asked, meeting Baralis' eye.

"Nothing at all." Baralis was so close now that Grift had to physically stop himself from moving back. Bodger had already done so and was now pinned against the back of the pew. "In fact," continued Baralis, "I hope you will be drinking tomorrow evening. I'll even send you the jugs myself—only the best, of course."

"Why would we want to drink tomorrow?" asked Grift. He was beginning to feel very wary.

"Because when you are drinking on the other side of the chapel doors, you will miss the passage of one man through them."

"Who is this man?"

Baralis' hand came up. "Ask no questions, my friend. Just do as I say." His voice was smooth, tempting. "Let the man pass and I will consider your debt repaid."

Grift knew he had little choice but to do as Baralis asked. The man could have them thrown out of the guard, whipped, tortured, poisoned, or worse. He cursed the day the king's chancellor had overheard them speaking. To be indebted to Baralis was the same as being indebted to the devil—both would take a man's soul given half a chance.

"You leave us little choice, Lord Baralis," he said.

"I see you're a sensible man. I trust your young companion there will also be sensible." He motioned toward Bodger.

"Bodger will do as I say."

"Good." Baralis brought his hands together. "Remember, not a word of this to anyone." He began to walk down the aisle.

Grift spoke up. "Will this man you speak of be coming through again?"

Baralis wheeled around. "Yes." He stood and considered for a moment. The expression on his face turned from thoughtfulness to pure cunning. "Raise the alarm when he does. I don't want him leaving the palace alive."

Thirty-five

N_o, Nessa," snapped Melli. "Not so tight. I won't be able to breathe, let alone walk up the aisle." She knew she was being a little harsh on the girl, but she was nervous. "Hand me the cup of wine." The servant dashed off to do her bidding. A moment later Melli heard footsteps behind her.

"My lady's wine." It was Tawl who held forth the cup, not Nessa.

Melli deliberately hid her pleasure at seeing him. "Where's Nessa?" she said, snatching the cup from him.

"She's slipped out for a moment. I think you wore her down." Tawl's voice was gently mocking. "You will make a beautiful bride, but hardly a serene one."

"I look beautiful?"

"Breathtaking."

Melli had to look away. There was too much truth in Tawl's eyes. "Will you be attending the wedding?" she asked, raising the cup to her lips.

"Yes. I will be escorting you and your husband back to your chambers."

Husband. Melli flinched at the word; she couldn't stop herself. Everything was happening so fast. Too fast. She felt as if she were caught up in something that she was now powerless to stop. It was as if the marriage had become a separate entity; it was a force unto itself, and its momentum was so great that it carried her along with it. Melli had been genuinely shocked when the duke had proposed such a quick marriage. She had been hoping for at least a few weeks warning, but it wasn't to be. The duke had insisted on marrying her today—in secret.

"Open the shutters," she said to Tawl. "Let me see what my wedding day promises."

Tawl, always so quick to do her bidding, was by the window in an instant. He pulled back the shutters to reveal a beautiful blue sky. Melli came and stood by him. The outside air was warm against her face. The great lake was as smooth as glass. "A perfect day," she murmured. Her hand felt for Tawl's. It was waiting for her.

The door opened and in strode her father. Tawl and Melli quickly pulled apart. Maybor was dressed in full splendor. Wearing the family colors of red and gold, he was bedecked from head to foot in rubies and silk. Even his shoes bore two matching stones. "Melliandra," he said, "you look beautiful. Beautiful."

She, too, wore red. A heavy satin dress of deepest crimson with a fortune's worth of pearls sewn upon the skirt. She had developed an almost superstitious dislike for the color, but she wasn't wearing it for herself. She wore it to honor her father. She stepped forward to meet him. Maybor caught her up in a huge bear hug. His smell was so familiar: expensive fragrances and lobanfern red. She felt like a child again.

Placing Melli down on the floor before him, Maybor said, "I am very proud this day, my daughter."

"Even though I'm not marrying a king?" There was so much more gray in his hair now, thought Melli. How much of it was she responsible for?

He took her hand and raised it to his lips. "You have made your own choice, and I'll tell you now: 'tis a better one than I made for you." It was her father's way of saying he was sorry.

"You should have known I would pick no pauper." She forced herself to smile. It was neither the time nor the place for tears.

"I am glad I am here today," said Maybor gently.

Melli nodded. She was glad, too. Her father's presence was a blessing; she drew strength from his nearness. After Catherine's outburst on the night of the wedding announcement, the only thing that had kept Melli sitting at the table was Maybor. He held her hand all night. She had wanted to run away from the accusations and the hostile stares of the court. Yet she couldn't let her father down. The great dignity he demonstrated that night had moved her deeply, and she had been determined to follow his example. People might have left that night shaking their heads over Catherine's behavior, but no one could find fault with Maybor and his daughter.

Melli would cherish the memory of her father's welcome to the end of her days. She had gone through her life thinking that Maybor did not love her, that he cared only for his sons, and that she was nothing but a possession to him. The Feast of First Sowing had shown her how wrong she had been. Oh, she was not stupid; of course he was thrilled that she was marrying the most powerful man in the north—things could not have worked out better from his point of view—but wealth and titles hadn't been on his mind when he leapt up to meet her that night. It had been love that was the strength behind those three mighty leaps. She was sure of it.

"Are you ready, my daughter?" Maybor offered her his arm.

Was it time already? Everything was moving so quickly. Since returning from the hunting lodge, she had hardly had time to catch her breath. Melli looked quickly toward Tawl, and then back to her father. If she were to back out now she would be failing both of them. She took Maybor's arm.

Nessa came back into the room and made the final adjustments to her dress. Melli smiled tenderly at her father, who kept patting her arm as if he still couldn't believe she was real. Tawl hadn't moved from the window. She didn't need to look at him to know that he was watching her.

When Nessa backed away, her task complete, Melli began to walk toward the door. Maybor pulled against her arm, halting her. Slipping his hand into his tunic, he pulled out a diamond and ruby necklace. Melli recognized it straightaway. It was her mother's: a wedding gift from Maybor to his new bride. The rubies were the size of cherries, and diamonds surrounded them like petals round a bud. "I brought it as a gift for Catherine," said Maybor. "But when it came time to give it to her, I found I could not do it. The necklace was always meant for you." With large, red hands that wouldn't stop shaking, Maybor fastened the necklace about Melli's neck.

"Let us go now, daughter," he said, smoothing her hair back in place. Melli nodded, unable to speak. Father and daughter walked toward the door. Somehow Tawl was in front of them now, opening the door, then placing a plain woolen cloak over Melli's shoulders. She caught his eye as she left the room. Perhaps Tawl would not have been disappointed if she had backed out of the wedding, after all.

"Tell me about your family, Jack," Stillfox requested.

Jack felt a quick flare of anger at the casual inquiry. He hated people asking about his family. And he hated himself for feeling ashamed. "Why do you need to know anything about my family?" he said. "I would never ask about yours."

Stillfox's eyebrows went up. "I didn't ask for curiosity's sake, Jack. I asked because I want to find out more about your powers: where they came from, if you inherited them from your father or mother."

They were sitting in Stillfox's cottage, close to the fire. It was a small place and boasted only two rooms: the kitchen and the storeroom.

Every shelf in the kitchen was crowded with jars and baskets containing herbs and spices. Sprigs of thyme and mistletoe hung from the rafters, drying slowly in the heat from the fire. Bowls of mushrooms and toadstools rested on the mantel, their pungent odors telling of various stages of decay. There was rosemary pickled in vinegar and sage pickled in brine. There were so many different plants and spices on show that Jack couldn't even begin to guess at the names of most of them. He might have been brought up in a kitchen, but he had never seen a selection as great as this.

"Do you get your powers from the herbs?" he asked, attempting to change the subject.

Stillfox shook his head. "No, lad. Certain herbs can enhance a man's powers, but they can't give him what he was not born with."

"So sorcery is passed down in the blood?" As Jack spoke he thought of his mother. It had been so long since she was last on his mind.

"Sorcery can come from three sources, Jack. Most commonly it is passed from parent to child, from generation to generation. Mostly, as time goes on, the amount of power lessens over time, so a mother with ability will usually give birth to a child with less power than herself. Of course there are exceptions, and if two people with sorcery in their blood join together and have a child, then that child might have greater ability than both of its parents." Stillfox made a sweeping gesture with his arm. "But nothing is certain.

"The second way a person can receive sorcery's gifts is at the exact moment of conception. On certain rare nights the air becomes heavy with fate and prophesy, and sorcery itself speeds the sending of the seed." The herbalist made a soft clicking sound in the back of his throat. "A child begot at such a time may be powerful indeed."

Without meeting Jack's eyes, he turned to the fire and basted the joint. It was a side of lamb that had been rubbed with mint and pepper. Fragrant cooking smells rose from the hearth like smoke.

Jack barely noticed the smell of the meat. He was trying to recall if his mother had ever done anything in his presence that might have been magical. All his memories brought him was guilt. He had been so careless, never listening, never watching, always taking her for granted. Except toward the end, when it had been too late. No, she had done nothing magical, but could he honestly say he would have noticed if she did?

"What is the third way a man can acquire sorcery?" he asked.

Stillfox was turning the spit. The joint was still browning and drops of fat fell sizzling to the flames. "There are some places where sorcery is in the earth itself. I don't claim to know much about such things—their time has long since passed—but there is one place I know of that still exists. An island where the rock, the soil, and even the sea that surrounds it is held in sorcery's thrall. It's the isle of Larn, where the seers are made.

"I don't know how the land became the way it is. Perhaps it was enchanted by a great sorcerer thousands of years ago, perhaps it has always been that way. I do not know. Its power continues on, though, that I know for sure." Stillfox's gaze shifted from Jack to the flames. The fat sizzled and flared, sending black smoke up the chimney with the gray.

When Stillfox spoke again, his voice was almost a whisper. The country lilt was heavy on his tongue. "I heard a tale about a girl who came from Larn once. Her mother was a servant to the priests. The powers that be on the island have ever been wary of feminine temptations and so only allow women who are disfigured at birth to serve them. Not only do they pay a cheap price for such girls, but they also eliminate the chance of one of their priests going astray. These girls are so horribly misshapen that no man would ever look at them.

"Still one man did. For the girl in the tale was born on the island. Her mother had either been raped or seduced by a priest. The baby girl she gave birth to grew up on Larn. Her developing body acted like a sponge, soaking up the magic of the isle, concentrating it in her blood and her tissue and her bone. Sorcery became part of her very soul.

"The magic of the island is what gives the seers their sight. The great hall of seeing is alive with sorcery; it runs through the rock like seams of crystal. It is said to be so powerful that the cavern actually glows with the force of it." Stillfox shook his head slowly. " 'Tis a sight I would love to see."

Jack shuddered. He never wanted to see such a place. "What happened to the girl?"

"She made the mistake of feeling pity for the seers. Each man is bound to a stone until the end of his days. They are tied for two reasons. First, to focus their minds, the seers are roped so tightly that they cannot move. All they can do is think and foretell. To escape their physical torment, they retreat to a world of delusion and insanity, and it is from there they catch glimpses of the future.

"Secondly, the very stone they are bound to gives them their power. It becomes theirs and theirs alone. A slice of the island bound to their backs. The sorcery is skin close: it creates the seers, drives them to madness, and then ultimately destroys them. The stone is their womb, their cradle, and their grave."

Hiss. More fat on the fire.

"No wonder the girl felt pity for them." Even though he was chilled to the bone, Jack drew his chair away from the hearth. The smell of cooking meat was making him feel sick.

"The girl would steal into the cavern and tend to the seers. She became friendly with one boy. Newly bound he was, barely old enough to be counted a man. She watched him slowly deteriorate, saw the rope bite against his flesh, saw the bleeding, the sores, the unbearable cramping of muscle. She watched it all with the eyes of a girl in love for the first time. She couldn't bear it. One day she went down to him and saw that the rope was no longer cutting through his flesh: it was part of it. Nestling underneath the skin, blood vessels had started to form around the rope as if it were bone. The sight of it drove the girl wild. She had just reached womanhood and her powers were flourishing with her body. She lost control. Her anger was focused against the stones, the cavern, the priests. The great hall of seering shook with her power.

"Then the priests came for her. She fought against them, kicking and screaming. Toward the end of the struggle, when she was close to being overpowered, she swore a terrible oath that one day she would destroy Larn.

"The priests carried her, bound and bleeding, from the hall, a wad of wet cloth thrust down her throat to stop the sorcererous flow. Barely able to breathe, she passed out. When she came to she found herself in a small, darkened room. The smell of incense in the air told her she was marked for death. It was her mother—a woman so badly deformed that she could use no muscles on the right side of her face, nor lift her right arm—who saved her. With her help the girl was cast adrift on a small boat in the treacherous waters that surround the island."

Jack was sitting very still. He had not moved or blinked the whole time Stillfox was speaking. "What happened to the girl?" he asked.

Stillfox shrugged. "She must have reached dry land, else I would not be here telling her tale. I don't know what became of her, though. It was many, many years ago now. The girl is probably long dead, her oath long forgotten. Larn still exists; as powerful and as deadly as ever."

Abruptly Jack stood up. The herbalist's cottage seemed small and confining. The smell of the lamb was unbearable.

"Where are you going?" Stillfox was one step behind him.

"Outside. I need some fresh air."

"No. You might be spotted."

Jack shook his head. He would not be hindered. His need to be alone was so great that nothing else mattered. "I will be careful," he said as he stepped through the door.

The herbalist's cottage was on the outskirts of a small village, the last house on the street before the rye fields. Jack headed over the plowed fields, down toward a distant copse of trees. The air was warm and the sky was blue and the soil beneath his feet was dry. He walked for over an hour, deliberately not thinking, just looking straight ahead.

Eventually Jack reached his destination. Sweating and out of breath, he slipped under the cool shade of the trees. Flies buzzed past his face and birds called softly, warning each other of his presence. He found the perfect tree: an oak old beyond telling, its branches low and heavy, its trunk as wide as three men. Jack sat beneath it, his feet resting upon its huge raised roots, the small of his back upon the bark. He bent forward, bringing his head down toward his knees, and took a deep breath. When he let it out, his emotions came with it.

Tarissa, Melli, the garrison, his mother, and strangely enough, the story of the girl from Larn—it was all too much. He sobbed quietly, thinking of Tarissa kneeling on the ground at his feet, begging him to take her along. As the tears ran down his face, his thoughts turned to the guard who had fallen from the battlements at the garrison, and he remembered how hard the man had struggled to touch him. Then there was his mother, sick and close to death, yet refusing the help of the physicians. He would never understand why.

Crying was a relief. He had been carrying so much inside for so long, trying to be brave. Only he wasn't brave, he was scared—frightened of what the future held. Jack wiped his eyes dry. That the future did hold something for him was a fact he no longer doubted.

He and Kylock were connected in some way. Even the mention of the new king's name was enough to send him reeling. Jack looked toward the deepest part of the wood. Kylock was evil. Had the vision that had shown him that been designed to shape his fate? Was his purpose to oppose Kylock?

Abruptly Jack stood up. He felt restless, overwhelmed with the desire to be doing something, to take action. Striking a path for the fields, he headed back toward the herbalist's cottage. The sun broke out from behind the clouds the moment he cleared the trees. Its warmth was an unmistakable blessing. Jack walked quickly; he was eager to get started. Stillfox had offered to teach him and it was time to learn all he could.

"And in God's holy presence, with the blessing of our savior, his beloved servant Borc, I hereby command those brought here to witness to step forth with their misgivings." The archbishop of Bren, a tall man with a high nasal voice, swept the room with his glance. No one moved.

Out of the corner of his eye, Tawl saw Catherine's expression. Hate in its purest, most vivid form was clearly written on her face. The other people gathered for the ceremony did not look especially pleased—except, of course, for Maybor, who was beaming ear to ear like a fisherman with a big catch—yet none of them dared show anything except politely frozen smiles.

Melli and the duke stood side by side at the altar, both facing the archbishop. A gaggle of clergy formed a half-circle around the group of three, prayer books and holy water in their hands. On one side of the church no less than four scribes were scribing, busy scratching away at their parchments, recording every detail of the ceremony. Later, when it was finished, all the witnesses—about twenty in number—would be asked to sign and date each account. The duke was taking no chances. Neither was Tawl: outside the chapel an entire company of troops was patrolling both entrances. There would be no uninvited guests at this wedding.

In her dress of crimson, with matching rubies sparkling at her throat, Melli looked impossibly regal. Every eye was upon her. Soon she would be a duchess. Later, if the duke had his way, she would be a queen. Tawl found he couldn't listen to the ceremony; the vows and prayers sounded false to his ears. He chose not to explore why, fearing that his thoughts might lead him into disloyalty.

Instead he concentrated on the security arrangements. The greatest danger today was the journey from the chapel to the duke's chamber. Once there the newlyweds should be safe. The duke's chamber was patrolled day and night by two guards. Tawl had increased the number to eight. There was only one entrance, and the fact that it was on a lower level than the actual living quarters made the whole place more secure. He personally had seen to all the food and drink preparation. Even as he sat here, two food tasters were sampling every dish from the wedding feast. At his suggestion, the duke and Melli would eat alone in their chambers, where they would be safe from the hostile intent of Lord Baralis and the court.

Tawl couldn't foresee any problems tonight, but tomorrow, when the whole of the city learned of the marriage, and when the duke and his new bride began to perform official duties in public together, the real problems would start. Protecting Melli would be a nightmare then.

Turning his attention back to the ceremony, Tawl was just in time to hear the archbishop pronounce the couple man and wife. As the duke embraced Melli, a cold chill ran down Tawl's spine. He stood up. He had no desire to look upon the happy couple. While everyone else was busy with congratulations, he made his way to the rear of the chapel. He settled back against a wooden beam and waited until the time came to escort the newlyweds to their chambers.

"From here you go alone," hissed Baralis.

Traff was not pleased. "You said you would show me to the passage-way." He did not trust him.

"Take the turn at the end of the corridor. At the bottom you will find a pair of double doors. Two guards will be at either side of it. They will let you pass unchallenged." Baralis drew his hood over his eyes. He was dressed in a cloak that matched the color of his shadow. "I must be off now."

"I thought you would wait for my return." Traff could see that Baralis was nervous; the great man did not want to be seen here with him.

"I will be back later." Baralis' voice was sharp. He kept looking from side to side. "I told you I will be waiting for you. You have my word on it. Now go."

Traff did not move. He was not about to be ordered around like a common servant. Besides, Baralis was lying: he would not wait for him.

"Stand there waiting any longer, my friend," said Baralis, becoming angry, "and the good duke will have broken in his new bride. Then dearest sweet Melliandra will be nothing more than used goods." Baralis drew closer. "Or is that the best a man like you can hope for?"

Traff went to strike him. His arm was stopped in mid-swing. He looked at Baralis; the man was smiling softly and shaking his head. "Come, come now, Traff," he said. "You should know better than to try and hurt me."

Struggling against the compulsion, Traff tried to move his arm. His muscles would not respond. The faint but unmistakable smell of hot metal filled the air. Then suddenly it was gone. His arm dropped down to his side; it felt heavy and sore.

Baralis turned the full force of his gaze upon him. "You know what to do. Now do it."

This time Traff moved. He turned and began to walk down the corridor. He did not look back. The muscle in his lower arm was cramping slightly, but he ignored it. He was used to pain. It was sorcery he couldn't deal with.

The passage curved around and a few seconds later he saw the double doors and the two guards. Both men were busy drinking. As soon as they spotted him, they got even busier, burying their faces in their cups, whilst turning away from the light. Traff fancied they looked familiar. He ignored them and opened one of the doors.

The mercenary found himself in a chapel. After sorcery, the thing Traff hated most was religion; he hated the scented candles, the long ceremonies, the self-satisfied priests. He reached in his tunic and brought out his snatch pouch. Pulling himself a fair portion, he slipped it between his lips. Even before it was soft, he spat a portion out. He felt a lot better after that; half the pleasure of snatch was the spitting. A man could say a lot with a spit. After a brief pause to grind the snatch into the chapel floor, Traff made his way behind the altar.

The middle panel, Baralis had said. He spoke the truth, for the panel swung to the side when Traff pressed on the left side of it. Looking inside the passageway, he hissed a curse. Like a fool, he hadn't realized it would be so dark. Grabbing one of the altar candles, Traff stepped into the passageway. Before he moved up the stairs, he pushed the panel back into place. As he did so, he tilted the candle and hot, fragrant wax fell on his forearm. This time he named Baralis in his curse: the wax had landed directly on the burn the man had given him many months ago in Castle Harvell. The skin was still tender and the memory still sharp. Traff shook his head grimly; he hated Baralis about as much as it was possible to hate a man. That wasn't important now; claiming Melli for his own was what counted. She was his, after all—her father had promised her to him. Only now it seemed that Lord Maybor had gone back on his word. Traff began to climb the stairs. Maybor, like Baralis, would have to be dealt with later.

The stairs spiraled upward toward the heart of the palace. With each step, Traff felt his excitement growing. Soon Melli would be his.

"I could have sworn that man was Traff, Bodger. What d'you think?"

"I think you're right, Grift. Looked a lot rougher than when I saw him last, though."

Grift shook his head. "This is trouble, Bodger. Real trouble. Traff is the sort who'd murder his own mother for a hundred golds."

"Best not ask any questions, Grift. Best not even talk about it."

Bodger was scared, thought Grift. He should have come here tonight on his own; there was no need for both of them to be outside the chapel. "Go down to the kitchens, Bodger. Grab yourself a bite of supper."

"No. I'm staying here with you, Grift. You don't know what will happen when Traff comes back."

"You're a good friend, Bodger." Grift looked at his companion for a moment. Bodger was too young to be involved in something like this, something that was going to end in disgrace either way. "You know what?"

"What Grift?"

"We're gonna be in trouble no matter what happens. If we stay here until Traff has done whatever he's supposed to, then raise the alarm, we'll be thrown out of the guard anyway. Everyone will say we were drunk on duty, and we'll have no choice but to go along with it."

"But what about Baralis, Grift? He's not a man you want to cross."

"What's Baralis up to, though, Bodger? Where does that tunnel lead?" Grift's voice was a whisper now. "What if it leads to the duke's chamber? We might as well slit our own throats here and now." Grift took a quick courage-giving swig of ale. "I say we take action, Bodger. We ain't got much to lose."

"What action, Grift?"

Grift thought for a long moment. "I say we run down to the kitchens, find young Nabber, tell him what's happened, and then let him fetch that tall blond warrior to deal with Traff."

"You mean the duke's champion, Grift?"

"Aye, Bodger, that's the one. Are you with me?"

"I'm with you, Grift."

Tawl was sitting in his room at the back of the kitchens. The wedding had gone according to plan. He had just escorted Melli and the duke safely back to their chambers. His intention had been to stand watch by the door all night, but with eight guards stationed there, it hardly seemed necessary. Besides, he didn't have the heart for it. Not tonight. He couldn't stand by the door to the duke's chambers and not think of what was going on inside: the wedding night, the wedding bed. No. Best to stay here and have a few quiet drinks on his own. And then perhaps a few more as the hours went by. There would be no sleep for him this night.

Just as he brought his ale to his lips, Nabber burst into the room.

"Tawl! Tawl," he cried. "Quickly. Follow me." The young pocket stood in the doorway, breath coming fast and furious. He had been running.

Tawl was on his feet in an instant. His hand slipped to his waist, checking for the reassuring presence of his blade. "What's happened?"

Nabber was so excited he could hardly get his words out. He stamped his feet impatiently. "Baralis has sent someone to murder the duke."

Tawl sprang across the room, pushing the pocket out of his way.

"No, Tawl. Don't head for the nobles' quarters. Follow me."

"Where?"

"There's a passage leading from the servants' chapel to the duke's chamber. The man went that way."

Tawl changed his course. He sprinted through the kitchens and the bakery. Dimly, he was aware that Nabber was following him. He made it to the chapel doors in less than a minute. Two guards were stationed outside. He wasted no words on them. Barging into the chapel, he looked around wildly.

"Where is the entrance?"

Nabber came padding up behind him. "Middle panel behind the altar."

Tawl was there before the words left Nabber's lips. He tore the panel from the wall. Complete darkness met his eyes. He went forward anyway—a candle would only slow him down. There was a single staircase leading upward. Tawl took the steps four at a time. Minutes later, the staircase came to an abrupt end.

Unable to see anything, Tawl felt the obstruction: wood. Probably some sort of door. Backing away for an instant, he slammed his shoulder into the panel. It cracked, sending splinters stabbing into his flesh. He hardly felt them. Again he brought his weight down. There was something heavy on the other side. He started kicking at the wood. Light began to steal in through the breaks in the door. Tawl made out the shape of a large desk. Someone had dragged it in front of the entrance.

His ear picked up the sound of a woman screaming. Melli! Gathering all the strength in his body, Tawl crashed into the door. The desk shifted back a hand's length. It was enough. He broke through the door and slipped into the space between the entrance and the desk. There was no screaming now. Grabbing hold of the desktop, he pushed it back, sending it thudding to the floor. Behind him he heard Nabber scrambling through the remains of the door.

"Stay where you are," he warned. The noise stopped instantly.

Tawl was in a small room. A body lay in a pool of blood beside the desk. A guard: his throat had been slit. Tawl had no time for the dead. He looked around. He wasn't familiar with the duke's chambers, but he'd seen enough to know that they were large, with many rooms. Taking a deep breath, he drew his blade, then made his way toward the door. He passed into a room he was familiar with: the duke's study. The large doors at the opposite side of the room marked the only entrance to the chambers. Or what he'd thought was the only entrance. The duke had been a fool not to tell him about the secret passageway.

Spinning around, Tawl turned to face the second door. It had to lead to the bedchamber. It was closed. He stepped lightly toward it. The screaming had stopped, which meant Melli was either injured, dead, or silenced by the assassin. Tawl guessed that the assassin knew he was in the chamber; the break-in had made a lot of noise. He proceeded cautiously.

He reached the door and pushed gently against it with his foot. As it swung back he stepped back against the wall, out of sight.

"Stay where you are," came a voice from inside. "Or I'll cut her open."

Her open? That meant the duke might already be dead. Tawl heard the sound of footsteps and the rustle of silk.

"Back away," said the voice. "I'm coming through and I've got the girl."

Slowly Tawl shifted away from the door. As he moved back, he knocked against a bureau. Reaching out a hand to prevent it falling over, Tawl's fingers brushed over a candlestick. Instinctively he grabbed hold of it, keeping it hidden behind his back.

Melli emerged first through the door. Tawl took a sharp intake of breath. Her face, neck, and chest were sprayed with blood. Her hair was tangled; there were dark stains on her dress. She stepped forward just enough for Tawl to see the knife at her back.

"Throw down your blade," said the one holding the knife. "Now!"

Tawl bent low. He sent the blade skittering forward. It landed at Melli's feet. She looked at him for one brief moment. Her eyes were bright with tears. She was shaking, terrified. Tawl nodded at her. She stepped forward and with her came the assassin. Turning his head, he spotted Tawl. "Get back," he screamed.

Behind his back, Tawl altered his grip on the candlestick. Just as he began to step away, out shot his arm. He flung the candlestick straight at the man's face. Tawl leapt after it. Landing right at Melli's side, he pushed her out of the way, sending her careening forward. "Go!" he cried.

Even as the syllable left his lips, he felt the knife in his side. Pain exploded in his body. Anger flared with it. He swung around and punched the assassin in the jaw. The blade was up again, but his fist was faster.

Elbow followed fist and the assassin was forced back against the door frame. Tawl felt hot blood running down his thigh. He grabbed hold of the man's wrist. His left arm pitted against the man's right. It was deadlock. The assassin's grip held firm.

An idea flashed through Tawl's mind. A second later he eased up his grip on the knife. The assassin smiled, thinking he'd got the better of him. The smile was Tawl's cue. Drawing back his head, he whipped it forward, butting the assassin squarely in the nose with his forehead. Bone cracked. Blood flared. The man screamed. Tawl slammed the assassin's wrist into the door frame, forcing him to drop the knife. Ignoring the reeling in his head, Tawl punched the man's face again—right on the broken nose, sending splinters of bone flying back toward his brain. The assassin swayed, loosing his footing. Tawl let him fall, using the time to snatch the knife from the floor.

By the time the assassin reached the ground he was dead, his own blade in his heart.

Tawl slumped against the door frame. Melli came rushing forward. "I told you to go," he said between ragged breaths.

She pushed past him, stepped over the assassin's body, and rushed through to the bedchamber. Turning around, Tawl saw her kneel by the body of the duke. He pressed his fist into the knife wound in his side and came to kneel beside her. Like the guard, the duke's throat had been cut.

"He's dead," he whispered, putting his arm around Melli's shoulder. "It was a clean blow."

Giant tears ran down Melli's cheeks. She didn't turn to look at him. She didn't say a word.

"Come with me," he said softly. "You can't stay here." Already his mind was racing ahead. Melli was in great danger. They would have to leave the palace tonight, before the body was discovered. He did not want to risk her being implicated in the murder; better by far for her to be safely away.

"He was waiting in the bedchamber for us." Her voice was devoid of emotion. "He just jumped out and . . ."

"Ssh." Tawl took hold of her hand. "Come with me. You're not safe here." He pulled, but she would not move. Her other hand was clasped around the duke's. She brought it to her lips and kissed each finger one by one. Gently she took them into her mouth and sucked upon the tips.

Tawl looked up to see Nabber standing in the doorway. "Get Lord Maybor," he mouthed to the boy. Melli was in shock; she needed someone familiar to help her round. Nabber scurried off. Tawl stood up and went over to the bed. Lilies and rose petals were strewn over the covers. The marriage had not been consummated—so legally it wasn't even a marriage. Melli would have no rights, everything would go to Catherine. Kylock would have Bren after all.

Grabbing hold of the top cover, he pulled it from the bed. Petals went flying into the air. Tawl crossed back to Melli and placed the blanket over her shoulders. She was sucking on the duke's thumb and didn't even acknowledge the gesture. Tawl brushed the hair from her face; it was sticky with blood. The bodice of her dress was wet with tears. There was nothing he could do to help her.

Feeling useless, Tawl left the room. He was impatient. He didn't know how much time they had. He doubted if any of the fighting or screaming had been overheard by the guards; they were one floor down, on the other side of two separate sets of doors. But the one who sent the assassin might raise the alarm. It was probably Baralis, acting with Catherine's help. In all likelihood the duke's daughter would have known about the secret passage. Tawl tore a strip from his tunic and bound it tightly around his side, stopping the flow of blood. If Catherine was somehow involved with the murder, then Melli was in even worse danger. Catherine hated her with a vengeance. She would have Melli imprisoned or executed. She was duchess of Bren now, she could do what she liked.

"Where is she?" It was Maybor, striding into the room with Nabber at his tail. "Where is Melliandra?"

"She is in the bedchamber with the duke," said Tawl, putting a restraining arm upon the lord. "Be gentle with her."

Maybor nodded. "I will."

Tawl and Nabber watched as Maybor stepped into the bedchamber. Tawl put his arm out and rubbed the pocket's hair. "You did well, Nabber. I'm proud of you."

Nabber looked grave. "No, Tawl. It was you who did the good stuff. I was just the messenger."

Tawl shook his head slowly. "I failed, Nabber. I failed again."

Maybor appeared in the doorway. Melli was at his side, leaning heavily against him. Her eyes were focused upon some distant point.

"Come on," said Tawl. "Let's go."

"Where are we going?" asked Maybor.

"We need to get Melli—" Tawl corrected himself "—Melliandra out of the palace. Her life is in danger if she stays here. Catherine will come after her once the news is out."

"You're right," said Maybor heavily. He pulled a piece of paper from his tunic. "I know of a place we can go." He handed it to Tawl.

Written upon it was an address. "Whose house is this?" Tawl asked.

"Lord Cravin's. It's on the south side of the city. He said I could use it if I ever had need."

"We'll head there, then." Tawl turned to Nabber. "Do you know any way we can get out of here without being spotted?" He wasn't at all surprised when the pocket nodded.

"Yes. By the entrance to the passage, on the opposite side of the stairs, there's a hole we can squeeze through. Once we're on the other side, I can have us out of this place in no time. The whole place is riddled with tunnels. Course some of them are a bit smelly, and old Lord Maybor here is going to have a hard time fitting through the gap." Nabber gave Maybor an appraising glance. "Reckon we'll have to make it bigger for him."

"Enough, Nabber." Tawl's voice was hard. "We'll manage. Now come on." He led the small party through the duke's chamber and then down the staircase. As Nabber predicted, the gap was too small for Maybor. Tawl took the hilt of his knife and chipped away at the stone piece by piece. Once through the ventilation hole, Nabber guided them out of the palace and into the darkness of the city.

It was a cold and moonless night in Bren. There were neither stars nor people to bear witness to their passing. The wind howled from the surface of the Great Lake, and as the four sped through the streets to safety, it seemed to push them on their way.

Thirty-six

*B*aralis sat at his new desk in his new apartments and smiled. Two weeks the old duke had been dead now. Two exquisitely perfect weeks.

Everything had worked out beautifully, better than he could have ever hoped. The duke was cold in his grave; Traff was dead, and so could tell no tales, or name no names; Melliandra had fled the palace—the marriage obviously not consummated, so not only was there no possibility of an heir, but she had no legal claim on the duke's estate either; and lastly, Maybor had gone with her. After all these months he'd finally succeeded in ridding himself of the vain and meddlesome lord. Fate was surely his partner for the dance.

As he thought, Baralis cut the string surrounding a bundle of books. Just this morning the courier had arrived from Bevlin's cottage, and resting on the desk before him lay the first of many deliveries. If he was lucky he might discover why the wiseman had sent the knight on a quest. If he was unlucky he simply received a few more books to add to his library. Baralis slipped off the leather wrapping and glanced at what lay beneath: some interesting books, indeed.

The knight and his little party were still somewhere in the city. On Baralis' instructions all the gates were being monitored closely, so he would know if they left. He had promised Larn that much. Tomorrow he intended to persuade the newly bereaved Catherine to mount a door-to-door search of the city. He doubted if they would be found that way, but it looked good nonetheless. The duchess should be seen to be actively pursuing her father's murderers. Or at least those suspected of it.

Oh, the theories abounded as to who had murdered the duke: a rogue assassin working alone; an old lover of Melliandra who couldn't bear to see her wed; Tawl, the duke's own champion on a mission from Valdis; and of course the lady herself, Maybor's daughter, who never really loved the duke, just craved his power and wealth. Traff's body had been found: the knife the duke had been killed with embedded deep within his heart. At this point in time the city of Bren didn't know whether to call the mysterious dead man a murderer or a hero. Baralis' lips shaped a slow smile. It really was most delicious.

The fact that Tawl and Melliandra had fled the murder scene added impetus to the rumors of their guilt. Innocent people stay and face their accusers; it is the guilty who need to hide. A commonly held misconception it may be, but one it was never wise to go against. Everyone in Bren was looking to blame the murder of their beloved duke on someone, and what better candidates than the two runaways, a traitorous knight and a foreign whore?

Baralis began to idly flick through Bevlin's books. Dealing with Catherine had been his greatest challenge. The morning after the murder she had come to him. Furious, confused, tears streaking down her beautiful face, she had demanded to know why her father had been killed. He had been expecting her. The wine he gave her was drugged. Nothing much: a mere relaxant with a little something extra added to ensure her pliability. The potion was a fitting accompaniment to his words. He told Catherine *his* account of the evening. He explained that when the assassin burst into the room ready to slit Melliandra's scrawny little throat, he found the duke already dead, and Melli abed with the duke's champion. Tawl and the assassin had fought, and the assassin had sadly lost.

Two things added weight to his tale: first, the duke's own physicians had concluded that the knife found in the assassin's heart was the murder weapon; and secondly, Catherine hated Tawl with a zealous frenzy. She was eager to believe his guilt: he had killed her lover. It did not take much to convince her that he had killed her father as well.

Catherine was now firmly in his court. The new duchess was allowing herself to be guided by him. Each day she would come to him, drink a glass of tainted wine, brush her plump lips against his cheek, and then listen eagerly to his advice. Her decisions were *his* decisions. Her orders were *his* orders. He was running Bren now. The marriage to Kylock would go ahead.

Once the official mourning period of forty days and forty nights was over, Catherine would wed Kylock here in the city. Nothing could stop his plans now. Nothing.

Even Kylock himself was playing his part well. Having conquered all of western Halcus, and taken the capital Helch, the young king had actually shown some restraint. Instead of continuing on and attempting to defeat the entire country, Kylock had sued for peace. The whole of the north had heaved a collective sigh of relief at the news. Baralis was well pleased. He could not have asked for better timing; this latest move of Kylock's had served to pacify Annis and Highwall. The two cities would now be less likely to hinder the joining of Bren and the kingdoms. Both powers had secretly been building up their armies for months and were in the position to raise powerful objections. War was inevitable, but it was far better that it be delayed until everything was in place. Annis and Highwall were still on their guard at the moment, after a few months of peace they would not be quite so alert.

Kylock would undoubtedly fare well in the coming peace talks with the Halcus. After his military success in the capital, he was in a strong position to negotiate and would doubtless come away from the parley with a good slice of enemy territory in his pocket. The Halcus warlords were no fools; they would rather give up a quarter of their domain than risk Kylock claiming all of it in yet another bloody war. The first meeting with the Halcus warlords was to take place this night, in Kylock's encampment just outside Helch. Baralis began flicking through another of Bevlin's books. It would be most interesting to see what the morning would bring.

Finding nothing of interest in the book he had just picked up, Baralis moved on to the next one. It was a very old copy of Marod's *Book of Words*. He very nearly decided not to bother with it at all—every minor clergyman and half-witted scholar in the Known Lands had a copy of Marod—but there was something about the delicate patina on the sheep's hide cover that caught his eye. The book was not merely old, it was ancient.

As he turned the pages, his excitement began to grow. Clearly discernible beneath the text lay ghosts of words: pale fragments of what had once been written and then later washed away. The paper had been twice used. A thrill of pure joy raced down Baralis' spine. This was one of the four original Galder copies. It was a well-known fact that Marod had died penniless and that Galder, his servant, unable to buy new paper, had been forced to write over old manuscripts. Baralis began to treat the book with a new respect; it was more valuable than a chest's worth of jewels.

Holding it up to the light, he began to examine the paper more thoroughly. As he tilted it toward the candle's flame, something slipped from the book. A marker. Baralis caught the silk ribbon before it fell out all the way. Holding it in his hand, he opened the book on the page it had marked. It was a verse. At first glance he thought he knew it, but as he read on, he realized that the version he was familiar with was subtly different from the one before him:

When men of honor lose sight of their cause
When three bloods are savored in one day
Two houses will meet in wedlock and wealth
And what forms at the join is decay
A man will come with neither father nor mother
But sister as lover
And stay the hand of the plague

The stones will be sundered, the temple will fall
The dark empire's expansion will end at his call
And only the fool knows the truth

By the time he had finished reading it, Baralis' heart was thumping like a drum. The verse spoke of the marriage between Catherine and Kylock. It predicted the empire he intended to build and it named a man who could destroy it. Baralis took a deep breath, trying to steady the shaking of his hand and the pounding of his heart. It was all here, written on this page. *Everything.* Three bloods were savored on the night of Kylock's begetting—*he* had tasted them. The men of honor were the knights—ever since Tyren had taken over the leadership gold had been their only cause.

Baralis stood up. Crossing over to the fire, he poured a slim measure of wine. He had to think. Bevlin had sent the knight to find the one in the prophecy: the man with neither father nor mother. The boy who Larn had said was to be found in the kingdoms. Trailing his fingers around the rim, Baralis stared into the cup. The wine was the color of blood. Who in the kingdoms could be the one?

A memory of a drawing skimmed across his brain. A drawing so strong that it had woken him from his sleep. He sent his mind further back in time to another drawing and eight score of loaves barely browned to a crust. Every fiber of Baralis' being was resonating, every hair on his body stirred at the root. The cup in his hands became a chalice and his fingers wove around it like a priest's. Jack the baker's boy. He was the one.

Tavalisk was in the kitchens choosing crabs. He and his cook were standing over a metal tank, putting the wily crustaceans through their paces. Choosing crabs was an art and the archbishop was a grand master. The secret to the perfect crab was neither size nor color: it was speed. The fastest crabs were the meatiest, the tastiest, and the most satisfying to the tongue. In order to judge the quickness of the various creatures before him, Tavalisk had devised a test. He would throw large heavy stones into the water, aiming for the greatest density of crabs. Those crabs who were crushed by the stones were pronounced unworthy, while the fortunate few who managed to scuttle away to safety were marked for the flame.

Tavalisk grimaced. The last stone had killed nearly half of them.

"Your Eminence," came a voice from behind.

"Yes, Gamil," said the archbishop turning round. "What is it?"

"Annis and Highwall have received the shipments of gold safely, Your Eminence."

"And the armaments?"

"They were sent out last week and so might take a little longer."

"I trust you made sure they were well guarded? I wouldn't want fifty wagons worth of steel and siege engines to fall into the wrong hands."

"A whole battalion rides along with the shipment, Your Eminence. And as a further precaution they are taking a lower pass. They will not come anywhere near Bren."

Tavalisk dropped another stone into the tank. "Good." The water splashed up against his sleeve. It was thick with crab spume. "So there's no chance of Baralis getting his eager little hands on them?"

"You mean the duchess Catherine."

"No, Gamil. I mean Baralis. It is perfectly obvious that *he* is ruling Bren now." The archbishop peered into the murky water. Another clump of dead crabs met his eyes.

"Does Your Eminence think it's wise to send arms to Annis and Highwall with peace looming on the horizon?"

"Peace!" Tavalisk snorted. "This so-called peace will last about as long as that crab over there." He pointed toward the corner of the tank where one of the few surviving crabs lay hiding in the shadows. The archbishop promptly dropped a stone upon it. The feisty little devil actually managed to run away. Tavalisk found compensation in the fact that its two surviving companions were agreeably flattened.

"May I ask why Your Eminence has been putting such great effort into rallying southern support for Annis and Highwall?"

"Certainly, Gamil. Kylock will now marry Catherine, that much is certain. With the duke out of the way, the kingdoms and Bren will become one. Already Kylock has secured the support of the knights." Tavalisk looked quickly at his aide. "Can't you see? The lines have now been drawn. It will only take the slightest provocation for the war to start, and the way things are at the moment, Annis and Highwall won't have a chance. They need our support, else before we know it Kylock will have all of the north to himself. That is something we simply cannot allow to happen. We all know where his ambitions will lead him next: south." The archbishop dropped another stone in the tank. "And the southern cities are hardly in a position to put up a fight. We don't go in for fortresses and high battlements like the north."

Gamil nodded. "Does this relate to Marod's prophecy, Your Eminence?"

"You remember that, do you?" Tavalisk rubbed his pink and hairless chin for a moment, considering whether to let Gamil in on his theory. The time was right: he had been modest for too long. Turning to his cook, he said, "Kindly excuse us, Master Bunyon. I will call you when I need you."

The cook, whose main duty at this point consisted of handing the archbishop stones on command, nodded and left.

The archbishop turned back to Gamil. His aide was looking decidedly sheepish. Taking a deep breath, Tavalisk began to recite the prophecy. He now knew it by heart:

"When men of honor trade in gold not grace
When two mighty powers join as one
The temples will fall
The dark empire will rise
And the world will come to ruin and waste

"One will come with neither father nor lover
But promised to another
Who will rid the land of its curse."

Tavalisk finished his recitation with a suitably dramatic flourish and then turned expectantly toward Gamil. "I trust everything is clear to you now?"

Gamil was cautious. "Not exactly, Your Eminence."

"Really, Gamil, and you call yourself a scholar!" The archbishop crooked a finger, beckoning his aide nearer. "Is it not obvious to you that the verse predicts the moral decay of the knights, Kylock's rise in the north, and the decline of the Church?"

"The decline of the Church, Your Eminence?"

"Yes, you dimwit. *The temples will fall.* Who besides the Church has temples, eh?"

Gamil nodded slowly. "Your Eminence could be right. Who then will be the one to rid the land of its curse?"

Tavalisk smiled like a rich widow. "It is I, Gamil. I am the one named in the verse."

"You!"

"Yes, me." The archbishop was not at all put out by the stupefied expression on his aide's face. "Think for a moment, Gamil. Consider the line: 'One will come with neither father nor lover'—I have no father, and my position prevents me from taking lovers. And then in the next line: 'But promised to another'—I am promised to another, Gamil. I am promised to God."

Gamil was looking at him as if he were mad. "What does Your Eminence intend to do about this?" he asked.

"I am already doing it, Gamil. It is obvious from Marod's prophecy that I have a sacred duty to put an end to Kylock's ascension in the north. I must do everything in my power to bring about the new king's downfall. It is my destiny. If I fail, then when Kylock comes south, he'll be bringing the knights with him. Before we know it Tyren will be burning our places of worship and forcing everyone to follow Valdis' creeds of belief. It would mark the end of the Church as we know it."

"It is certainly a great responsibility, Your Eminence." Gamil's eyes narrowed. "Will you gain anything personally by it?"

"Nothing for myself, Gamil." Tavalisk shrugged. "But if the Church felt the need to repay me in some small way by offering me the title of He Who Is Most Holy, then I could hardly refuse, could I?"

"Of course not, Your Eminence."

Tavalisk clapped his hands together. "You may go now, Gamil. Send Master Bunyon back in. Oh, and be sure to keep an ear out for news of Kylock's peace meeting. It happens this night, does it not?"

"Yes, Your Eminence. The north will rest easier in its bed after tonight." Gamil bowed and left.

Tavalisk felt a moment of misgiving as he watched his aide walk away. Should he have confided in the man? The archbishop shrugged. He could always have Gamil silenced or certified if he started spreading rumors. Feeling immediately cheered by that thought, Tavalisk turned his mind to food. He watched as his cook scooped the one surviving crab from the tank. Perhaps the peace would outlive the crab after all. He certainly hoped it would, for Master Bunyon was about to put the resilient little creature over a very hot flame.

Strange that a night in midspring should be so cold. Kylock's breath whitened in the air, quickly dispersing before it reached the shadow's end. His hands were gloved, not against the chill, but against the all-pervasive filth. In the silk beneath the leather, he could feel his fingers sweating. The sensation sickened him.

Kylock stood within the folds of his tent and watched the arrival of the Halcus warlords. On massive horses they came, decked out in their ceremonial armor, torches in their free hands, swords buckled at their waists. Men of bearing and experience they were. Noble fighting men with gray in their hair; their necks and arms thick with muscle. Real muscle, formed in real battles, not the cultivated artifice of the tourney field. These men were veterans of many campaigns; they knew of blood and pain and victory. They were the power behind the Halcus throne.

And tonight they had come to talk of peace.

Their faces were grim as they approached the camp. They came alone, their escort—a full company of guards—positioned at a fitting distance from the camp. They were proud men, riding to meet their enemy with conscious dignity. Proud, but not foolish, thought Kylock. The camp was undoubtedly ringed with their troops: swordsmen lying belly-flat in the mud, and archers training their bows in the darkness behind bush and tree. Kylock ran a gloved finger along the roughness of the tent. He was not worried. He had rings around the rings.

Twelve men, he counted. Some of their faces were familiar, some not. Lord Herven and Lord Kilstaff dismounted their horses. They had fought against him at the border and so were the first to witness his success. Lord Angus, Helch's chief protector, was deep in conversation with Gerheart of Asketh; both men looked tense. They stood close and spoke in whispers. As Kylock looked on, the great Lord Tymouth himself rode up. Responsible for the defense of the realm, Tymouth answered only to the king.

Kylock slipped through the shadows and entered his tent. Lord Vernal stood waiting. Kylock nodded once. "They have arrived," he said.

Vernal looked nervous. Kylock would have preferred him not to be here, not tonight. But the one-time military leader of the kingdoms was a respected man in Halcus, and his name and reputation was what brought the warlords together this night. They trusted Vernal. He was a man of his word.

"If all is ready, I will go to them," said Vernal. His expression was unreadable, his tone guarded. He drank the last of his brandy. "I will expect you to follow after me. I know these men, it is not wise to keep them waiting."

"Lord Vernal, I don't believe I asked for your advice." Kylock's voice was deceptively light. "Go now. Greet my guests. Soften them up with brandy and tales of the good old days of stalemate."

"I warn you now, Kylock. Do not treat these men with contempt. You may have beaten them, but they deserve respect. They were fighting in campaigns before you were born."

Anger flared within Kylock. No one but Vernal dared to treat him like this. The leather of his glove crackled as he curled his fingers into a fist. With one sudden sharp movement, he brought his fist down upon the desk. The sound was violent, satisfying. "I think you'd better go, Lord Vernal," said Kylock very softly. "Those in the negotiating tent await you."

He had the satisfaction of seeing fear in Vernal's eyes. Fear and something else. Comprehension, perhaps? Kylock waved an arm in dismissal, then turned his back on the man. It was too late now. There was nothing Vernal could do.

As soon as the man left, Kylock picked up the cup he had drunk from. He held it by the base, careful not to touch the rim, and carried it out of the tent. Slipping around the back, he tossed it onto the fire. He would drink from nobody's cup but his own.

Quickly, he returned to his position in the folds of the tent. His lip twisted into a sneer as he watched Vernal greet the Halcus warlords. There was much arm grasping and back patting, and even a little good-natured banter. Kylock clearly heard Vernal inviting the men into the tent. Lord Tymouth shook his head and said something that silenced all present immediately. Kylock felt a measure of foreboding. His eyes slanted across to the far side of the camp, where another waited in the shadows. Kedrac, son of Lord Maybor, and Kylock's most trusted companion, raised his arm in acknowledgment of the glance. It was a small gesture loaded with meaning. Wait, it said, let us see what this latest development brings. Kylock was well pleased: Maybor's son was keeping his nerve.

Three horsemen approached the camp. Two carried torches, the third, the figure in the middle, was misshapen, one shoulder clearly higher than the other. Kylock sucked in his breath. It was the king.

Hirayus, King of Halcus. Hunchback and tyrant. Feared by his enemies, worshipped by his people. Forty of his fifty years had been spent on the throne. At the age of ten the physicians pronounced him too weak to survive his eleventh year. The only reason he lived today was to spite them. Hirayus was a legend in the north. His determination, his willpower, and his single-minded devotion to his country had made a giant from a cripple.

The warlords turned to meet him, swords drawn in respect, blades pointing to the earth in subjugation. Vernal came forward. Words were exchanged. Hirayus dismounted his horse.

On the far side of the camp, Kedrac's hand was up. Kylock returned the motion, arm wavering with apprehension. *The king was not supposed to be here.* Tymouth had been chosen to handle the peace negotiations. Tymouth and the warlords. Kylock drew deeper into folds. His heart was racing. The silk around his fingers was as warm and wet as the womb. He couldn't bear it. Pulling the gloves off, he threw them onto the ground. As the cool night air dried the sweat from his fingers, Kylock grew calm. So the king was here. Did it really make any difference?

He turned his attention back to the negotiating party. Vernal was escorting Hirayus into the tent. Any minute now they would be expecting him to follow.

Wood smoke stole into his nostrils and Kylock was glad of it. The smell was almost cleansing. The king had come to parley; that meant at least another company on the lee of the hill and double that amount concealed around the camp. Nothing that couldn't be dealt with. Hirayus probably thought he had done a clever thing by turning up here unannounced. Kylock lifted his fingers to his nose: his mother's stench was still upon them. Hirayus had not been clever at all. In fact, he had just made the biggest mistake of his life.

Out came Kylock's hand from the shadows. The pale skin reflected the moonlight like glass. His long elegant fingers were stretched full out, his palm faced outward toward Kedrac. Slowly, very slowly, he tilted his palm downward to face the ground.

Even as shadow took the place of moonlight upon his flesh, Kylock heard the archers stringing their longbows. He heard swords being drawn from leather and the movement of men leaving Kedrac's tent. The cry went up and the carnage began.

One hundred barbed arrows were loosed upon the tent. They ripped through the fabric as if it were linen. The instant the arrows met their target, the swordsmen went in. Their orders were simple: kill all who remained alive. Kylock heard the screams of men and horses, he heard blade clashing against blade. In the distance the noise of battle began as the two Halcus companies tried to gain the camp. None would reach here alive. In the distance, on the hillsides and in the woods, his men were closing in, taking out Hirayus' archers one by one.

Kylock stepped out into the moonlight. The action in the negotiating tent was drawing to a close. The fabric flapped no more. Kylock took a torch from its metal stand and walked forward. The last of the swordsmen emerged from the tent. He met the eyes of his king. "All are dead, sire."

Kylock nodded. Drawing close, he set the torch against the tent. The fabric was ready for the flame, catching light on first contact. It crackled and blazed, spreading upward in sheets. He backed away, better to admire the fire. "Burn brightly, this night, King Hirayus," he murmured. "May the flames of your corpse be a warning to the north. Kylock has not done with you yet."

The End of Book II

CPSIA information can be obtained
at www.ICGtesting.com
Printed in the USA
LVOW03s2345060318
568947LV00001B/179/P